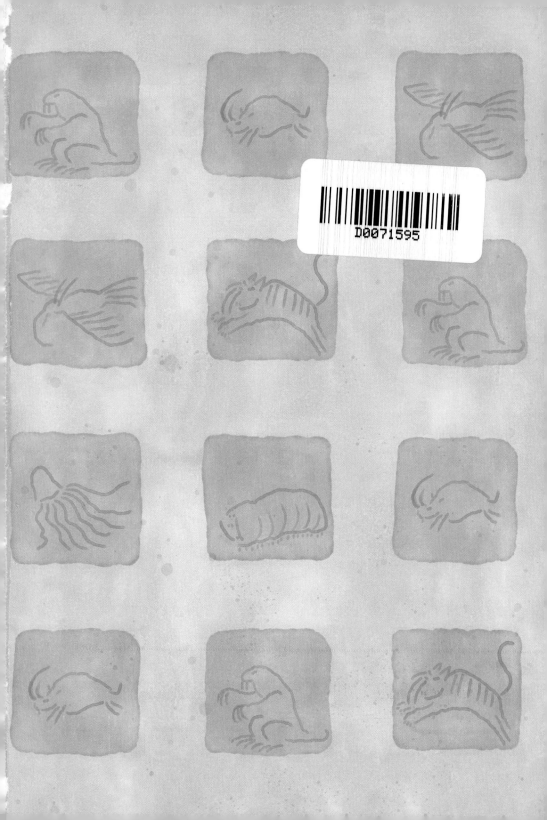

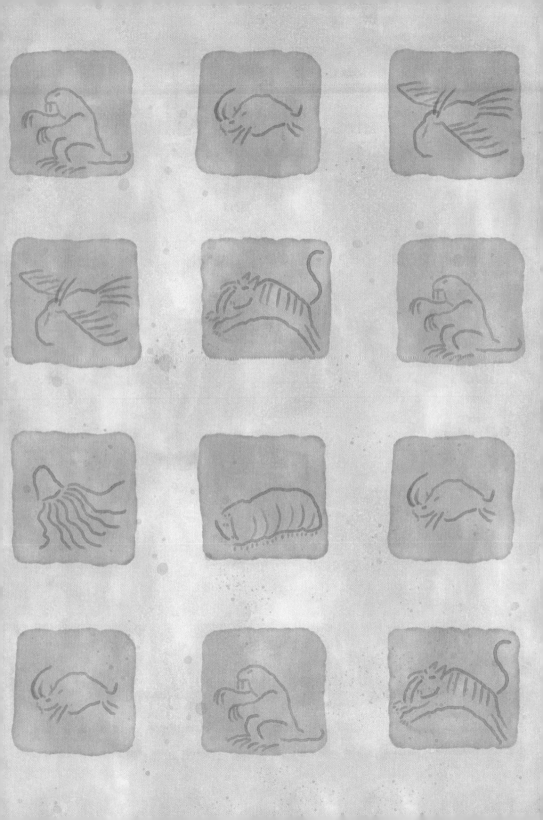

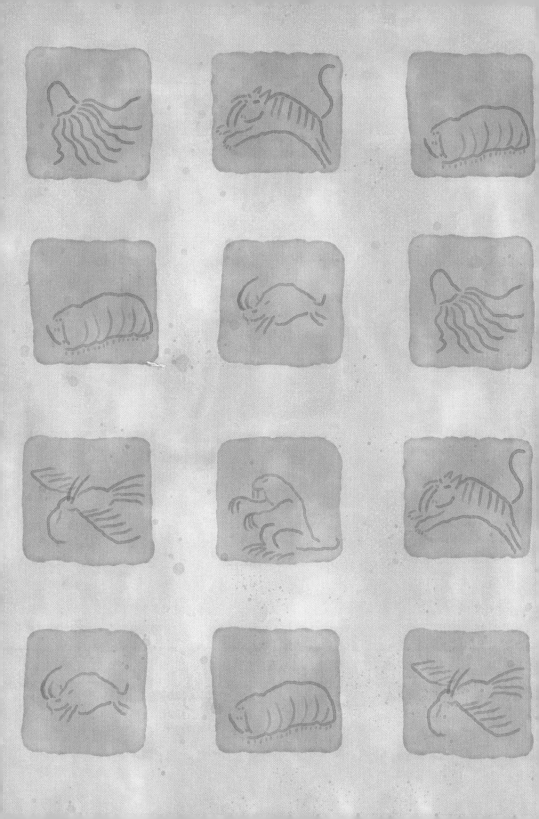

CAVEBOY DAVE

MORE SCRAWNY THAN BRAWNY

by Aaron Reynolds

illustrated by Phil McAndrew

VIKING

VIKING
An imprint of Penguin Random House LLC
375 Hudson Street
New York, New York 10014

First published in the United States of America by Viking,
an imprint of Penguin Random House LLC, 2016

Text copyright © 2016 by Aaron Reynolds
Illustrations copyright © 2016 by Phil McAndrew

LIBRARY OF CONGRESS CATALOGING-IN-PUBLICATION DATA
Names: Reynolds, Aaron, 1970–author. | McAndrew, Phil, illustrator.
Title: Caveboy Dave : more scrawny than brawny / Aaron Reynolds ; illustrated by Phil McAndrew.
Other titles: More scrawny than brawny
Description: New York : Viking Books for Young Readers, 2016. | Series: Caveboy Dave ; 1 | Summary: "A young caveman named Dave must complete a dangerous rite of passage with his peers"—Provided by publisher.
Identifiers: LCCN 2016003728| ISBN 9780147516589 (paperback)
ISBN 9780451475473 (hardcover)
Subjects: LCSH: Graphic novels. | CYAC: Graphic novels. | Prehistoric peoples—Fiction. | Humorous stories. | BISAC: JUVENILE FICTION / Comics & Graphic Novels / General. | JUVENILE FICTION / Animals / Dinosaurs & Prehistoric Creatures. | JUVENILE FICTION / Humorous Stories.
Classification: LCC PZ7.7.R49 Cav 2016 | DDC 741.5/973—dc23 LC record available at https://lccn.loc.gov/2016003728

Manufactured in China

3   5   7   9   10   8   6   4

To Lori Kilkelly, cool chick, great friend,
and more brawny than scrawny. - A. R.

For my mother, Joelle, and my father, Mike,
who taught me to hunt and invent. - P. M.

CAVEBOY DAVE

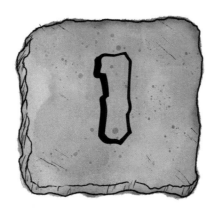

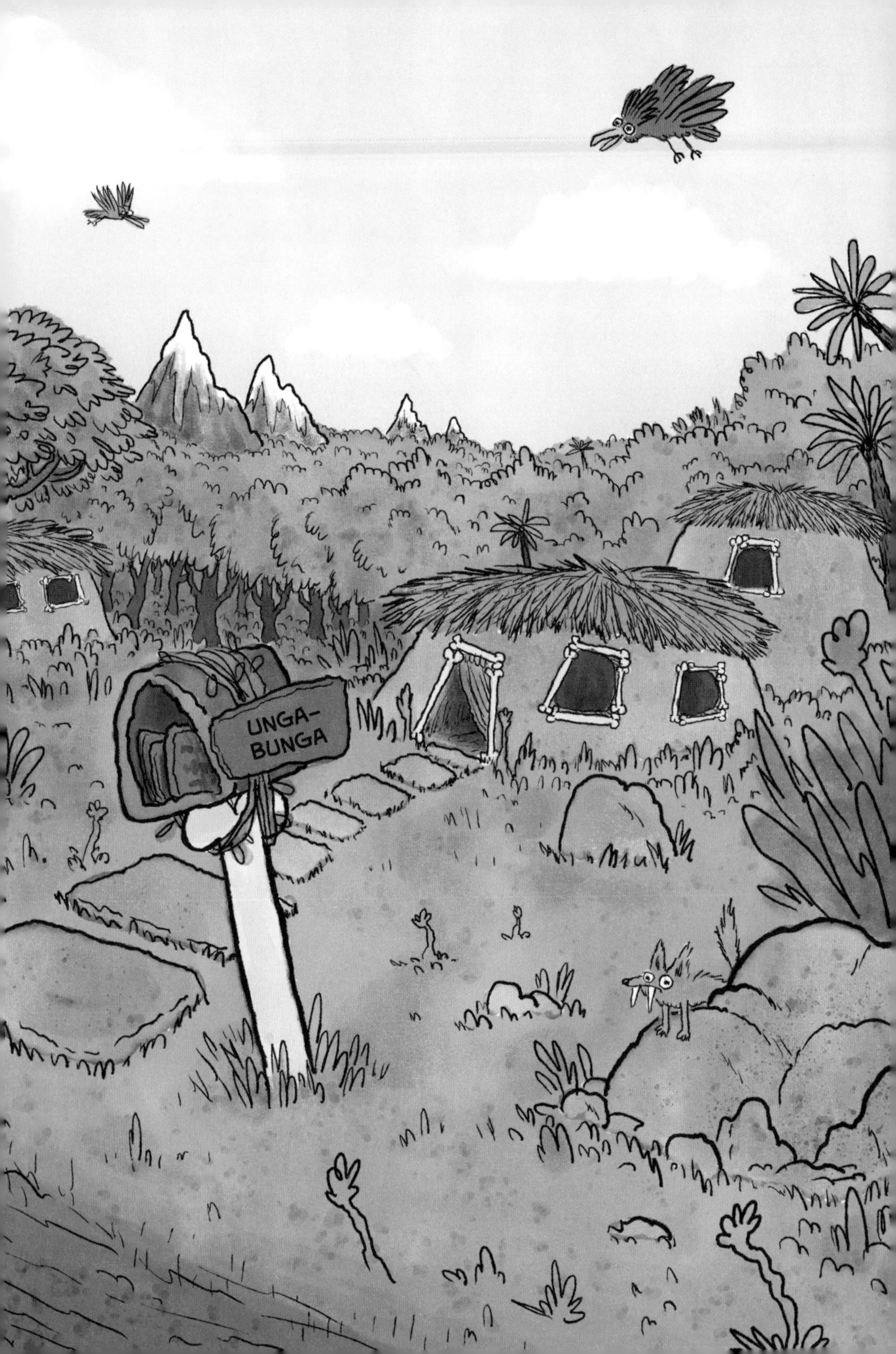
UNGA-
BUNGA

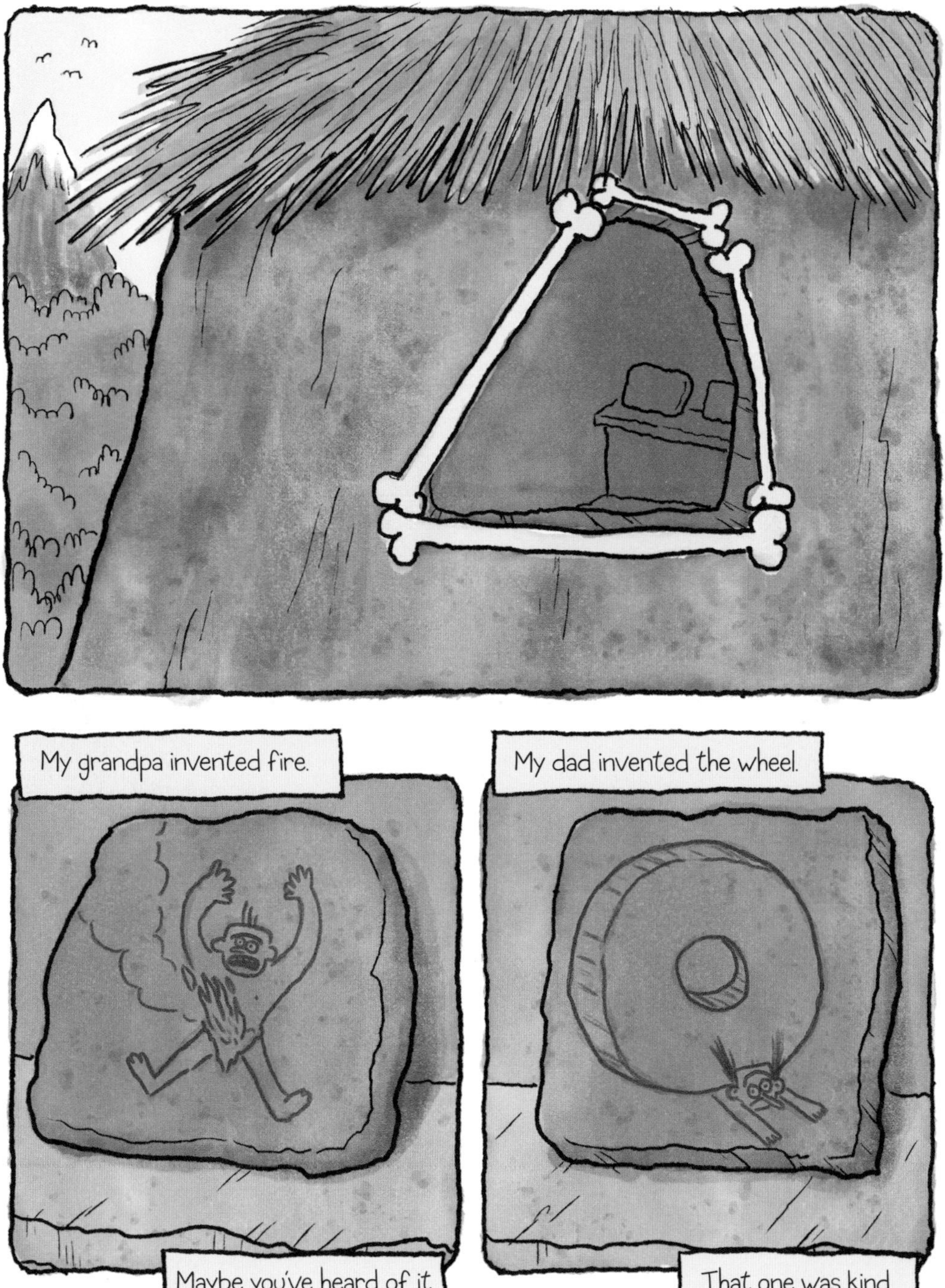
My grandpa invented fire.
Maybe you've heard of it.
My dad invented the wheel.
That one was kind of a big deal.

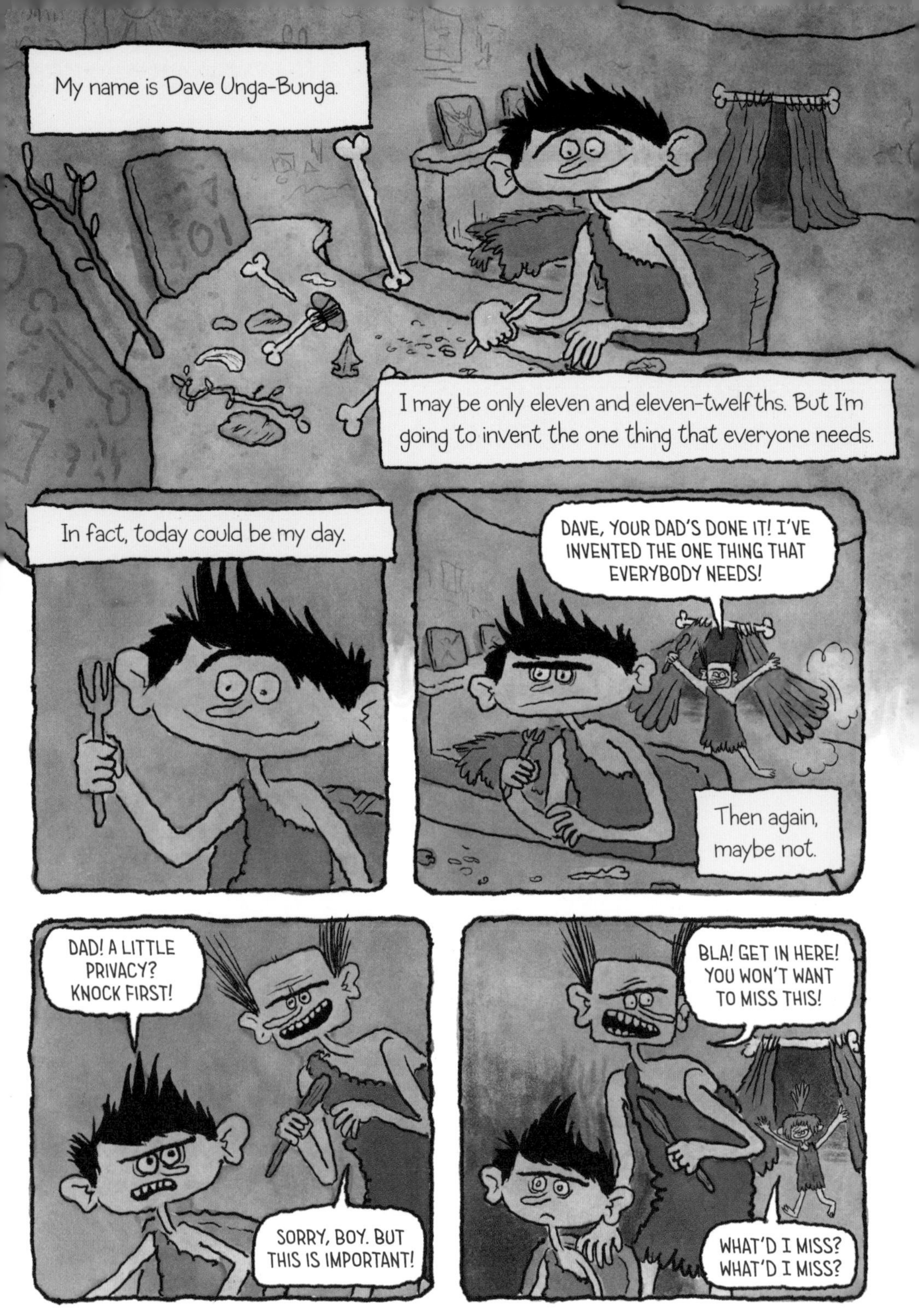
My name is Dave Unga-Bunga.
I may be only eleven and eleven-twelfths. But I'm going to invent the one thing that everyone needs.
In fact, today could be my day.
DAVE, YOUR DAD'S DONE IT! I'VE INVENTED THE ONE THING THAT EVERYBODY NEEDS!
Then again, maybe not.
DAD! A LITTLE PRIVACY? KNOCK FIRST!
SORRY, BOY. BUT THIS IS IMPORTANT!
BLA! GET IN HERE! YOU WON'T WANT TO MISS THIS!
WHAT'D I MISS? WHAT'D I MISS?

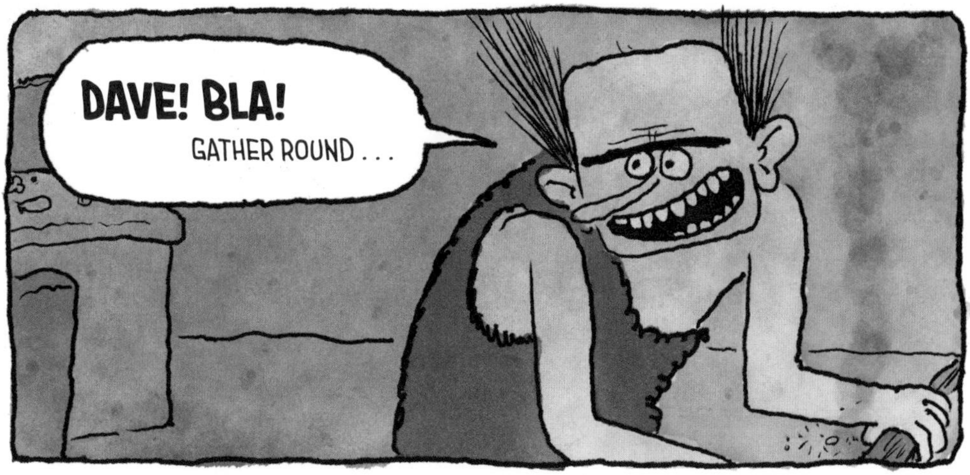
DAVE! BLA!
GATHER ROUND . . .

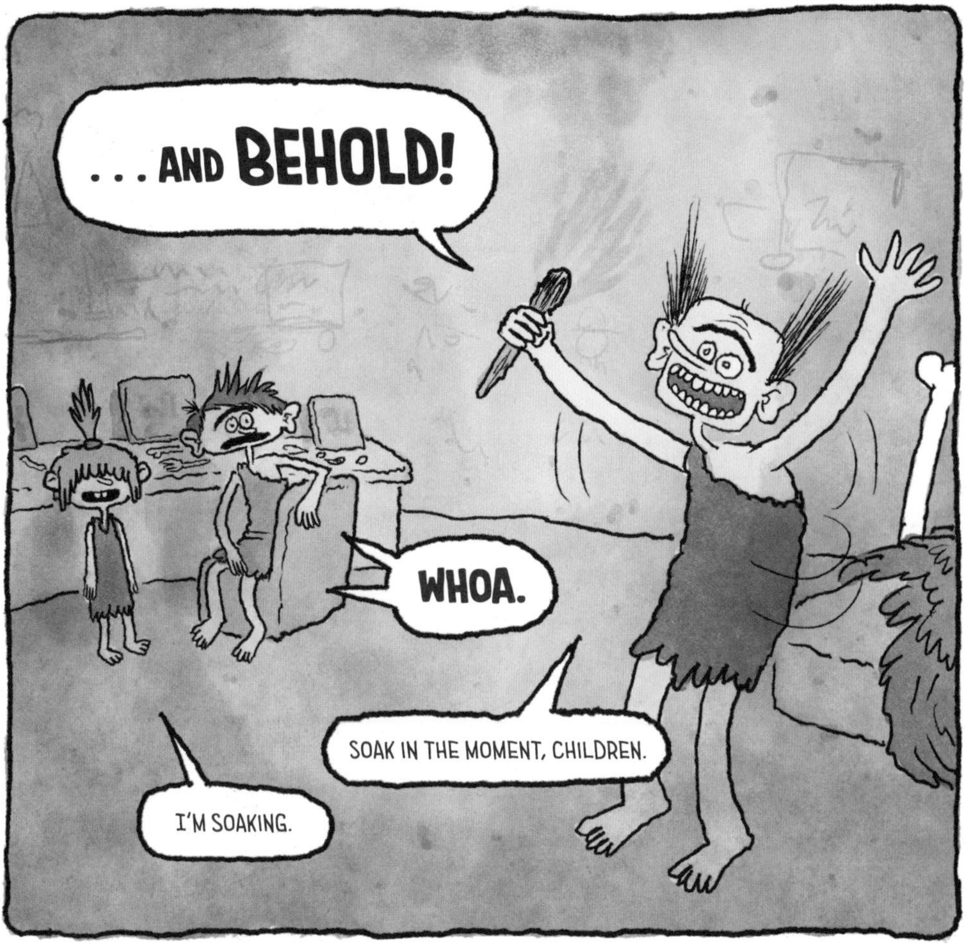
. . . AND BEHOLD!
WHOA.
SOAK IN THE MOMENT, CHILDREN.
I'M SOAKING.

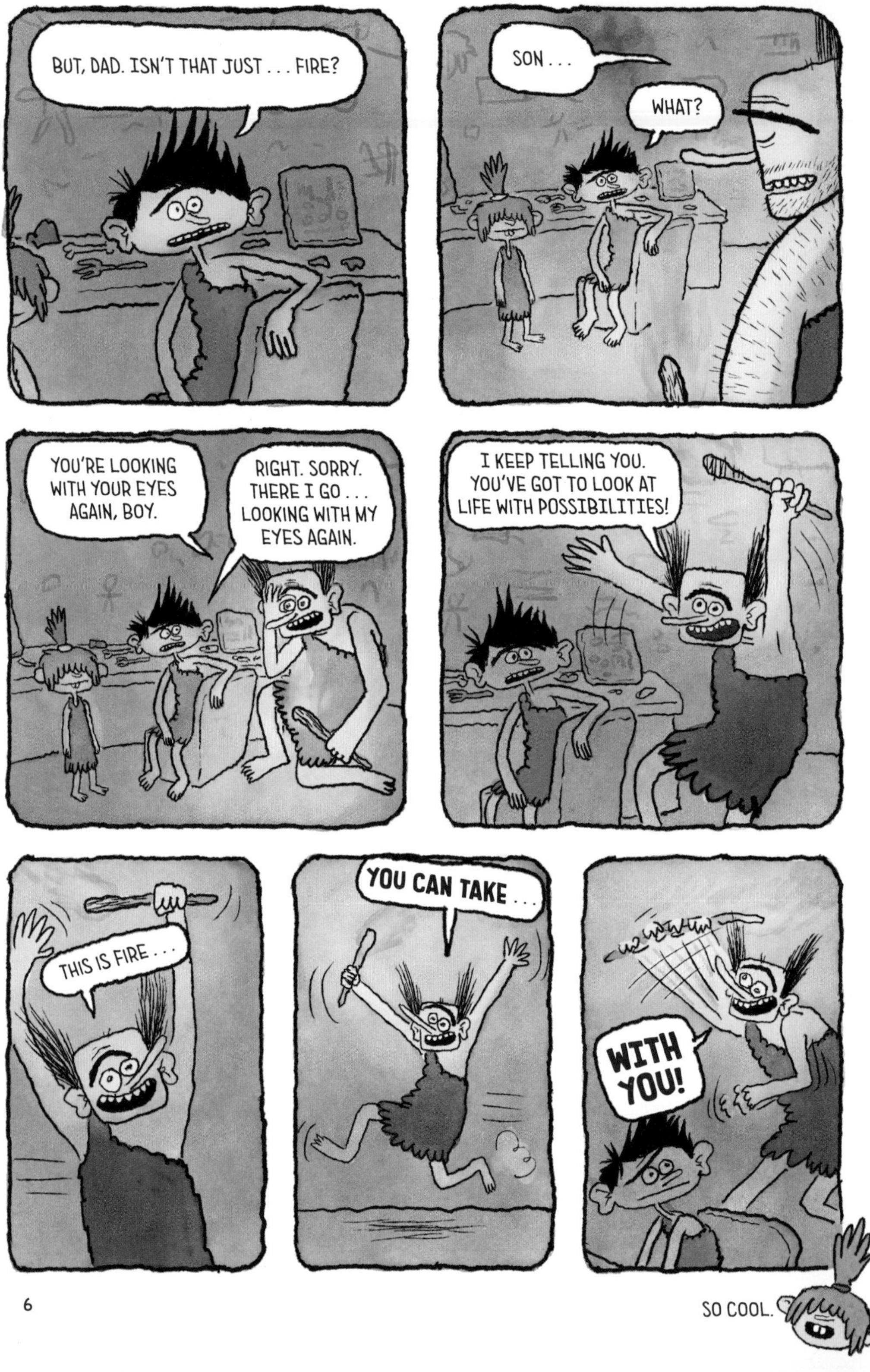
BUT, DAD. ISN'T THAT JUST . . . FIRE?
SON . . .
WHAT?
YOU'RE LOOKING WITH YOUR EYES AGAIN, BOY.
RIGHT. SORRY. THERE I GO . . . LOOKING WITH MY EYES AGAIN.
I KEEP TELLING YOU. YOU'VE GOT TO LOOK AT LIFE WITH POSSIBILITIES!
THIS IS FIRE . . .
YOU CAN TAKE . . .
WITH YOU!
SO COOL.

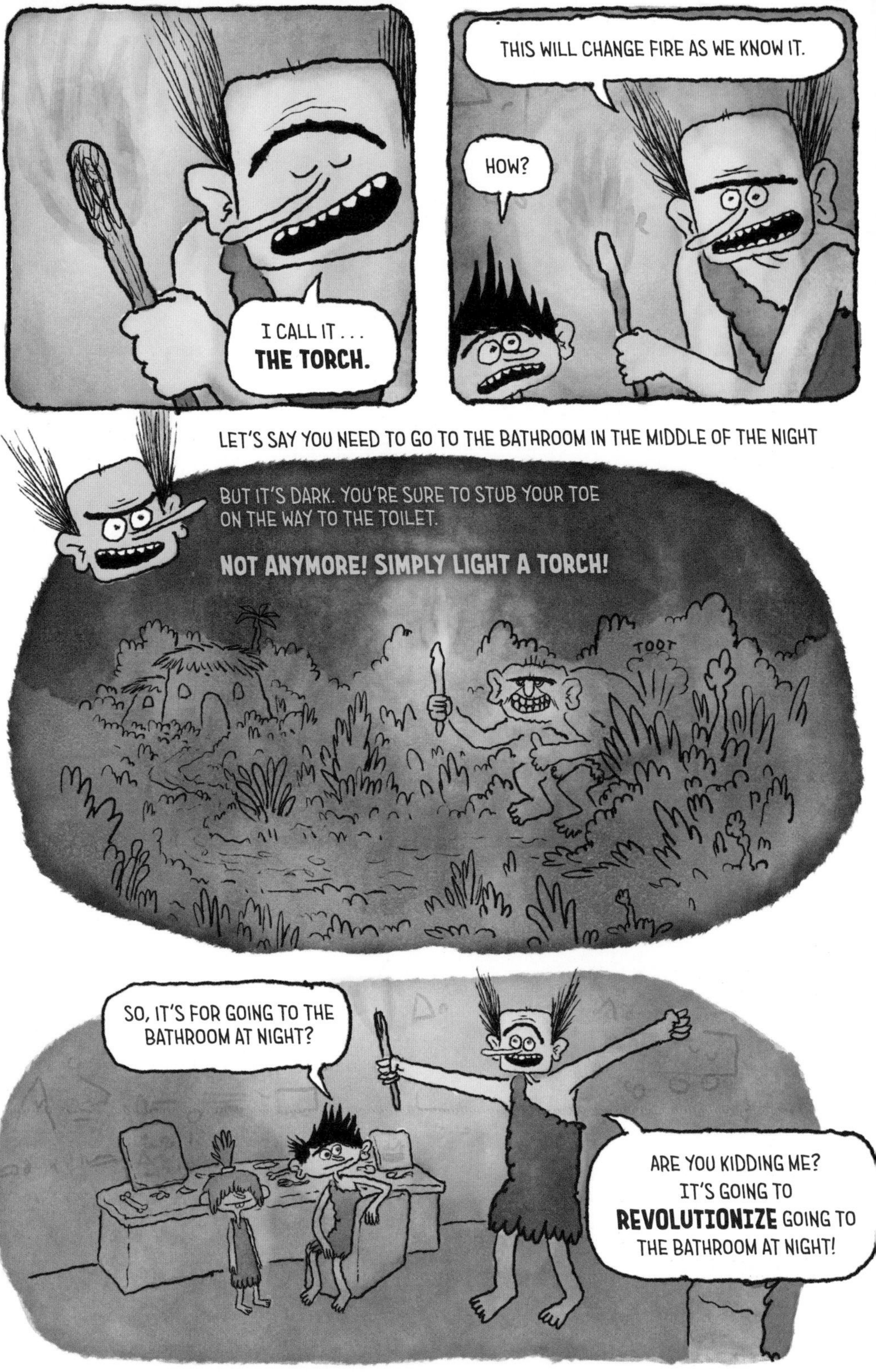
I CALL IT . . .
THE TORCH.
THIS WILL CHANGE FIRE AS WE KNOW IT.
HOW?
LET'S SAY YOU NEED TO GO TO THE BATHROOM IN THE MIDDLE OF THE NIGHT
BUT IT'S DARK. YOU'RE SURE TO STUB YOUR TOE ON THE WAY TO THE TOILET.
NOT ANYMORE! SIMPLY LIGHT A TORCH!
TOOT
SO, IT'S FOR GOING TO THE BATHROOM AT NIGHT?
ARE YOU KIDDING ME? IT'S GOING TO REVOLUTIONIZE GOING TO THE BATHROOM AT NIGHT!

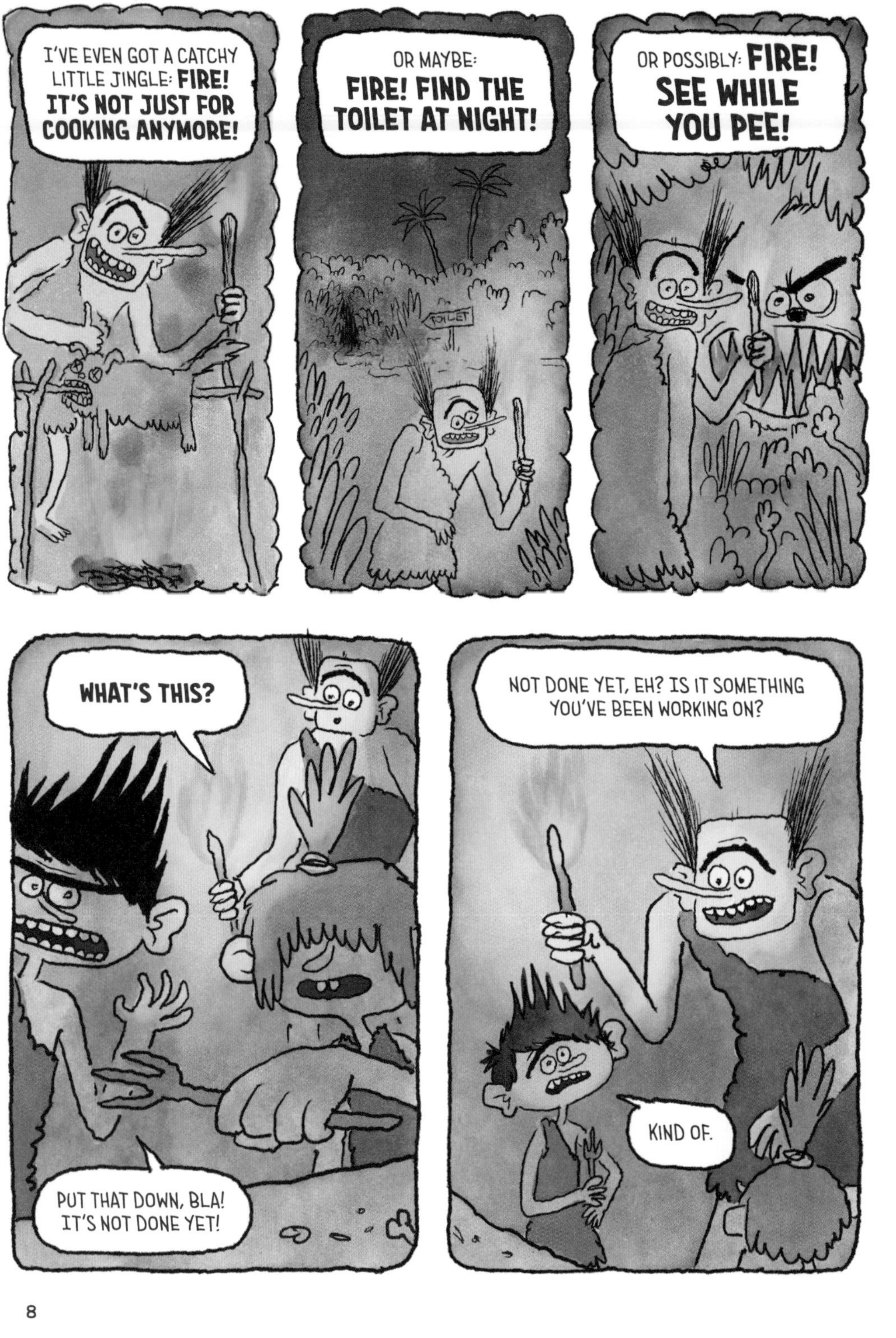
I'VE EVEN GOT A CATCHY LITTLE JINGLE: **FIRE! IT'S NOT JUST FOR COOKING ANYMORE!**
OR MAYBE: **FIRE! FIND THE TOILET AT NIGHT!**
TOILET
OR POSSIBLY: **FIRE! SEE WHILE YOU PEE!**
WHAT'S THIS?
PUT THAT DOWN, BLA! IT'S NOT DONE YET!
NOT DONE YET, EH? IS IT SOMETHING YOU'VE BEEN WORKING ON?
KIND OF.

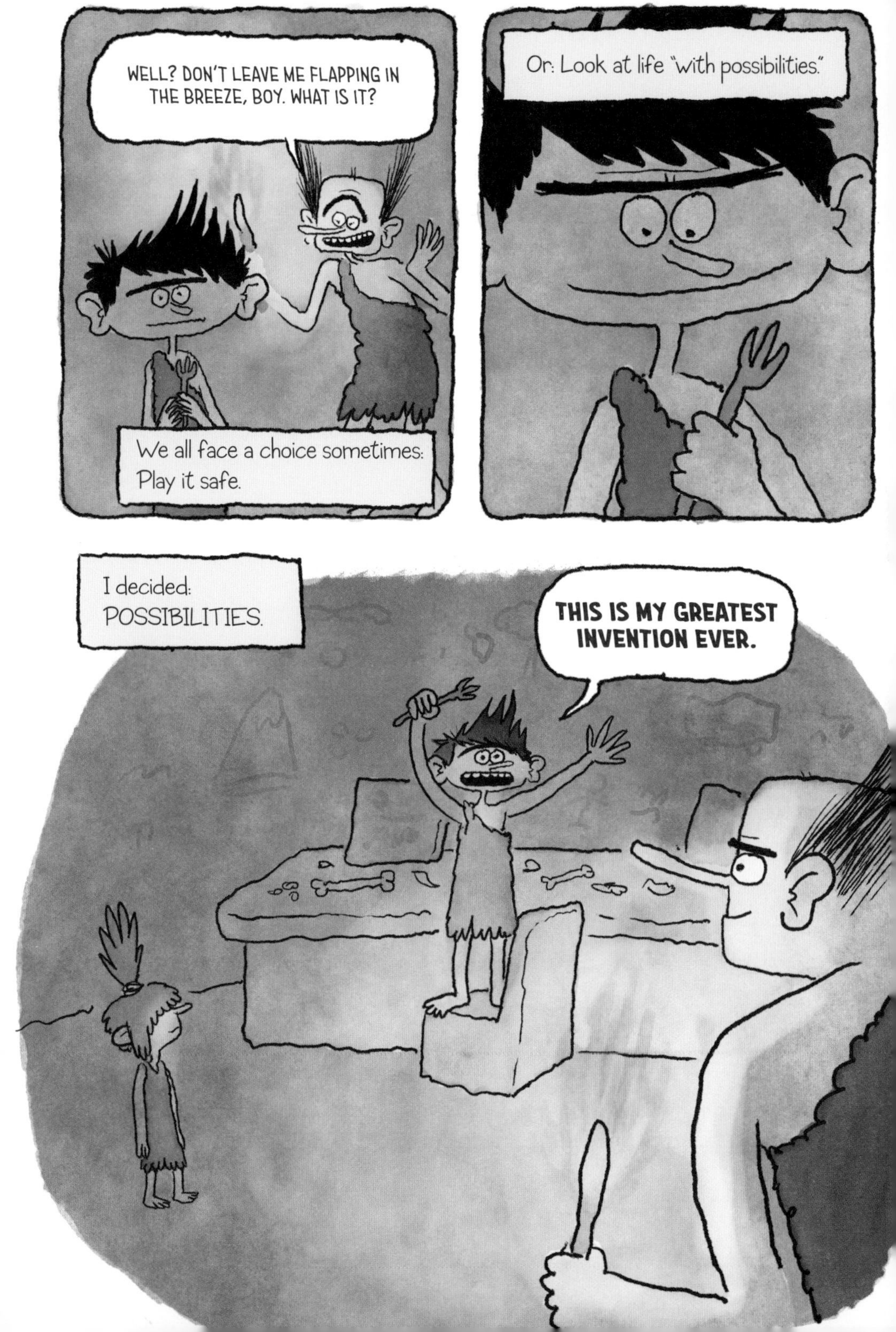
WELL? DON'T LEAVE ME FLAPPING IN THE BREEZE, BOY. WHAT IS IT?
We all face a choice sometimes: Play it safe.
Or: Look at life "with possibilities."
I decided: POSSIBILITIES.
THIS IS MY GREATEST INVENTION EVER.

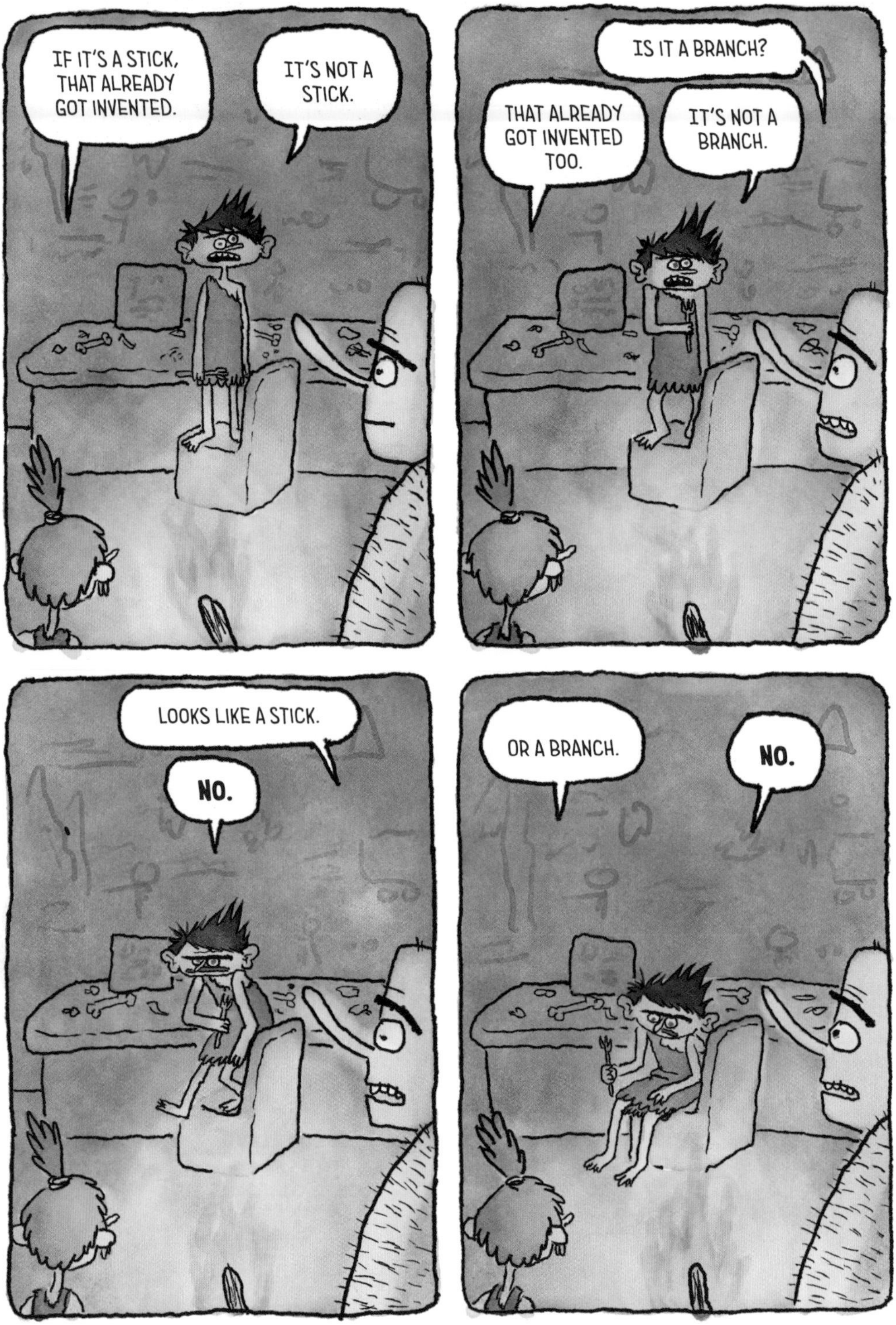
IF IT'S A STICK, THAT ALREADY GOT INVENTED.
IT'S NOT A STICK.
IS IT A BRANCH?
THAT ALREADY GOT INVENTED TOO.
IT'S NOT A BRANCH.
LOOKS LIKE A STICK.
NO.
OR A BRANCH.
NO.

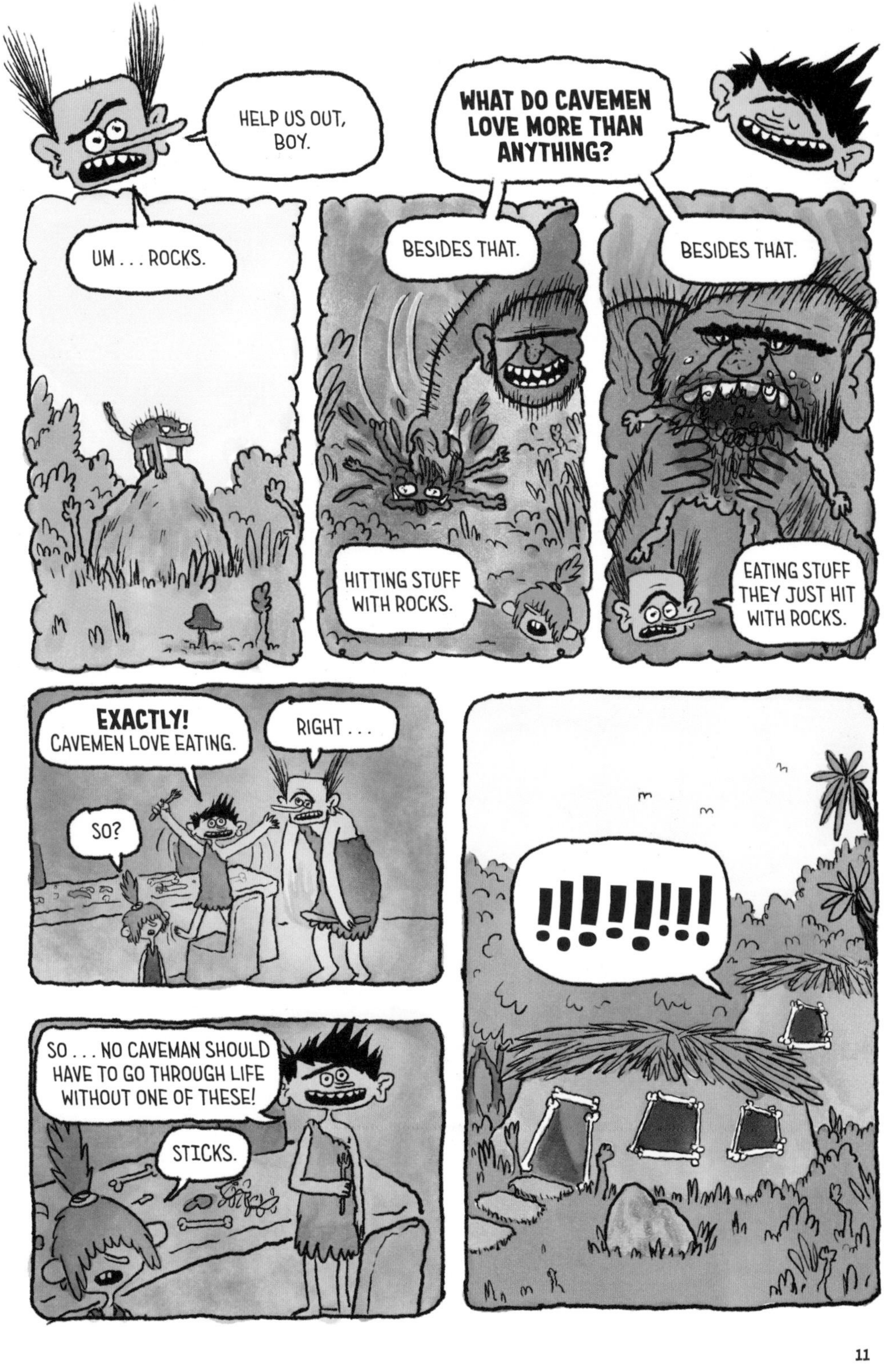
HELP US OUT, BOY.
WHAT DO CAVEMEN LOVE MORE THAN ANYTHING?
UM . . . ROCKS.
BESIDES THAT.
HITTING STUFF WITH ROCKS.
BESIDES THAT.
EATING STUFF THEY JUST HIT WITH ROCKS.
EXACTLY! CAVEMEN LOVE EATING.
RIGHT . . .
SO?
SO . . . NO CAVEMAN SHOULD HAVE TO GO THROUGH LIFE WITHOUT ONE OF THESE!
STICKS.
!!!!!!!!

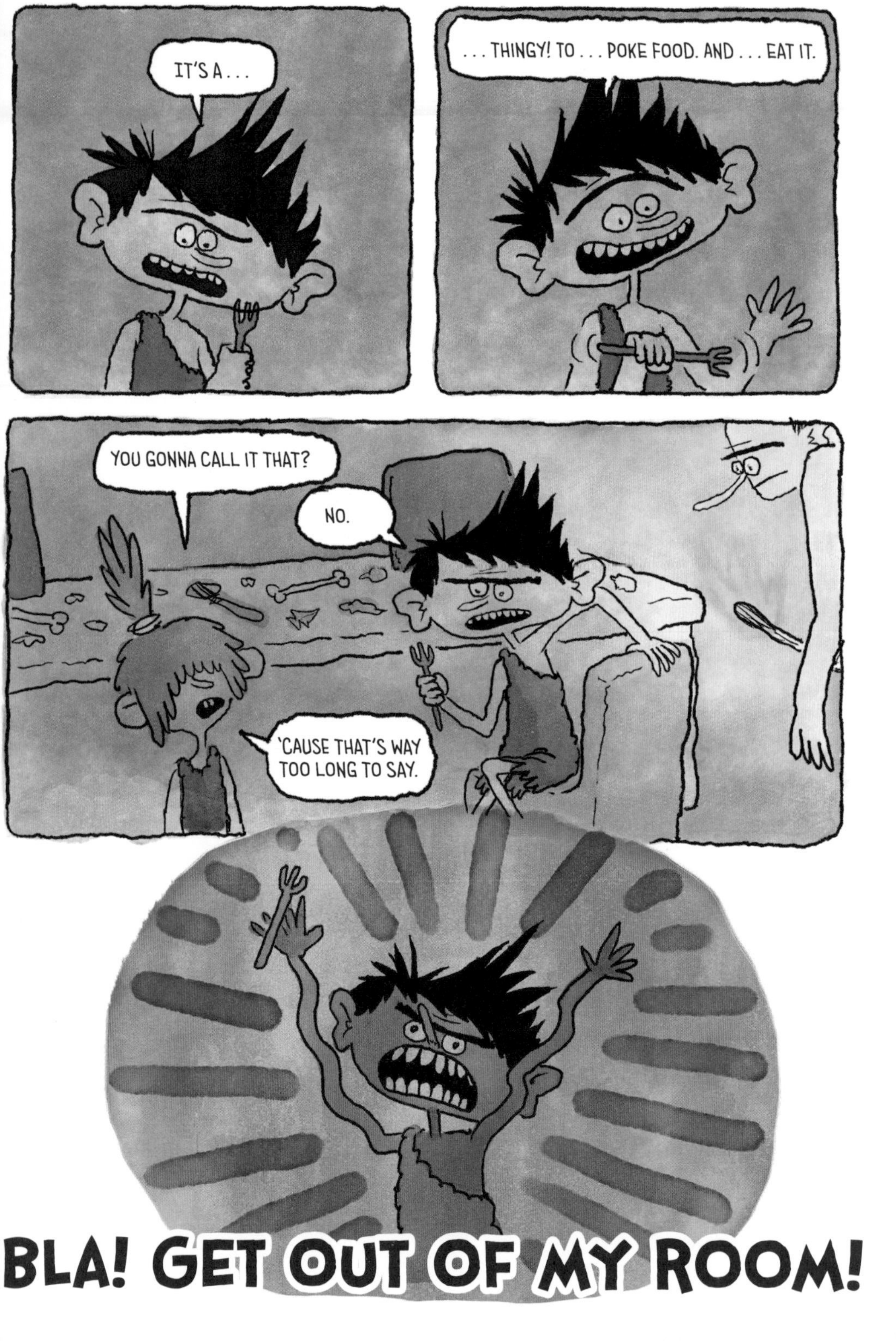
IT'S A . . .
. . . THINGY! TO . . . POKE FOOD. AND . . . EAT IT.
YOU GONNA CALL IT THAT?
NO.
'CAUSE THAT'S WAY TOO LONG TO SAY.
BLA! GET OUT OF MY ROOM!

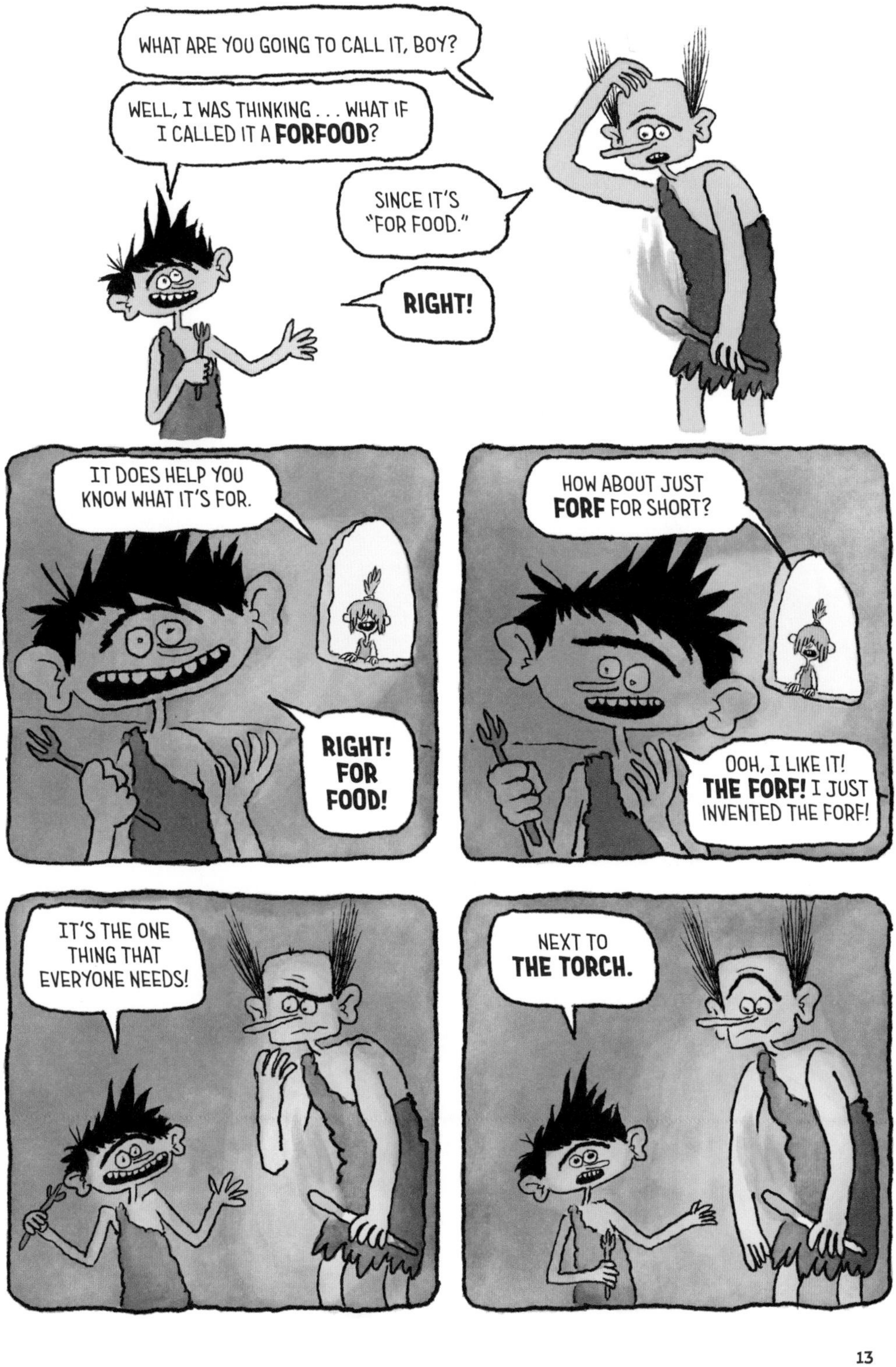

WHAT ARE YOU GOING TO CALL IT, BOY?
WELL, I WAS THINKING . . . WHAT IF I CALLED IT A **FORFOOD**?
SINCE IT'S "FOR FOOD."
RIGHT!
IT DOES HELP YOU KNOW WHAT IT'S FOR.
RIGHT! FOR FOOD!
HOW ABOUT JUST **FORF** FOR SHORT?
OOH, I LIKE IT! **THE FORF!** I JUST INVENTED THE FORF!
IT'S THE ONE THING THAT EVERYONE NEEDS!
NEXT TO **THE TORCH.**

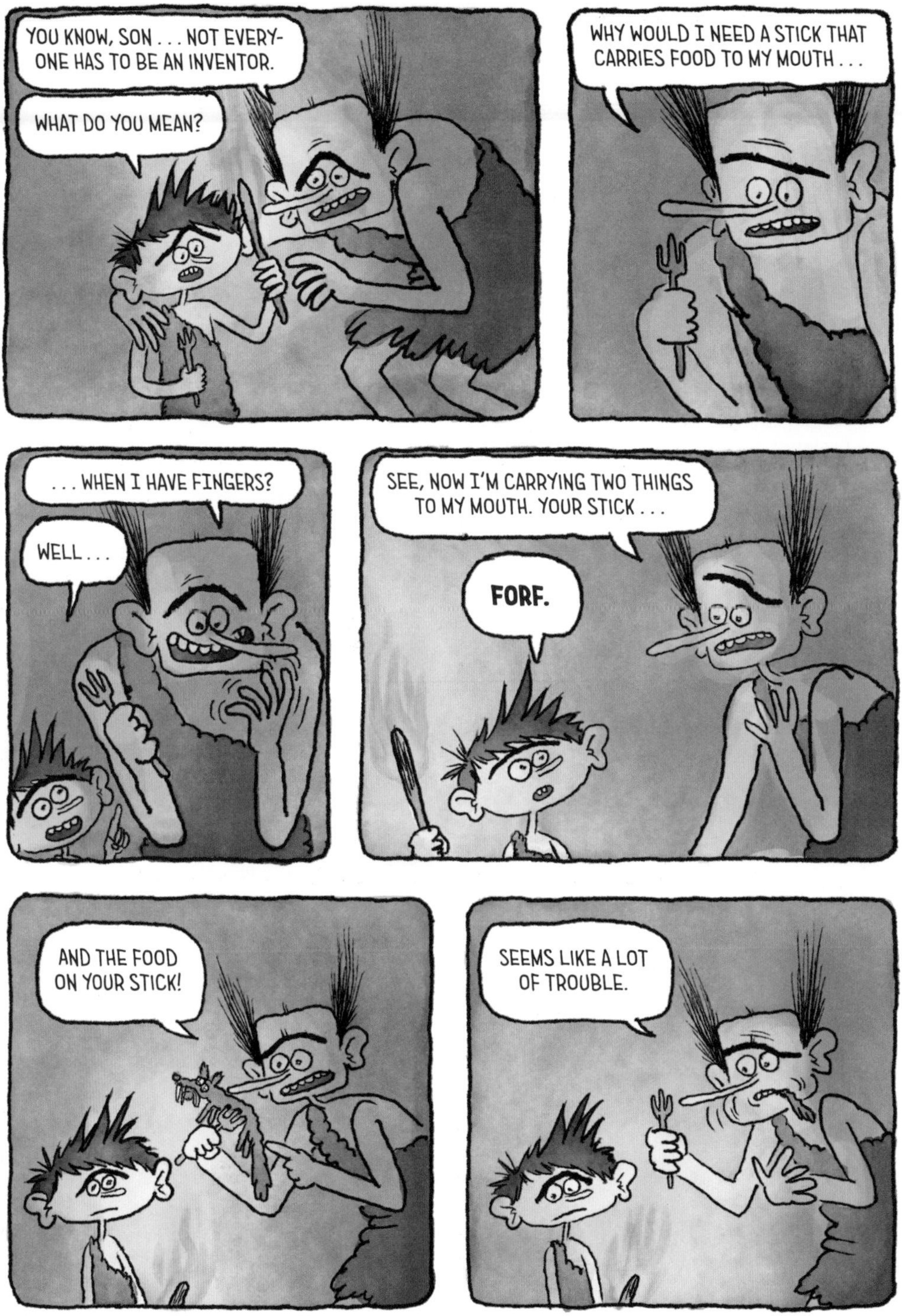
YOU KNOW, SON . . . NOT EVERY-ONE HAS TO BE AN INVENTOR.
WHAT DO YOU MEAN?
WHY WOULD I NEED A STICK THAT CARRIES FOOD TO MY MOUTH . . .
. . . WHEN I HAVE FINGERS?
WELL . . .
SEE, NOW I'M CARRYING TWO THINGS TO MY MOUTH. YOUR STICK . . .
FORF.
AND THE FOOD ON YOUR STICK!
SEEMS LIKE A LOT OF TROUBLE.

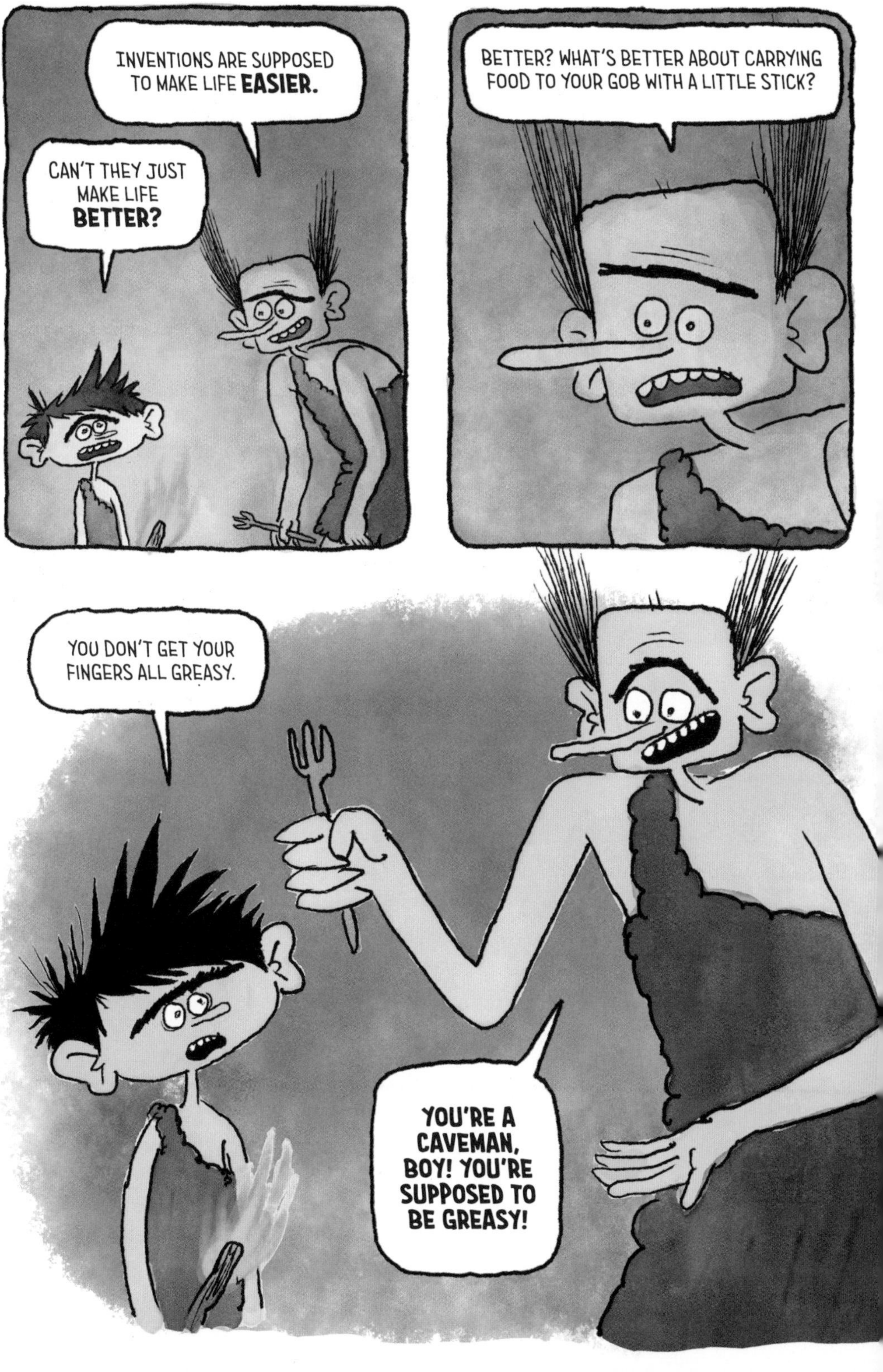
INVENTIONS ARE SUPPOSED TO MAKE LIFE **EASIER.**
CAN'T THEY JUST MAKE LIFE **BETTER?**
BETTER? WHAT'S BETTER ABOUT CARRYING FOOD TO YOUR GOB WITH A LITTLE STICK?
YOU DON'T GET YOUR FINGERS ALL GREASY.
YOU'RE A CAVEMAN, BOY! YOU'RE SUPPOSED TO BE GREASY!

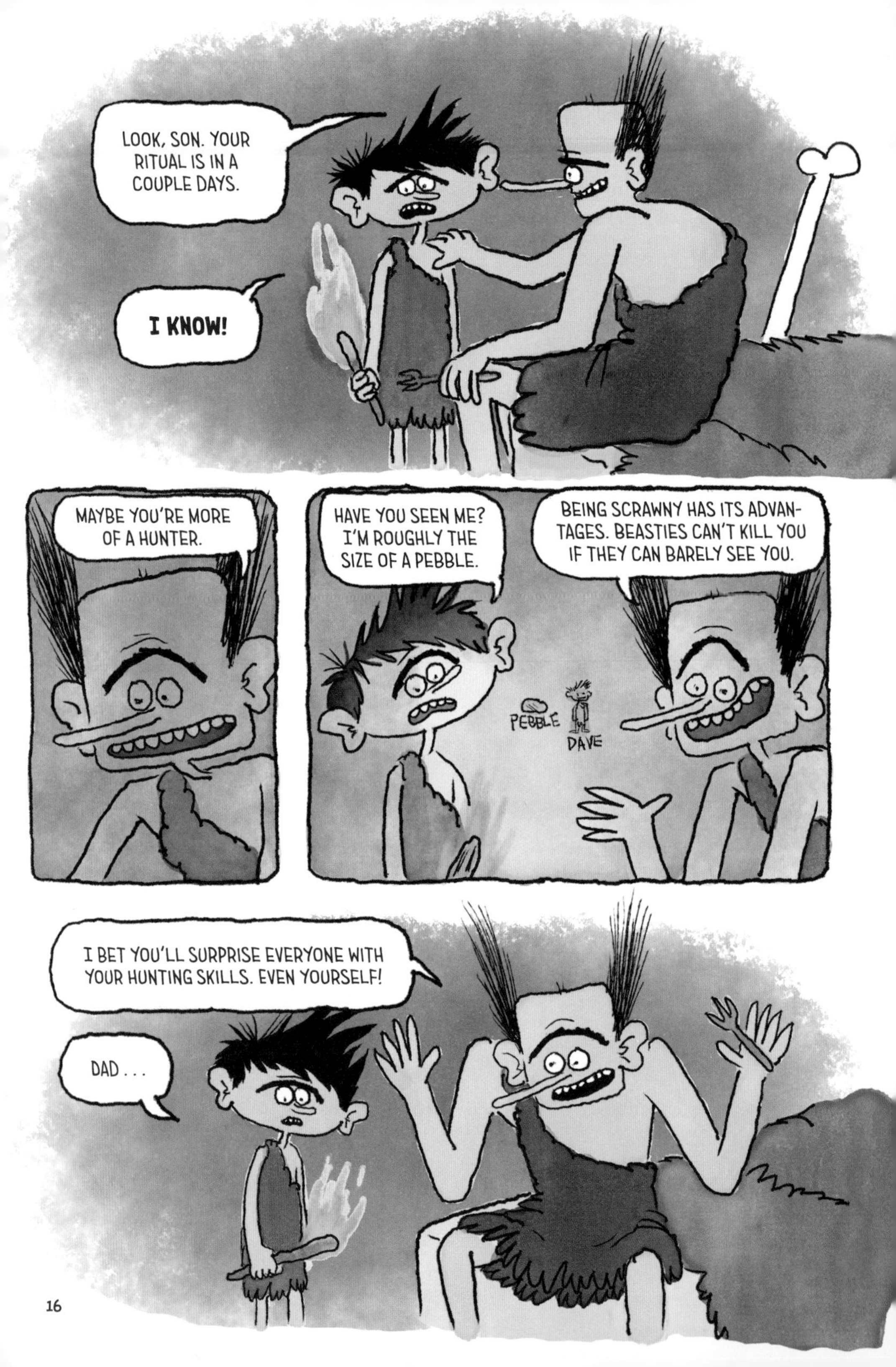
LOOK, SON. YOUR RITUAL IS IN A COUPLE DAYS.
I KNOW!
MAYBE YOU'RE MORE OF A HUNTER.
HAVE YOU SEEN ME? I'M ROUGHLY THE SIZE OF A PEBBLE.
PEBBLE
DAVE
BEING SCRAWNY HAS ITS ADVANTAGES. BEASTIES CAN'T KILL YOU IF THEY CAN BARELY SEE YOU.
I BET YOU'LL SURPRISE EVERYONE WITH YOUR HUNTING SKILLS. EVEN YOURSELF!
DAD . . .

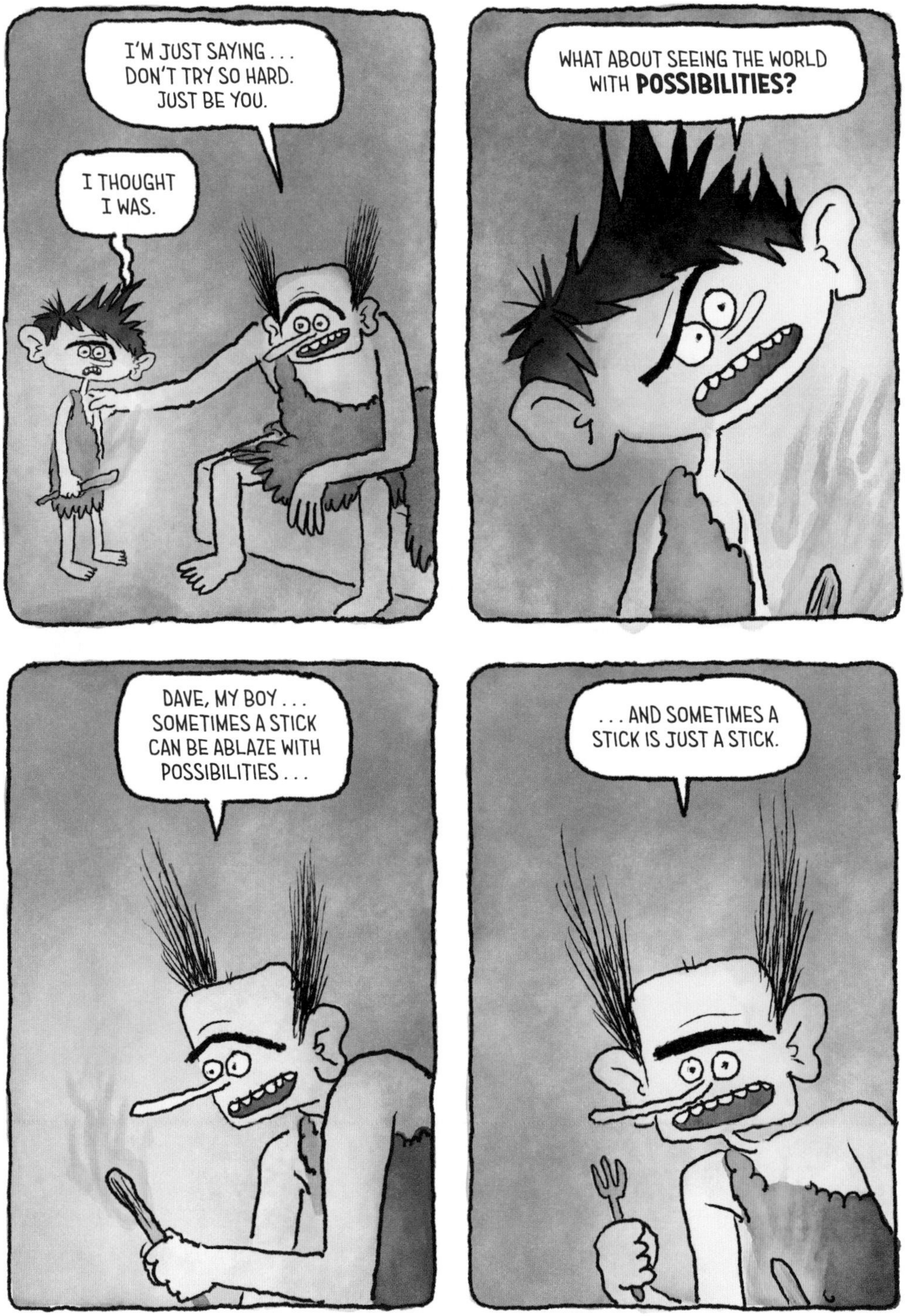
I'M JUST SAYING . . .
DON'T TRY SO HARD.
JUST BE YOU.
I THOUGHT
I WAS.
WHAT ABOUT SEEING THE WORLD
WITH POSSIBILITIES?
DAVE, MY BOY . . .
SOMETIMES A STICK
CAN BE ABLAZE WITH
POSSIBILITIES . . .
. . . AND SOMETIMES A
STICK IS JUST A STICK.

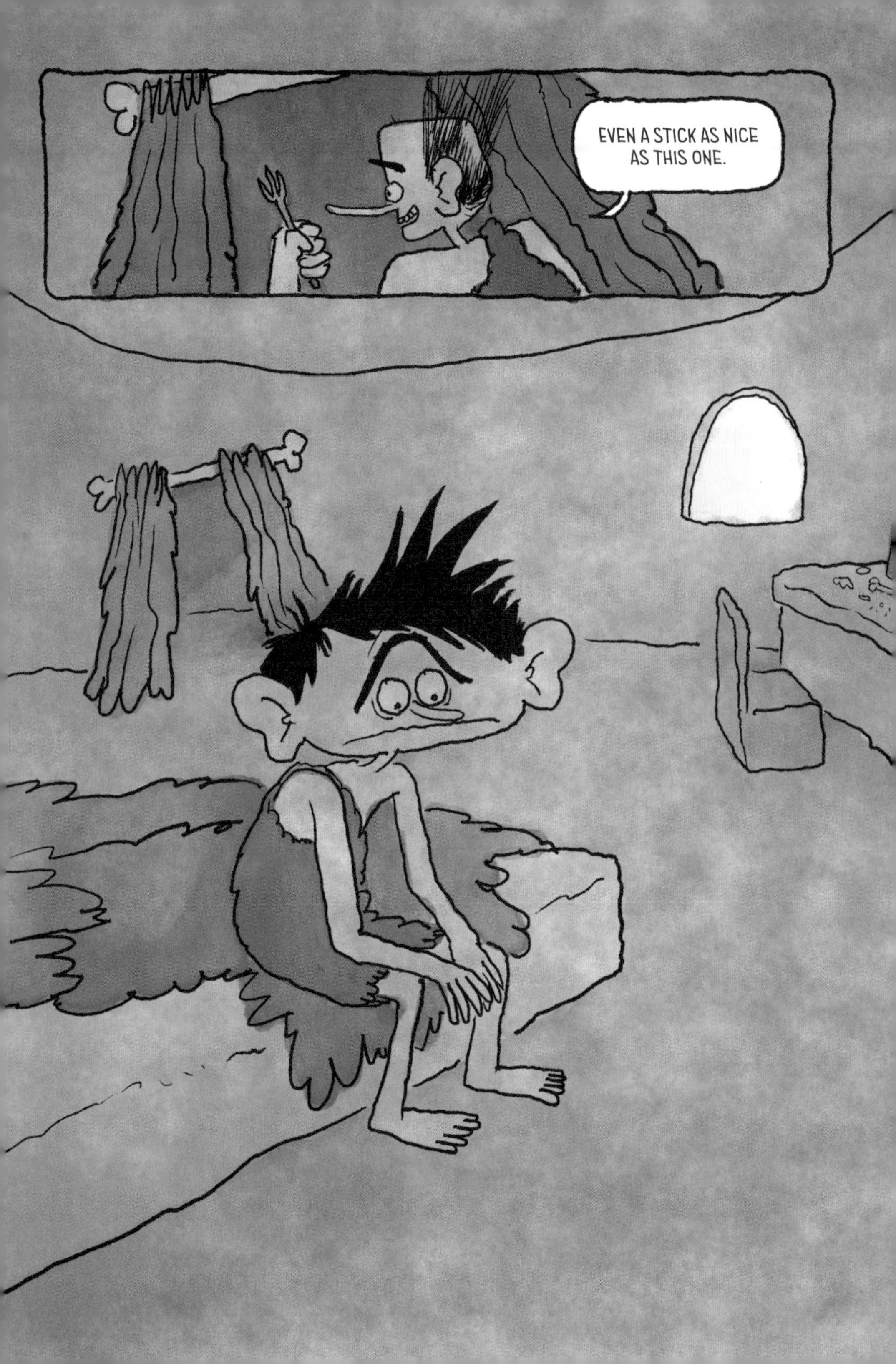
EVEN A STICK AS NICE AS THIS ONE.

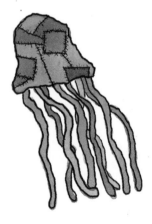

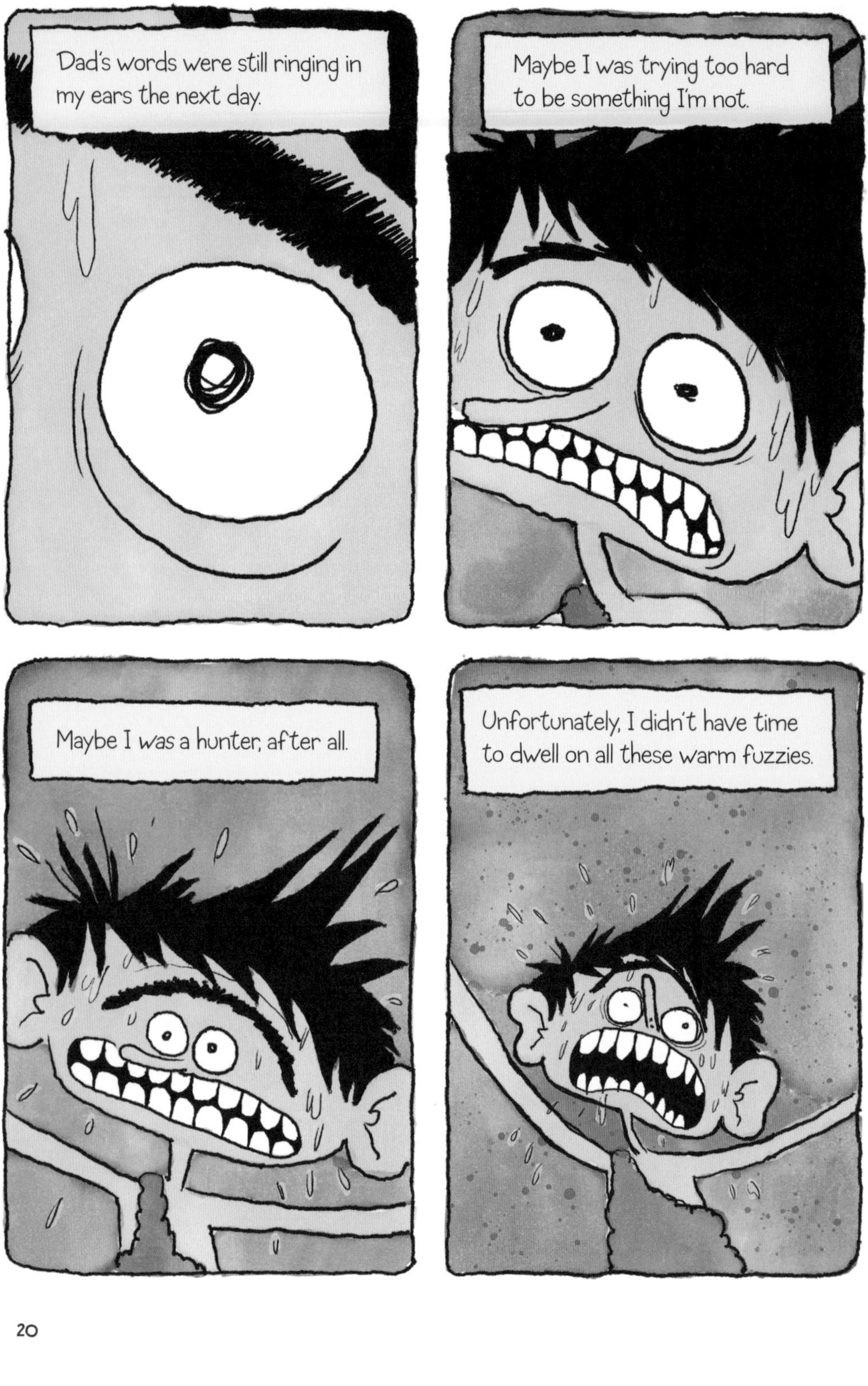
Dad's words were still ringing in my ears the next day.
Maybe I was trying too hard to be something I'm not.
Maybe I *was* a hunter, after all.
Unfortunately, I didn't have time to dwell on all these warm fuzzies.

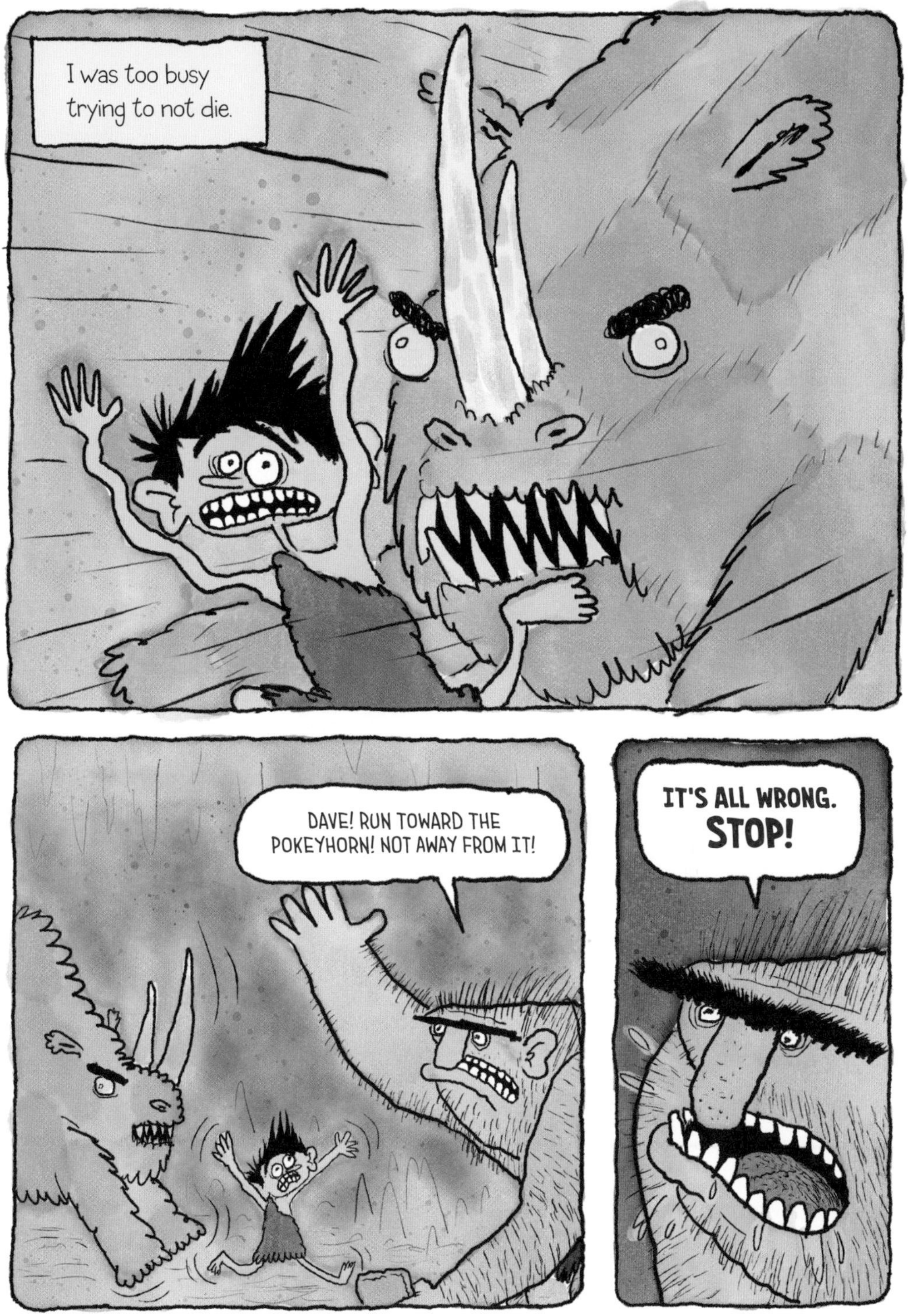
I was too busy trying to not die.
DAVE! RUN TOWARD THE POKEYHORN! NOT AWAY FROM IT!
IT'S ALL WRONG. STOP!

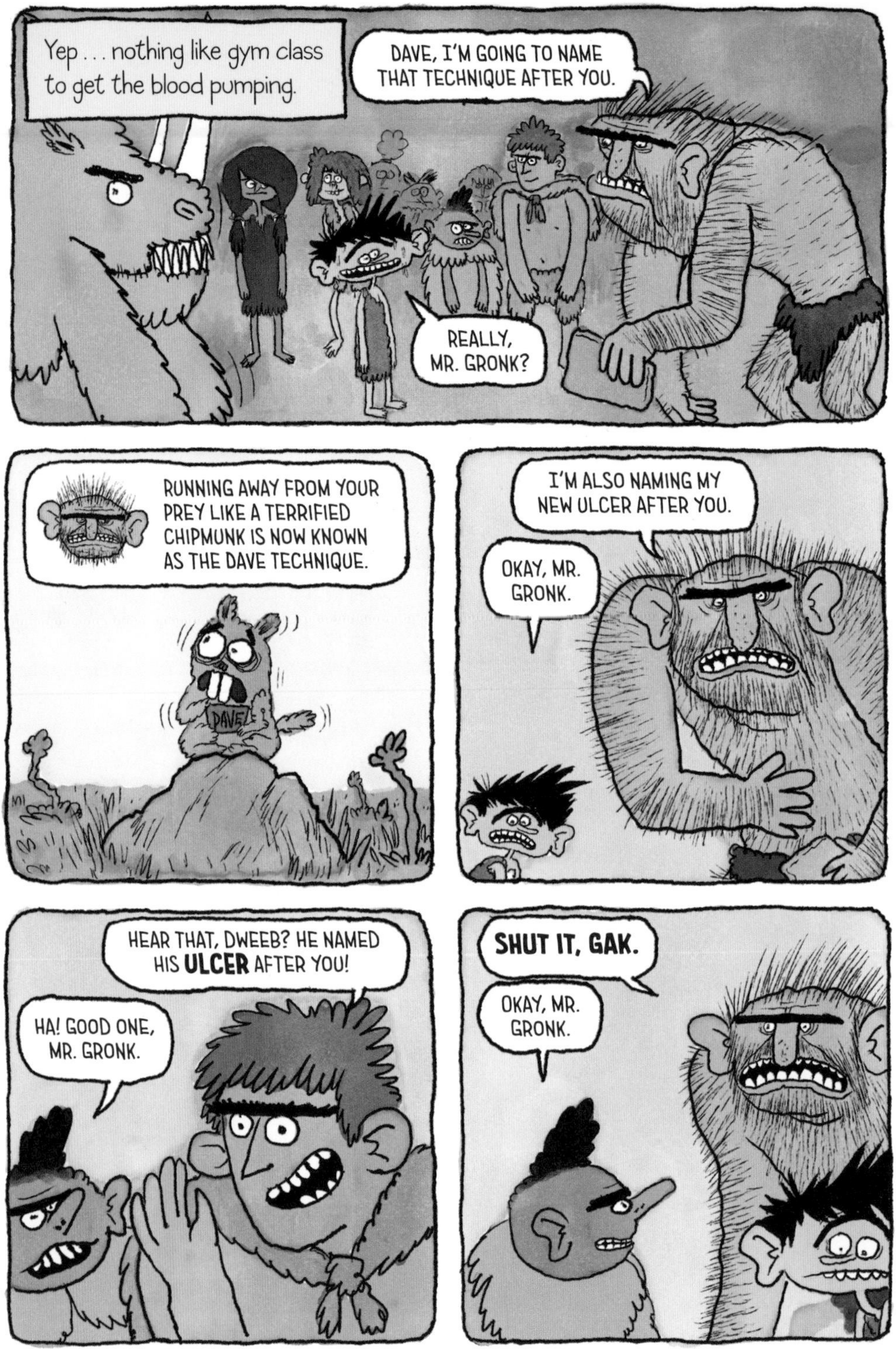
Yep . . . nothing like gym class to get the blood pumping.
DAVE, I'M GOING TO NAME THAT TECHNIQUE AFTER YOU.
REALLY, MR. GRONK?
RUNNING AWAY FROM YOUR PREY LIKE A TERRIFIED CHIPMUNK IS NOW KNOWN AS THE DAVE TECHNIQUE.
DAVE
I'M ALSO NAMING MY NEW ULCER AFTER YOU.
OKAY, MR. GRONK.
HEAR THAT, DWEEB? HE NAMED HIS **ULCER** AFTER YOU!
HA! GOOD ONE, MR. GRONK.
SHUT IT, GAK.
OKAY, MR. GRONK.

THIS IS **HUNTING 101**, NOT RUNNY-RUNNY CLASS.

YOUR BABY-GO-BOOM RITUAL IS TOMORROW! **TOMORROW!**

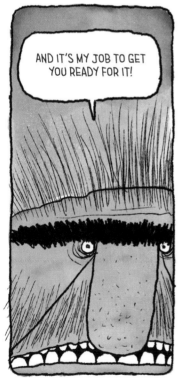

AND IT'S MY JOB TO GET YOU READY FOR IT!

LIKE IT OR NOT, YOU'RE THE NEW GENERATION OF MEAT-BRINGERS.

MEAT-BRINGERS

AND THE **BEST** MEAT . . . THE **ONLY** MEAT . . . COMES FROM THE **BIG SIX**.

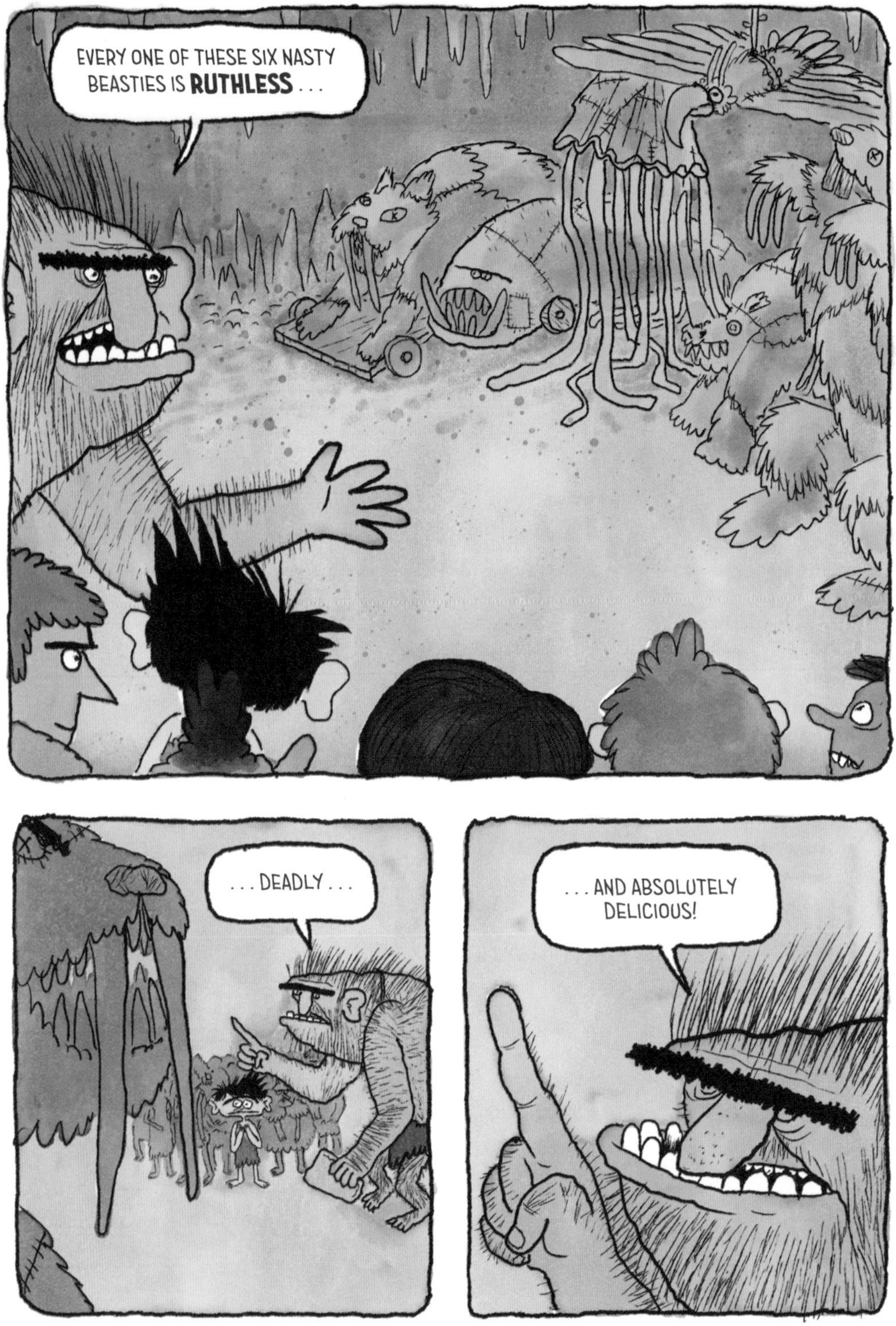
EVERY ONE OF THESE SIX NASTY BEASTIES IS **RUTHLESS** . . .
. . . DEADLY . . .
. . . AND ABSOLUTELY DELICIOUS!

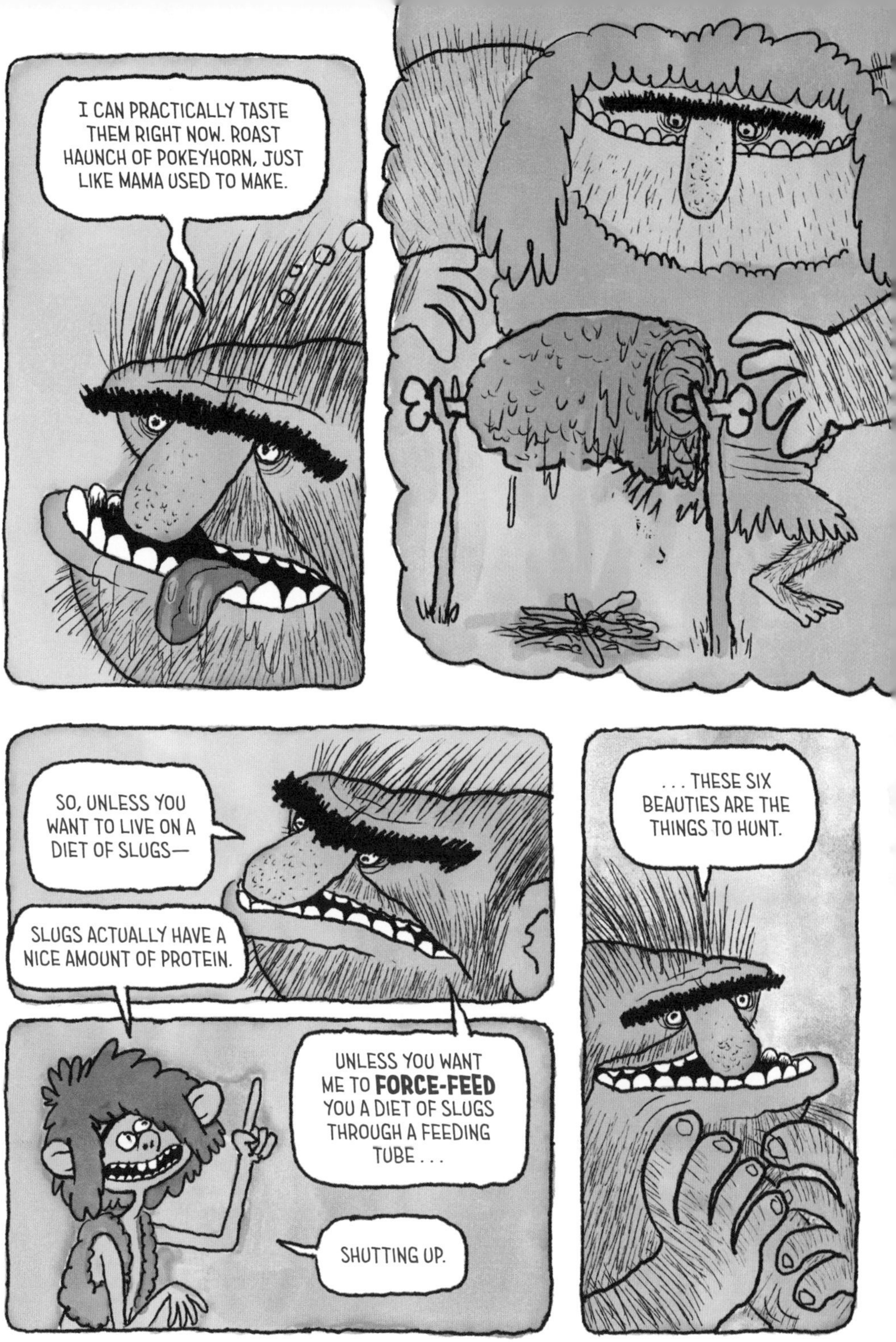
I CAN PRACTICALLY TASTE THEM RIGHT NOW. ROAST HAUNCH OF POKEYHORN, JUST LIKE MAMA USED TO MAKE.
SO, UNLESS YOU WANT TO LIVE ON A DIET OF SLUGS—
SLUGS ACTUALLY HAVE A NICE AMOUNT OF PROTEIN.
UNLESS YOU WANT ME TO **FORCE-FEED** YOU A DIET OF SLUGS THROUGH A FEEDING TUBE . . .
SHUTTING UP.
. . . THESE SIX BEAUTIES ARE THE THINGS TO HUNT.

NUMBER SIX: THE BUCK-TOOTHED **SLOTHOPOD**.

NUMBER FIVE: THE BLOODTHIRSTY **POKEYHORN**, A MEAT-BRINGER FAVORITE.

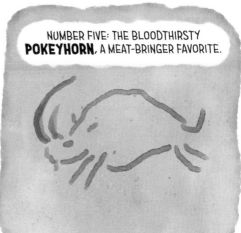

NUMBER FOUR: THE FLYING **RIPPY-BEAK**.

NUMBER THREE: THE GIANT **BLOBBY-GOO**.

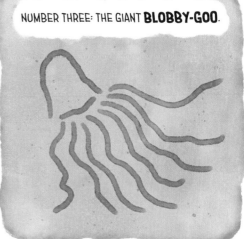

NUMBER TWO: THE **SLUGASAURUS**.

AND NASTY NUMBER ONE . . . THE **STABBY-CAT**.

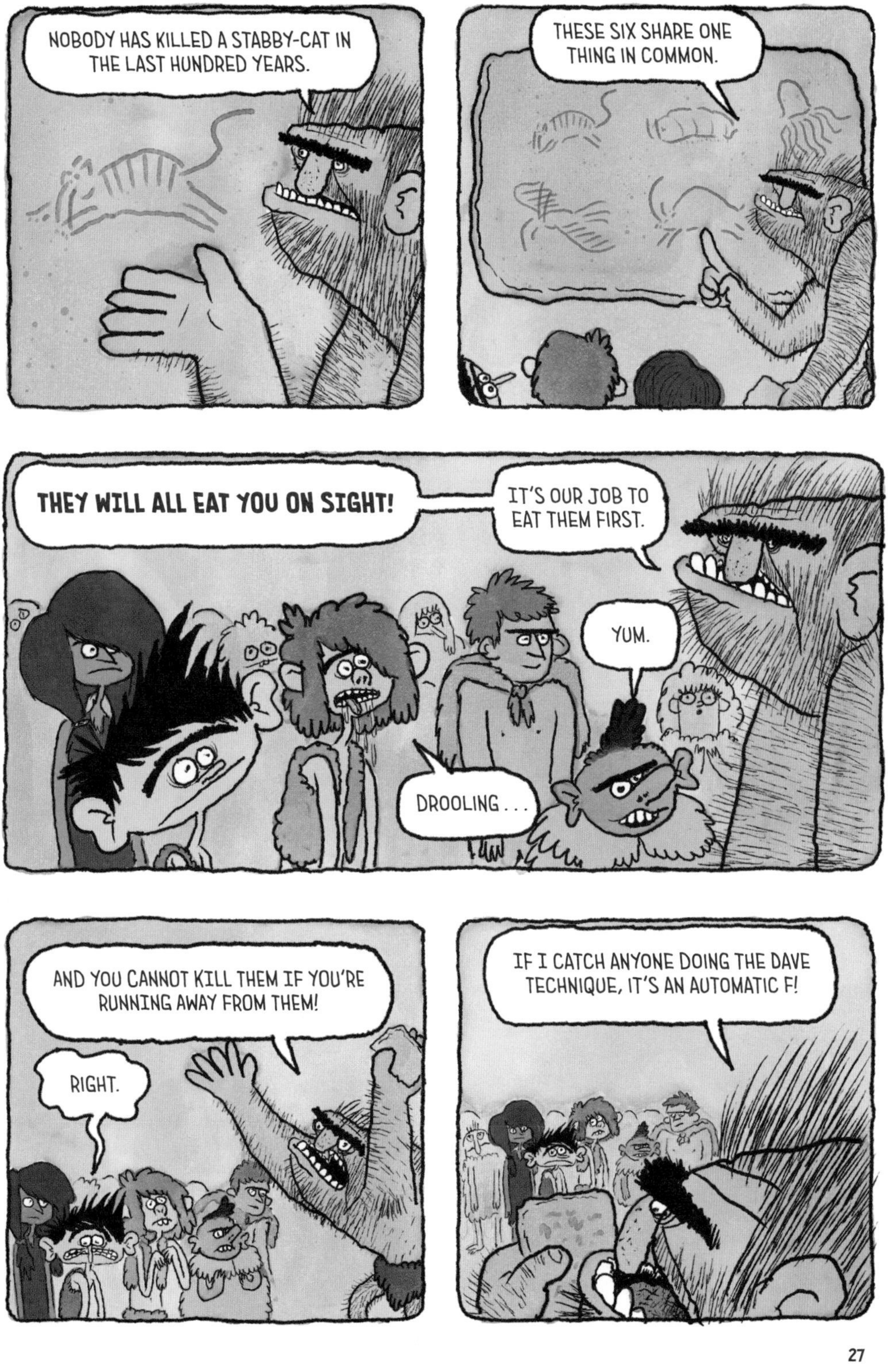
NOBODY HAS KILLED A STABBY-CAT IN THE LAST HUNDRED YEARS.
THESE SIX SHARE ONE THING IN COMMON.
THEY WILL ALL EAT YOU ON SIGHT!
IT'S OUR JOB TO EAT THEM FIRST.
YUM.
DROOLING . . .
AND YOU CANNOT KILL THEM IF YOU'RE RUNNING AWAY FROM THEM!
RIGHT.
IF I CATCH ANYONE DOING THE DAVE TECHNIQUE, IT'S AN AUTOMATIC F!

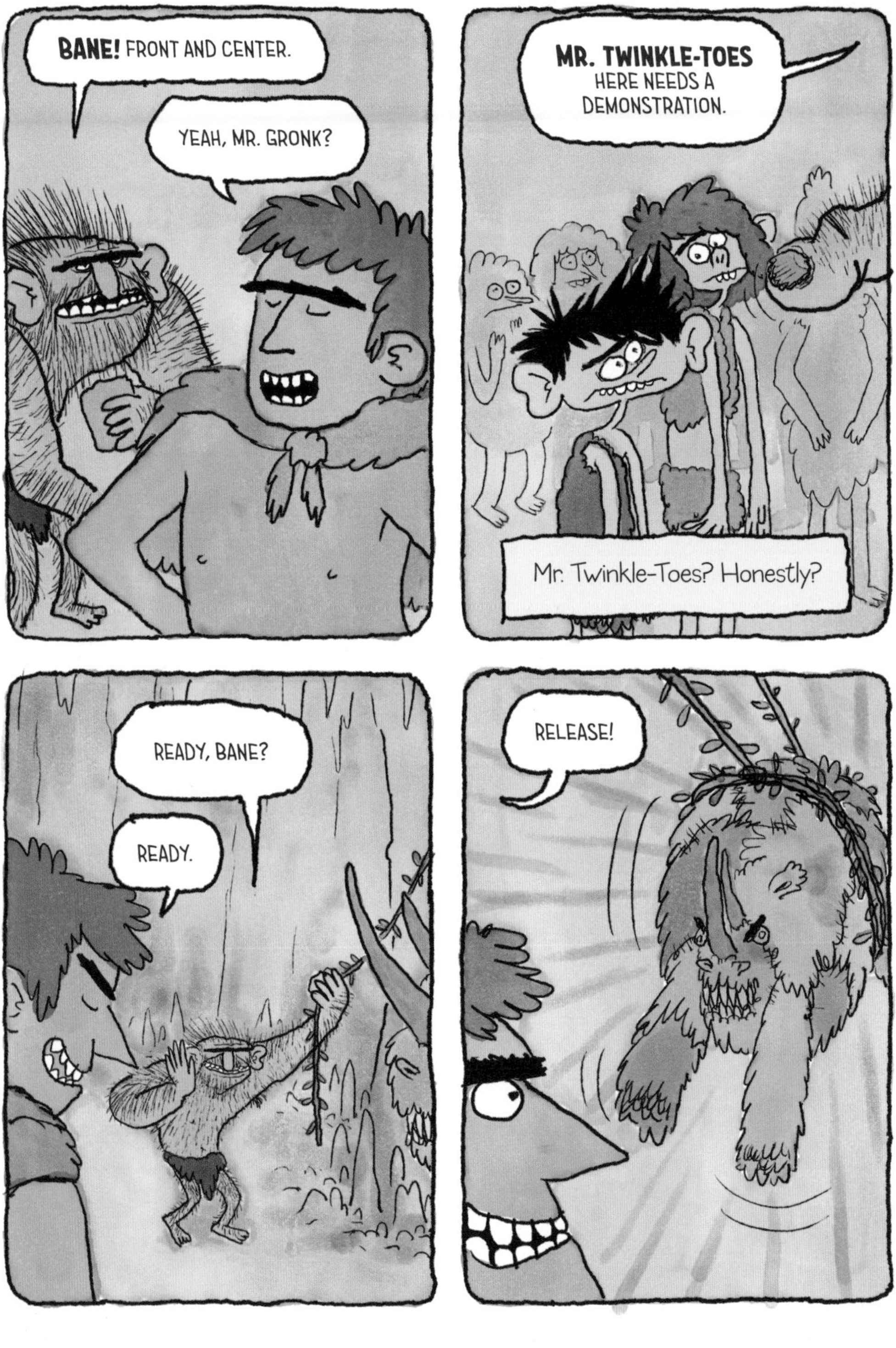
BANE! FRONT AND CENTER.
YEAH, MR. GRONK?
MR. TWINKLE-TOES HERE NEEDS A DEMONSTRATION.
Mr. Twinkle-Toes? Honestly?
READY, BANE?
READY.
RELEASE!

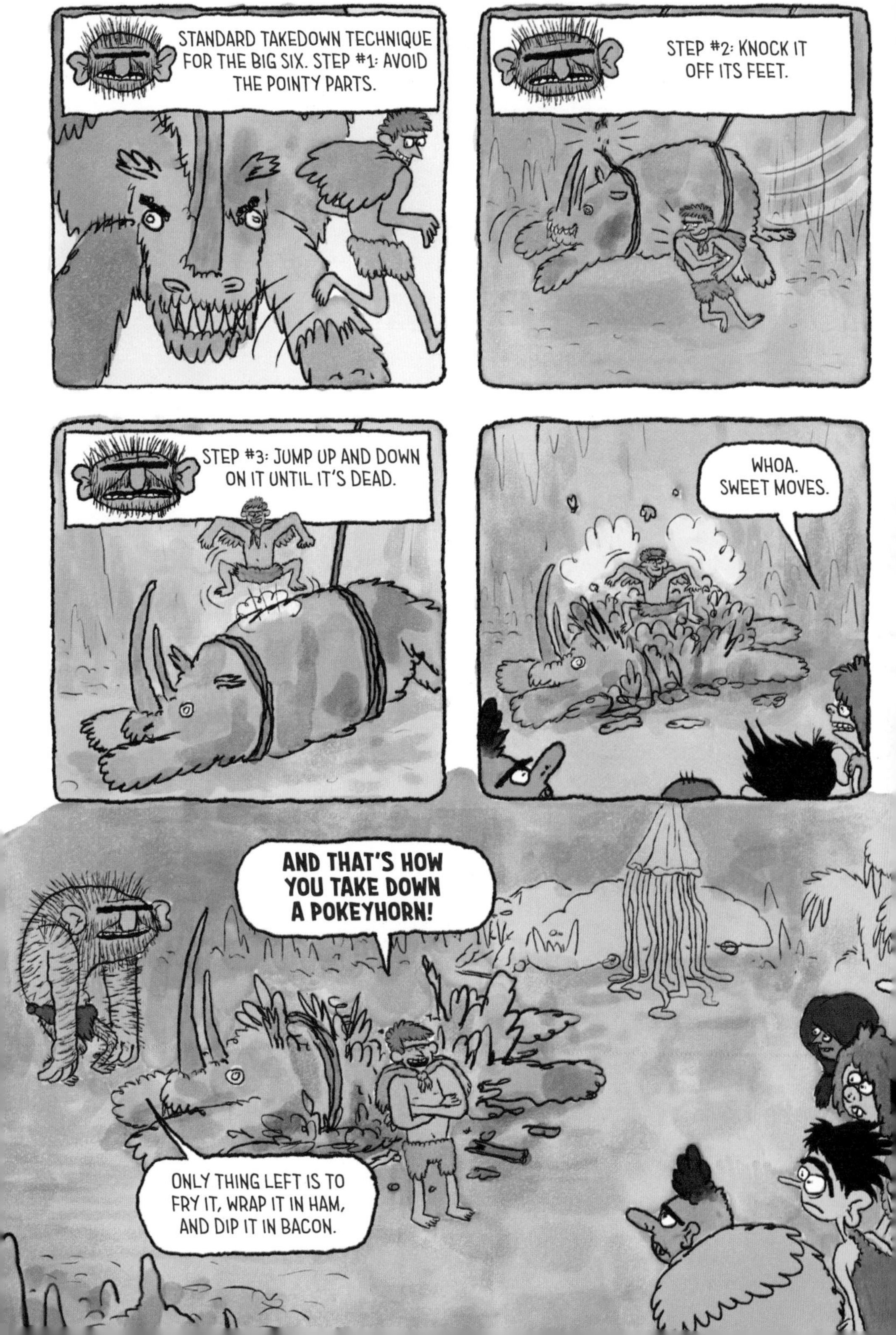
STANDARD TAKEDOWN TECHNIQUE FOR THE BIG SIX. STEP #1: AVOID THE POINTY PARTS.
STEP #2: KNOCK IT OFF ITS FEET.
STEP #3: JUMP UP AND DOWN ON IT UNTIL IT'S DEAD.
WHOA. SWEET MOVES.
AND THAT'S HOW YOU TAKE DOWN A POKEYHORN!
ONLY THING LEFT IS TO FRY IT, WRAP IT IN HAM, AND DIP IT IN BACON.

YOUR TURN, KID. A GIANT BLOBBY-GOO ATTACKS. THINK FAST!

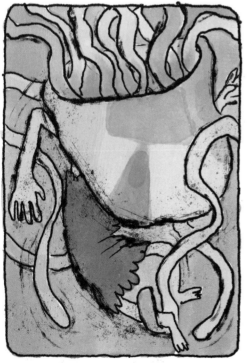

OW.

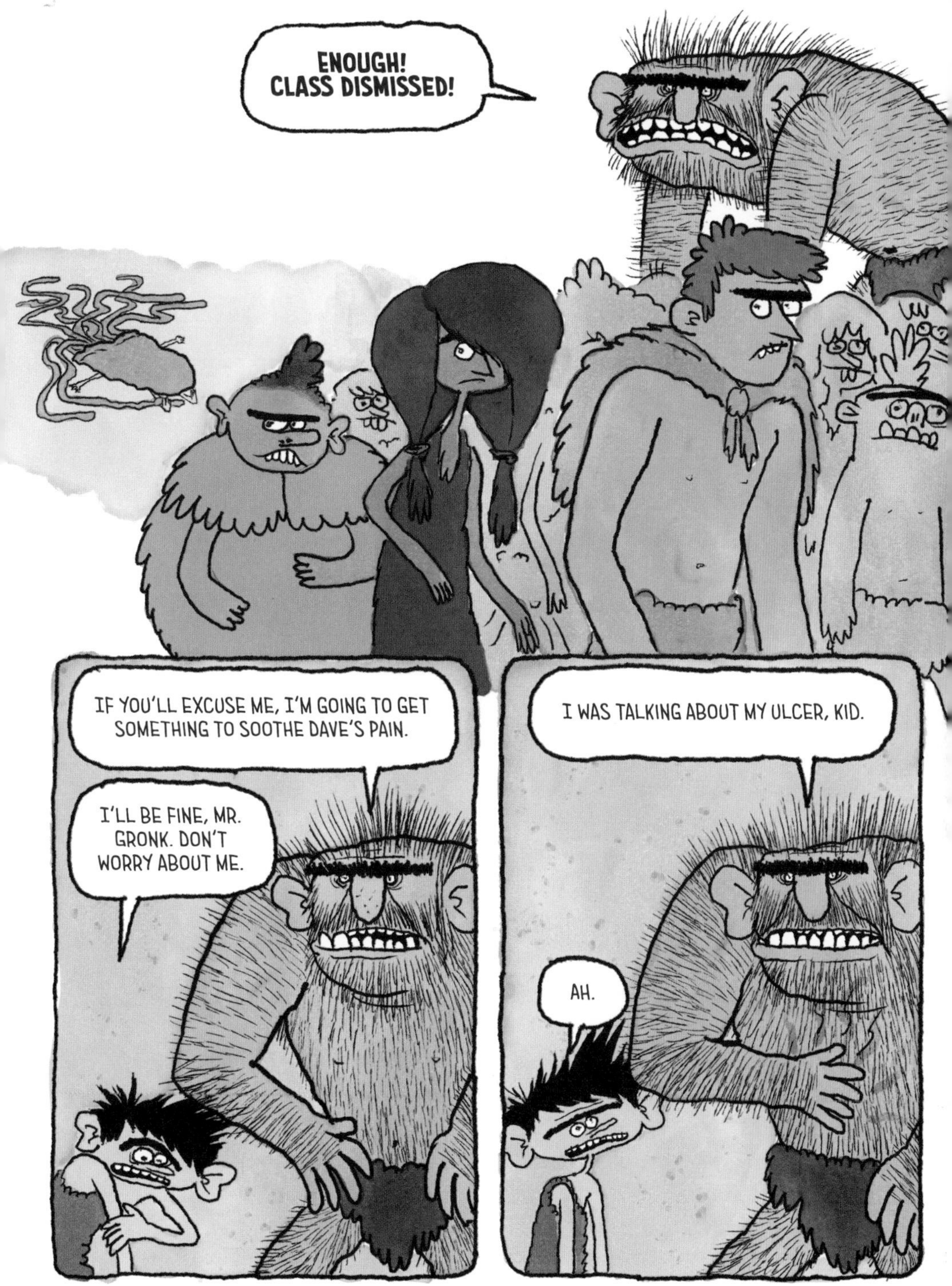
ENOUGH! CLASS DISMISSED!
IF YOU'LL EXCUSE ME, I'M GOING TO GET SOMETHING TO SOOTHE DAVE'S PAIN.
I'LL BE FINE, MR. GRONK. DON'T WORRY ABOUT ME.
I WAS TALKING ABOUT MY ULCER, KID.
AH.

ROAST POKEYHORN

(JUST LIKE MAMA USED TO MAKE)

STEP ONE: MAKE FIRE. FIRE GOOD.

STEP TWO: TIE UP POKEYHORN WITH VINES. ROLL IN BUGS FOR EXTRA CRUNCH.

STEP THREE: FIND BIG STICK. HANG POKEYHORN ON STICK.

STEP FOUR: REMEMBER FIRE? FIRE GOOD. PUT POKEYHORN OVER THE FIRE.

STEP FIVE (OPTIONAL): ATTACH BACON TO POKEYHORN FROM WARTHOG YOU CAUGHT. (YOU REAL GOOD HUNTER!)

STEP SIX: COOK POKEYHORN UNTIL BROWN AND SIZZLY. BE PATIENT. MAYBE GO DO SOMETHING ELSE TO TAKE MIND OFF TENDER, SUCCULENT POKEYHORN YOU NOT EATING. TRY A GAME OF HIT ROCK WITH STICK. ALWAYS FUN.

STEP SEVEN: EAT POKEYHORN. GET GREASY. BURP LOTS. YOU CAVEMAN, AFTER ALL.

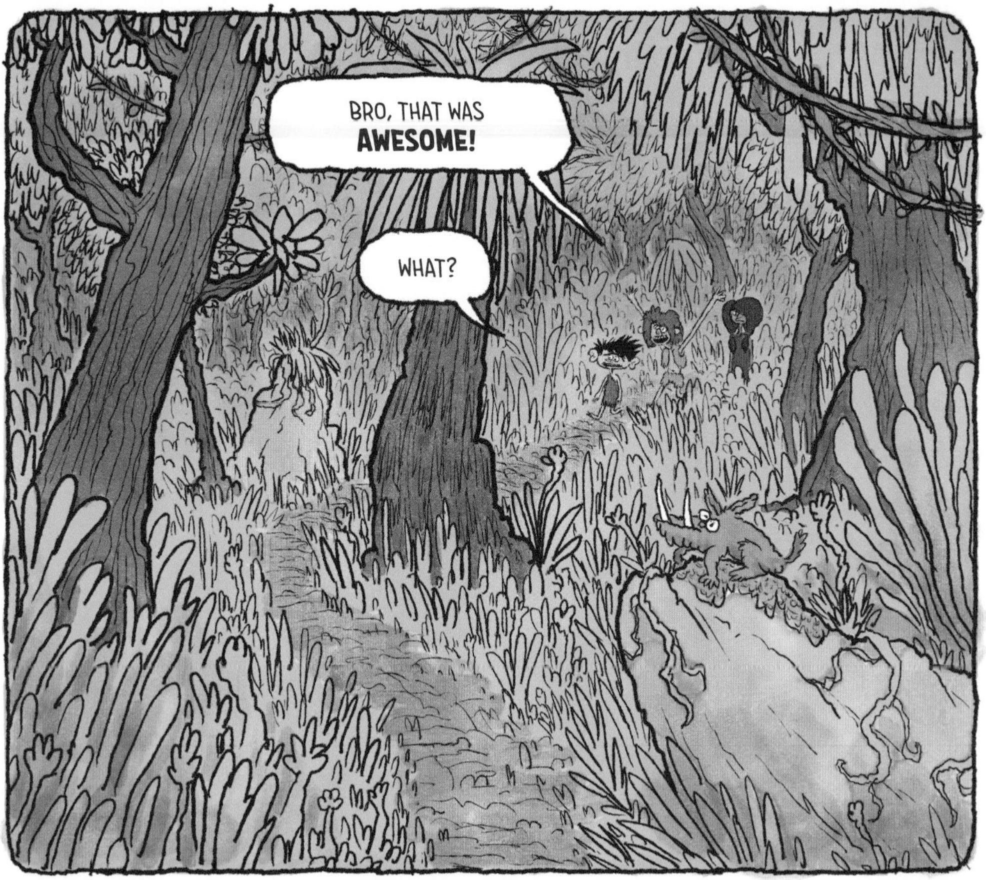
BRO, THAT WAS **AWESOME!**
WHAT?
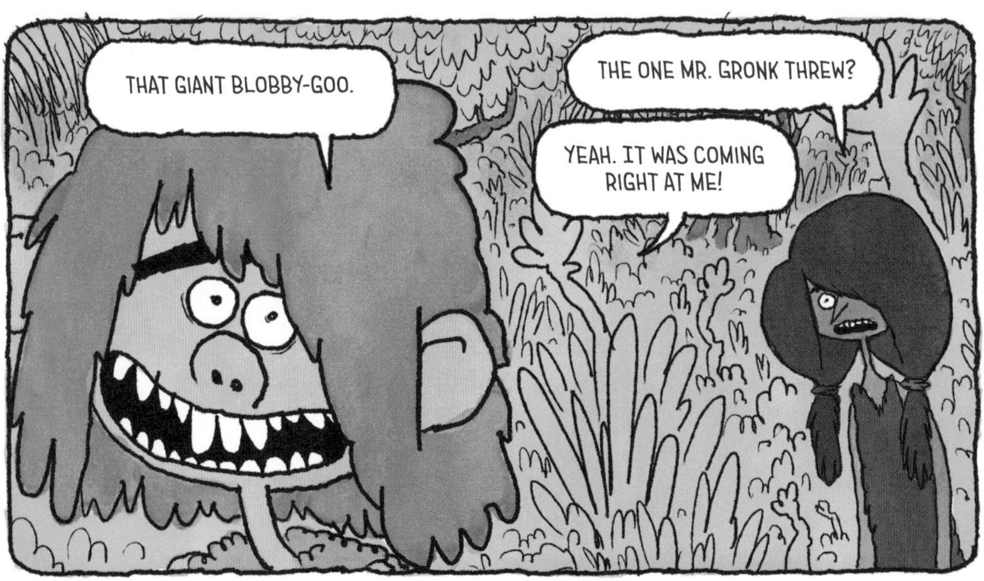
THAT GIANT BLOBBY-GOO.
THE ONE MR. GRONK THREW?
YEAH. IT WAS COMING RIGHT AT ME!

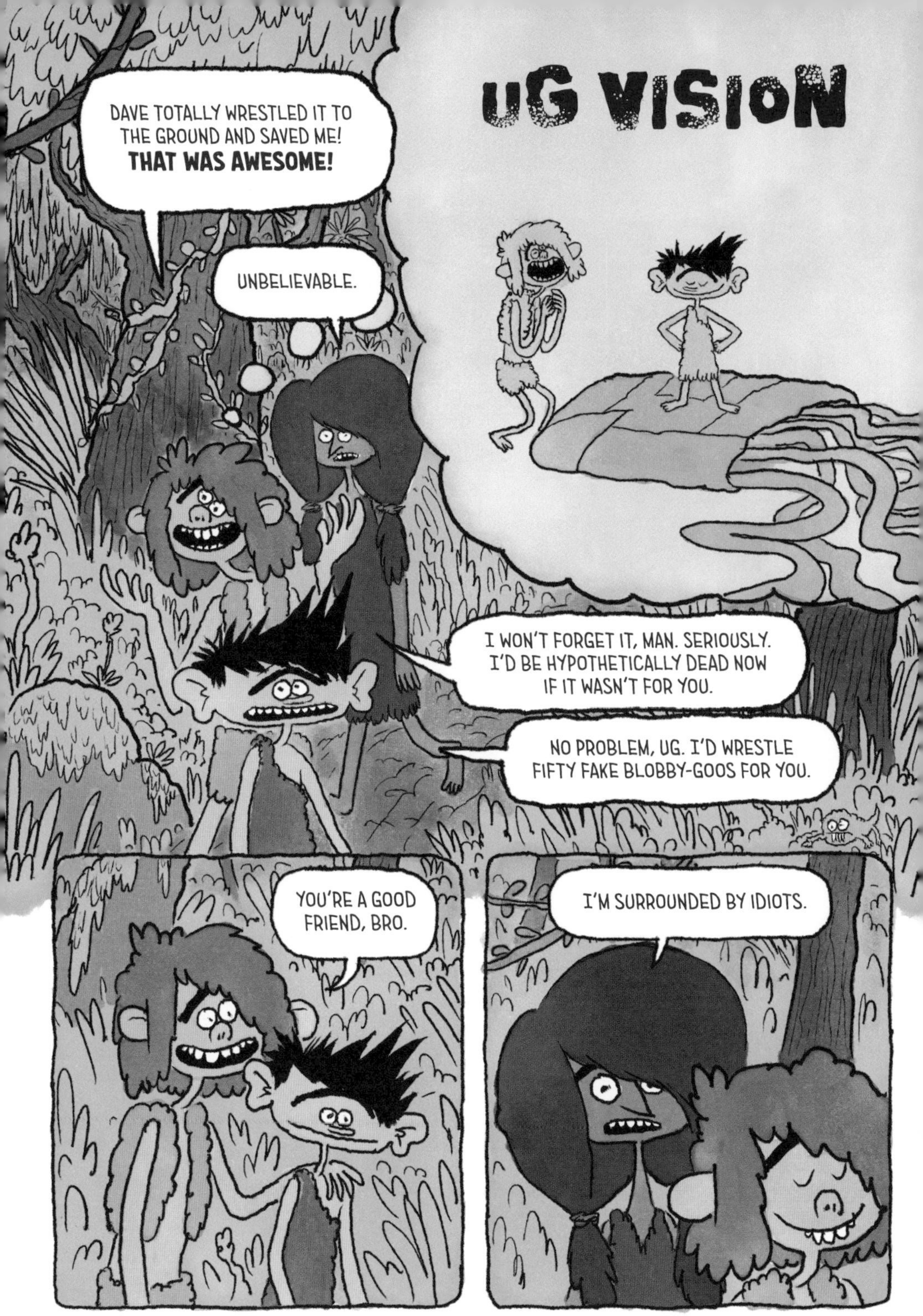
UG VISION
DAVE TOTALLY WRESTLED IT TO THE GROUND AND SAVED ME! **THAT WAS AWESOME!**
UNBELIEVABLE.
I WON'T FORGET IT, MAN. SERIOUSLY. I'D BE HYPOTHETICALLY DEAD NOW IF IT WASN'T FOR YOU.
NO PROBLEM, UG. I'D WRESTLE FIFTY FAKE BLOBBY-GOOS FOR YOU.
YOU'RE A GOOD FRIEND, BRO.
I'M SURROUNDED BY IDIOTS.

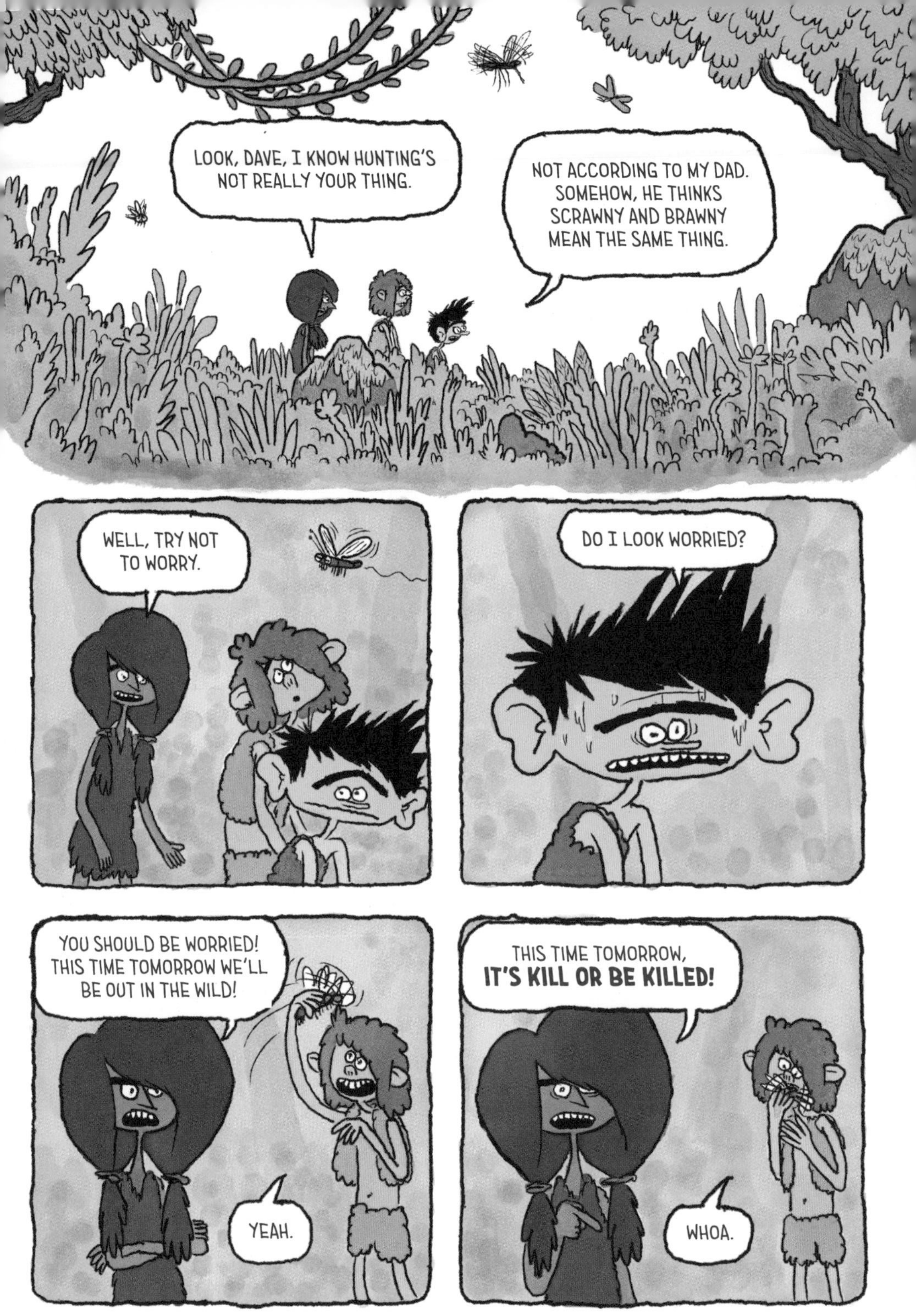
LOOK, DAVE, I KNOW HUNTING'S NOT REALLY YOUR THING.
NOT ACCORDING TO MY DAD. SOMEHOW, HE THINKS SCRAWNY AND BRAWNY MEAN THE SAME THING.
WELL, TRY NOT TO WORRY.
DO I LOOK WORRIED?
YOU SHOULD BE WORRIED! THIS TIME TOMORROW WE'LL BE OUT IN THE WILD!
YEAH.
THIS TIME TOMORROW, **IT'S KILL OR BE KILLED!**
WHOA.

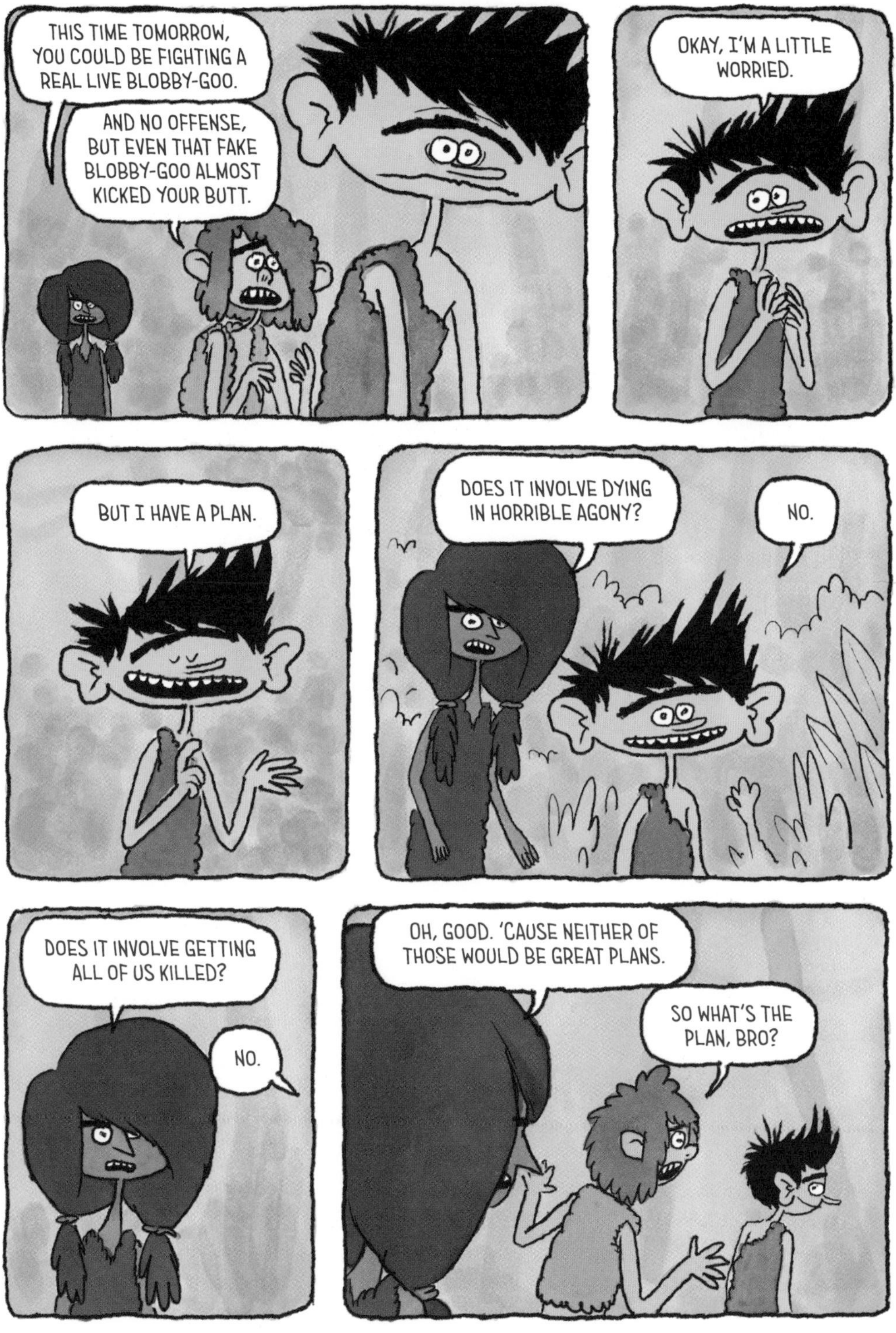
THIS TIME TOMORROW, YOU COULD BE FIGHTING A REAL LIVE BLOBBY-GOO.
AND NO OFFENSE, BUT EVEN THAT FAKE BLOBBY-GOO ALMOST KICKED YOUR BUTT.
OKAY, I'M A LITTLE WORRIED.
BUT I HAVE A PLAN.
DOES IT INVOLVE DYING IN HORRIBLE AGONY?
NO.
DOES IT INVOLVE GETTING ALL OF US KILLED?
NO.
OH, GOOD. 'CAUSE NEITHER OF THOSE WOULD BE GREAT PLANS.
SO WHAT'S THE PLAN, BRO?

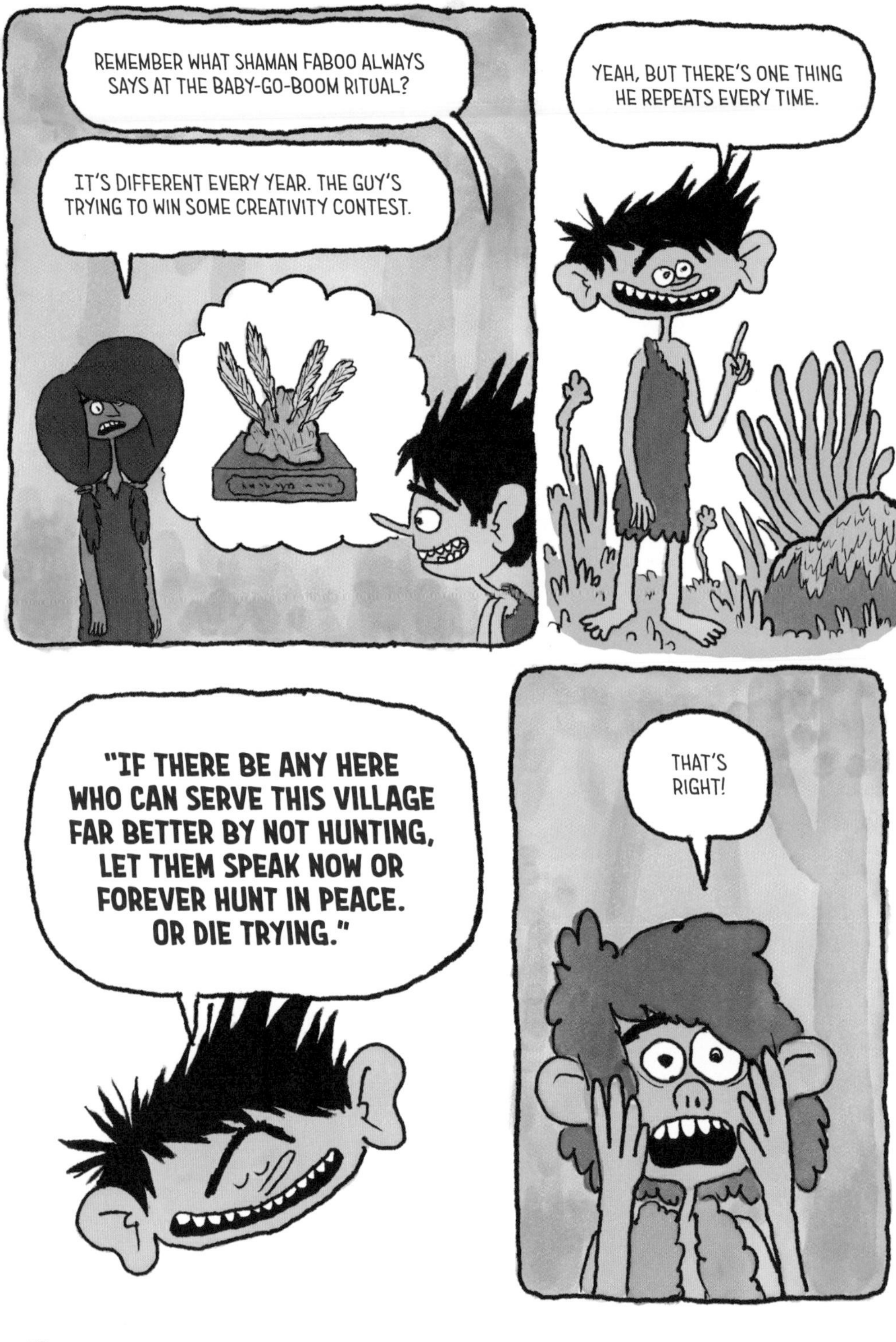
REMEMBER WHAT SHAMAN FABOO ALWAYS SAYS AT THE BABY-GO-BOOM RITUAL?
IT'S DIFFERENT EVERY YEAR. THE GUY'S TRYING TO WIN SOME CREATIVITY CONTEST.
YEAH, BUT THERE'S ONE THING HE REPEATS EVERY TIME.
"IF THERE BE ANY HERE WHO CAN SERVE THIS VILLAGE FAR BETTER BY NOT HUNTING, LET THEM SPEAK NOW OR FOREVER HUNT IN PEACE. OR DIE TRYING."
THAT'S RIGHT!

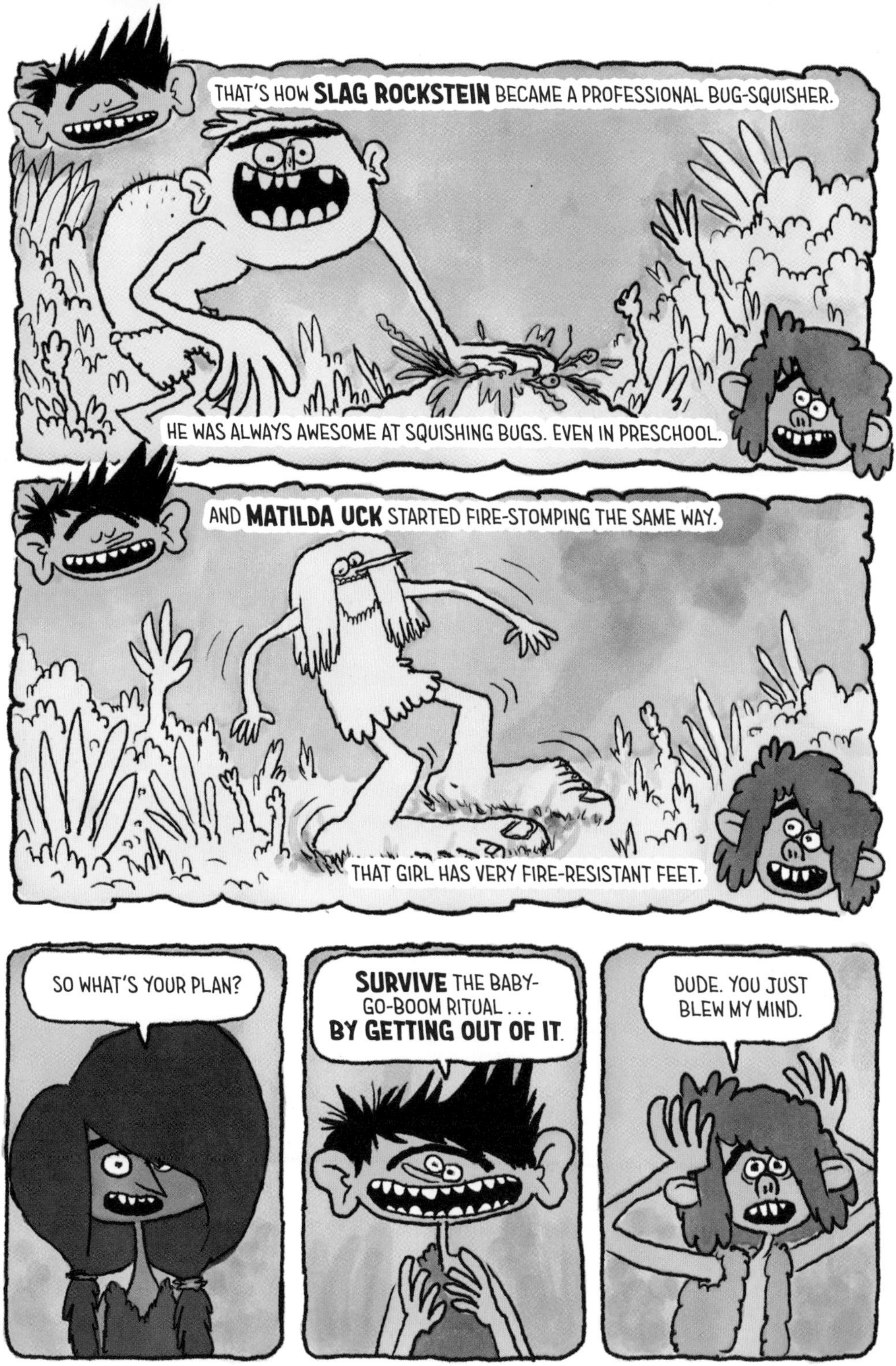
THAT'S HOW SLAG ROCKSTEIN BECAME A PROFESSIONAL BUG-SQUISHER.
HE WAS ALWAYS AWESOME AT SQUISHING BUGS. EVEN IN PRESCHOOL.
AND MATILDA UCK STARTED FIRE-STOMPING THE SAME WAY.
THAT GIRL HAS VERY FIRE-RESISTANT FEET.
SO WHAT'S YOUR PLAN?
SURVIVE THE BABY-GO-BOOM RITUAL . . . BY GETTING OUT OF IT.
DUDE. YOU JUST BLEW MY MIND.

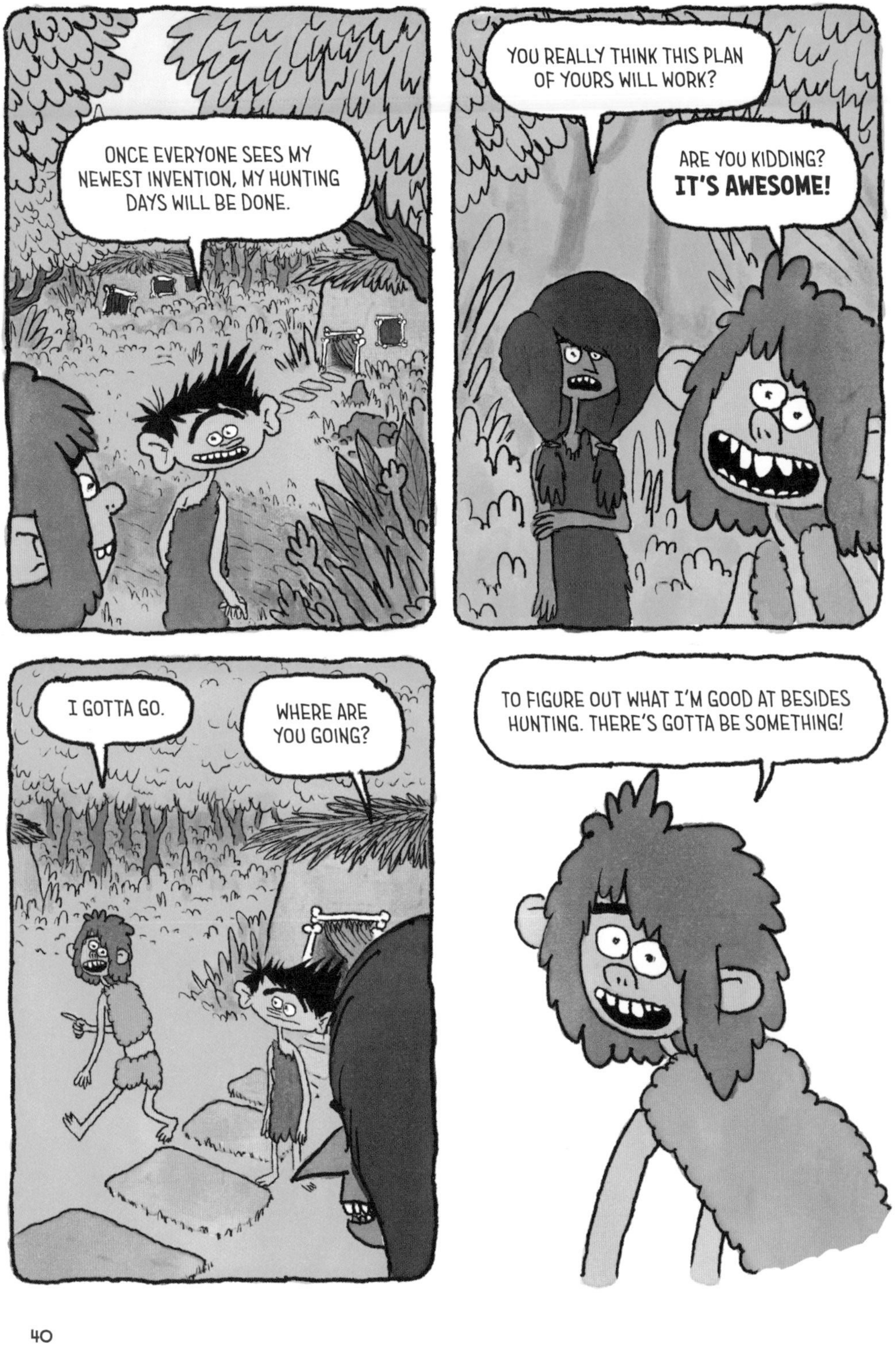
ONCE EVERYONE SEES MY NEWEST INVENTION, MY HUNTING DAYS WILL BE DONE.
YOU REALLY THINK THIS PLAN OF YOURS WILL WORK?
ARE YOU KIDDING? **IT'S AWESOME!**
I GOTTA GO.
WHERE ARE YOU GOING?
TO FIGURE OUT WHAT I'M GOOD AT BESIDES HUNTING. THERE'S GOTTA BE SOMETHING!

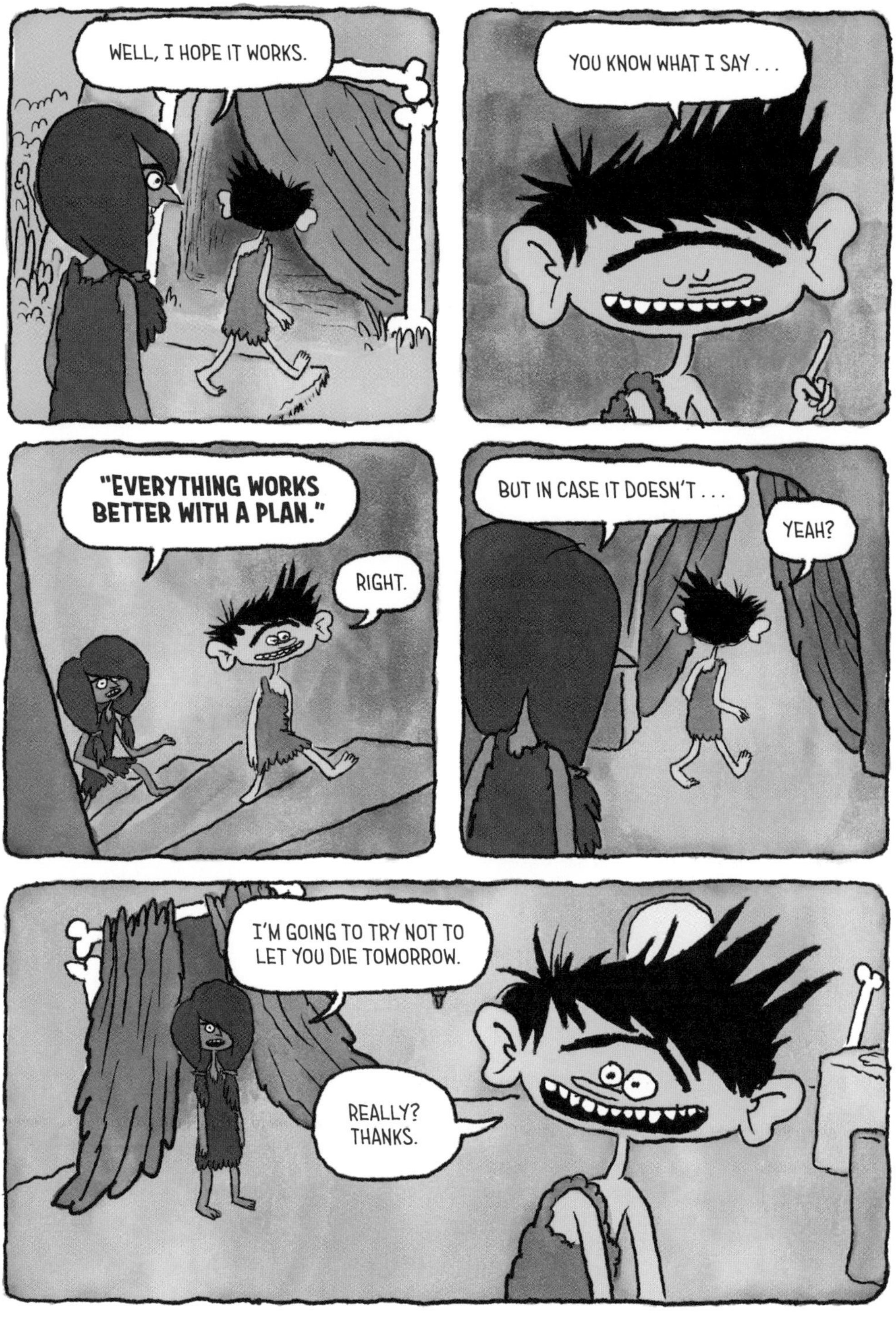
WELL, I HOPE IT WORKS.
YOU KNOW WHAT I SAY . . .
"EVERYTHING WORKS BETTER WITH A PLAN."
RIGHT.
BUT IN CASE IT DOESN'T . . .
YEAH?
I'M GOING TO TRY NOT TO LET YOU DIE TOMORROW.
REALLY? THANKS.

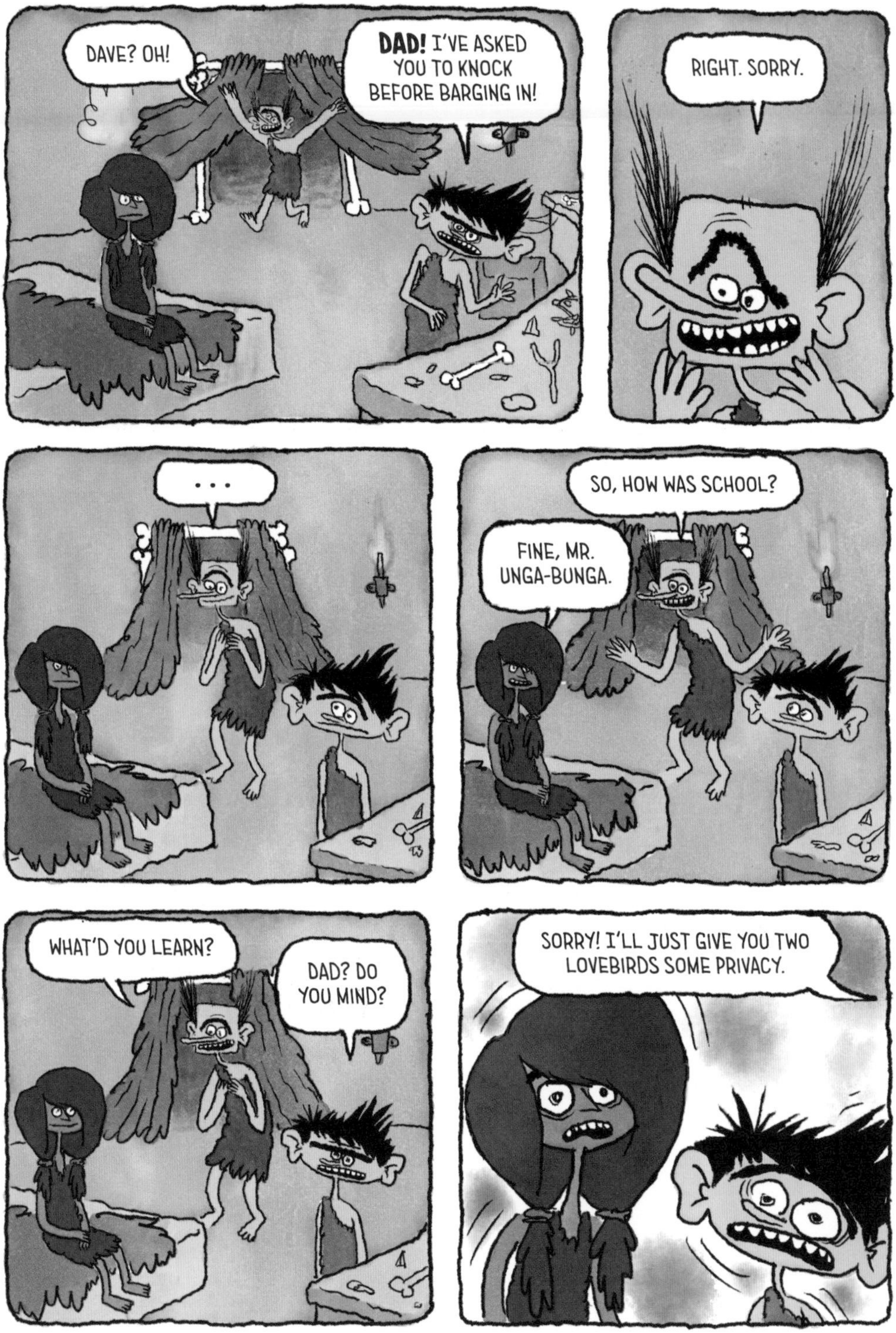
DAVE? OH!
DAD! I'VE ASKED YOU TO KNOCK BEFORE BARGING IN!
RIGHT. SORRY.
. . .
SO, HOW WAS SCHOOL?
FINE, MR. UNGA-BUNGA.
WHAT'D YOU LEARN?
DAD? DO YOU MIND?
SORRY! I'LL JUST GIVE YOU TWO LOVEBIRDS SOME PRIVACY.

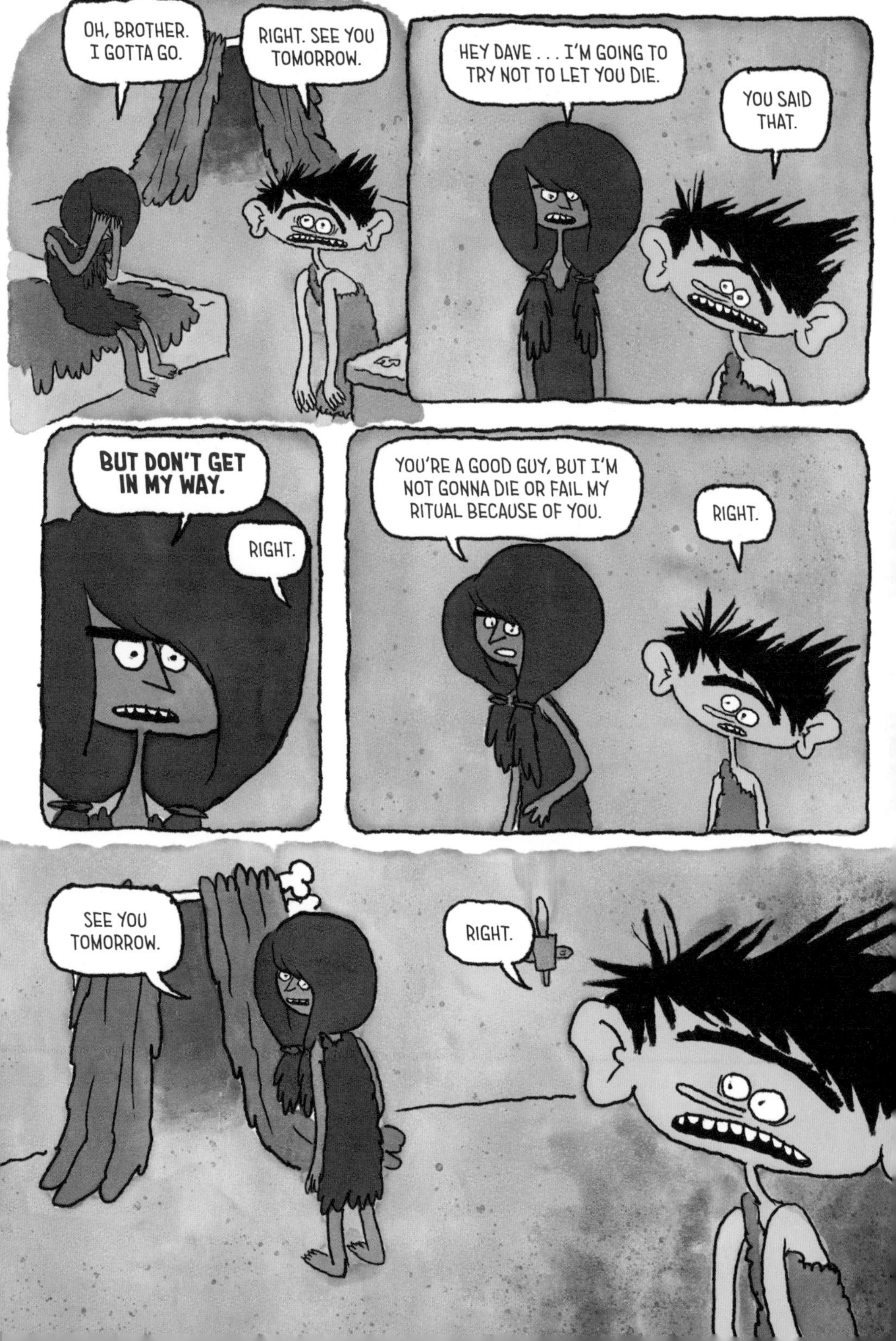
OH, BROTHER. I GOTTA GO.
RIGHT. SEE YOU TOMORROW.
HEY DAVE . . . I'M GOING TO TRY NOT TO LET YOU DIE.
YOU SAID THAT.
BUT DON'T GET IN MY WAY.
RIGHT.
YOU'RE A GOOD GUY, BUT I'M NOT GONNA DIE OR FAIL MY RITUAL BECAUSE OF YOU.
RIGHT.
SEE YOU TOMORROW.
RIGHT.

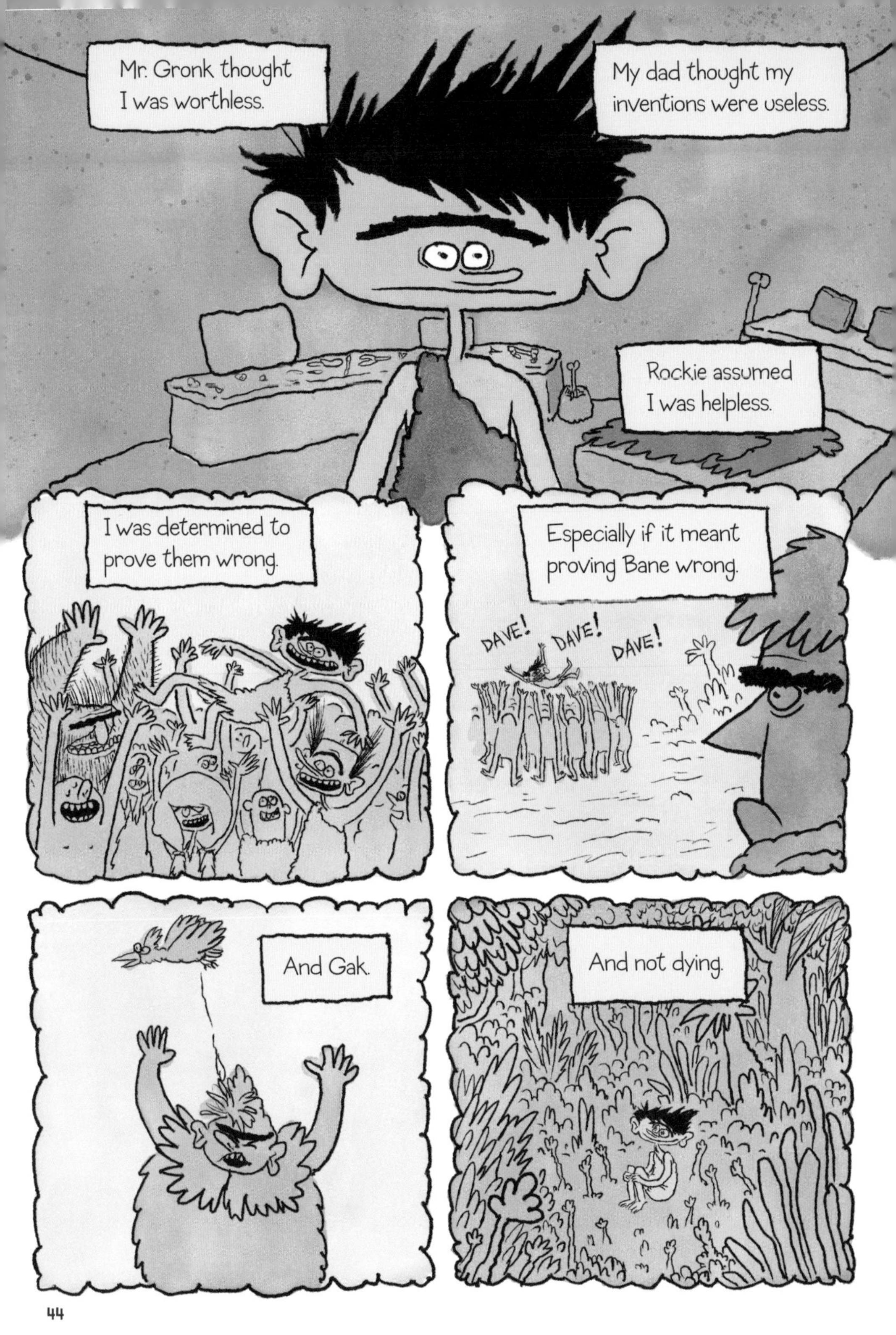
Mr. Gronk thought
I was worthless.
My dad thought my
inventions were useless.
Rockie assumed
I was helpless.
I was determined to
prove them wrong.
Especially if it meant
proving Bane wrong.
DAVE!
DAVE!
DAVE!
And Gak.
And not dying.

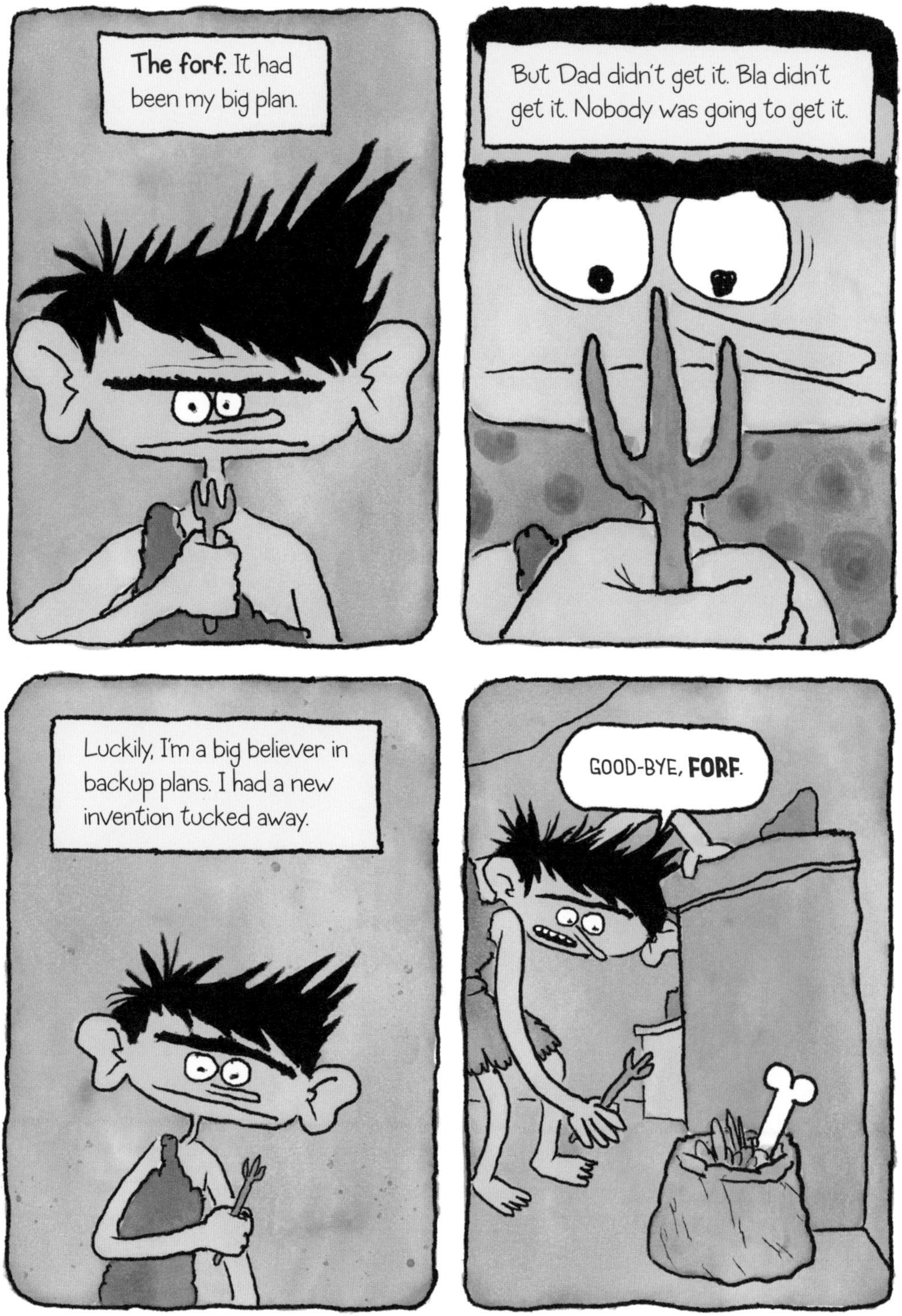
The forf. It had been my big plan.
But Dad didn't get it. Bla didn't get it. Nobody was going to get it.
Luckily, I'm a big believer in backup plans. I had a new invention tucked away.
GOOD-BYE, FORF.

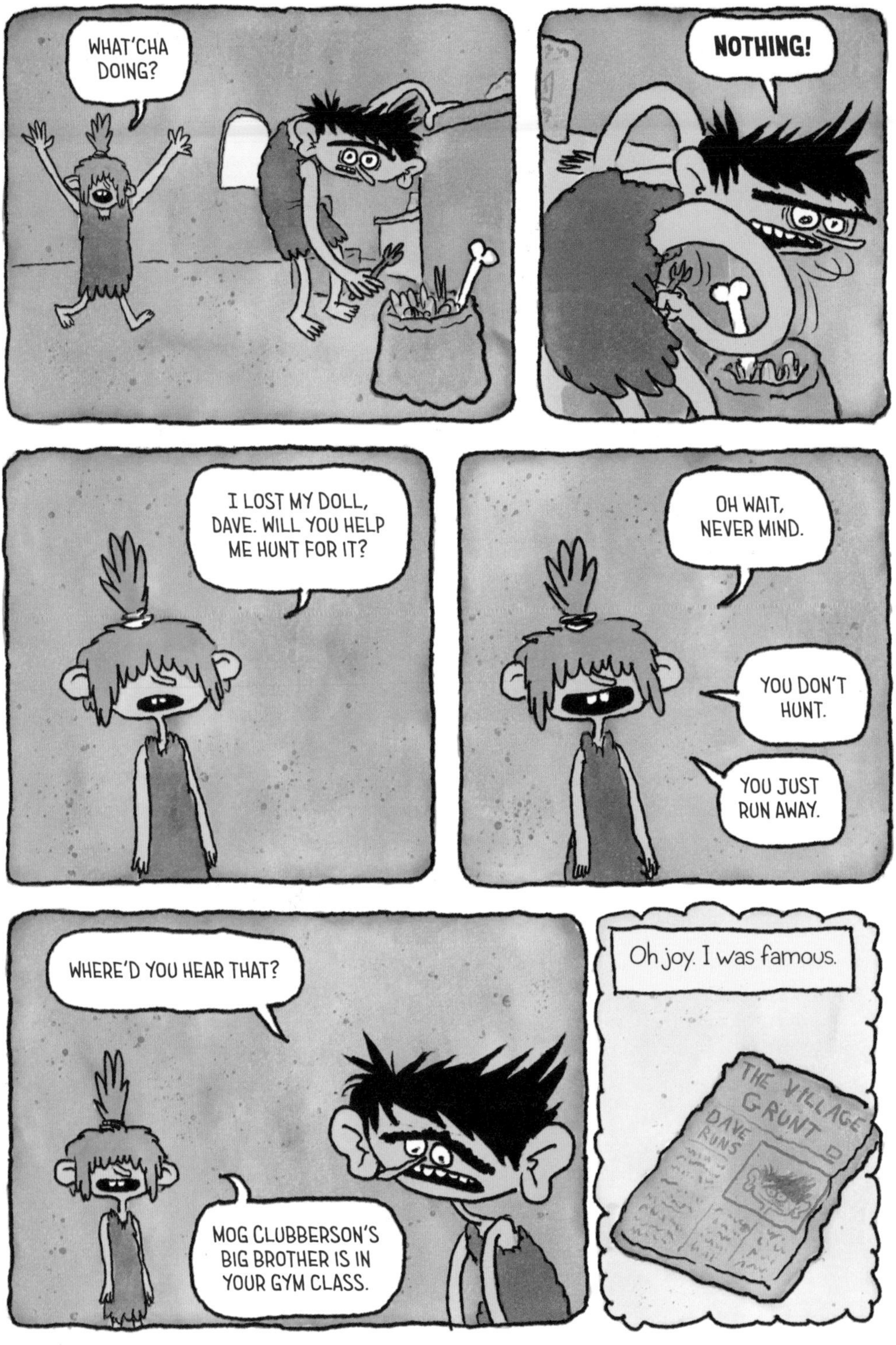
WHAT'CHA DOING?
NOTHING!
I LOST MY DOLL, DAVE. WILL YOU HELP ME HUNT FOR IT?
OH WAIT, NEVER MIND.
YOU DON'T HUNT.
YOU JUST RUN AWAY.
WHERE'D YOU HEAR THAT?
MOG CLUBBERSON'S BIG BROTHER IS IN YOUR GYM CLASS.
Oh joy. I was famous.
THE VILLAGE GRUNT
DAVE RUNS

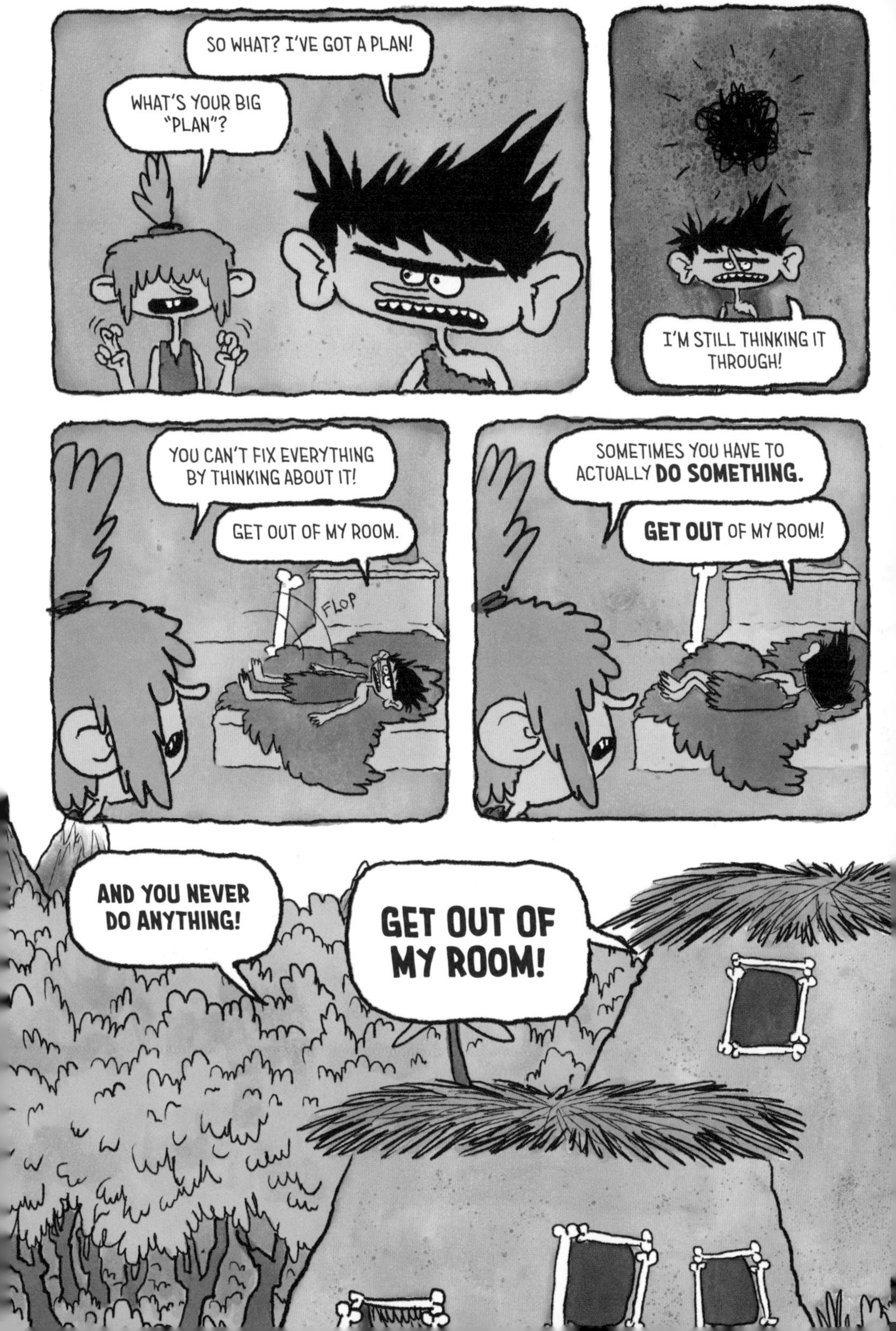
SO WHAT? I'VE GOT A PLAN!
WHAT'S YOUR BIG "PLAN"?
I'M STILL THINKING IT THROUGH!
YOU CAN'T FIX EVERYTHING BY THINKING ABOUT IT!
GET OUT OF MY ROOM.
FLOP
SOMETIMES YOU HAVE TO ACTUALLY **DO SOMETHING.**
GET OUT OF MY ROOM!
AND YOU NEVER DO ANYTHING!
GET OUT OF MY ROOM!

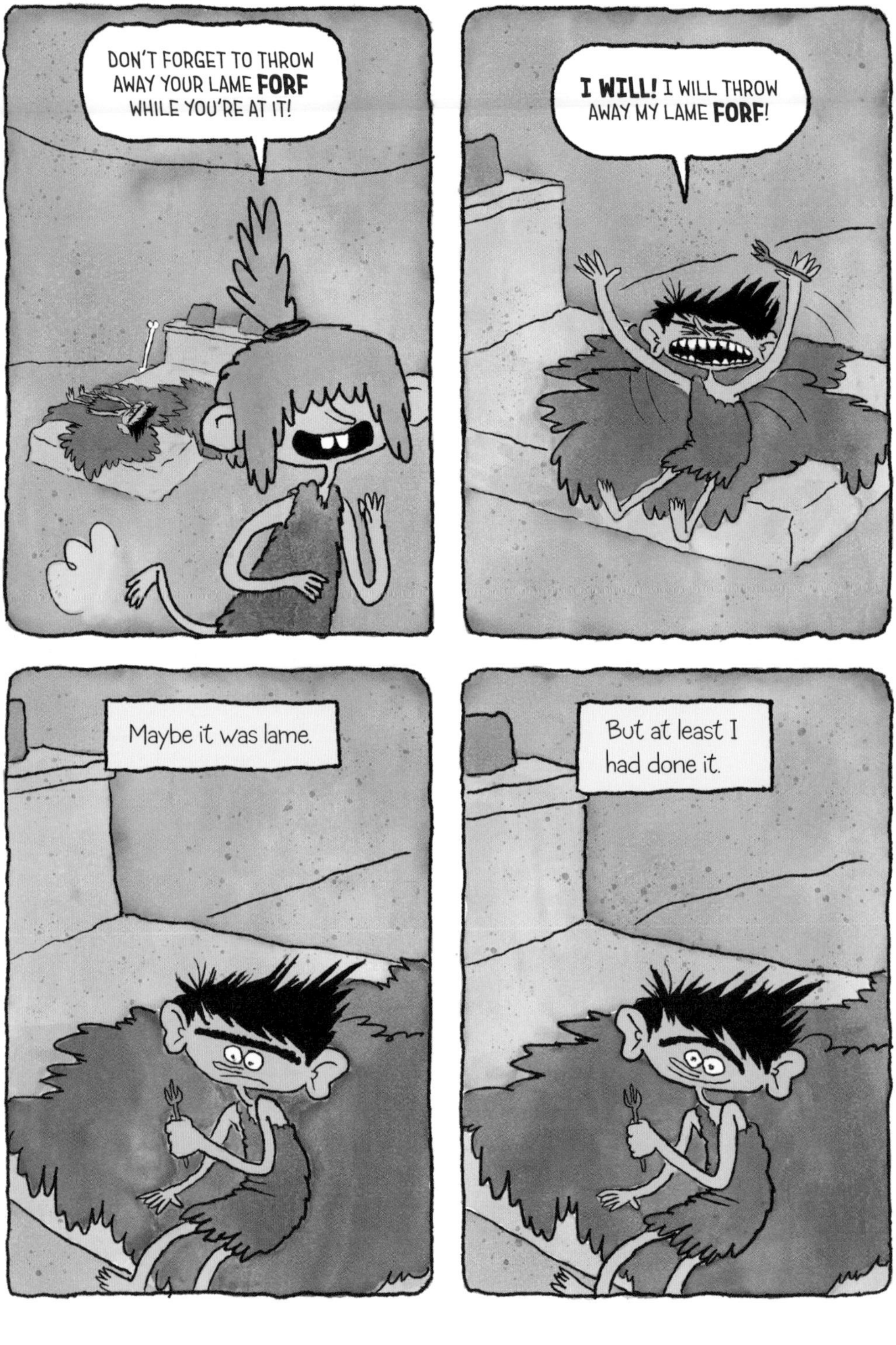
DON'T FORGET TO THROW AWAY YOUR LAME **FORF** WHILE YOU'RE AT IT!
I WILL! I WILL THROW AWAY MY LAME **FORF**!
Maybe it was lame.
But at least I had done it.

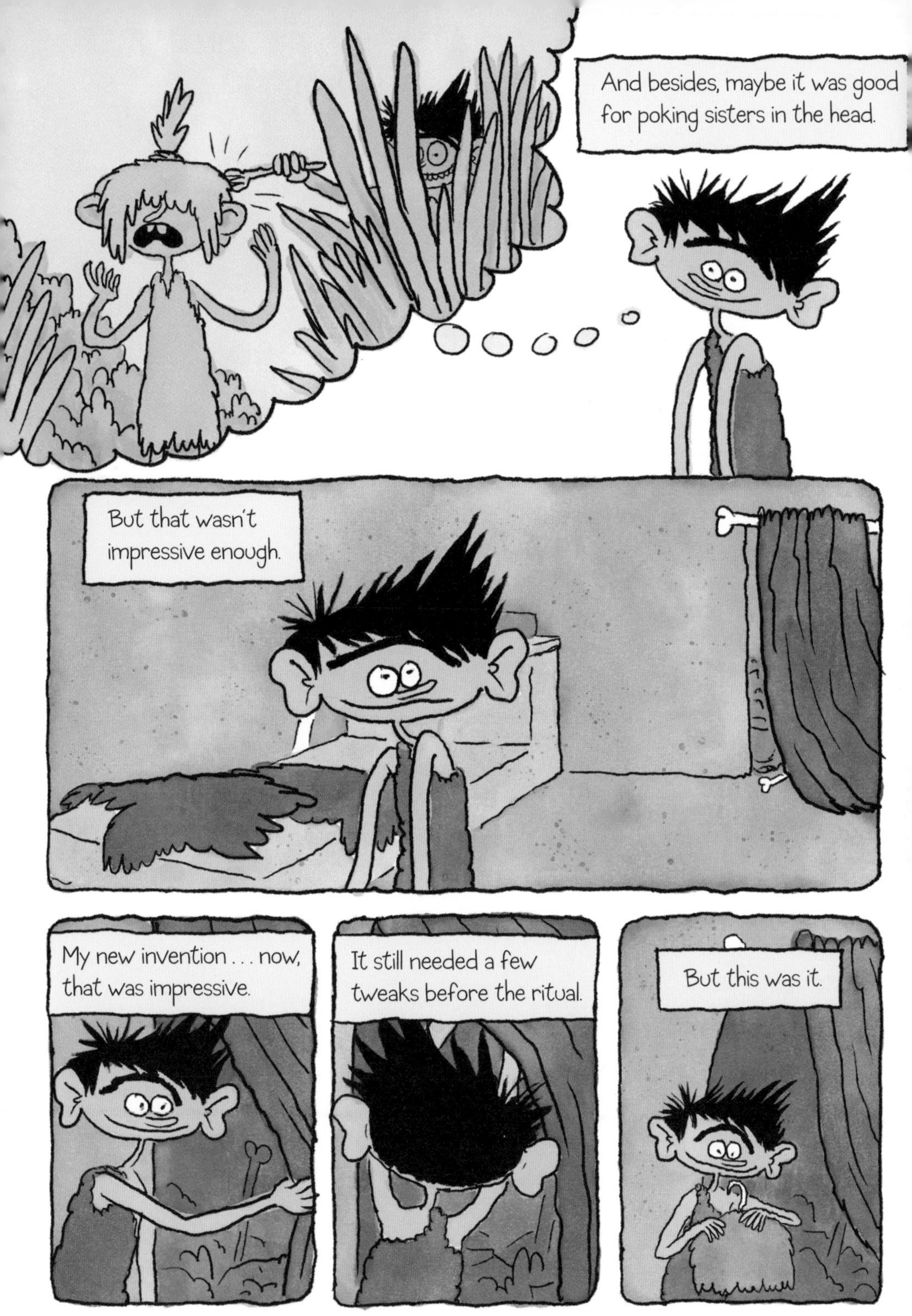
And besides, maybe it was good for poking sisters in the head.
But that wasn't impressive enough.
My new invention . . . now, that was impressive.
It still needed a few tweaks before the ritual.
But this was it.

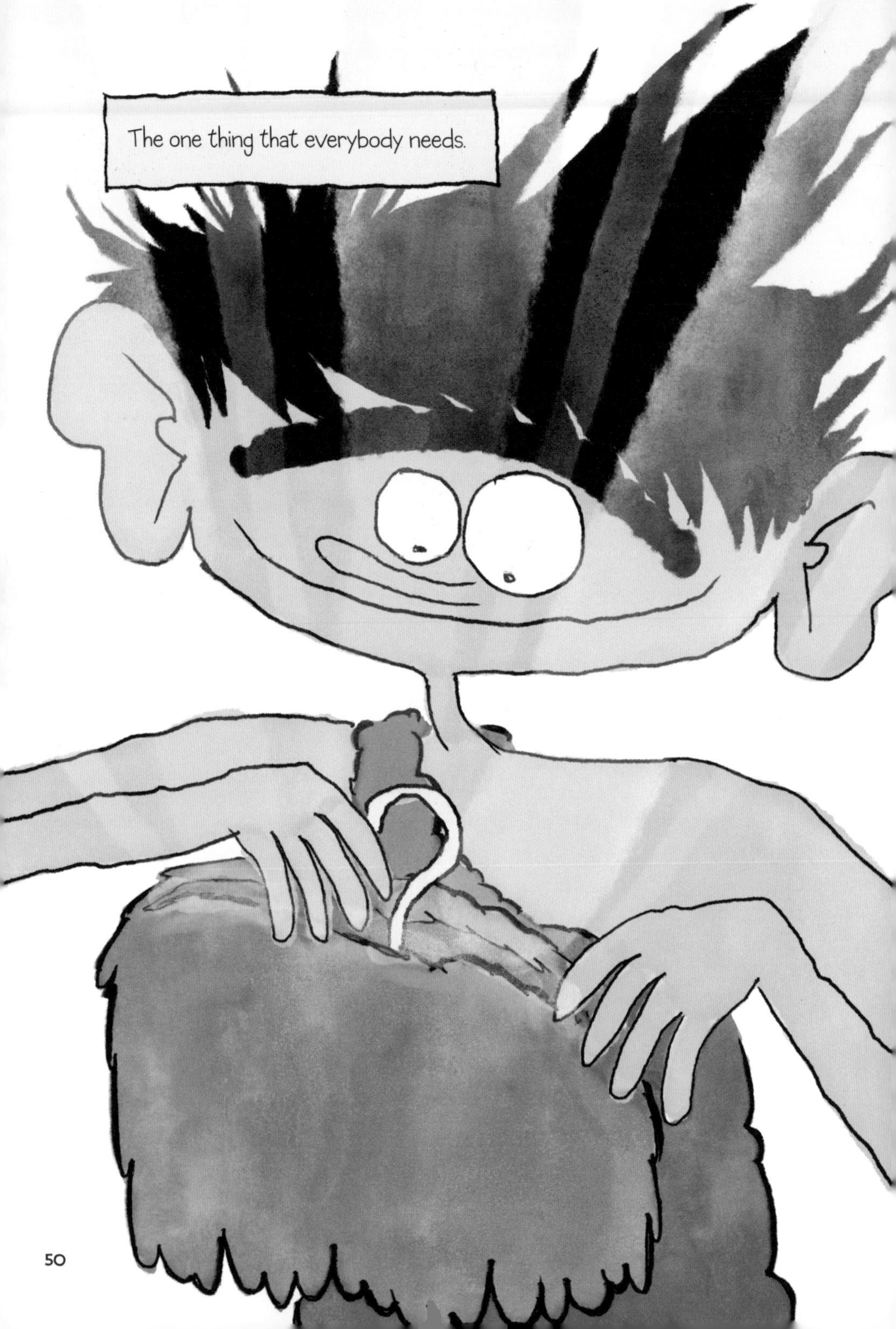
The one thing that everybody needs.

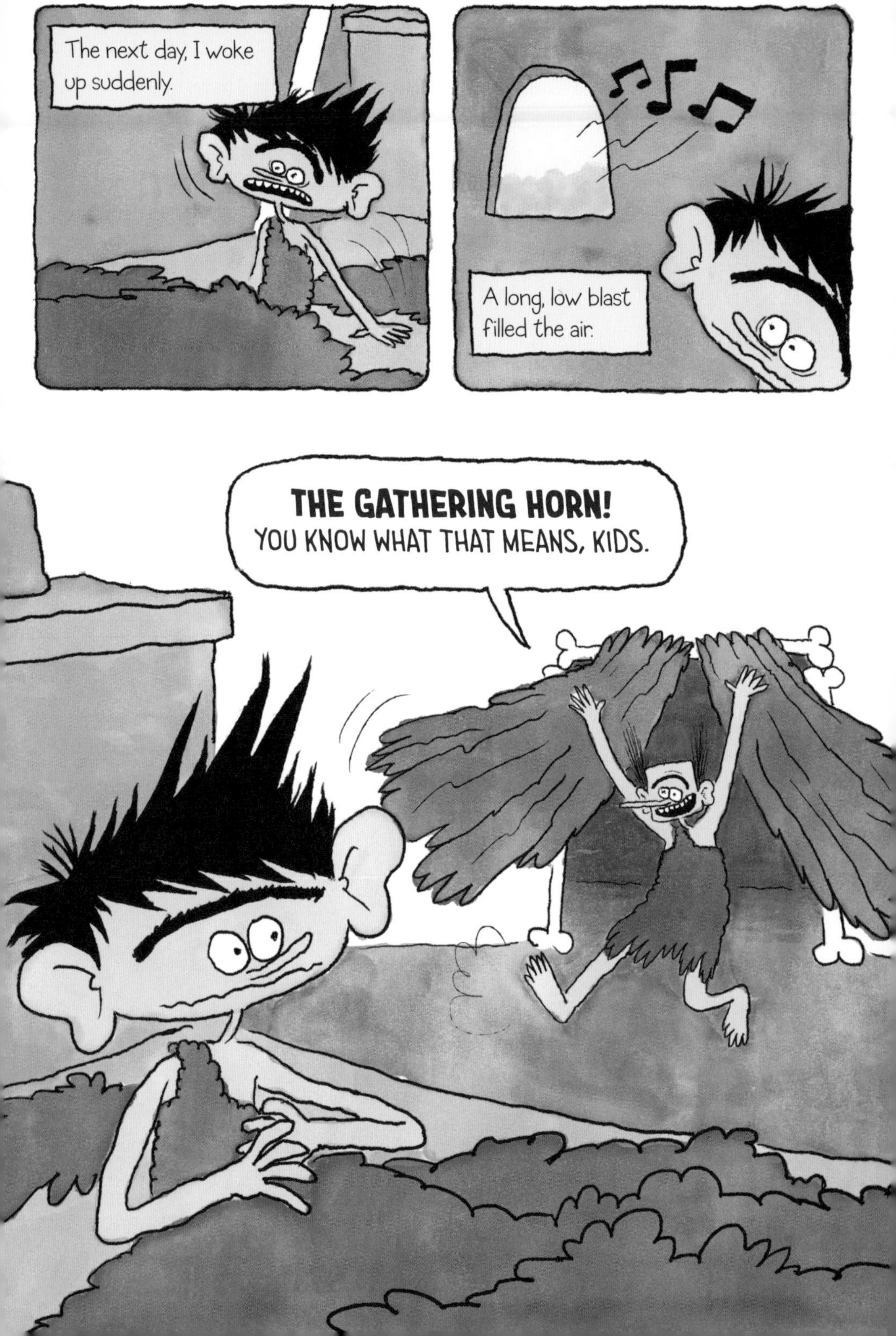

The next day, I woke up suddenly.
A long, low blast filled the air.
THE GATHERING HORN!
YOU KNOW WHAT THAT MEANS, KIDS.

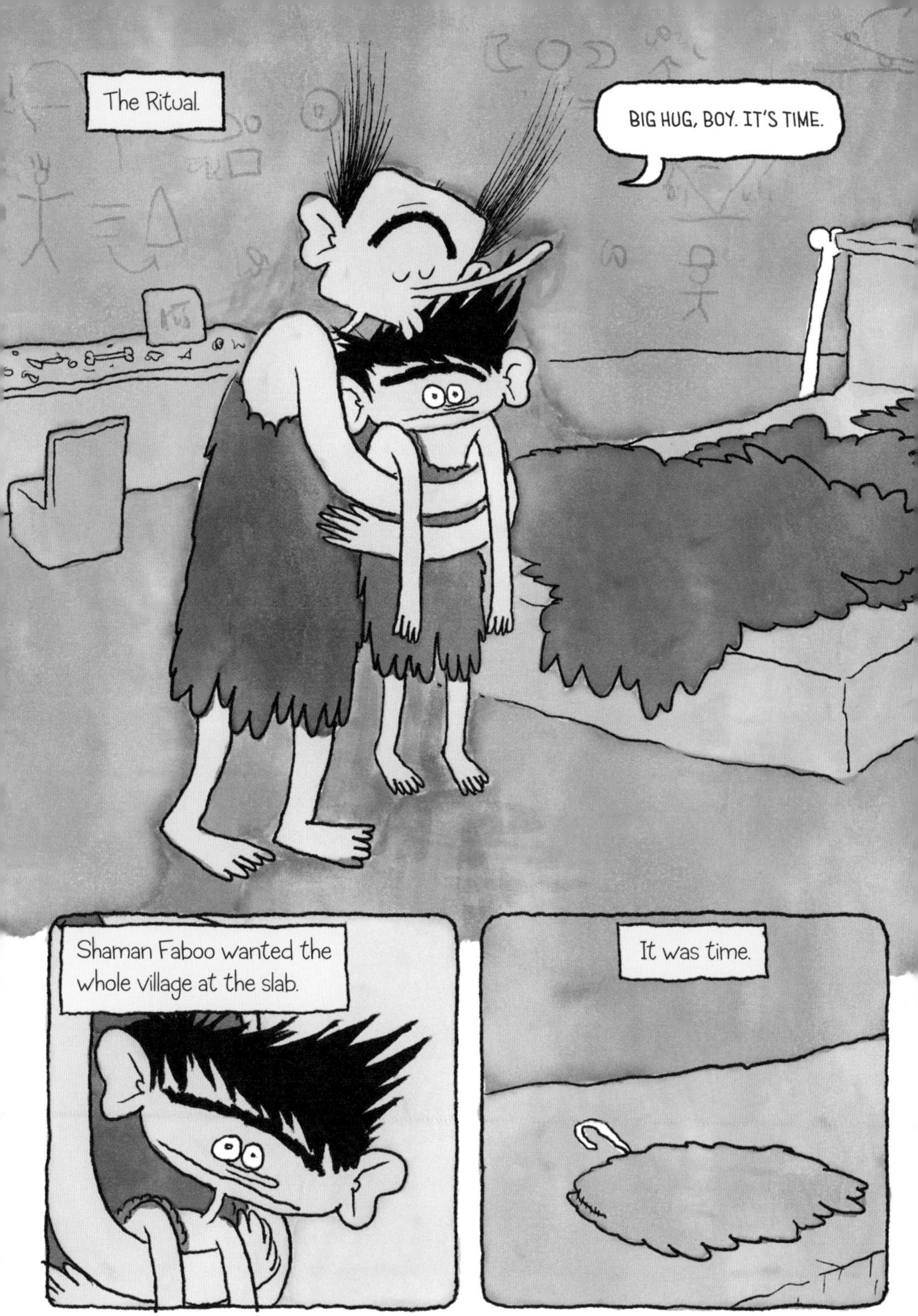
The Ritual.
BIG HUG, BOY. IT'S TIME.
Shaman Faboo wanted the whole village at the slab.
It was time.

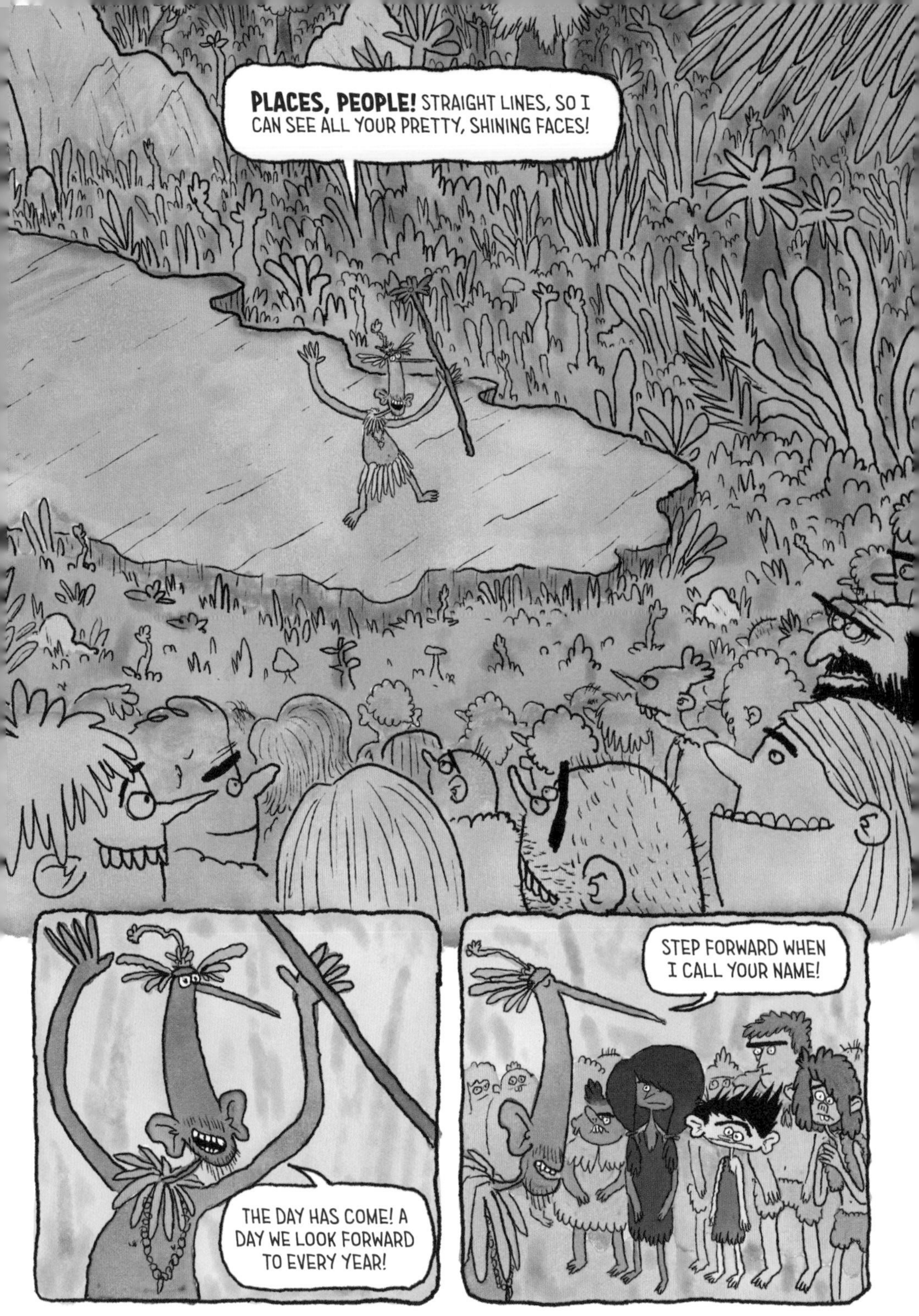

PLACES, PEOPLE! STRAIGHT LINES, SO I CAN SEE ALL YOUR PRETTY, SHINING FACES!
THE DAY HAS COME! A DAY WE LOOK FORWARD TO EVERY YEAR!
STEP FORWARD WHEN I CALL YOUR NAME!

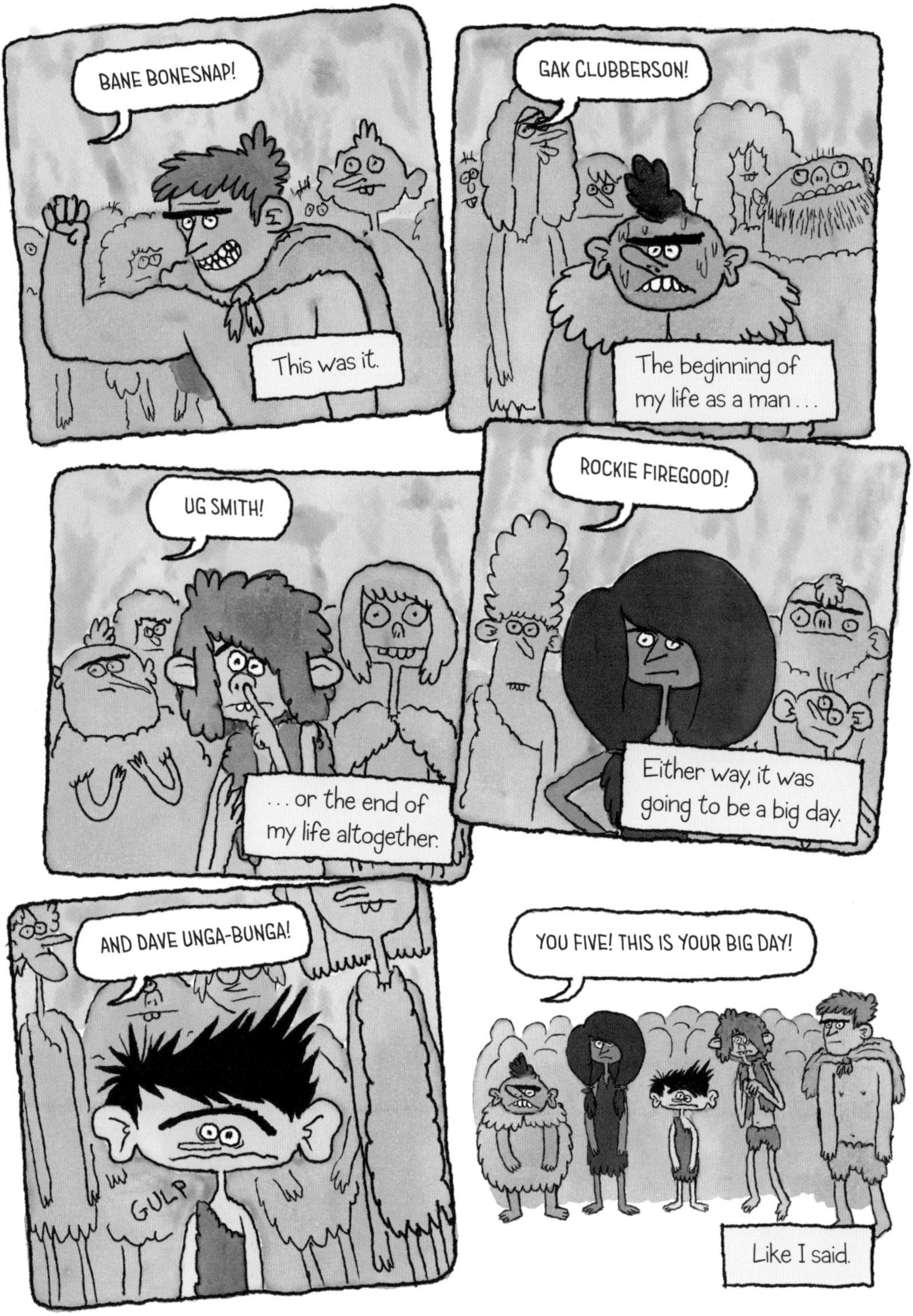
BANE BONESNAP!
This was it.
GAK CLUBBERSON!
The beginning of my life as a man . . .
UG SMITH!
. . . or the end of my life altogether.
ROCKIE FIREGOOD!
Either way, it was going to be a big day.
AND DAVE UNGA-BUNGA!
GULP
YOU FIVE! THIS IS YOUR BIG DAY!
Like I said.

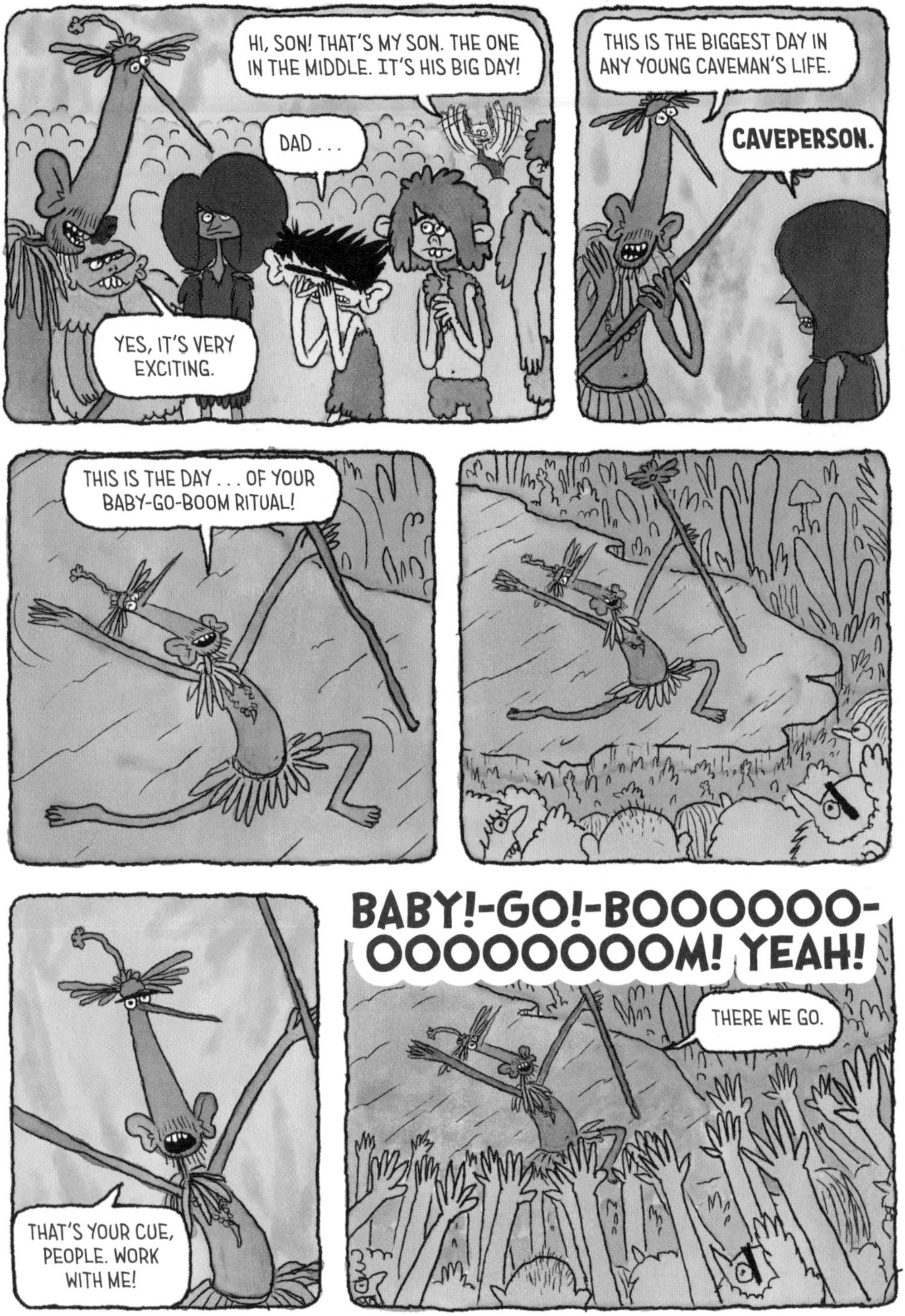
HI, SON! THAT'S MY SON. THE ONE IN THE MIDDLE. IT'S HIS BIG DAY!
DAD . . .
YES, IT'S VERY EXCITING.
THIS IS THE BIGGEST DAY IN ANY YOUNG CAVEMAN'S LIFE.
CAVEPERSON.
THIS IS THE DAY . . . OF YOUR BABY-GO-BOOM RITUAL!
THAT'S YOUR CUE, PEOPLE. WORK WITH ME!
BABY!-GO!-BOOOOOO-OOOOOOOOM! YEAH!
THERE WE GO.

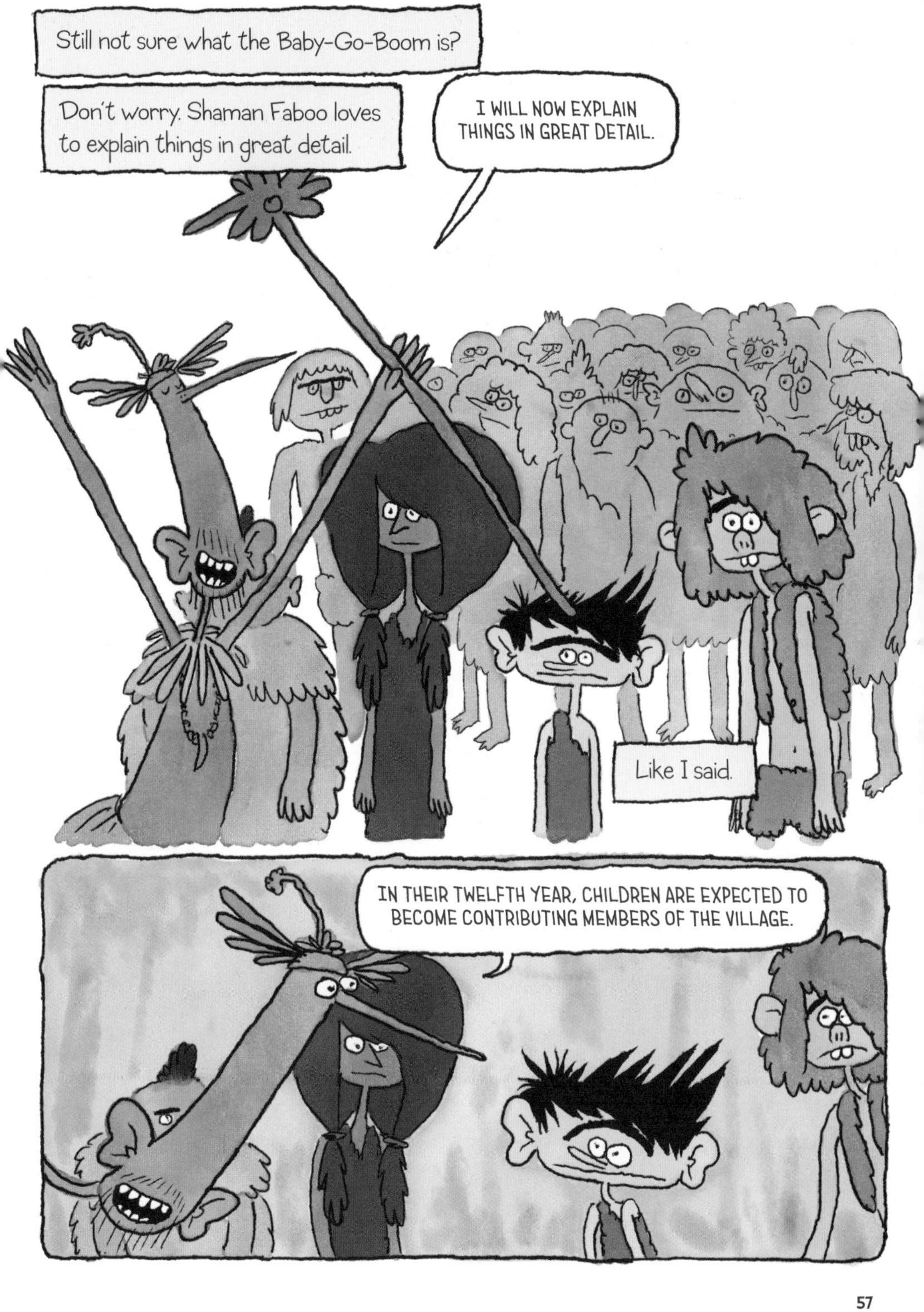
Still not sure what the Baby-Go-Boom is?
Don't worry. Shaman Faboo loves to explain things in great detail.
I WILL NOW EXPLAIN THINGS IN GREAT DETAIL.
Like I said.
IN THEIR TWELFTH YEAR, CHILDREN ARE EXPECTED TO BECOME CONTRIBUTING MEMBERS OF THE VILLAGE.

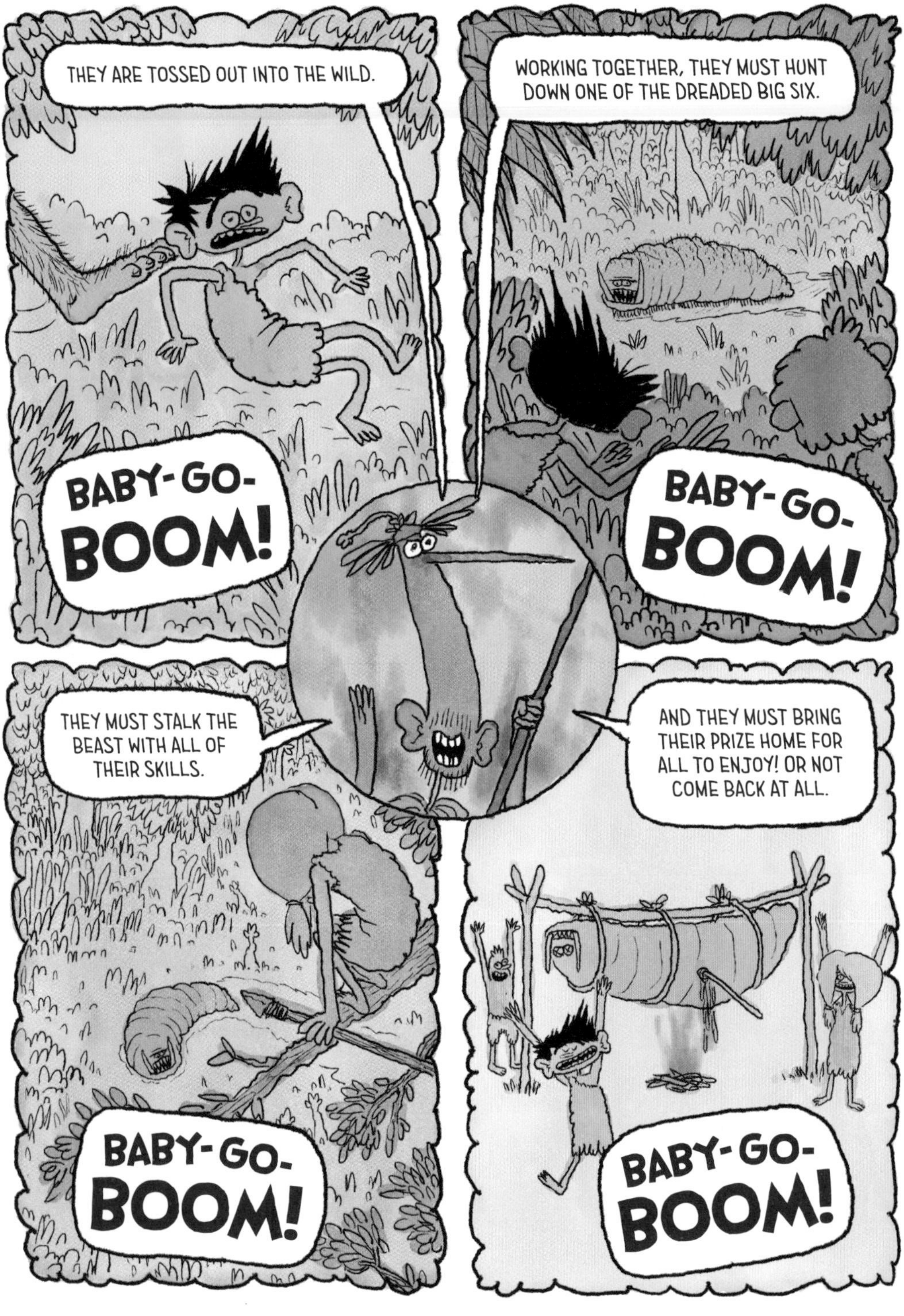
THEY ARE TOSSED OUT INTO THE WILD.
BABY-GO-BOOM!
WORKING TOGETHER, THEY MUST HUNT DOWN ONE OF THE DREADED BIG SIX.
BABY-GO-BOOM!
THEY MUST STALK THE BEAST WITH ALL OF THEIR SKILLS.
BABY-GO-BOOM!
AND THEY MUST BRING THEIR PRIZE HOME FOR ALL TO ENJOY! OR NOT COME BACK AT ALL.
BABY-GO-BOOM!

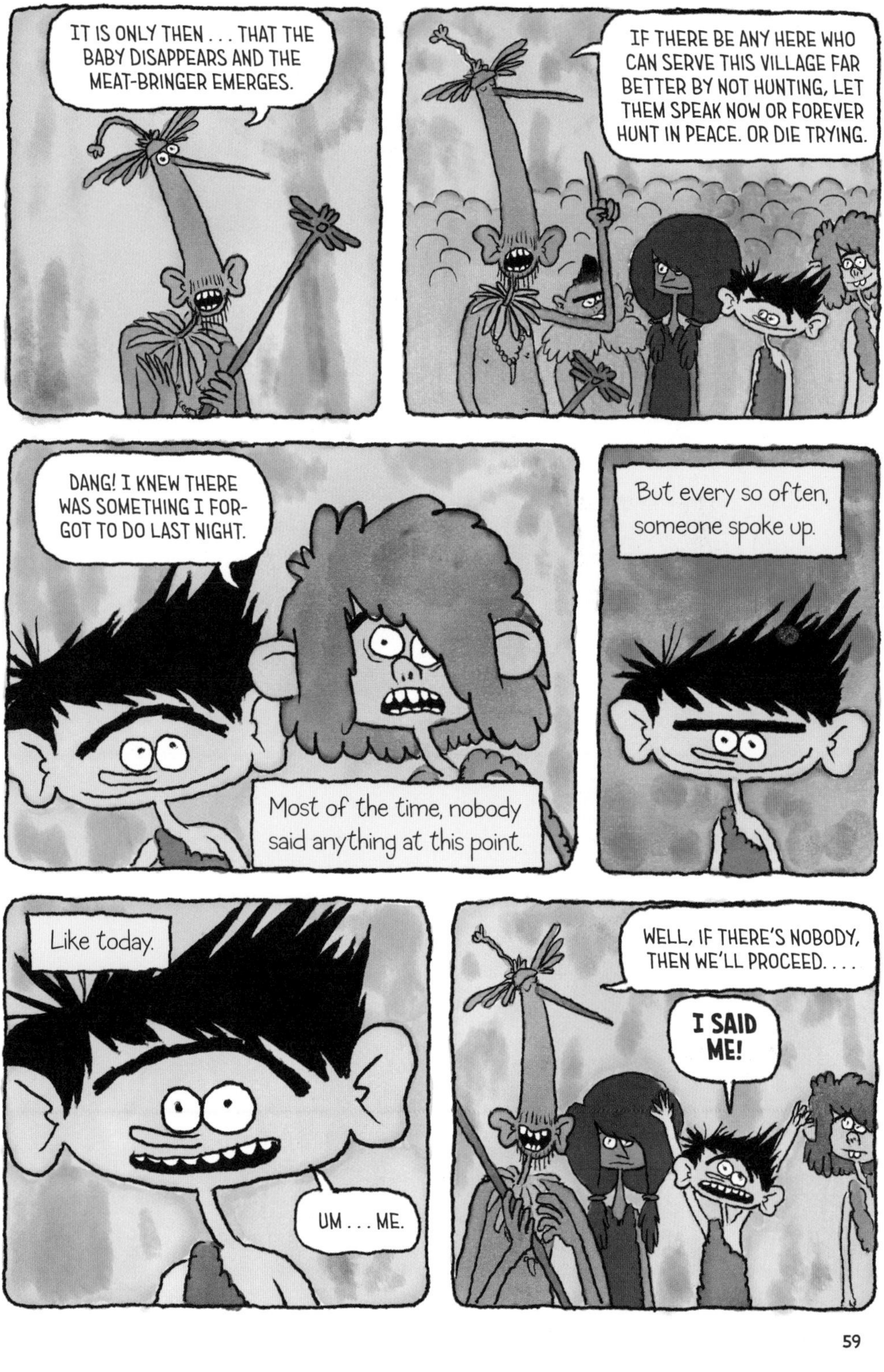
IT IS ONLY THEN . . . THAT THE BABY DISAPPEARS AND THE MEAT-BRINGER EMERGES.
IF THERE BE ANY HERE WHO CAN SERVE THIS VILLAGE FAR BETTER BY NOT HUNTING, LET THEM SPEAK NOW OR FOREVER HUNT IN PEACE. OR DIE TRYING.
DANG! I KNEW THERE WAS SOMETHING I FOR-GOT TO DO LAST NIGHT.
Most of the time, nobody said anything at this point.
But every so often, someone spoke up.
Like today.
UM . . . ME.
WELL, IF THERE'S NOBODY, THEN WE'LL PROCEED. . . .
I SAID ME!

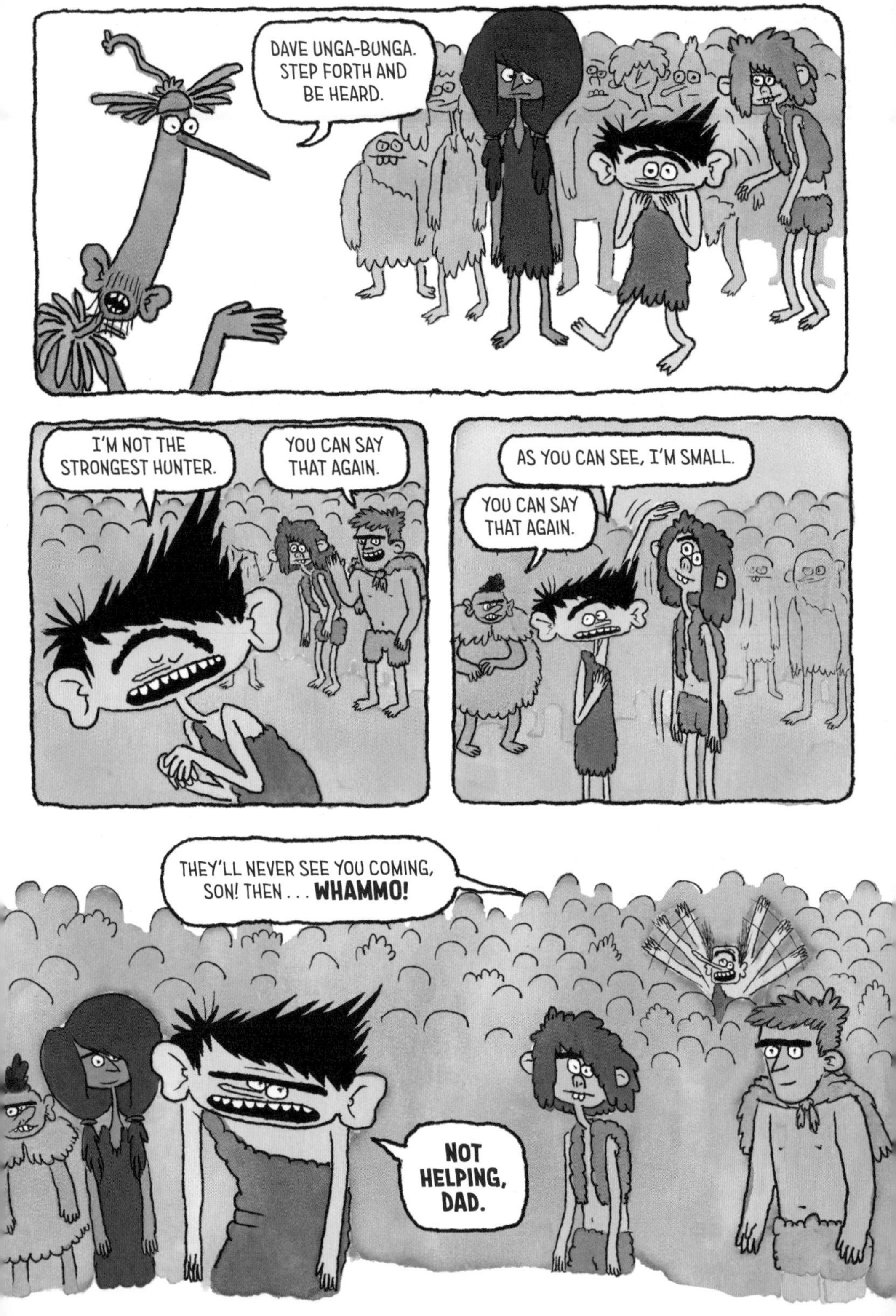
DAVE UNGA-BUNGA. STEP FORTH AND BE HEARD.
I'M NOT THE STRONGEST HUNTER.
YOU CAN SAY THAT AGAIN.
AS YOU CAN SEE, I'M SMALL.
YOU CAN SAY THAT AGAIN.
THEY'LL NEVER SEE YOU COMING, SON! THEN . . . **WHAMMO!**
NOT HELPING, DAD.

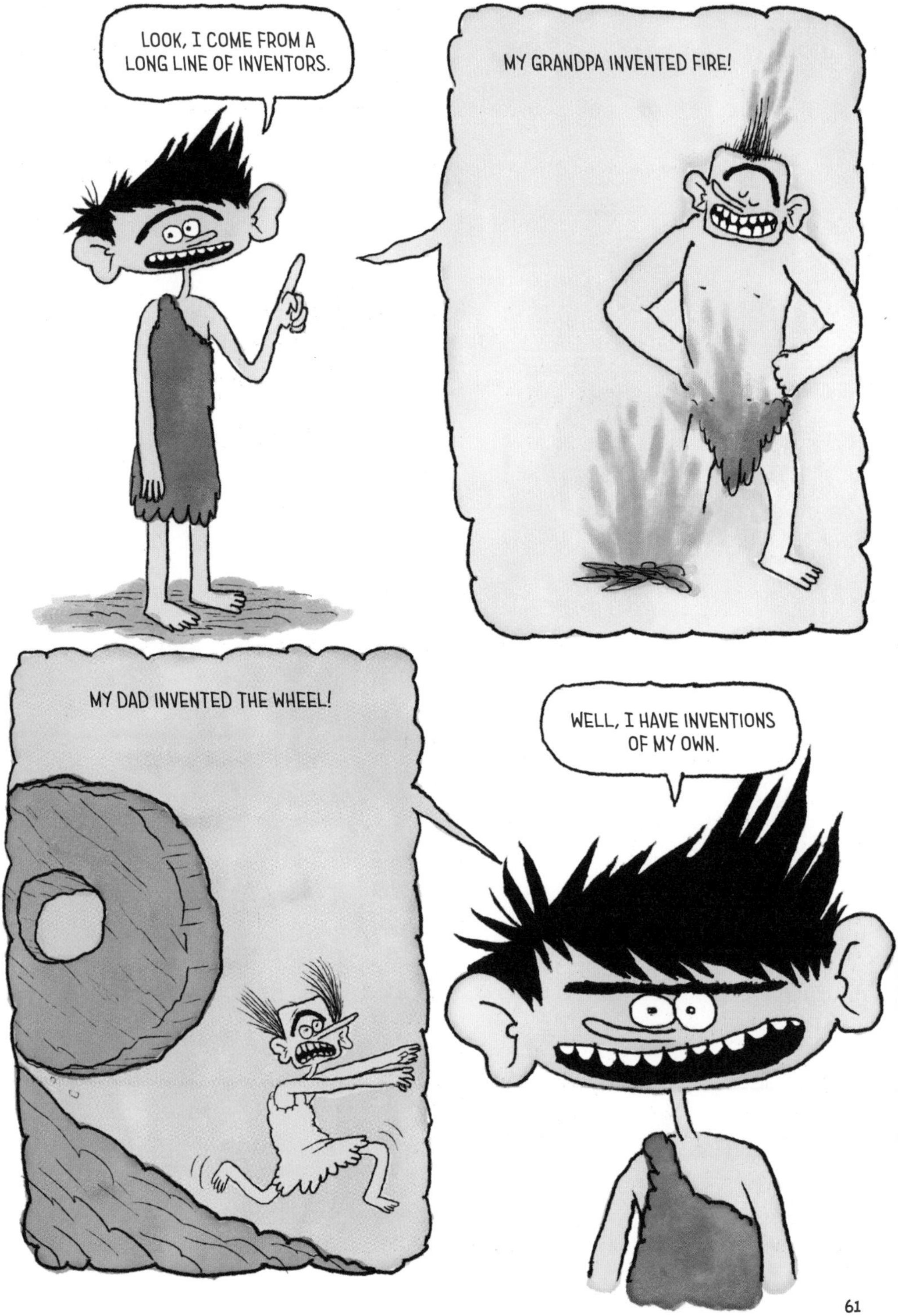
LOOK, I COME FROM A LONG LINE OF INVENTORS.
MY GRANDPA INVENTED FIRE!
MY DAD INVENTED THE WHEEL!
WELL, I HAVE INVENTIONS OF MY OWN.

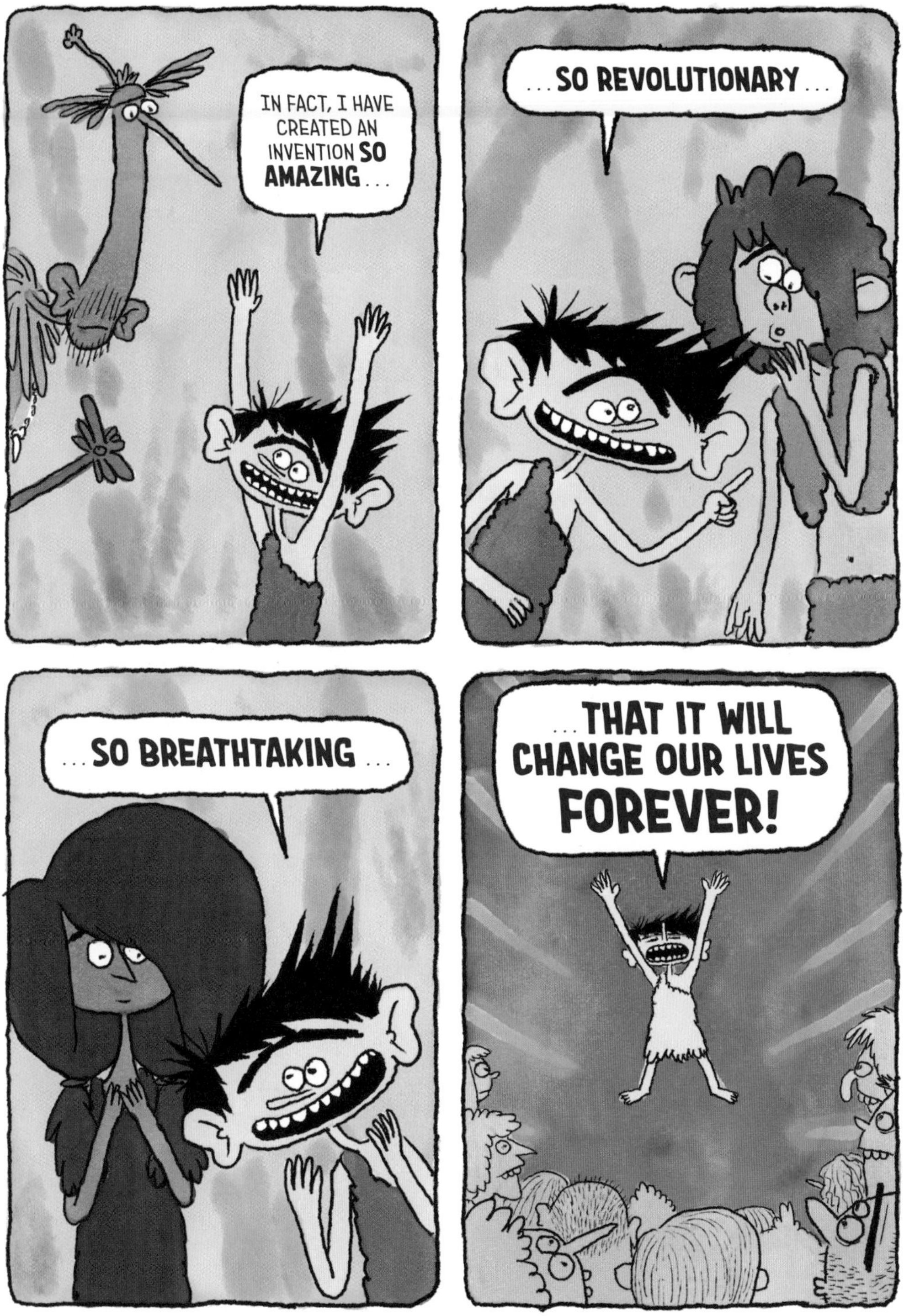
IN FACT, I HAVE CREATED AN INVENTION SO AMAZING . . .
. . . SO REVOLUTIONARY . . .
. . . SO BREATHTAKING . . .
. . . THAT IT WILL CHANGE OUR LIVES FOREVER!

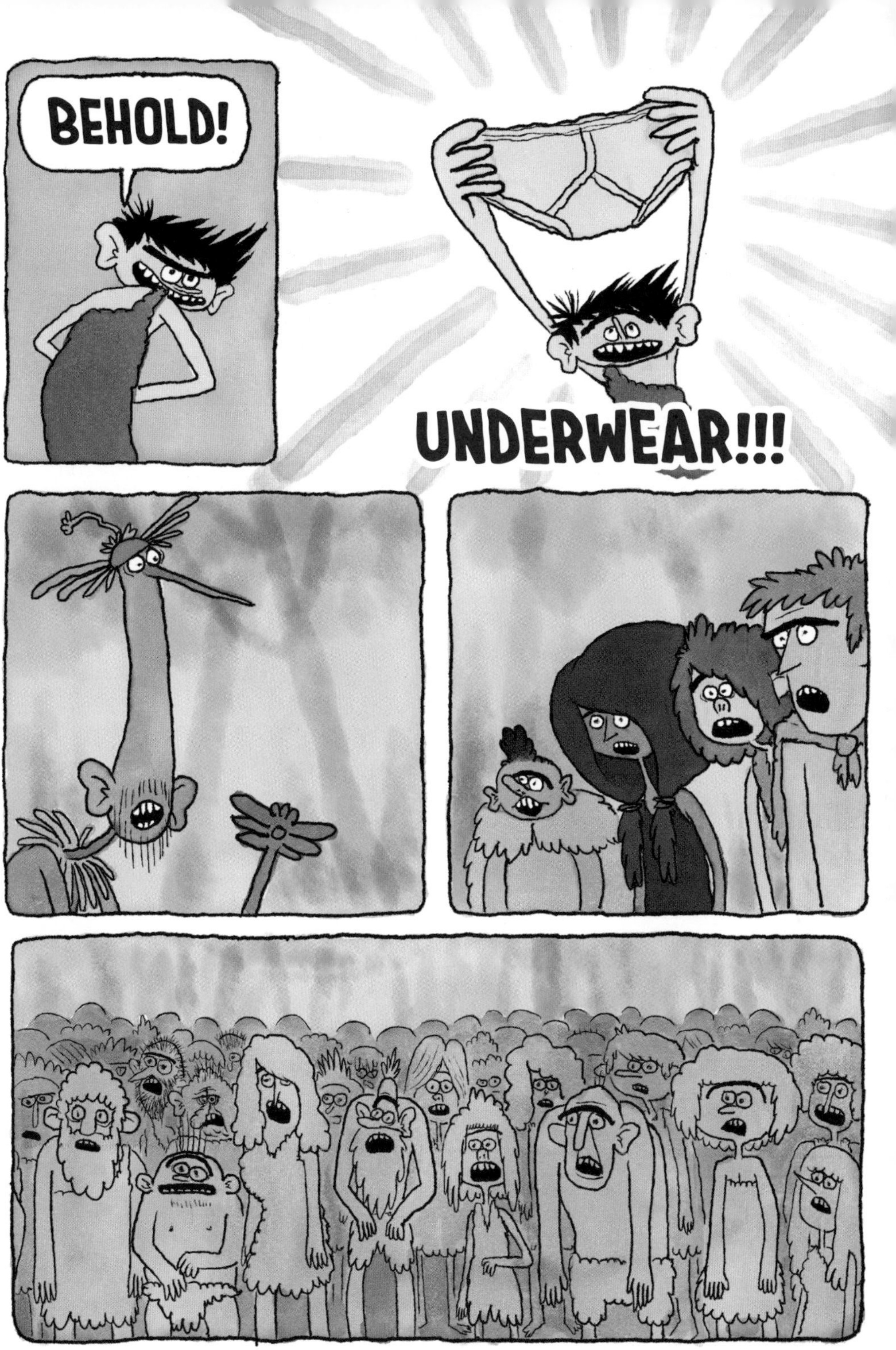
BEHOLD!
UNDERWEAR!!!

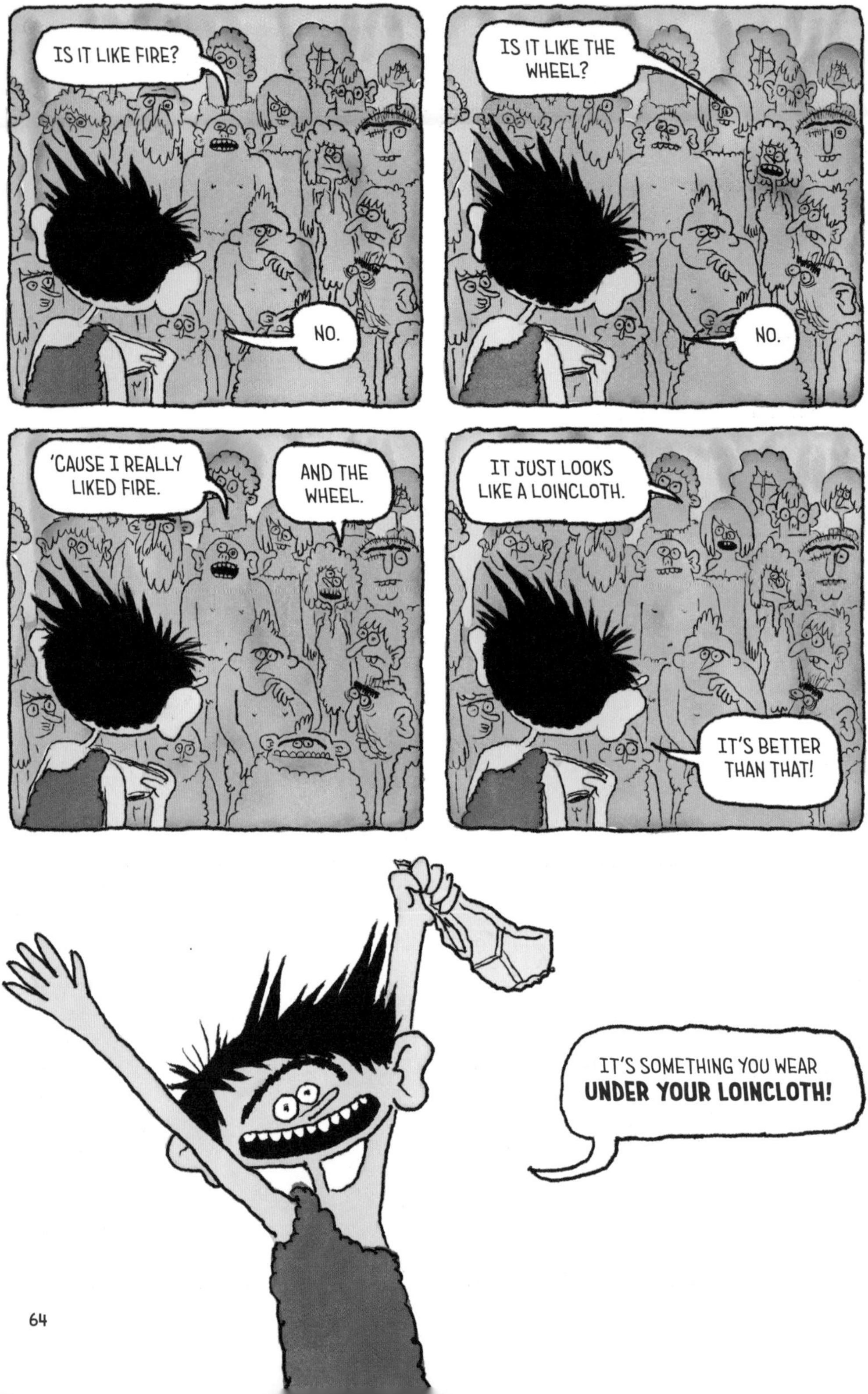
IS IT LIKE FIRE?
NO.
IS IT LIKE THE WHEEL?
NO.
'CAUSE I REALLY LIKED FIRE.
AND THE WHEEL.
IT JUST LOOKS LIKE A LOINCLOTH.
IT'S BETTER THAN THAT!
IT'S SOMETHING YOU WEAR **UNDER YOUR LOINCLOTH!**

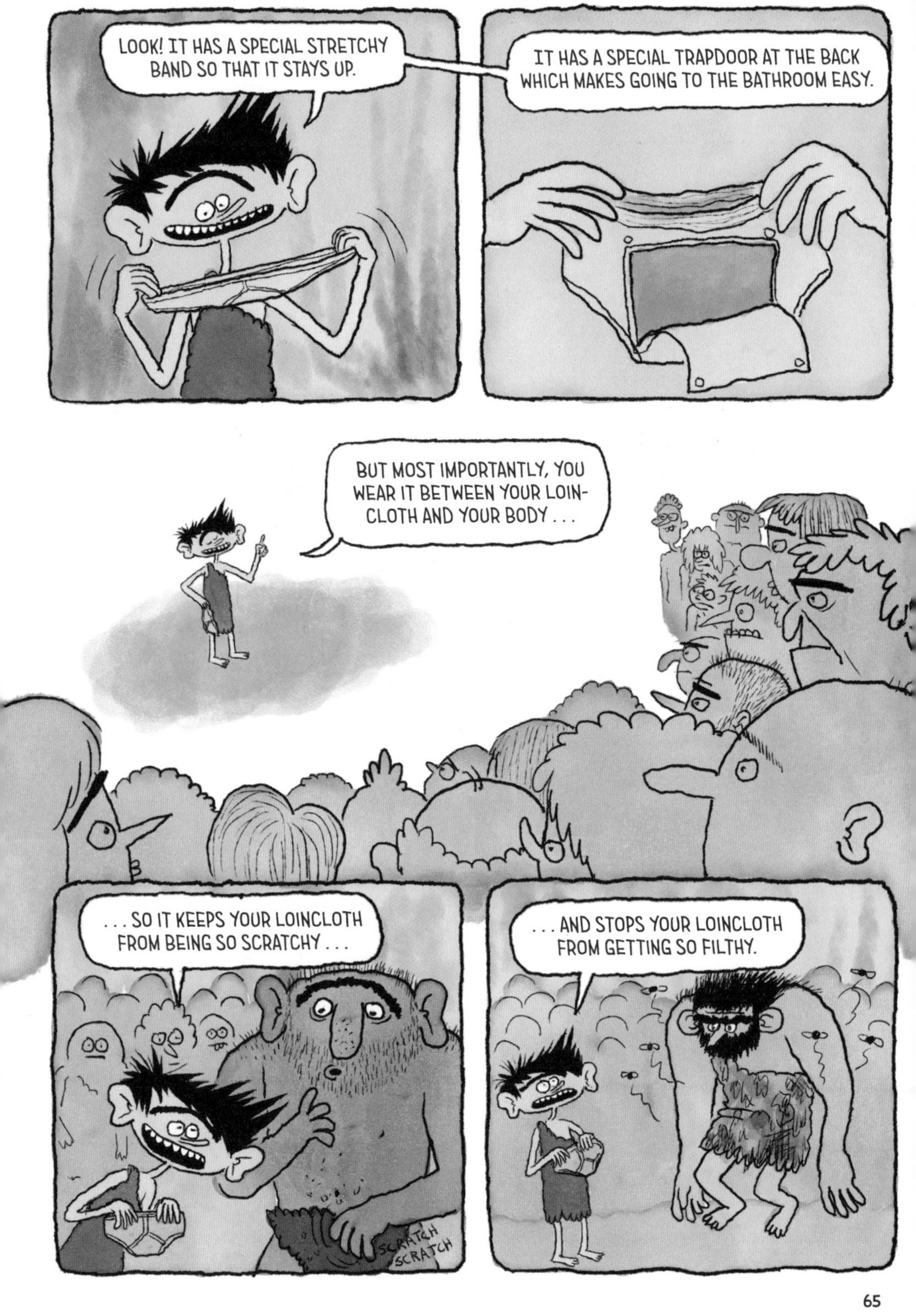
LOOK! IT HAS A SPECIAL STRETCHY BAND SO THAT IT STAYS UP.
IT HAS A SPECIAL TRAPDOOR AT THE BACK WHICH MAKES GOING TO THE BATHROOM EASY.
BUT MOST IMPORTANTLY, YOU WEAR IT BETWEEN YOUR LOIN-CLOTH AND YOUR BODY . . .
. . . SO IT KEEPS YOUR LOINCLOTH FROM BEING SO SCRATCHY . . .
SCRATCH SCRATCH
. . . AND STOPS YOUR LOINCLOTH FROM GETTING SO FILTHY.

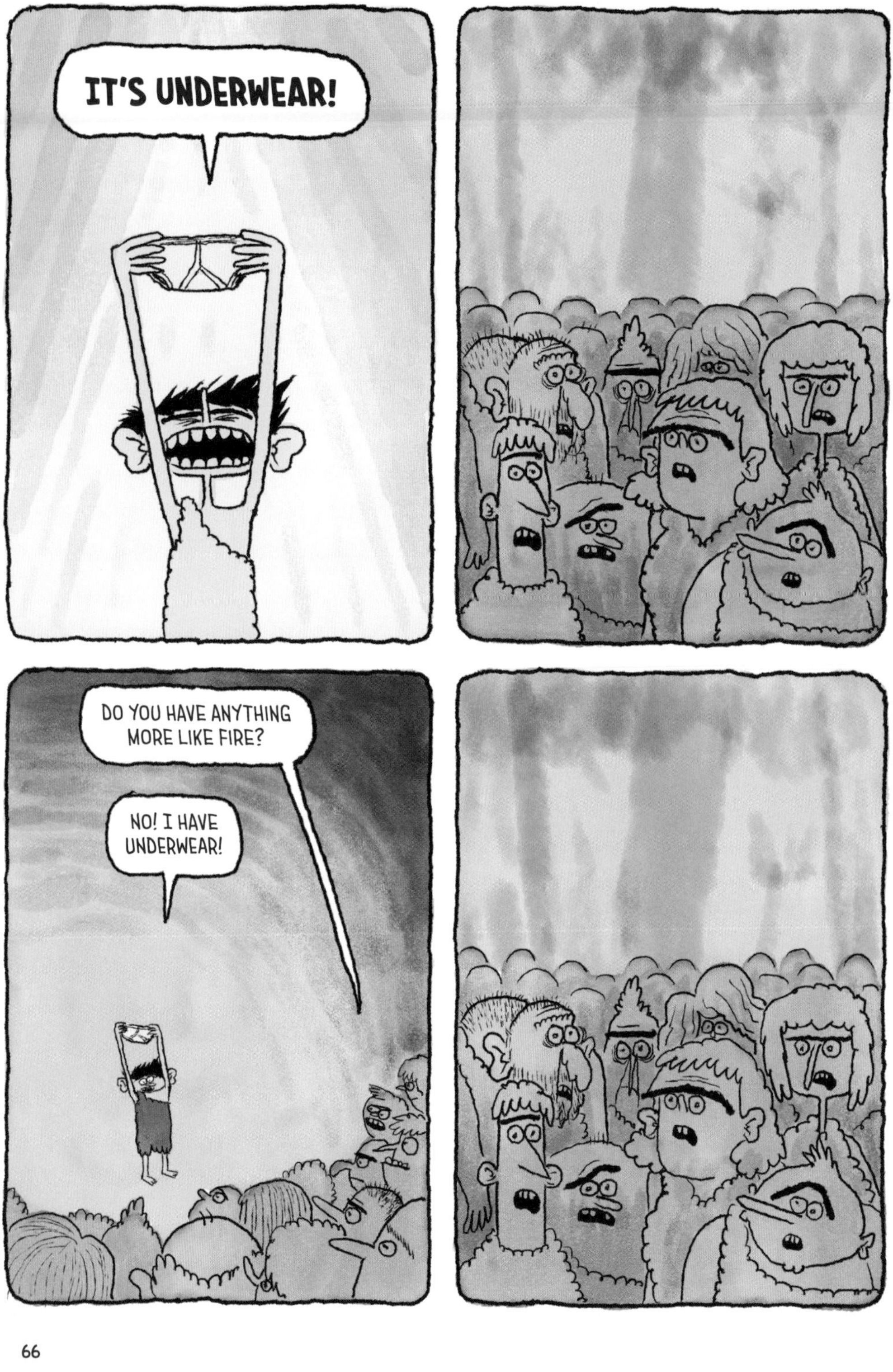
IT'S UNDERWEAR!
DO YOU HAVE ANYTHING MORE LIKE FIRE?
NO! I HAVE UNDERWEAR!

THANK YOU, DAVE. IT'S TRULY AN INTERESTING... UNDERWEAR.

WE MUST DETERMINE THE VALUE OF THIS CONTRIBUTION.

ARE THERE ANY HERE THAT WOULD LIKE TO HAVE THIS UNDERWEAR?

I WOULD. THAT STUFF LOOKS SUPER COMFY!

ARE THERE ANY HERE WHO BELIEVE THIS IS A BETTER CONTRIBUTION THAN MEAT-BRINGING?

I THINK I'D RATHER JUST HAVE THE MEAT.

BUT CAN'T YOU SEE? UNDERWEAR IS BETTER THAN NO UNDERWEAR!

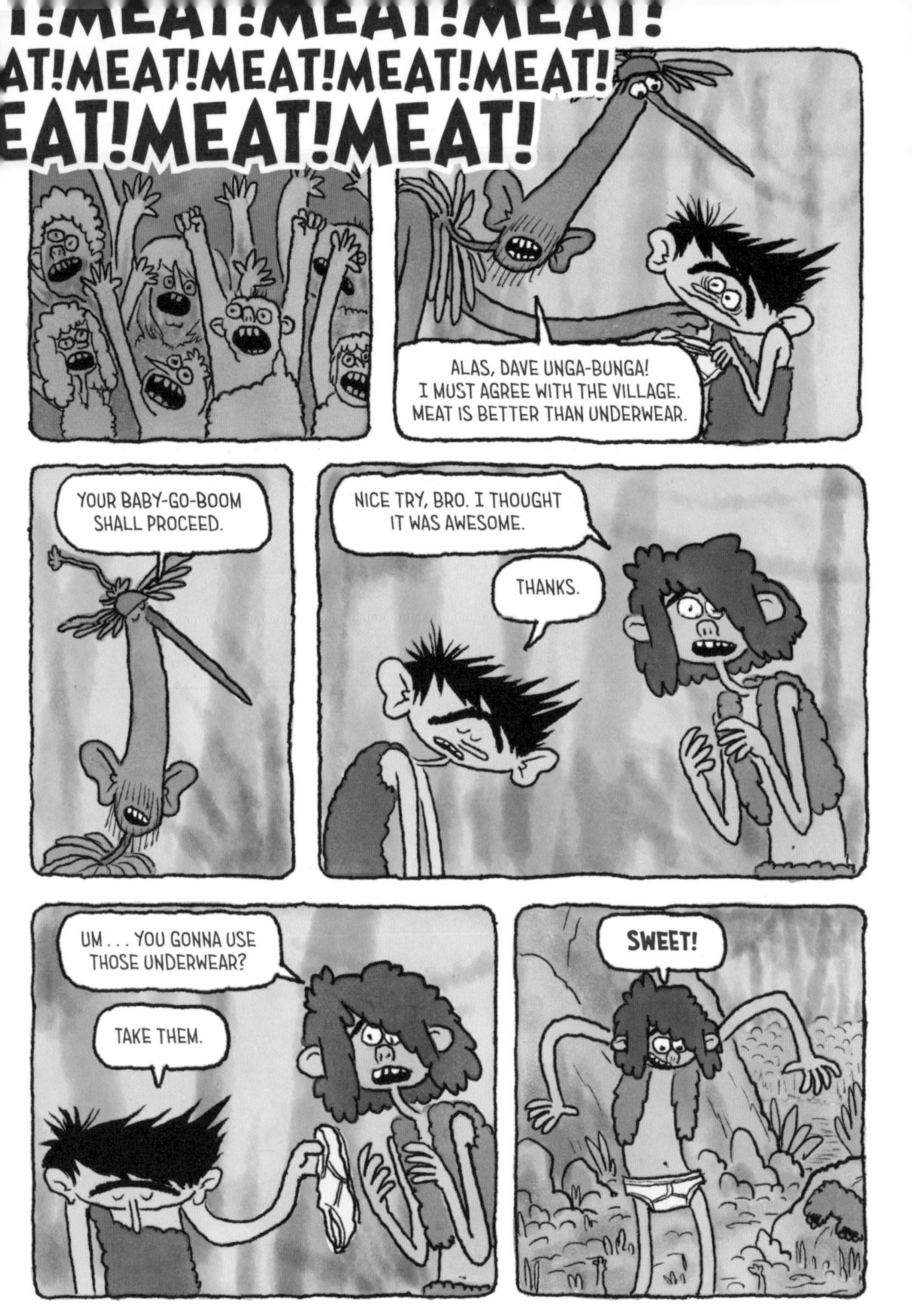
AT!MEAT!MEAT!MEAT!MEAT!
EAT!MEAT!MEAT!
ALAS, DAVE UNGA-BUNGA! I MUST AGREE WITH THE VILLAGE. MEAT IS BETTER THAN UNDERWEAR.
YOUR BABY-GO-BOOM SHALL PROCEED.
NICE TRY, BRO. I THOUGHT IT WAS AWESOME.
THANKS.
UM . . . YOU GONNA USE THOSE UNDERWEAR?
TAKE THEM.
SWEET!

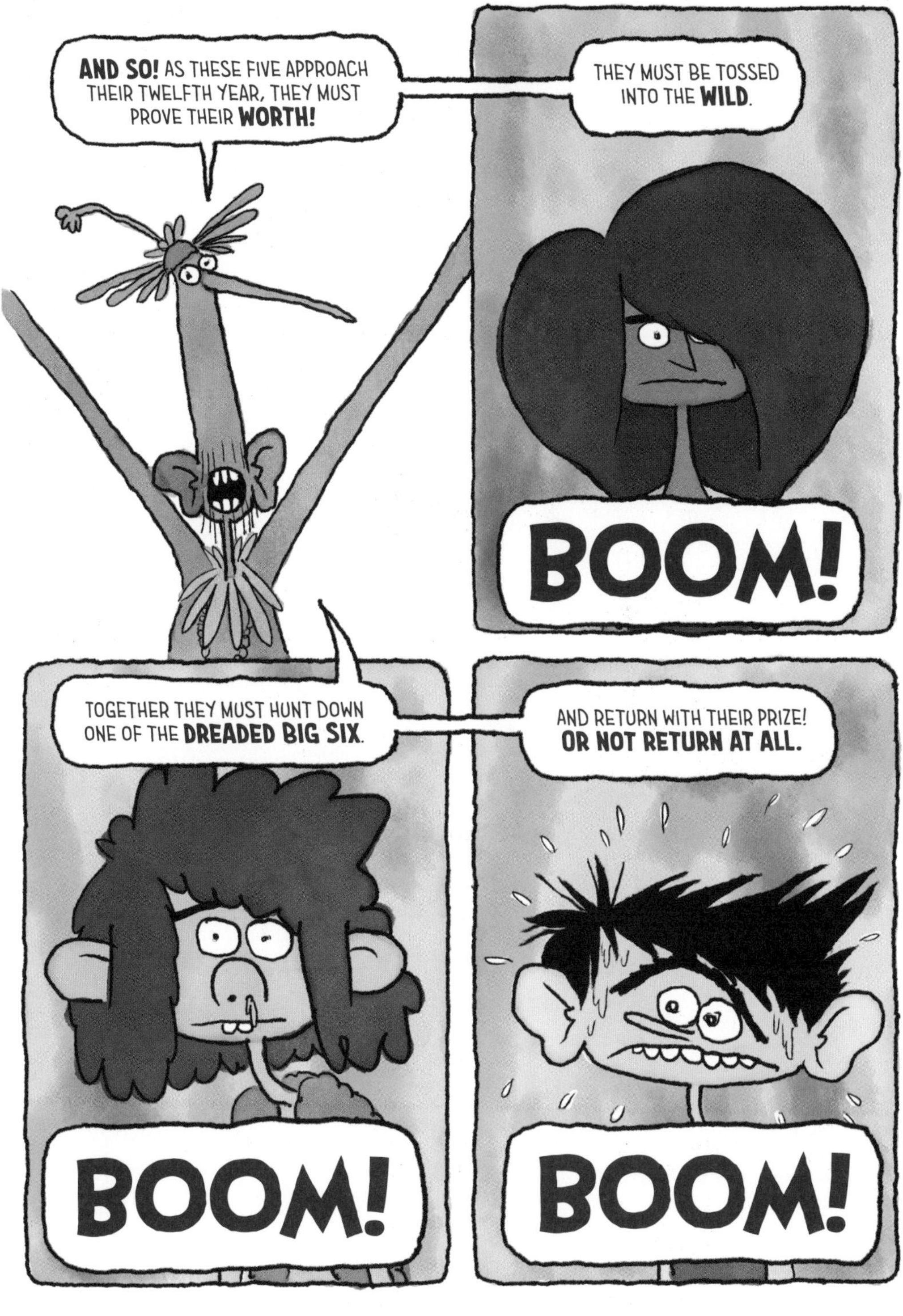
AND SO! AS THESE FIVE APPROACH THEIR TWELFTH YEAR, THEY MUST PROVE THEIR WORTH!
THEY MUST BE TOSSED INTO THE WILD.
BOOM!
TOGETHER THEY MUST HUNT DOWN ONE OF THE DREADED BIG SIX.
AND RETURN WITH THEIR PRIZE! OR NOT RETURN AT ALL.
BOOM!
BOOM!

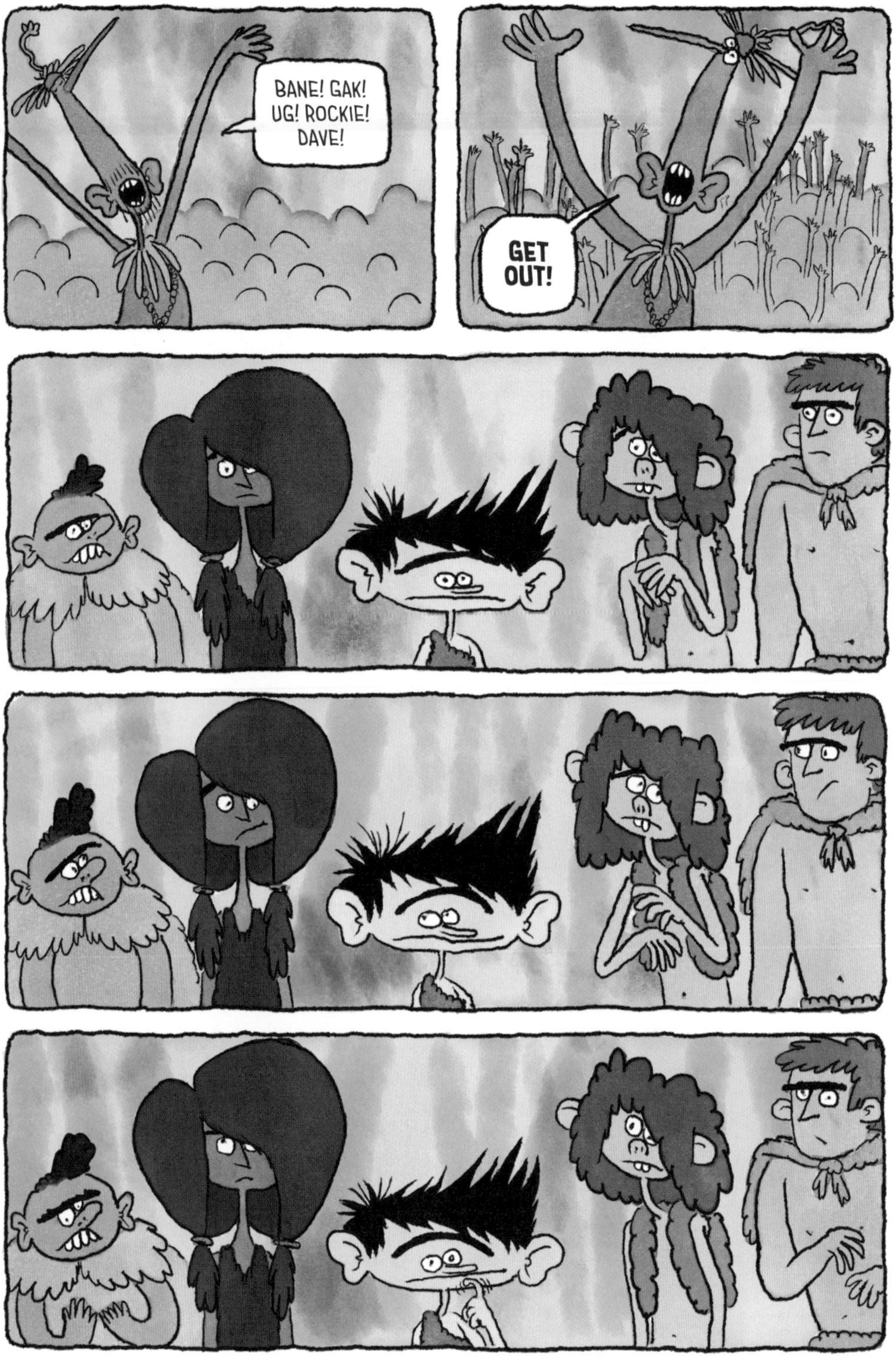
BANE! GAK!
UG! ROCKIE!
DAVE!
GET
OUT!

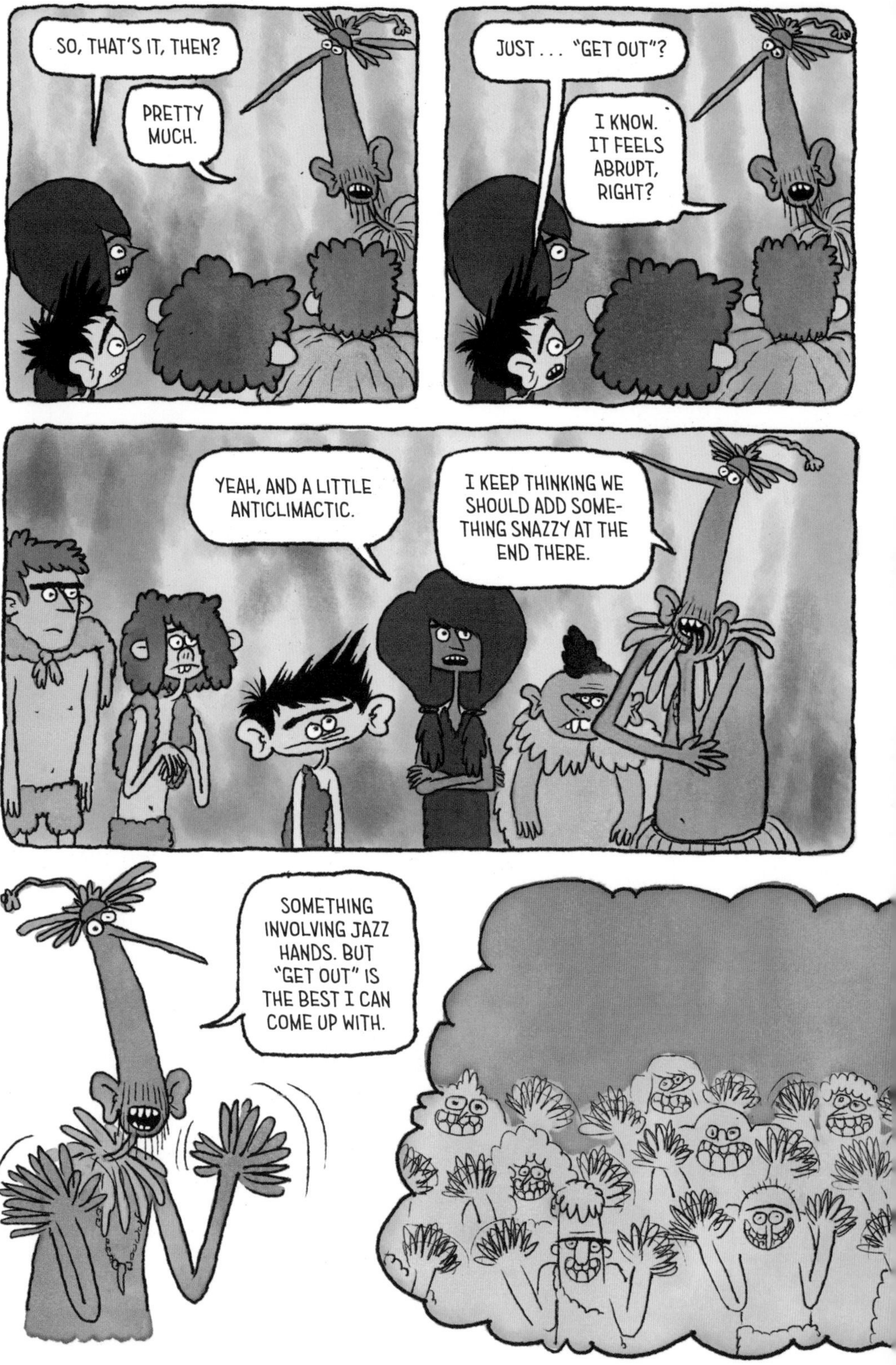
SO, THAT'S IT, THEN?
PRETTY MUCH.
JUST . . . "GET OUT"?
I KNOW. IT FEELS ABRUPT, RIGHT?
YEAH, AND A LITTLE ANTICLIMACTIC.
I KEEP THINKING WE SHOULD ADD SOME-THING SNAZZY AT THE END THERE.
SOMETHING INVOLVING JAZZ HANDS. BUT "GET OUT" IS THE BEST I CAN COME UP WITH.

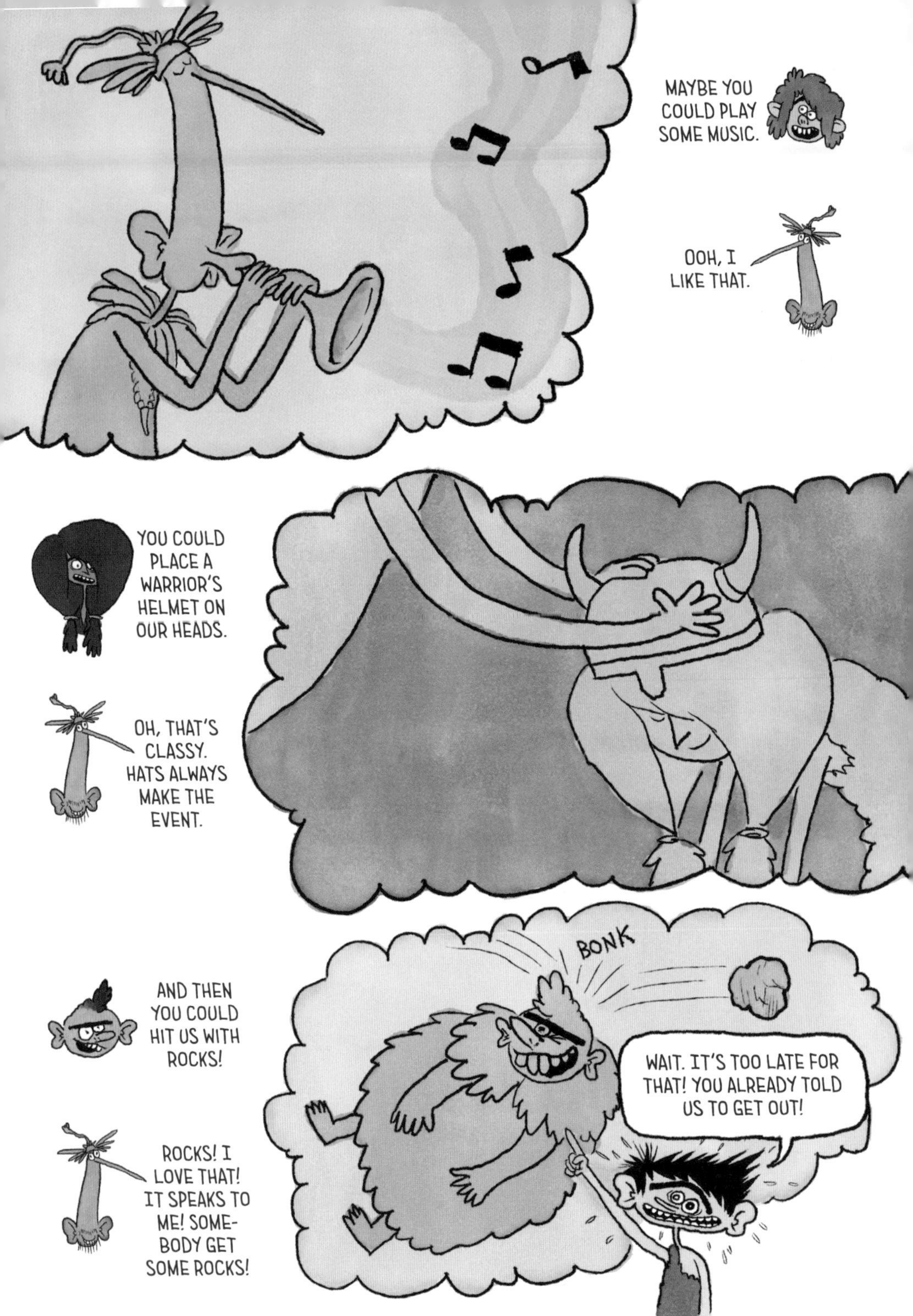
MAYBE YOU COULD PLAY SOME MUSIC.
OOH, I LIKE THAT.
YOU COULD PLACE A WARRIOR'S HELMET ON OUR HEADS.
OH, THAT'S CLASSY. HATS ALWAYS MAKE THE EVENT.
AND THEN YOU COULD HIT US WITH ROCKS!
ROCKS! I LOVE THAT! IT SPEAKS TO ME! SOME-BODY GET SOME ROCKS!
BONK
WAIT. IT'S TOO LATE FOR THAT! YOU ALREADY TOLD US TO GET OUT!

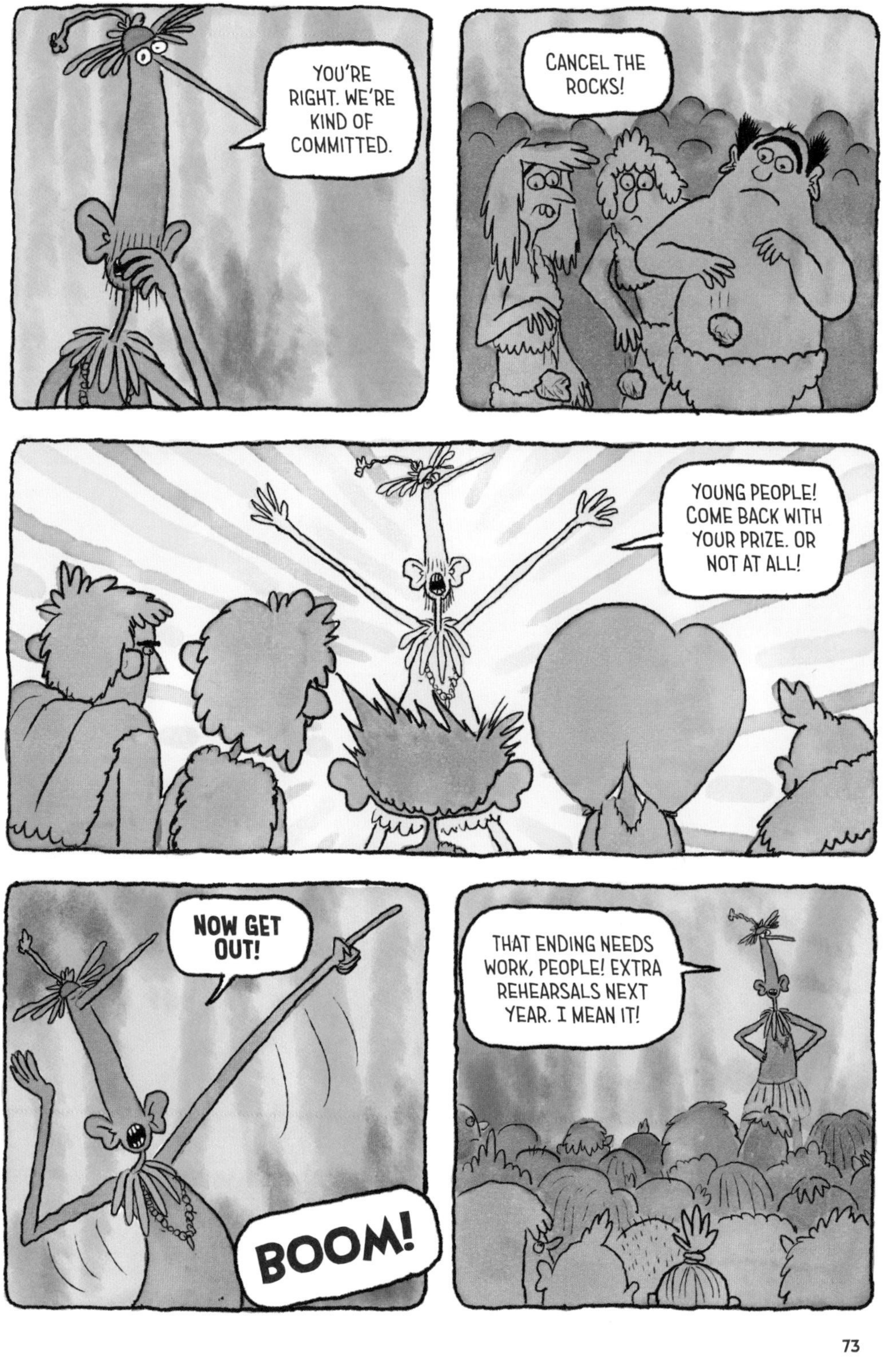
YOU'RE RIGHT. WE'RE KIND OF COMMITTED.
CANCEL THE ROCKS!
YOUNG PEOPLE! COME BACK WITH YOUR PRIZE. OR NOT AT ALL!
NOW GET OUT!
BOOM!
THAT ENDING NEEDS WORK, PEOPLE! EXTRA REHEARSALS NEXT YEAR. I MEAN IT!

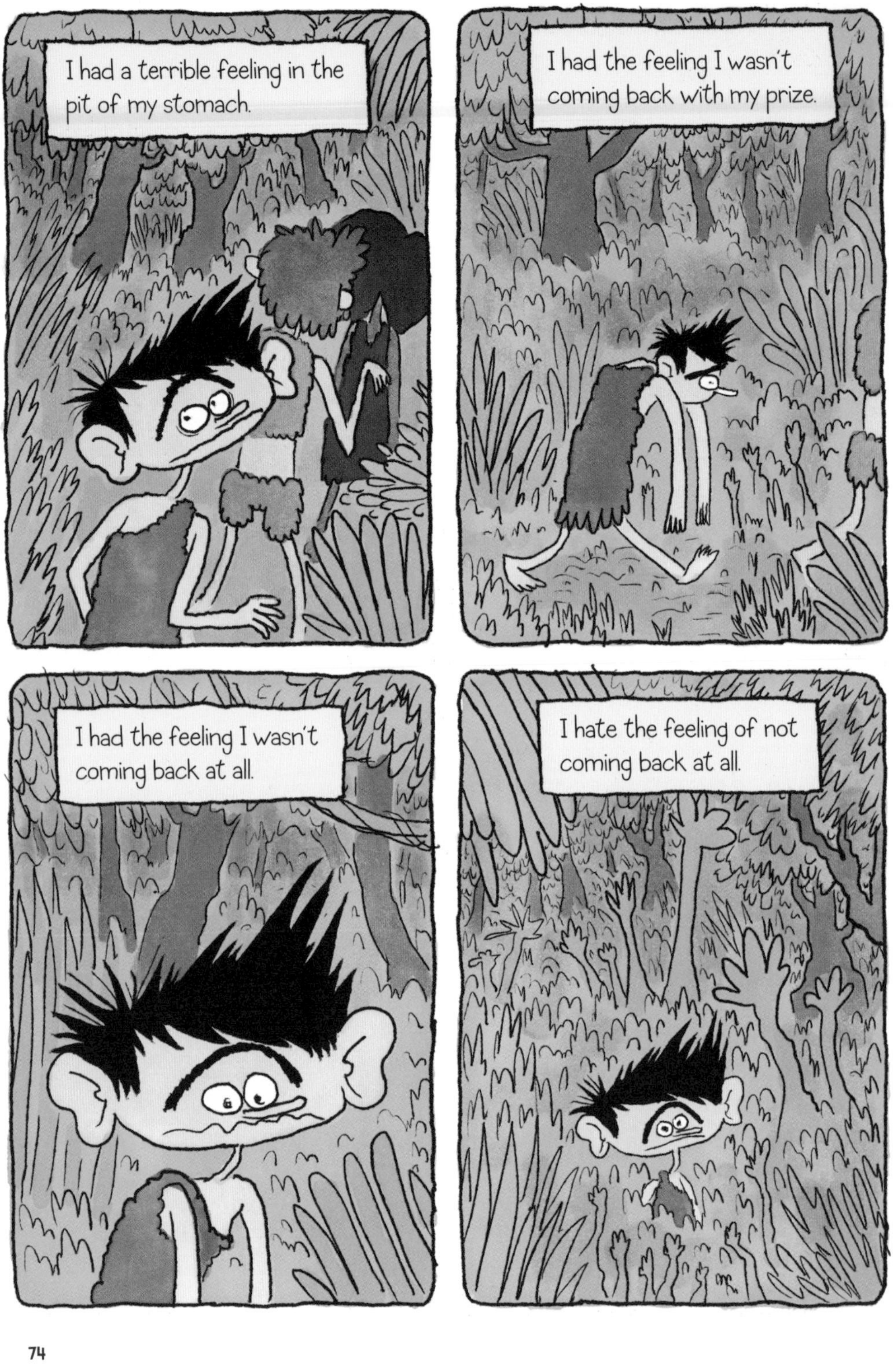
I had a terrible feeling in the pit of my stomach.
I had the feeling I wasn't coming back with my prize.
I had the feeling I wasn't coming back at all.
I hate the feeling of not coming back at all.

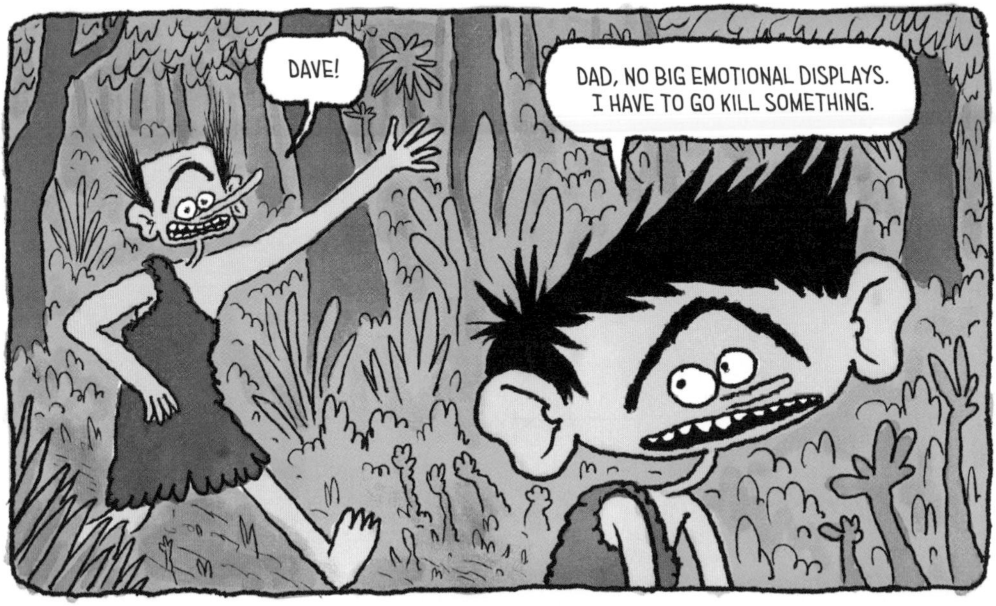
DAVE!
DAD, NO BIG EMOTIONAL DISPLAYS. I HAVE TO GO KILL SOMETHING.

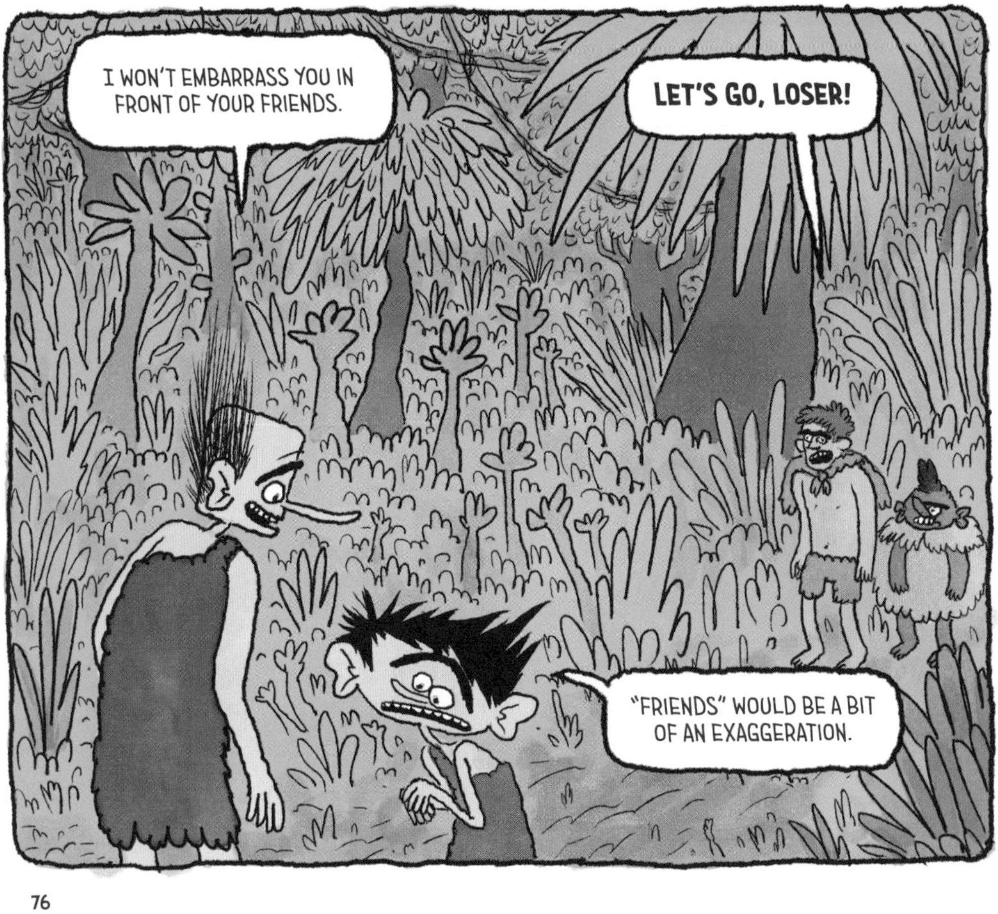
I WON'T EMBARRASS YOU IN FRONT OF YOUR FRIENDS.
LET'S GO, LOSER!
"FRIENDS" WOULD BE A BIT OF AN EXAGGERATION.

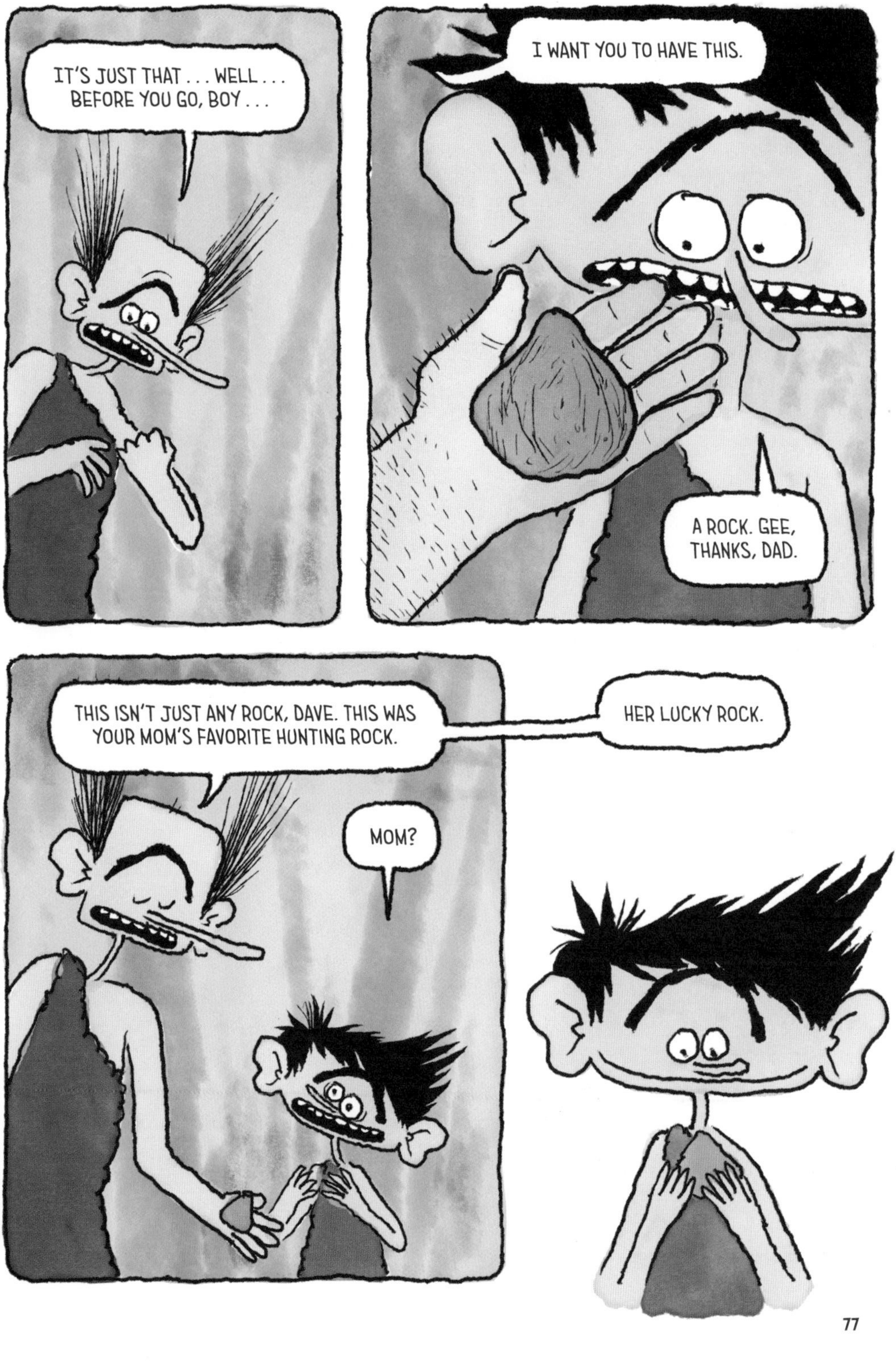
IT'S JUST THAT . . . WELL . . . BEFORE YOU GO, BOY . . .
I WANT YOU TO HAVE THIS.
A ROCK. GEE, THANKS, DAD.
THIS ISN'T JUST ANY ROCK, DAVE. THIS WAS YOUR MOM'S FAVORITE HUNTING ROCK.
HER LUCKY ROCK.
MOM?

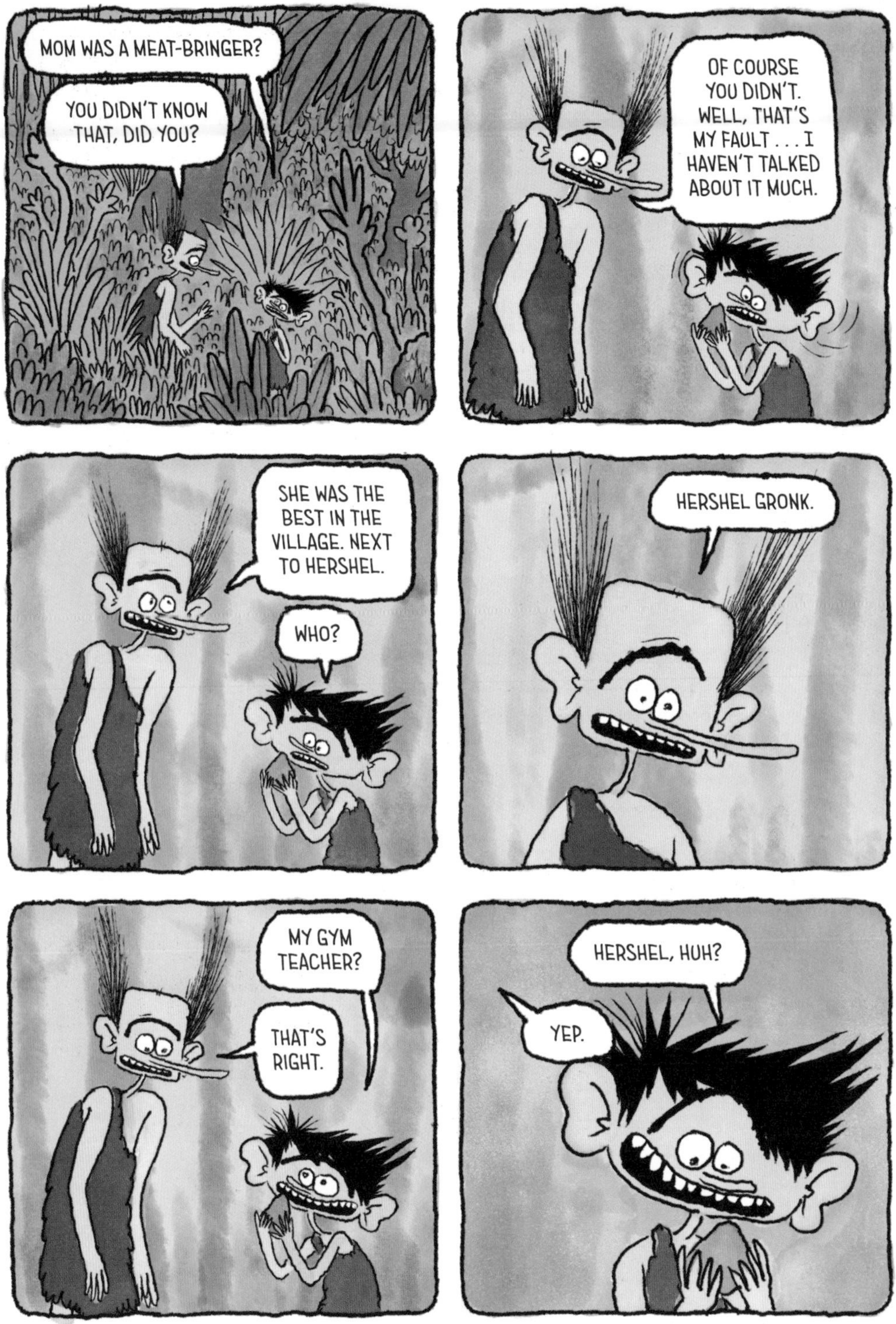
MOM WAS A MEAT-BRINGER?
YOU DIDN'T KNOW THAT, DID YOU?
OF COURSE YOU DIDN'T. WELL, THAT'S MY FAULT . . . I HAVEN'T TALKED ABOUT IT MUCH.
SHE WAS THE BEST IN THE VILLAGE. NEXT TO HERSHEL.
WHO?
HERSHEL GRONK.
MY GYM TEACHER?
THAT'S RIGHT.
HERSHEL, HUH?
YEP.

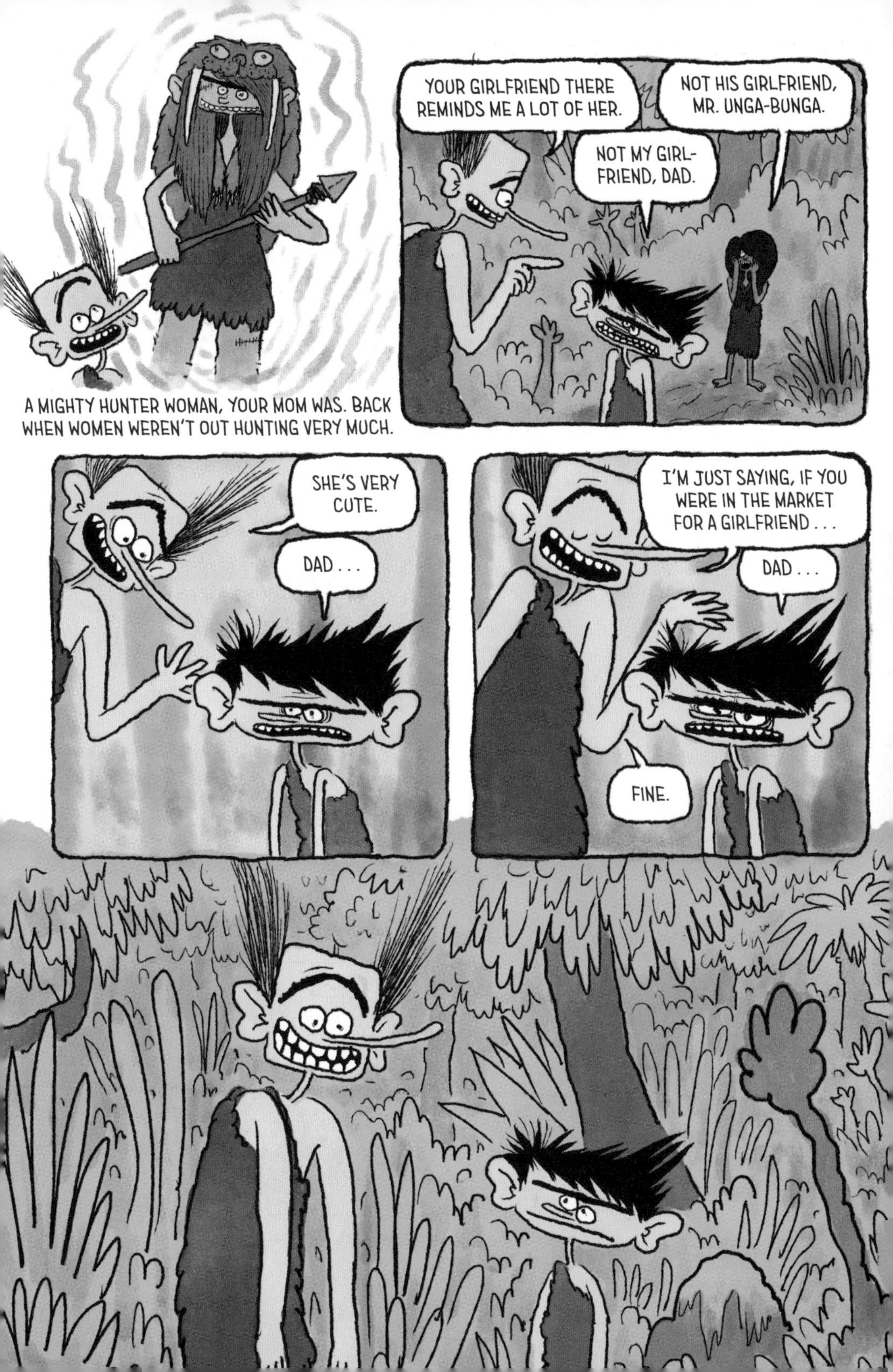
A MIGHTY HUNTER WOMAN, YOUR MOM WAS. BACK WHEN WOMEN WEREN'T OUT HUNTING VERY MUCH.
YOUR GIRLFRIEND THERE REMINDS ME A LOT OF HER.
NOT MY GIRL-FRIEND, DAD.
NOT HIS GIRLFRIEND, MR. UNGA-BUNGA.
SHE'S VERY CUTE.
DAD . . .
I'M JUST SAYING, IF YOU WERE IN THE MARKET FOR A GIRLFRIEND . . .
DAD . . .
FINE.

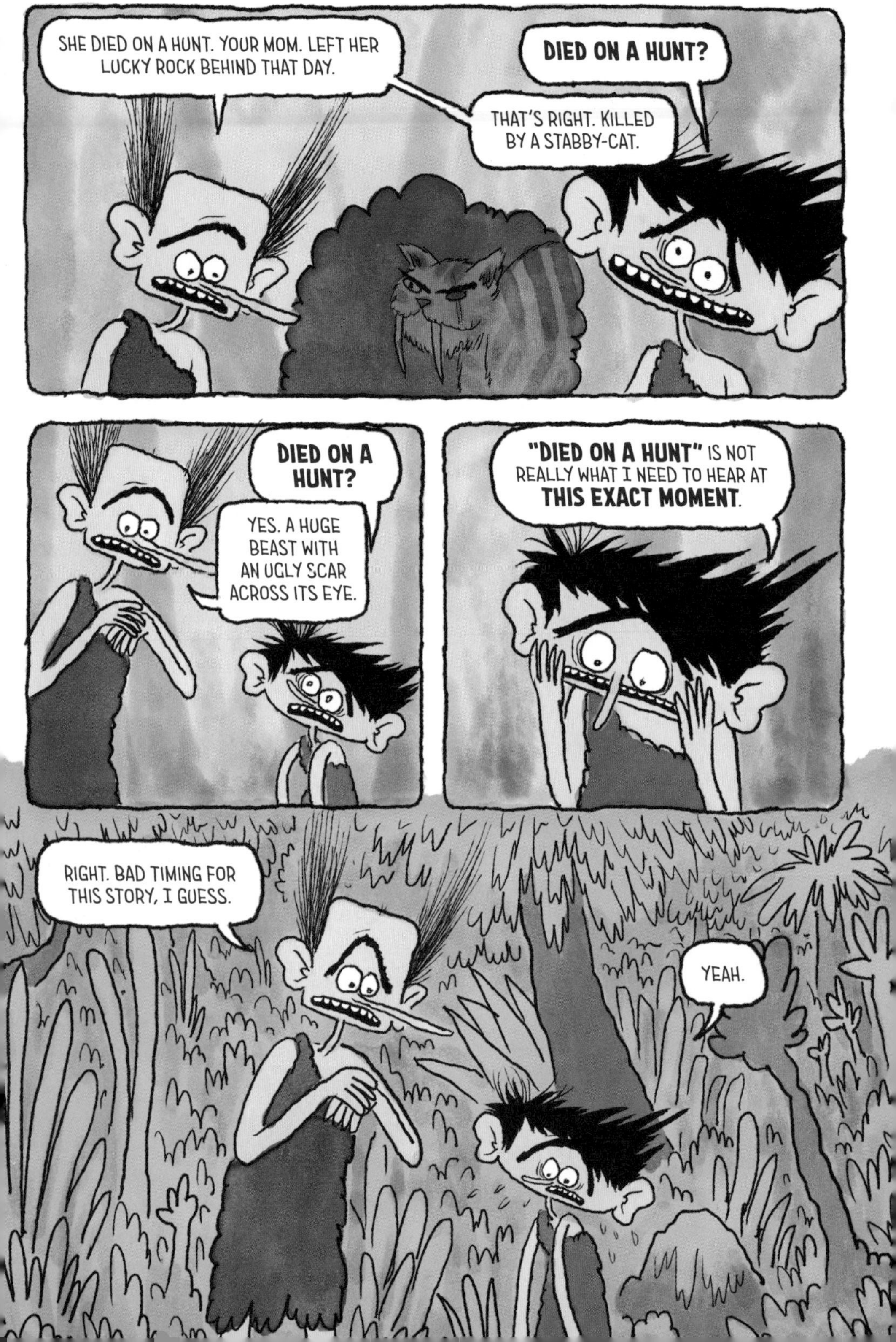

SHE DIED ON A HUNT. YOUR MOM. LEFT HER LUCKY ROCK BEHIND THAT DAY.
DIED ON A HUNT?
THAT'S RIGHT. KILLED BY A STABBY-CAT.
DIED ON A HUNT?
YES. A HUGE BEAST WITH AN UGLY SCAR ACROSS ITS EYE.
"DIED ON A HUNT" IS NOT REALLY WHAT I NEED TO HEAR AT THIS EXACT MOMENT.
RIGHT. BAD TIMING FOR THIS STORY, I GUESS.
YEAH.

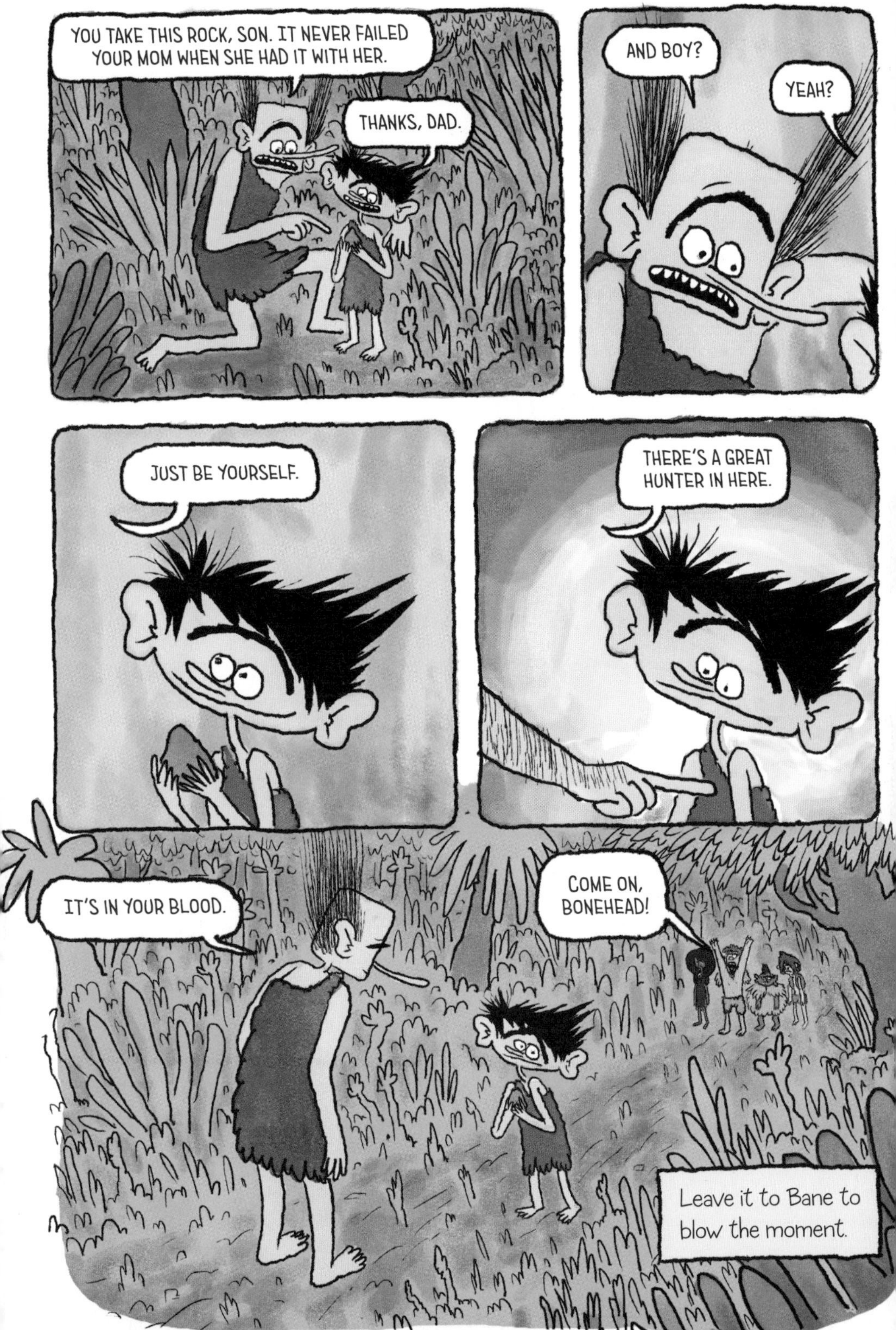
YOU TAKE THIS ROCK, SON. IT NEVER FAILED YOUR MOM WHEN SHE HAD IT WITH HER.
THANKS, DAD.
AND BOY?
YEAH?
JUST BE YOURSELF.
THERE'S A GREAT HUNTER IN HERE.
IT'S IN YOUR BLOOD.
COME ON, BONEHEAD!
Leave it to Bane to blow the moment.

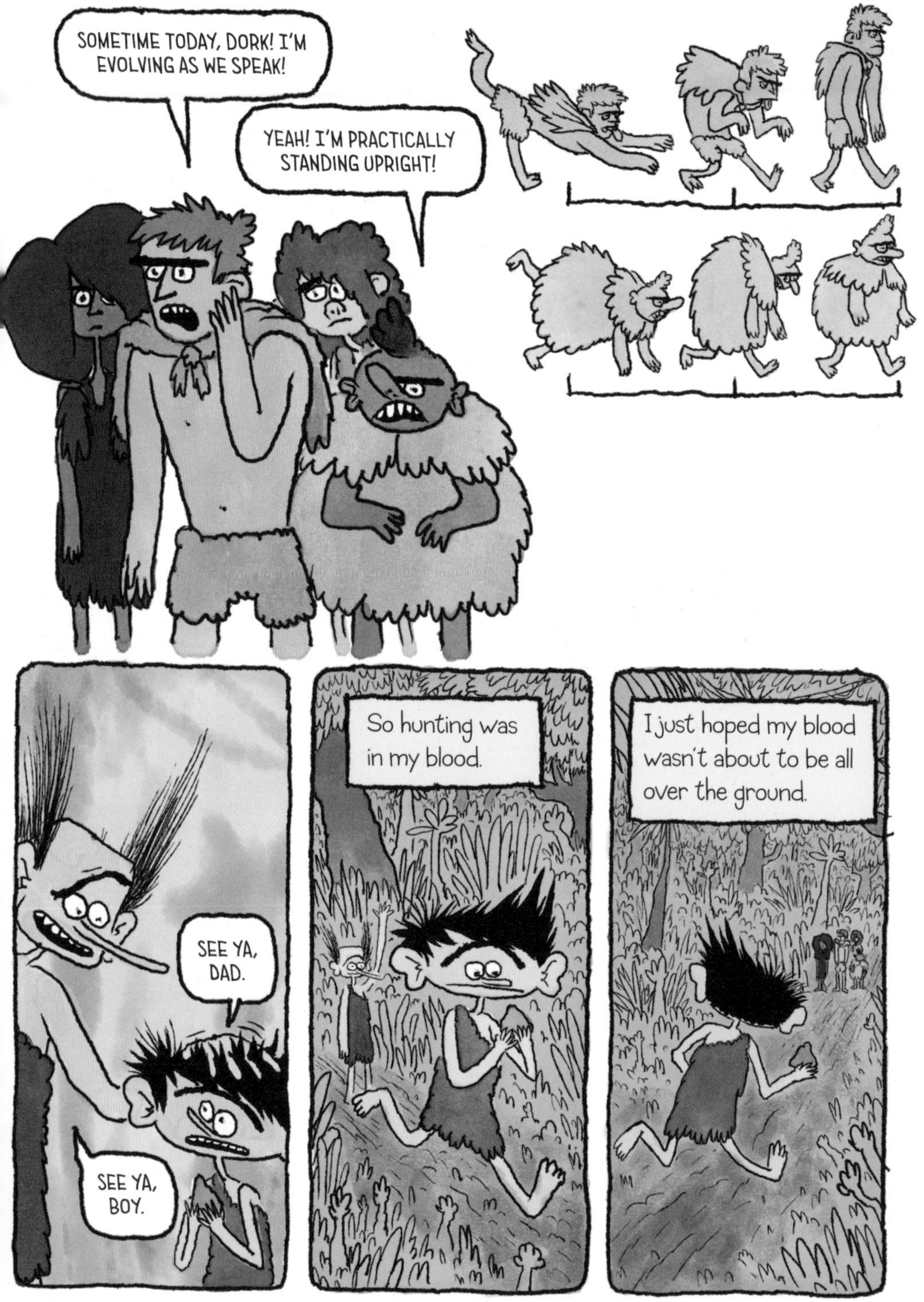
SOMETIME TODAY, DORK! I'M EVOLVING AS WE SPEAK!
YEAH! I'M PRACTICALLY STANDING UPRIGHT!
SEE YA, DAD.
SEE YA, BOY.
So hunting was in my blood.
I just hoped my blood wasn't about to be all over the ground.

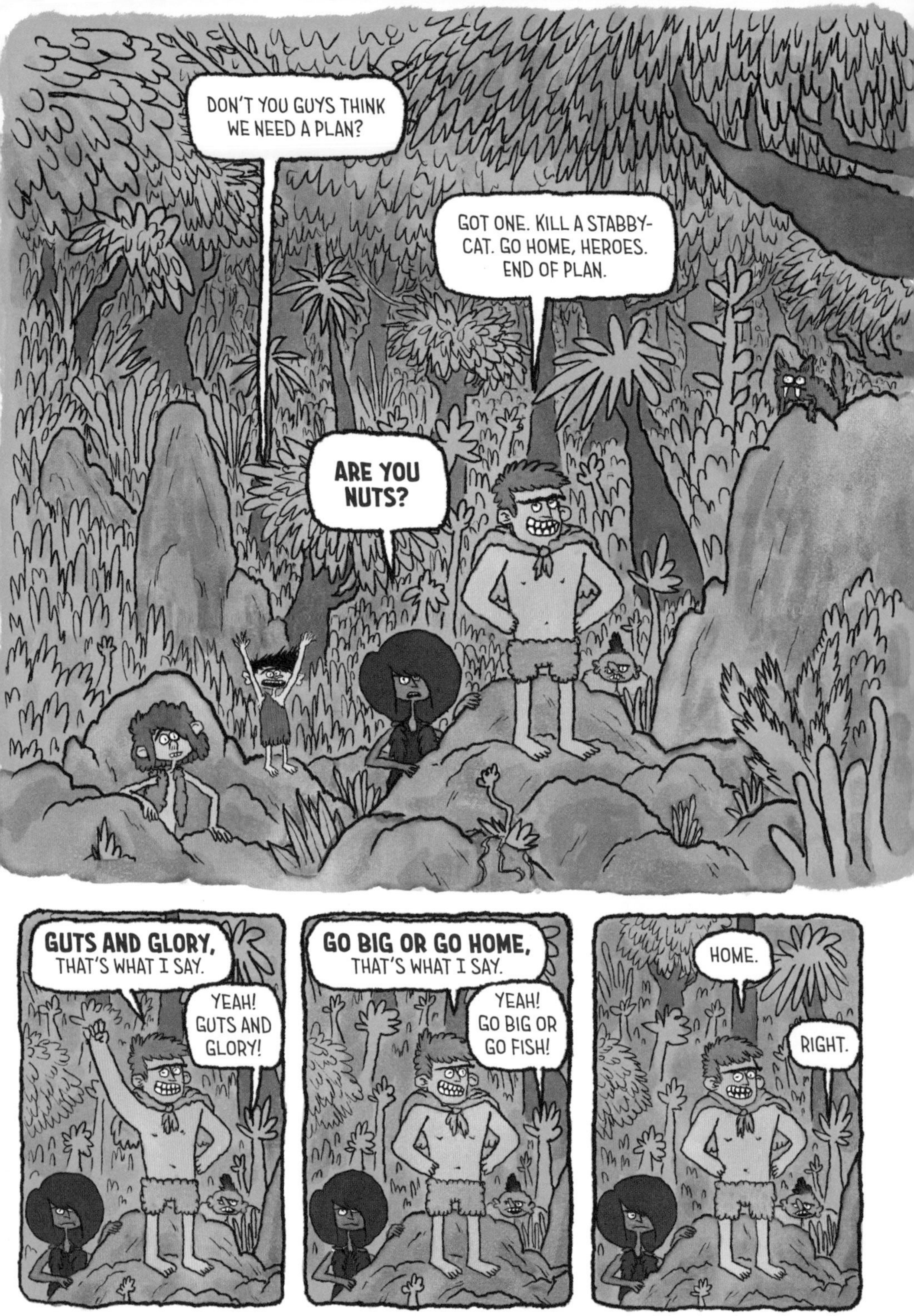
DON'T YOU GUYS THINK WE NEED A PLAN?
GOT ONE. KILL A STABBY-CAT. GO HOME, HEROES. END OF PLAN.
ARE YOU NUTS?
GUTS AND GLORY, THAT'S WHAT I SAY.
YEAH! GUTS AND GLORY!
GO BIG OR GO HOME, THAT'S WHAT I SAY.
YEAH! GO BIG OR GO FISH!
HOME.
RIGHT.

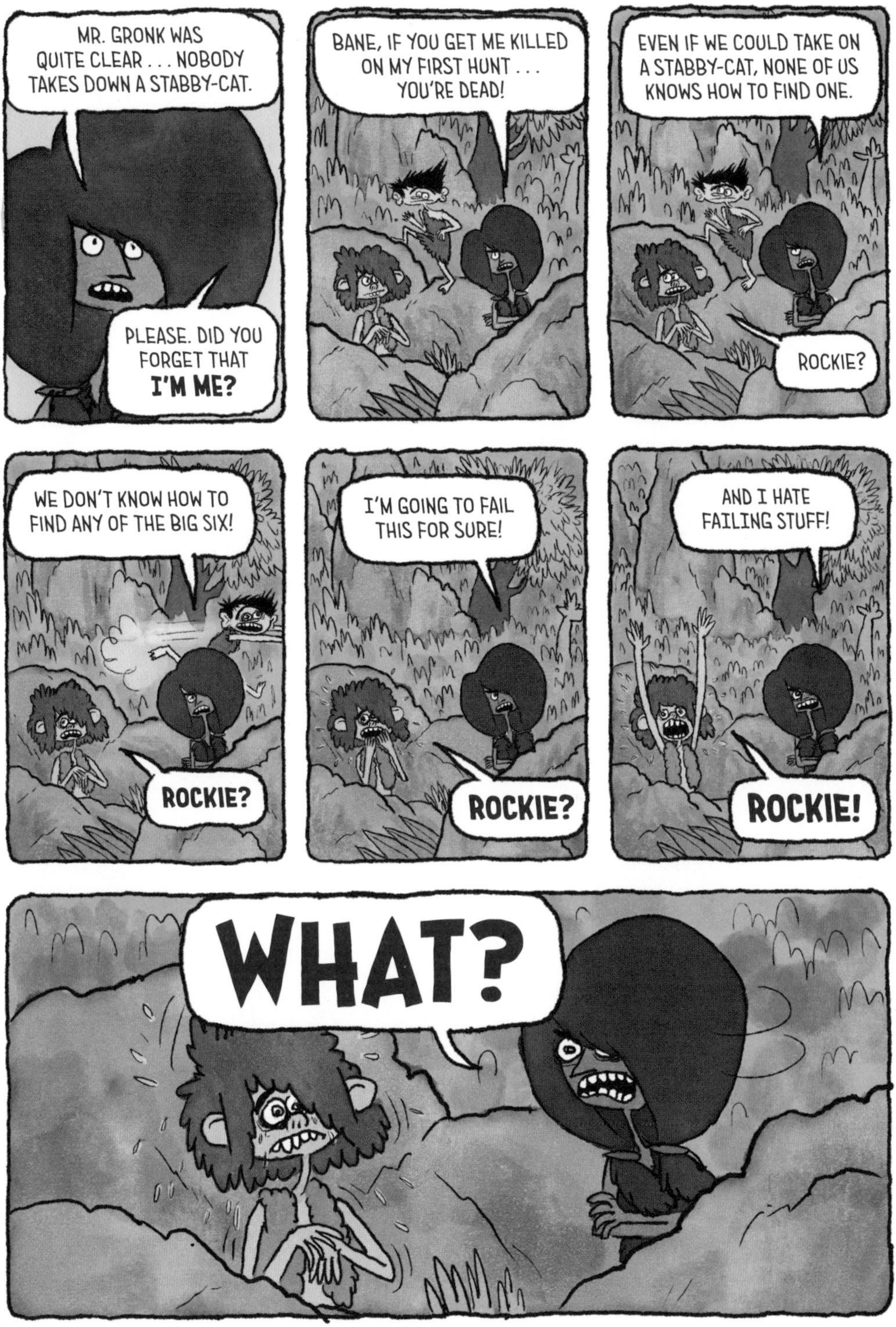
MR. GRONK WAS QUITE CLEAR . . . NOBODY TAKES DOWN A STABBY-CAT.
PLEASE. DID YOU FORGET THAT **I'M ME?**
BANE, IF YOU GET ME KILLED ON MY FIRST HUNT . . . YOU'RE DEAD!
EVEN IF WE COULD TAKE ON A STABBY-CAT, NONE OF US KNOWS HOW TO FIND ONE.
ROCKIE?
WE DON'T KNOW HOW TO FIND ANY OF THE BIG SIX!
ROCKIE?
I'M GOING TO FAIL THIS FOR SURE!
ROCKIE?
AND I HATE FAILING STUFF!
ROCKIE!
WHAT?

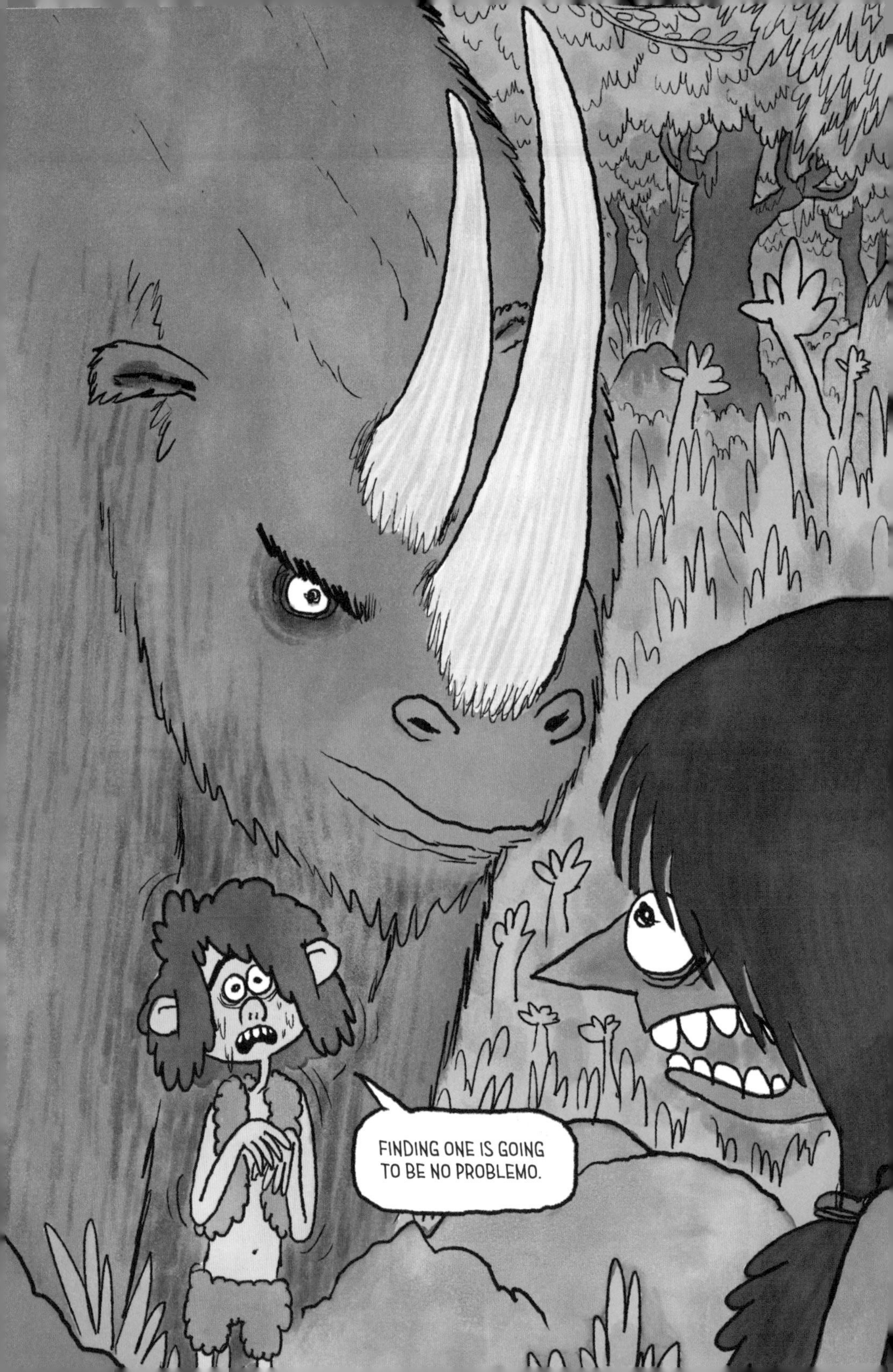
FINDING ONE IS GOING TO BE NO PROBLEMO.

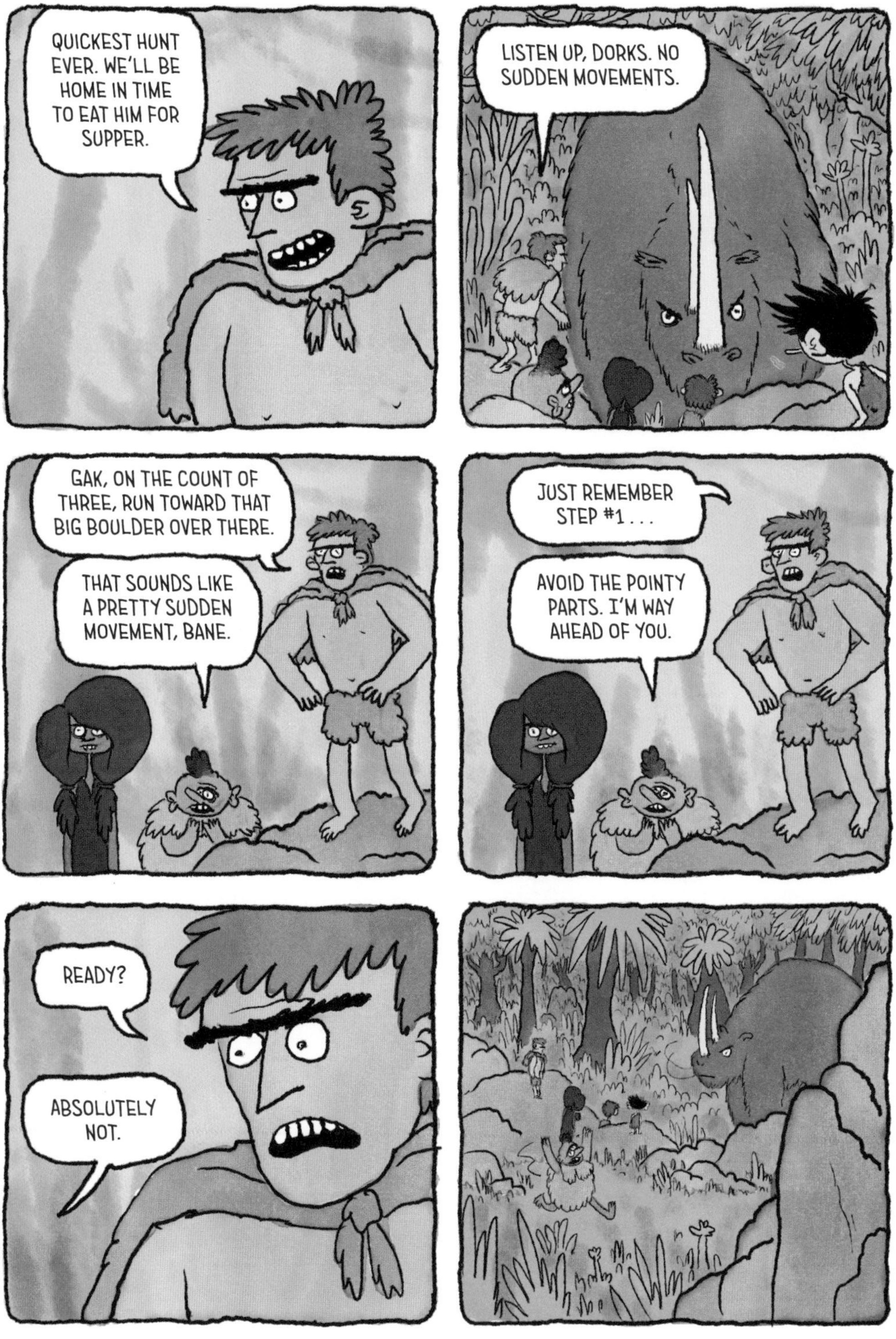
QUICKEST HUNT EVER. WE'LL BE HOME IN TIME TO EAT HIM FOR SUPPER.
LISTEN UP, DORKS. NO SUDDEN MOVEMENTS.
GAK, ON THE COUNT OF THREE, RUN TOWARD THAT BIG BOULDER OVER THERE.
THAT SOUNDS LIKE A PRETTY SUDDEN MOVEMENT, BANE.
JUST REMEMBER STEP #1 . . .
AVOID THE POINTY PARTS. I'M WAY AHEAD OF YOU.
READY?
ABSOLUTELY NOT.

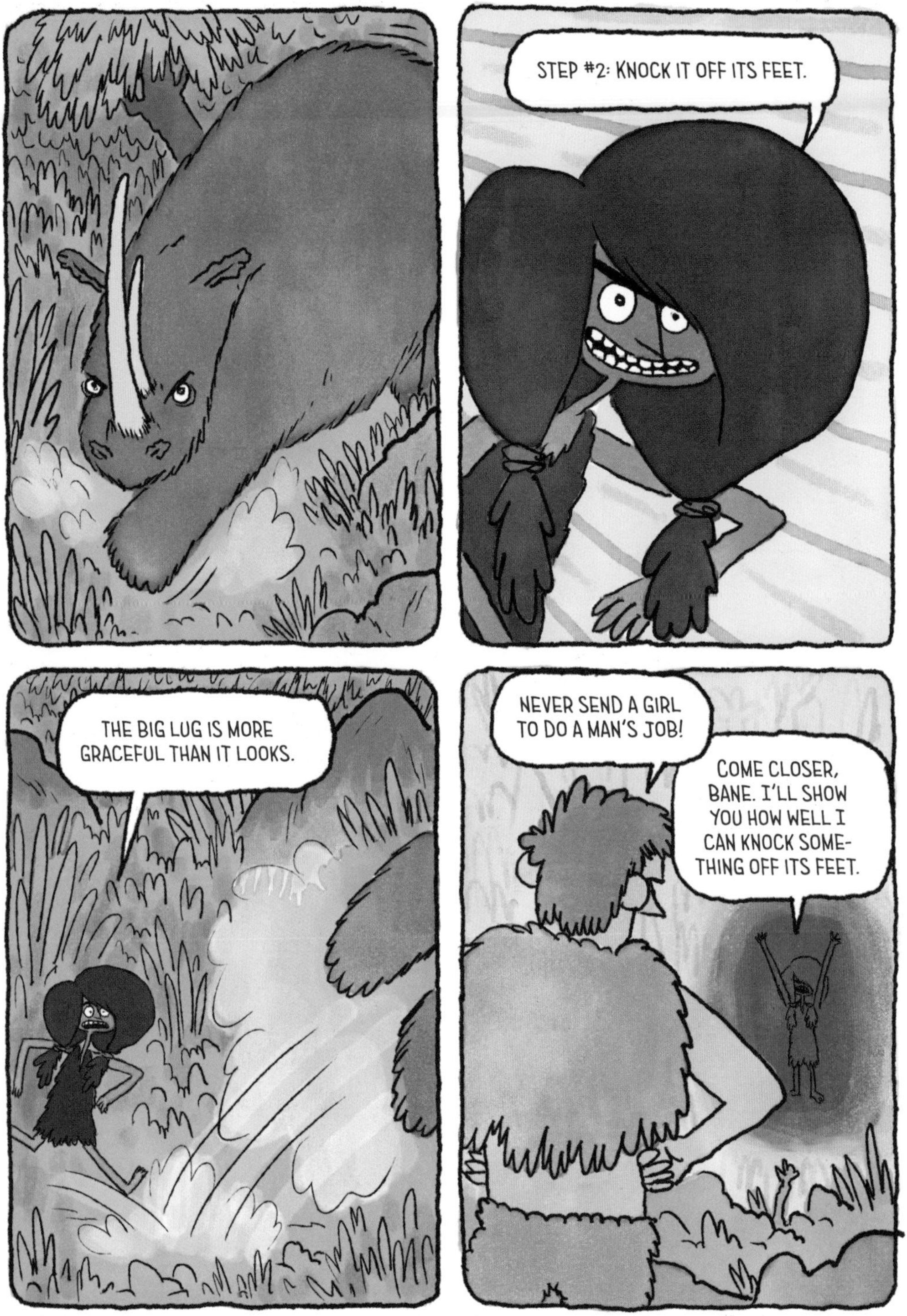
STEP #2: KNOCK IT OFF ITS FEET.
THE BIG LUG IS MORE GRACEFUL THAN IT LOOKS.
NEVER SEND A GIRL TO DO A MAN'S JOB!
COME CLOSER, BANE. I'LL SHOW YOU HOW WELL I CAN KNOCK SOME-THING OFF ITS FEET.

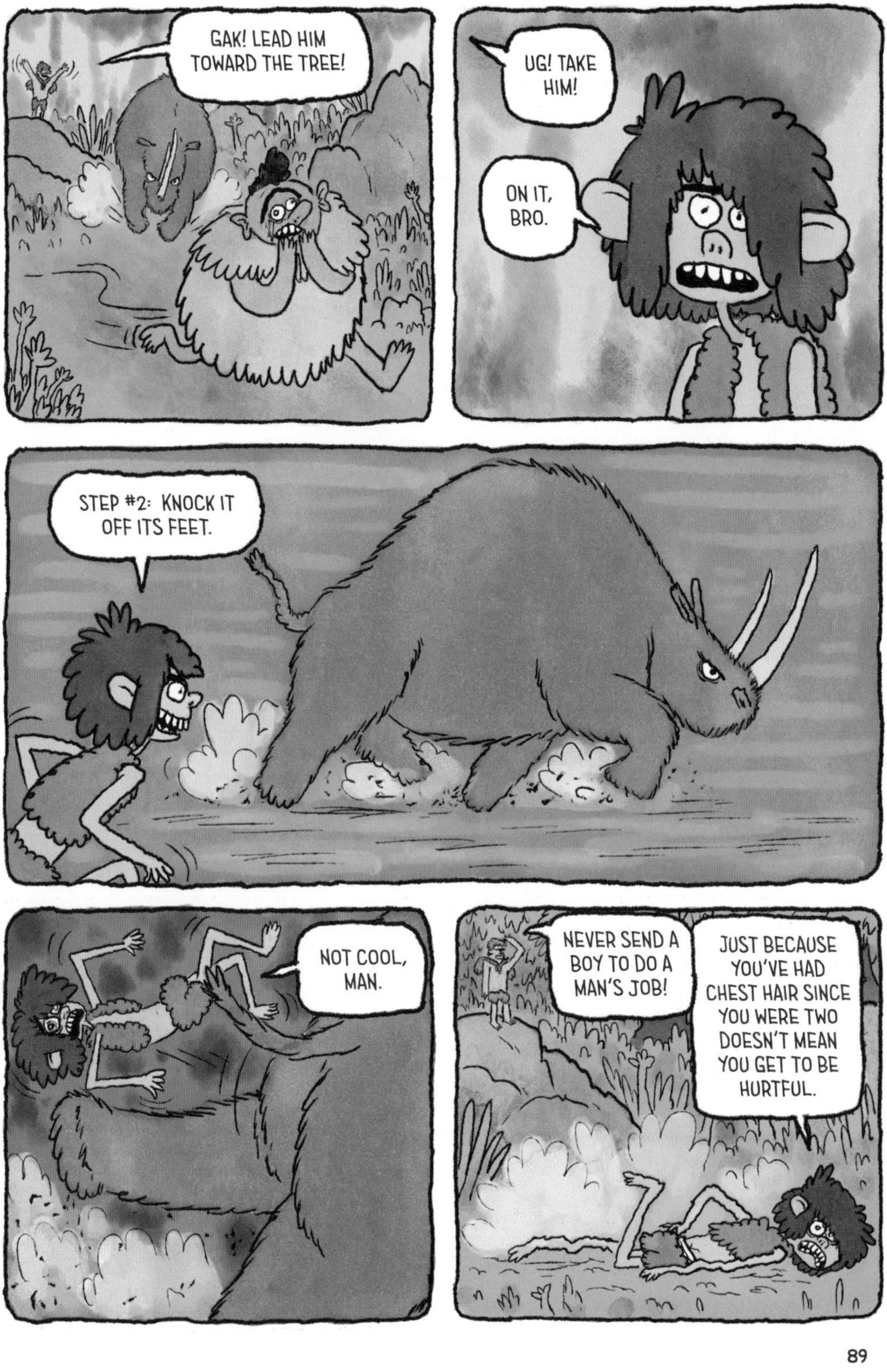
GAK! LEAD HIM TOWARD THE TREE!
UG! TAKE HIM!
ON IT, BRO.
STEP #2: KNOCK IT OFF ITS FEET.
NOT COOL, MAN.
NEVER SEND A BOY TO DO A MAN'S JOB!
JUST BECAUSE YOU'VE HAD CHEST HAIR SINCE YOU WERE TWO DOESN'T MEAN YOU GET TO BE HURTFUL.

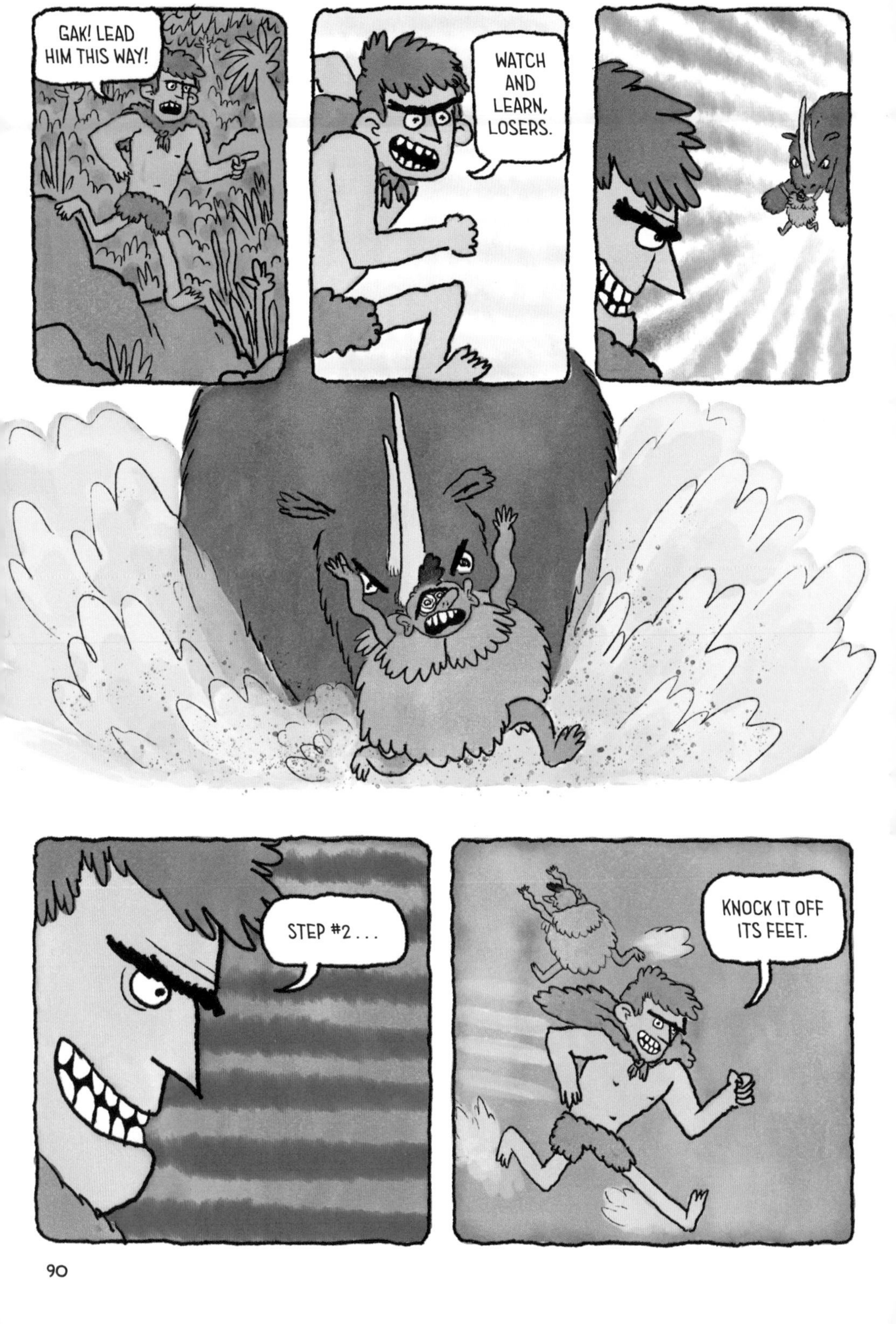
GAK! LEAD HIM THIS WAY!
WATCH AND LEARN, LOSERS.
STEP #2 . . .
KNOCK IT OFF ITS FEET.

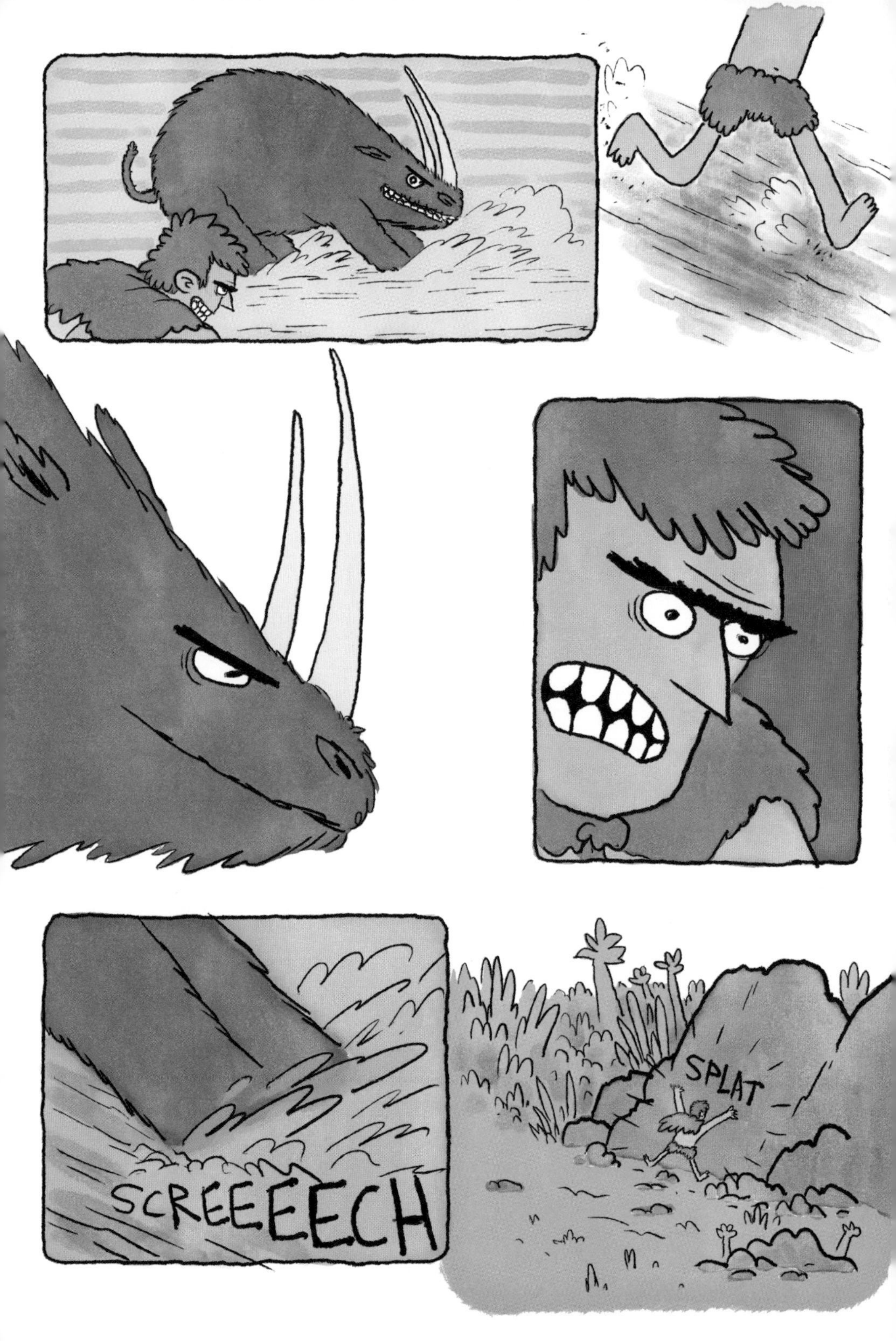
SCREEEECH
SPLAT

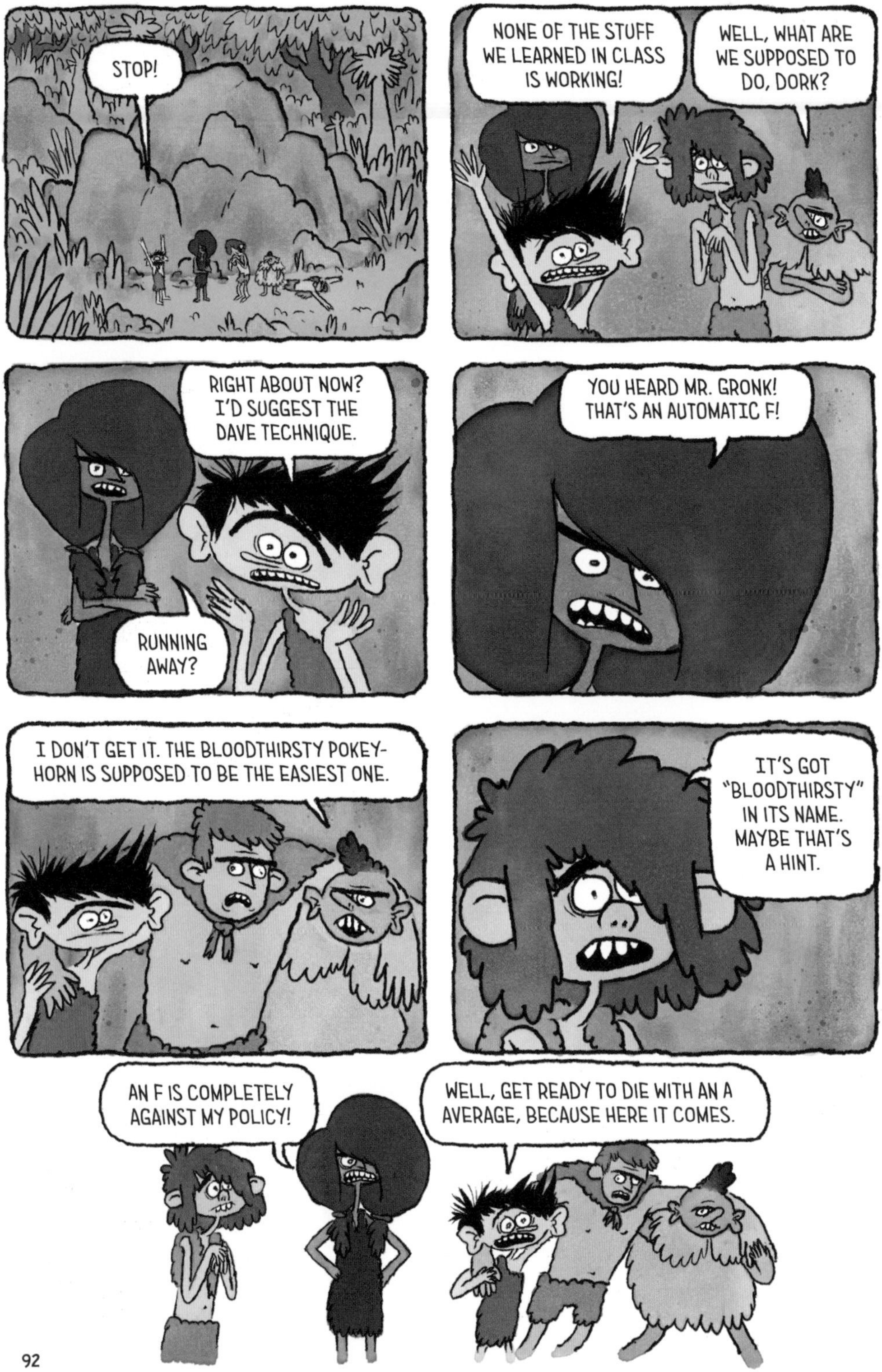
STOP!
NONE OF THE STUFF WE LEARNED IN CLASS IS WORKING!
WELL, WHAT ARE WE SUPPOSED TO DO, DORK?
RIGHT ABOUT NOW? I'D SUGGEST THE DAVE TECHNIQUE.
RUNNING AWAY?
YOU HEARD MR. GRONK! THAT'S AN AUTOMATIC F!
I DON'T GET IT. THE BLOODTHIRSTY POKEY-HORN IS SUPPOSED TO BE THE EASIEST ONE.
IT'S GOT "BLOODTHIRSTY" IN ITS NAME. MAYBE THAT'S A HINT.
AN F IS COMPLETELY AGAINST MY POLICY!
WELL, GET READY TO DIE WITH AN A AVERAGE, BECAUSE HERE IT COMES.

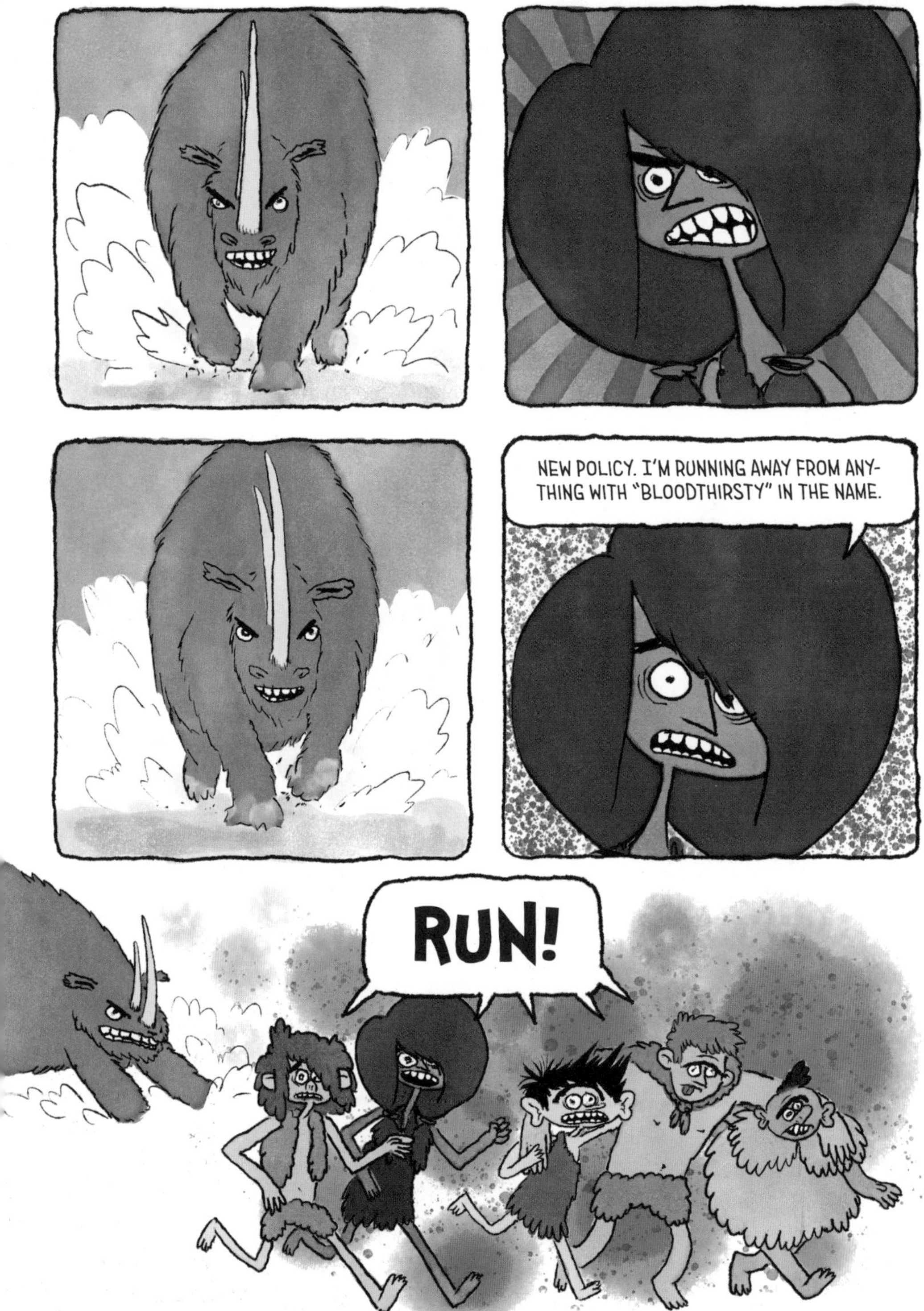

NEW POLICY. I'M RUNNING AWAY FROM ANY-THING WITH "BLOODTHIRSTY" IN THE NAME.
RUN!

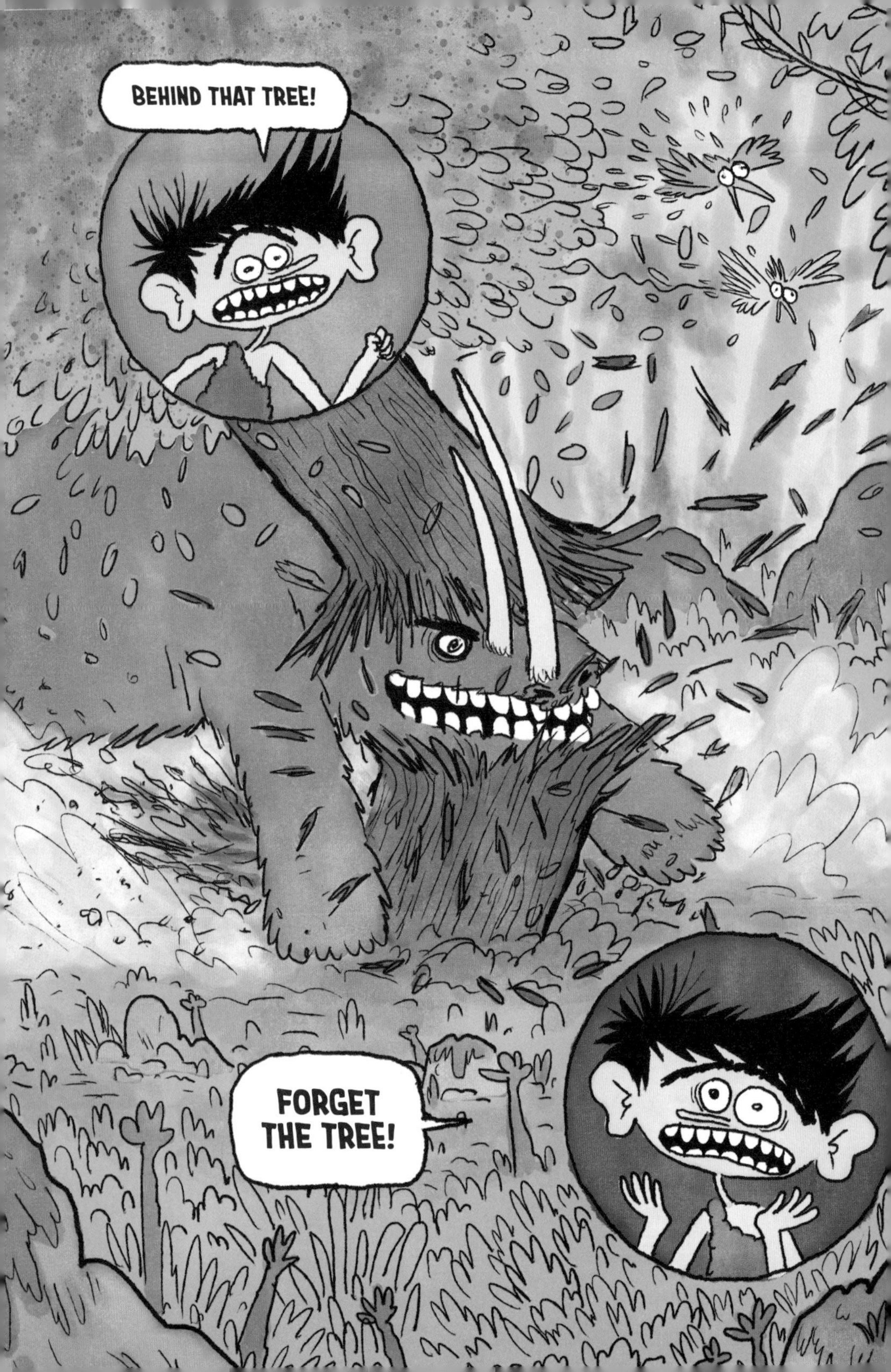
BEHIND THAT TREE!
FORGET THE TREE!

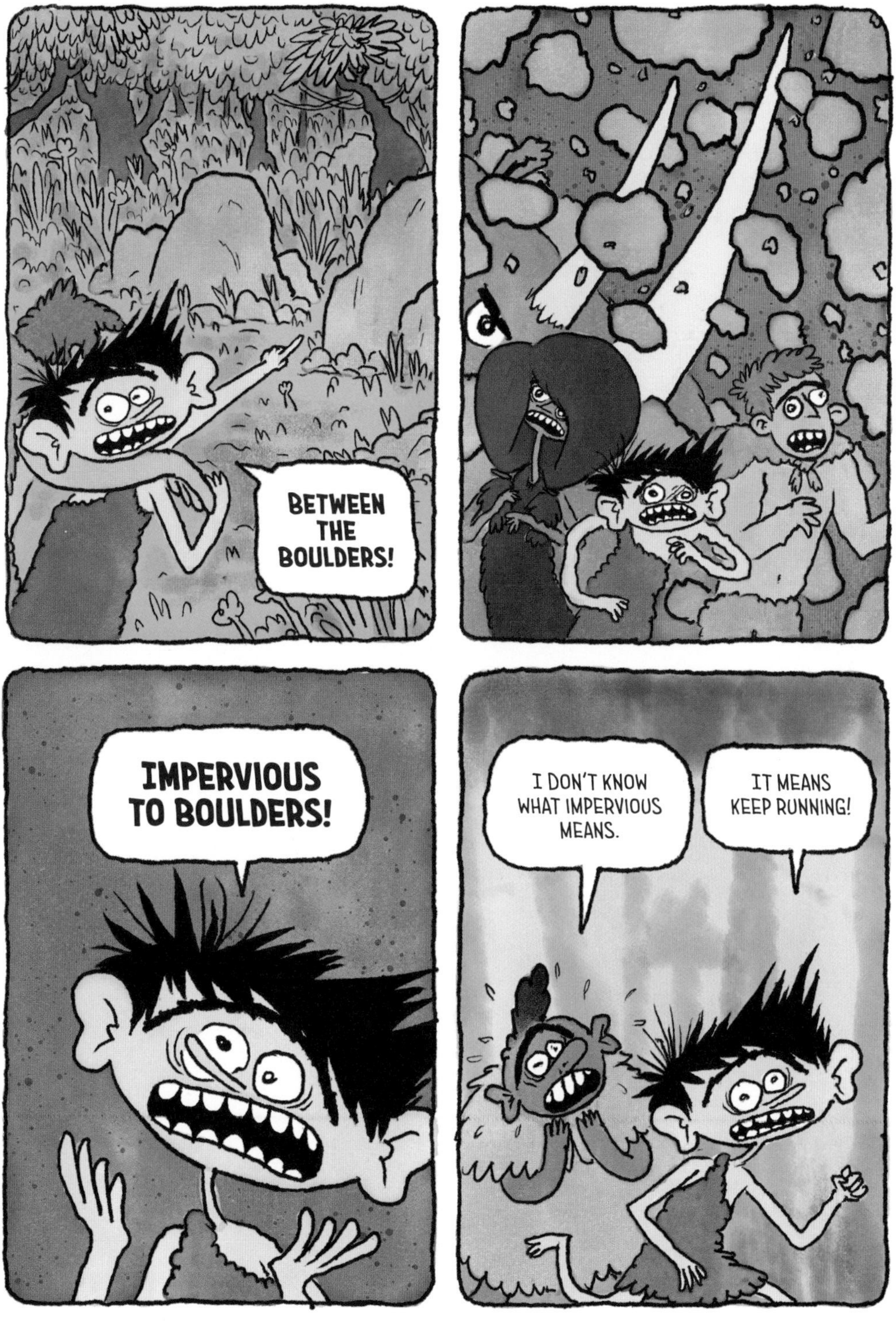
BETWEEN THE BOULDERS!
IMPERVIOUS TO BOULDERS!
I DON'T KNOW WHAT IMPERVIOUS MEANS.
IT MEANS KEEP RUNNING!

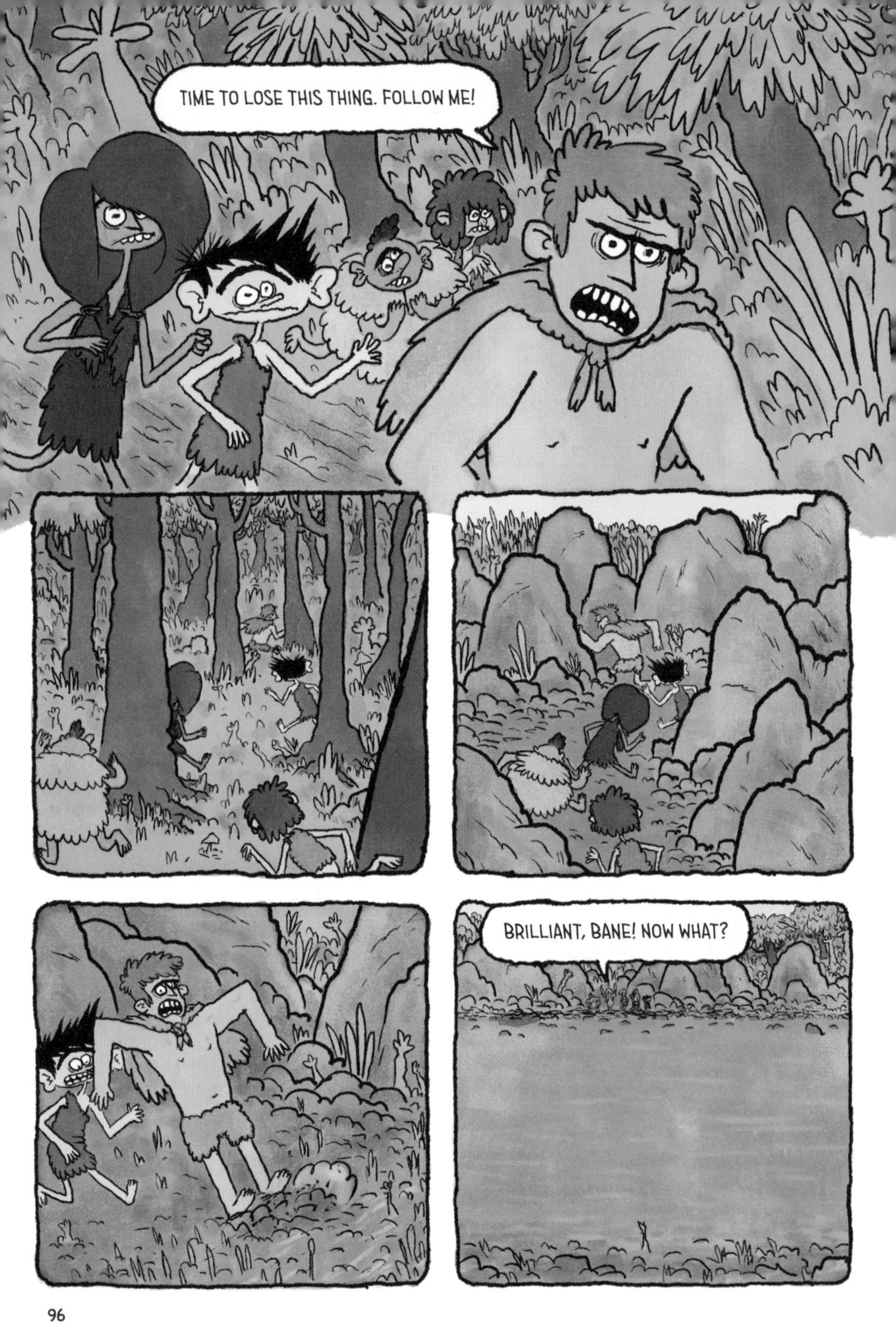
TIME TO LOSE THIS THING. FOLLOW ME!
BRILLIANT, BANE! NOW WHAT?

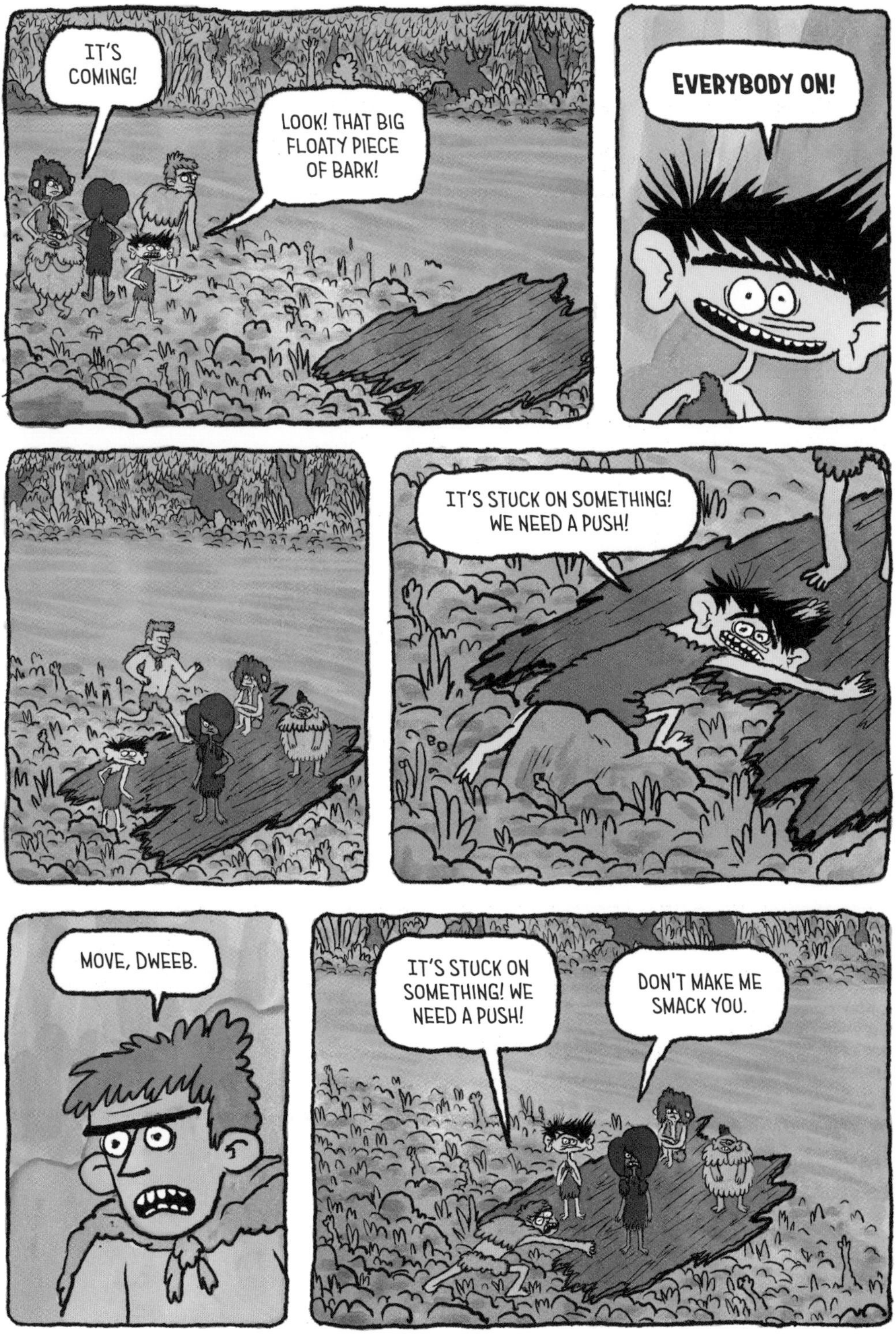
IT'S COMING!
LOOK! THAT BIG FLOATY PIECE OF BARK!
EVERYBODY ON!
IT'S STUCK ON SOMETHING! WE NEED A PUSH!
MOVE, DWEEB.
IT'S STUCK ON SOMETHING! WE NEED A PUSH!
DON'T MAKE ME SMACK YOU.

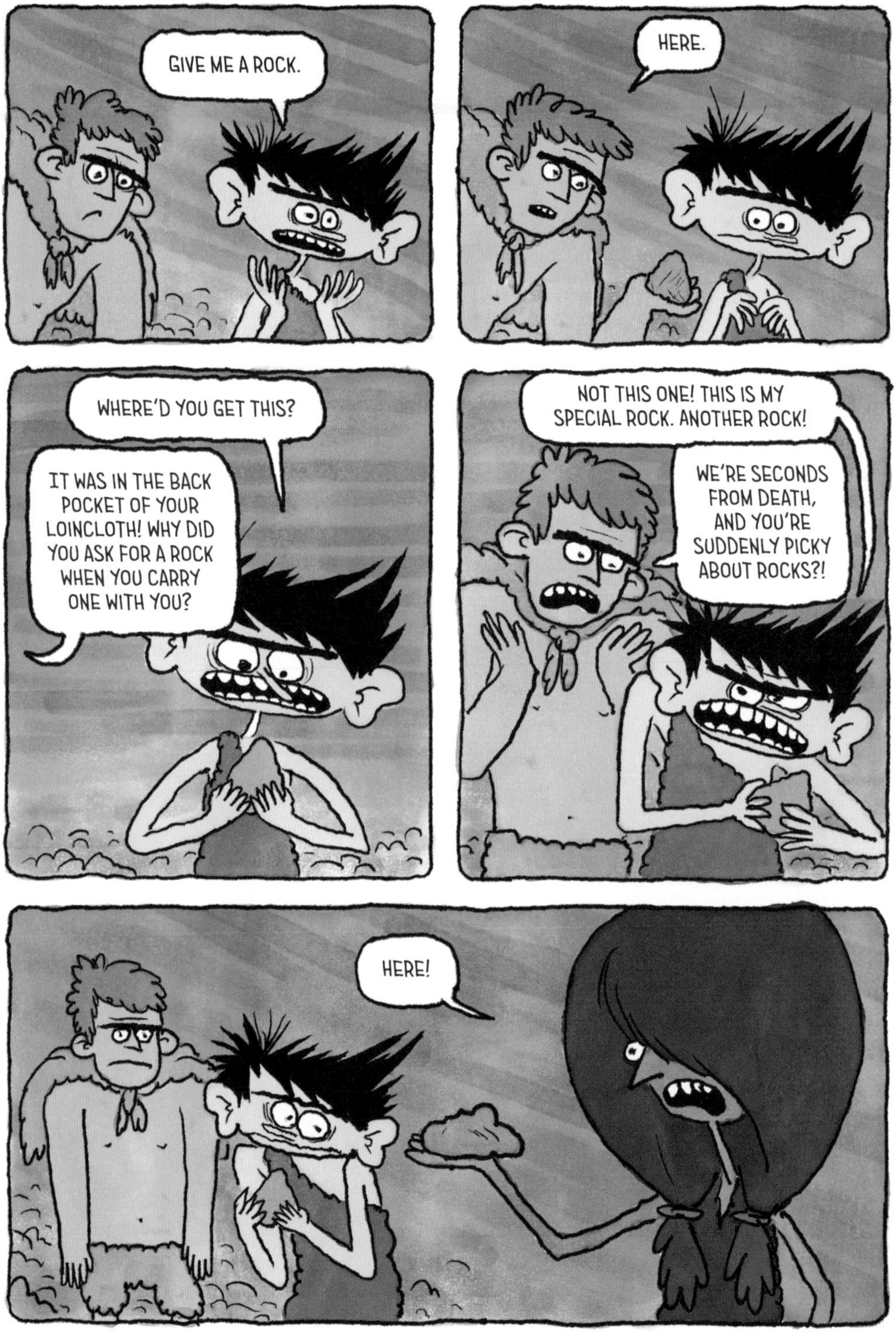
GIVE ME A ROCK.
HERE.
WHERE'D YOU GET THIS?
IT WAS IN THE BACK POCKET OF YOUR LOINCLOTH! WHY DID YOU ASK FOR A ROCK WHEN YOU CARRY ONE WITH YOU?
NOT THIS ONE! THIS IS MY SPECIAL ROCK. ANOTHER ROCK!
WE'RE SECONDS FROM DEATH, AND YOU'RE SUDDENLY PICKY ABOUT ROCKS?!
HERE!

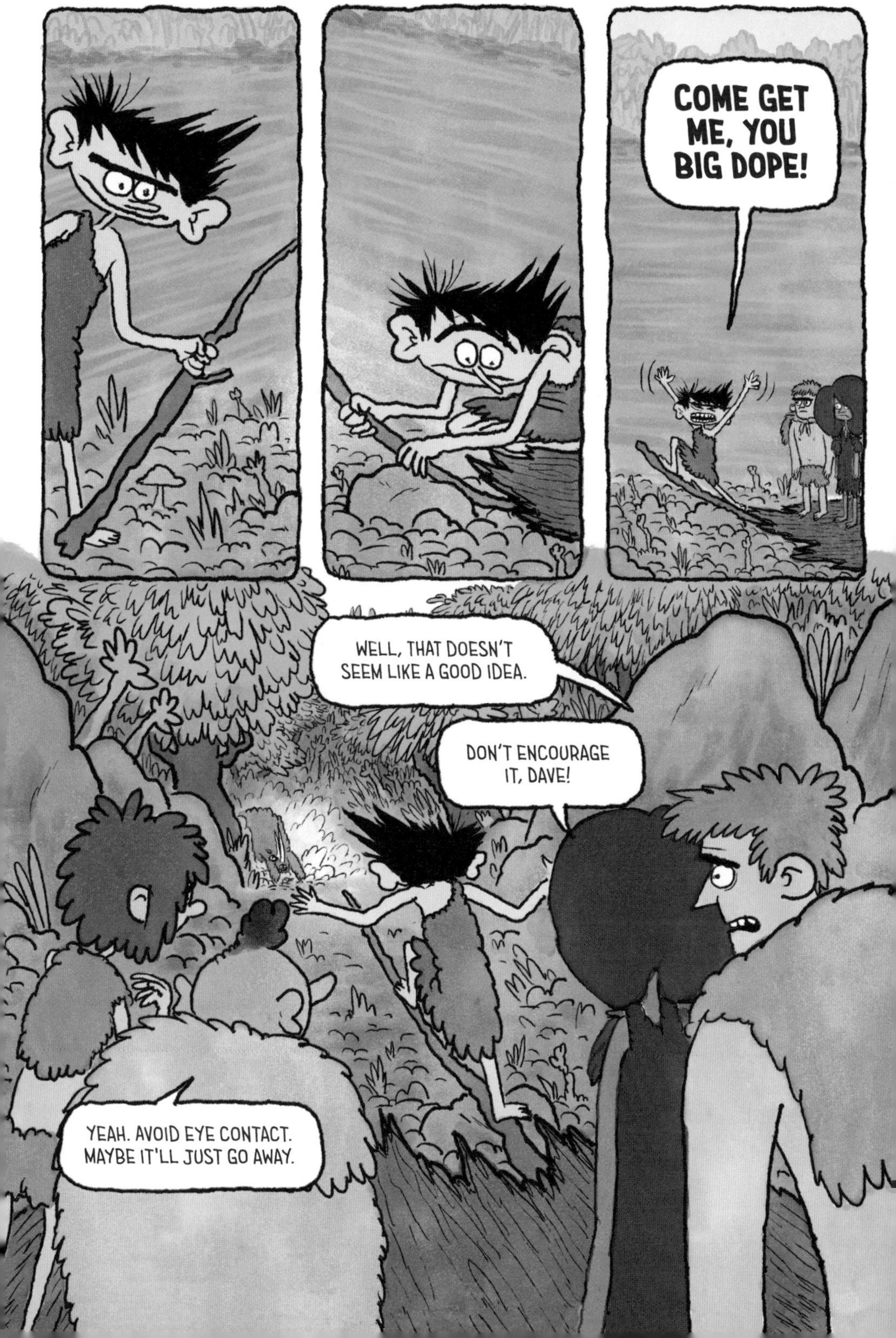
COME GET ME, YOU BIG DOPE!
WELL, THAT DOESN'T SEEM LIKE A GOOD IDEA.
DON'T ENCOURAGE IT, DAVE!
YEAH. AVOID EYE CONTACT. MAYBE IT'LL JUST GO AWAY.

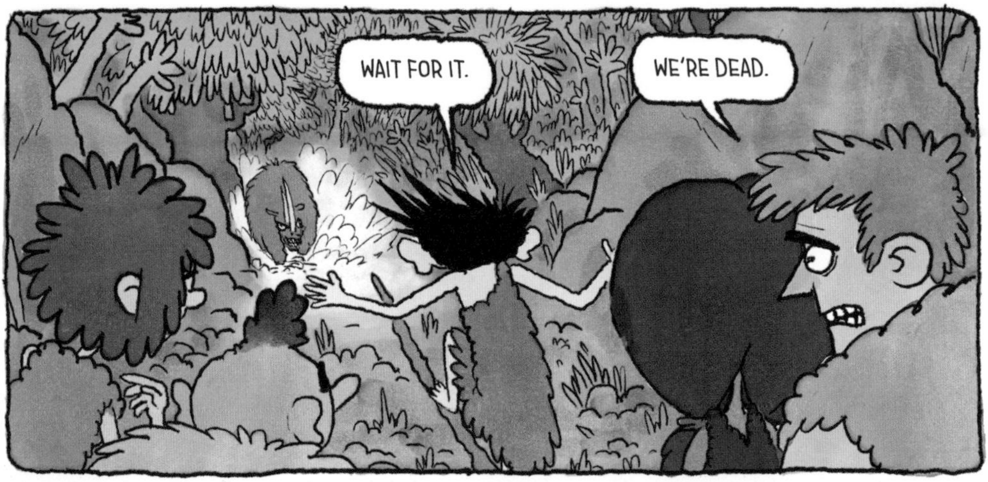
WAIT FOR IT.
WE'RE DEAD.

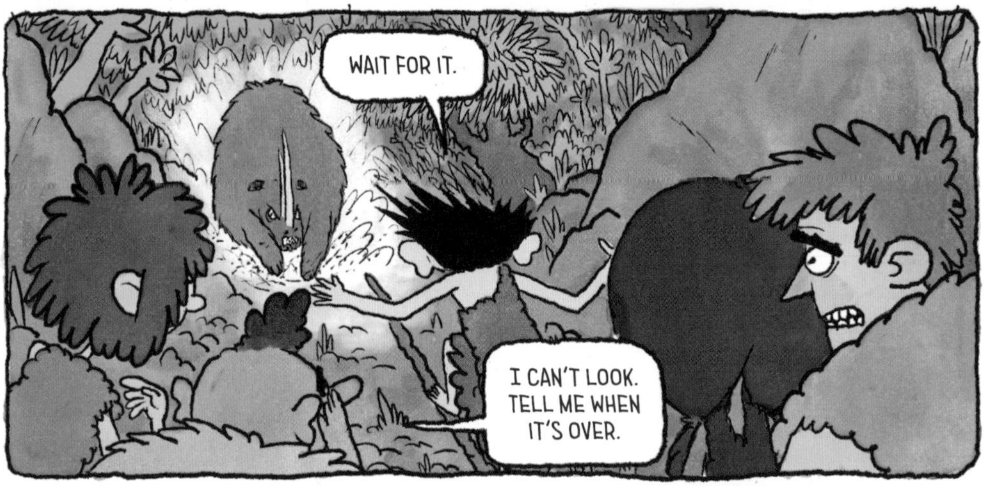
WAIT FOR IT.
I CAN'T LOOK. TELL ME WHEN IT'S OVER.

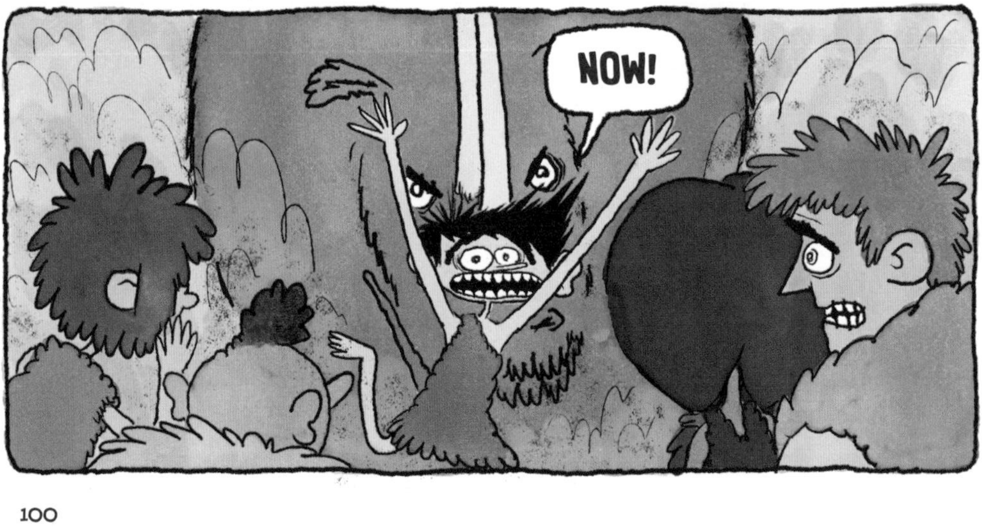
NOW!

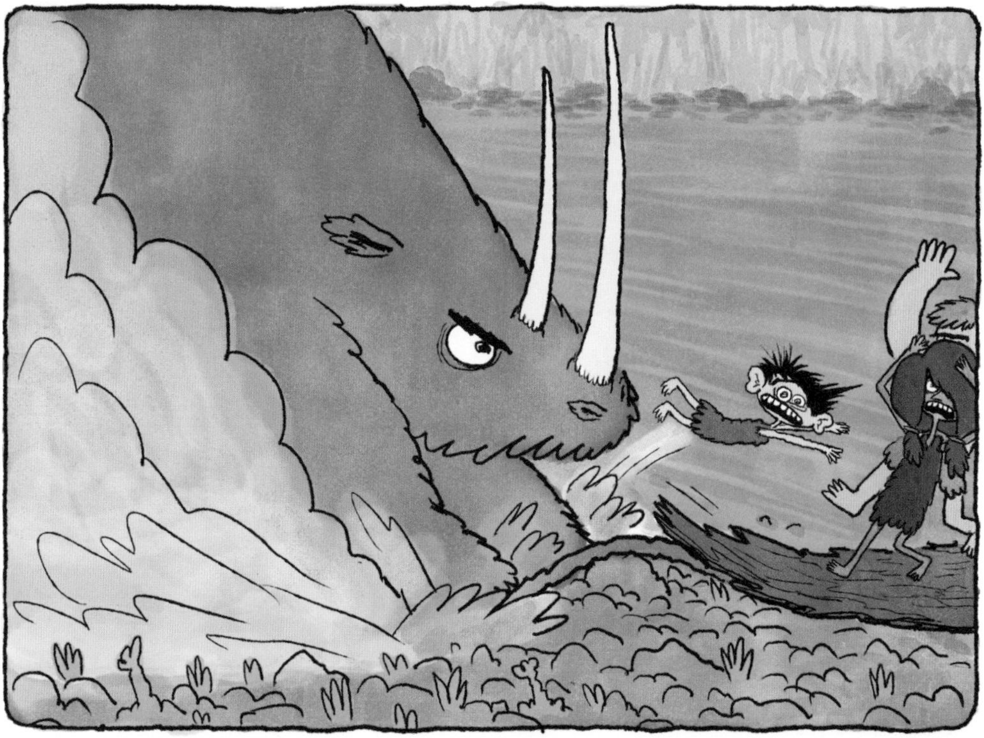

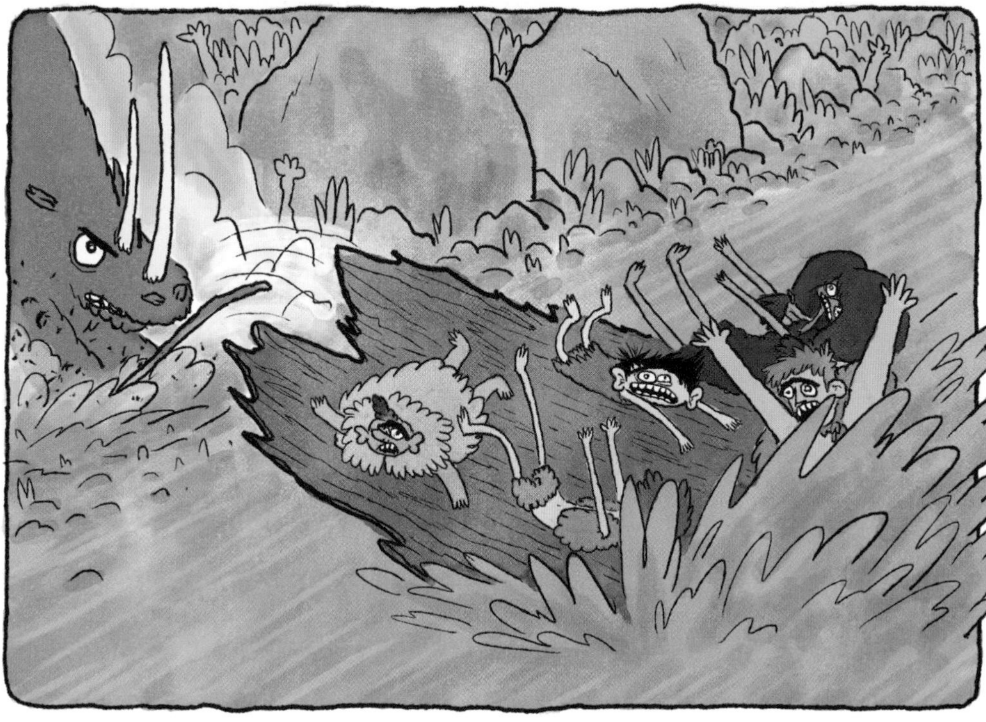

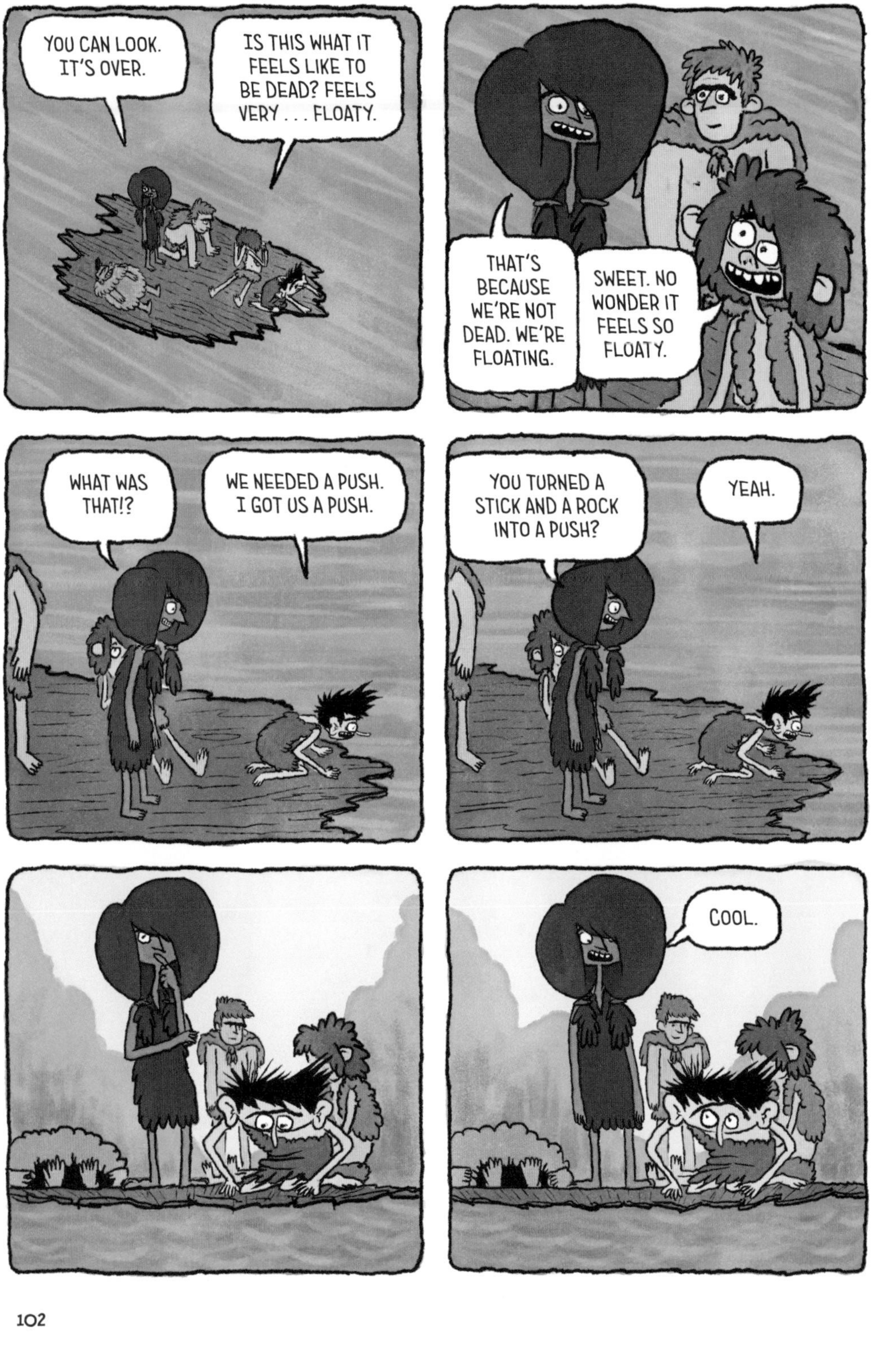
YOU CAN LOOK. IT'S OVER.
IS THIS WHAT IT FEELS LIKE TO BE DEAD? FEELS VERY . . . FLOATY.
THAT'S BECAUSE WE'RE NOT DEAD. WE'RE FLOATING.
SWEET. NO WONDER IT FEELS SO FLOATY.
WHAT WAS THAT!?
WE NEEDED A PUSH. I GOT US A PUSH.
YOU TURNED A STICK AND A ROCK INTO A PUSH?
YEAH.
COOL.

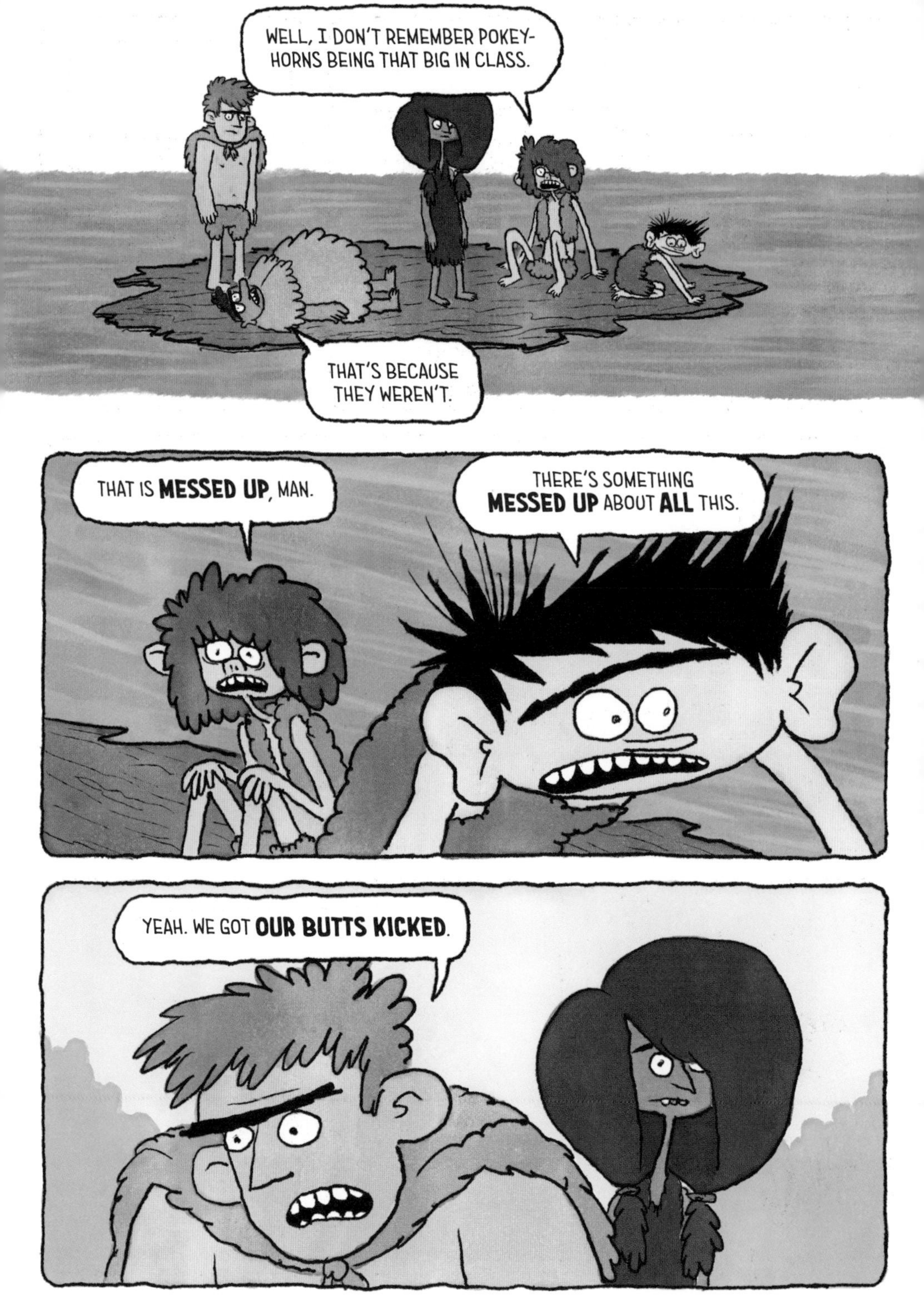
WELL, I DON'T REMEMBER POKEY-HORNS BEING THAT BIG IN CLASS.
THAT'S BECAUSE THEY WEREN'T.
THAT IS **MESSED UP**, MAN.
THERE'S SOMETHING **MESSED UP** ABOUT **ALL** THIS.
YEAH. WE GOT **OUR BUTTS KICKED**.

ROCKIE DID THE TAKEDOWN TECHNIQUE PERFECTLY. JUST LIKE IN CLASS.

AND YET HERE WE ARE, FLOATING ON A RIVER INSTEAD OF EATING ROAST POKEYHORN.

MAYBE THEY'RE NOT AS DUMB AS WE THOUGHT.

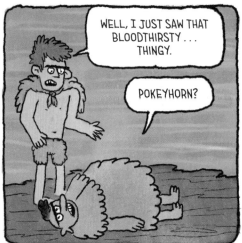

WELL, I JUST SAW THAT BLOODTHIRSTY . . . THINGY.

POKEYHORN?

RIGHT. AND THAT WAS ONE DUMB . . . THINGY!

POKEYHORN?

QUIT SAYING POKEY-HORN!!!

ALL I KNOW IS THAT WE JUST FAILED MISERABLY.

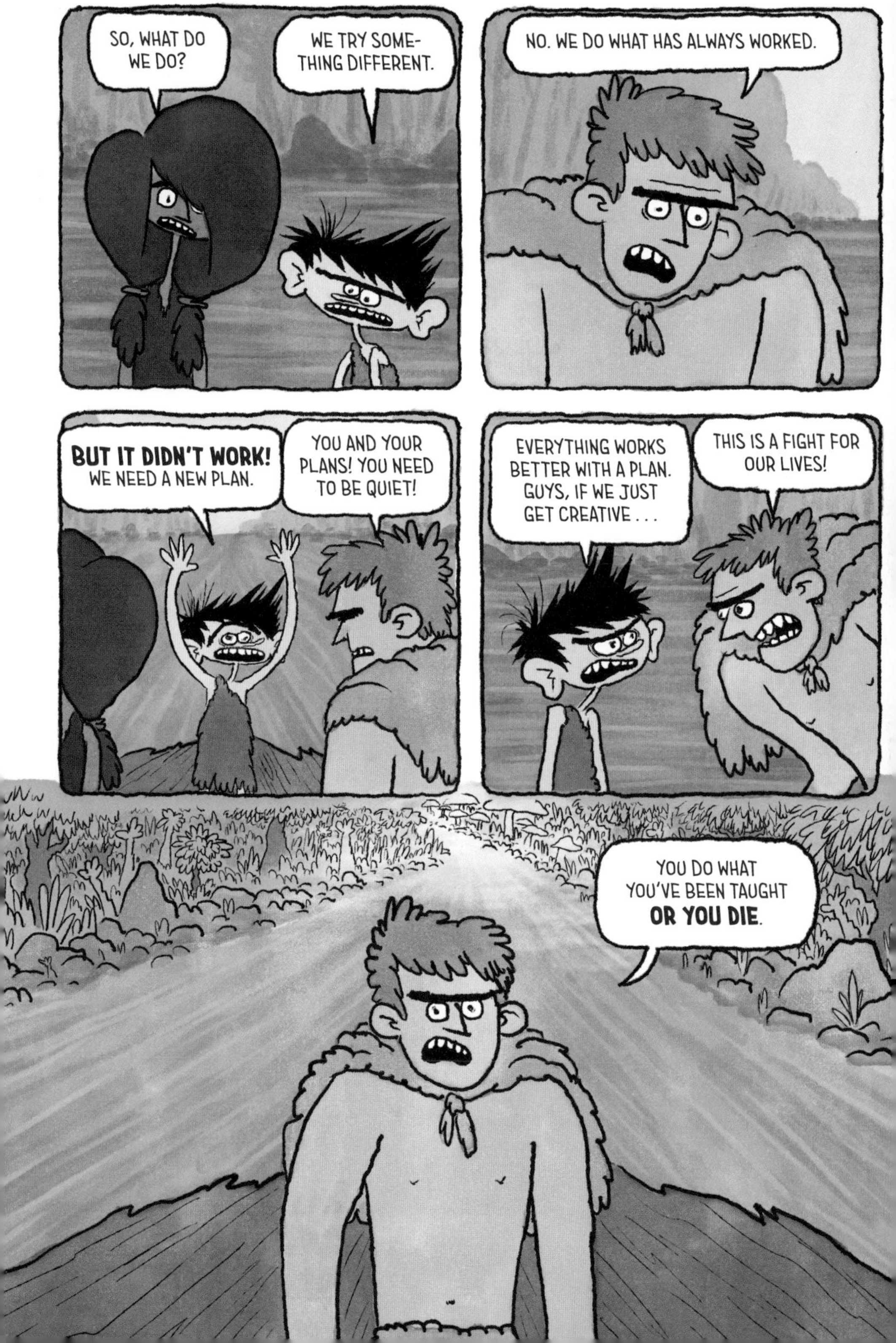
SO, WHAT DO WE DO?
WE TRY SOMETHING DIFFERENT.
NO. WE DO WHAT HAS ALWAYS WORKED.
BUT IT DIDN'T WORK! WE NEED A NEW PLAN.
YOU AND YOUR PLANS! YOU NEED TO BE QUIET!
EVERYTHING WORKS BETTER WITH A PLAN. GUYS, IF WE JUST GET CREATIVE . . .
THIS IS A FIGHT FOR OUR LIVES!
YOU DO WHAT YOU'VE BEEN TAUGHT **OR YOU DIE**.

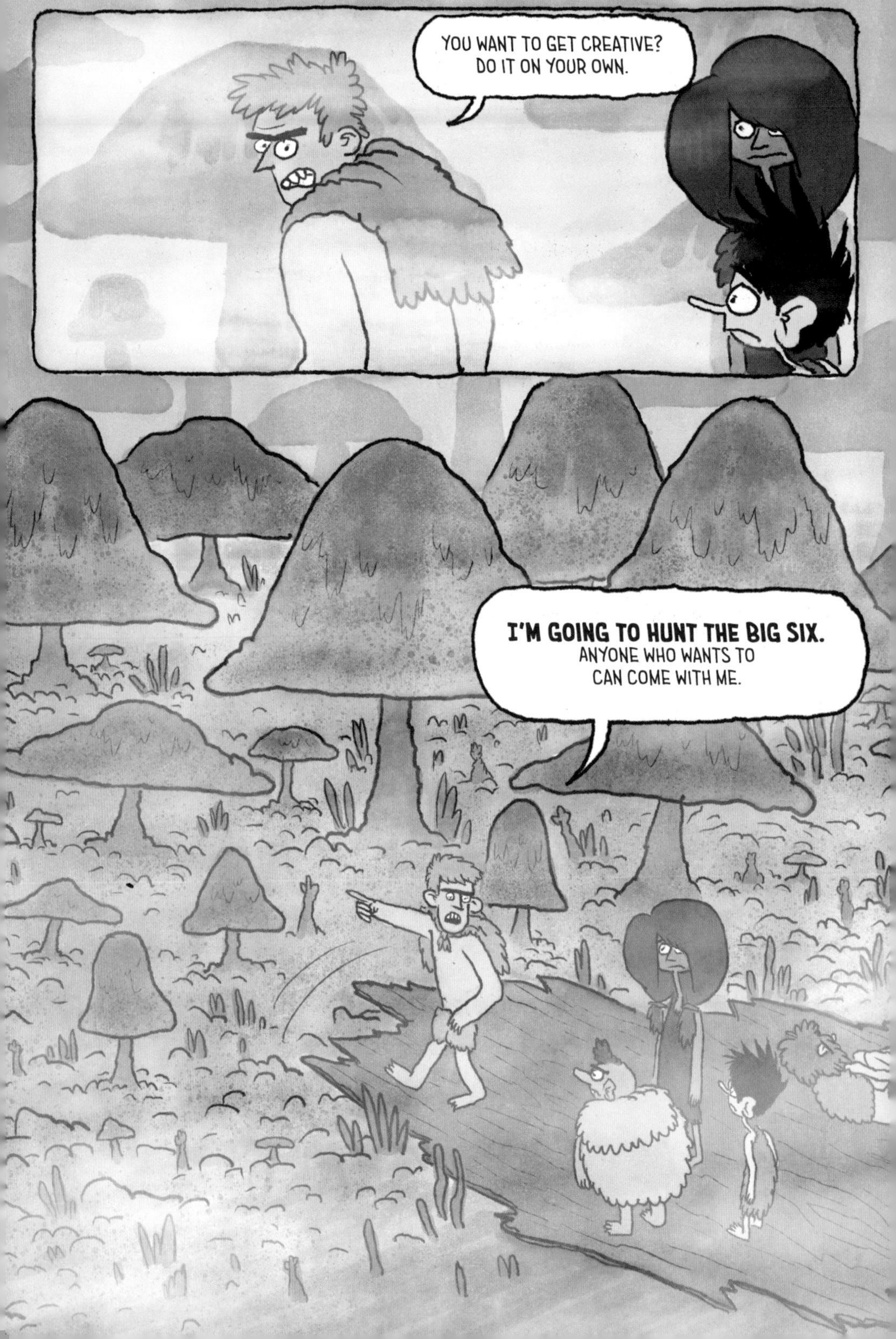
YOU WANT TO GET CREATIVE? DO IT ON YOUR OWN.
I'M GOING TO HUNT THE BIG SIX.
ANYONE WHO WANTS TO CAN COME WITH ME.

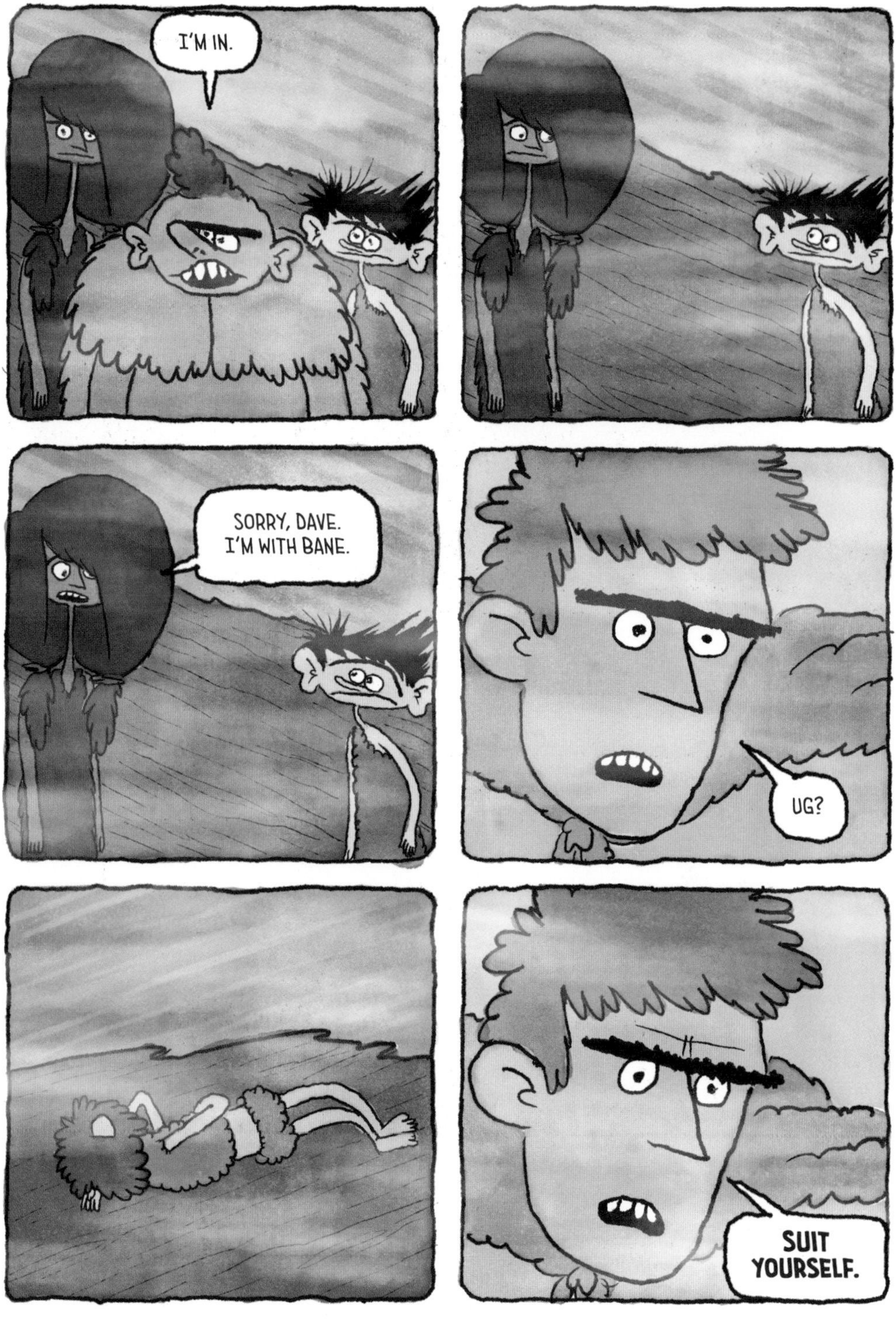
I'M IN.
SORRY, DAVE.
I'M WITH BANE.
UG?
SUIT
YOURSELF.

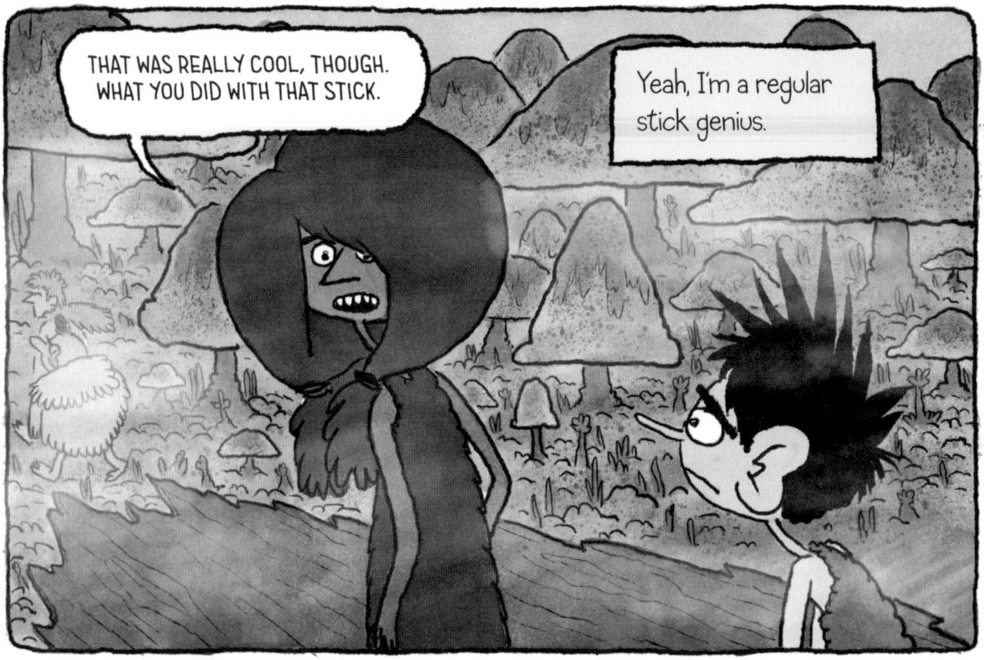
THAT WAS REALLY COOL, THOUGH. WHAT YOU DID WITH THAT STICK.
Yeah, I'm a regular stick genius.

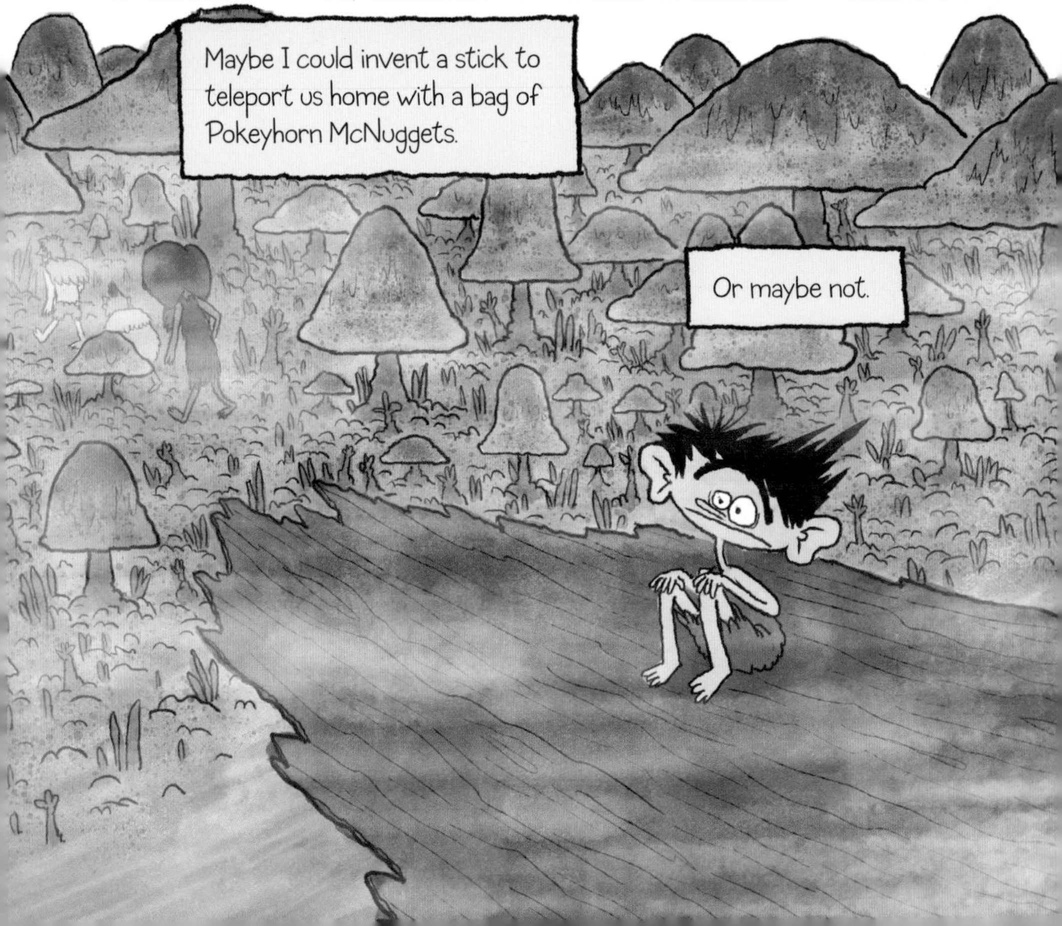
Maybe I could invent a stick to teleport us home with a bag of Pokeyhorn McNuggets.
Or maybe not.

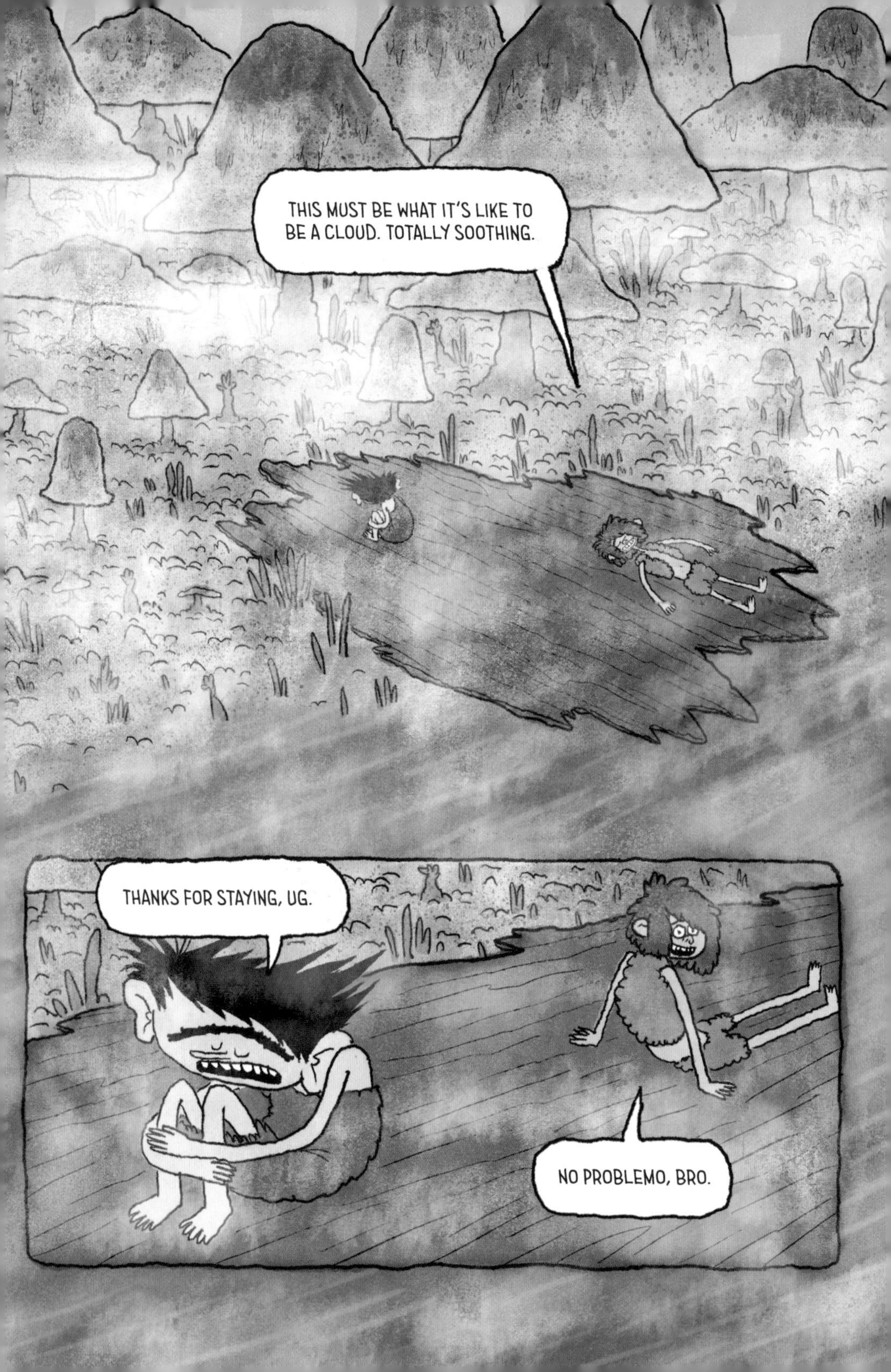
THIS MUST BE WHAT IT'S LIKE TO BE A CLOUD. TOTALLY SOOTHING.
THANKS FOR STAYING, UG.
NO PROBLEMO, BRO.

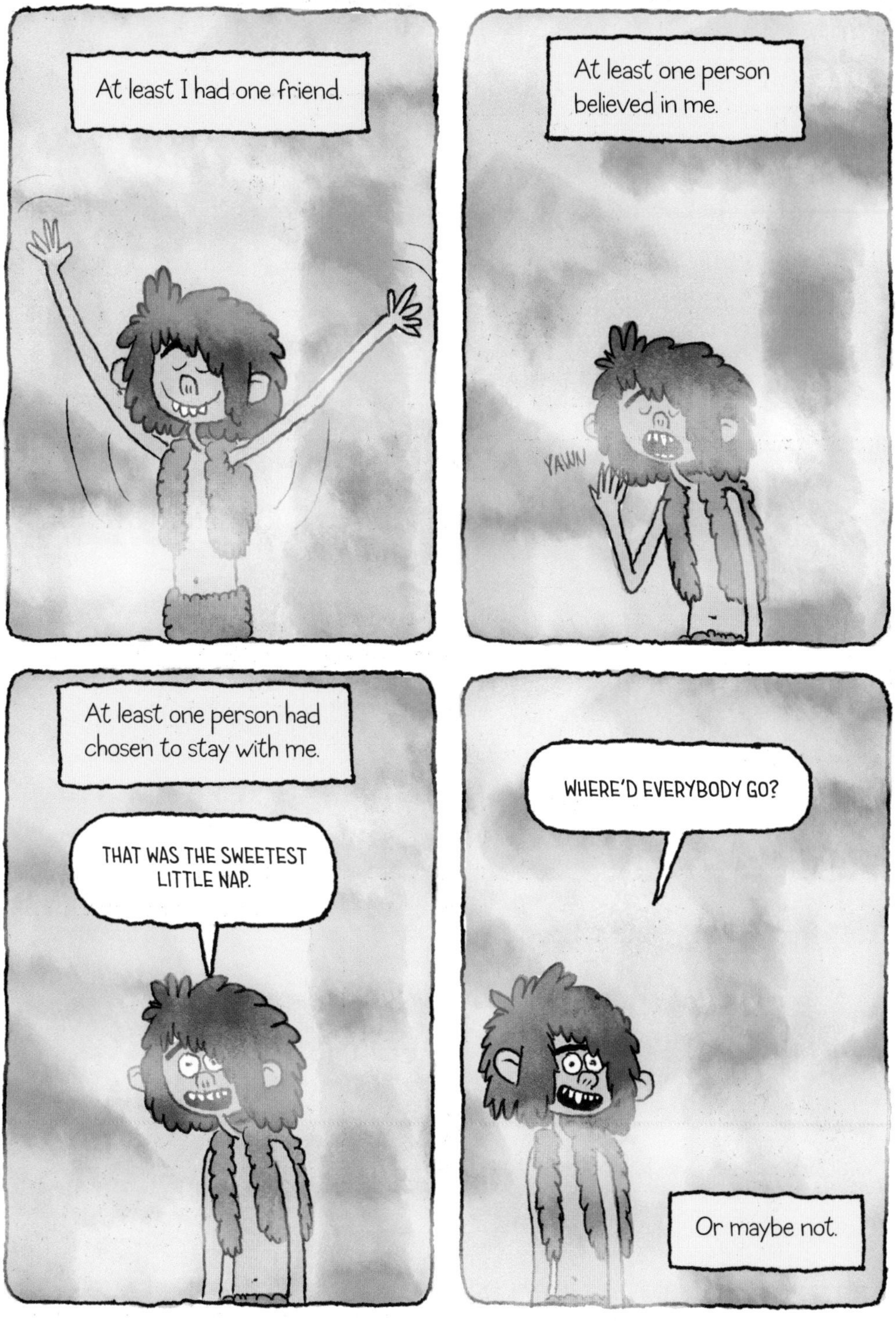
At least I had one friend.
At least one person believed in me.
YAWN
At least one person had chosen to stay with me.
THAT WAS THE SWEETEST LITTLE NAP.
WHERE'D EVERYBODY GO?
Or maybe not.

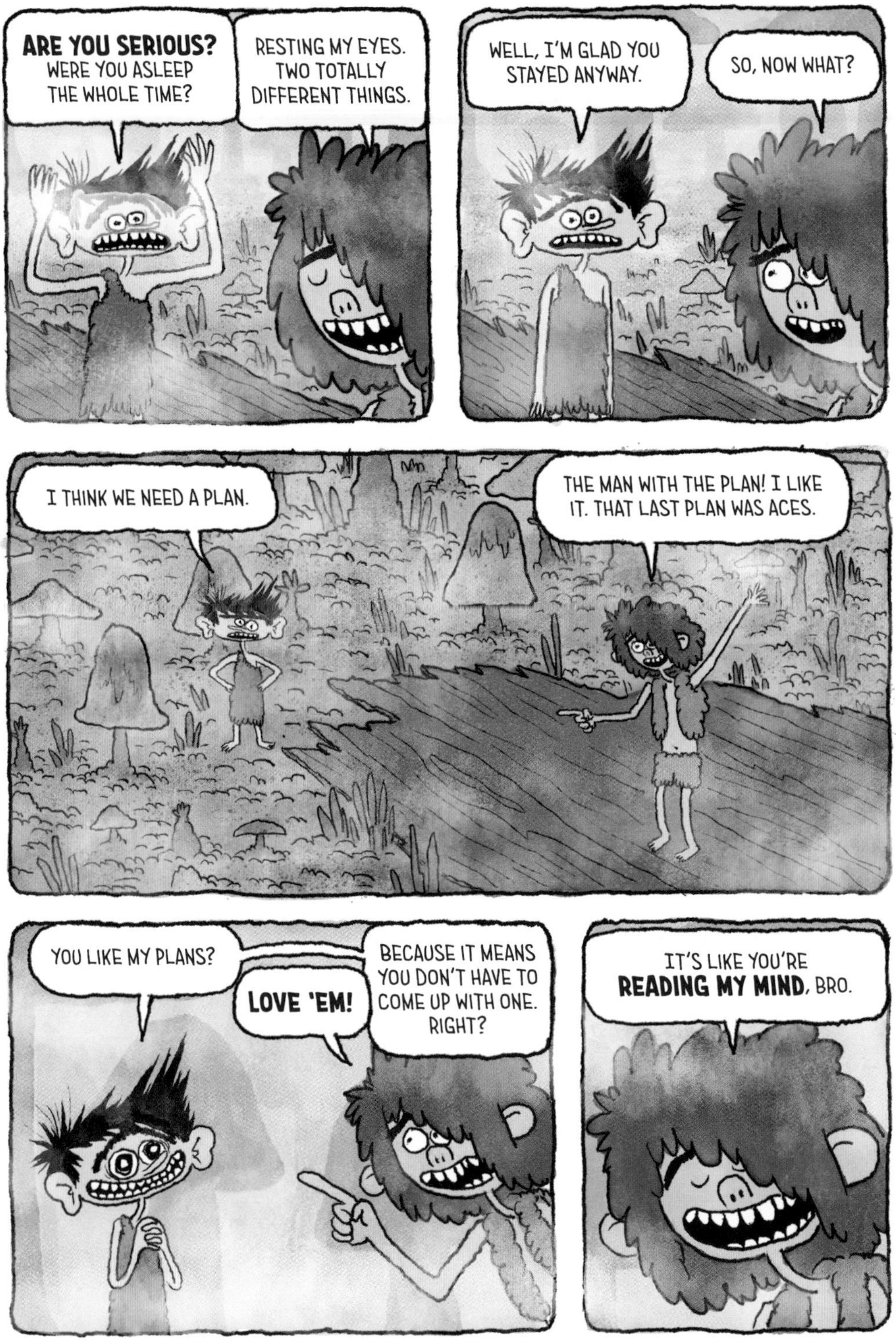
ARE YOU SERIOUS? WERE YOU ASLEEP THE WHOLE TIME?
RESTING MY EYES. TWO TOTALLY DIFFERENT THINGS.
WELL, I'M GLAD YOU STAYED ANYWAY.
SO, NOW WHAT?
I THINK WE NEED A PLAN.
THE MAN WITH THE PLAN! I LIKE IT. THAT LAST PLAN WAS ACES.
YOU LIKE MY PLANS?
LOVE 'EM!
BECAUSE IT MEANS YOU DON'T HAVE TO COME UP WITH ONE. RIGHT?
IT'S LIKE YOU'RE **READING MY MIND**, BRO.

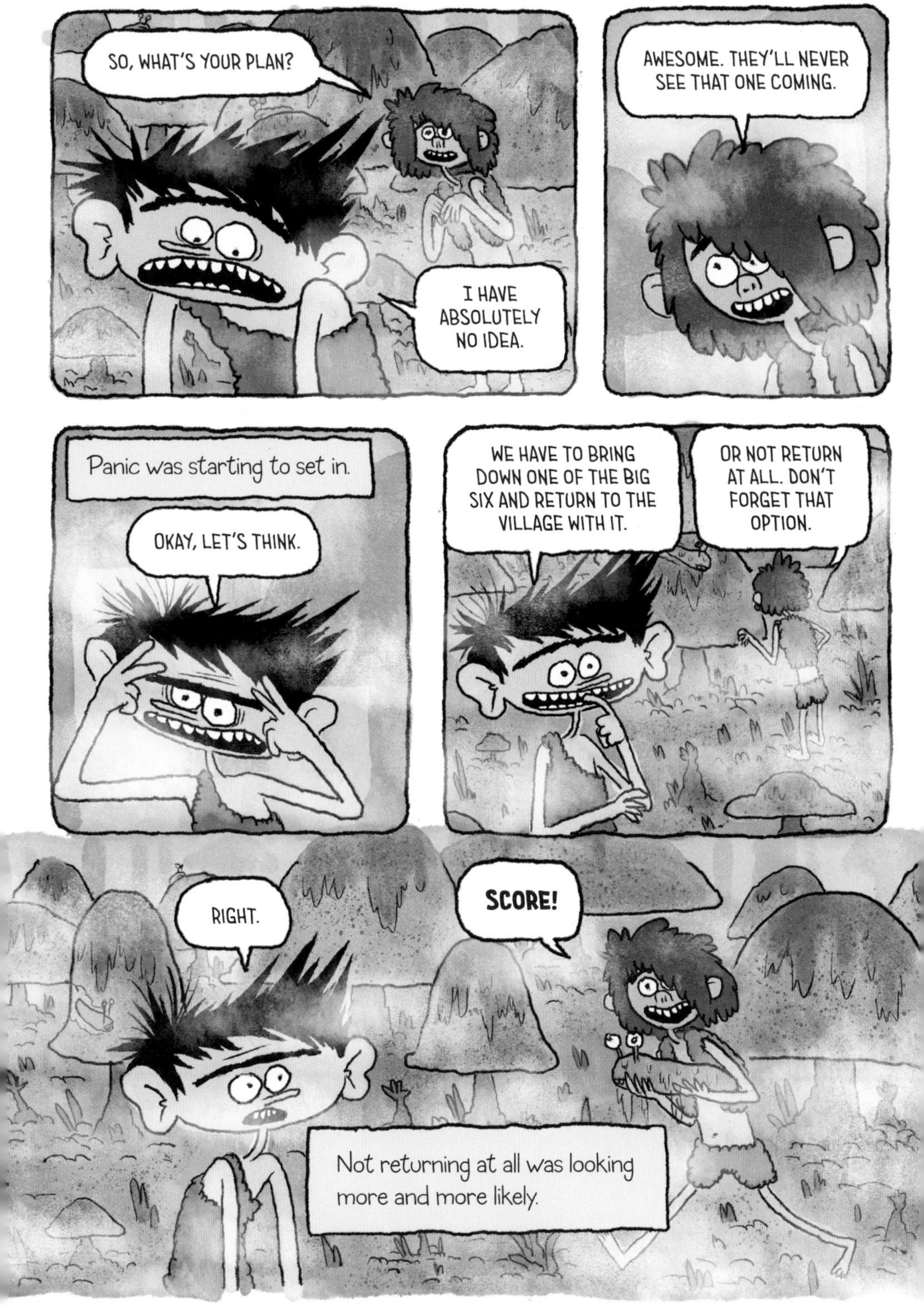
SO, WHAT'S YOUR PLAN?
I HAVE ABSOLUTELY NO IDEA.
AWESOME. THEY'LL NEVER SEE THAT ONE COMING.
Panic was starting to set in.
OKAY, LET'S THINK.
WE HAVE TO BRING DOWN ONE OF THE BIG SIX AND RETURN TO THE VILLAGE WITH IT.
OR NOT RETURN AT ALL. DON'T FORGET THAT OPTION.
RIGHT.
SCORE!
Not returning at all was looking more and more likely.

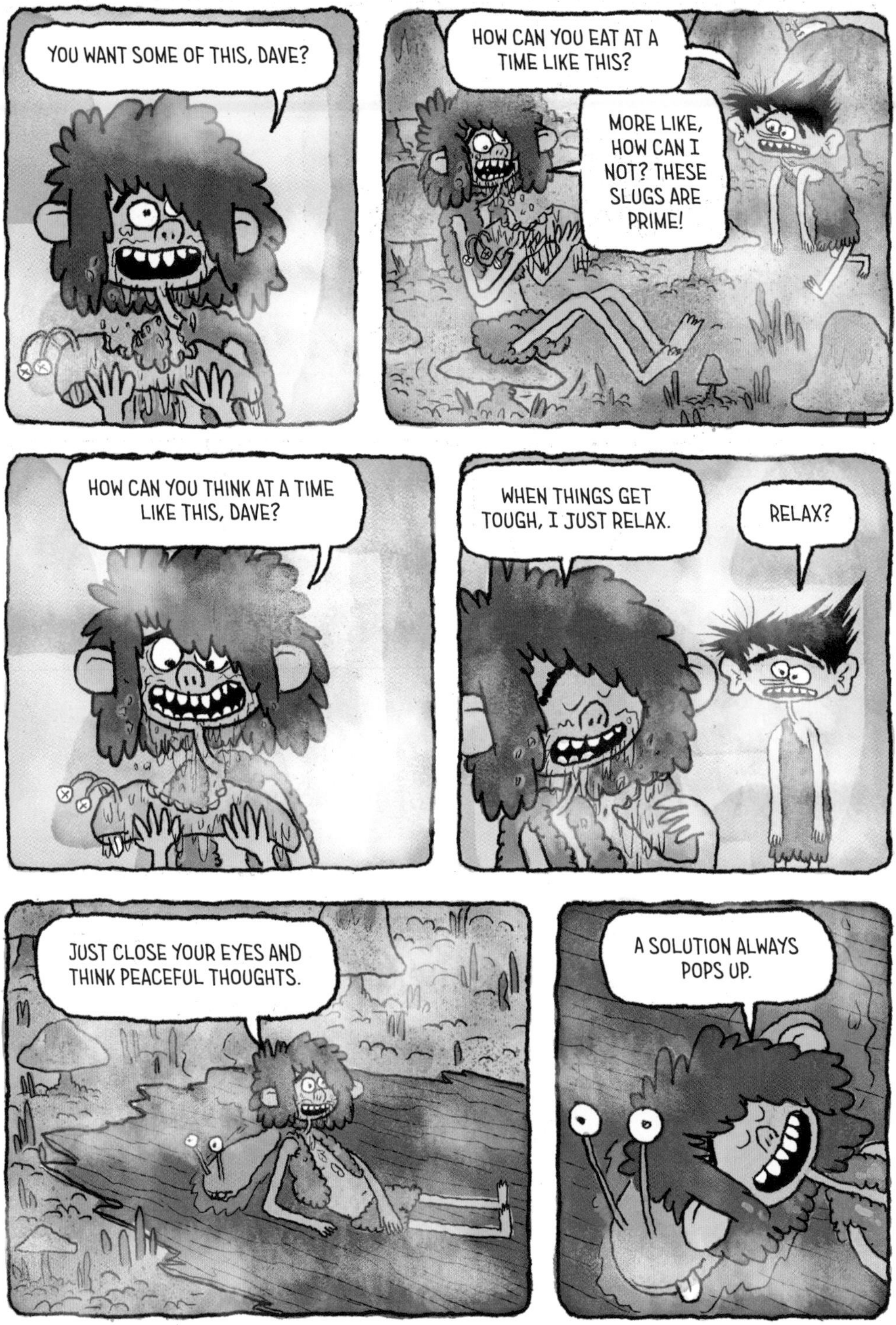
YOU WANT SOME OF THIS, DAVE?
HOW CAN YOU EAT AT A TIME LIKE THIS?
MORE LIKE, HOW CAN I NOT? THESE SLUGS ARE PRIME!
HOW CAN YOU THINK AT A TIME LIKE THIS, DAVE?
WHEN THINGS GET TOUGH, I JUST RELAX.
RELAX?
JUST CLOSE YOUR EYES AND THINK PEACEFUL THOUGHTS.
A SOLUTION ALWAYS POPS UP.

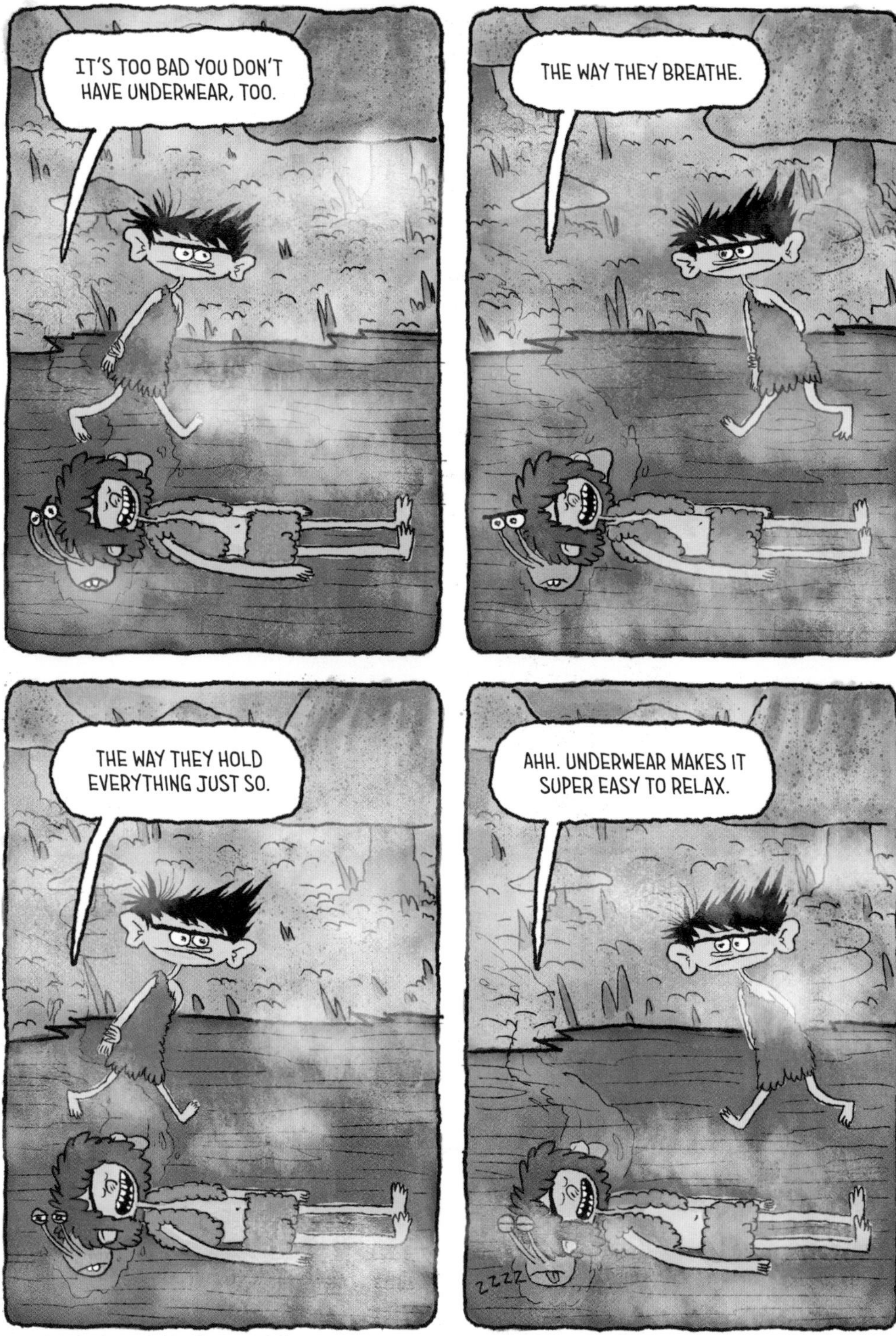
IT'S TOO BAD YOU DON'T HAVE UNDERWEAR, TOO.
THE WAY THEY BREATHE.
THE WAY THEY HOLD EVERYTHING JUST SO.
AHH. UNDERWEAR MAKES IT SUPER EASY TO RELAX.
ZZZZ

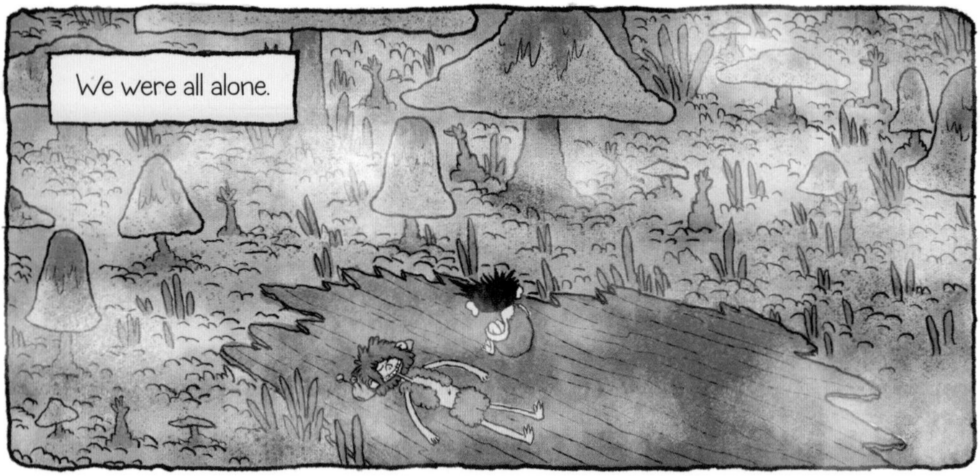
We were all alone.

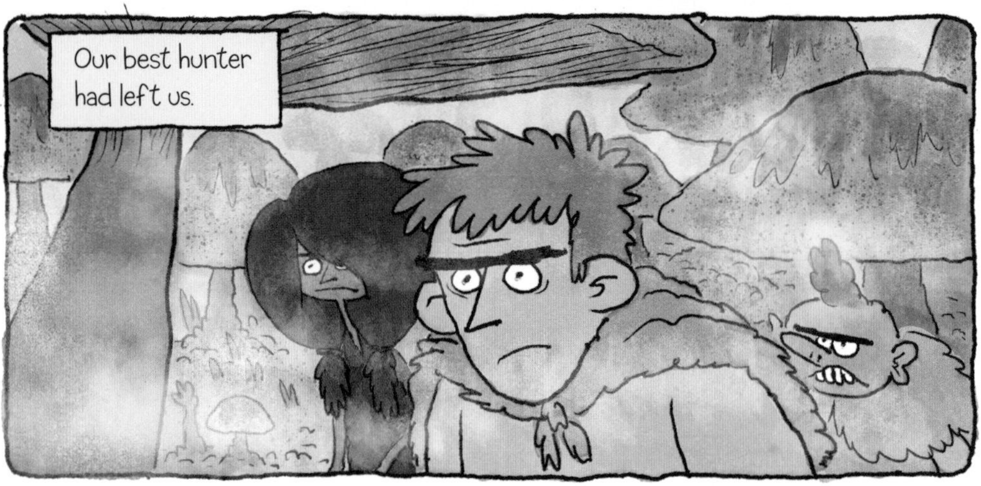
Our best hunter had left us.

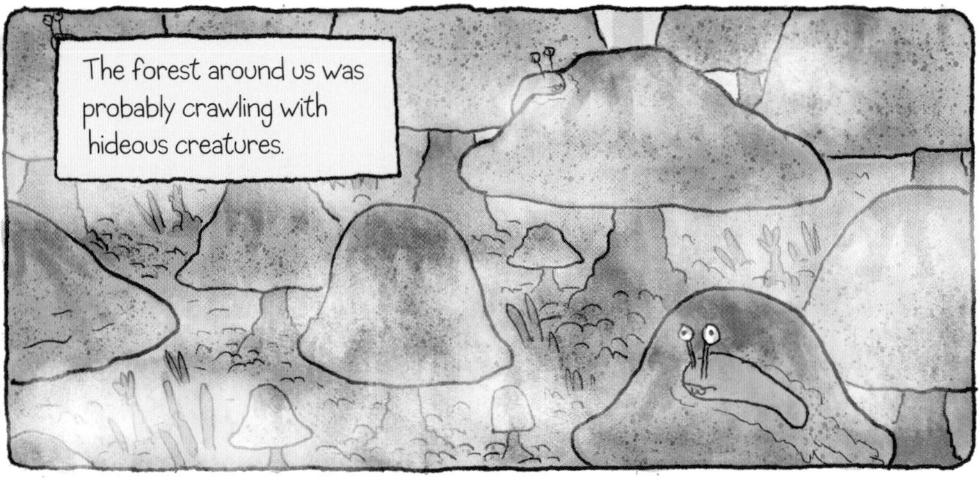
The forest around us was probably crawling with hideous creatures.

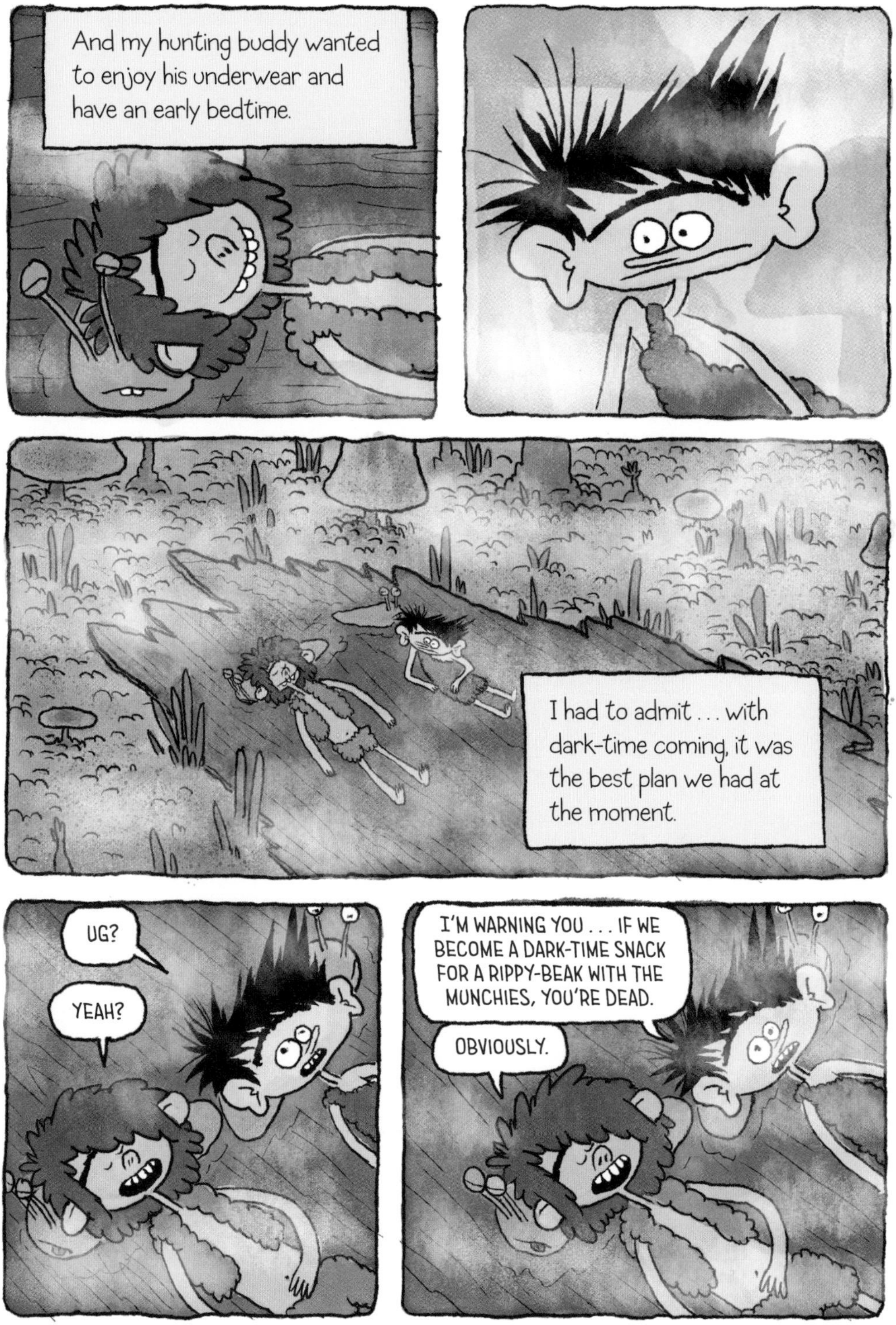

And my hunting buddy wanted to enjoy his underwear and have an early bedtime.
I had to admit . . . with dark-time coming, it was the best plan we had at the moment.
UG?
YEAH?
I'M WARNING YOU . . . IF WE BECOME A DARK-TIME SNACK FOR A RIPPY-BEAK WITH THE MUNCHIES, YOU'RE DEAD.
OBVIOUSLY.

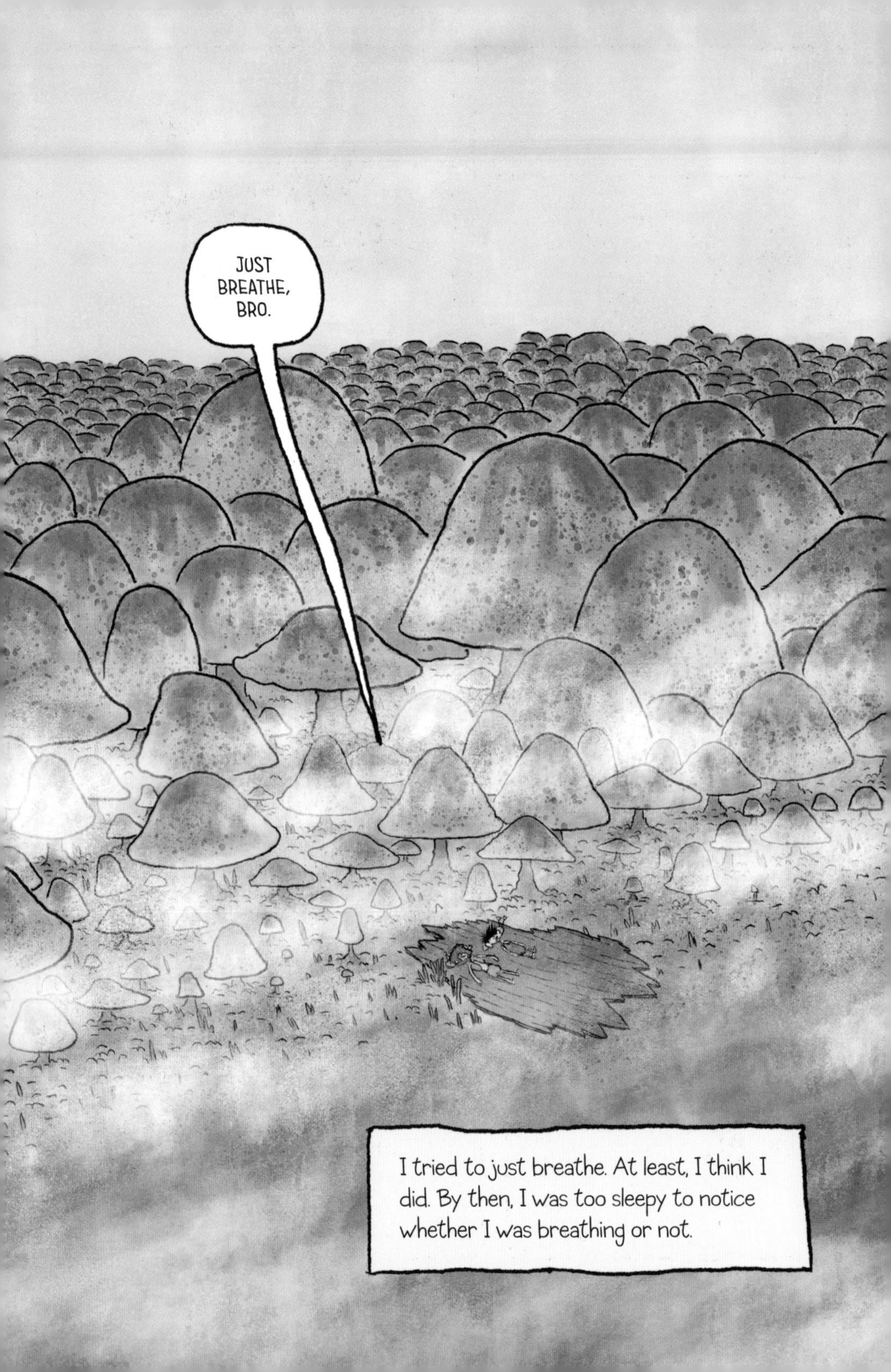
JUST BREATHE, BRO.
I tried to just breathe. At least, I think I did. By then, I was too sleepy to notice whether I was breathing or not.

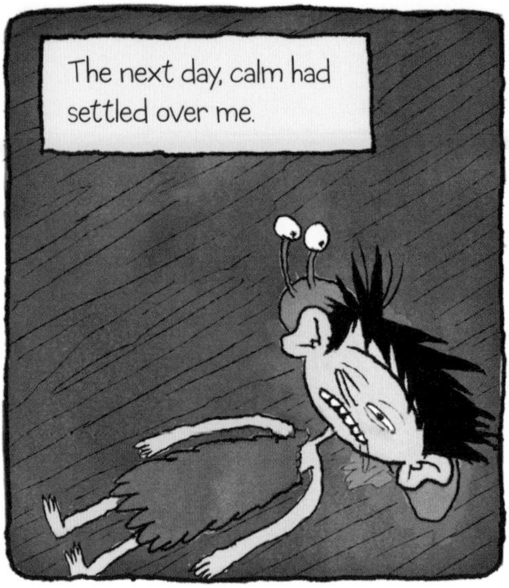
The next day, calm had settled over me.

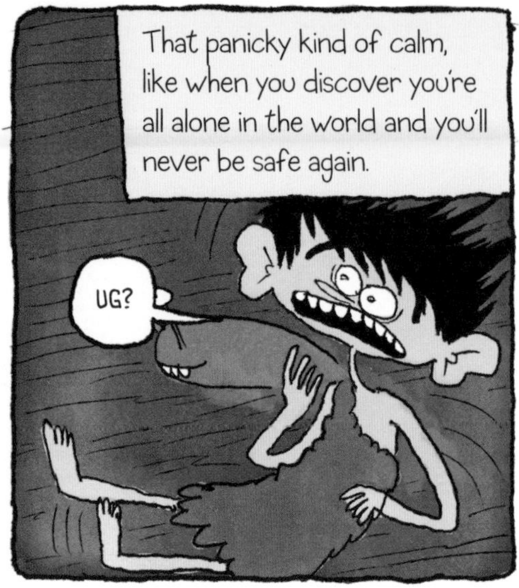
That panicky kind of calm, like when you discover you're all alone in the world and you'll never be safe again.
UG?

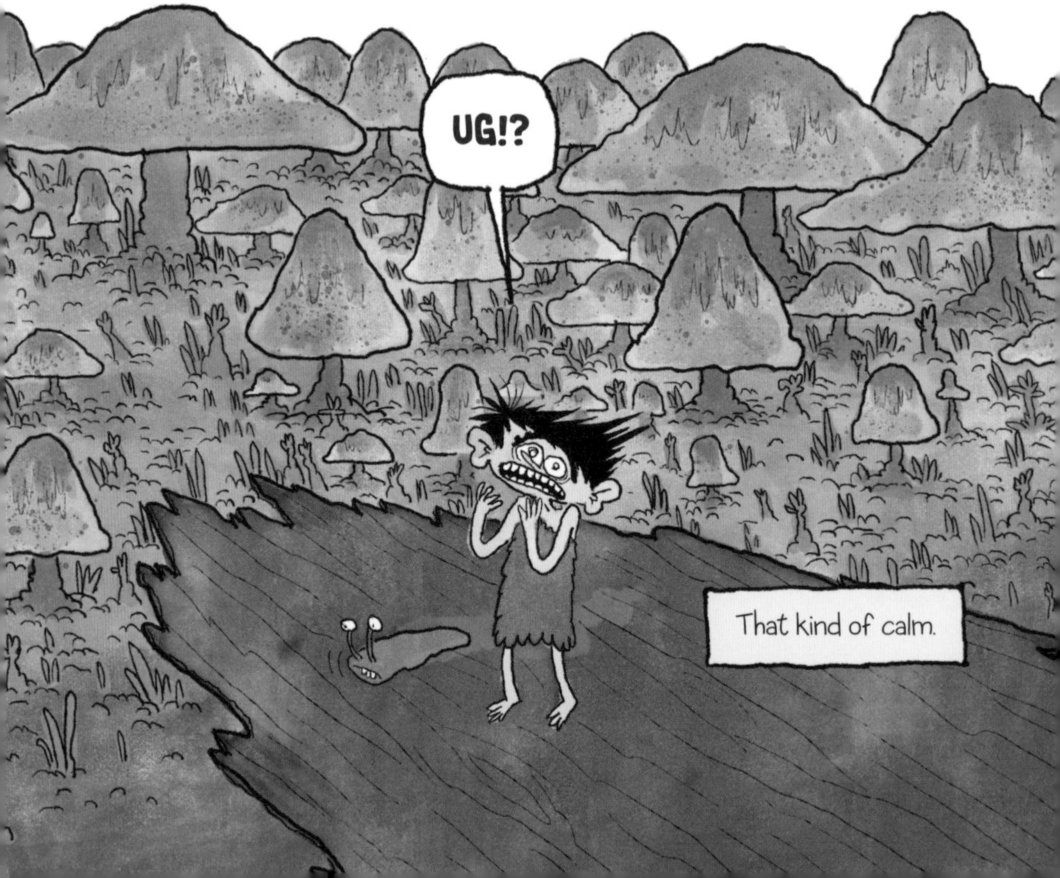
UG!?
That kind of calm.

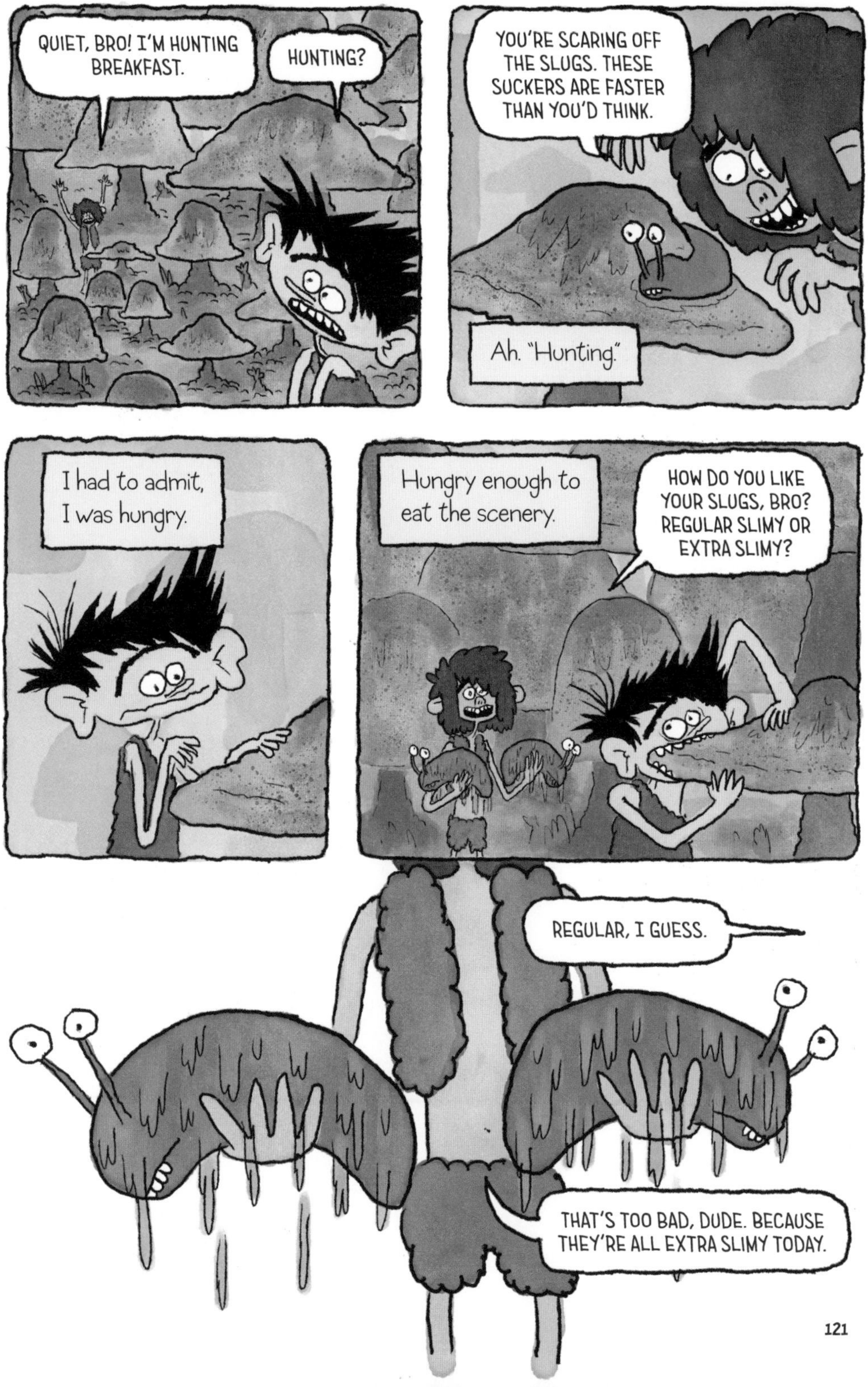
QUIET, BRO! I'M HUNTING BREAKFAST.
HUNTING?
YOU'RE SCARING OFF THE SLUGS. THESE SUCKERS ARE FASTER THAN YOU'D THINK.
Ah. "Hunting."
I had to admit, I was hungry.
Hungry enough to eat the scenery.
HOW DO YOU LIKE YOUR SLUGS, BRO? REGULAR SLIMY OR EXTRA SLIMY?
REGULAR, I GUESS.
THAT'S TOO BAD, DUDE. BECAUSE THEY'RE ALL EXTRA SLIMY TODAY.

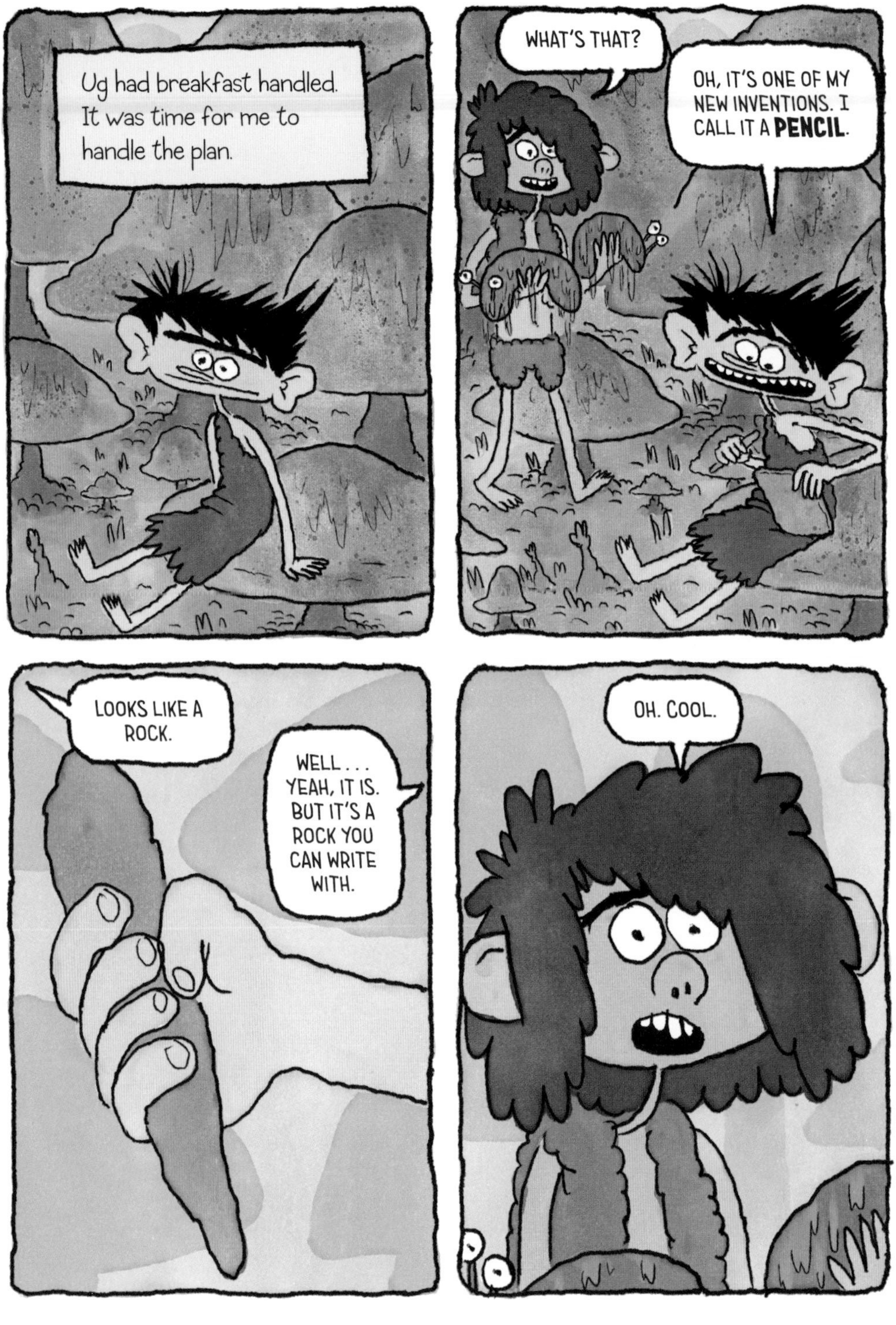
Ug had breakfast handled. It was time for me to handle the plan.
WHAT'S THAT?
OH, IT'S ONE OF MY NEW INVENTIONS. I CALL IT A **PENCIL**.
LOOKS LIKE A ROCK.
WELL . . . YEAH, IT IS. BUT IT'S A ROCK YOU CAN WRITE WITH.
OH. COOL.

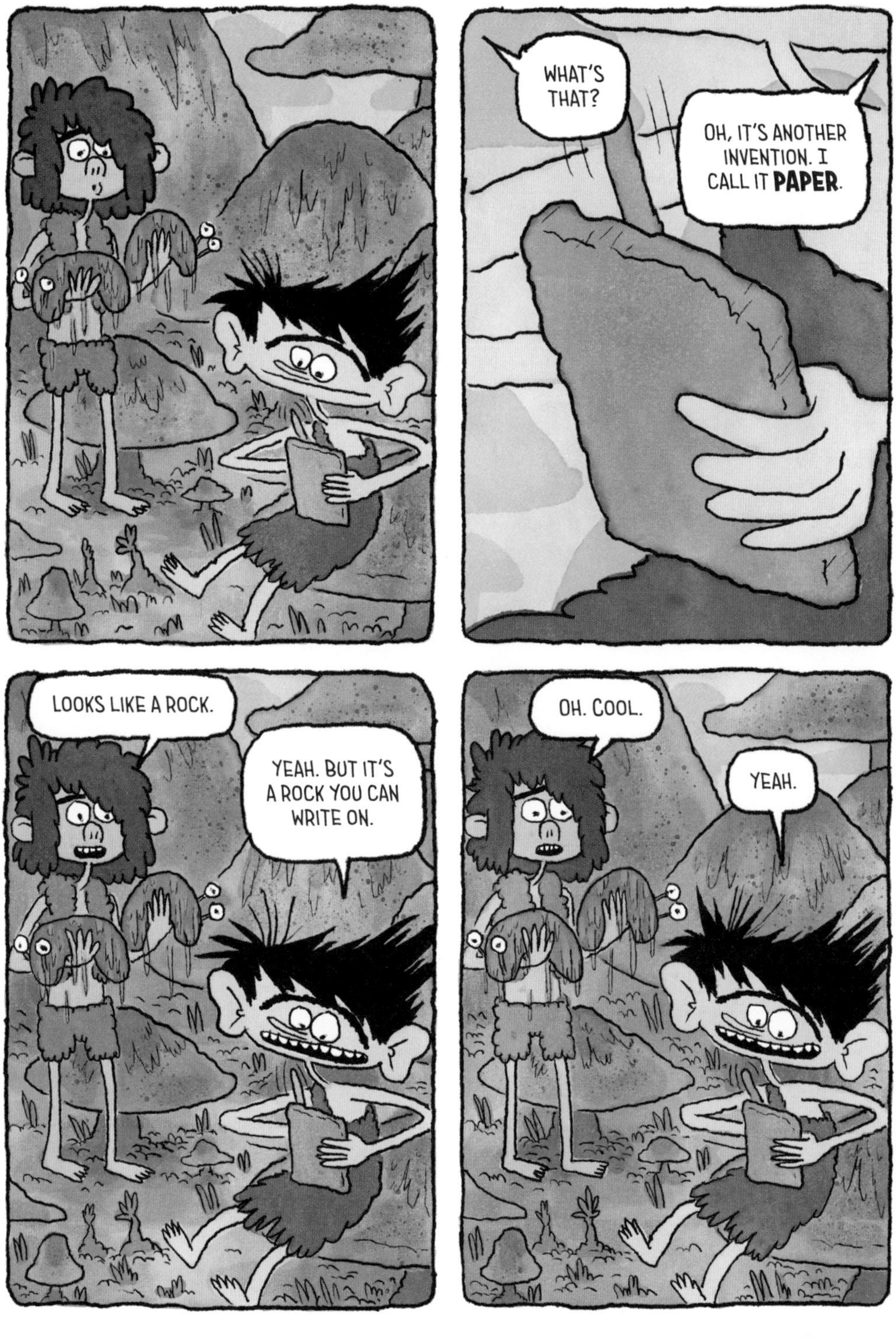
WHAT'S THAT?
OH, IT'S ANOTHER INVENTION. I CALL IT **PAPER**.
LOOKS LIKE A ROCK.
YEAH. BUT IT'S A ROCK YOU CAN WRITE ON.
OH. COOL.
YEAH.

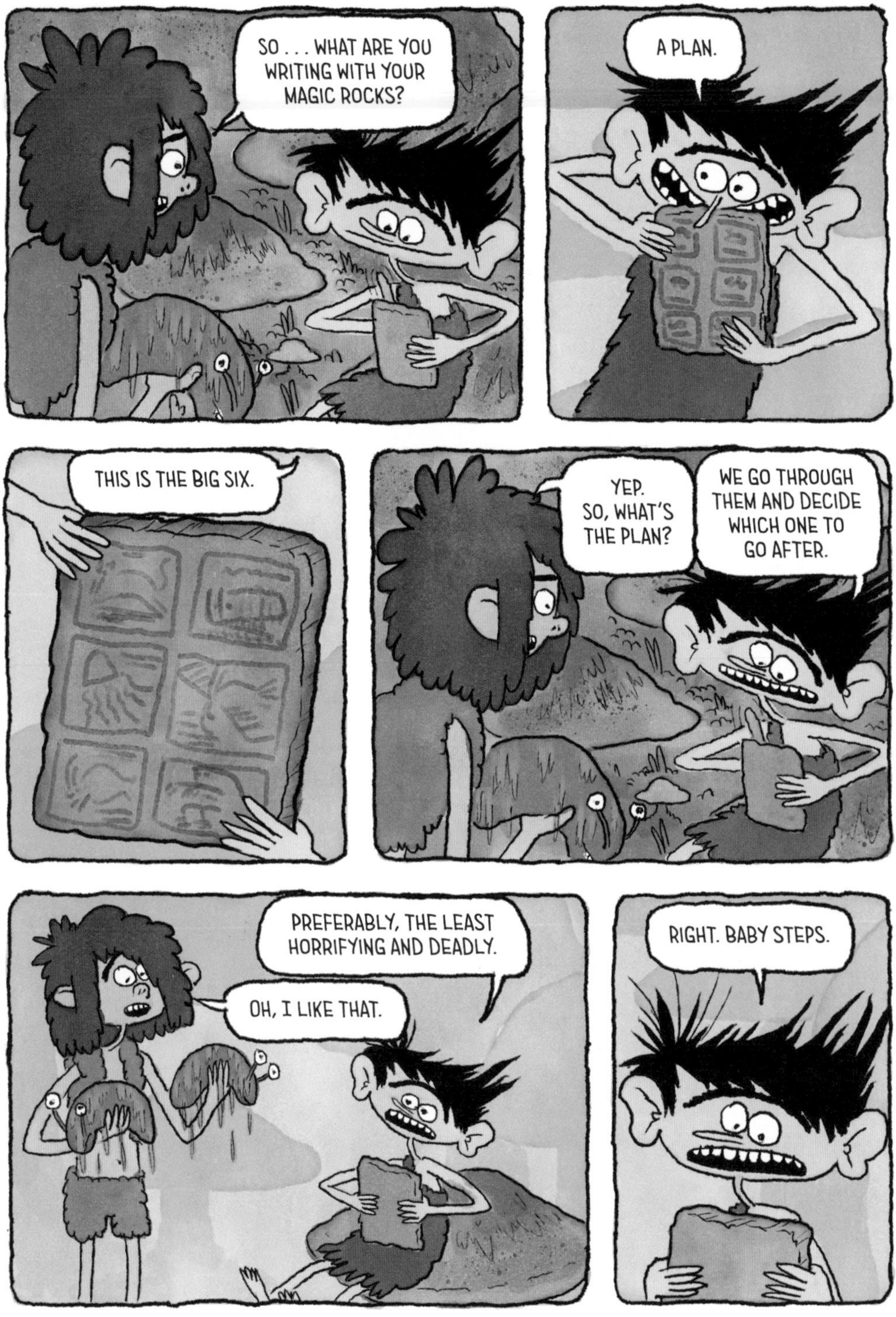
SO . . . WHAT ARE YOU WRITING WITH YOUR MAGIC ROCKS?
A PLAN.
THIS IS THE BIG SIX.
YEP. SO, WHAT'S THE PLAN?
WE GO THROUGH THEM AND DECIDE WHICH ONE TO GO AFTER.
PREFERABLY, THE LEAST HORRIFYING AND DEADLY.
OH, I LIKE THAT.
RIGHT. BABY STEPS.

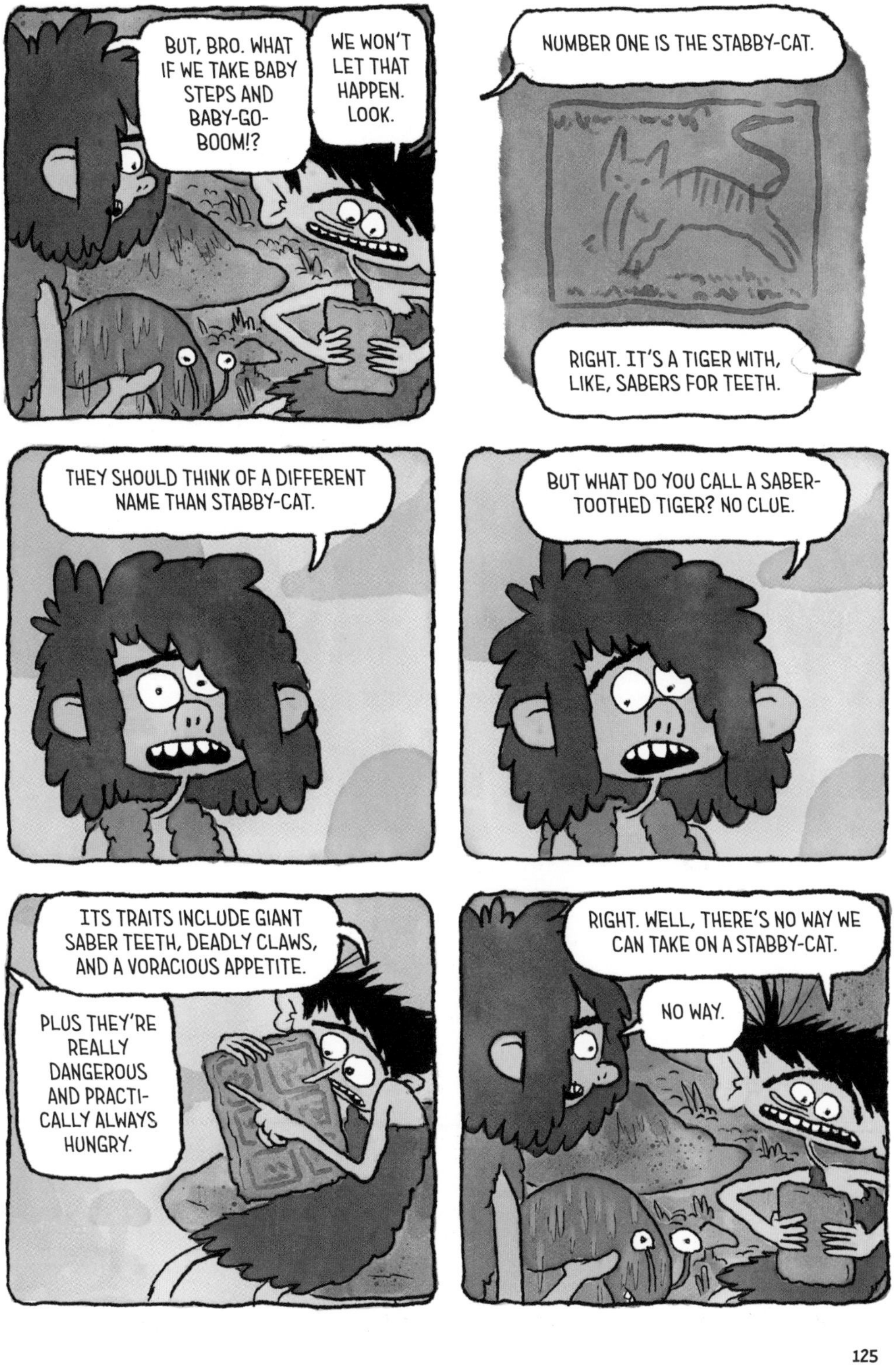
BUT, BRO. WHAT IF WE TAKE BABY STEPS AND BABY-GO-BOOM!?
WE WON'T LET THAT HAPPEN. LOOK.
NUMBER ONE IS THE STABBY-CAT.
RIGHT. IT'S A TIGER WITH, LIKE, SABERS FOR TEETH.
THEY SHOULD THINK OF A DIFFERENT NAME THAN STABBY-CAT.
BUT WHAT DO YOU CALL A SABER-TOOTHED TIGER? NO CLUE.
ITS TRAITS INCLUDE GIANT SABER TEETH, DEADLY CLAWS, AND A VORACIOUS APPETITE.
PLUS THEY'RE REALLY DANGEROUS AND PRACTI-CALLY ALWAYS HUNGRY.
RIGHT. WELL, THERE'S NO WAY WE CAN TAKE ON A STABBY-CAT.
NO WAY.

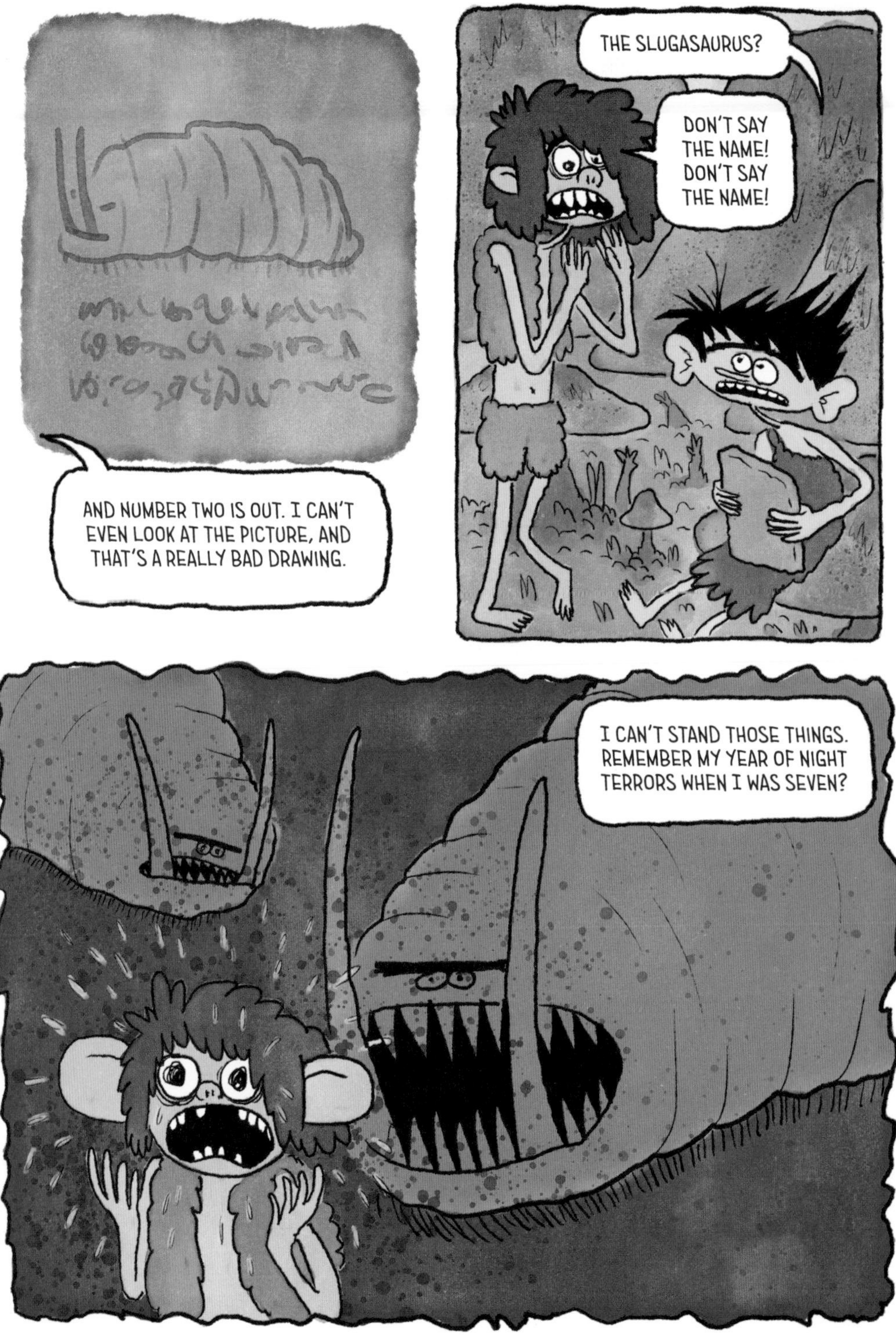
AND NUMBER TWO IS OUT. I CAN'T EVEN LOOK AT THE PICTURE, AND THAT'S A REALLY BAD DRAWING.
THE SLUGASAURUS?
DON'T SAY THE NAME! DON'T SAY THE NAME!
I CAN'T STAND THOSE THINGS. REMEMBER MY YEAR OF NIGHT TERRORS WHEN I WAS SEVEN?

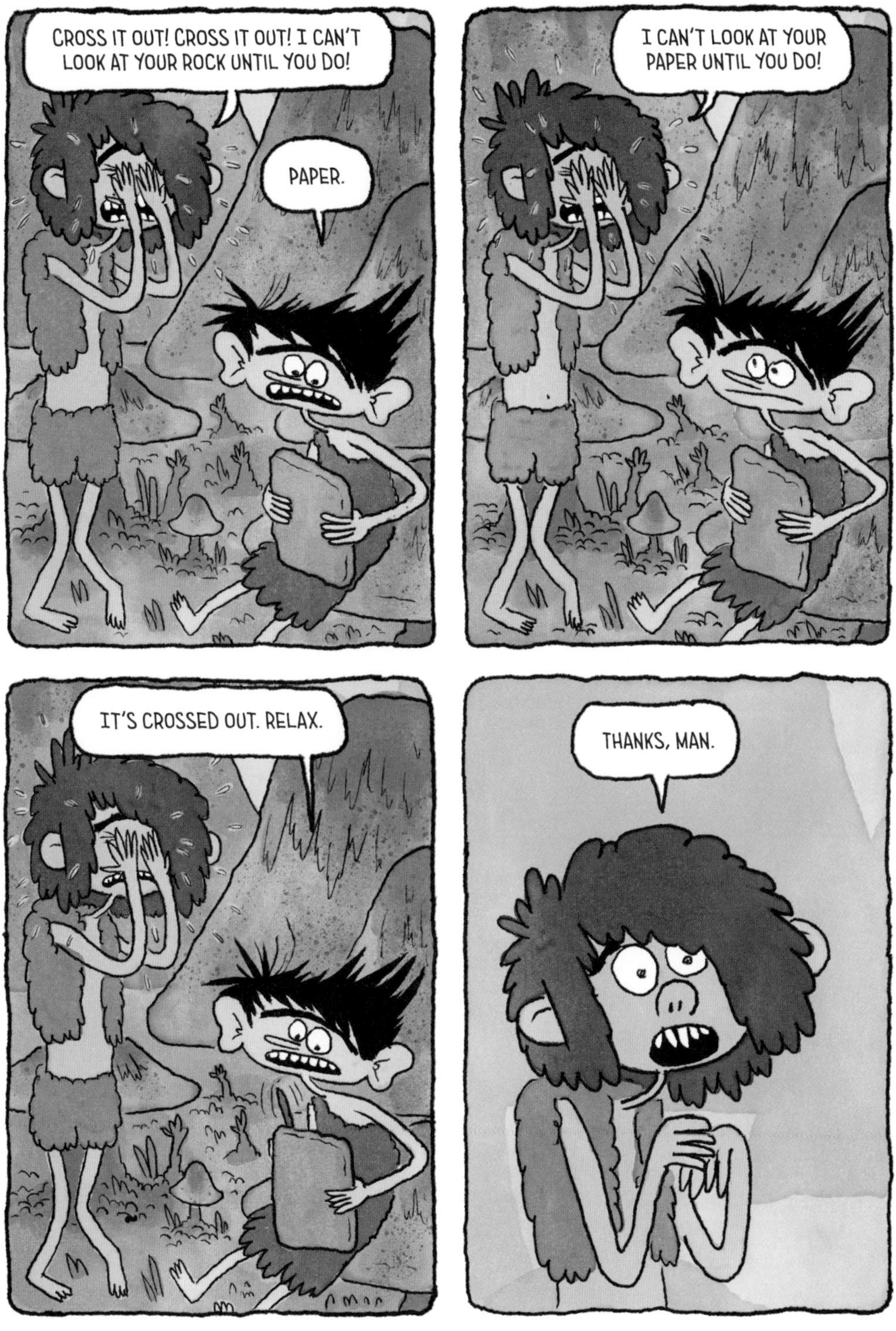
CROSS IT OUT! CROSS IT OUT! I CAN'T LOOK AT YOUR ROCK UNTIL YOU DO!
PAPER.
I CAN'T LOOK AT YOUR PAPER UNTIL YOU DO!
IT'S CROSSED OUT. RELAX.
THANKS, MAN.

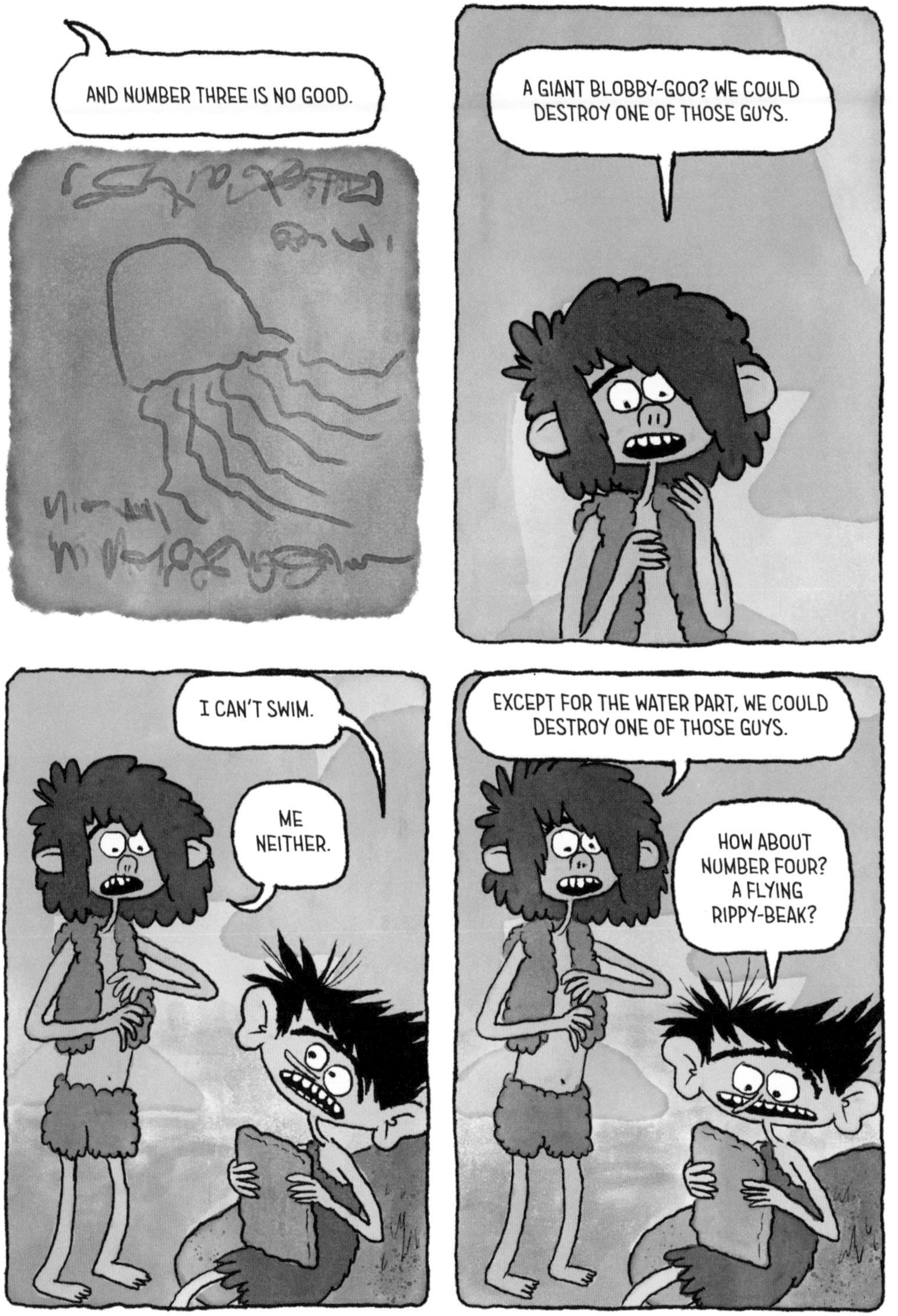
AND NUMBER THREE IS NO GOOD.
A GIANT BLOBBY-GOO? WE COULD DESTROY ONE OF THOSE GUYS.
I CAN'T SWIM.
ME NEITHER.
EXCEPT FOR THE WATER PART, WE COULD DESTROY ONE OF THOSE GUYS.
HOW ABOUT NUMBER FOUR? A FLYING RIPPY-BEAK?

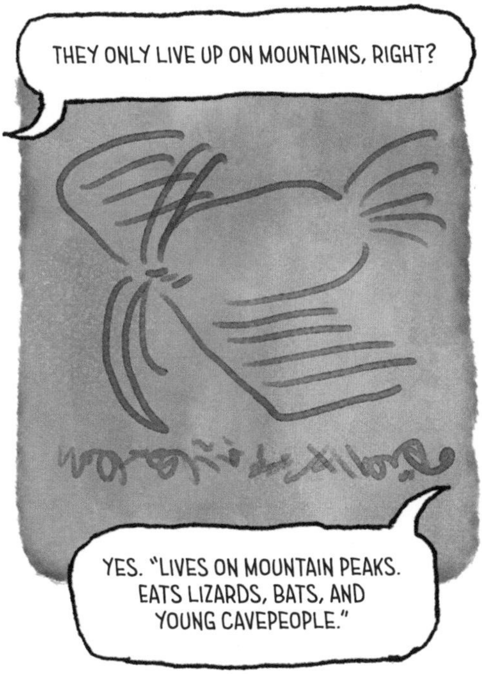
THEY ONLY LIVE UP ON MOUNTAINS, RIGHT?
YES. "LIVES ON MOUNTAIN PEAKS. EATS LIZARDS, BATS, AND YOUNG CAVEPEOPLE."

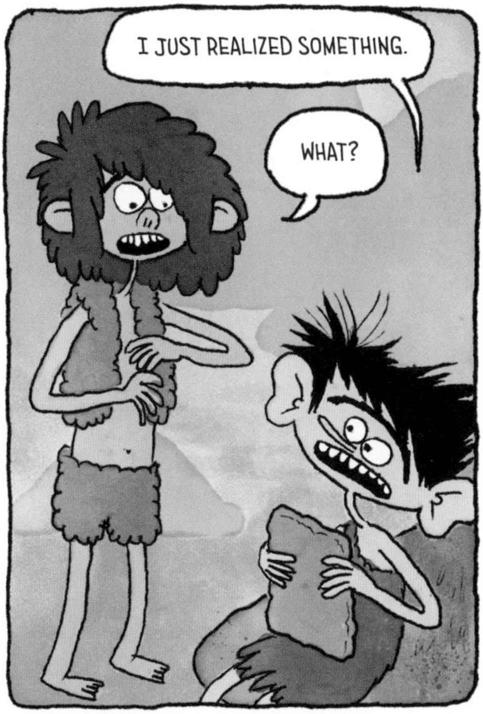
I JUST REALIZED SOMETHING.
WHAT?

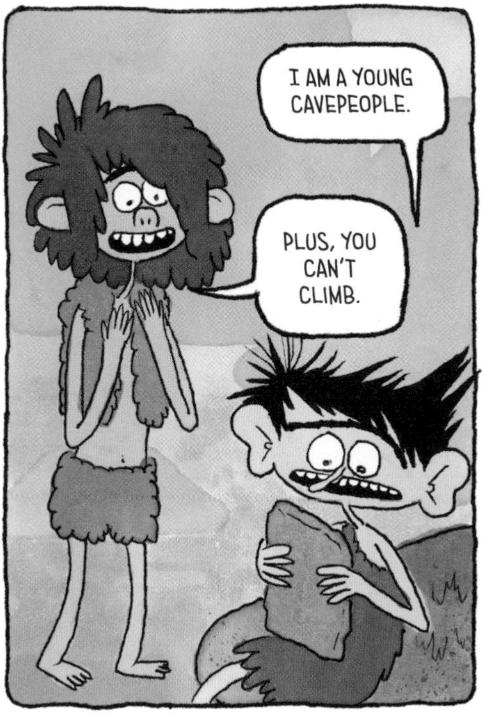
I AM A YOUNG CAVEPEOPLE.
PLUS, YOU CAN'T CLIMB.

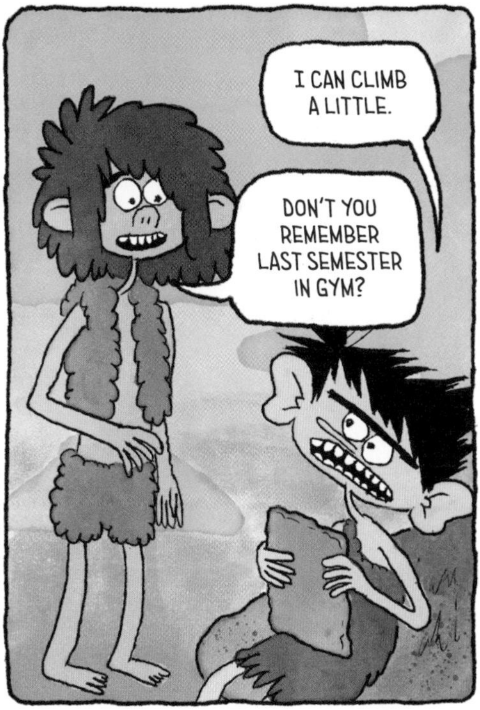
I CAN CLIMB A LITTLE.
DON'T YOU REMEMBER LAST SEMESTER IN GYM?

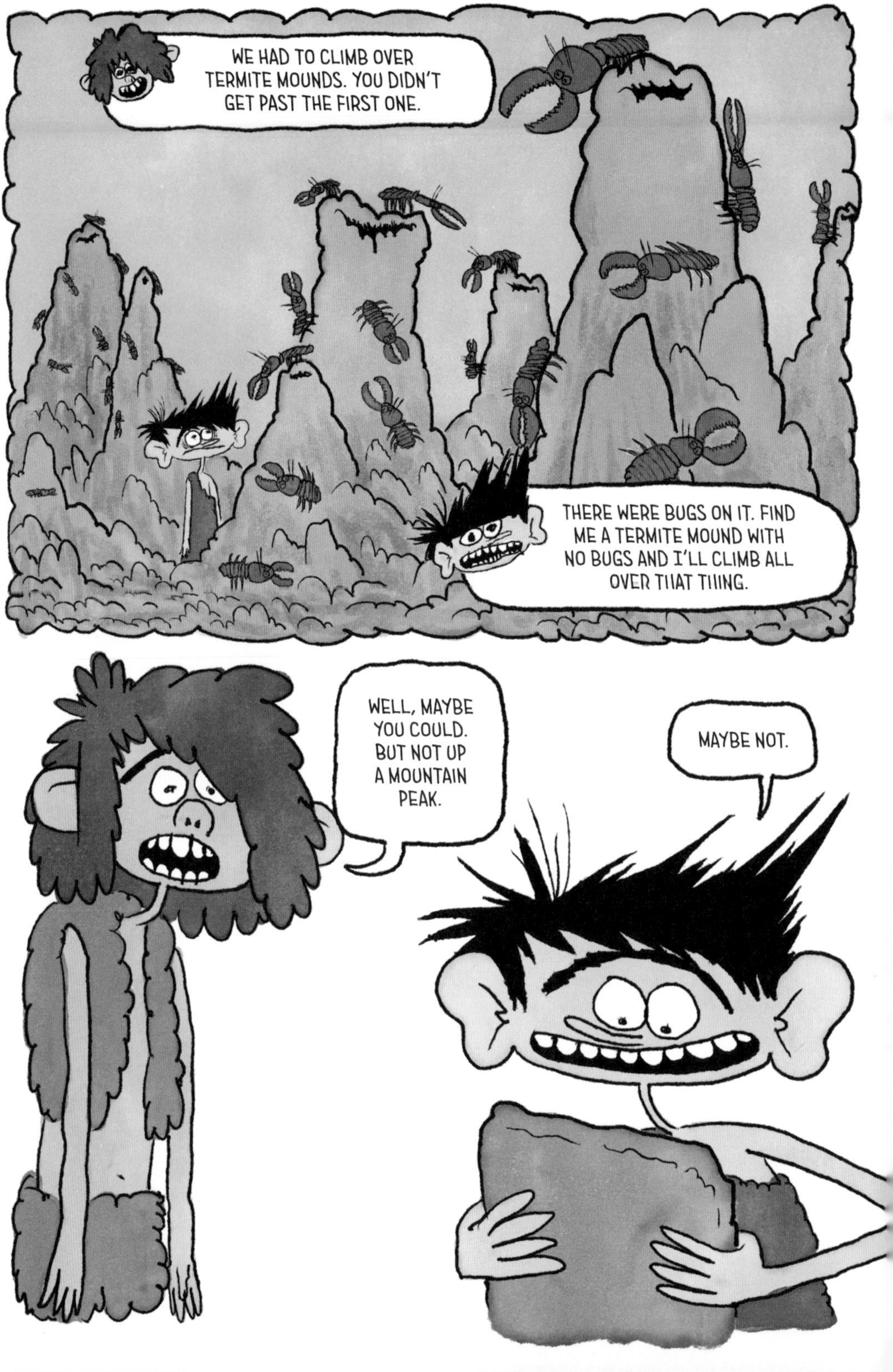
WE HAD TO CLIMB OVER TERMITE MOUNDS. YOU DIDN'T GET PAST THE FIRST ONE.
THERE WERE BUGS ON IT. FIND ME A TERMITE MOUND WITH NO BUGS AND I'LL CLIMB ALL OVER THAT THING.
WELL, MAYBE YOU COULD. BUT NOT UP A MOUNTAIN PEAK.
MAYBE NOT.

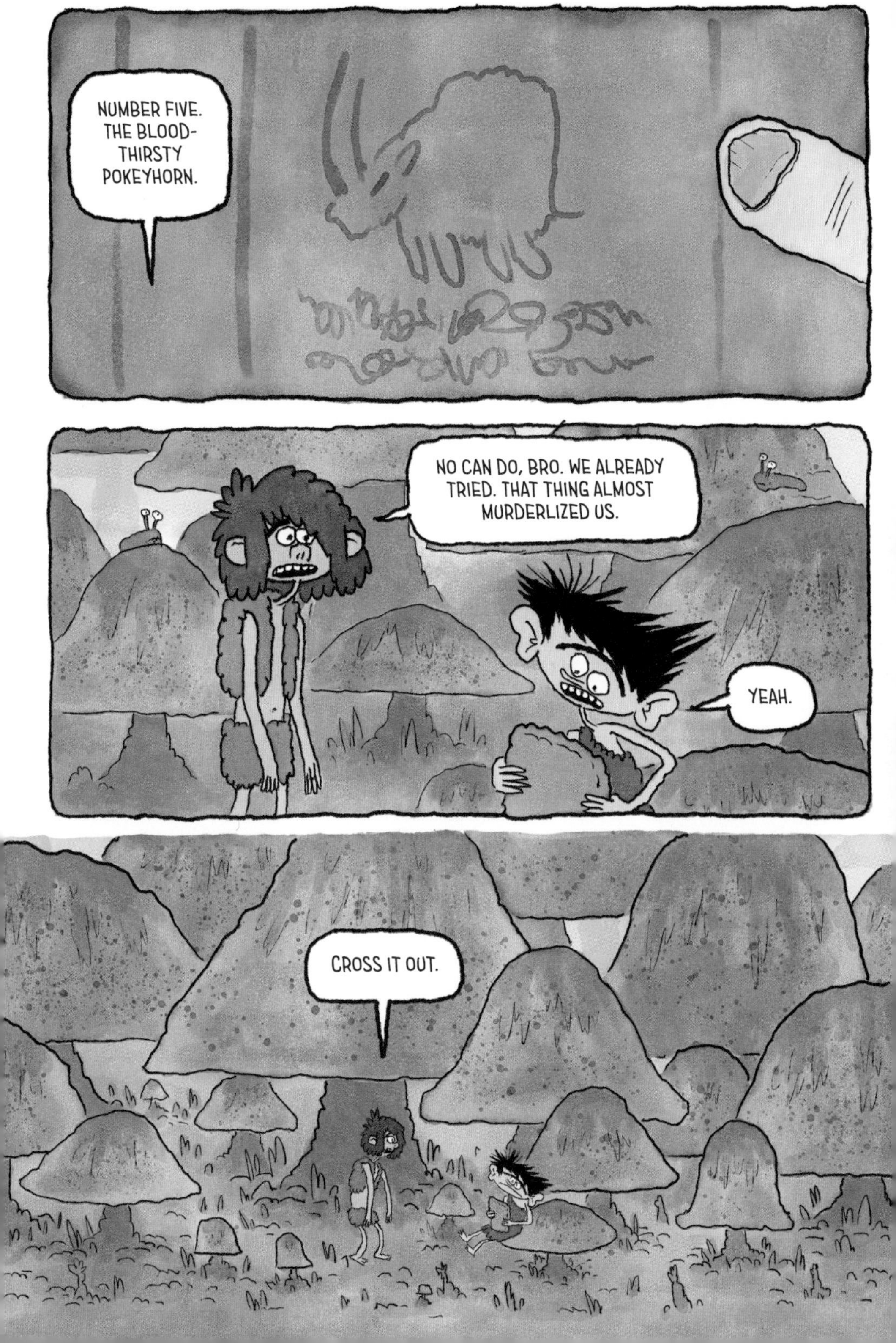
NUMBER FIVE. THE BLOOD-THIRSTY POKEYHORN.
NO CAN DO, BRO. WE ALREADY TRIED. THAT THING ALMOST MURDERLIZED US.
YEAH.
CROSS IT OUT.

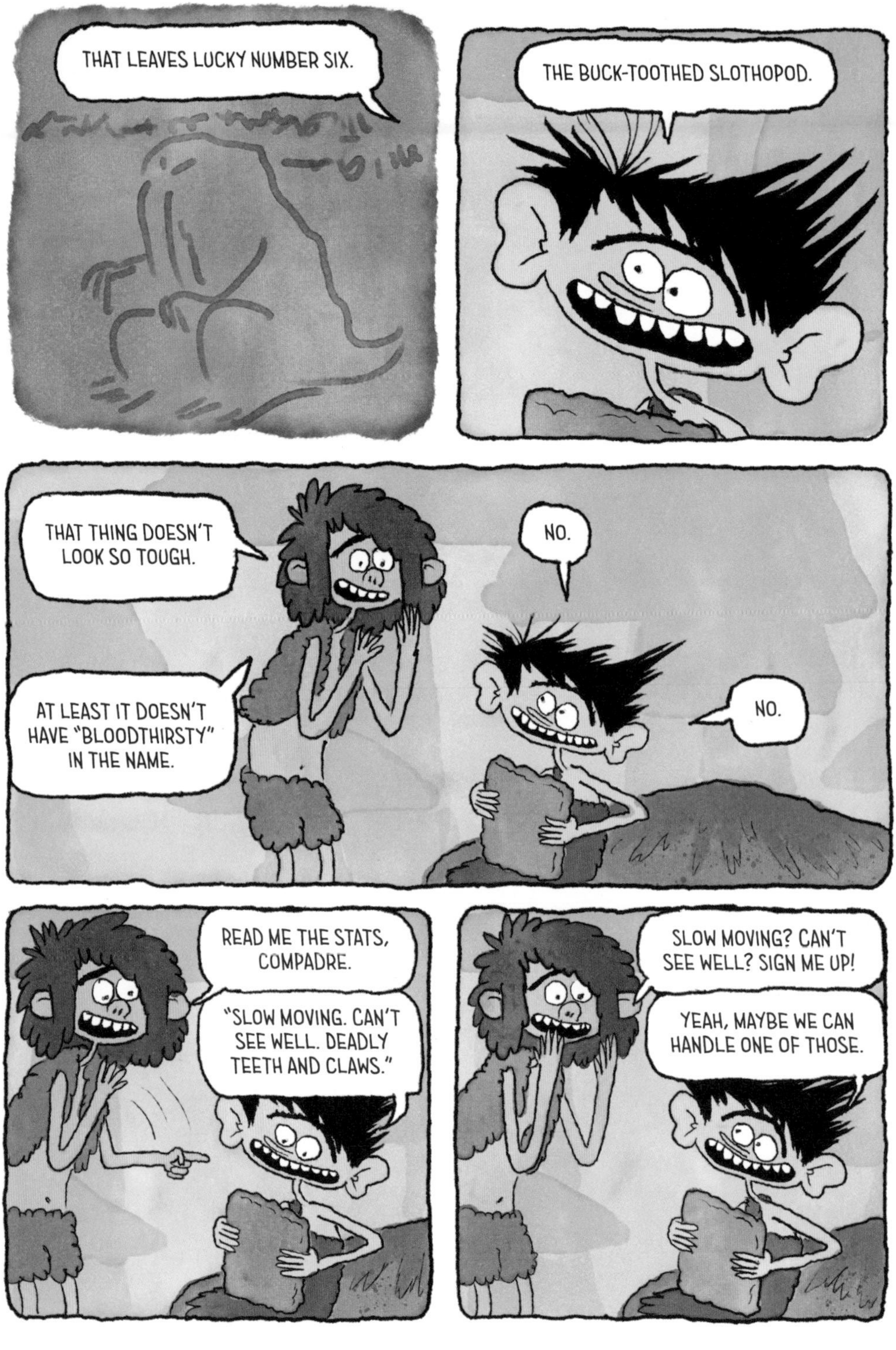
THAT LEAVES LUCKY NUMBER SIX.
THE BUCK-TOOTHED SLOTHOPOD.
THAT THING DOESN'T LOOK SO TOUGH.
NO.
AT LEAST IT DOESN'T HAVE "BLOODTHIRSTY" IN THE NAME.
NO.
READ ME THE STATS, COMPADRE.
"SLOW MOVING. CAN'T SEE WELL. DEADLY TEETH AND CLAWS."
SLOW MOVING? CAN'T SEE WELL? SIGN ME UP!
YEAH, MAYBE WE CAN HANDLE ONE OF THOSE.

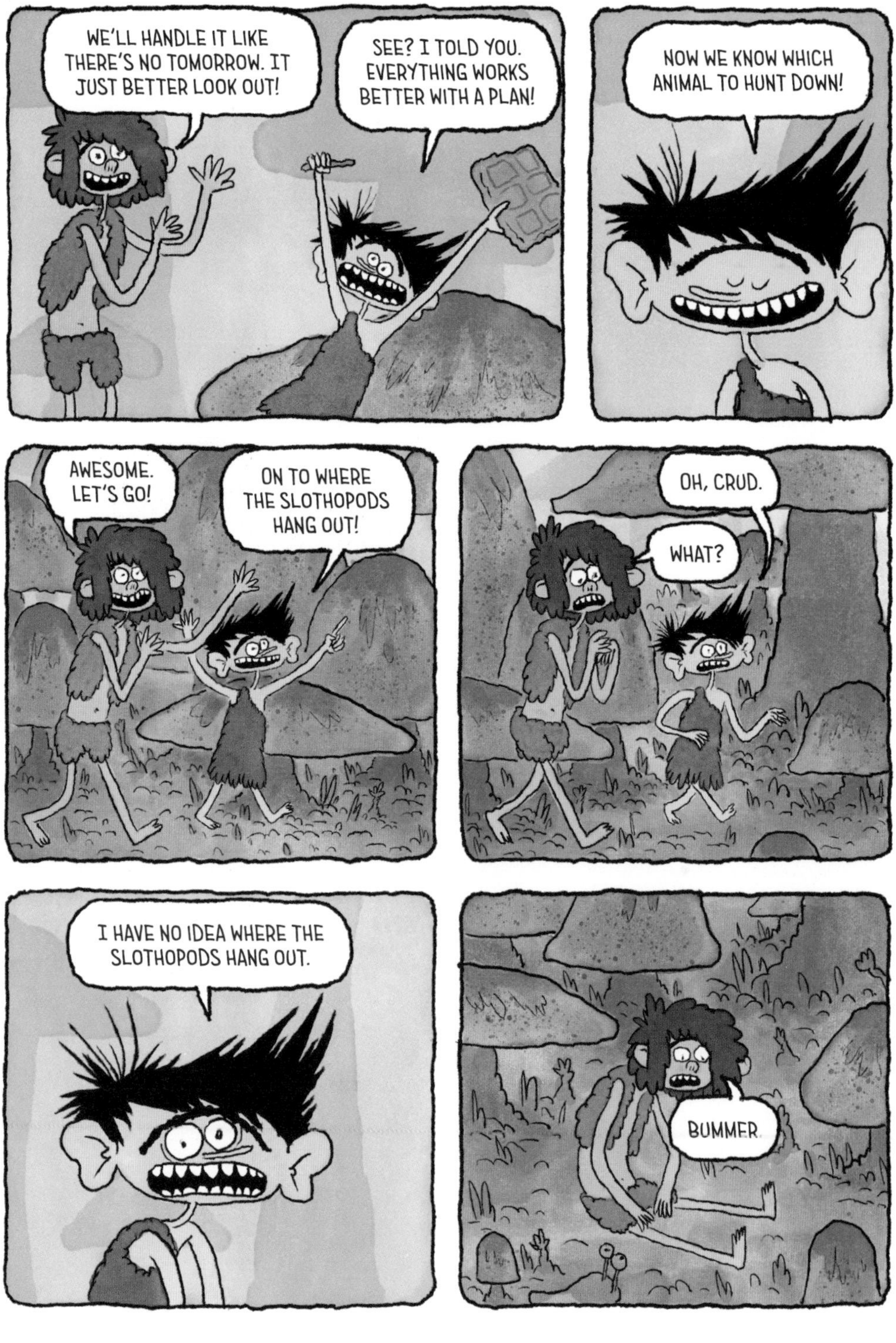
WE'LL HANDLE IT LIKE THERE'S NO TOMORROW. IT JUST BETTER LOOK OUT!
SEE? I TOLD YOU. EVERYTHING WORKS BETTER WITH A PLAN!
NOW WE KNOW WHICH ANIMAL TO HUNT DOWN!
AWESOME. LET'S GO!
ON TO WHERE THE SLOTHOPODS HANG OUT!
OH, CRUD.
WHAT?
I HAVE NO IDEA WHERE THE SLOTHOPODS HANG OUT.
BUMMER.

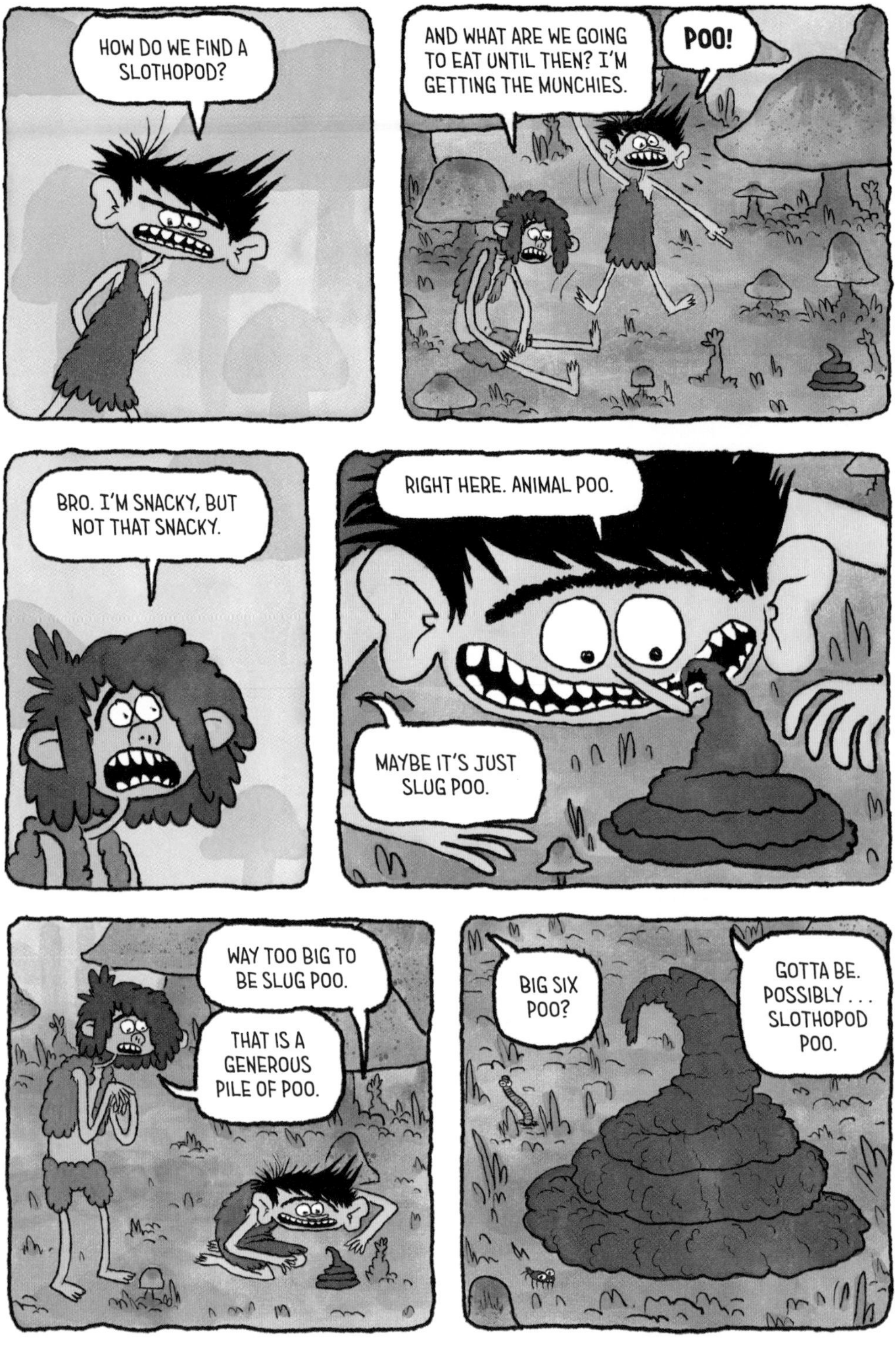
HOW DO WE FIND A SLOTHOPOD?
AND WHAT ARE WE GOING TO EAT UNTIL THEN? I'M GETTING THE MUNCHIES.
POO!
BRO. I'M SNACKY, BUT NOT THAT SNACKY.
RIGHT HERE. ANIMAL POO.
MAYBE IT'S JUST SLUG POO.
WAY TOO BIG TO BE SLUG POO.
THAT IS A GENEROUS PILE OF POO.
BIG SIX POO?
GOTTA BE. POSSIBLY . . . SLOTHOPOD POO.

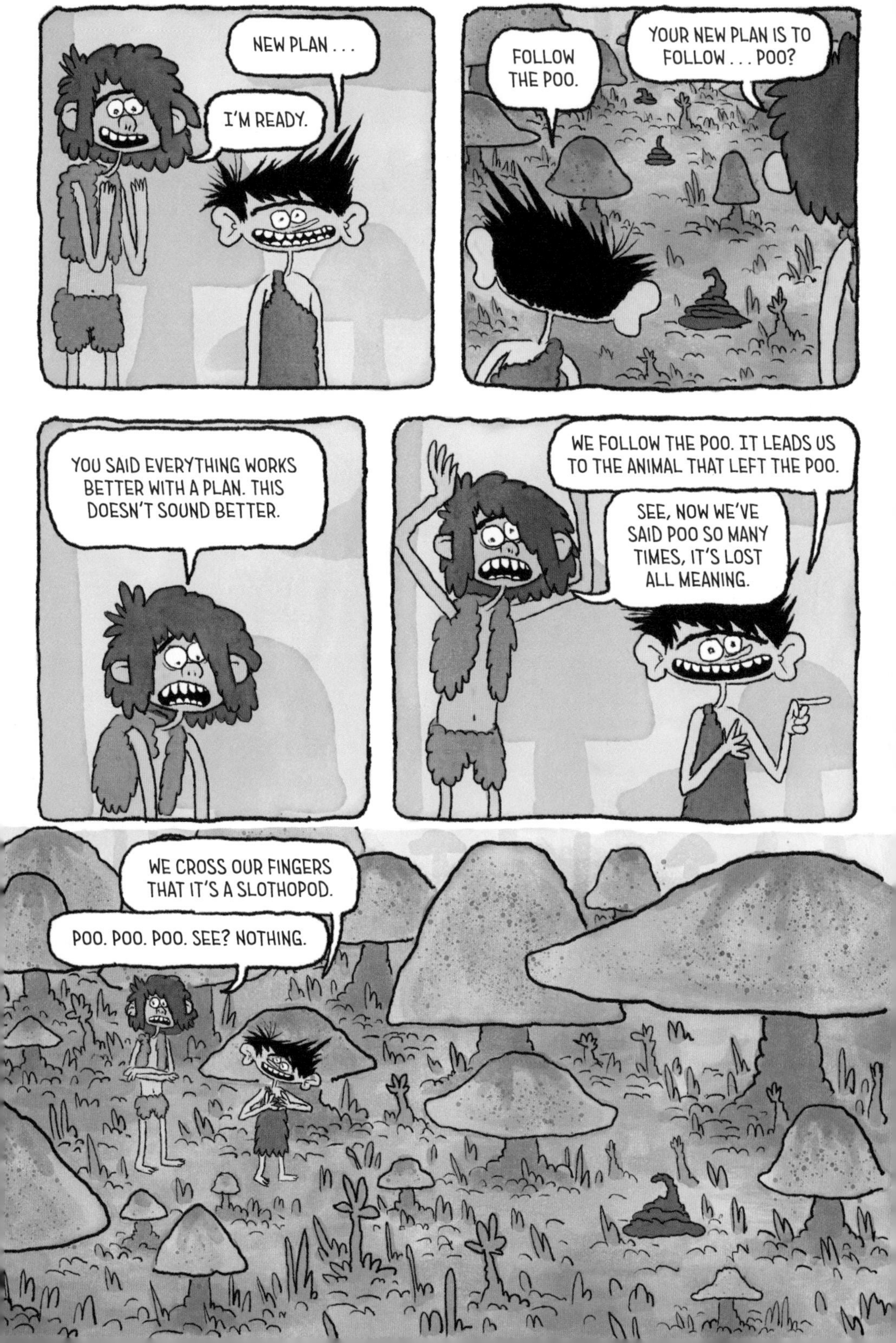
NEW PLAN . . .
I'M READY.
FOLLOW THE POO.
YOUR NEW PLAN IS TO FOLLOW . . . POO?
YOU SAID EVERYTHING WORKS BETTER WITH A PLAN. THIS DOESN'T SOUND BETTER.
WE FOLLOW THE POO. IT LEADS US TO THE ANIMAL THAT LEFT THE POO.
SEE, NOW WE'VE SAID POO SO MANY TIMES, IT'S LOST ALL MEANING.
WE CROSS OUR FINGERS THAT IT'S A SLOTHOPOD.
POO. POO. POO. SEE? NOTHING.

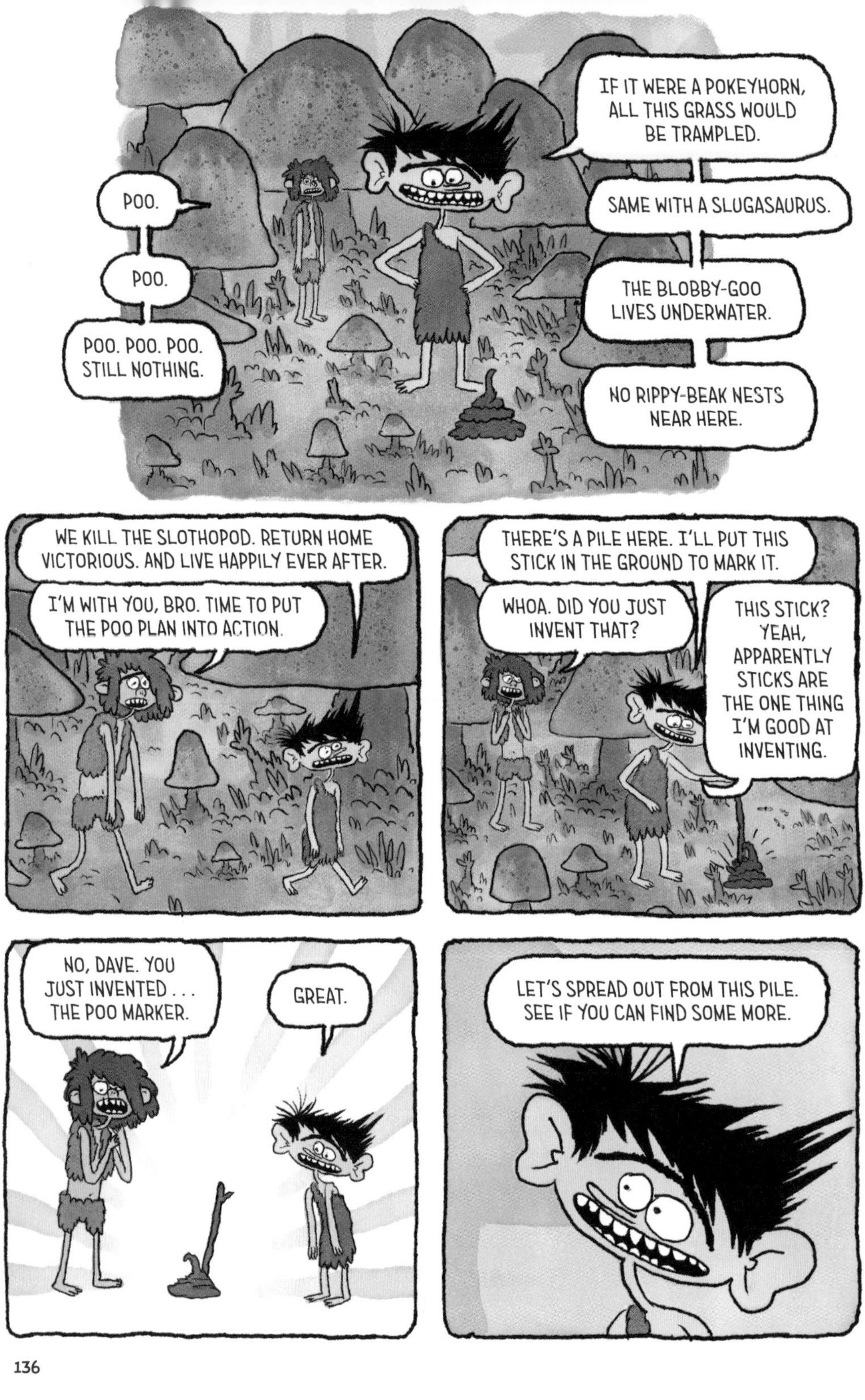
IF IT WERE A POKEYHORN, ALL THIS GRASS WOULD BE TRAMPLED.
POO.
SAME WITH A SLUGASAURUS.
POO.
THE BLOBBY-GOO LIVES UNDERWATER.
POO. POO. POO. STILL NOTHING.
NO RIPPY-BEAK NESTS NEAR HERE.
WE KILL THE SLOTHOPOD. RETURN HOME VICTORIOUS. AND LIVE HAPPILY EVER AFTER.
I'M WITH YOU, BRO. TIME TO PUT THE POO PLAN INTO ACTION.
THERE'S A PILE HERE. I'LL PUT THIS STICK IN THE GROUND TO MARK IT.
WHOA. DID YOU JUST INVENT THAT?
THIS STICK? YEAH, APPARENTLY STICKS ARE THE ONE THING I'M GOOD AT INVENTING.
NO, DAVE. YOU JUST INVENTED . . . THE POO MARKER.
GREAT.
LET'S SPREAD OUT FROM THIS PILE. SEE IF YOU CAN FIND SOME MORE.

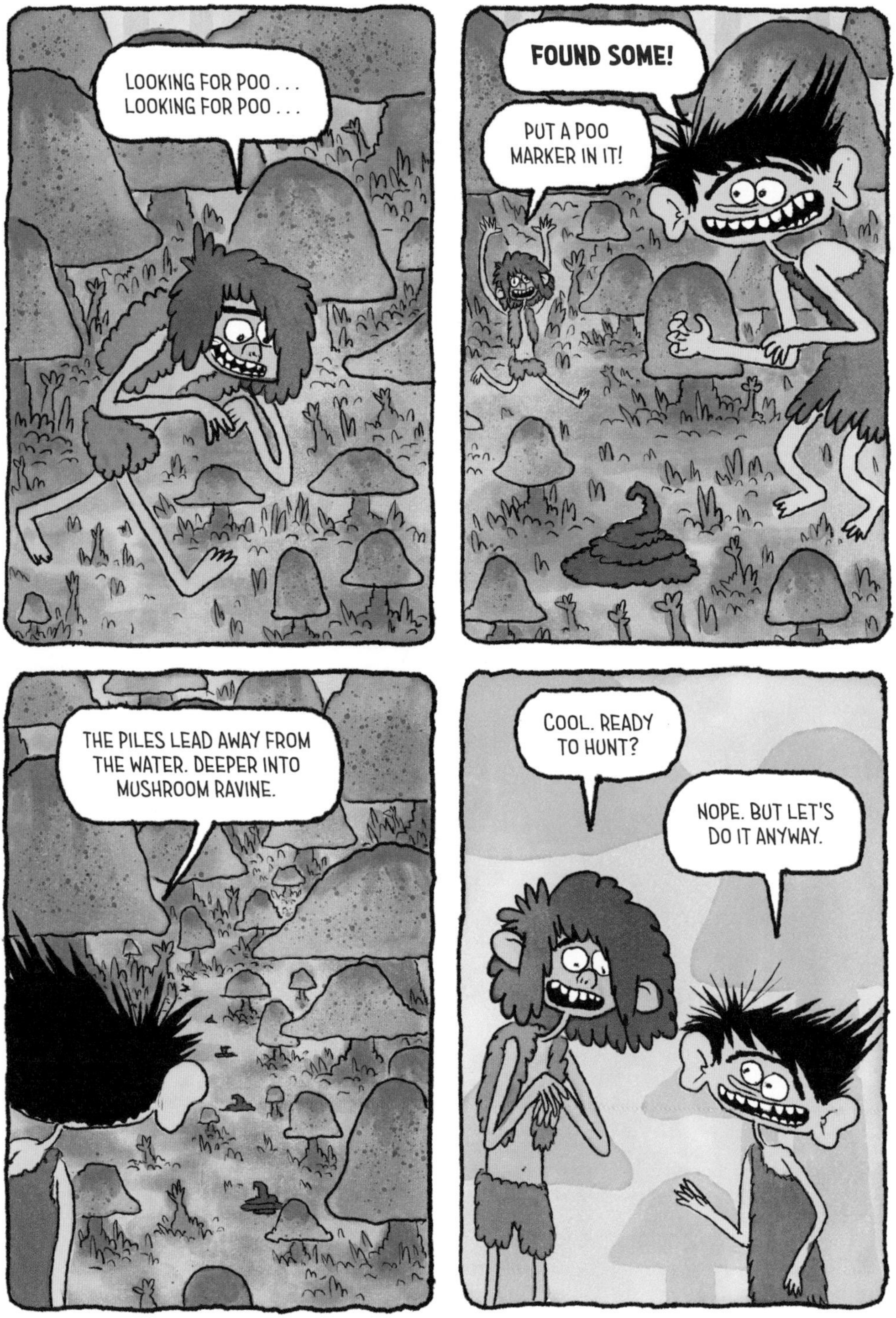
LOOKING FOR POO . . .
LOOKING FOR POO . . .
FOUND SOME!
PUT A POO MARKER IN IT!
THE PILES LEAD AWAY FROM THE WATER. DEEPER INTO MUSHROOM RAVINE.
COOL. READY TO HUNT?
NOPE. BUT LET'S DO IT ANYWAY.

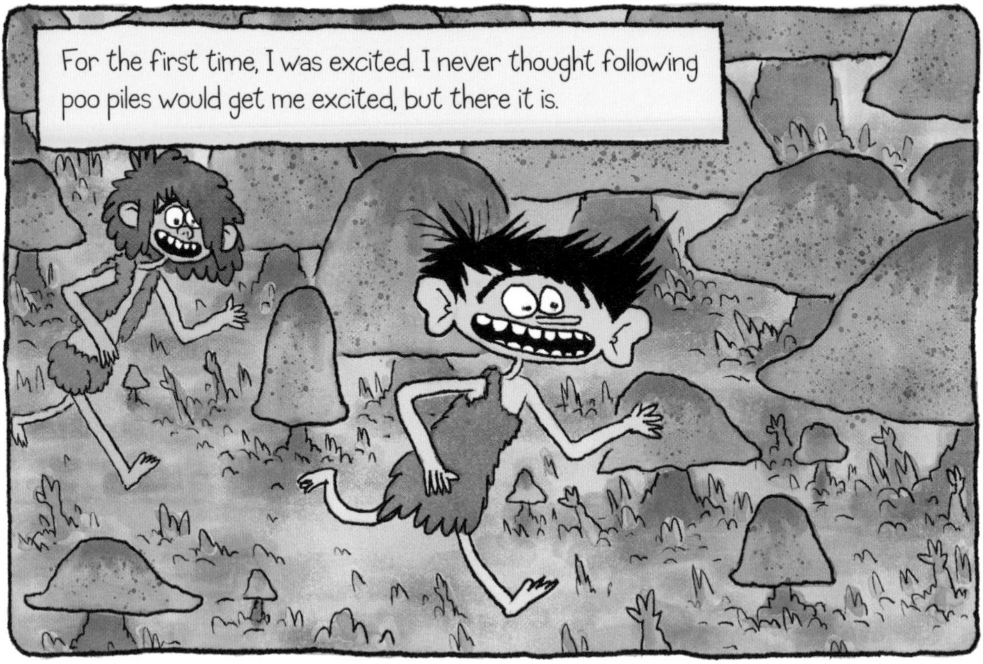
For the first time, I was excited. I never thought following poo piles would get me excited, but there it is.

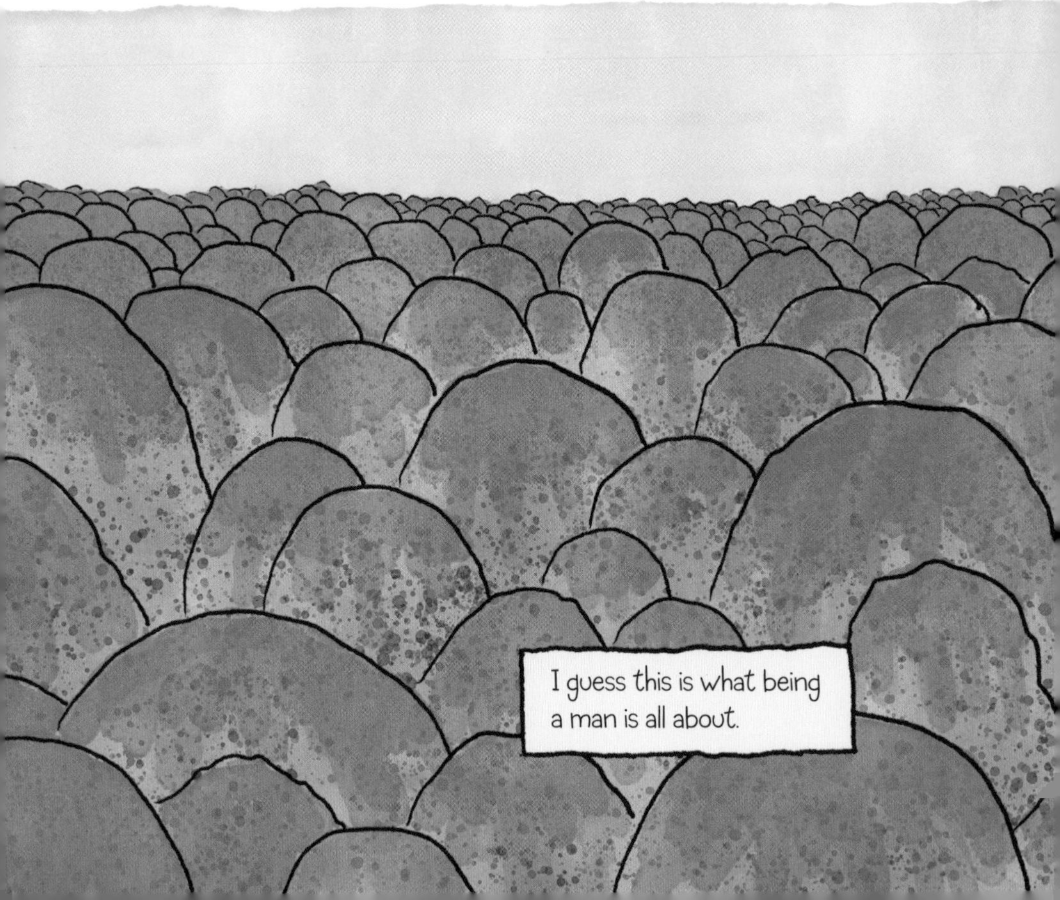
I guess this is what being a man is all about.

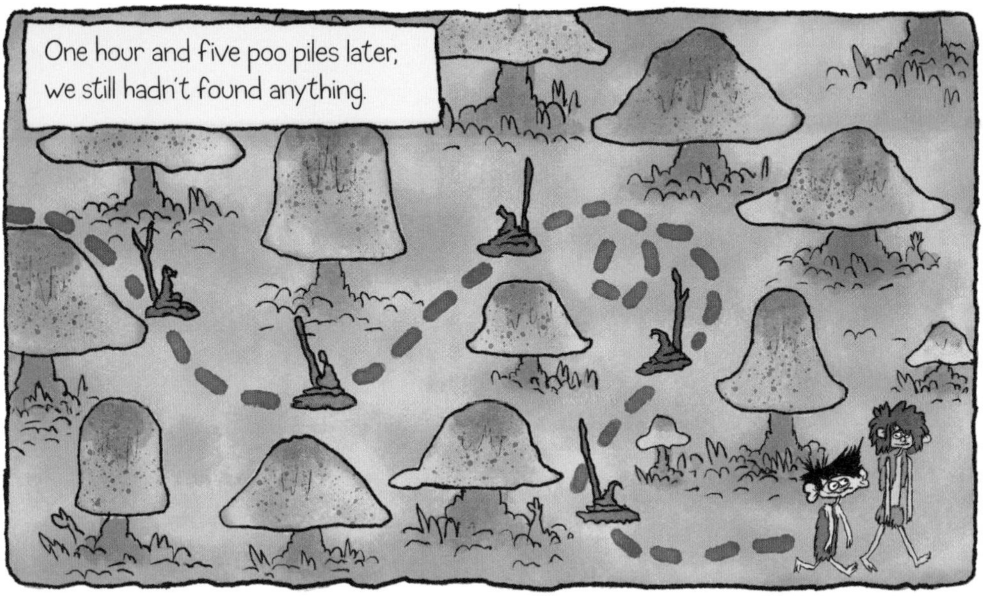
One hour and five poo piles later, we still hadn't found anything.

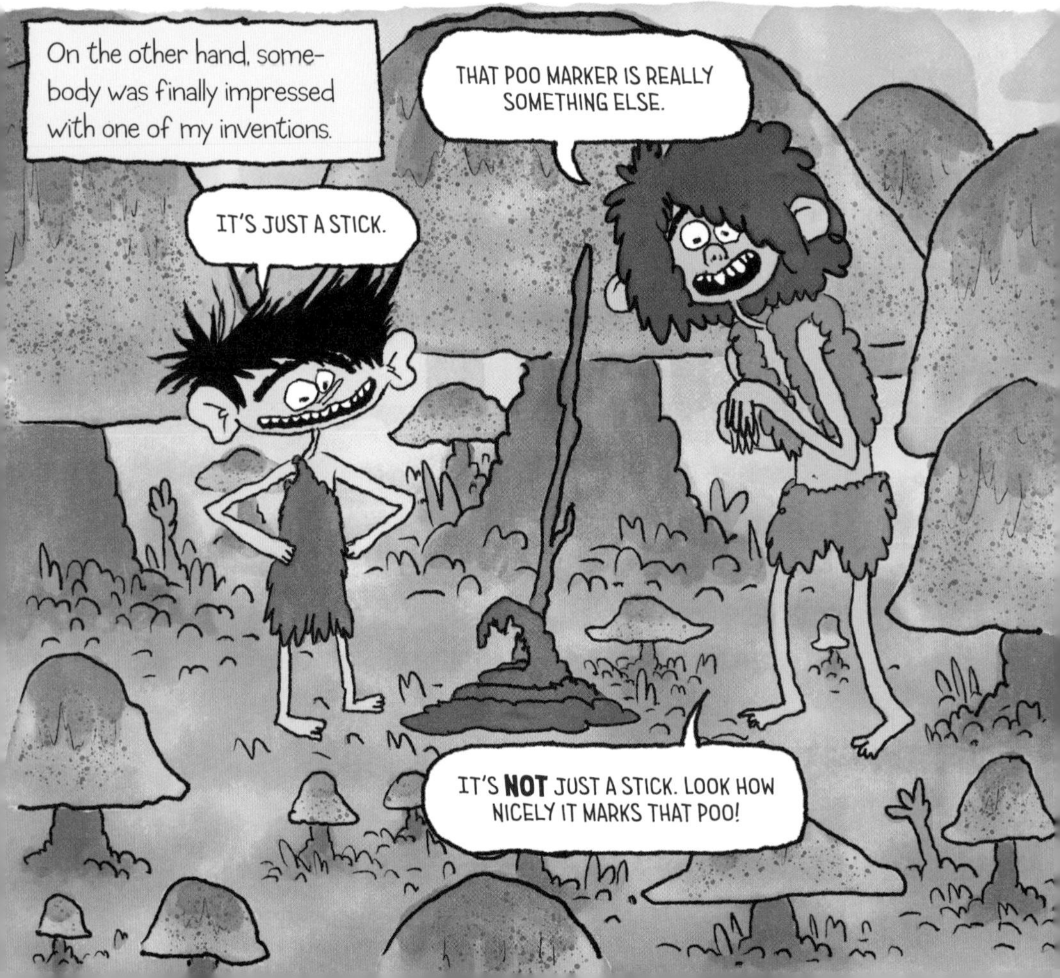
On the other hand, some-body was finally impressed with one of my inventions.
THAT POO MARKER IS REALLY SOMETHING ELSE.
IT'S JUST A STICK.
IT'S **NOT** JUST A STICK. LOOK HOW NICELY IT MARKS THAT POO!

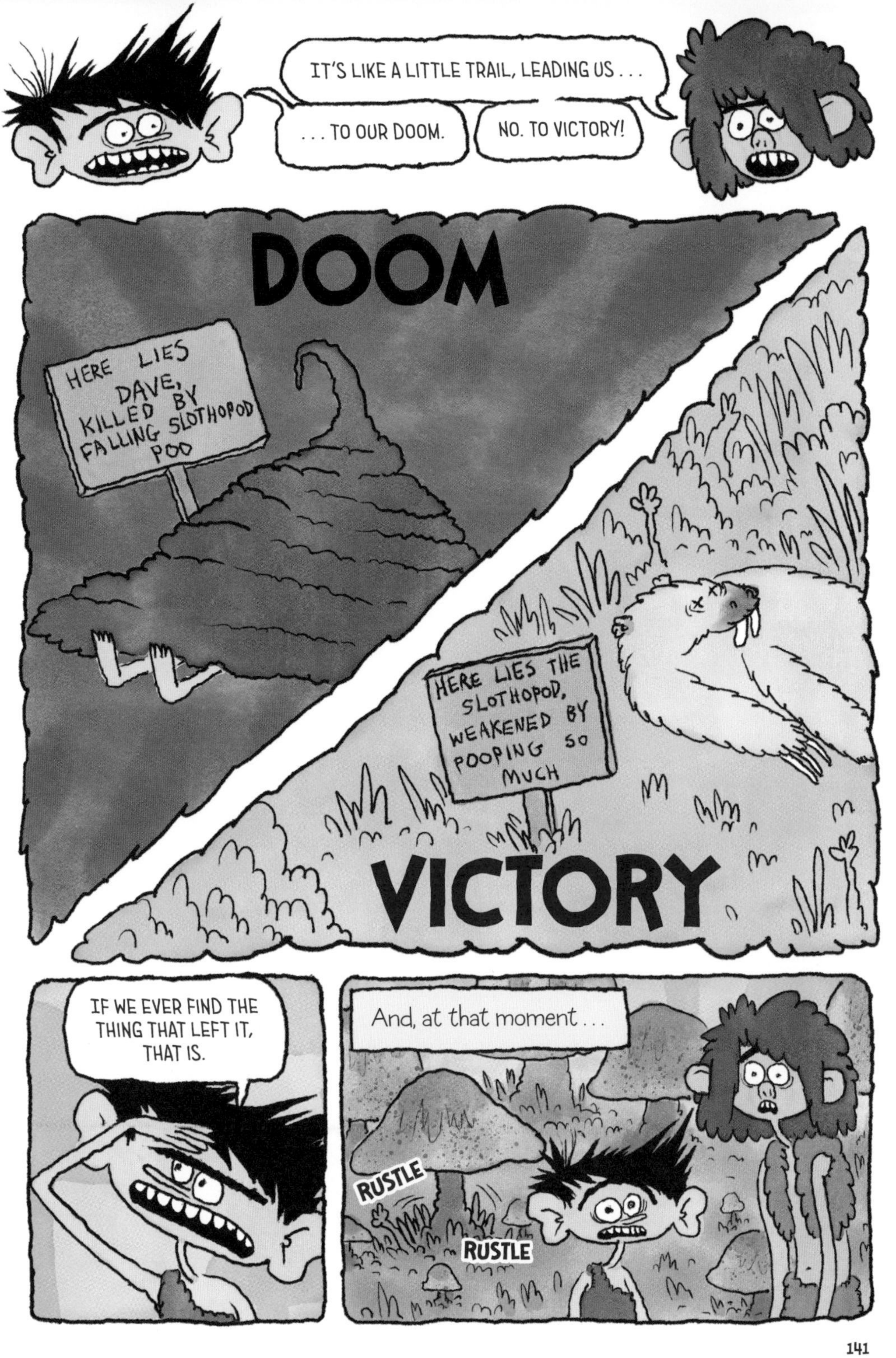

IT'S LIKE A LITTLE TRAIL, LEADING US . . .
. . . TO OUR DOOM.
NO. TO VICTORY!
DOOM
HERE LIES DAVE, KILLED BY FALLING SLOTHOPOD POO
HERE LIES THE SLOTHOPOD, WEAKENED BY POOPING SO MUCH
VICTORY
IF WE EVER FIND THE THING THAT LEFT IT, THAT IS.
And, at that moment . . .
RUSTLE
RUSTLE

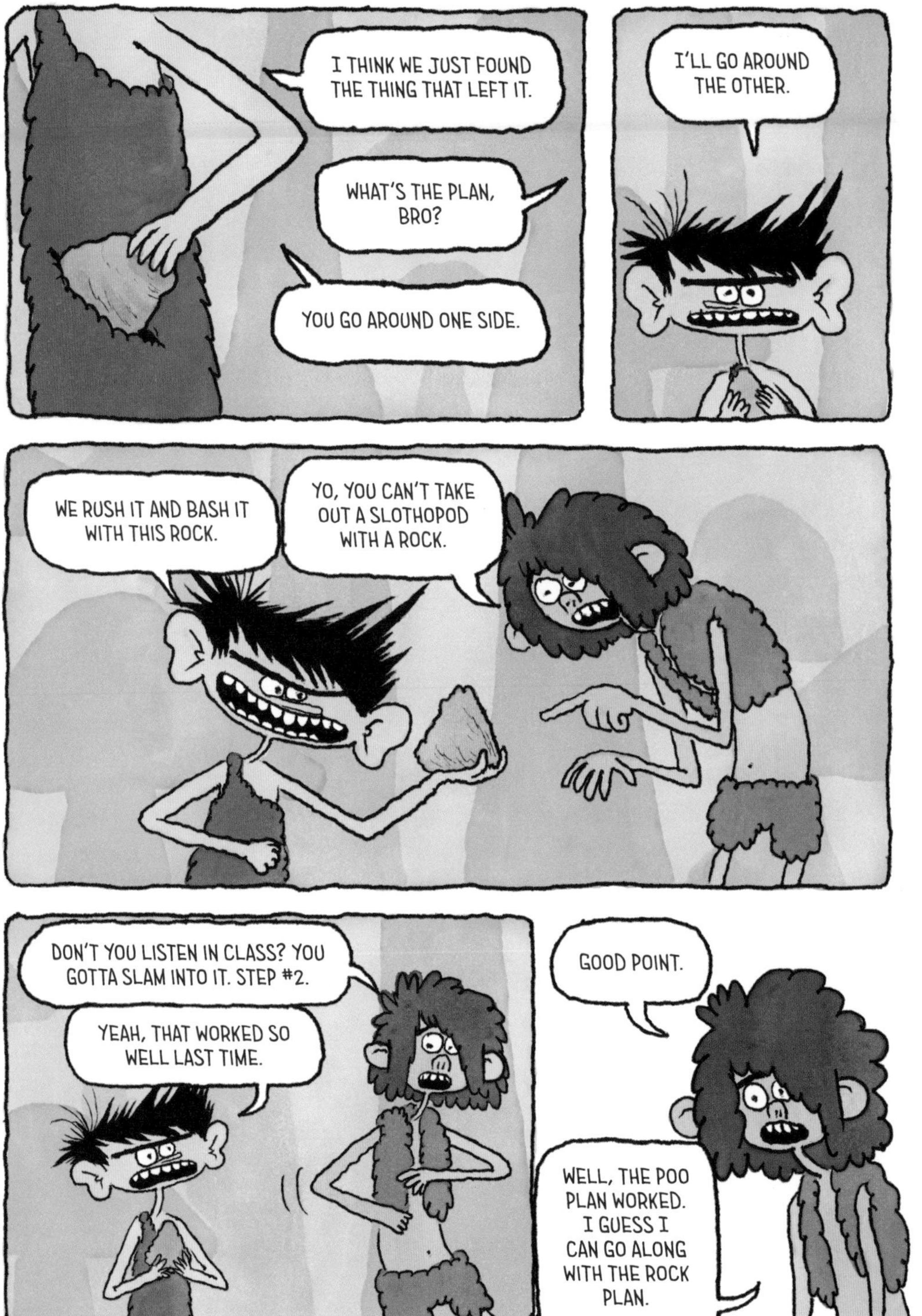
I THINK WE JUST FOUND THE THING THAT LEFT IT.
WHAT'S THE PLAN, BRO?
YOU GO AROUND ONE SIDE.
I'LL GO AROUND THE OTHER.
WE RUSH IT AND BASH IT WITH THIS ROCK.
YO, YOU CAN'T TAKE OUT A SLOTHOPOD WITH A ROCK.
DON'T YOU LISTEN IN CLASS? YOU GOTTA SLAM INTO IT. STEP #2.
YEAH, THAT WORKED SO WELL LAST TIME.
GOOD POINT.
WELL, THE POO PLAN WORKED. I GUESS I CAN GO ALONG WITH THE ROCK PLAN.

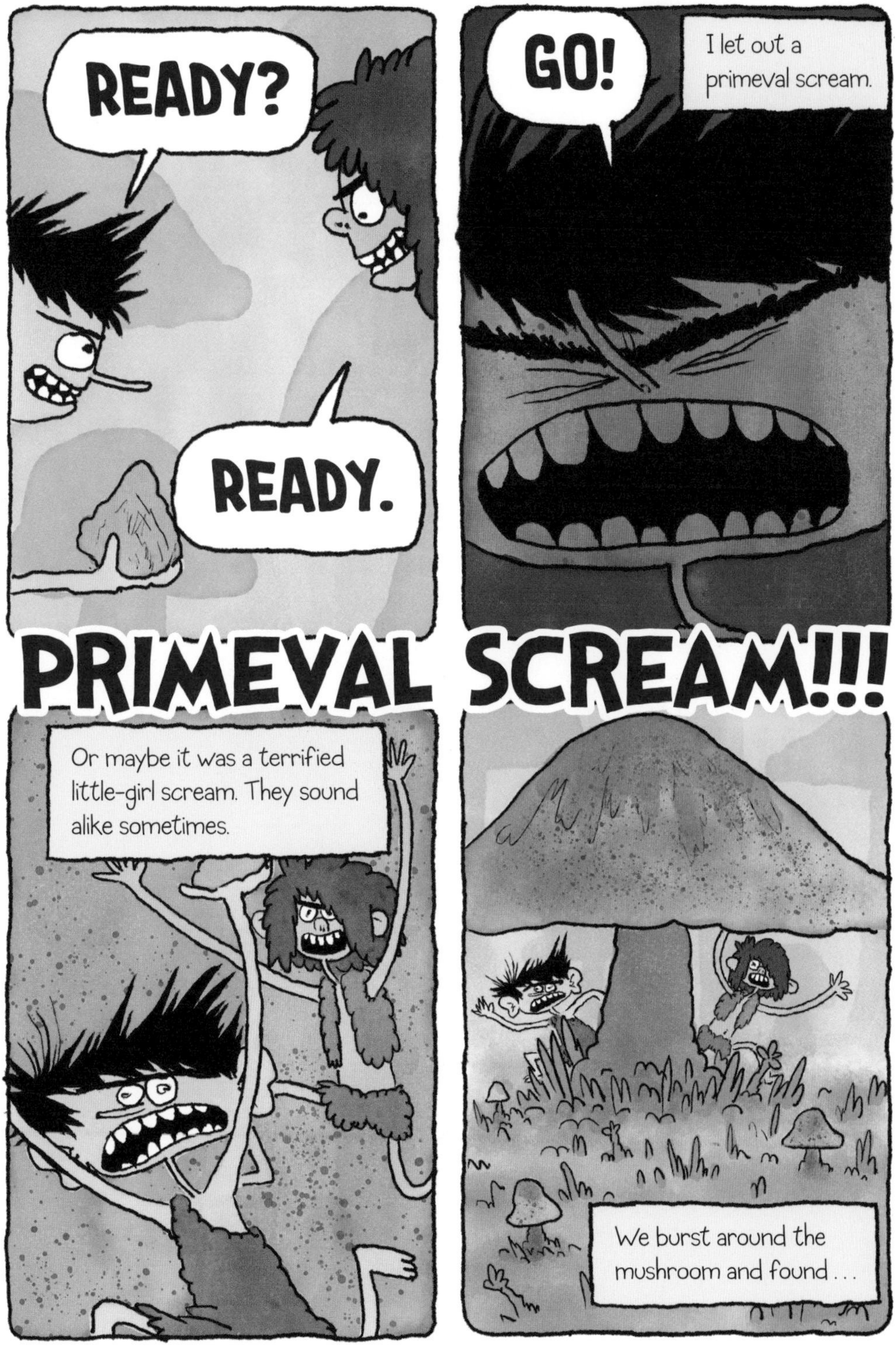
READY?
READY.
GO!
I let out a primeval scream.
PRIMEVAL SCREAM!!!
Or maybe it was a terrified little-girl scream. They sound alike sometimes.
We burst around the mushroom and found . . .

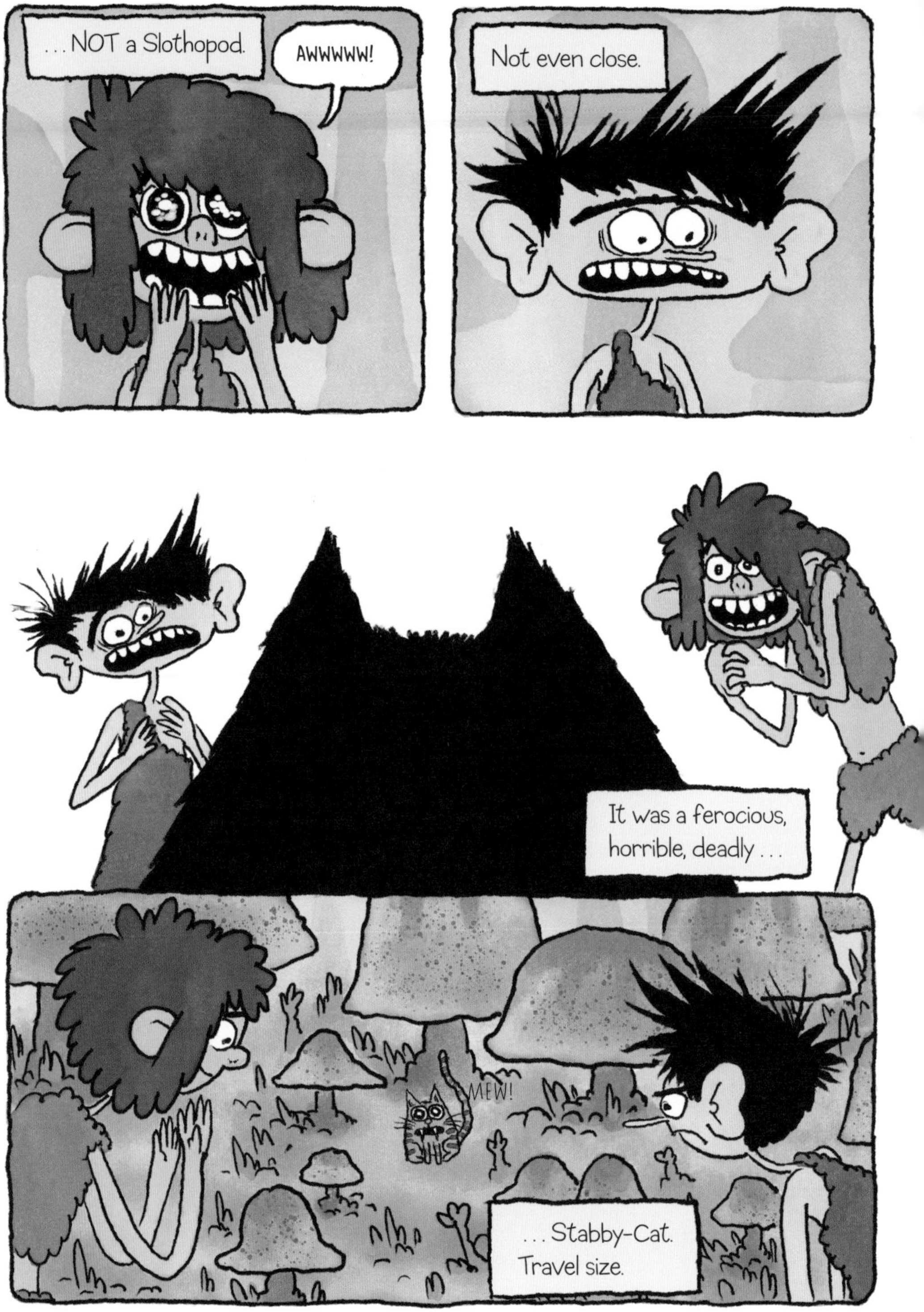
. . . NOT a Slothopod.
AWWWWW!
Not even close.
It was a ferocious,
horrible, deadly . . .
MEW!
. . . Stabby-Cat.
Travel size.

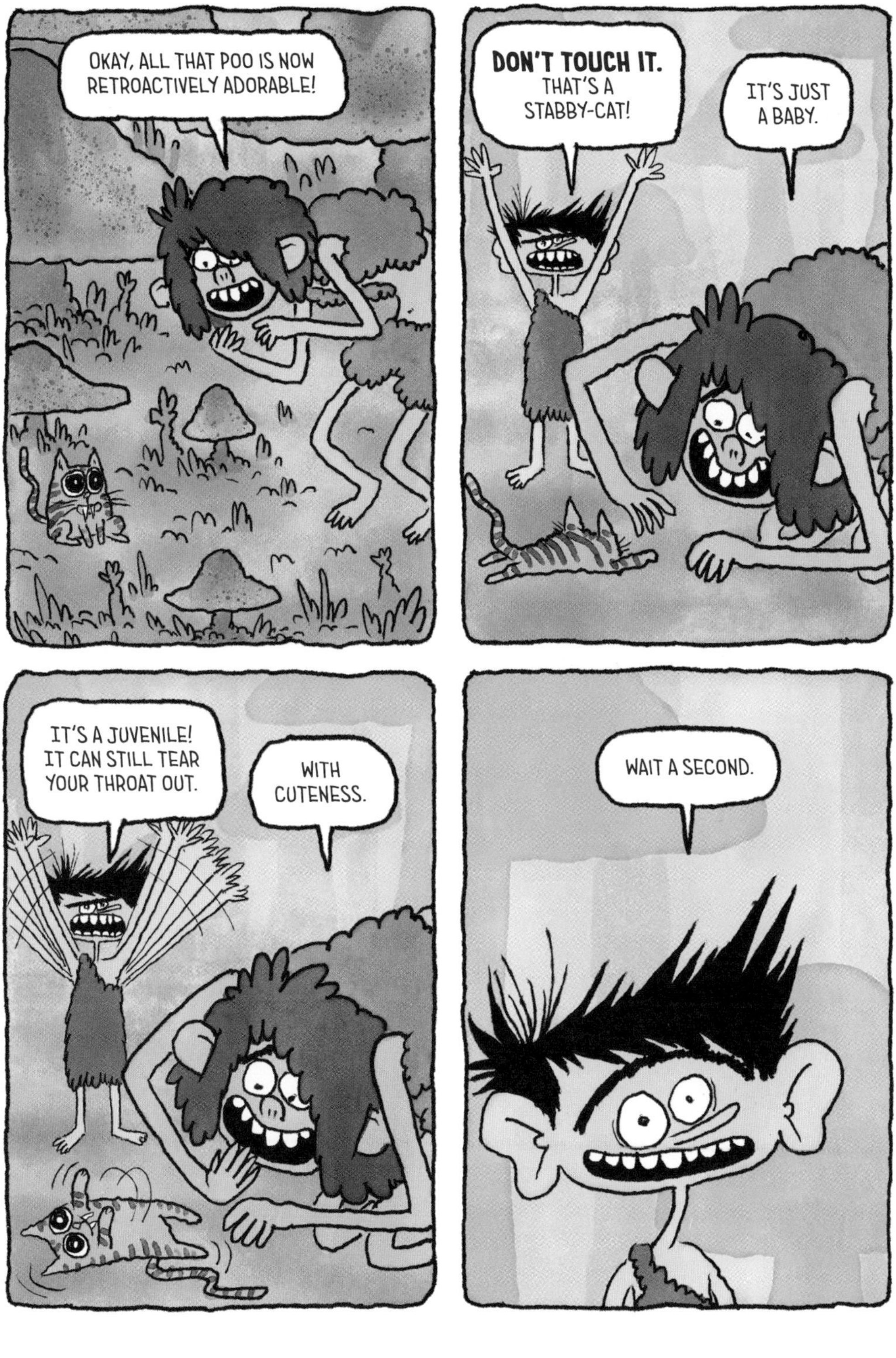
OKAY, ALL THAT POO IS NOW RETROACTIVELY ADORABLE!
DON'T TOUCH IT. THAT'S A STABBY-CAT!
IT'S JUST A BABY.
IT'S A JUVENILE! IT CAN STILL TEAR YOUR THROAT OUT.
WITH CUTENESS.
WAIT A SECOND.

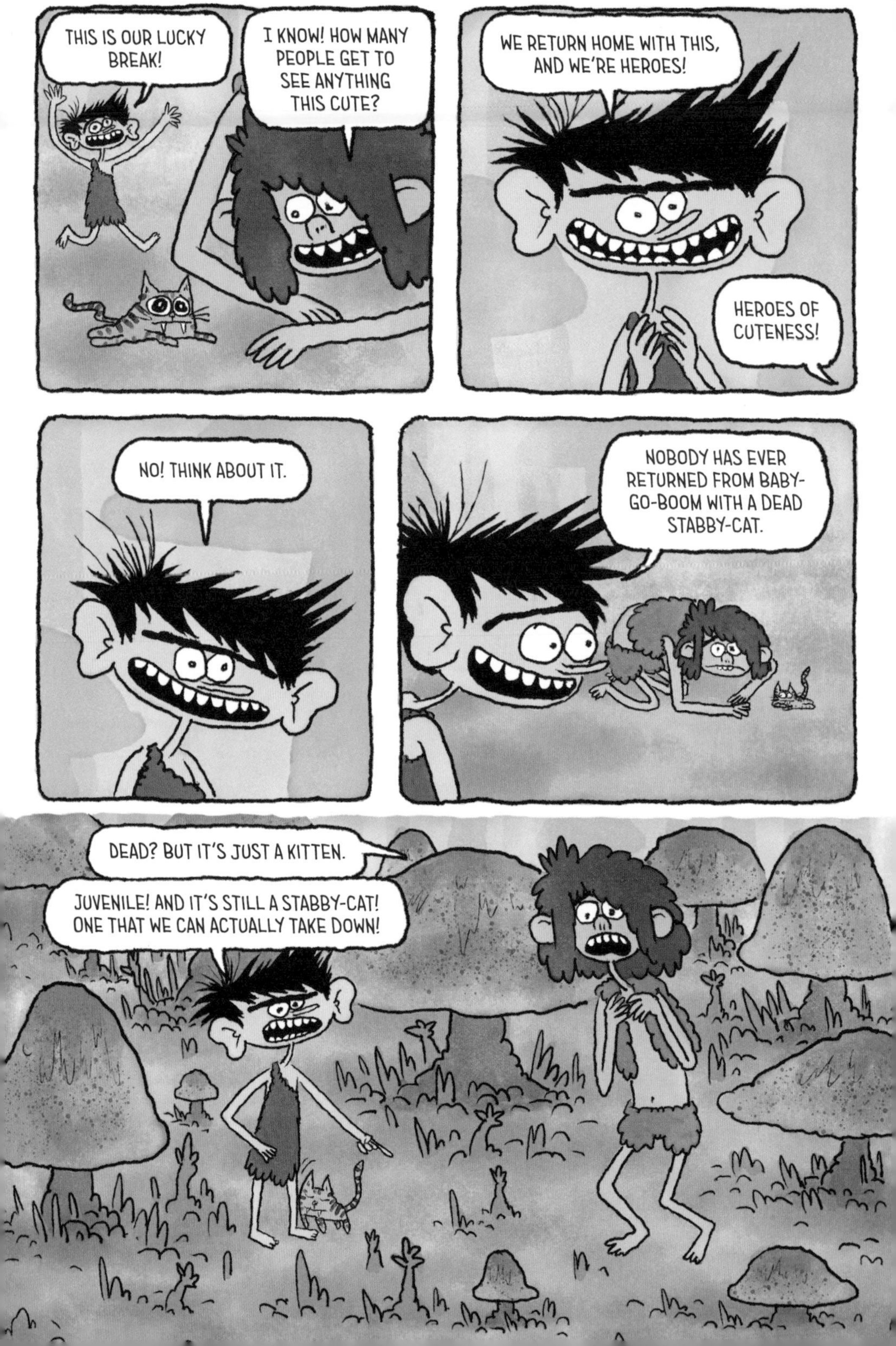

THIS IS OUR LUCKY BREAK!
I KNOW! HOW MANY PEOPLE GET TO SEE ANYTHING THIS CUTE?
WE RETURN HOME WITH THIS, AND WE'RE HEROES!
HEROES OF CUTENESS!
NO! THINK ABOUT IT.
NOBODY HAS EVER RETURNED FROM BABY-GO-BOOM WITH A DEAD STABBY-CAT.
DEAD? BUT IT'S JUST A KITTEN.
JUVENILE! AND IT'S STILL A STABBY-CAT! ONE THAT WE CAN ACTUALLY TAKE DOWN!

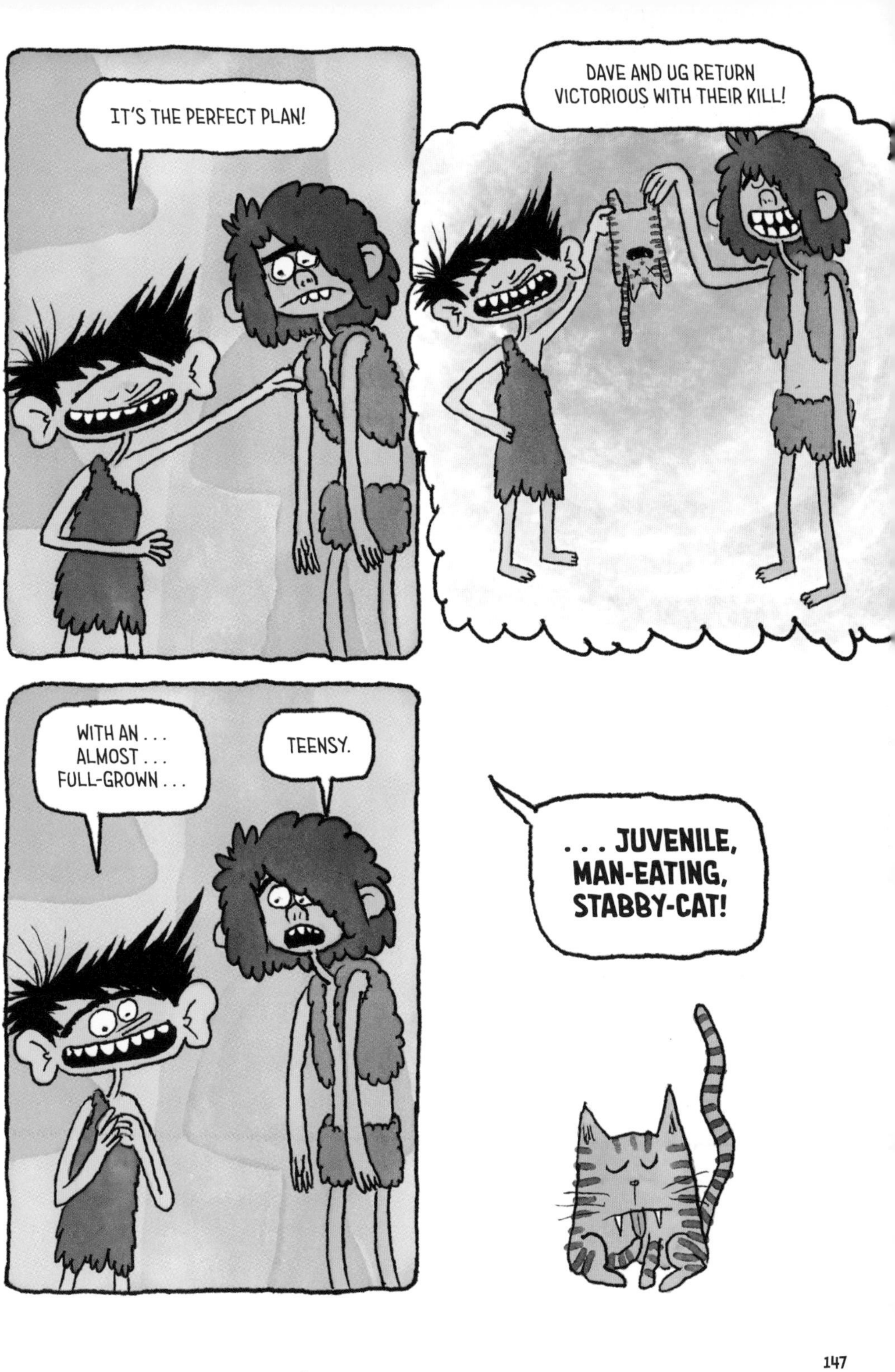
IT'S THE PERFECT PLAN!
DAVE AND UG RETURN VICTORIOUS WITH THEIR KILL!
WITH AN . . . ALMOST . . . FULL-GROWN . . .
TEENSY.
. . . JUVENILE, MAN-EATING, STABBY-CAT!

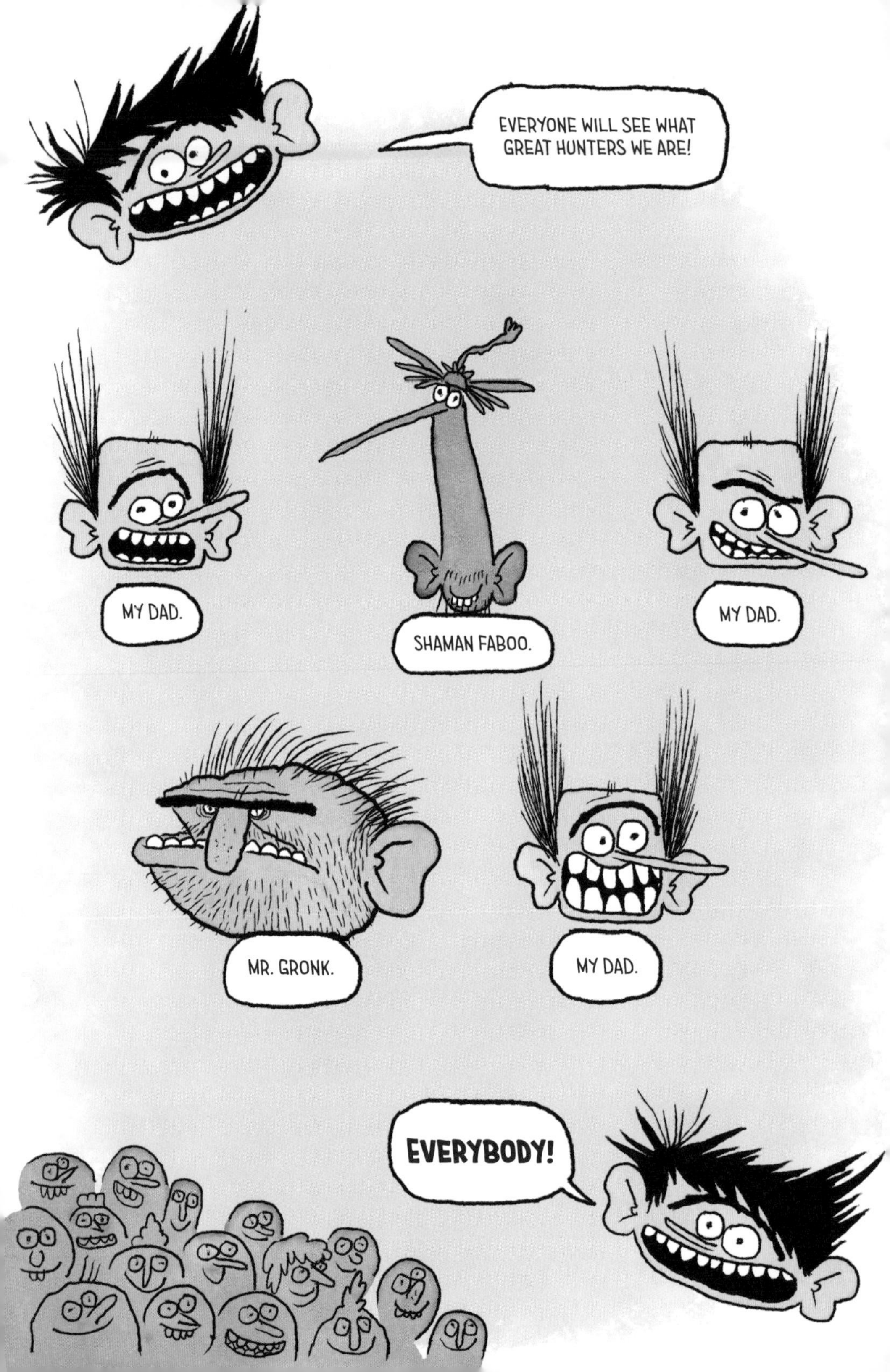
EVERYONE WILL SEE WHAT GREAT HUNTERS WE ARE!
MY DAD.
SHAMAN FABOO.
MY DAD.
MR. GRONK.
MY DAD.
EVERYBODY!

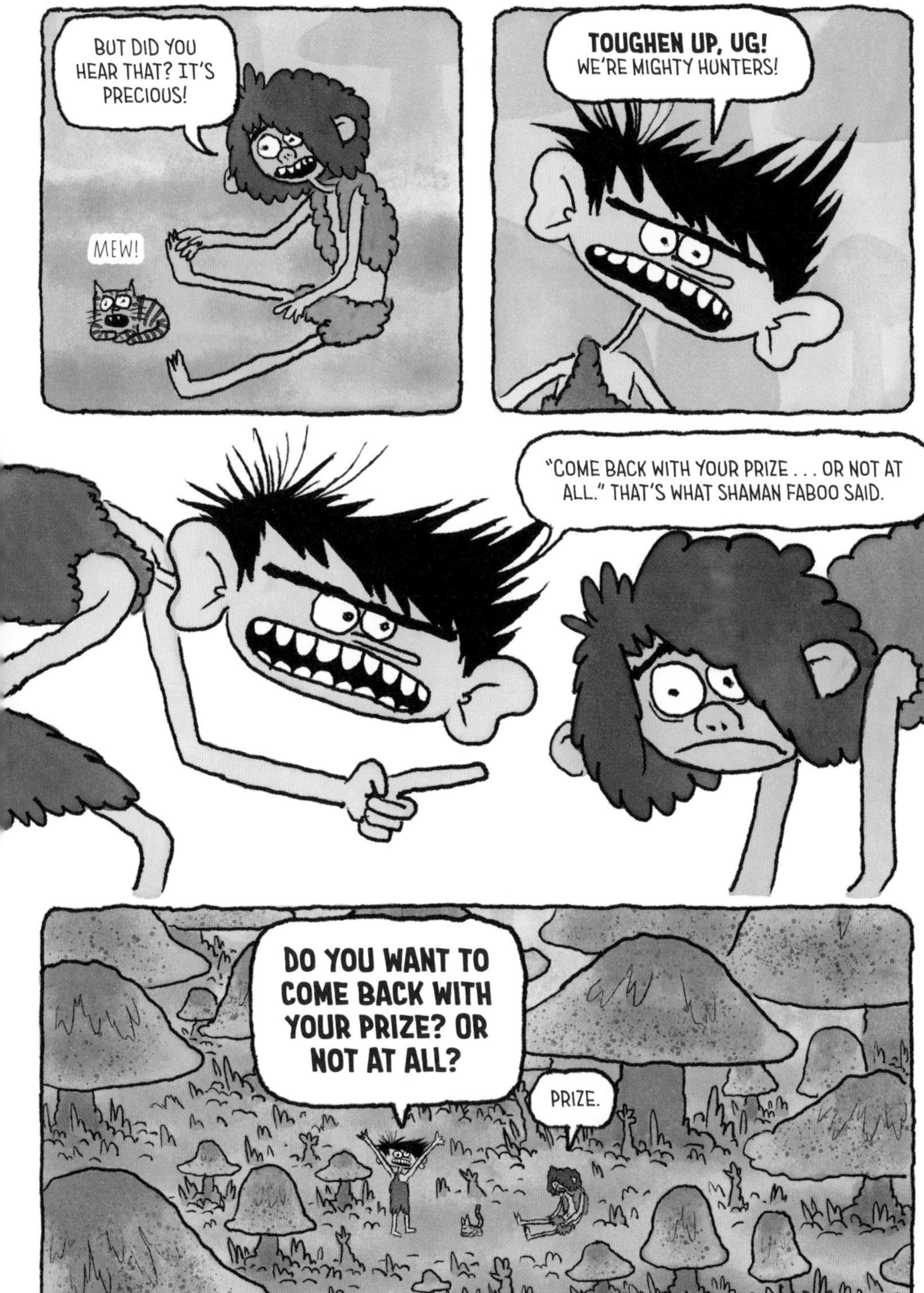
BUT DID YOU HEAR THAT? IT'S PRECIOUS!
MEW!
TOUGHEN UP, UG! WE'RE MIGHTY HUNTERS!
"COME BACK WITH YOUR PRIZE . . . OR NOT AT ALL." THAT'S WHAT SHAMAN FABOO SAID.
DO YOU WANT TO COME BACK WITH YOUR PRIZE? OR NOT AT ALL?
PRIZE.

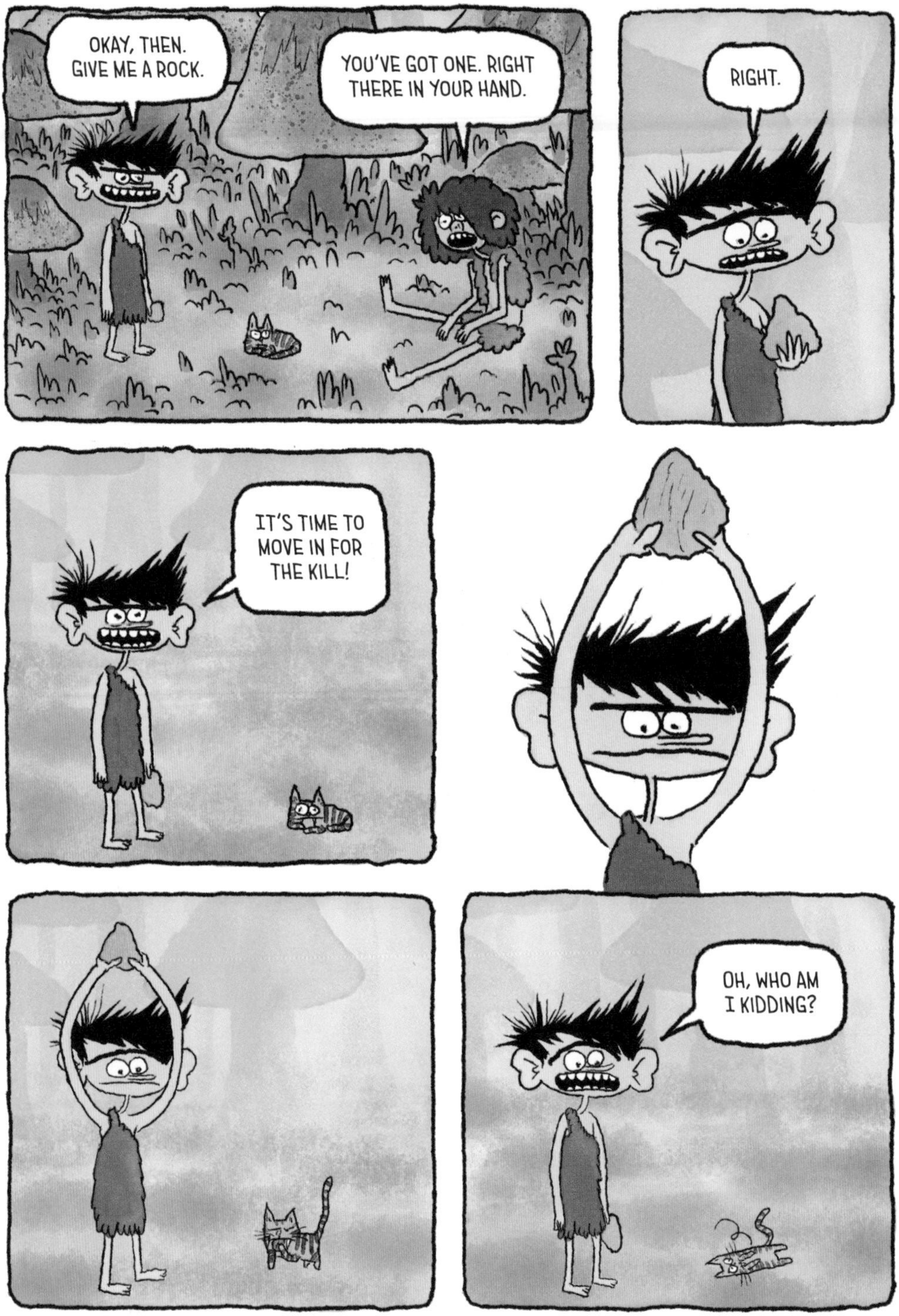
OKAY, THEN. GIVE ME A ROCK.
YOU'VE GOT ONE. RIGHT THERE IN YOUR HAND.
RIGHT.
IT'S TIME TO MOVE IN FOR THE KILL!
OH, WHO AM I KIDDING?

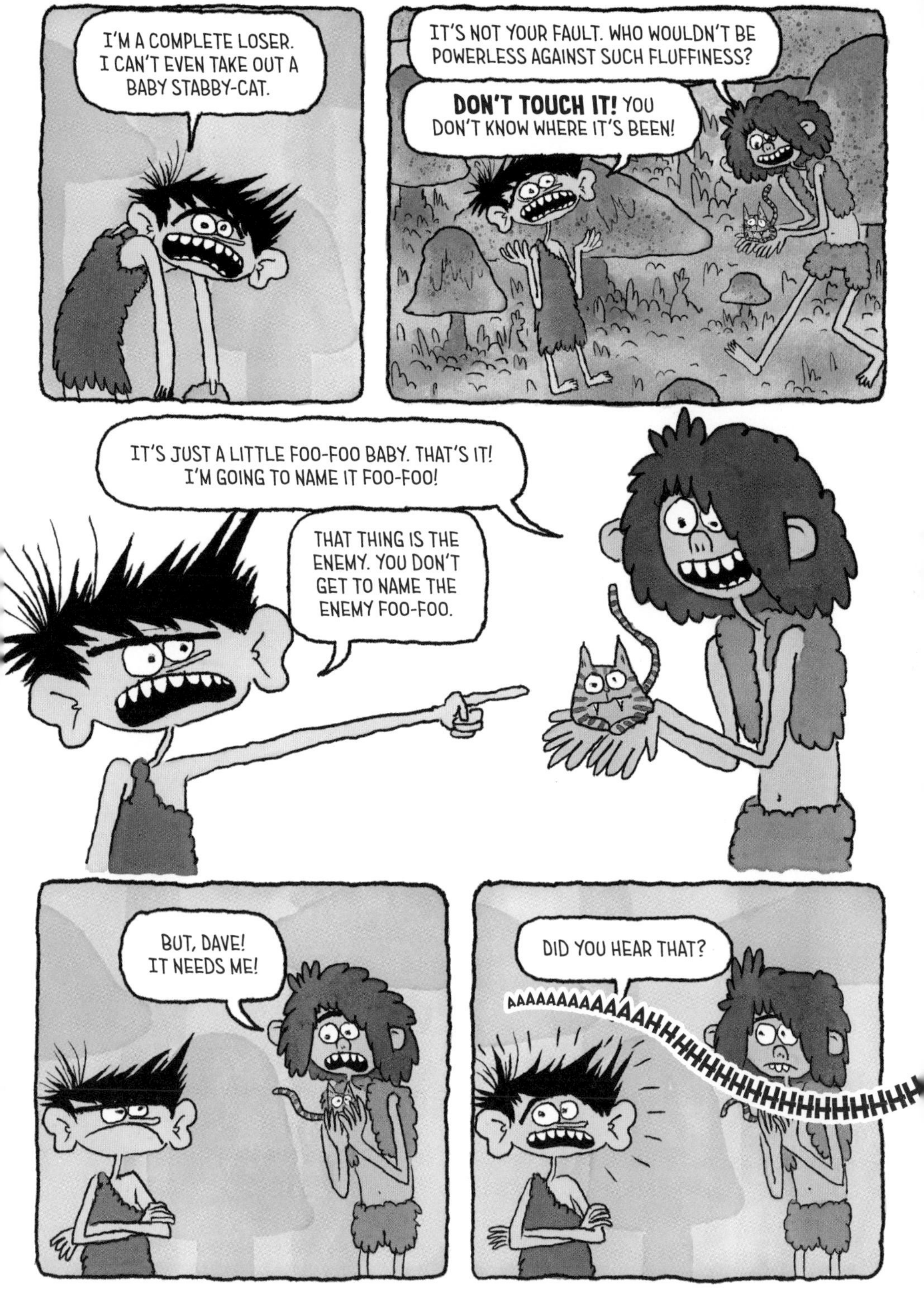
I'M A COMPLETE LOSER. I CAN'T EVEN TAKE OUT A BABY STABBY-CAT.
IT'S NOT YOUR FAULT. WHO WOULDN'T BE POWERLESS AGAINST SUCH FLUFFINESS?
DON'T TOUCH IT! YOU DON'T KNOW WHERE IT'S BEEN!
IT'S JUST A LITTLE FOO-FOO BABY. THAT'S IT! I'M GOING TO NAME IT FOO-FOO!
THAT THING IS THE ENEMY. YOU DON'T GET TO NAME THE ENEMY FOO-FOO.
BUT, DAVE! IT NEEDS ME!
DID YOU HEAR THAT?
AAAAAAAAAAAAAHHHHHHHHHHHHHHHHHHH

ALL I HEAR IS MY HEART BREAKING AT THE THOUGHT OF LEAVING FOO-FOO BEHIND.

AAAAAAAAAAAAHHHHHHHHHHHHHHHHHHHH

I HEARD THAT.

Someone was screaming for help.

And it sounded like . . .

GAK.

COME ON!

We raced up the ridge, following the voice.

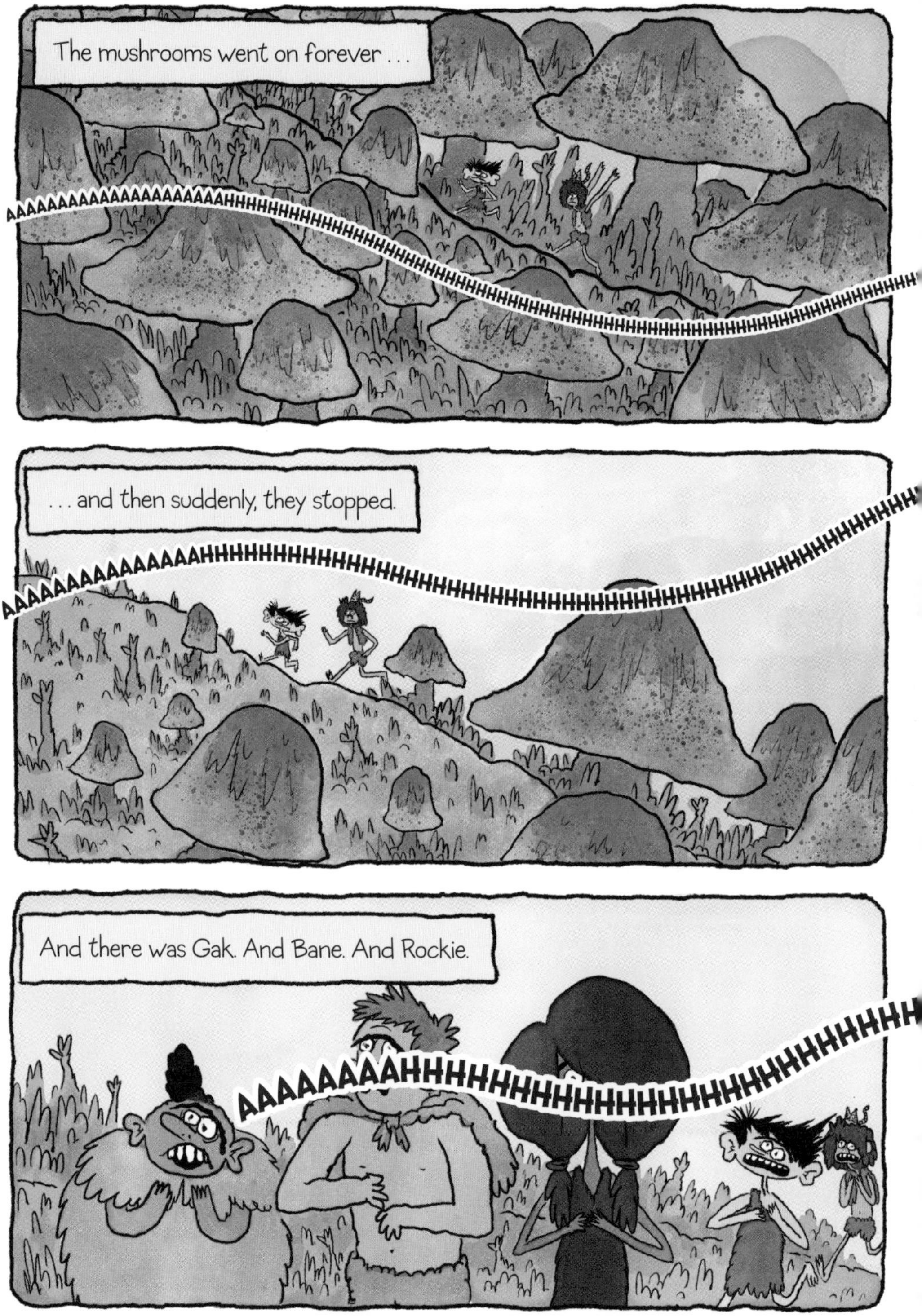
The mushrooms went on forever . . .
. . . and then suddenly, they stopped.
And there was Gak. And Bane. And Rockie.

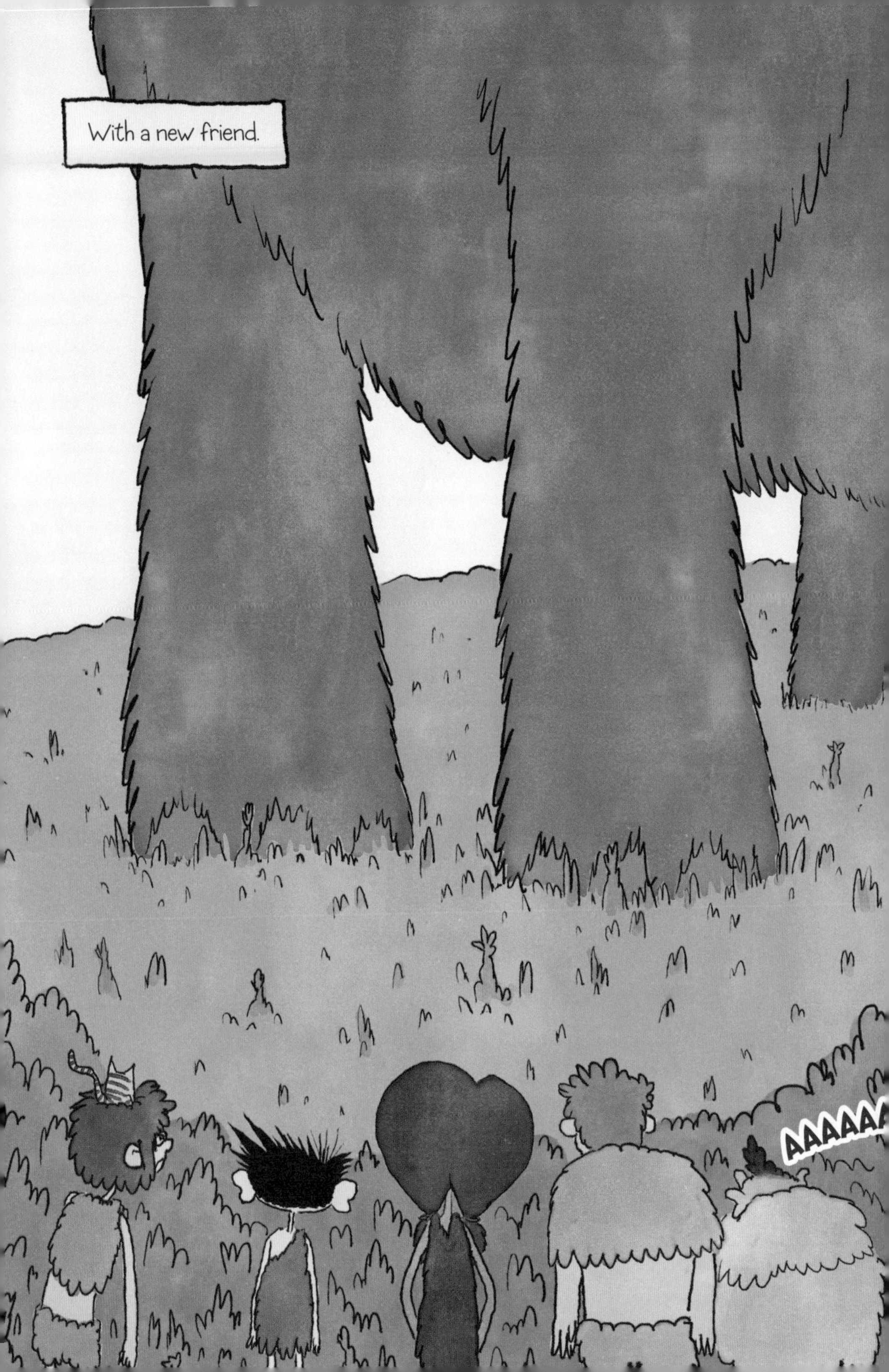
With a new friend.
AAAAAA

10

UNLIKE
ANYTHING
EVER SEEN

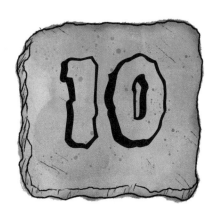

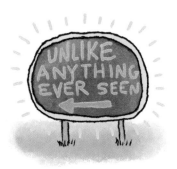

HHHHHHHHHH!!!

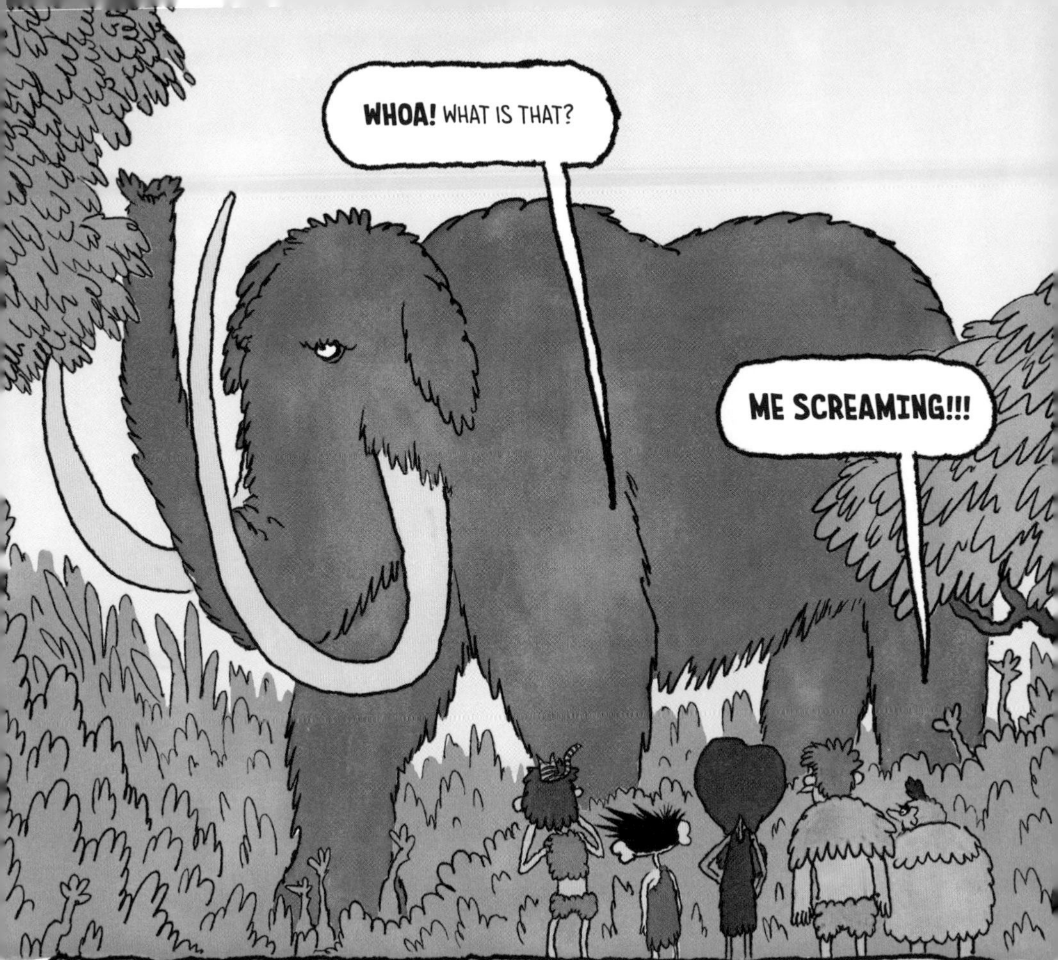
WHOA! WHAT IS THAT?
ME SCREAMING!!!

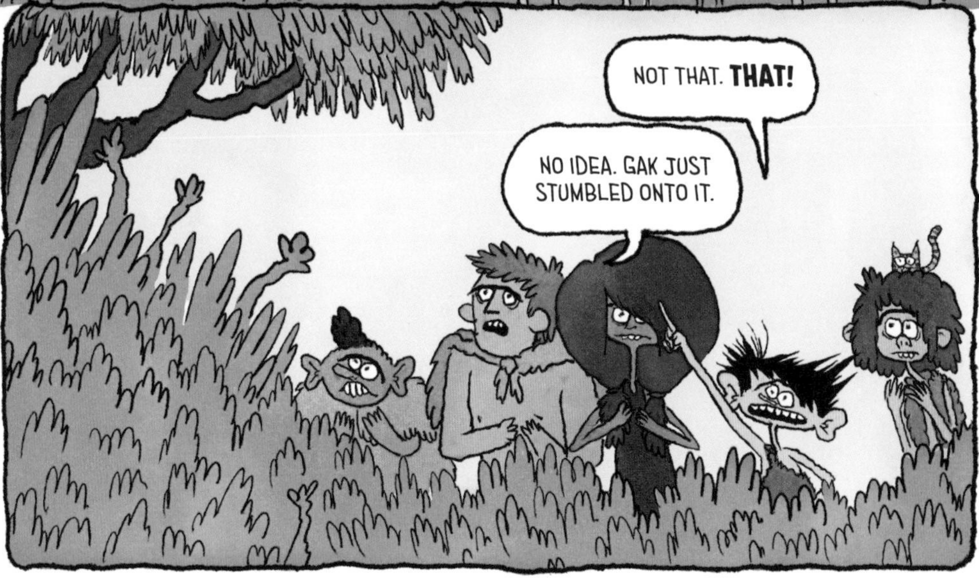
NOT THAT. THAT!
NO IDEA. GAK JUST STUMBLED ONTO IT.

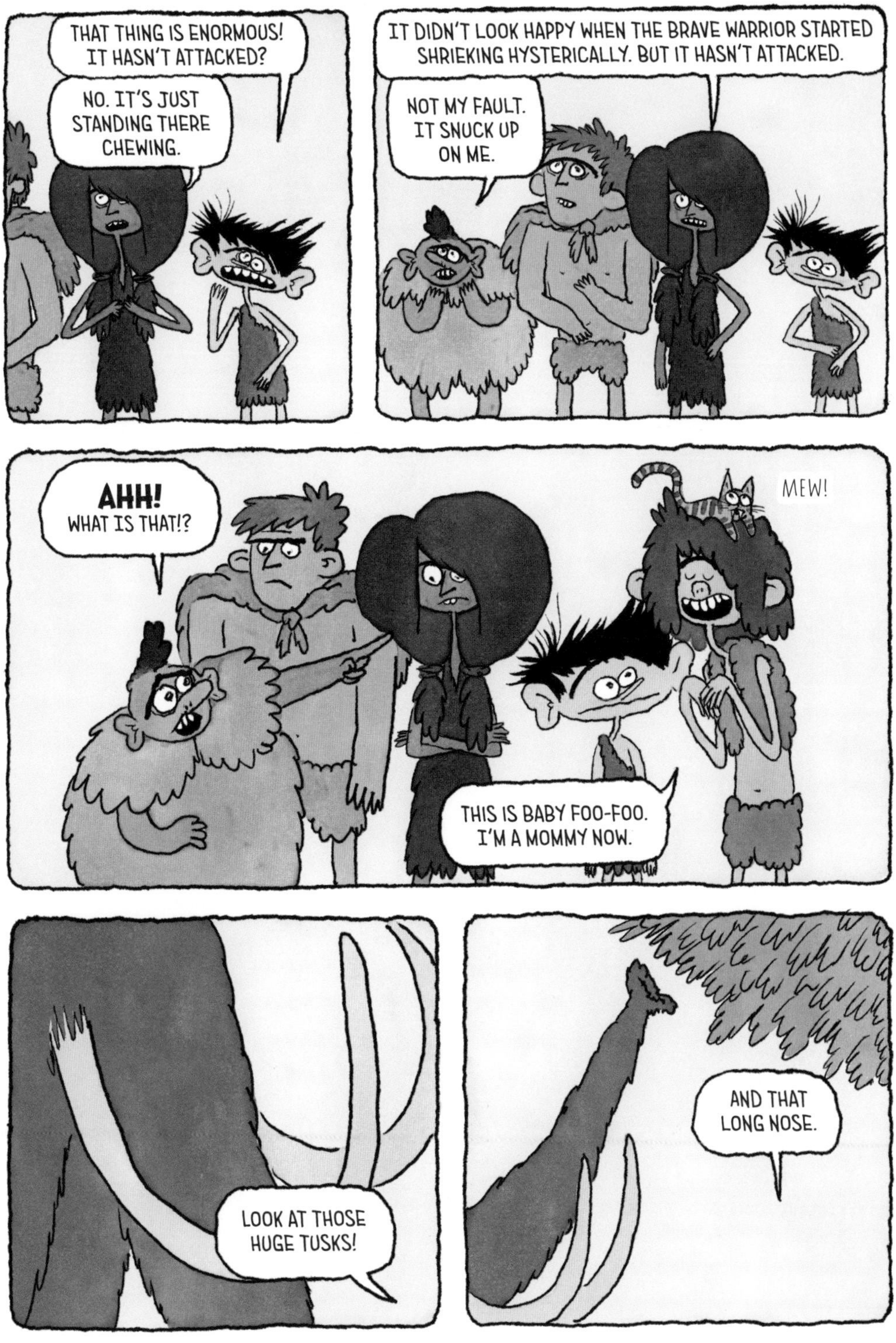
THAT THING IS ENORMOUS! IT HASN'T ATTACKED?
NO. IT'S JUST STANDING THERE CHEWING.
IT DIDN'T LOOK HAPPY WHEN THE BRAVE WARRIOR STARTED SHRIEKING HYSTERICALLY. BUT IT HASN'T ATTACKED.
NOT MY FAULT. IT SNUCK UP ON ME.
AHH! WHAT IS THAT!?
MEW!
THIS IS BABY FOO-FOO. I'M A MOMMY NOW.
LOOK AT THOSE HUGE TUSKS!
AND THAT LONG NOSE.

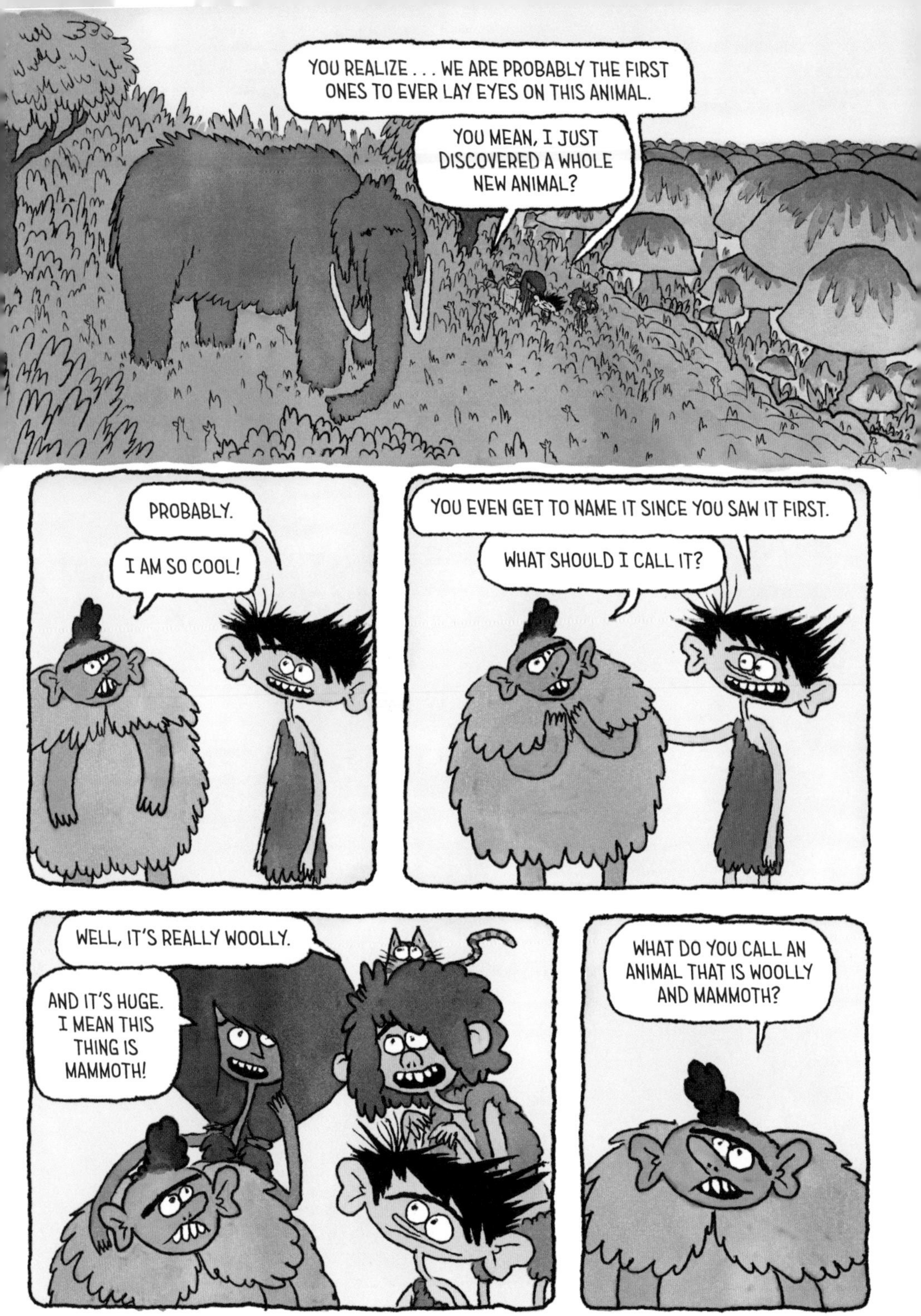

YOU REALIZE . . . WE ARE PROBABLY THE FIRST ONES TO EVER LAY EYES ON THIS ANIMAL.
YOU MEAN, I JUST DISCOVERED A WHOLE NEW ANIMAL?
PROBABLY.
I AM SO COOL!
YOU EVEN GET TO NAME IT SINCE YOU SAW IT FIRST.
WHAT SHOULD I CALL IT?
WELL, IT'S REALLY WOOLLY.
AND IT'S HUGE. I MEAN THIS THING IS MAMMOTH!
WHAT DO YOU CALL AN ANIMAL THAT IS WOOLLY AND MAMMOTH?

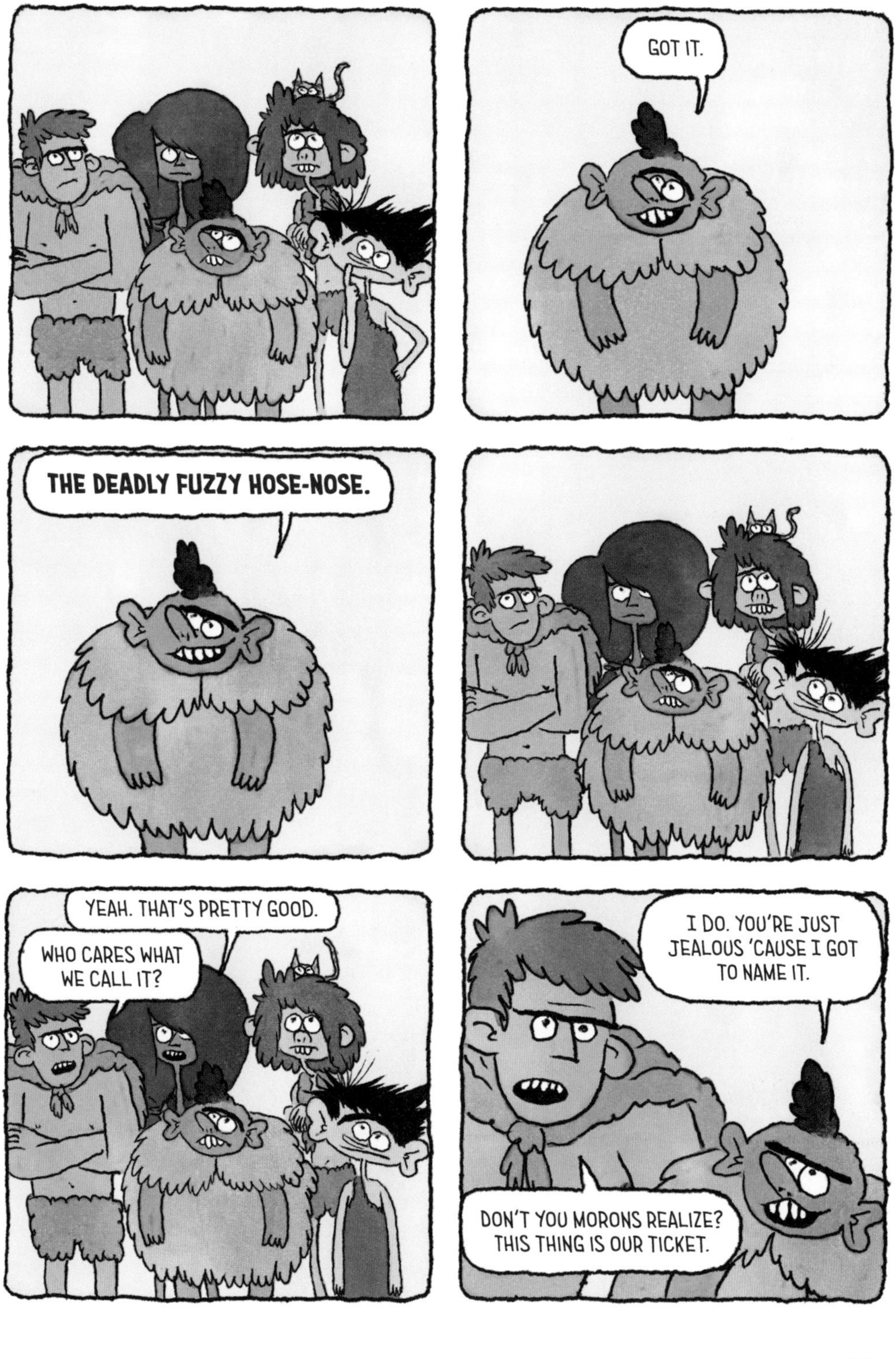
GOT IT.
THE DEADLY FUZZY HOSE-NOSE.
YEAH. THAT'S PRETTY GOOD.
WHO CARES WHAT WE CALL IT?
I DO. YOU'RE JUST JEALOUS 'CAUSE I GOT TO NAME IT.
DON'T YOU MORONS REALIZE? THIS THING IS OUR TICKET.

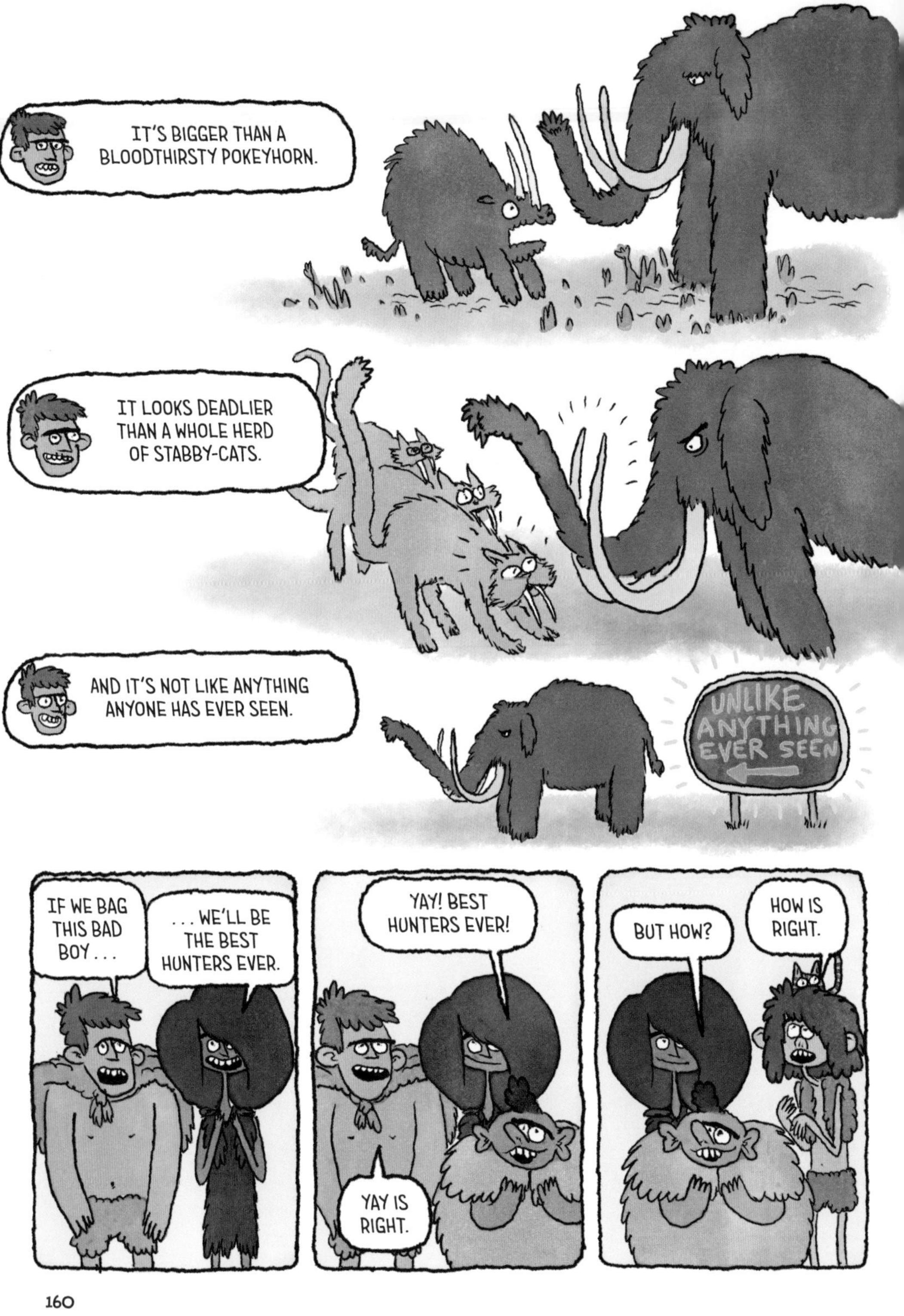
IT'S BIGGER THAN A BLOODTHIRSTY POKEYHORN.
IT LOOKS DEADLIER THAN A WHOLE HERD OF STABBY-CATS.
AND IT'S NOT LIKE ANYTHING ANYONE HAS EVER SEEN.
UNLIKE ANYTHING EVER SEEN
IF WE BAG THIS BAD BOY . . .
. . . WE'LL BE THE BEST HUNTERS EVER.
YAY! BEST HUNTERS EVER!
YAY IS RIGHT.
BUT HOW?
HOW IS RIGHT.

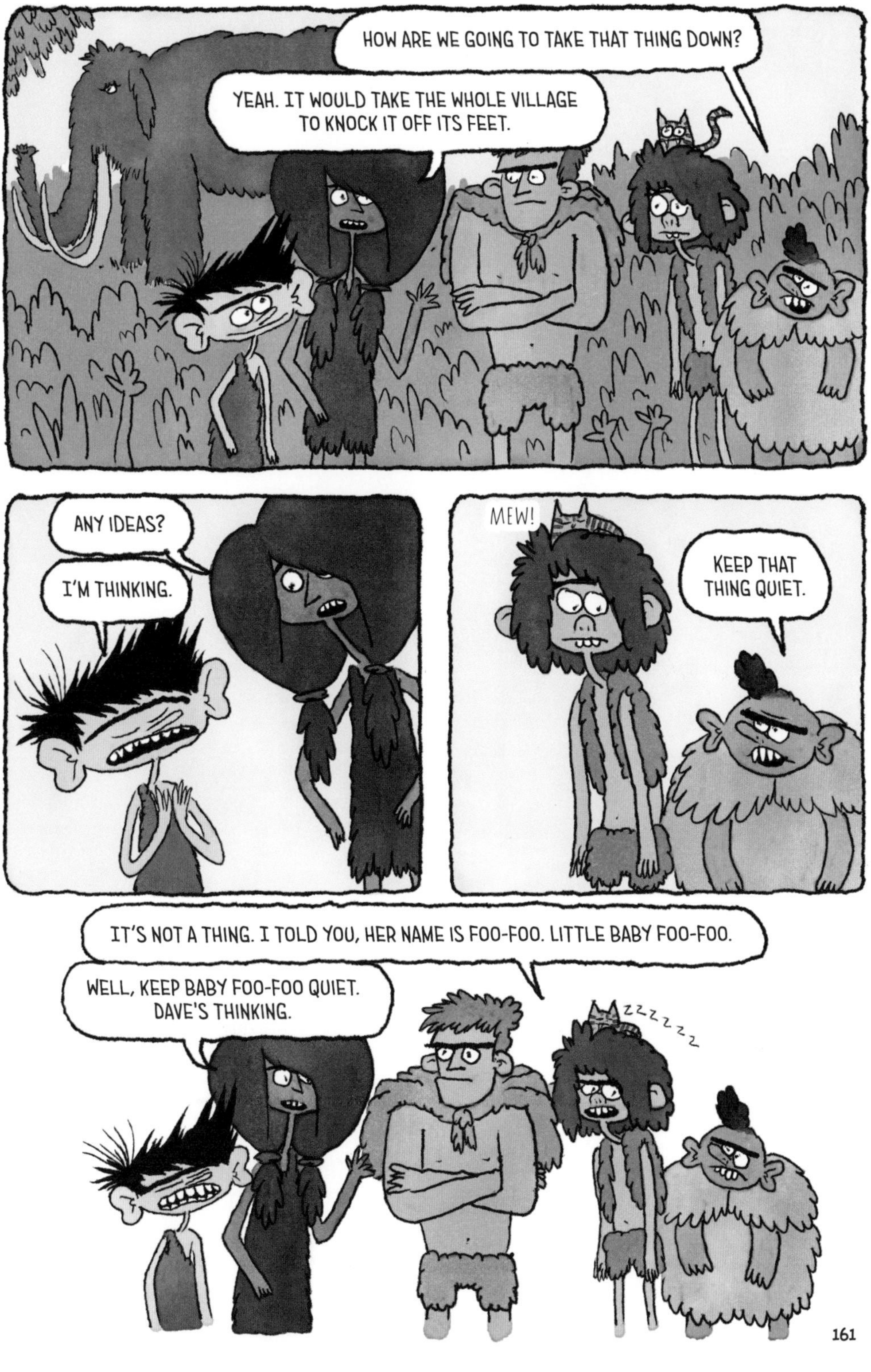
HOW ARE WE GOING TO TAKE THAT THING DOWN?
YEAH. IT WOULD TAKE THE WHOLE VILLAGE TO KNOCK IT OFF ITS FEET.
ANY IDEAS?
I'M THINKING.
MEW!
KEEP THAT THING QUIET.
IT'S NOT A THING. I TOLD YOU, HER NAME IS FOO-FOO. LITTLE BABY FOO-FOO.
WELL, KEEP BABY FOO-FOO QUIET. DAVE'S THINKING.
ZZZZZZZ

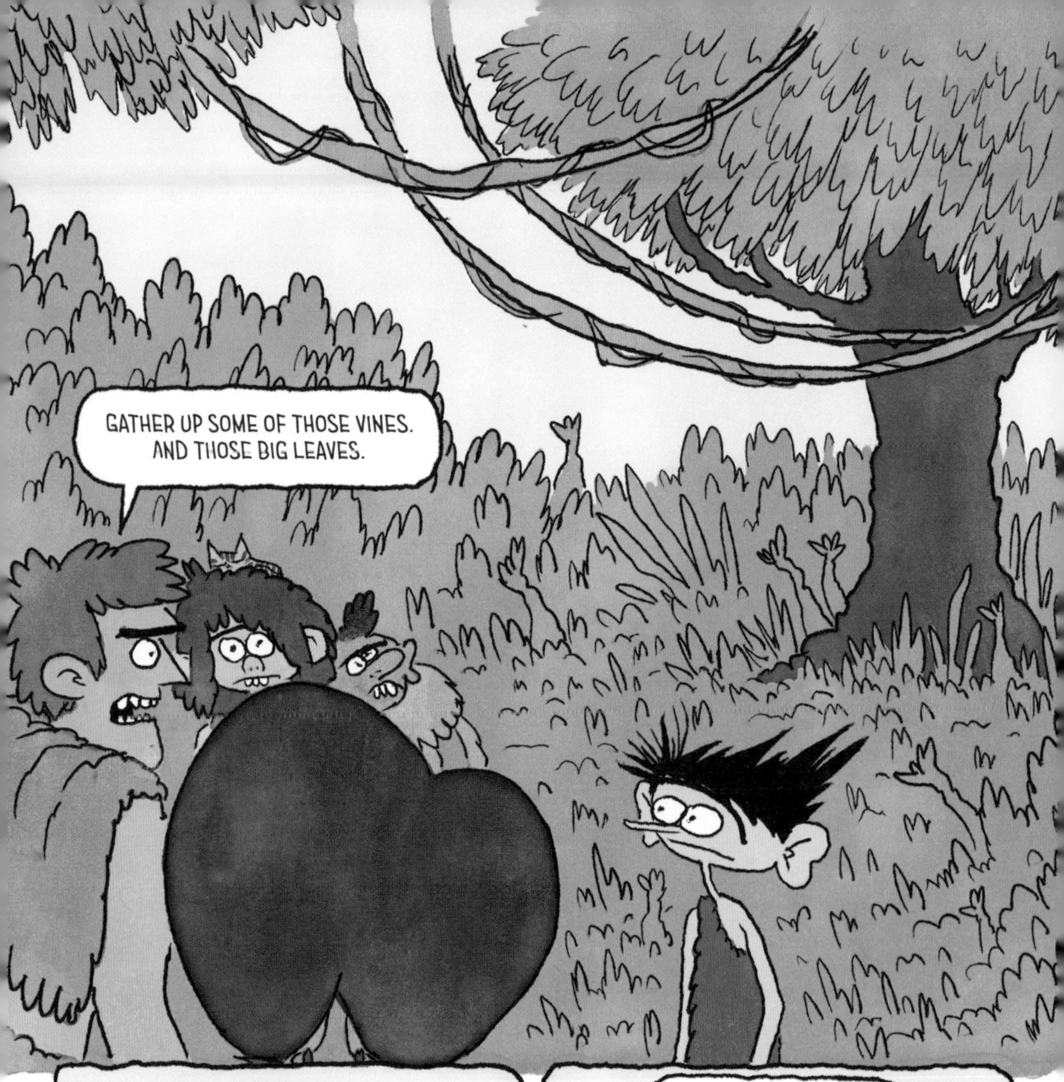
GATHER UP SOME OF THOSE VINES.
AND THOSE BIG LEAVES.

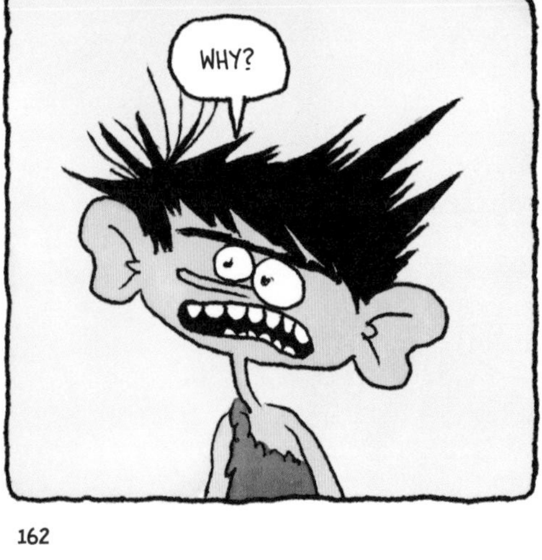
WHY?

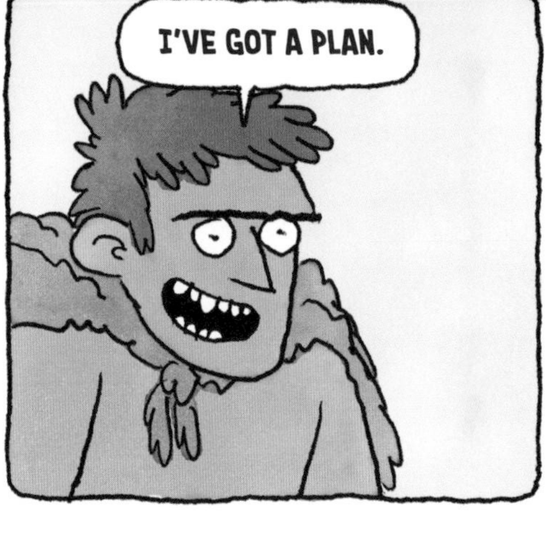
I'VE GOT A PLAN.

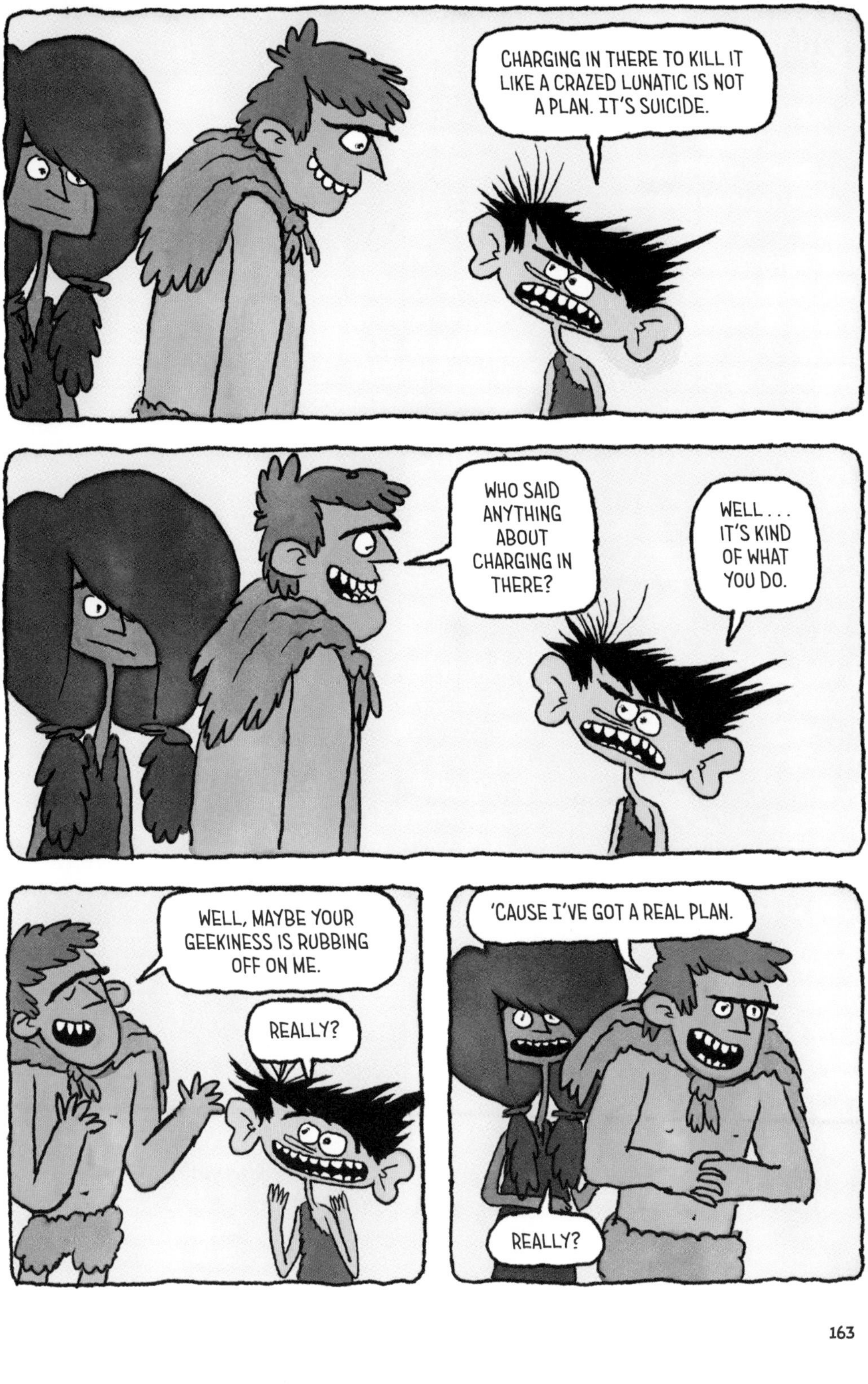
CHARGING IN THERE TO KILL IT LIKE A CRAZED LUNATIC IS NOT A PLAN. IT'S SUICIDE.
WHO SAID ANYTHING ABOUT CHARGING IN THERE?
WELL . . . IT'S KIND OF WHAT YOU DO.
WELL, MAYBE YOUR GEEKINESS IS RUBBING OFF ON ME.
REALLY?
'CAUSE I'VE GOT A REAL PLAN.
REALLY?

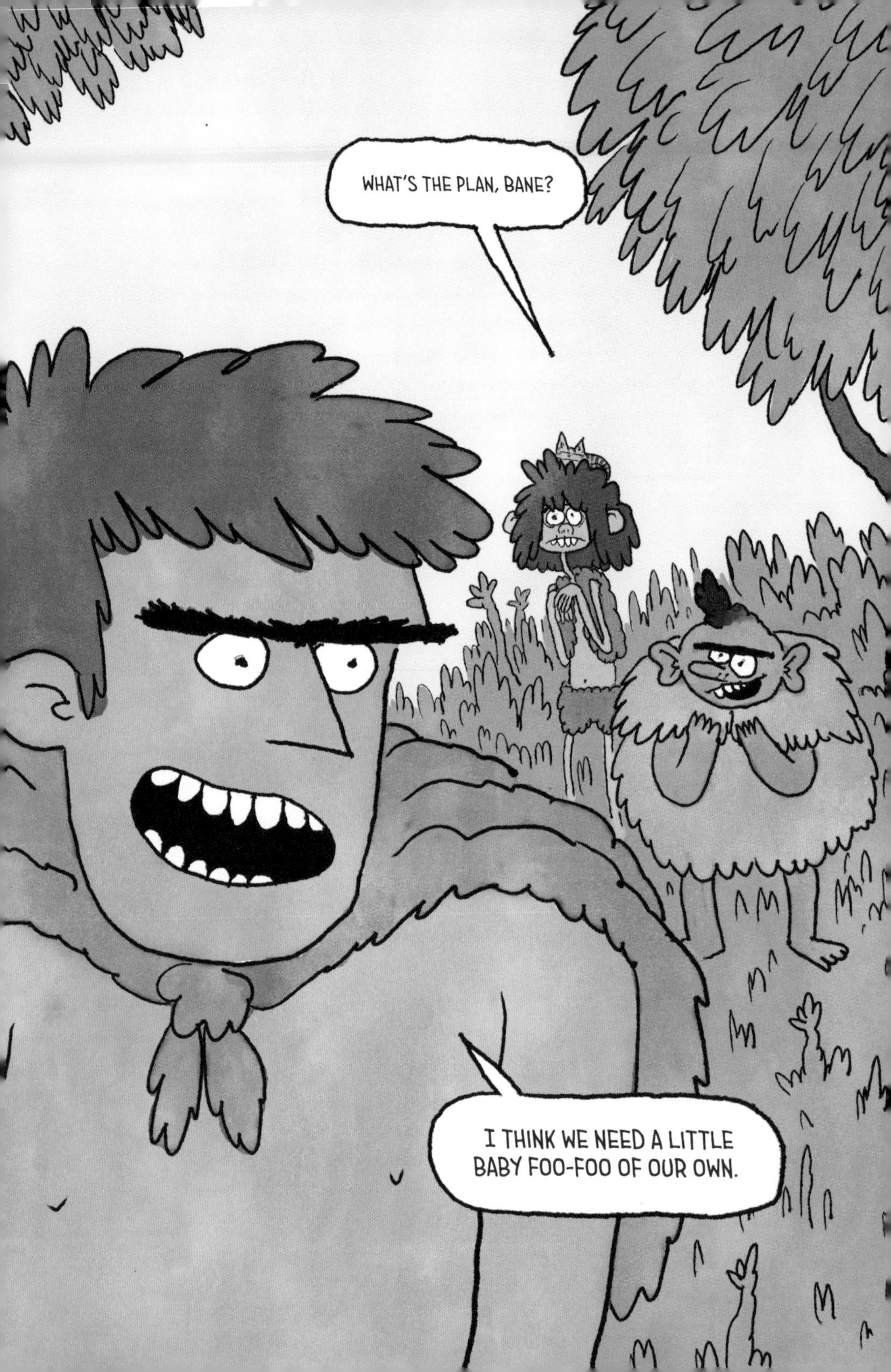
WHAT'S THE PLAN, BANE?
I THINK WE NEED A LITTLE BABY FOO-FOO OF OUR OWN.

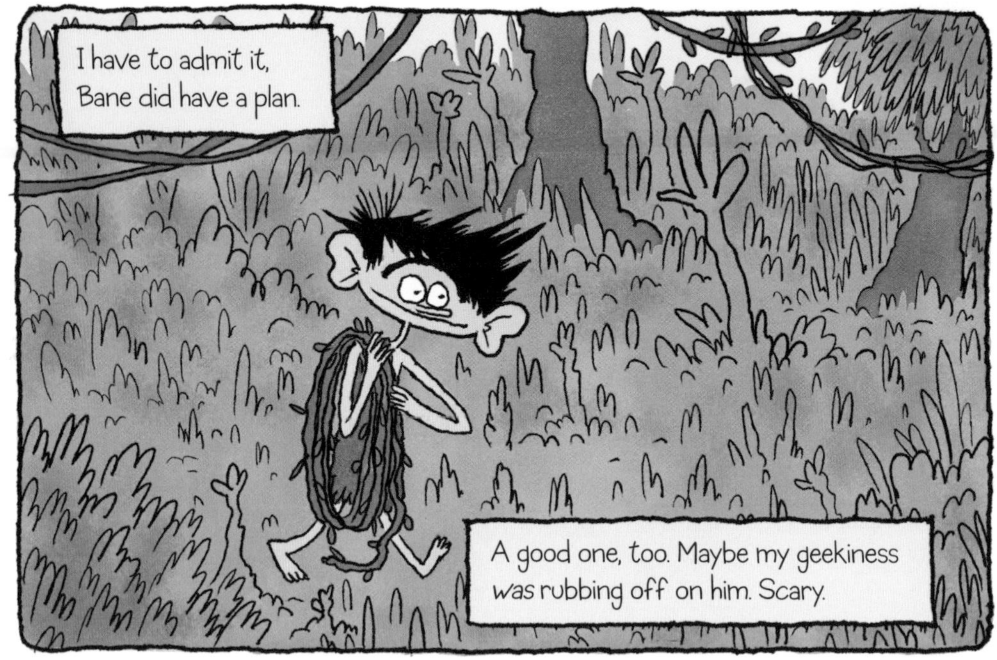
I have to admit it,
Bane did have a plan.
A good one, too. Maybe my geekiness *was* rubbing off on him. Scary.

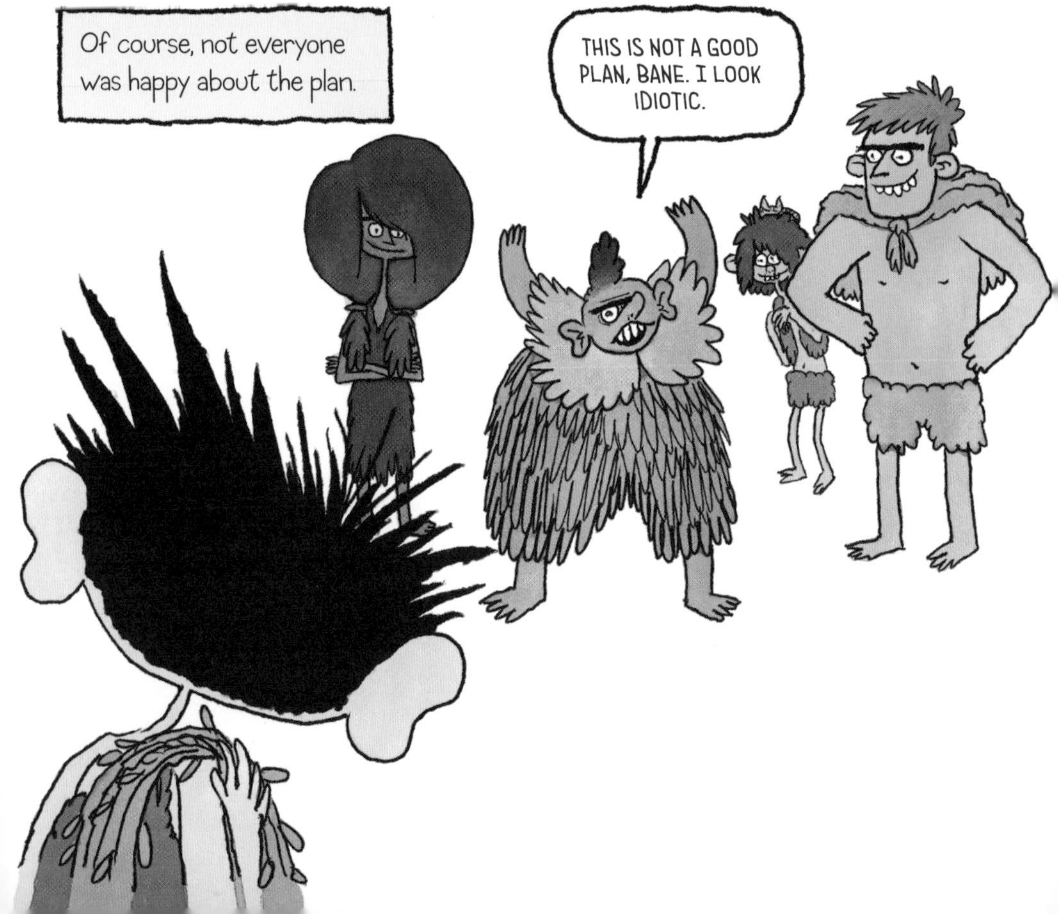
Of course, not everyone was happy about the plan.
THIS IS NOT A GOOD PLAN, BANE. I LOOK IDIOTIC.

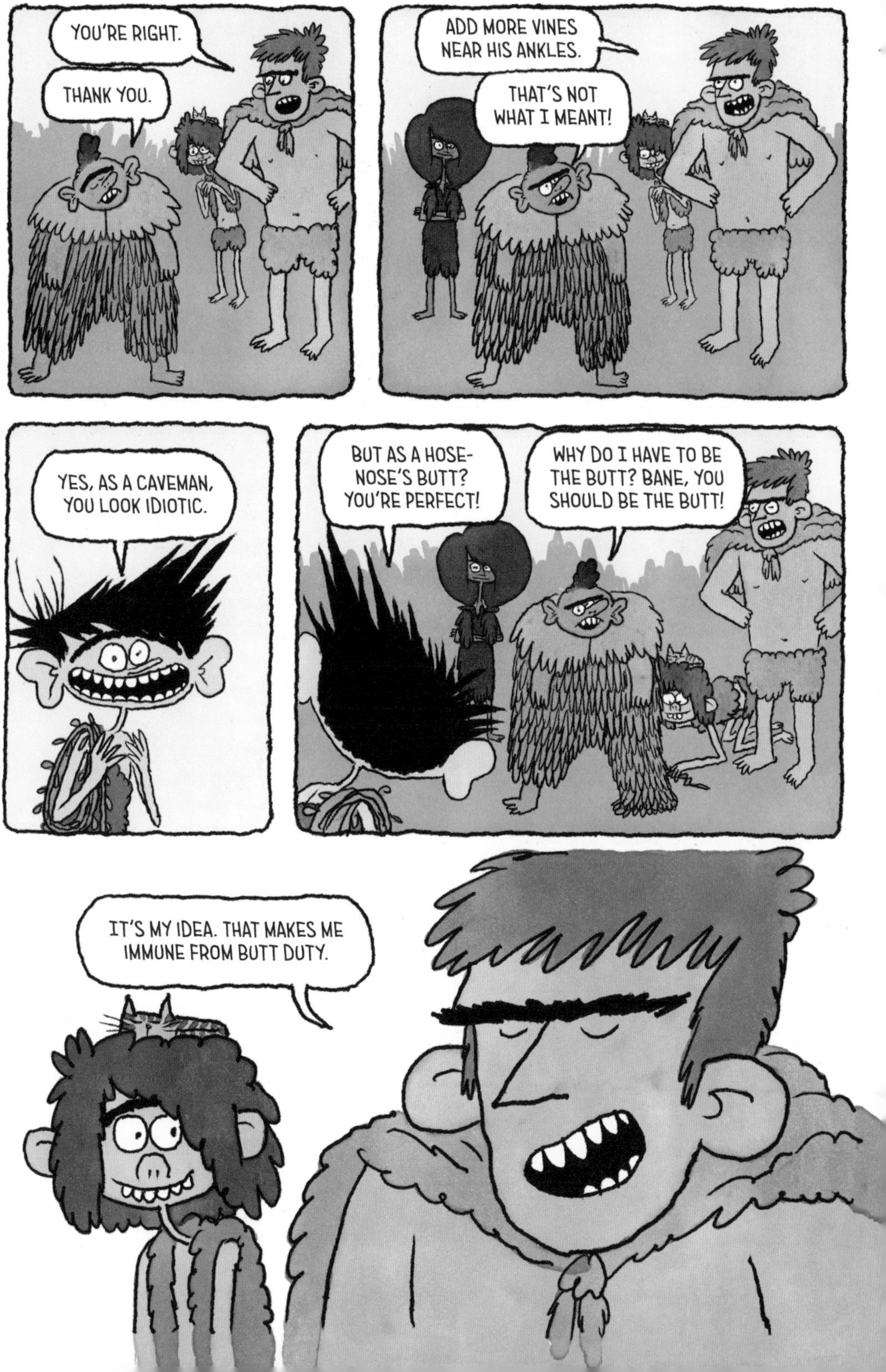
YOU'RE RIGHT.
THANK YOU.
ADD MORE VINES NEAR HIS ANKLES.
THAT'S NOT WHAT I MEANT!
YES, AS A CAVEMAN, YOU LOOK IDIOTIC.
BUT AS A HOSE-NOSE'S BUTT? YOU'RE PERFECT!
WHY DO I HAVE TO BE THE BUTT? BANE, YOU SHOULD BE THE BUTT!
IT'S MY IDEA. THAT MAKES ME IMMUNE FROM BUTT DUTY.

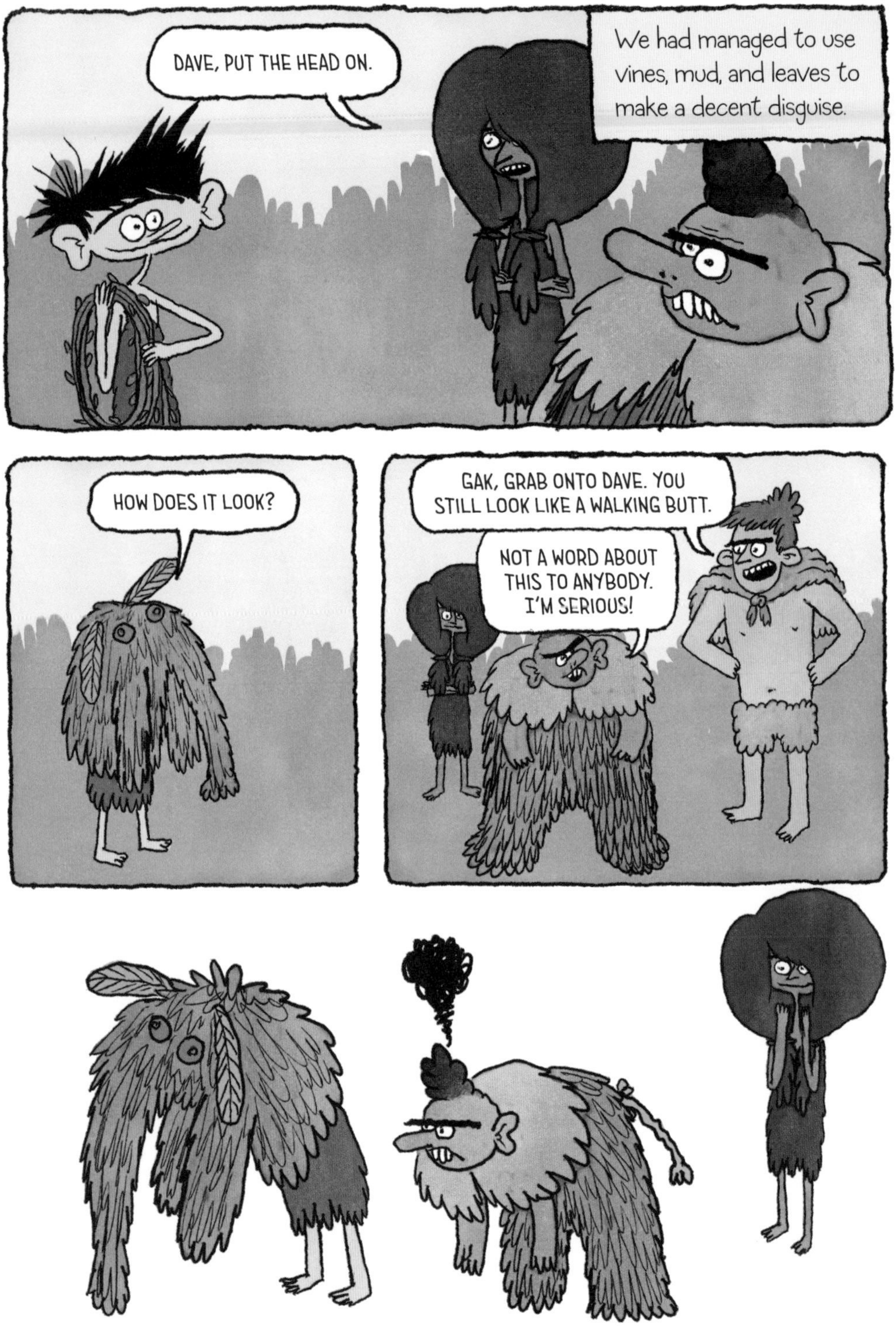
DAVE, PUT THE HEAD ON.
We had managed to use vines, mud, and leaves to make a decent disguise.
HOW DOES IT LOOK?
GAK, GRAB ONTO DAVE. YOU STILL LOOK LIKE A WALKING BUTT.
NOT A WORD ABOUT THIS TO ANYBODY. I'M SERIOUS!

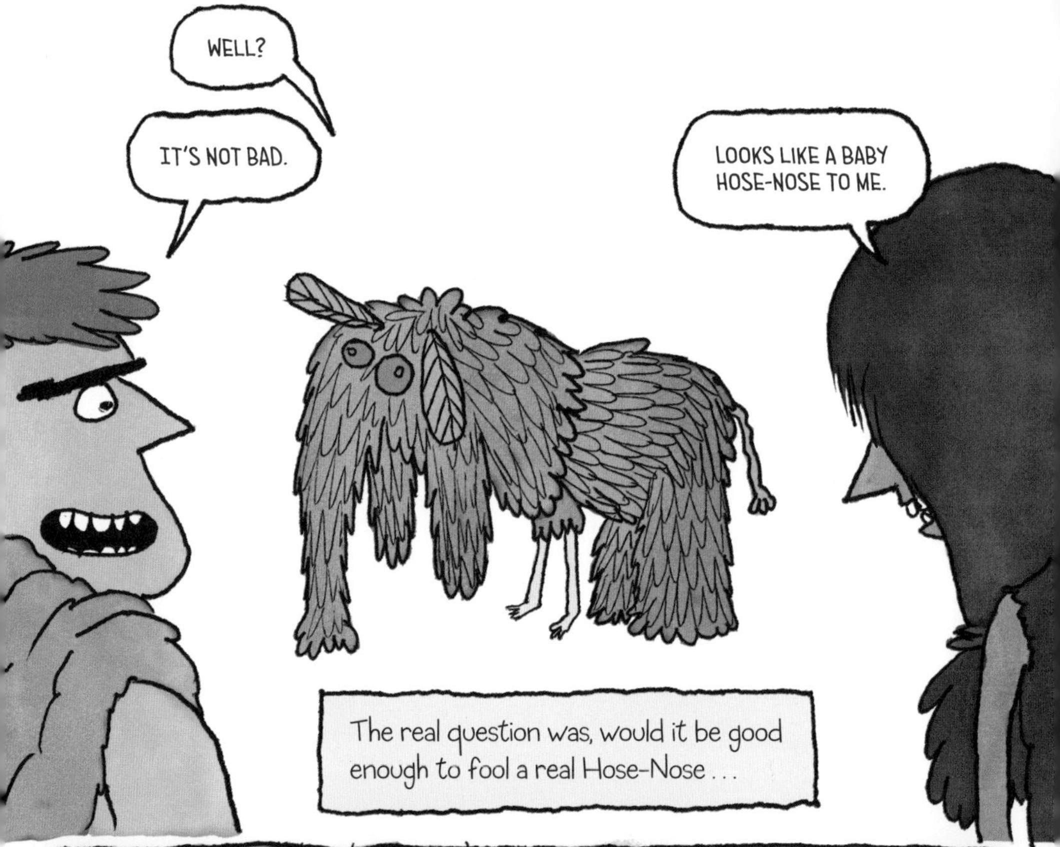
WELL?
IT'S NOT BAD.
LOOKS LIKE A BABY HOSE-NOSE TO ME.
The real question was, would it be good enough to fool a real Hose-Nose . . .

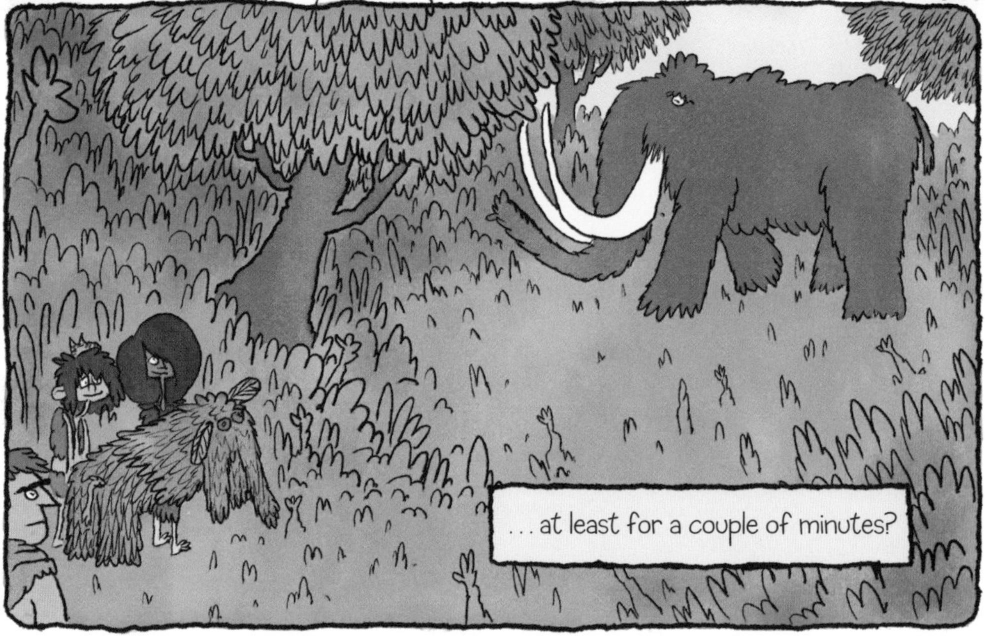
. . . at least for a couple of minutes?

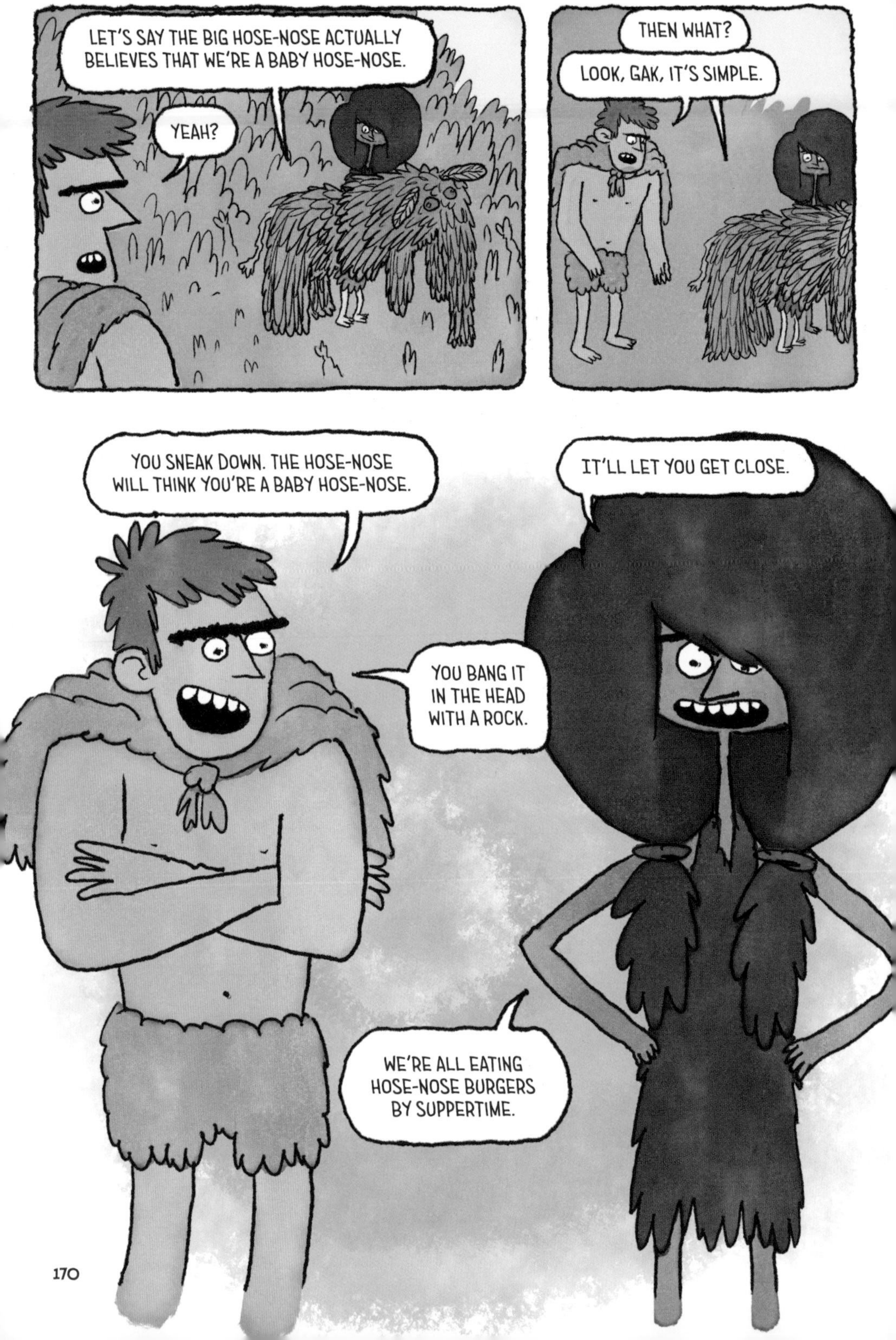
LET'S SAY THE BIG HOSE-NOSE ACTUALLY BELIEVES THAT WE'RE A BABY HOSE-NOSE.
YEAH?
THEN WHAT?
LOOK, GAK, IT'S SIMPLE.
YOU SNEAK DOWN. THE HOSE-NOSE WILL THINK YOU'RE A BABY HOSE-NOSE.
IT'LL LET YOU GET CLOSE.
YOU BANG IT IN THE HEAD WITH A ROCK.
WE'RE ALL EATING HOSE-NOSE BURGERS BY SUPPERTIME.

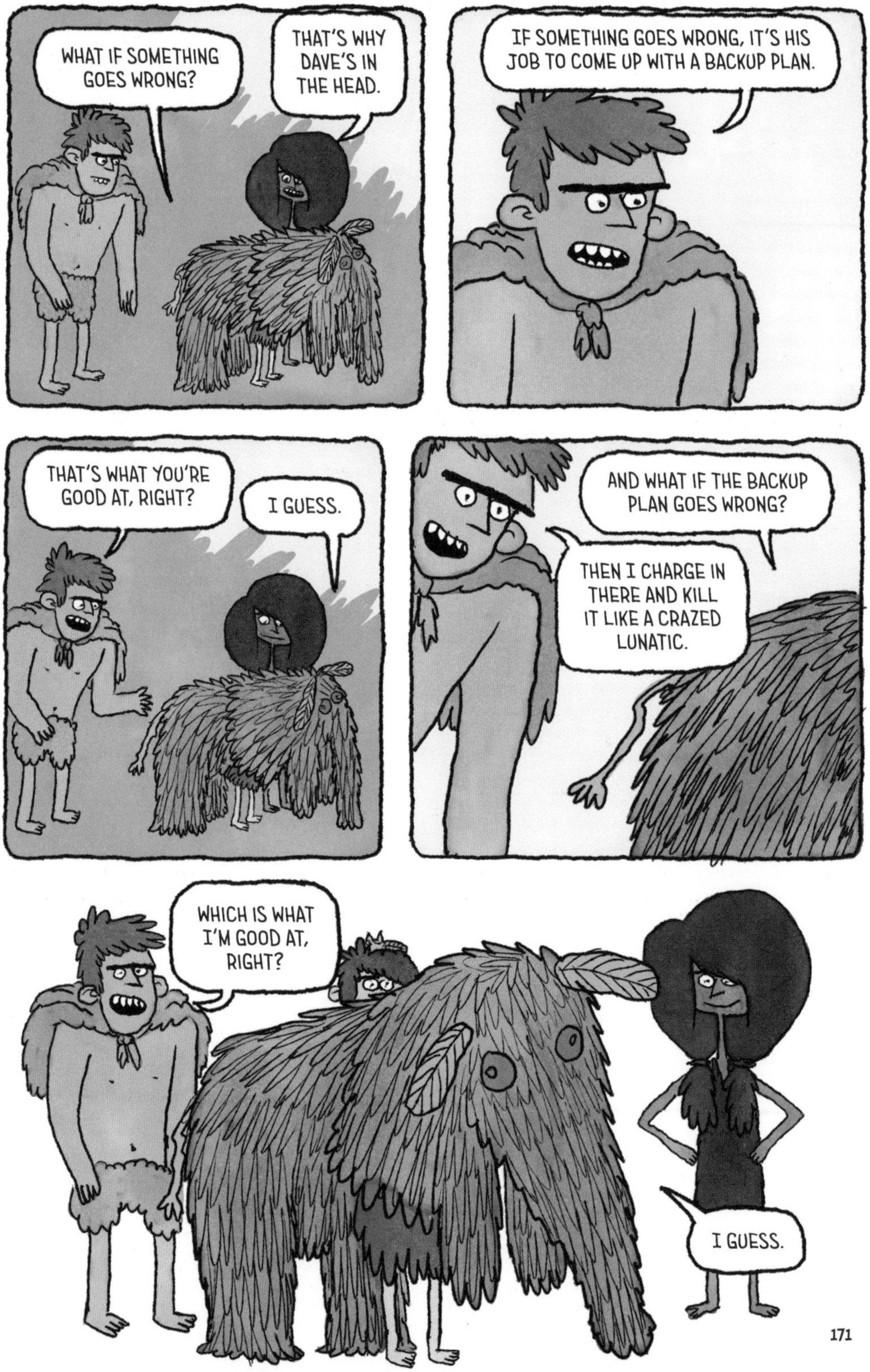
WHAT IF SOMETHING GOES WRONG?
THAT'S WHY DAVE'S IN THE HEAD.
IF SOMETHING GOES WRONG, IT'S HIS JOB TO COME UP WITH A BACKUP PLAN.
THAT'S WHAT YOU'RE GOOD AT, RIGHT?
I GUESS.
AND WHAT IF THE BACKUP PLAN GOES WRONG?
THEN I CHARGE IN THERE AND KILL IT LIKE A CRAZED LUNATIC.
WHICH IS WHAT I'M GOOD AT, RIGHT?
I GUESS.

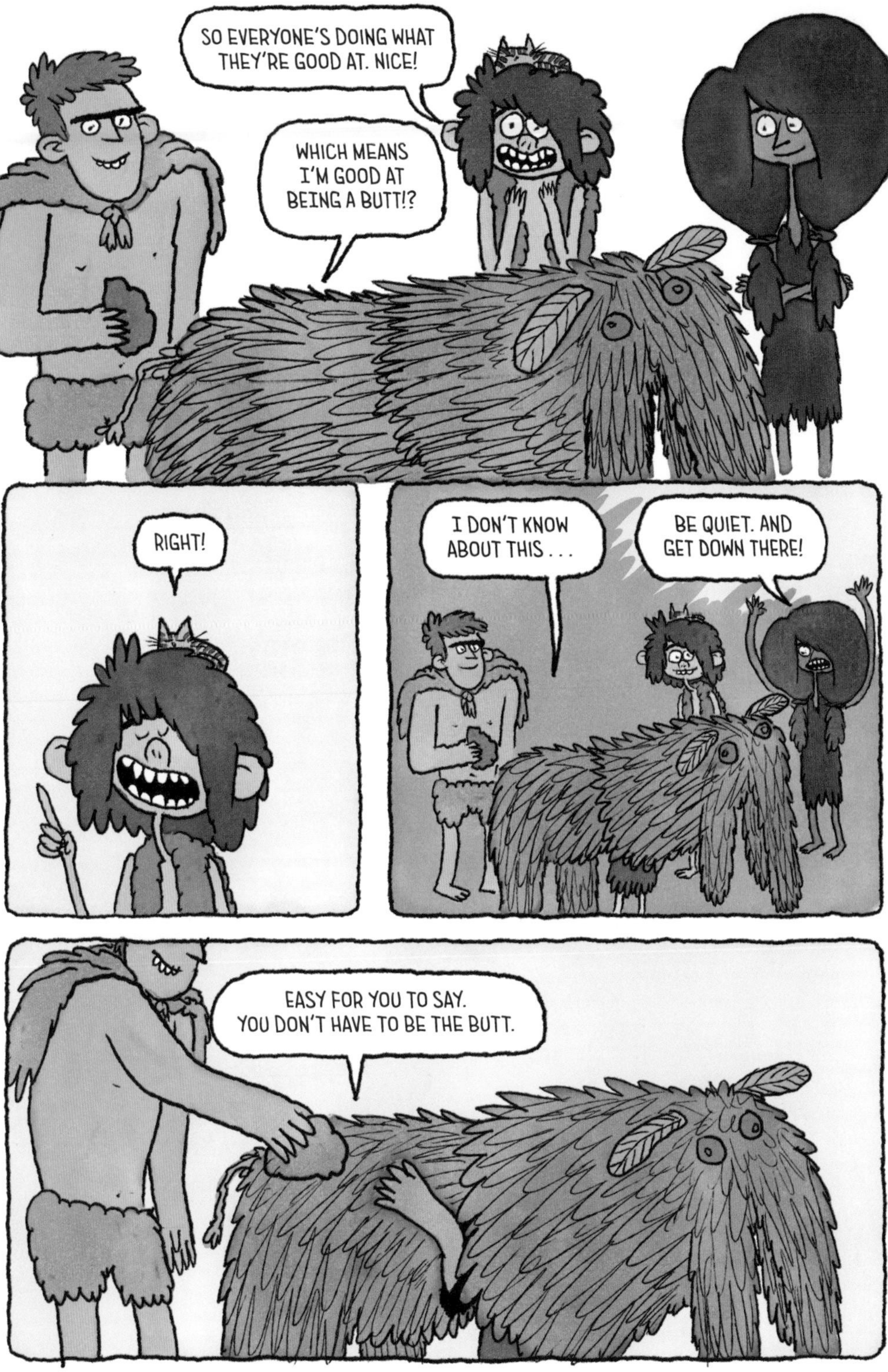
SO EVERYONE'S DOING WHAT THEY'RE GOOD AT. NICE!
WHICH MEANS I'M GOOD AT BEING A BUTT!?
RIGHT!
I DON'T KNOW ABOUT THIS . . .
BE QUIET. AND GET DOWN THERE!
EASY FOR YOU TO SAY. YOU DON'T HAVE TO BE THE BUTT.

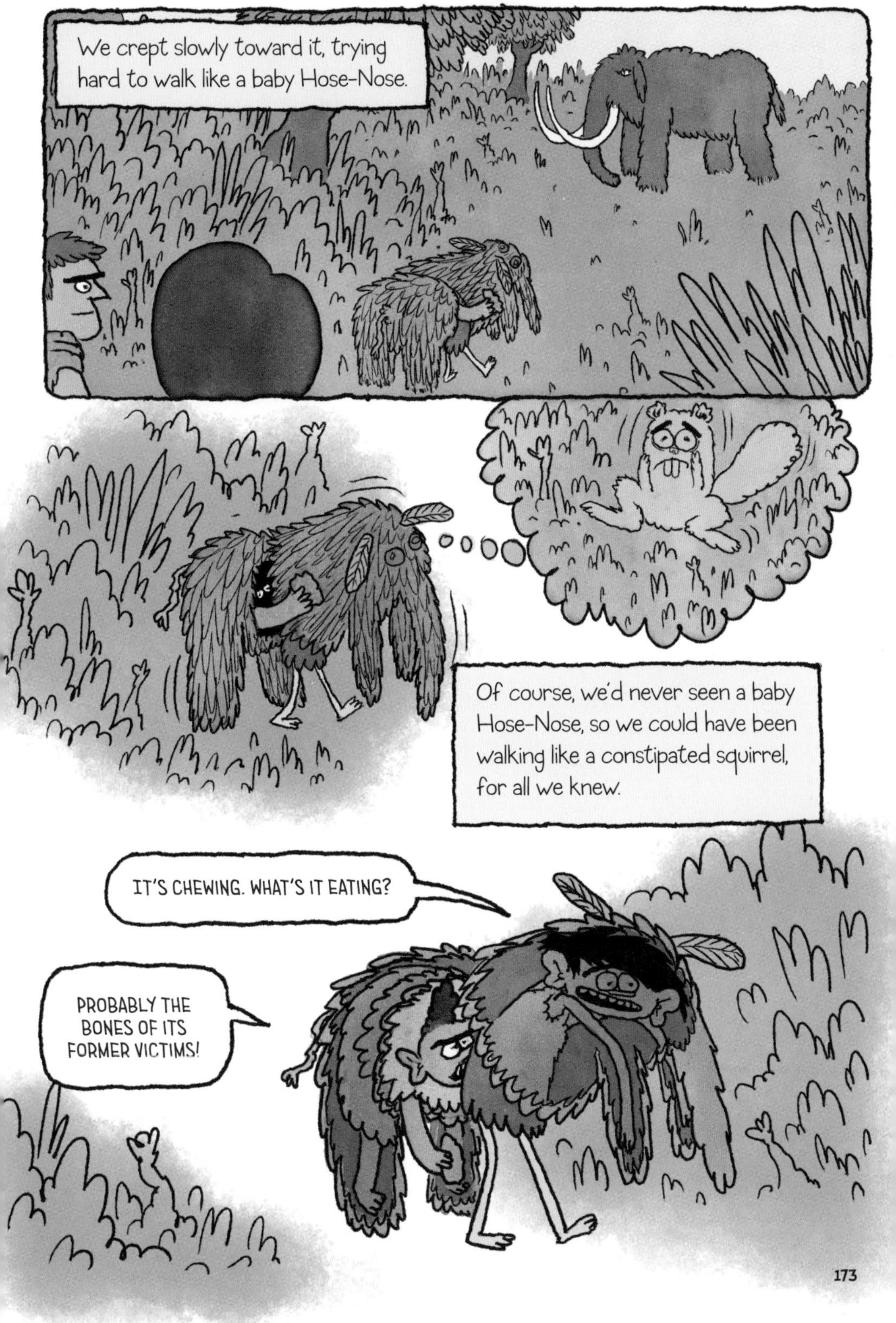

We crept slowly toward it, trying hard to walk like a baby Hose-Nose.
Of course, we'd never seen a baby Hose-Nose, so we could have been walking like a constipated squirrel, for all we knew.
IT'S CHEWING. WHAT'S IT EATING?
PROBABLY THE BONES OF ITS FORMER VICTIMS!

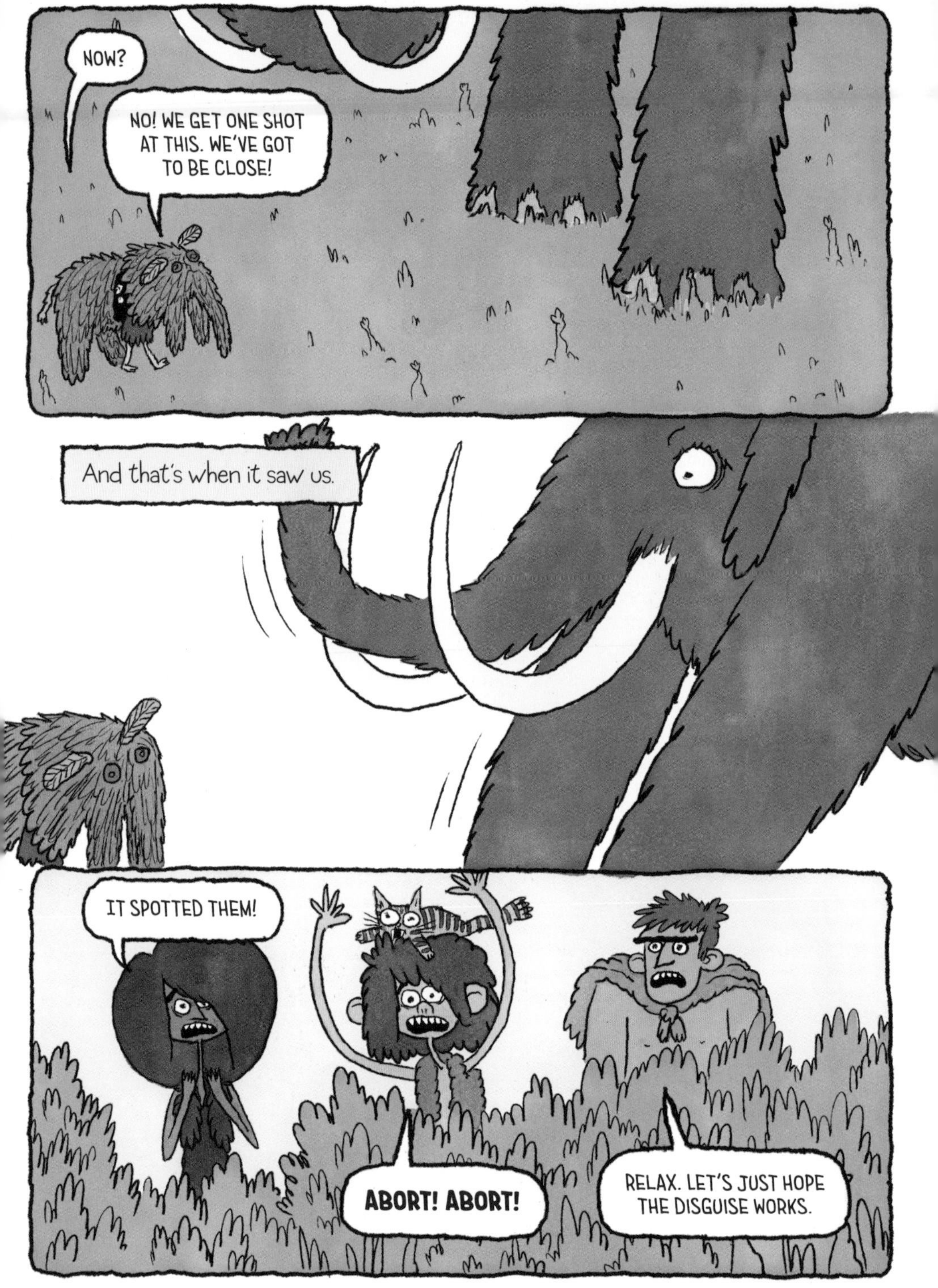
NOW?
NO! WE GET ONE SHOT AT THIS. WE'VE GOT TO BE CLOSE!
And that's when it saw us.
IT SPOTTED THEM!
ABORT! ABORT!
RELAX. LET'S JUST HOPE THE DISGUISE WORKS.

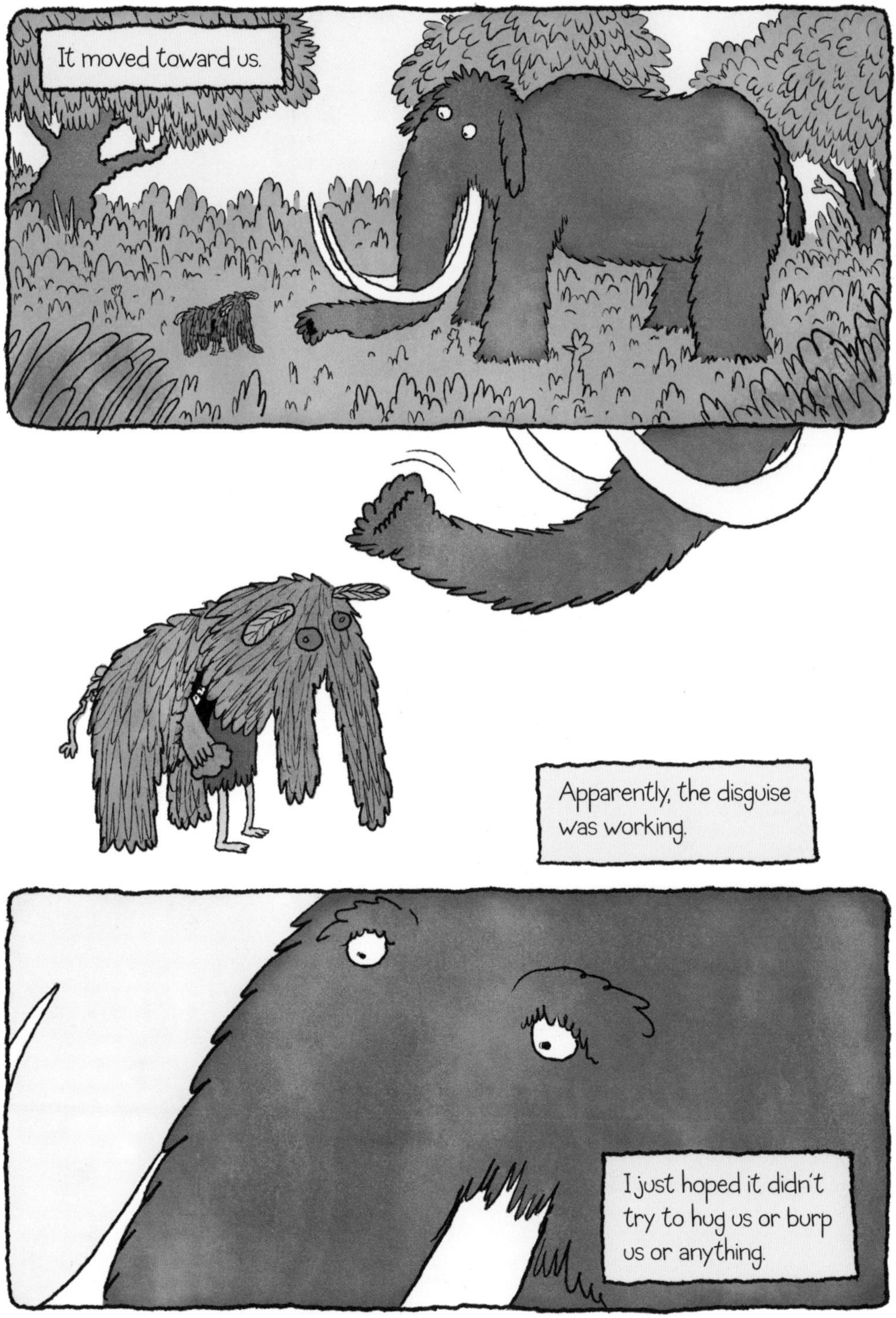
It moved toward us.
Apparently, the disguise was working.
I just hoped it didn't try to hug us or burp us or anything.

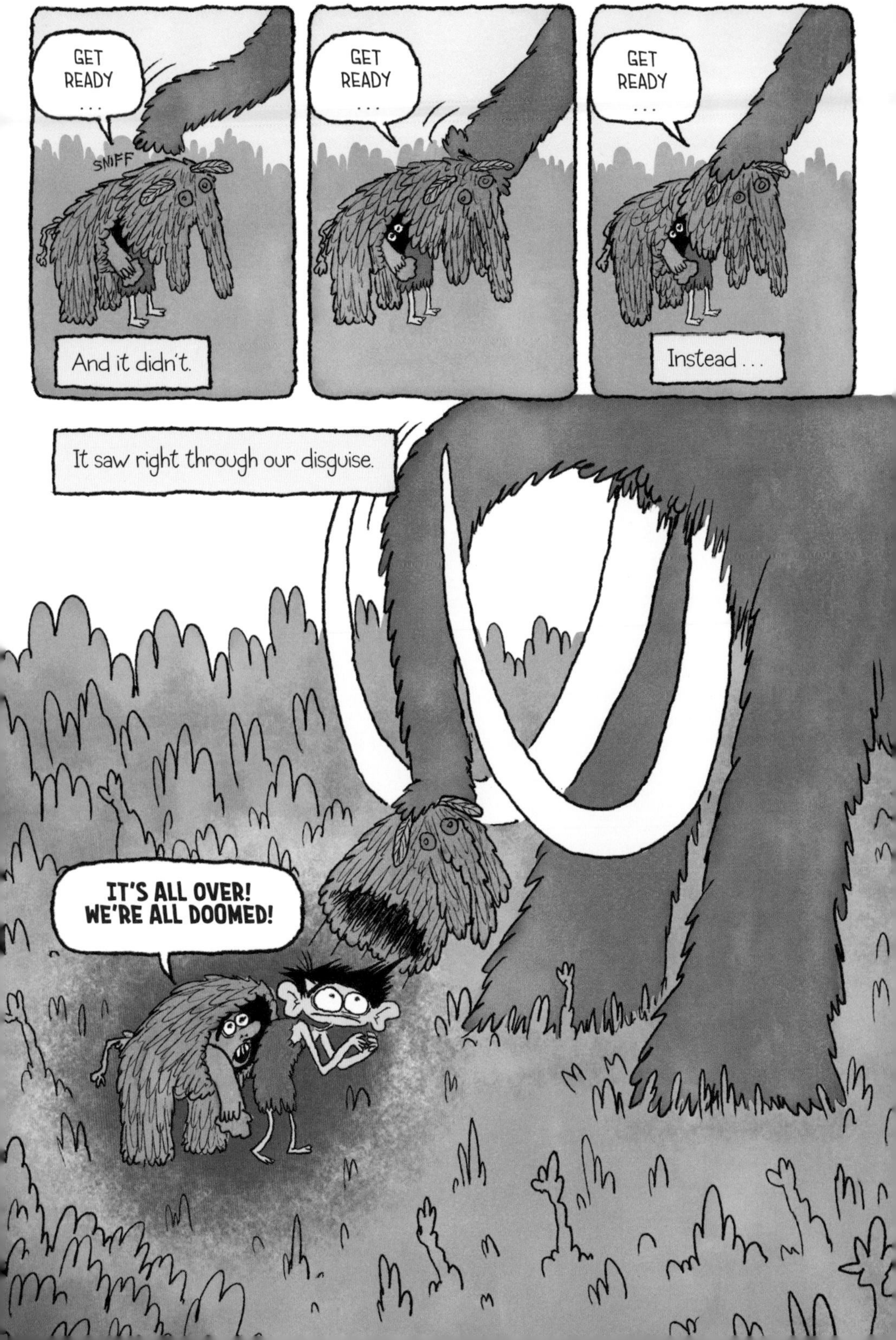

GET READY . . .
SNIFF
And it didn't.
GET READY . . .
GET READY . . .
Instead . . .
It saw right through our disguise.
IT'S ALL OVER! WE'RE ALL DOOMED!

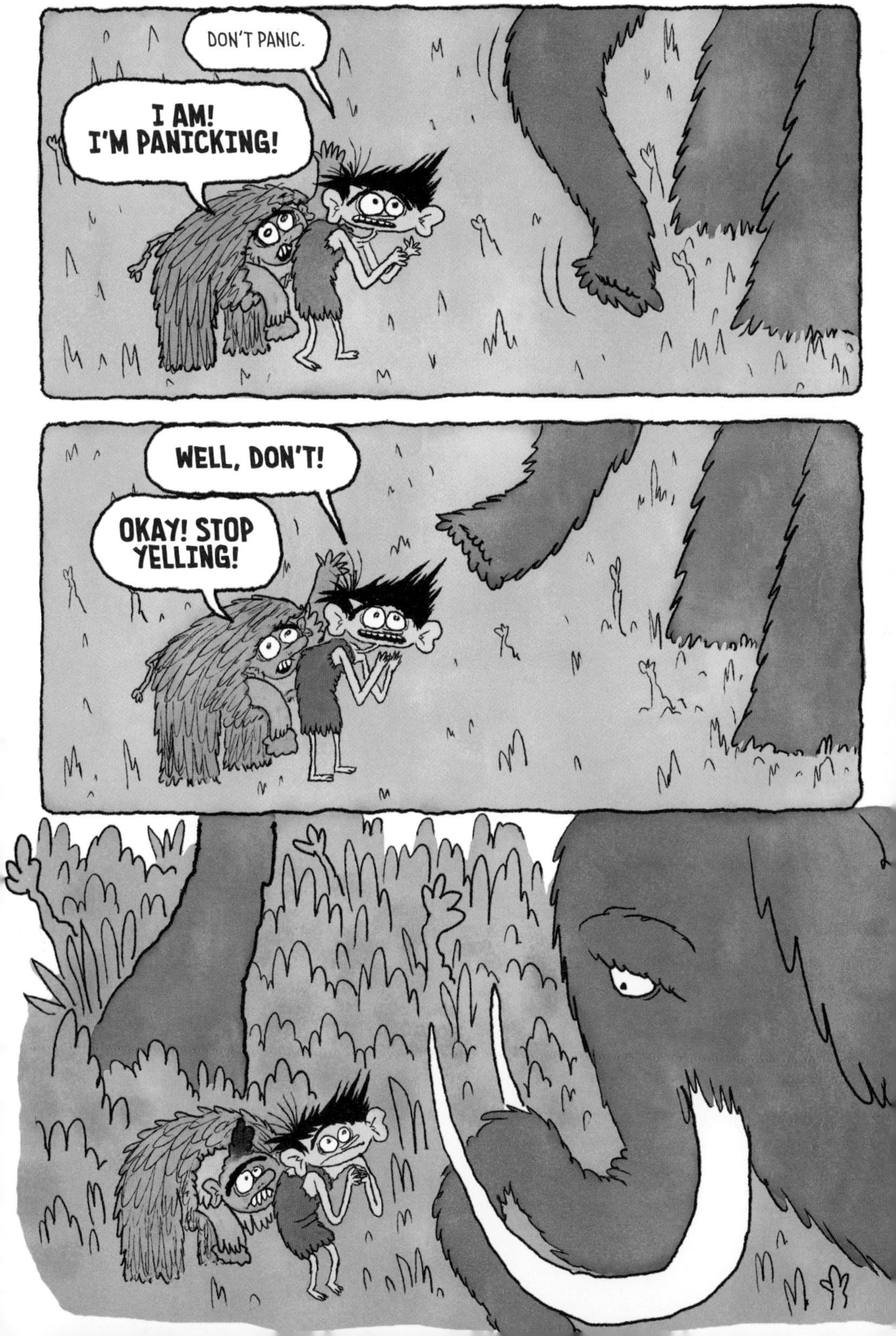
DON'T PANIC.
I AM! I'M PANICKING!
WELL, DON'T!
OKAY! STOP YELLING!

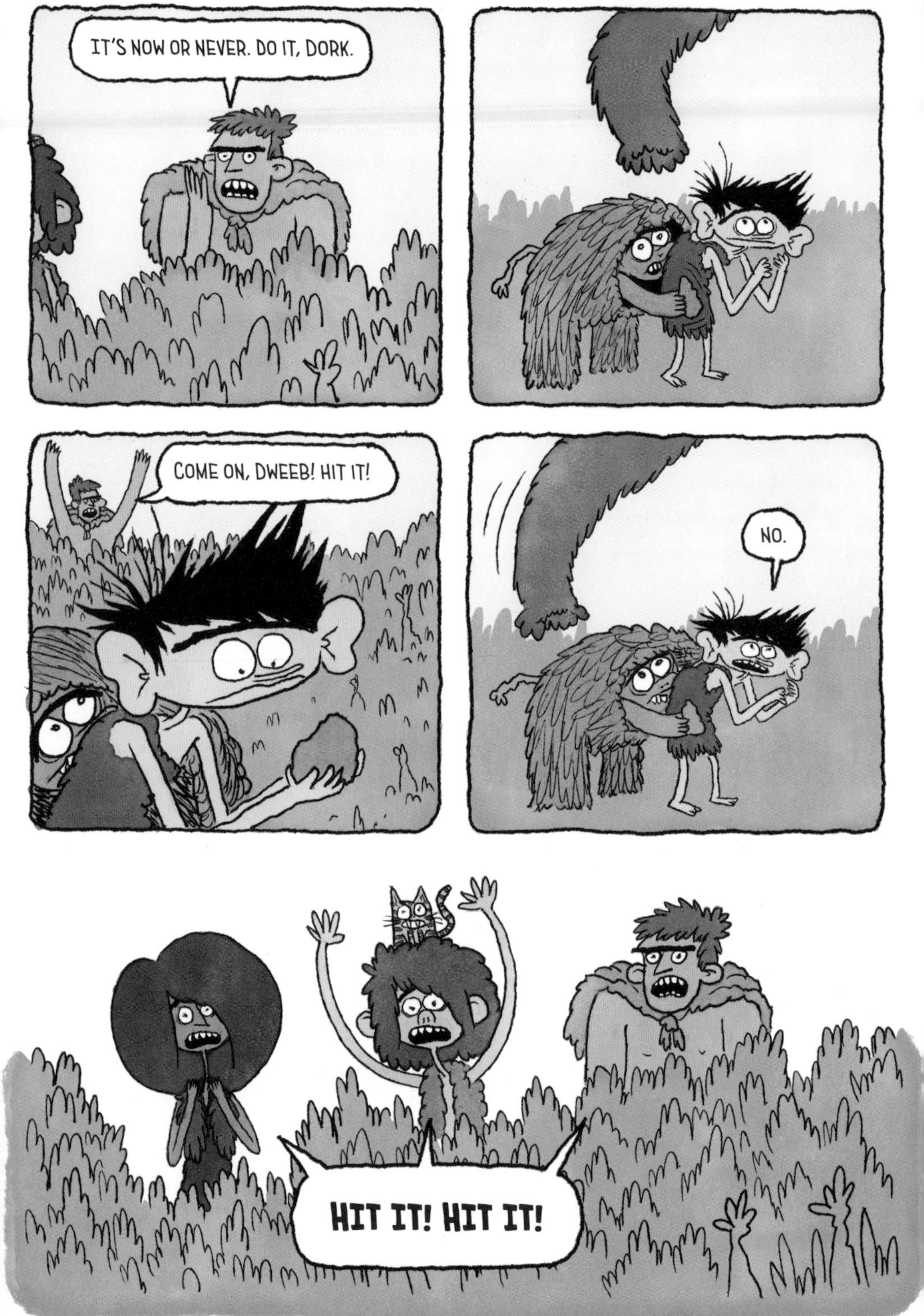
IT'S NOW OR NEVER. DO IT, DORK.
COME ON, DWEEB! HIT IT!
NO.
HIT IT! HIT IT!

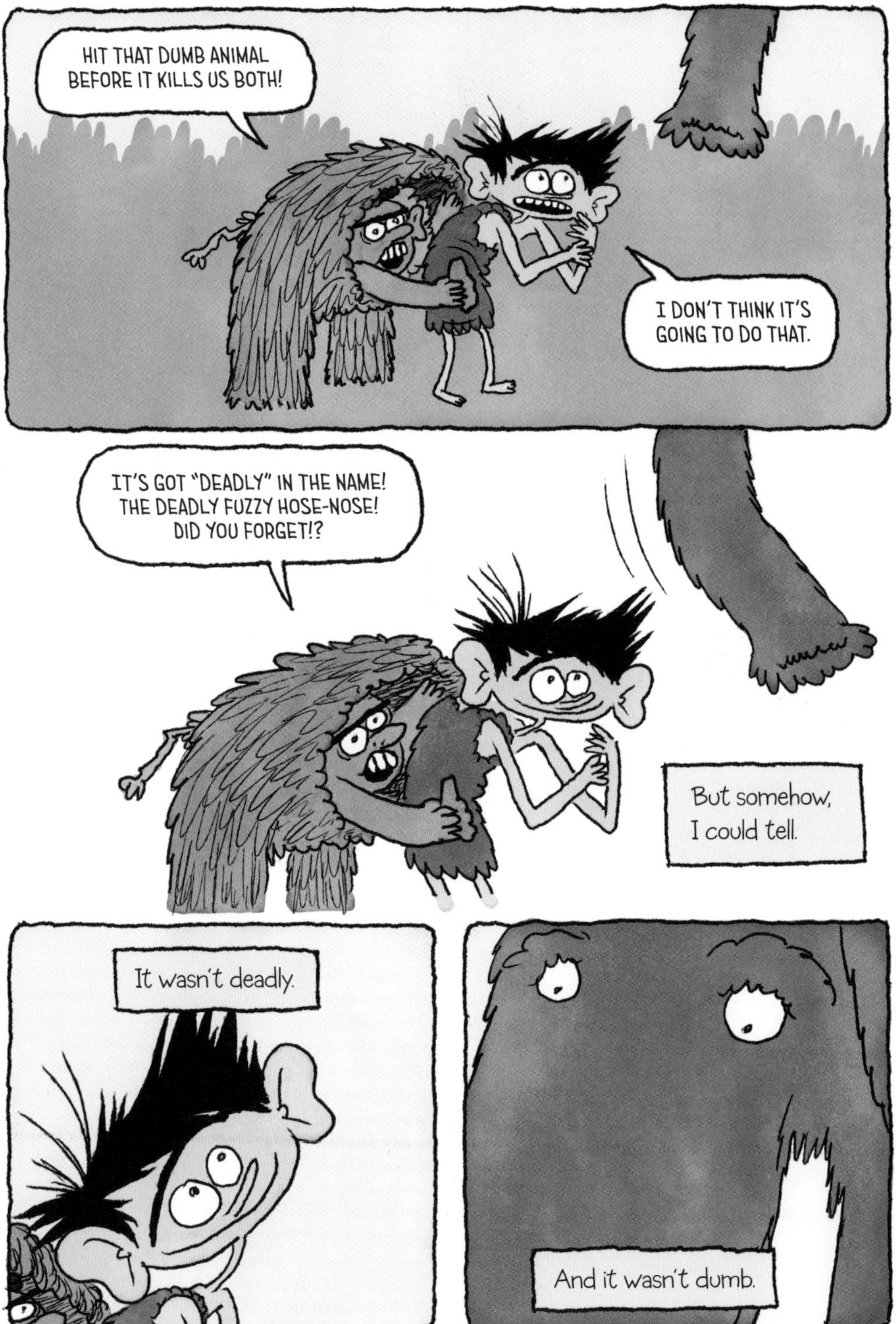
HIT THAT DUMB ANIMAL BEFORE IT KILLS US BOTH!
I DON'T THINK IT'S GOING TO DO THAT.
IT'S GOT "DEADLY" IN THE NAME! THE DEADLY FUZZY HOSE-NOSE! DID YOU FORGET!?
But somehow, I could tell.
It wasn't deadly.
And it wasn't dumb.

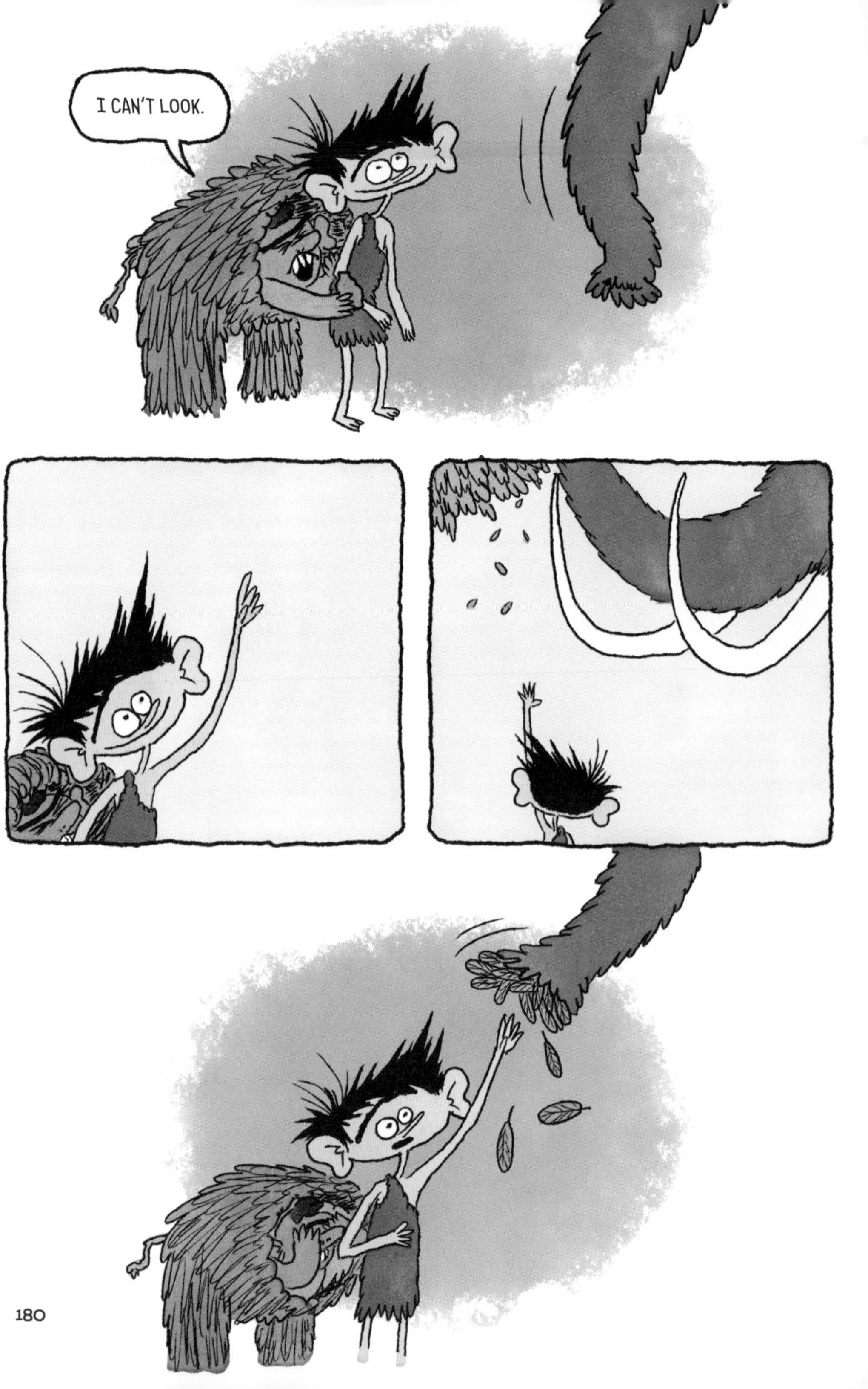
I CAN'T LOOK.

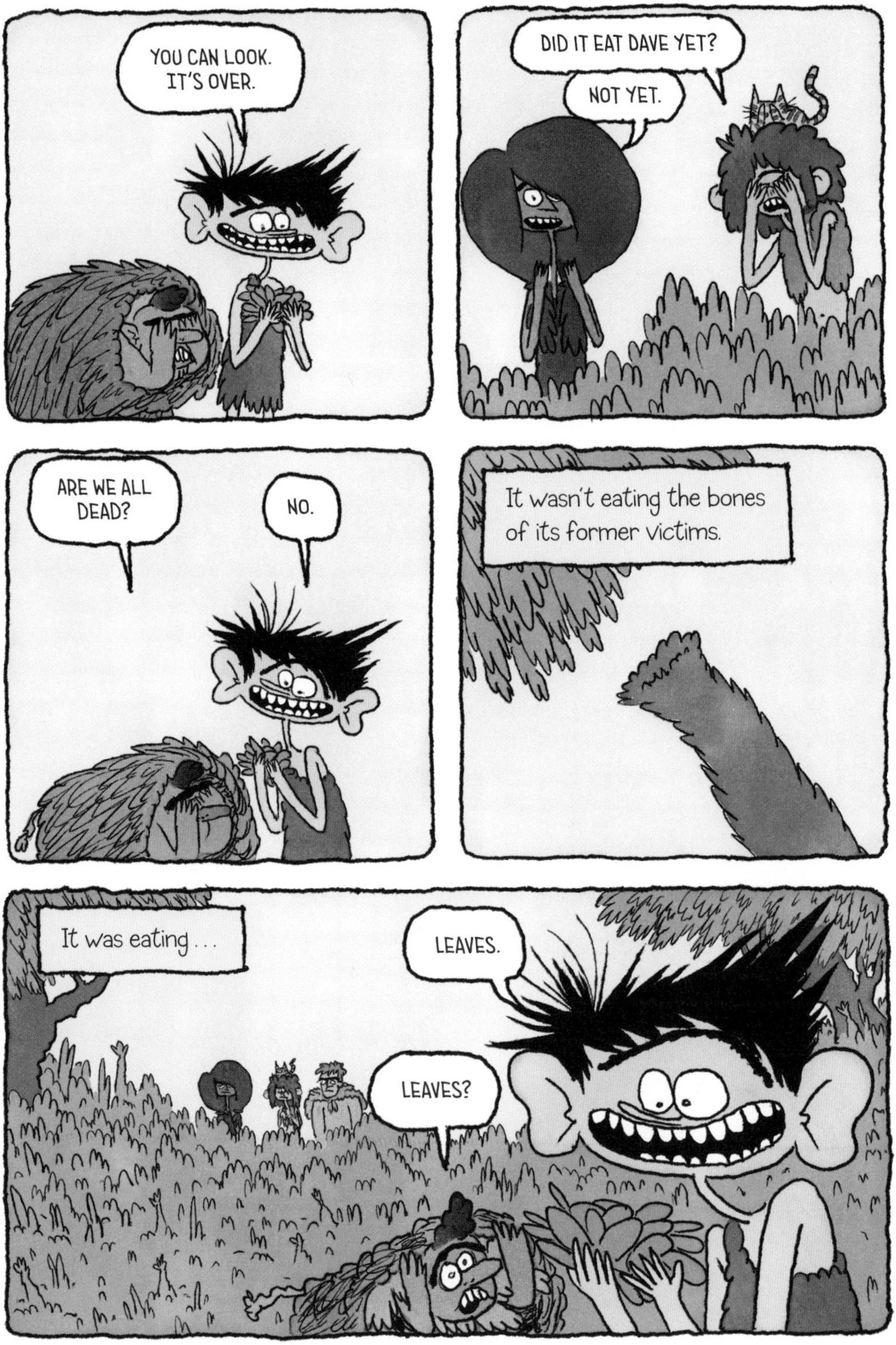
YOU CAN LOOK. IT'S OVER.
DID IT EAT DAVE YET?
NOT YET.
ARE WE ALL DEAD?
NO.
It wasn't eating the bones of its former victims.
It was eating . . .
LEAVES.
LEAVES?

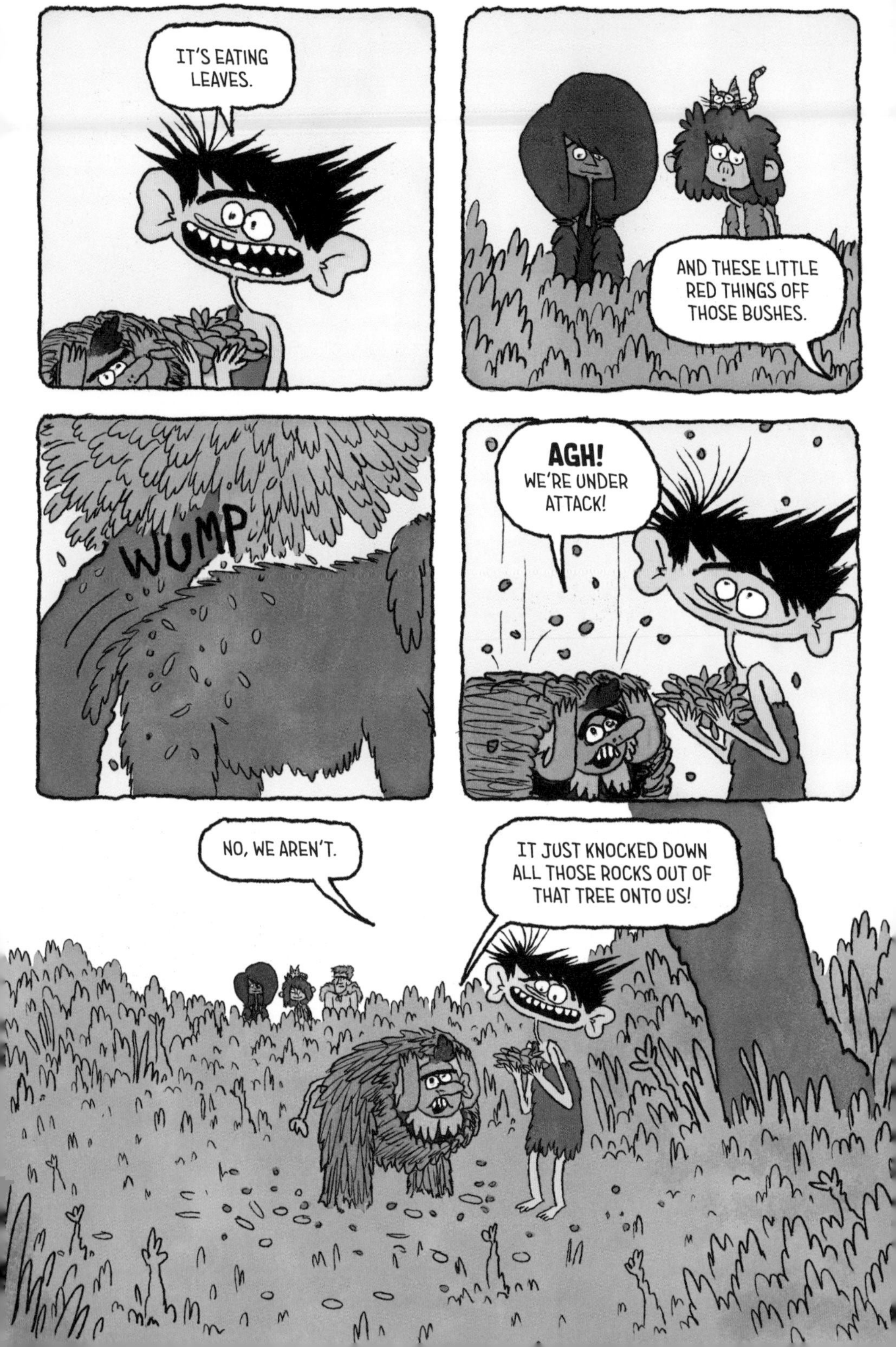
IT'S EATING LEAVES.
AND THESE LITTLE RED THINGS OFF THOSE BUSHES.
WUMP
AGH! WE'RE UNDER ATTACK!
NO, WE AREN'T.
IT JUST KNOCKED DOWN ALL THOSE ROCKS OUT OF THAT TREE ONTO US!

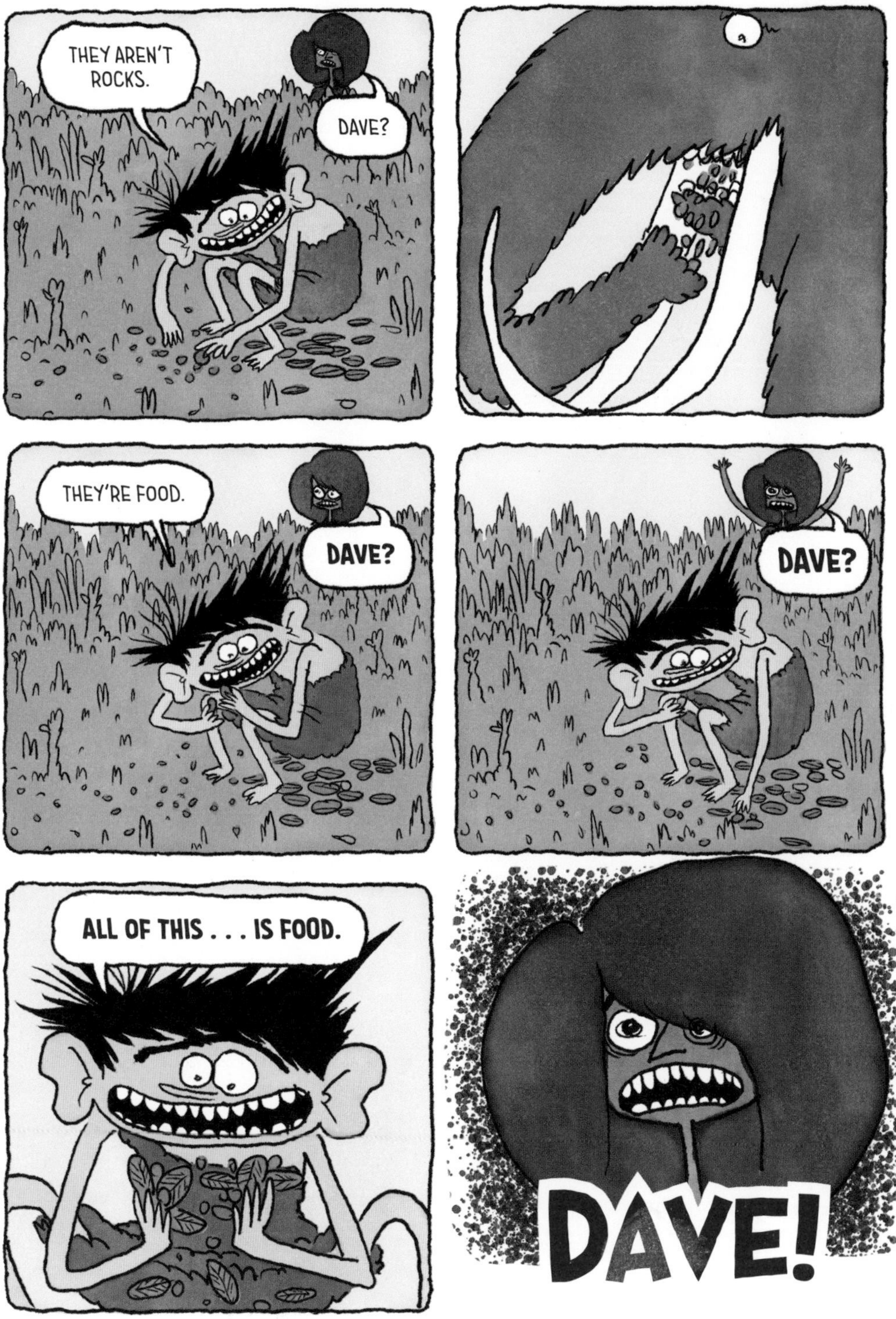
THEY AREN'T ROCKS.
DAVE?
THEY'RE FOOD.
DAVE?
DAVE?
ALL OF THIS . . . IS FOOD.
DAVE!

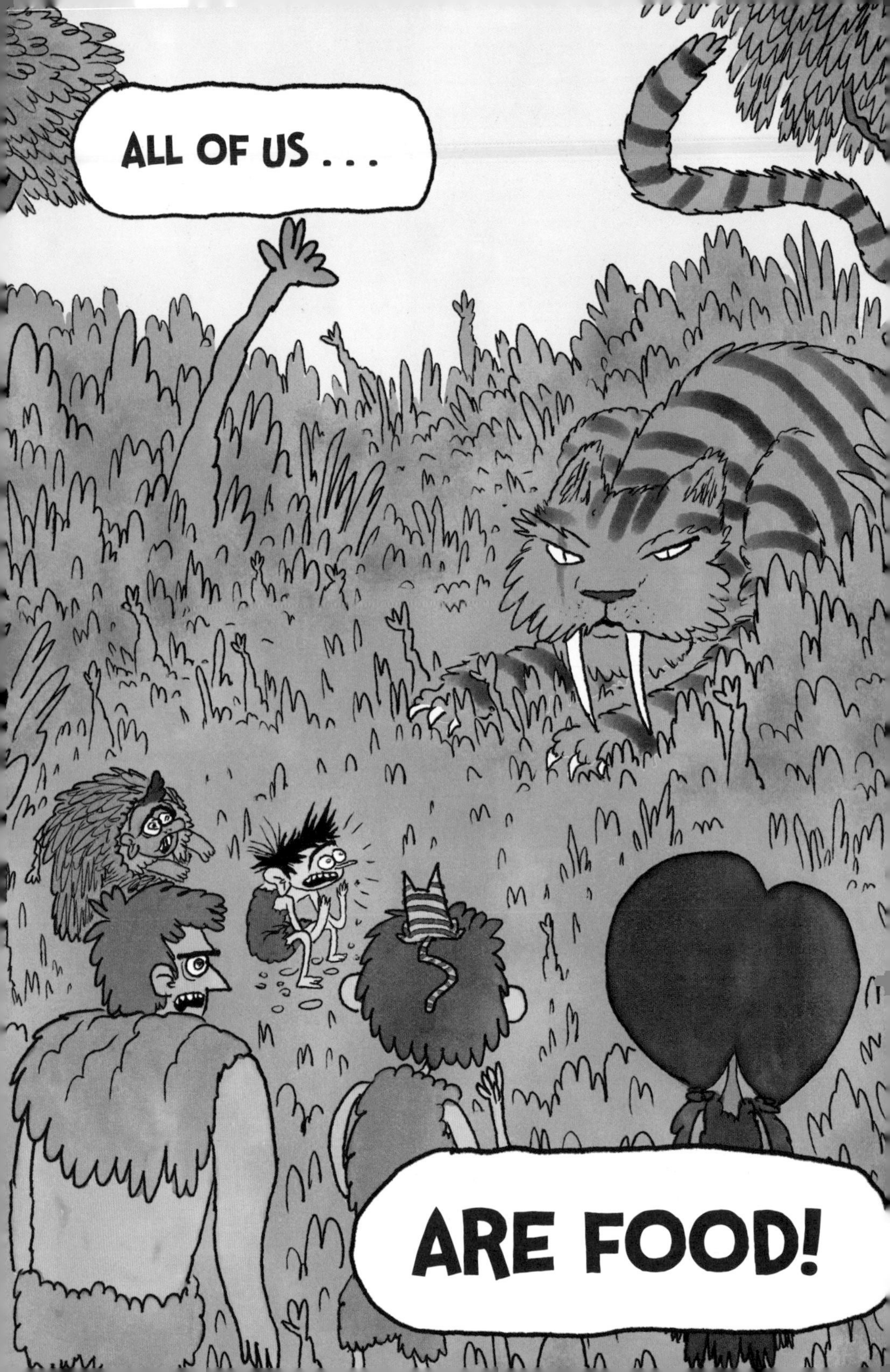
ALL OF US . . .
ARE FOOD!

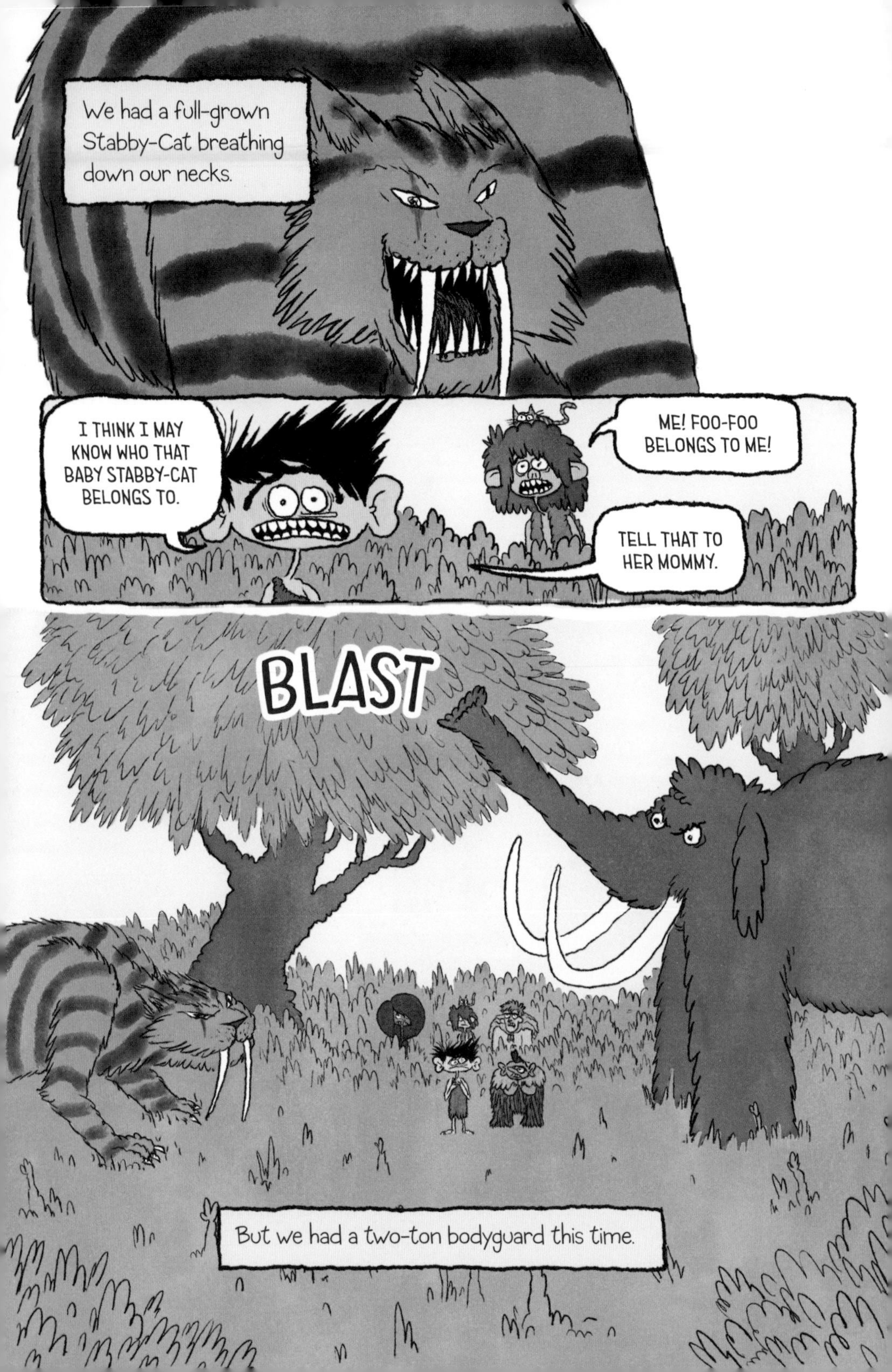

We had a full-grown Stabby-Cat breathing down our necks.
I THINK I MAY KNOW WHO THAT BABY STABBY-CAT BELONGS TO.
ME! FOO-FOO BELONGS TO ME!
TELL THAT TO HER MOMMY.
BLAST
But we had a two-ton bodyguard this time.

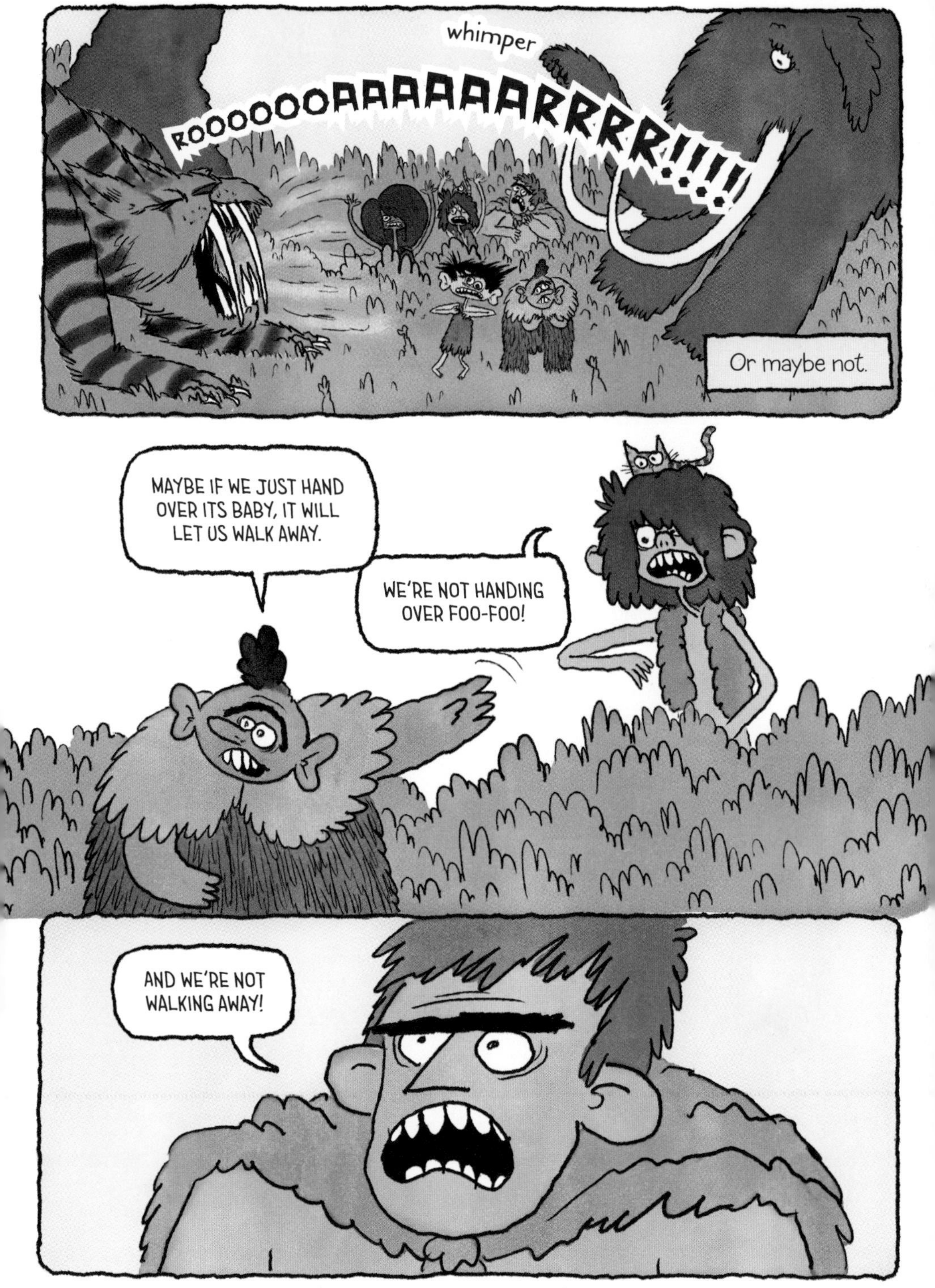
whimper
ROOOOOOAAAAAAAARRRRR!!!!
Or maybe not.
MAYBE IF WE JUST HAND OVER ITS BABY, IT WILL LET US WALK AWAY.
WE'RE NOT HANDING OVER FOO-FOO!
AND WE'RE NOT WALKING AWAY!

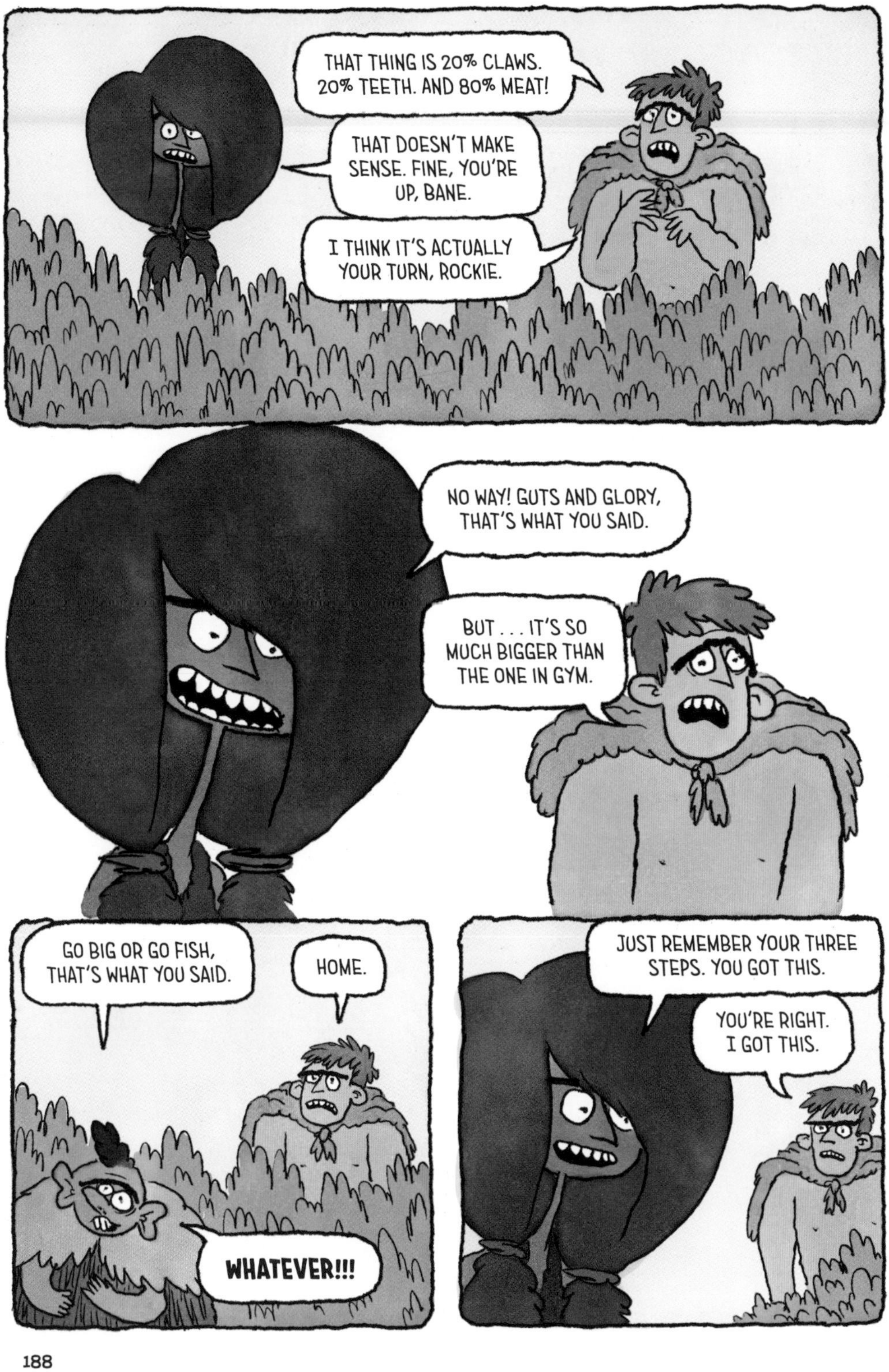
THAT THING IS 20% CLAWS. 20% TEETH. AND 80% MEAT!
THAT DOESN'T MAKE SENSE. FINE, YOU'RE UP, BANE.
I THINK IT'S ACTUALLY YOUR TURN, ROCKIE.
NO WAY! GUTS AND GLORY, THAT'S WHAT YOU SAID.
BUT . . . IT'S SO MUCH BIGGER THAN THE ONE IN GYM.
GO BIG OR GO FISH, THAT'S WHAT YOU SAID.
HOME.
WHATEVER!!!
JUST REMEMBER YOUR THREE STEPS. YOU GOT THIS.
YOU'RE RIGHT. I GOT THIS.

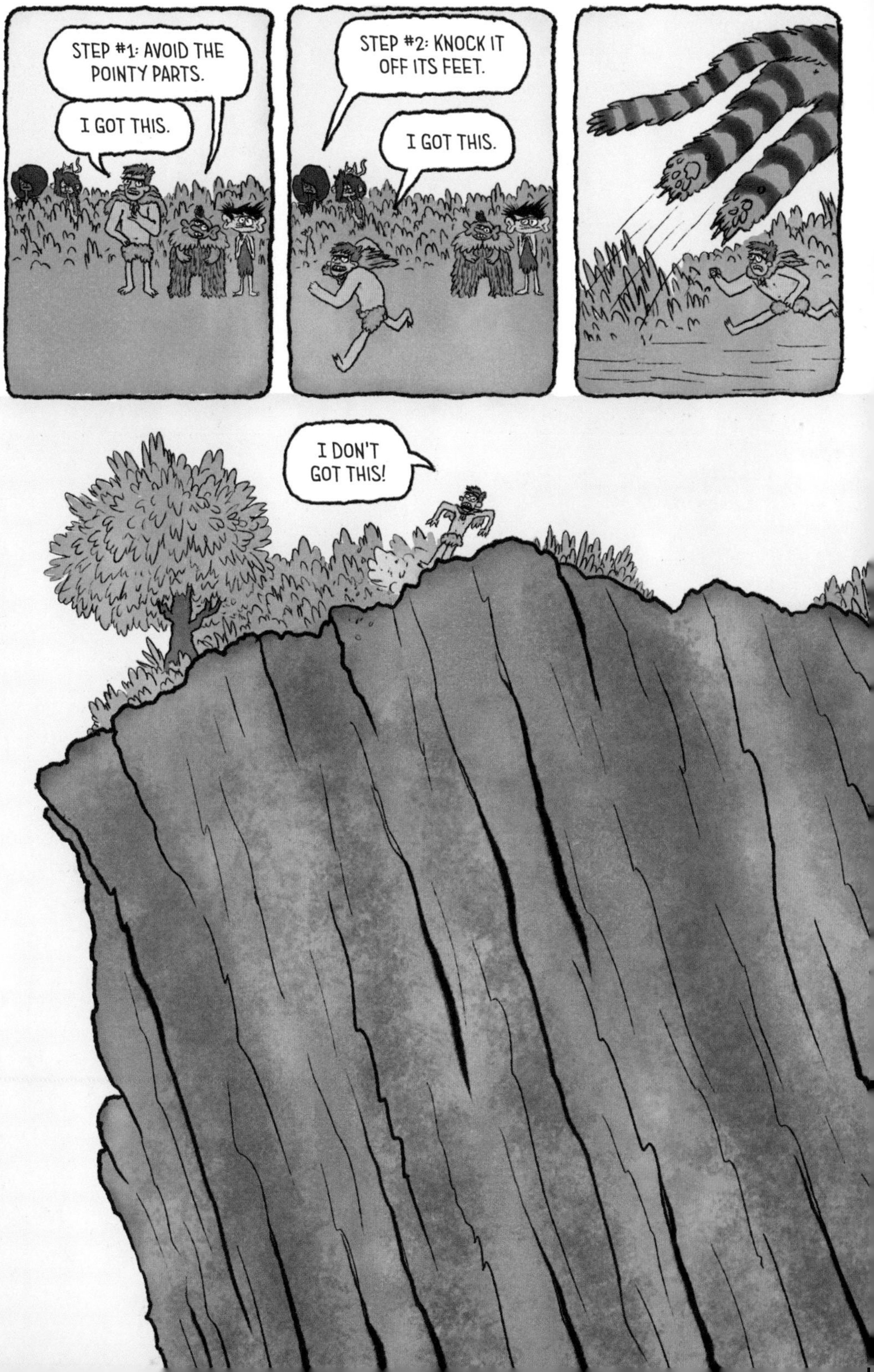
STEP #1: AVOID THE POINTY PARTS.
I GOT THIS.
STEP #2: KNOCK IT OFF ITS FEET.
I GOT THIS.
I DON'T GOT THIS!

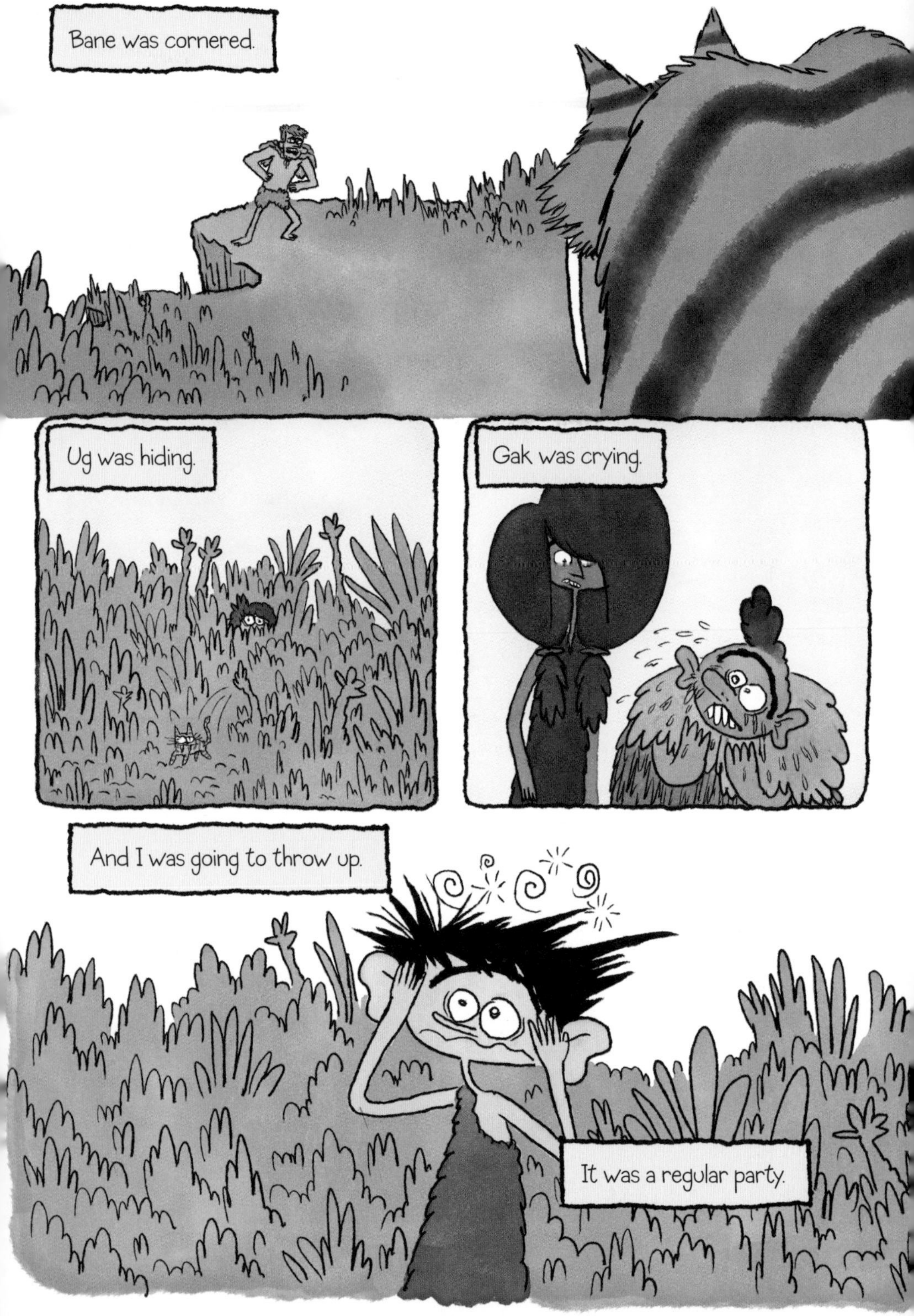

Bane was cornered.
Ug was hiding.
Gak was crying.
And I was going to throw up.
It was a regular party.

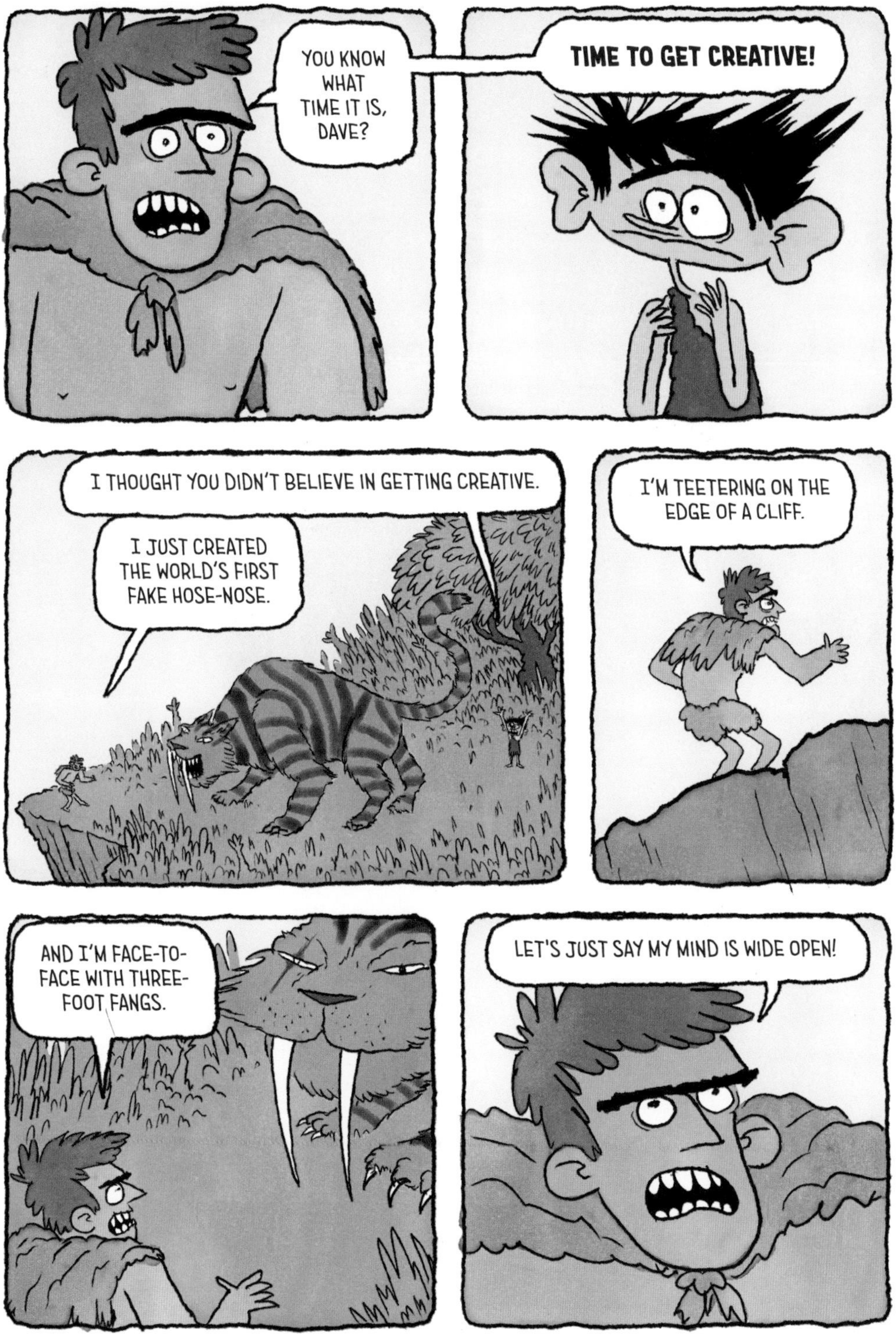

YOU KNOW WHAT TIME IT IS, DAVE?
TIME TO GET CREATIVE!
I THOUGHT YOU DIDN'T BELIEVE IN GETTING CREATIVE.
I JUST CREATED THE WORLD'S FIRST FAKE HOSE-NOSE.
I'M TEETERING ON THE EDGE OF A CLIFF.
AND I'M FACE-TO-FACE WITH THREE-FOOT FANGS.
LET'S JUST SAY MY MIND IS WIDE OPEN!

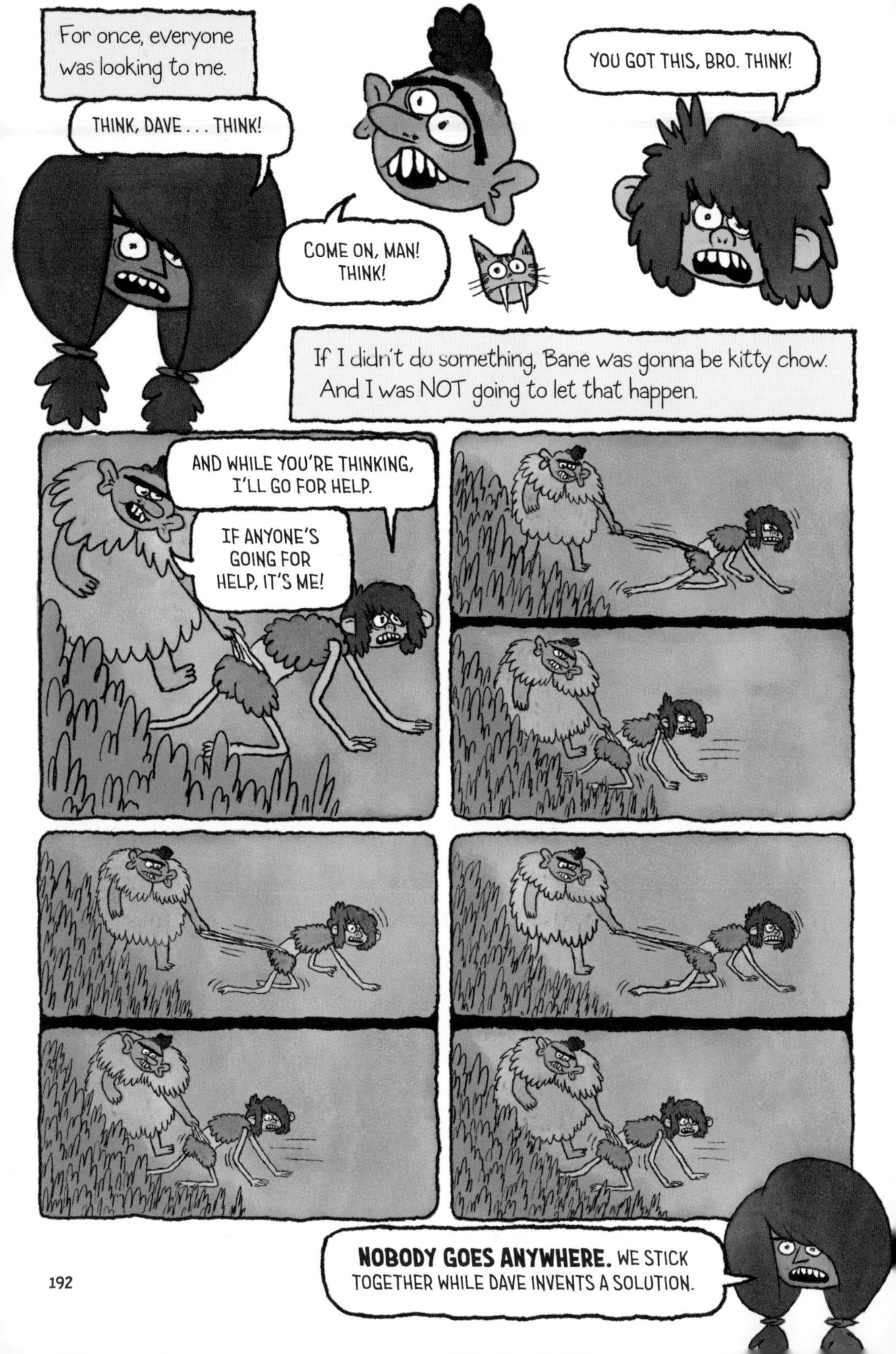

For once, everyone was looking to me.
THINK, DAVE . . . THINK!
COME ON, MAN! THINK!
YOU GOT THIS, BRO. THINK!
If I didn't do something, Bane was gonna be kitty chow. And I was NOT going to let that happen.
AND WHILE YOU'RE THINKING, I'LL GO FOR HELP.
IF ANYONE'S GOING FOR HELP, IT'S ME!
NOBODY GOES ANYWHERE. WE STICK TOGETHER WHILE DAVE INVENTS A SOLUTION.

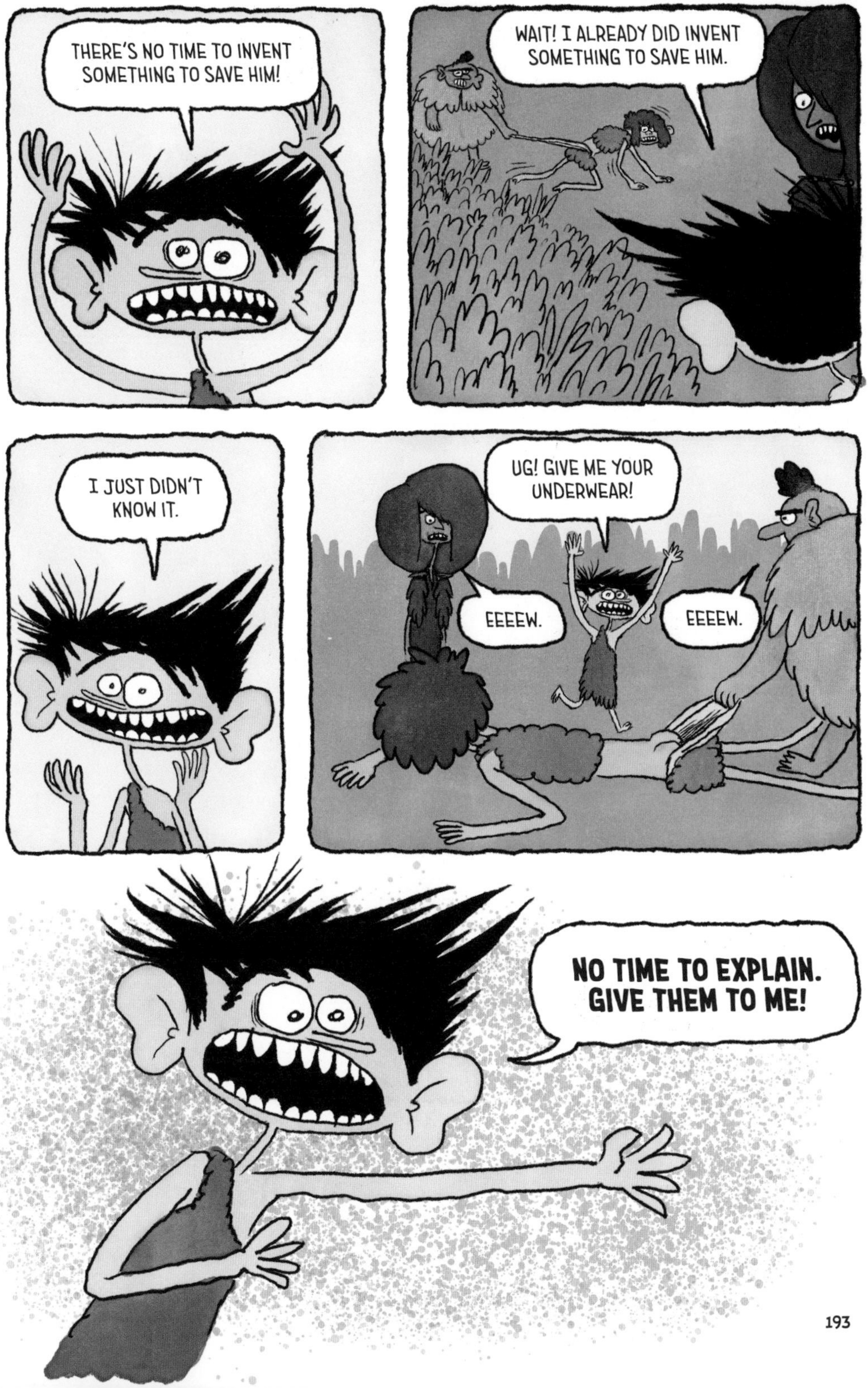
THERE'S NO TIME TO INVENT SOMETHING TO SAVE HIM!
WAIT! I ALREADY DID INVENT SOMETHING TO SAVE HIM.
I JUST DIDN'T KNOW IT.
UG! GIVE ME YOUR UNDERWEAR!
EEEEW.
EEEEW.
NO TIME TO EXPLAIN. GIVE THEM TO ME!

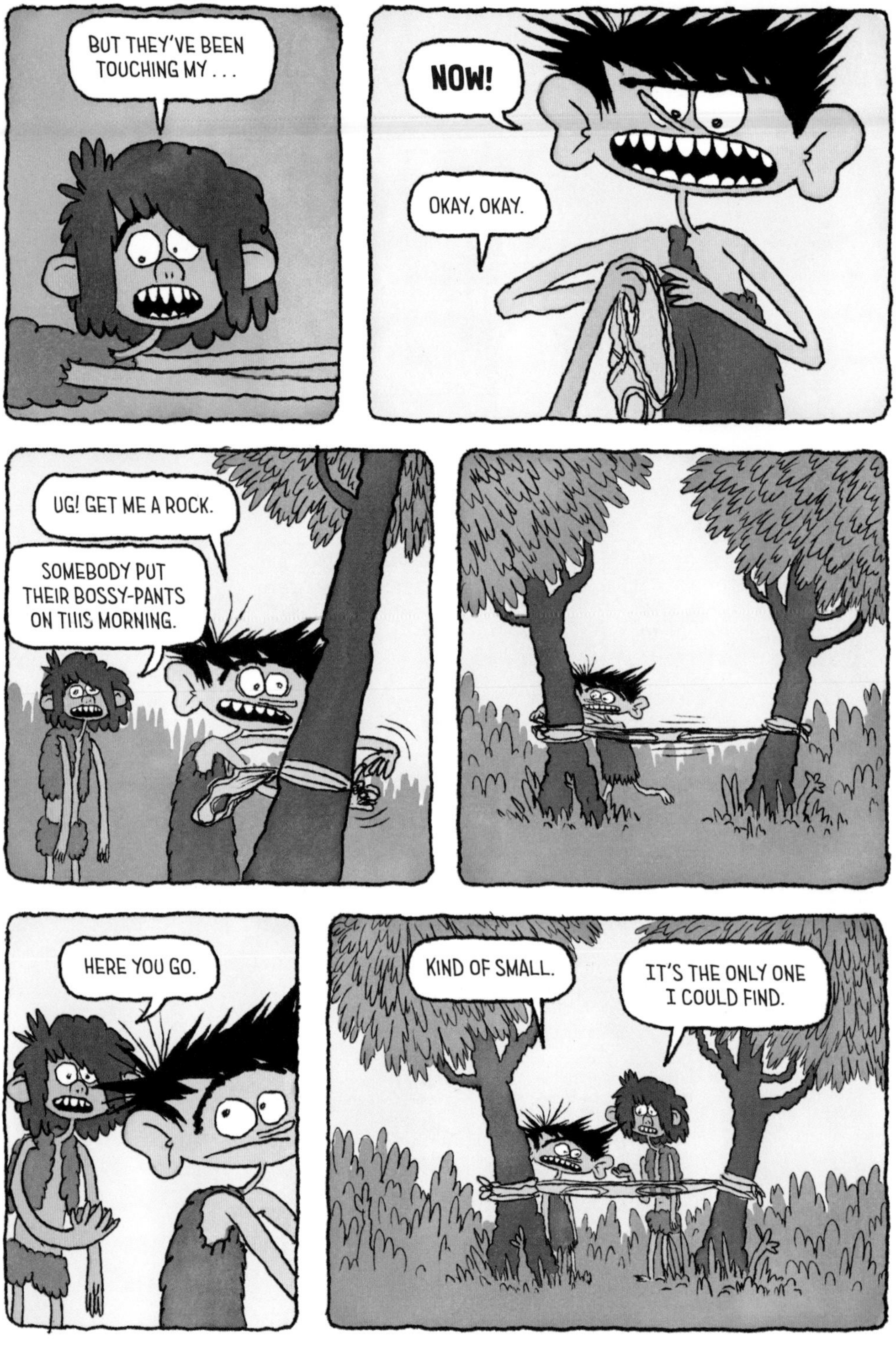
BUT THEY'VE BEEN TOUCHING MY . . .
NOW!
OKAY, OKAY.
UG! GET ME A ROCK.
SOMEBODY PUT THEIR BOSSY-PANTS ON THIS MORNING.
HERE YOU GO.
KIND OF SMALL.
IT'S THE ONLY ONE I COULD FIND.

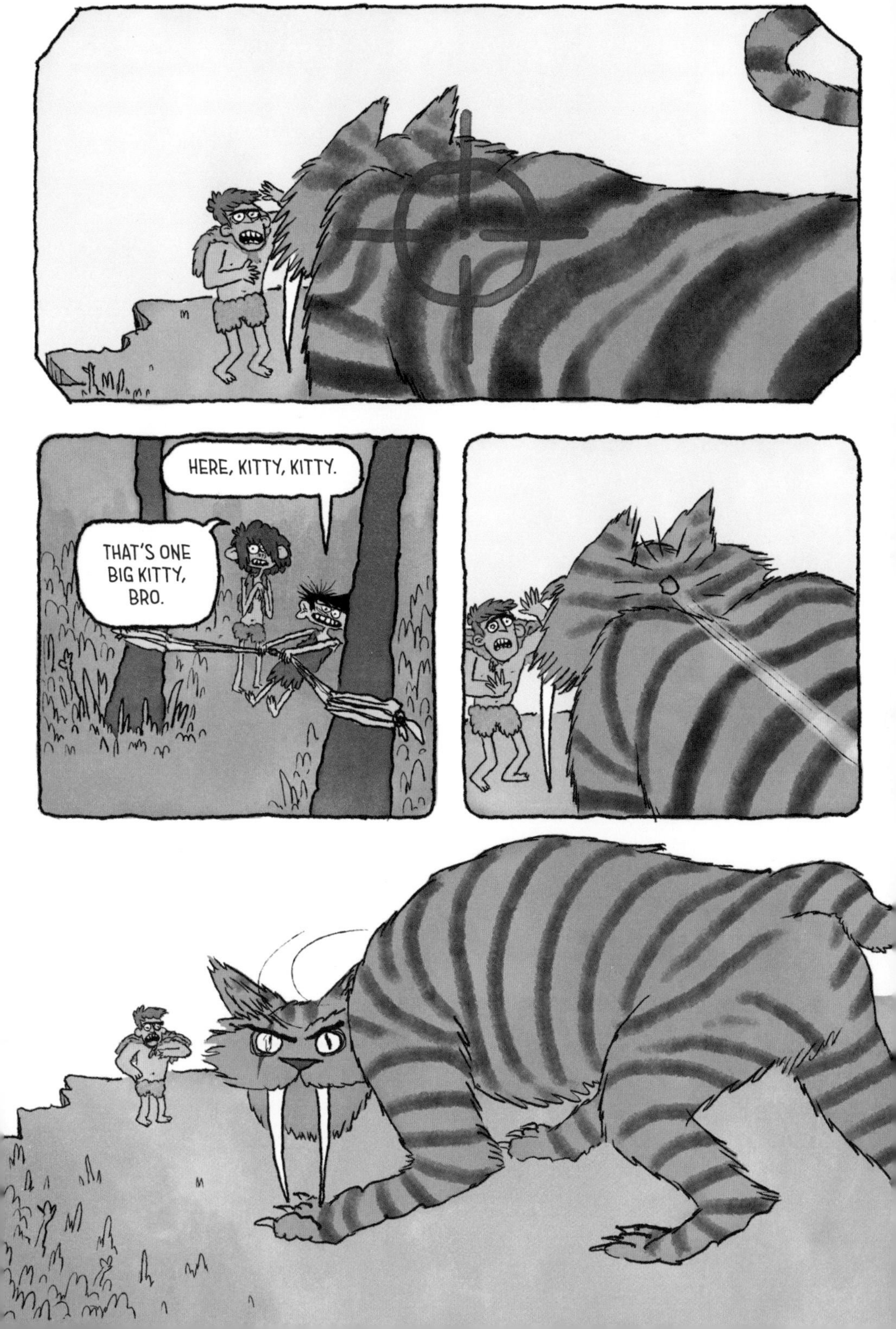
HERE, KITTY, KITTY.
THAT'S ONE BIG KITTY, BRO.

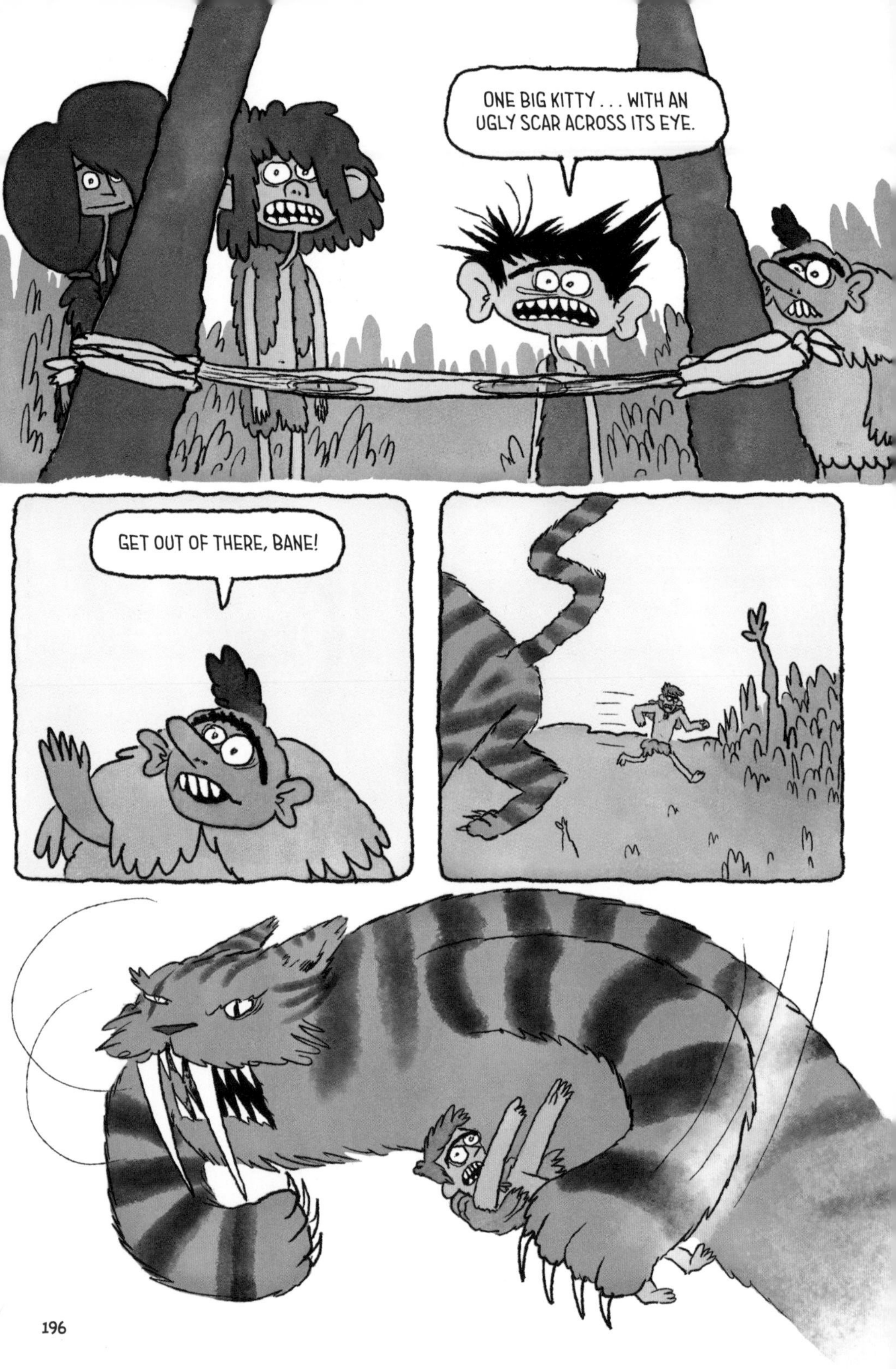
ONE BIG KITTY . . . WITH AN UGLY SCAR ACROSS ITS EYE.
GET OUT OF THERE, BANE!

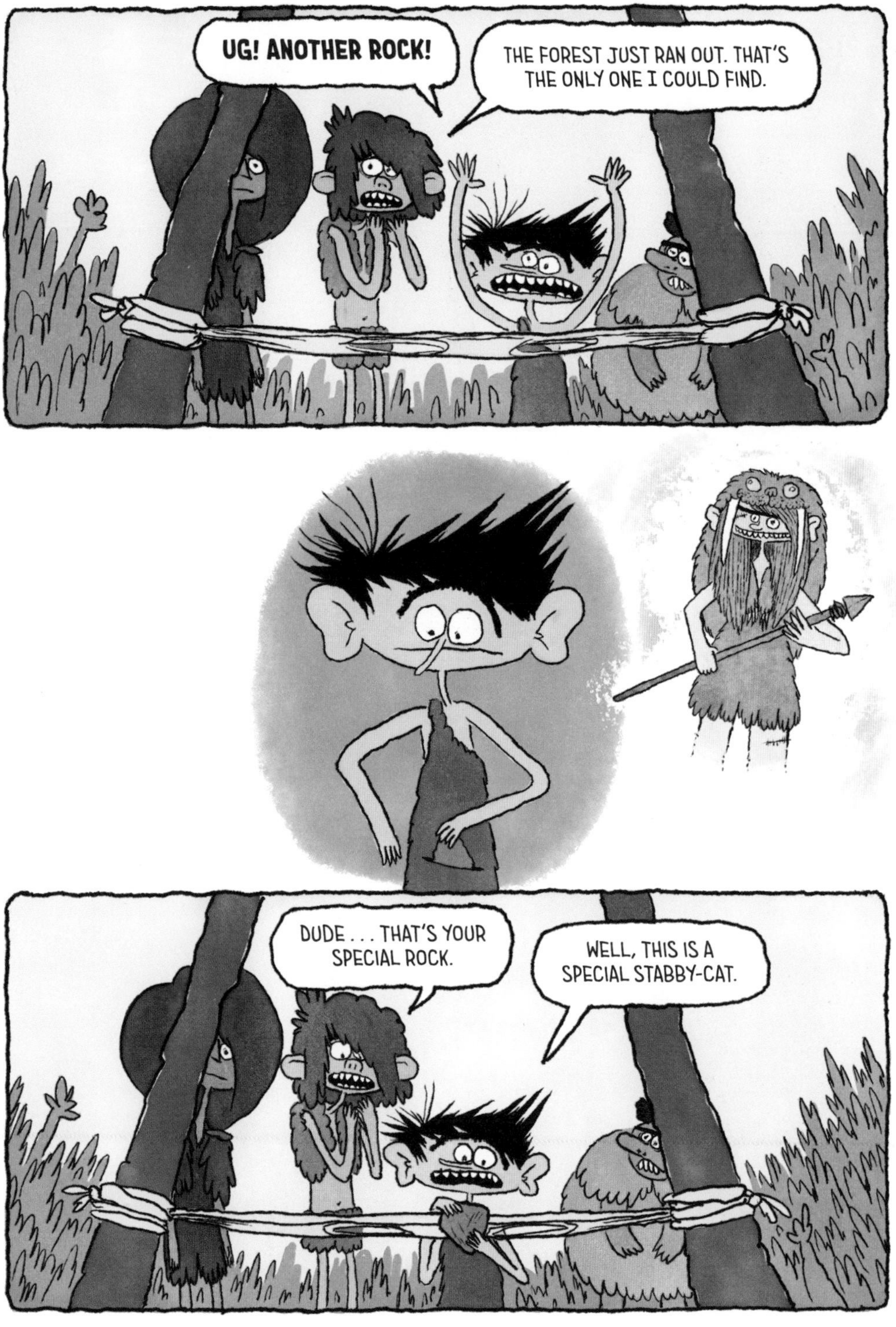
UG! ANOTHER ROCK!
THE FOREST JUST RAN OUT. THAT'S THE ONLY ONE I COULD FIND.
DUDE . . . THAT'S YOUR SPECIAL ROCK.
WELL, THIS IS A SPECIAL STABBY-CAT.

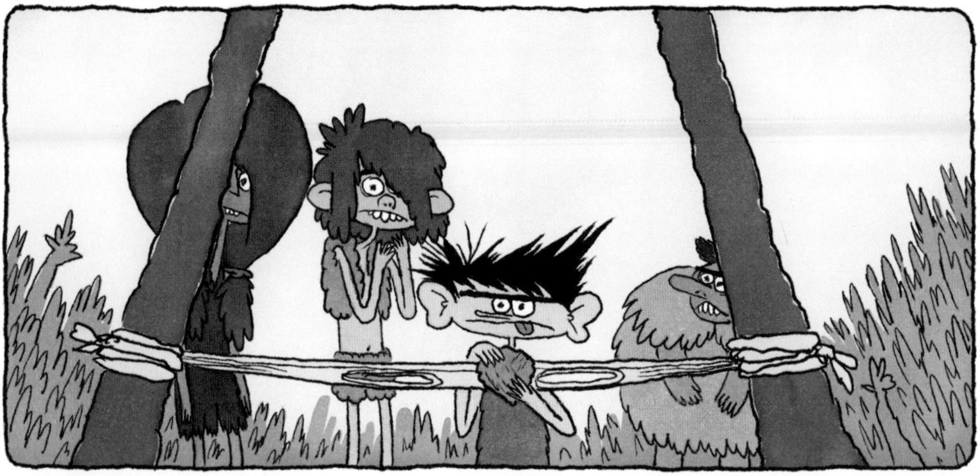
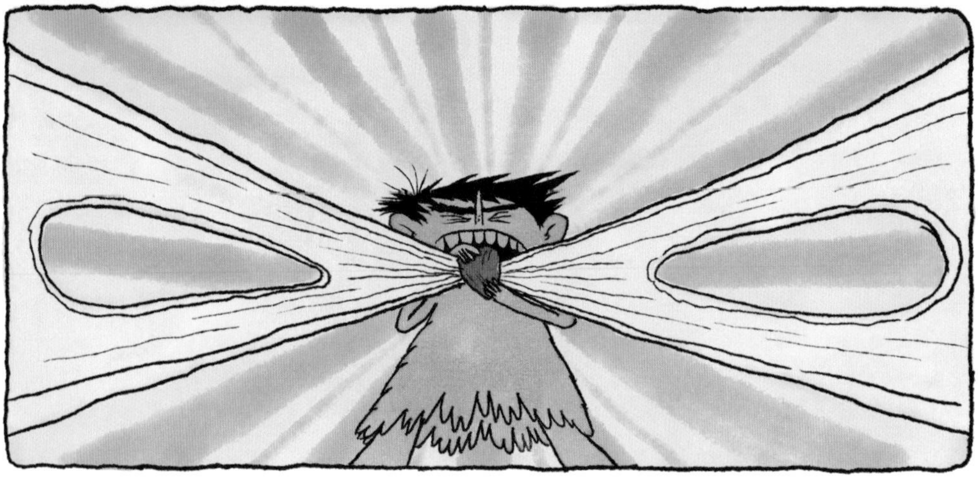
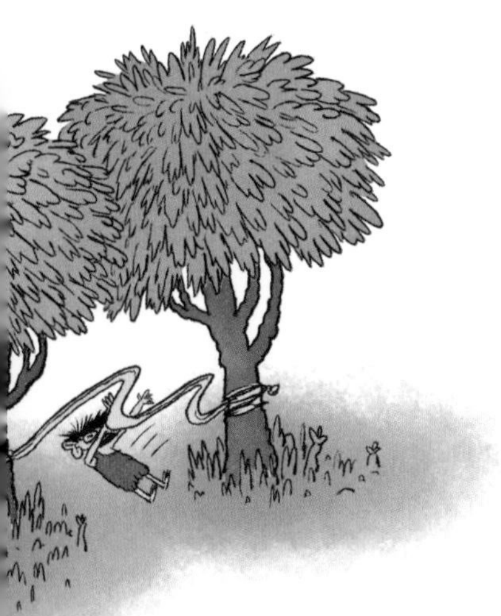

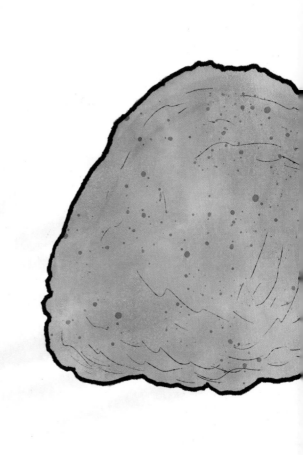

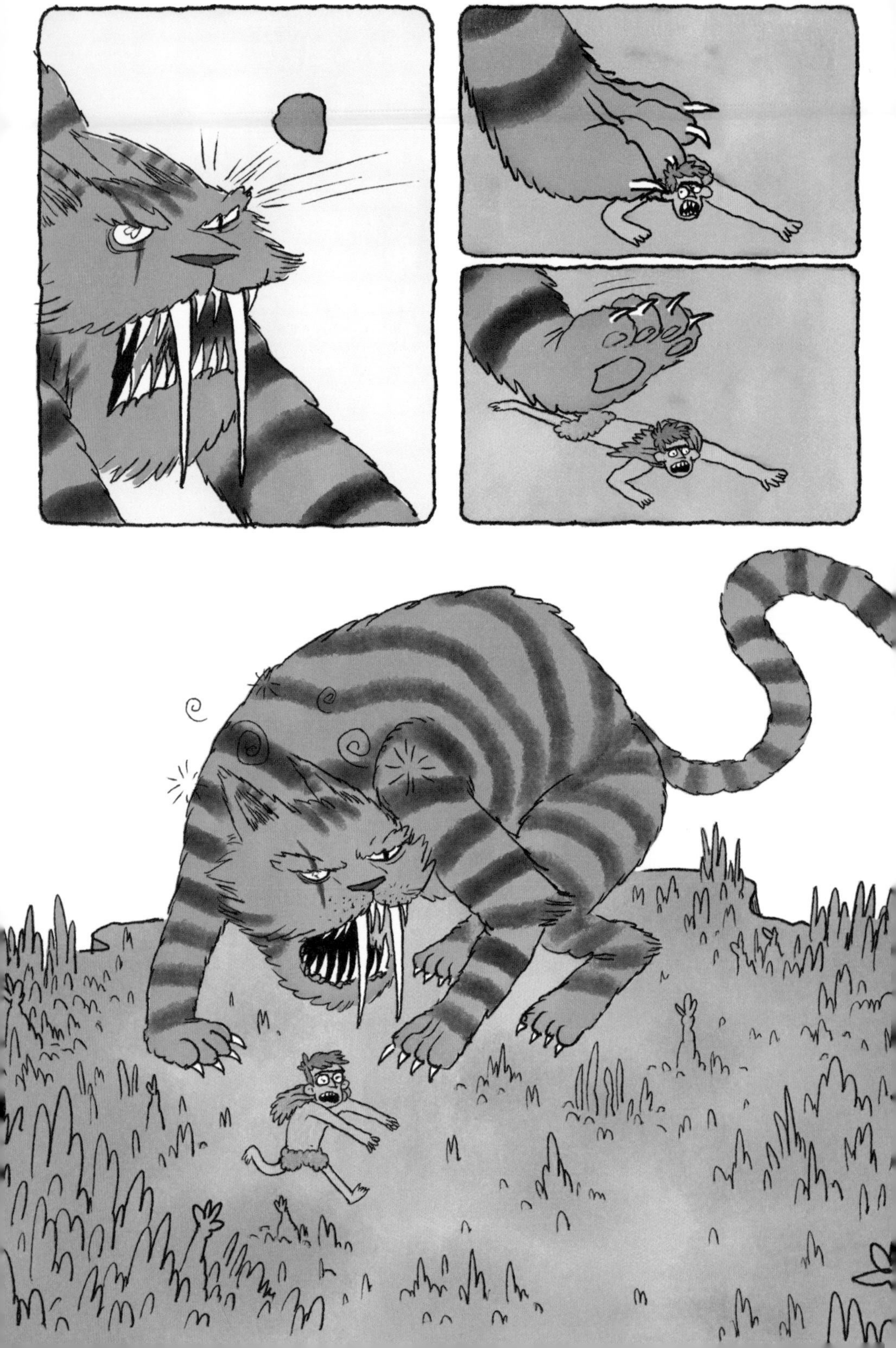

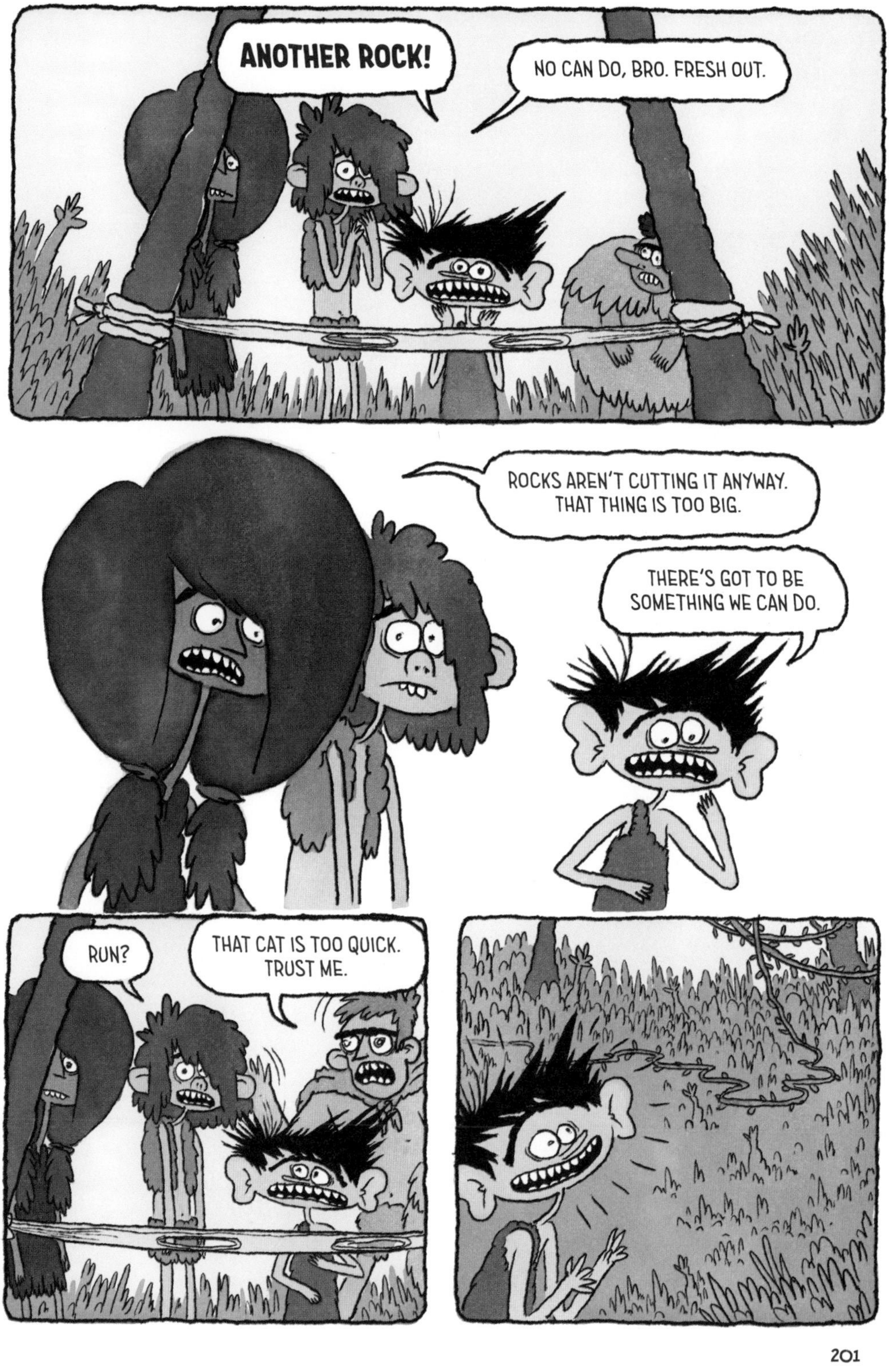
ANOTHER ROCK!
NO CAN DO, BRO. FRESH OUT.
ROCKS AREN'T CUTTING IT ANYWAY. THAT THING IS TOO BIG.
THERE'S GOT TO BE SOMETHING WE CAN DO.
RUN?
THAT CAT IS TOO QUICK. TRUST ME.

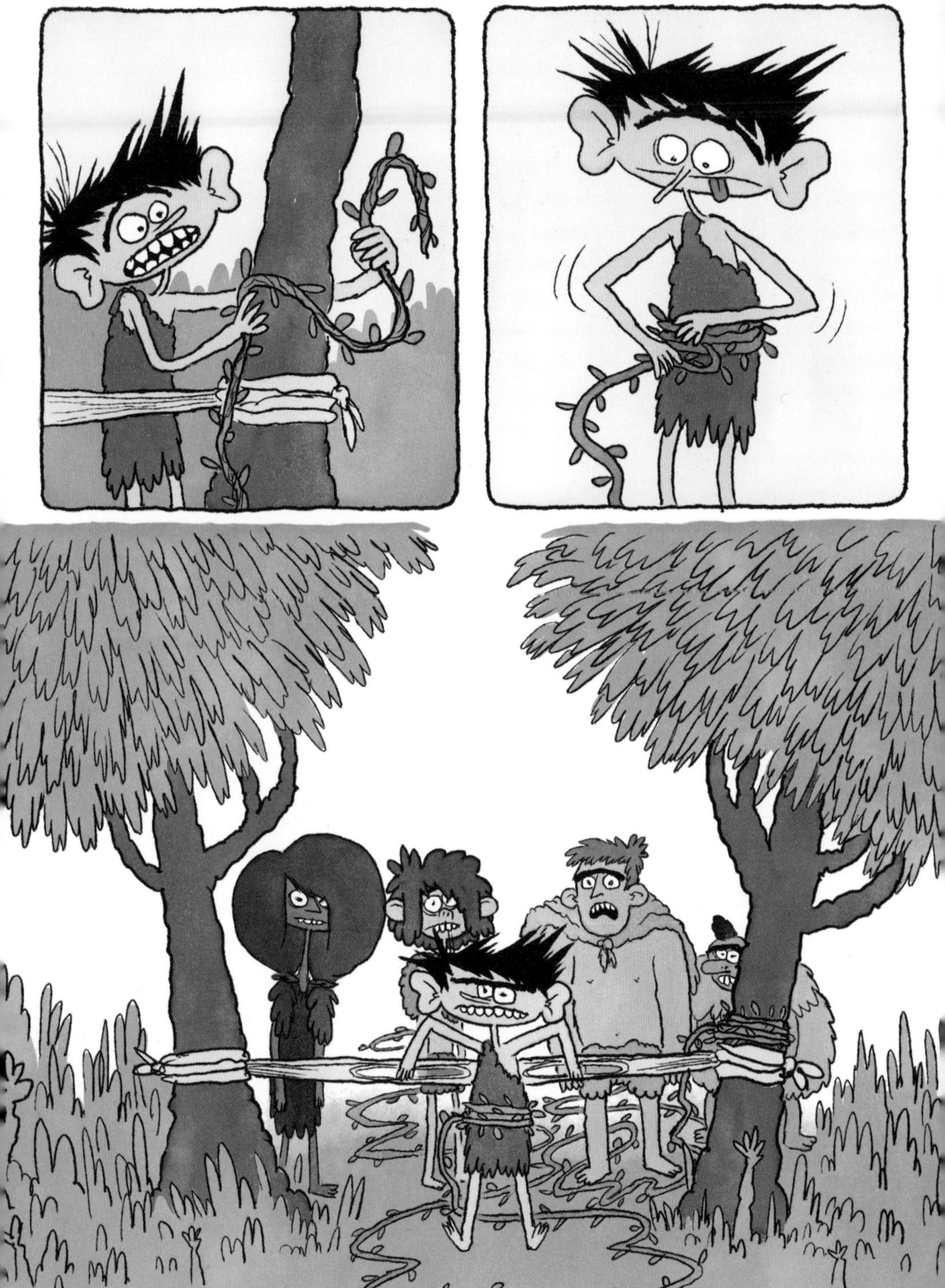

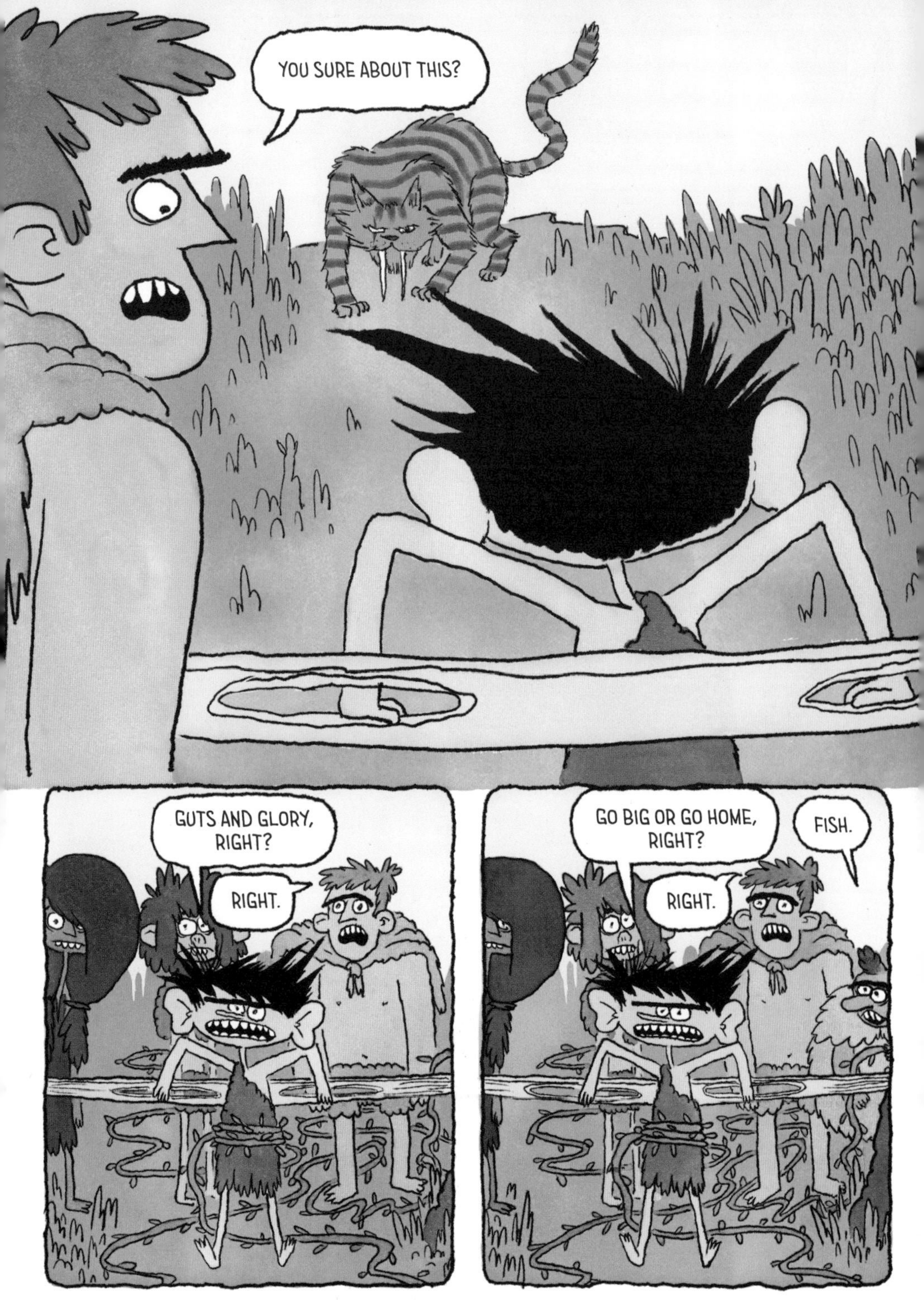
YOU SURE ABOUT THIS?
GUTS AND GLORY, RIGHT?
RIGHT.
GO BIG OR GO HOME, RIGHT?
RIGHT.
FISH.

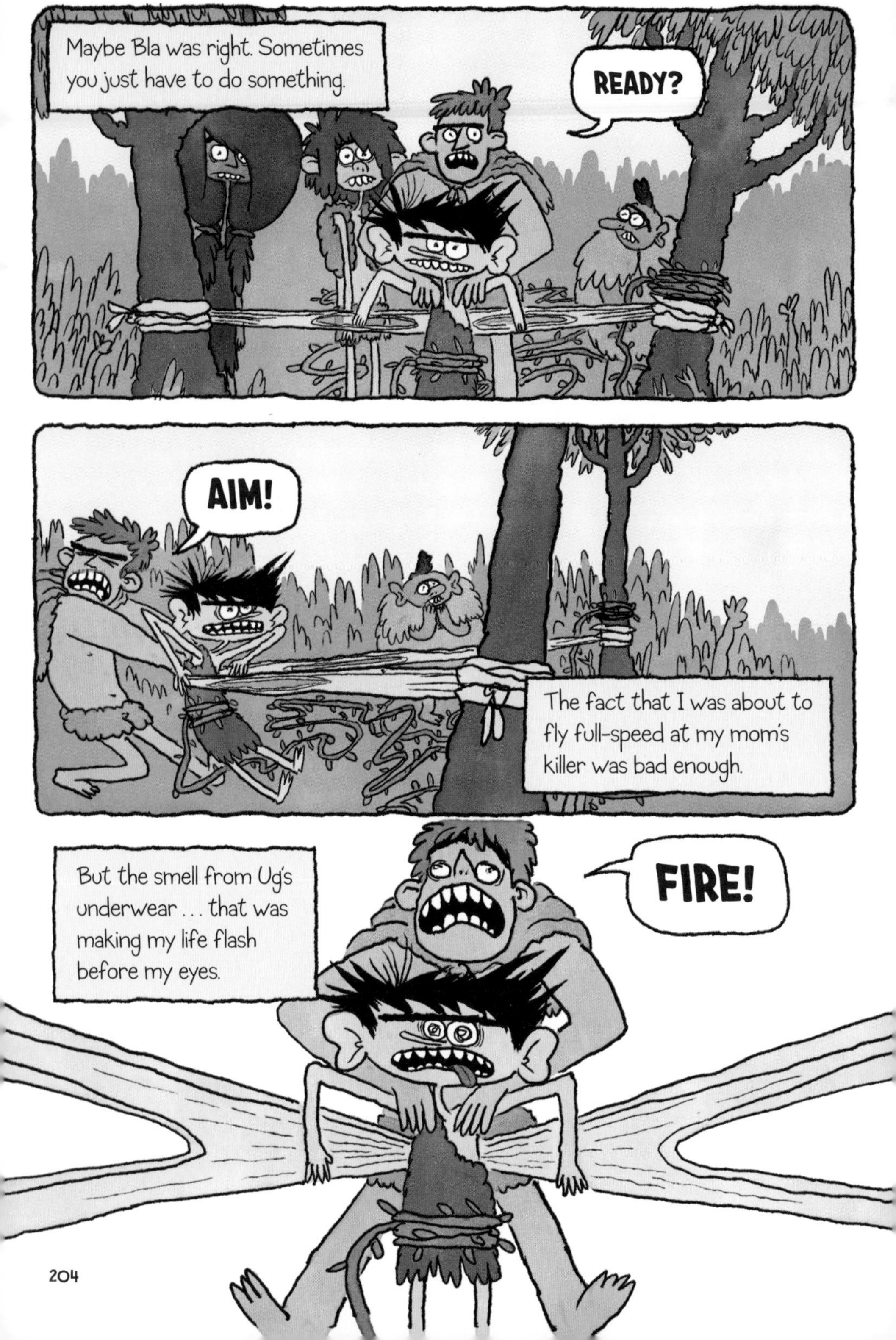
Maybe Bla was right. Sometimes you just have to do something.
READY?
AIM!
The fact that I was about to fly full-speed at my mom's killer was bad enough.
But the smell from Ug's underwear . . . that was making my life flash before my eyes.
FIRE!

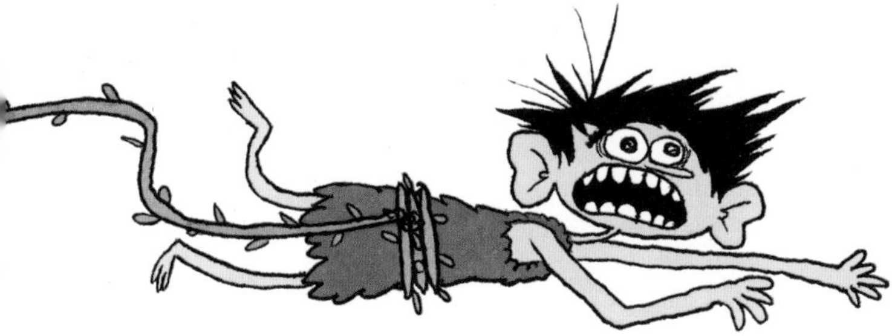

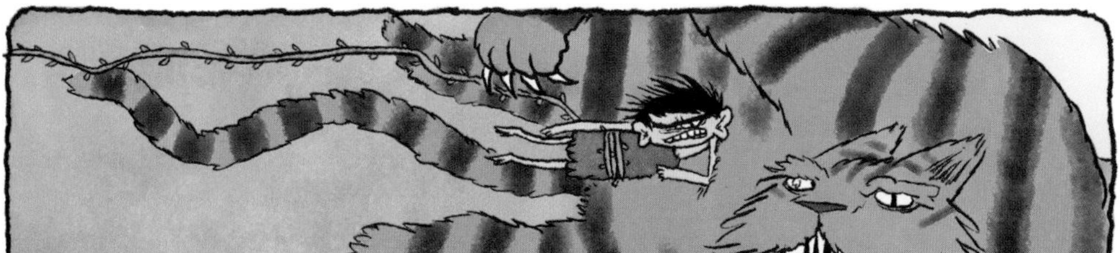

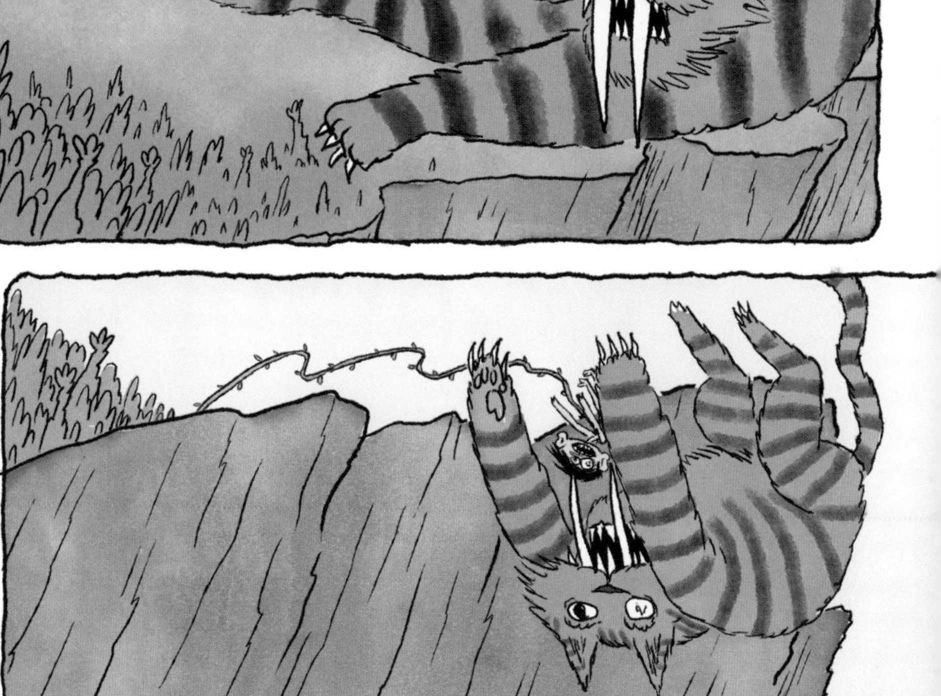

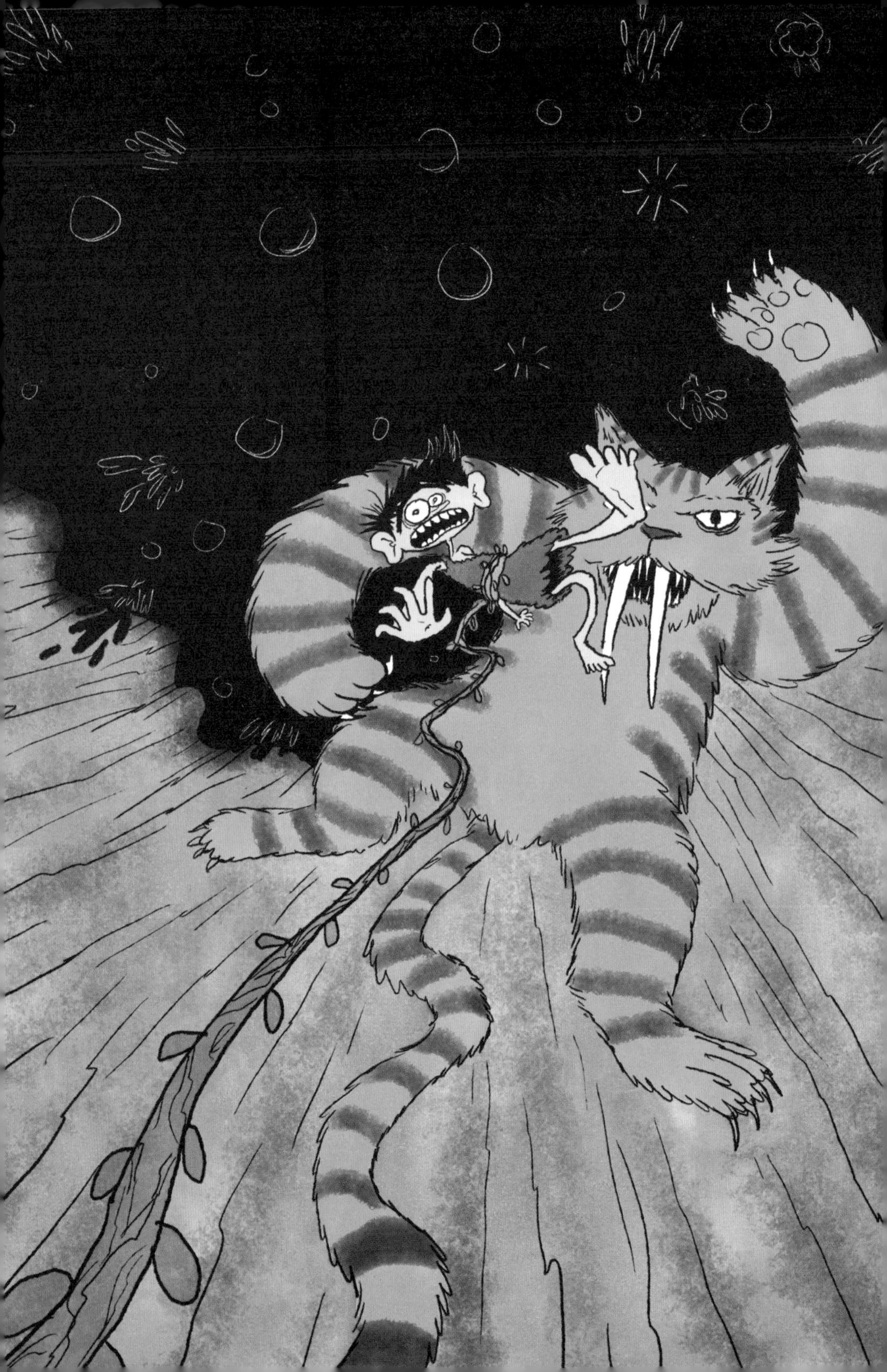

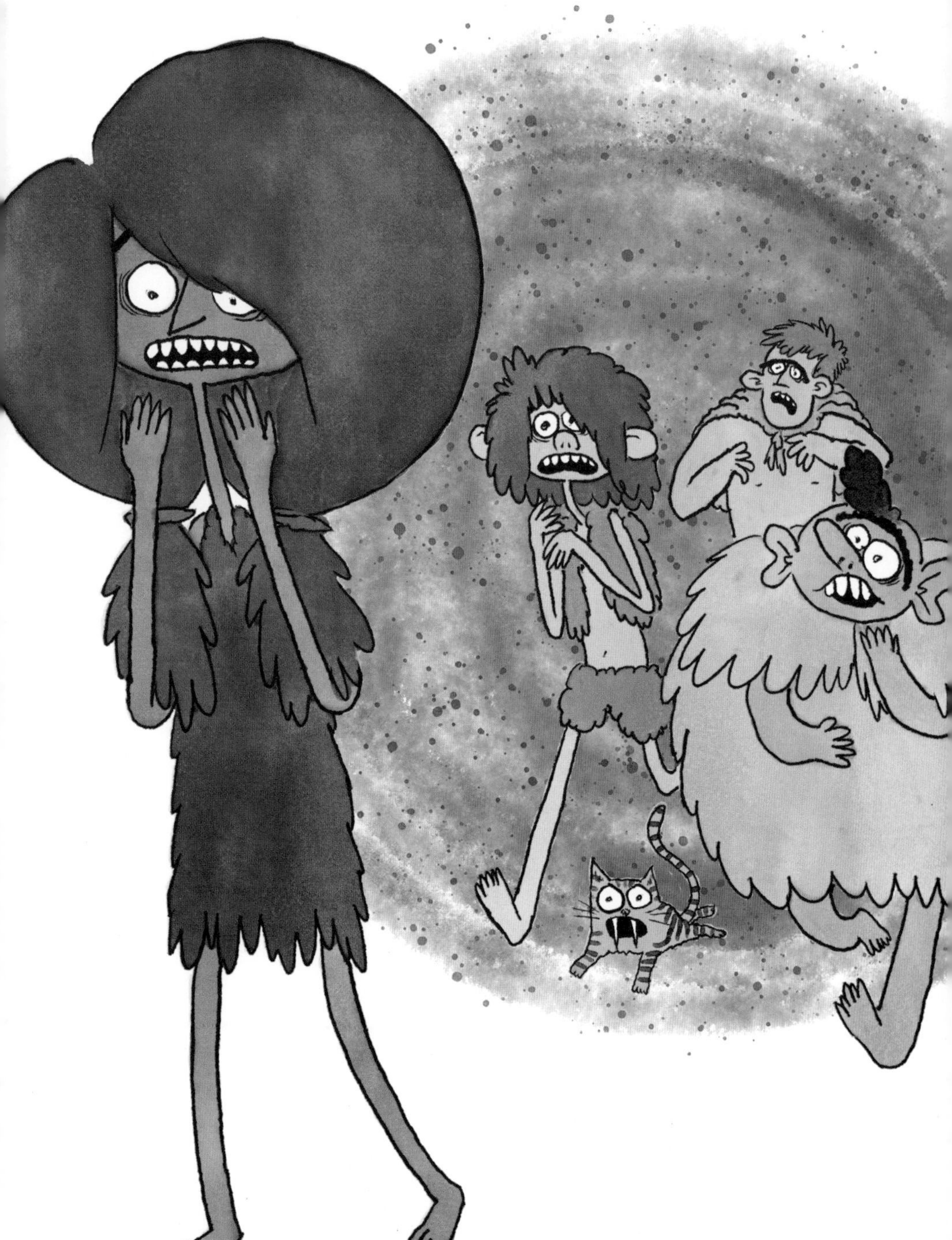

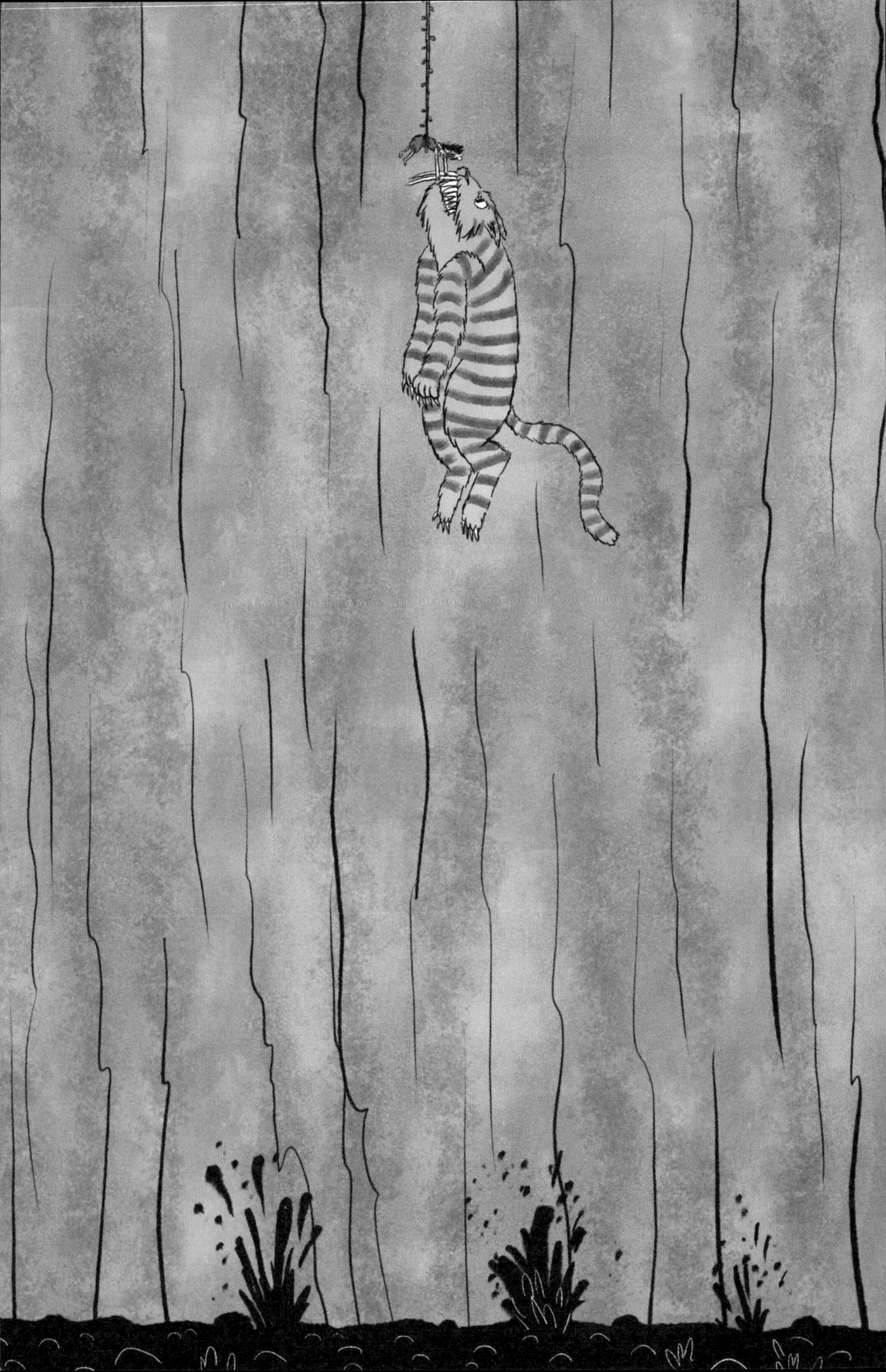

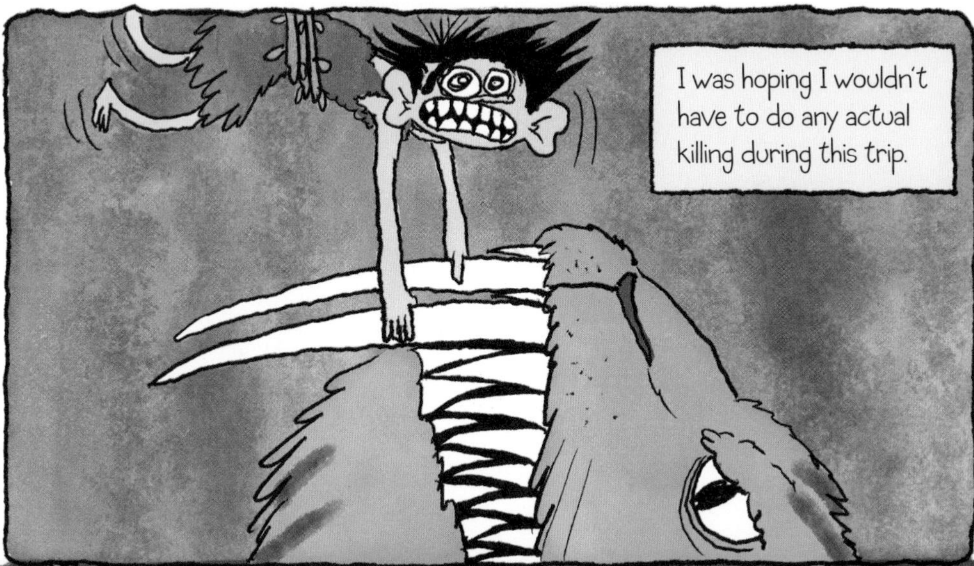
I was hoping I wouldn't have to do any actual killing during this trip.

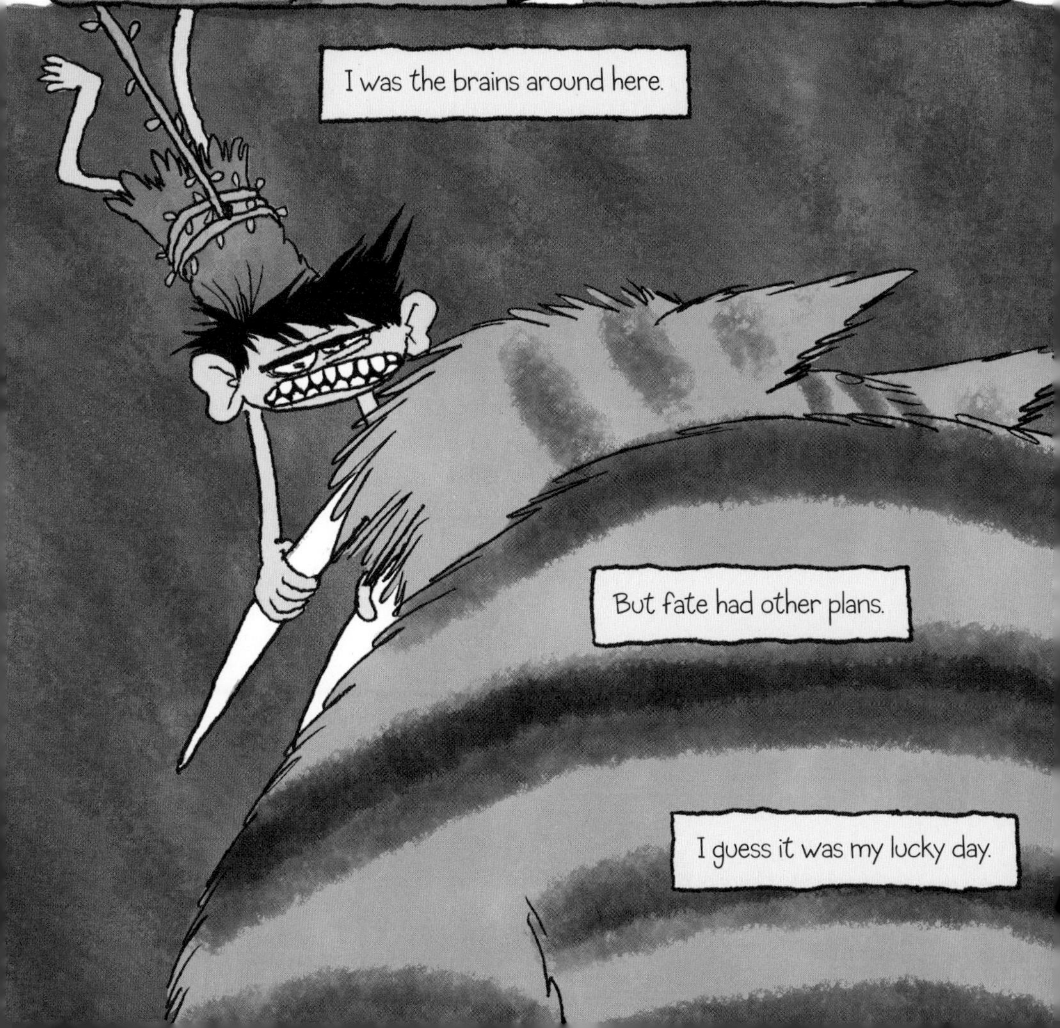
I was the brains around here.
But fate had other plans.
I guess it was my lucky day.

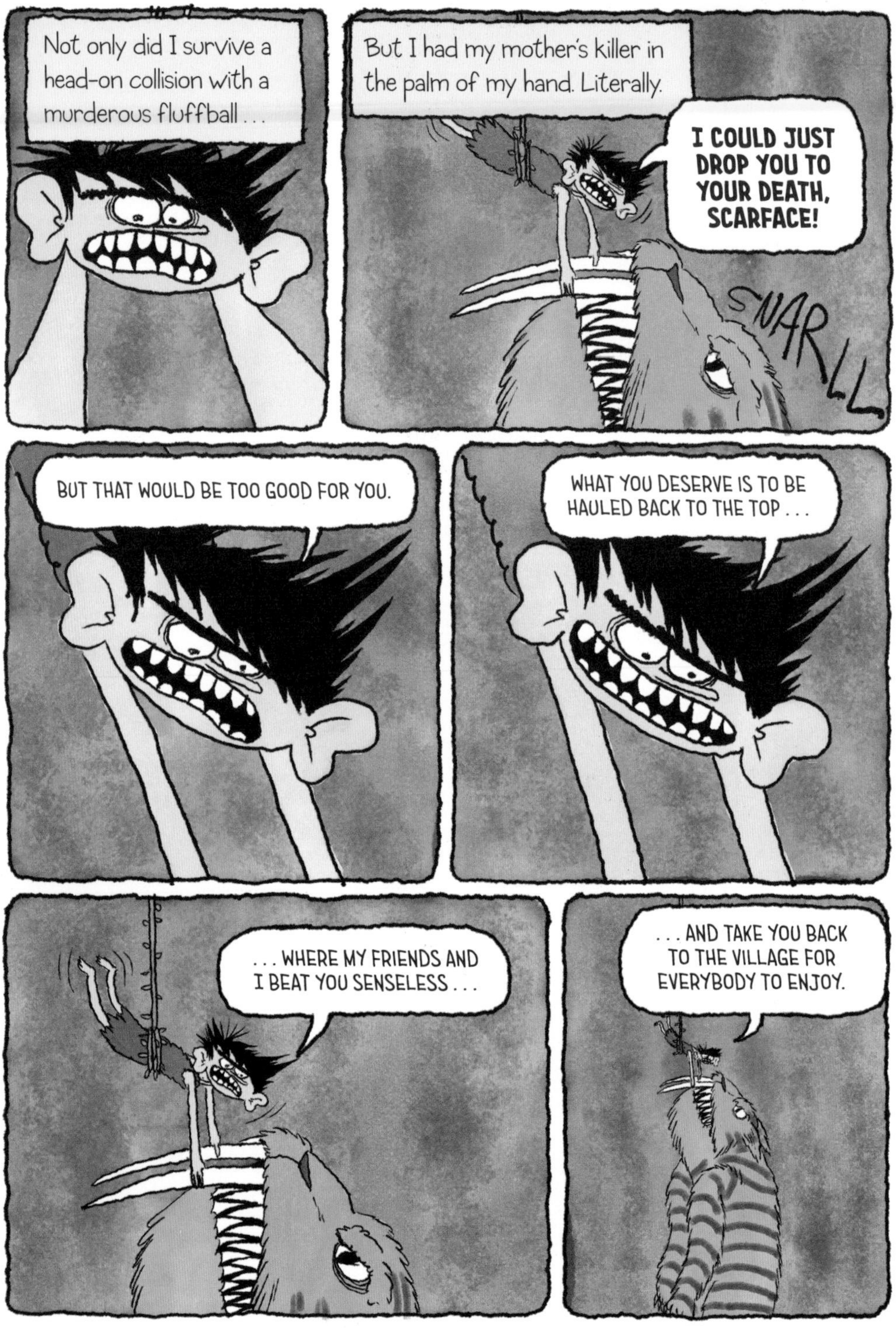
Not only did I survive a head-on collision with a murderous fluffball . . .
But I had my mother's killer in the palm of my hand. Literally.
I COULD JUST DROP YOU TO YOUR DEATH, SCARFACE!
SNARLL
BUT THAT WOULD BE TOO GOOD FOR YOU.
WHAT YOU DESERVE IS TO BE HAULED BACK TO THE TOP . . .
. . . WHERE MY FRIENDS AND I BEAT YOU SENSELESS . . .
. . . AND TAKE YOU BACK TO THE VILLAGE FOR EVERYBODY TO ENJOY.

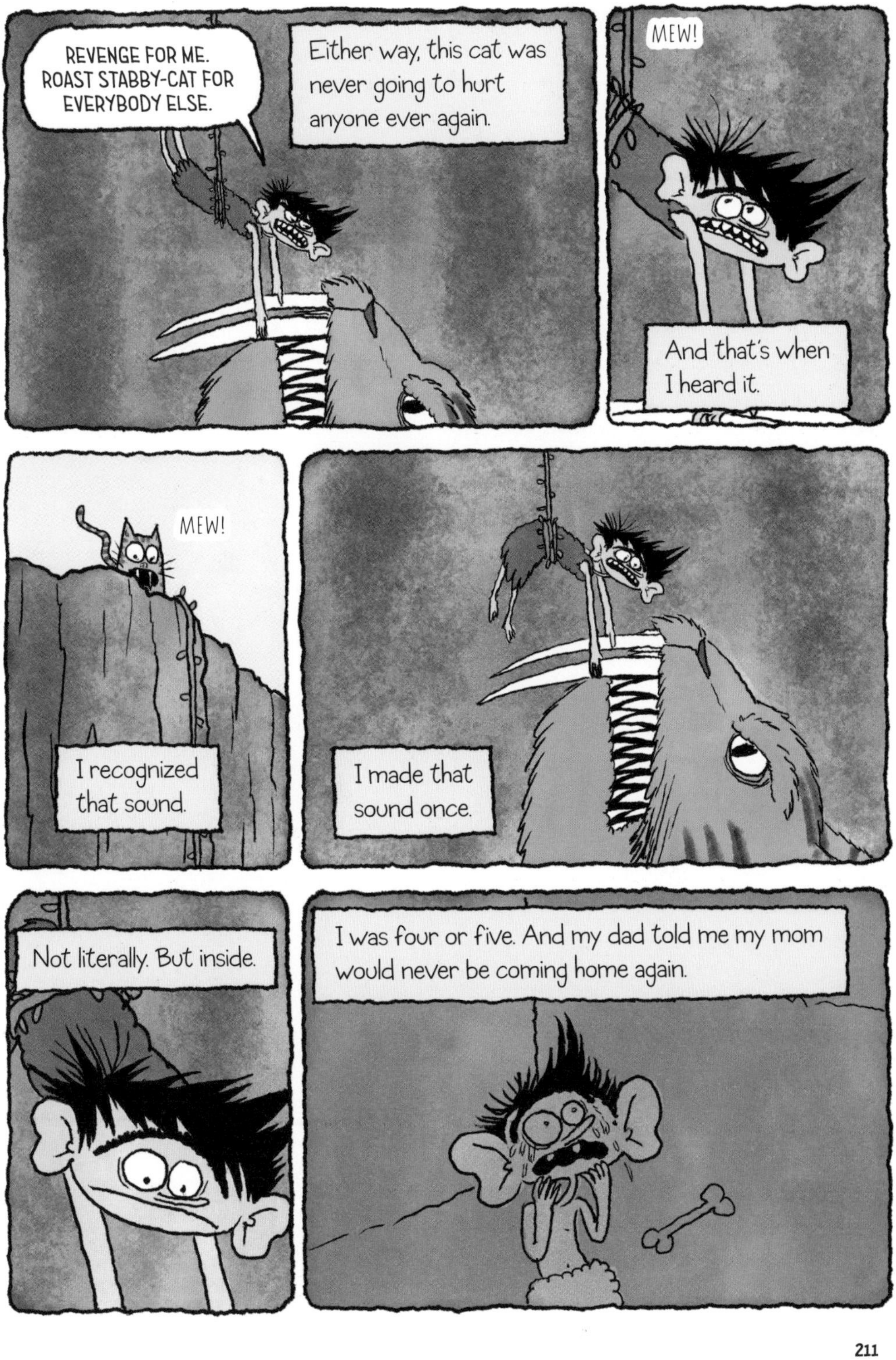

REVENGE FOR ME. ROAST STABBY-CAT FOR EVERYBODY ELSE.
Either way, this cat was never going to hurt anyone ever again.
MEW!
And that's when I heard it.
MEW!
I recognized that sound.
I made that sound once.
Not literally. But inside.
I was four or five. And my dad told me my mom would never be coming home again.

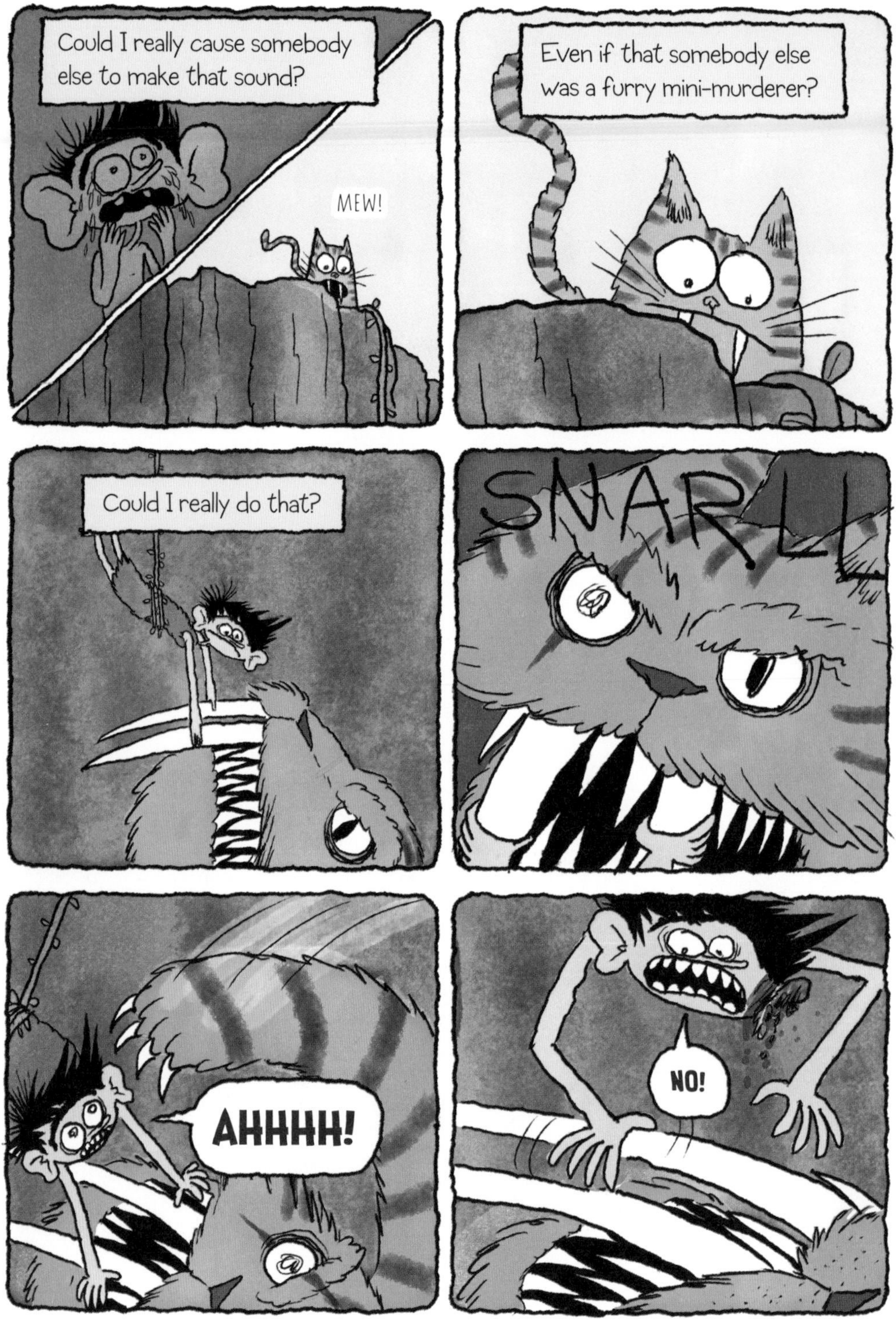
Could I really cause somebody else to make that sound?
MEW!
Even if that somebody else was a furry mini-murderer?
Could I really do that?
SNARLL
AHHHH!
NO!

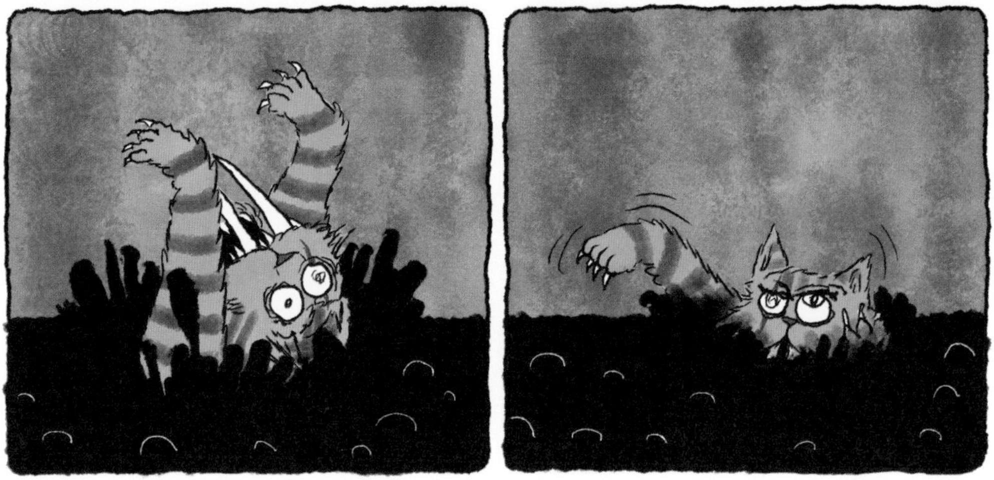

I guess I could.

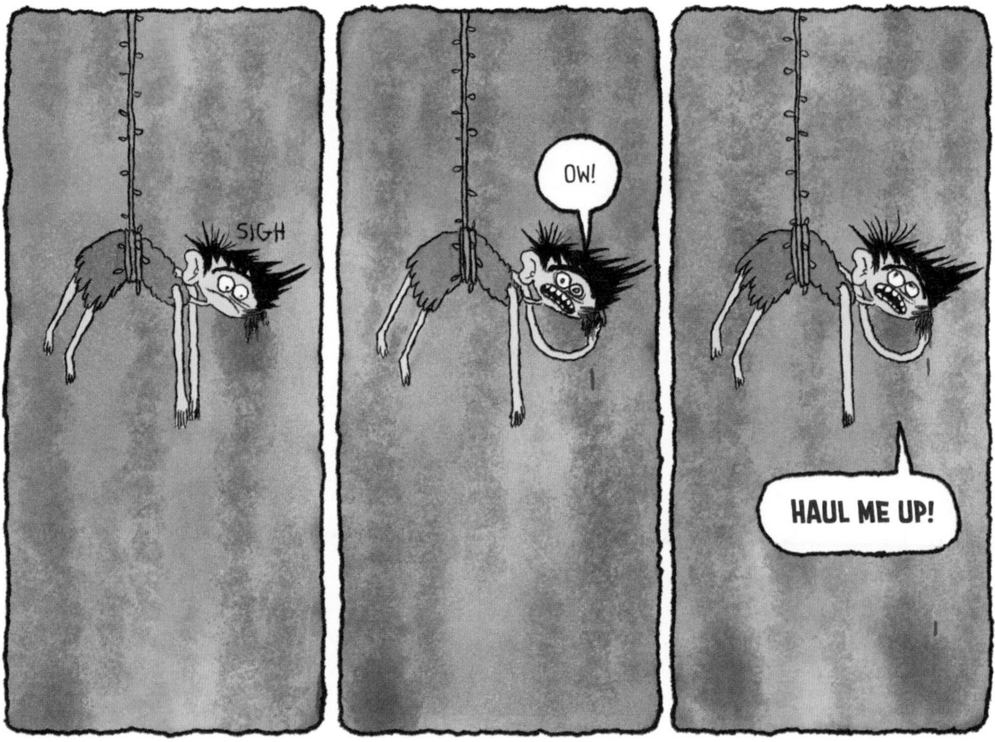
SIGH
OW!
HAUL ME UP!

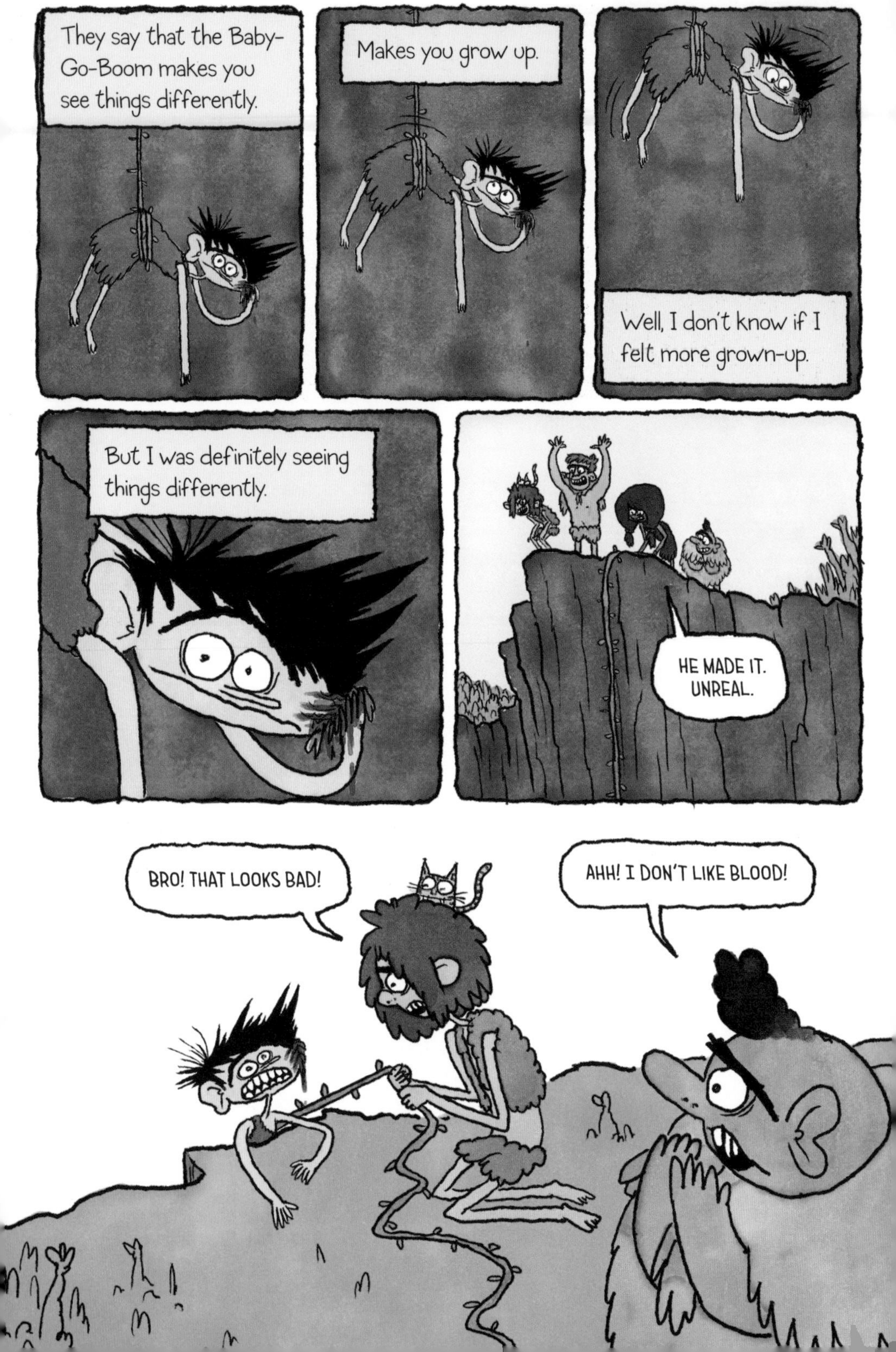
They say that the Baby-Go-Boom makes you see things differently.
Makes you grow up.
Well, I don't know if I felt more grown-up.
But I was definitely seeing things differently.
HE MADE IT. UNREAL.
BRO! THAT LOOKS BAD!
AHH! I DON'T LIKE BLOOD!

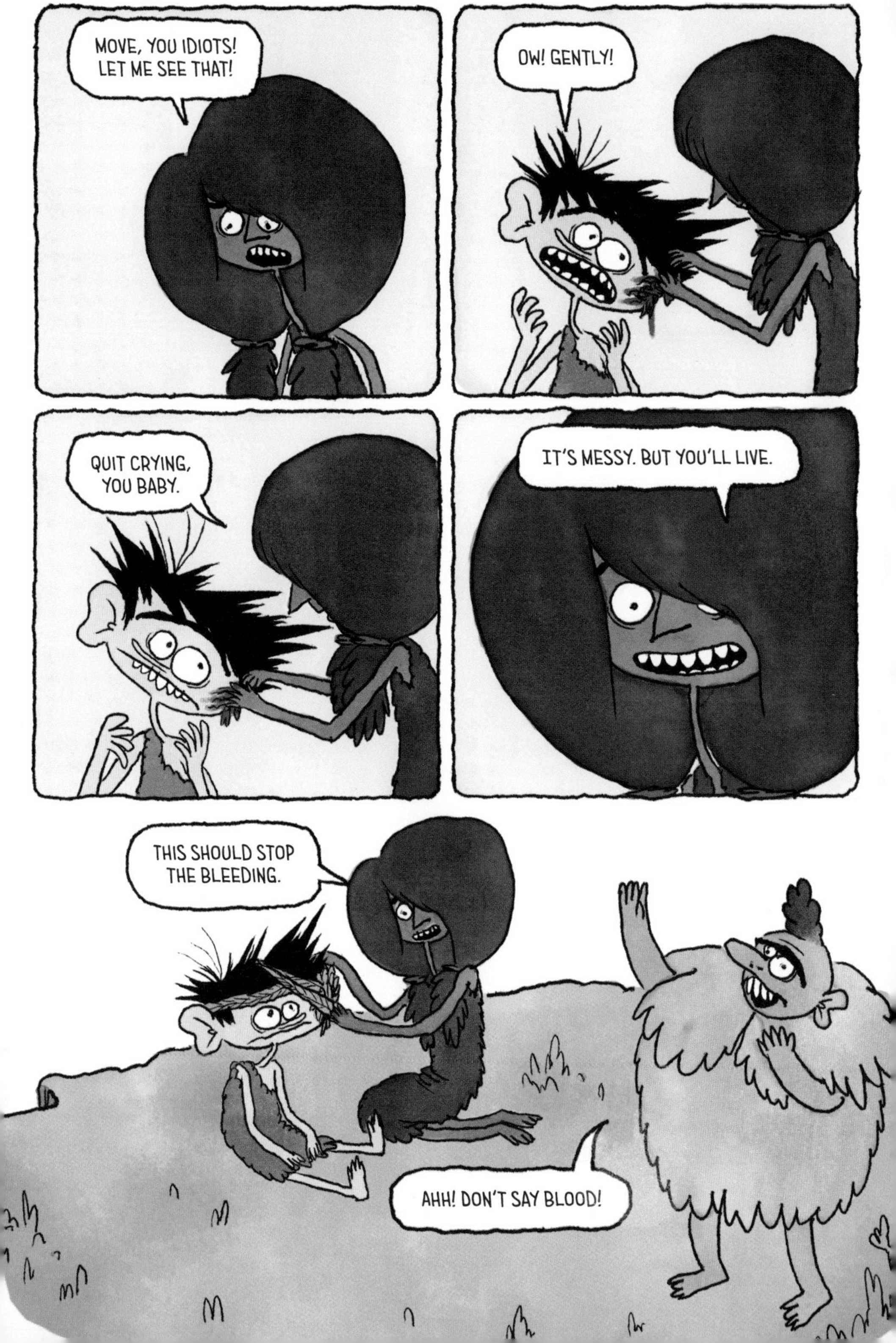
MOVE, YOU IDIOTS! LET ME SEE THAT!
OW! GENTLY!
QUIT CRYING, YOU BABY.
IT'S MESSY. BUT YOU'LL LIVE.
THIS SHOULD STOP THE BLEEDING.
AHH! DON'T SAY BLOOD!

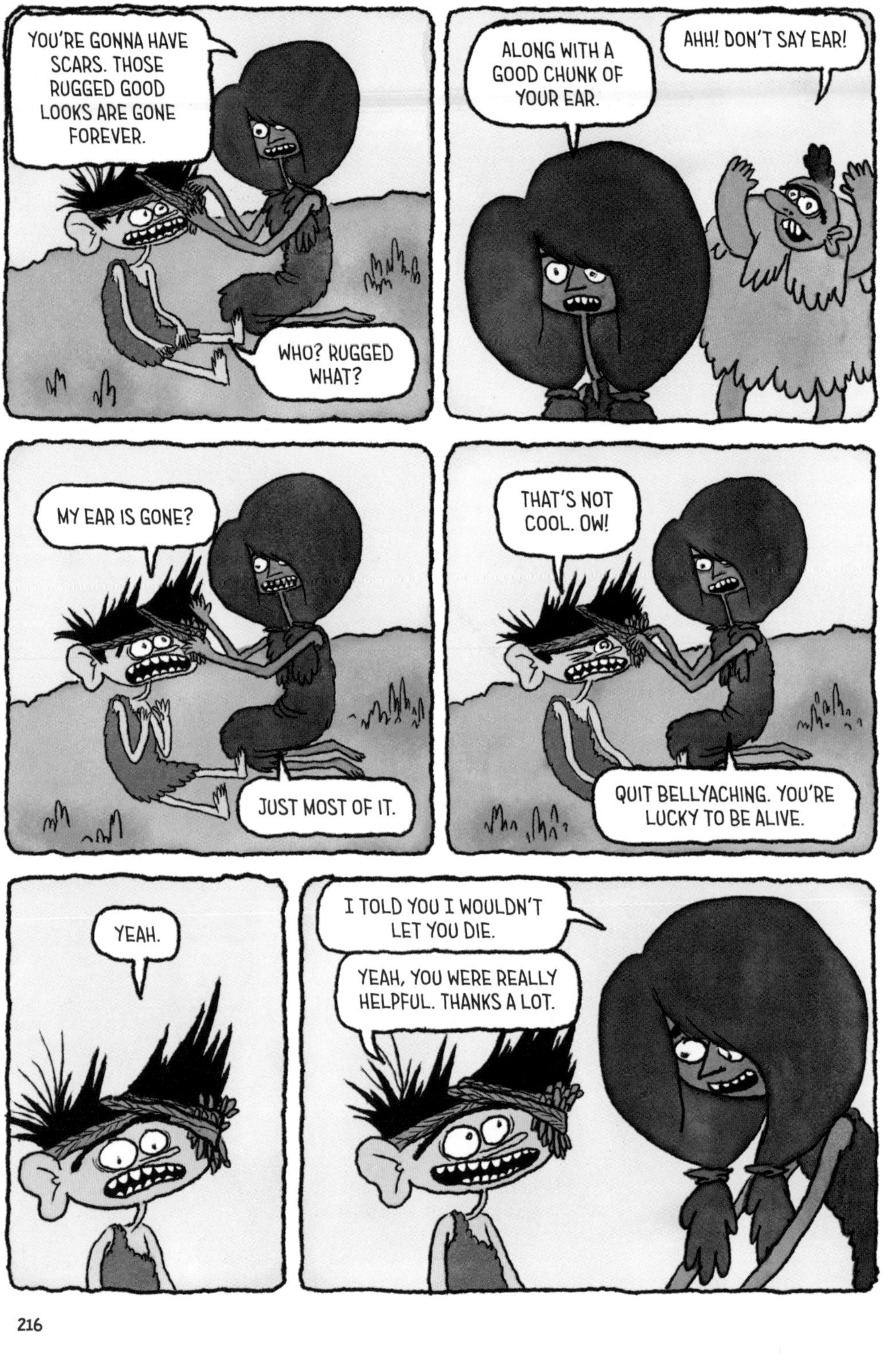
YOU'RE GONNA HAVE SCARS. THOSE RUGGED GOOD LOOKS ARE GONE FOREVER.
WHO? RUGGED WHAT?
ALONG WITH A GOOD CHUNK OF YOUR EAR.
AHH! DON'T SAY EAR!
MY EAR IS GONE?
JUST MOST OF IT.
THAT'S NOT COOL. OW!
QUIT BELLYACHING. YOU'RE LUCKY TO BE ALIVE.
YEAH.
I TOLD YOU I WOULDN'T LET YOU DIE.
YEAH, YOU WERE REALLY HELPFUL. THANKS A LOT.

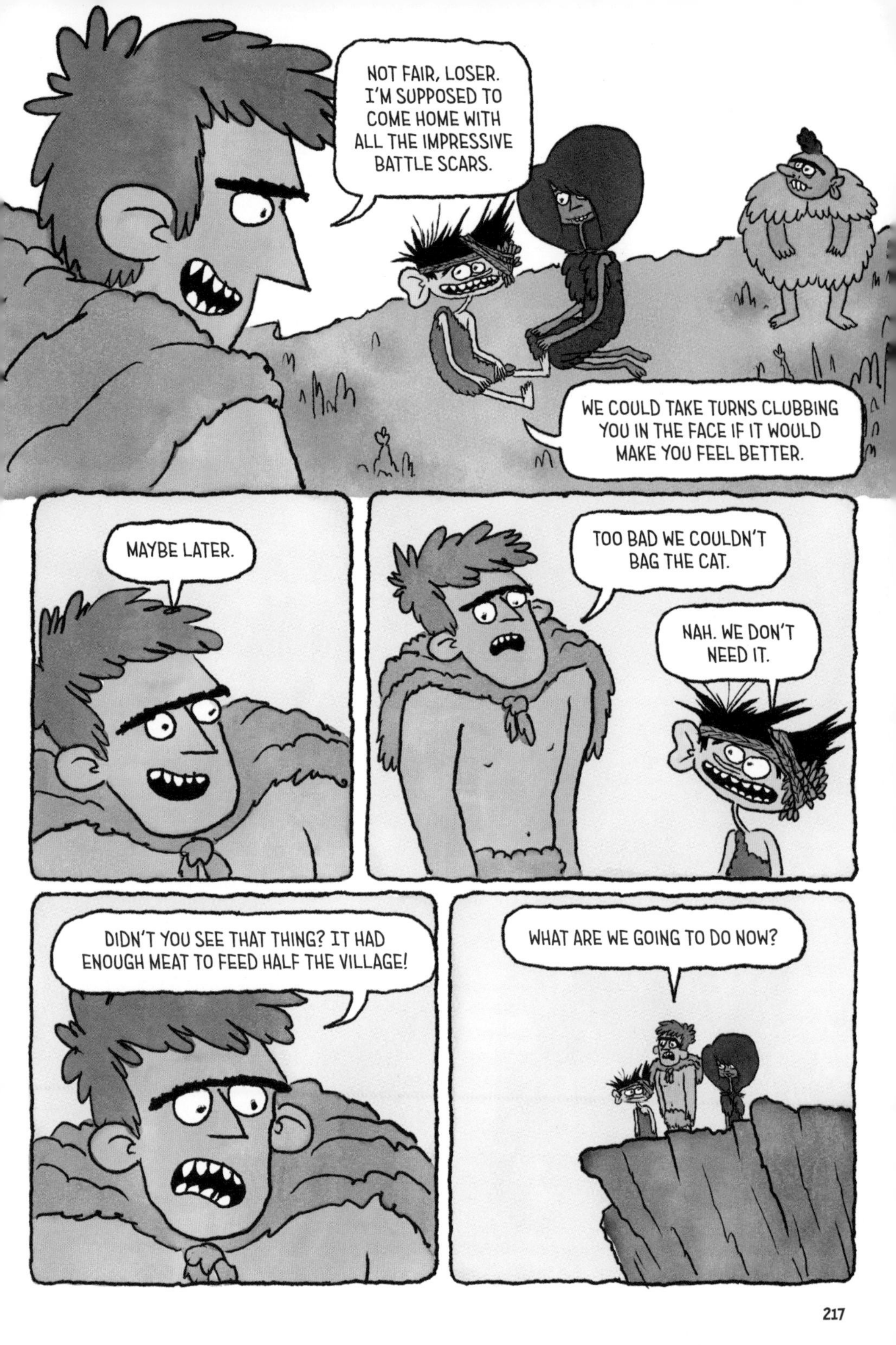
NOT FAIR, LOSER. I'M SUPPOSED TO COME HOME WITH ALL THE IMPRESSIVE BATTLE SCARS.
WE COULD TAKE TURNS CLUBBING YOU IN THE FACE IF IT WOULD MAKE YOU FEEL BETTER.
MAYBE LATER.
TOO BAD WE COULDN'T BAG THE CAT.
NAH. WE DON'T NEED IT.
DIDN'T YOU SEE THAT THING? IT HAD ENOUGH MEAT TO FEED HALF THE VILLAGE!
WHAT ARE WE GOING TO DO NOW?

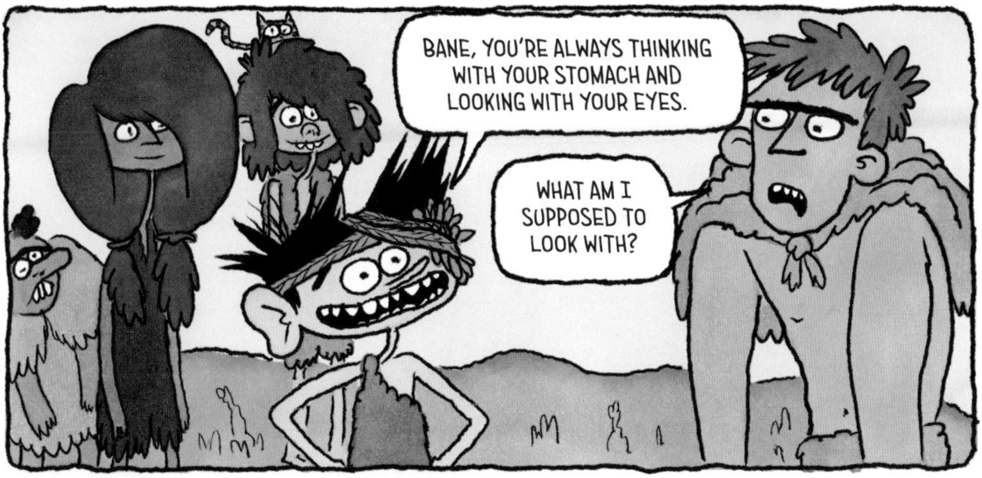
BANE, YOU'RE ALWAYS THINKING WITH YOUR STOMACH AND LOOKING WITH YOUR EYES.
WHAT AM I SUPPOSED TO LOOK WITH?

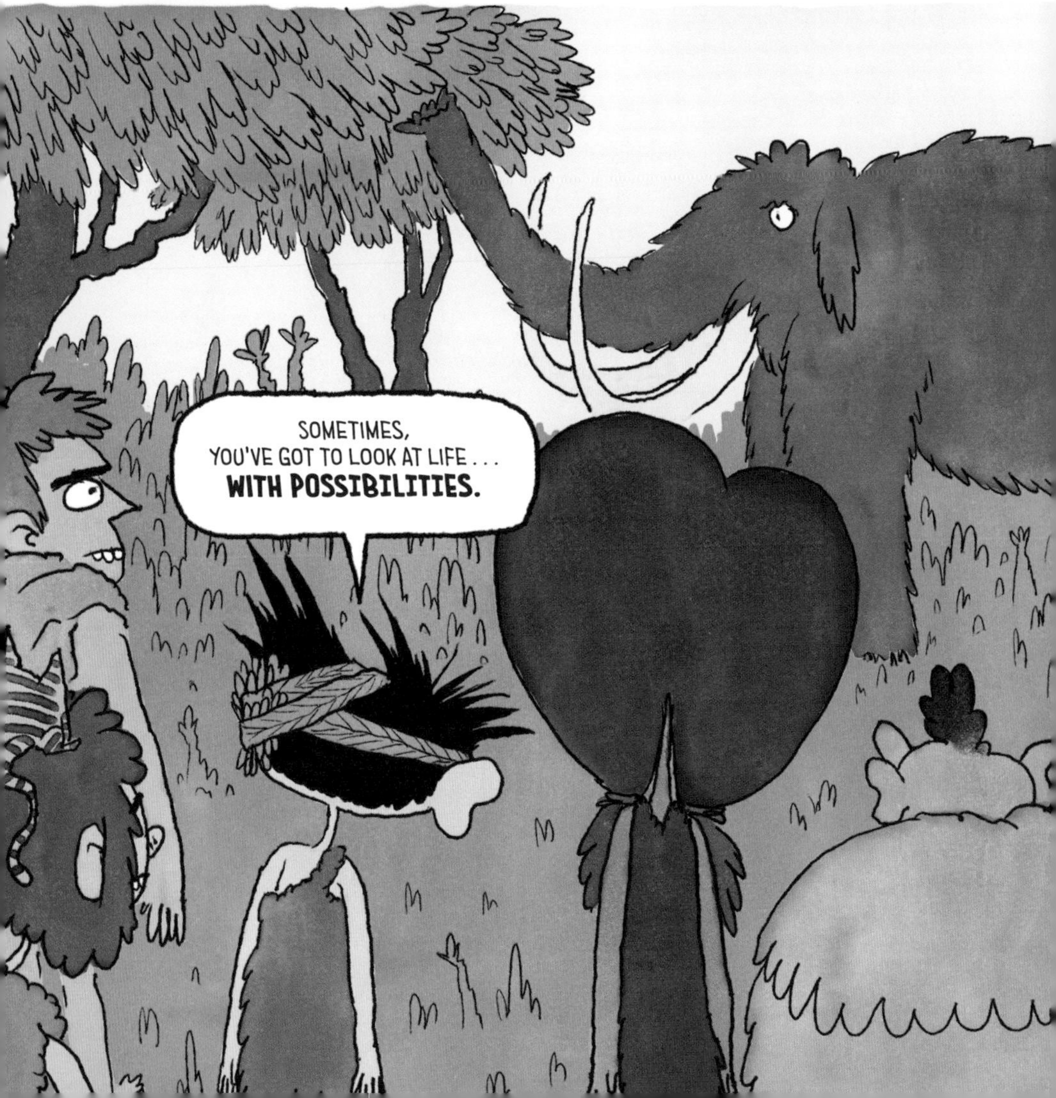
SOMETIMES, YOU'VE GOT TO LOOK AT LIFE . . . **WITH POSSIBILITIES.**

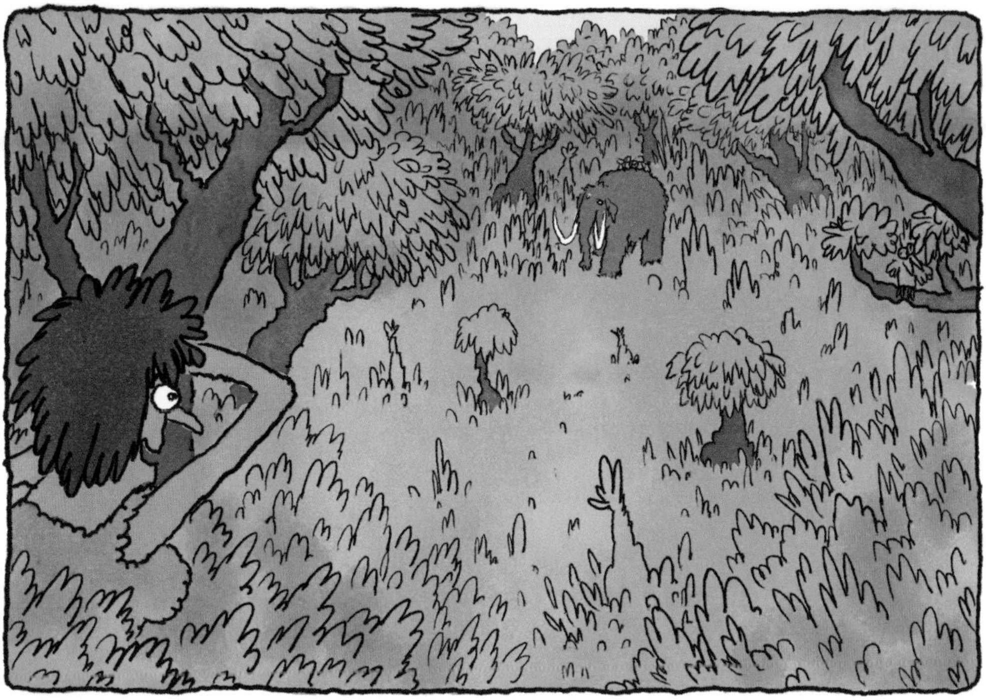

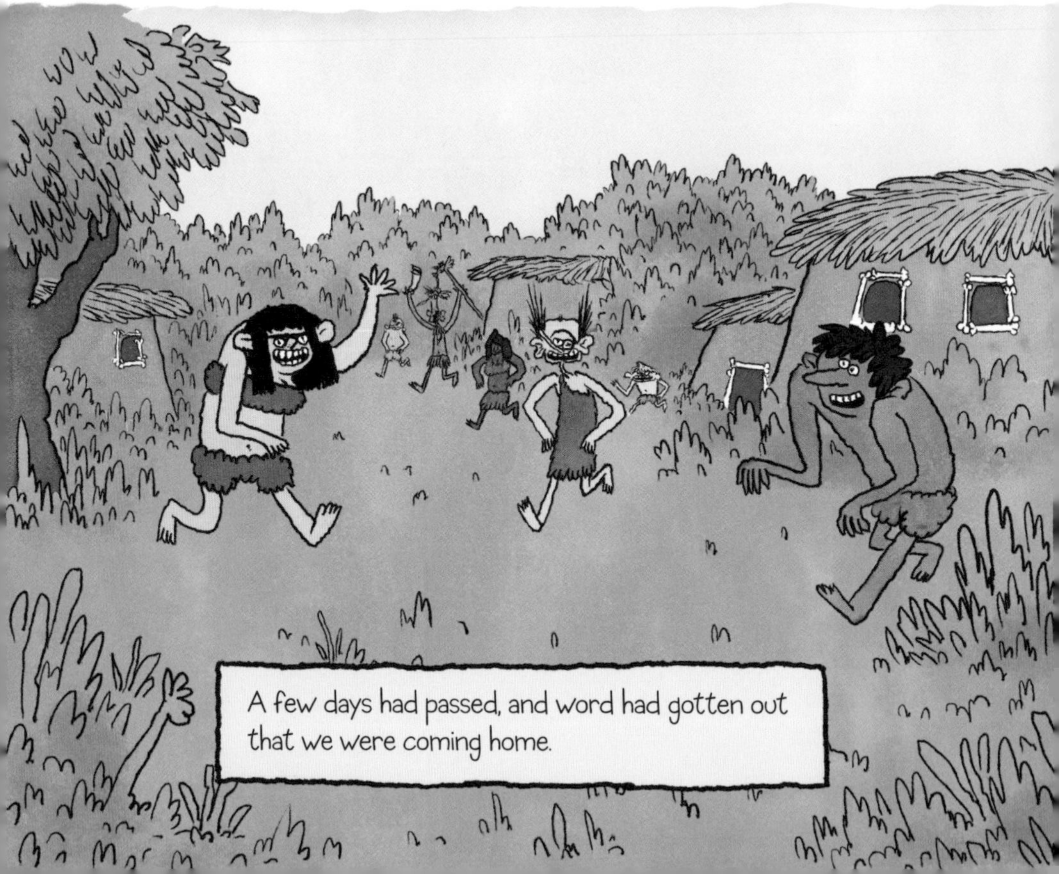
A few days had passed, and word had gotten out that we were coming home.

Everyone had gathered to see the mighty hunters return with their kill.

What they actually saw ... they never expected.

IT'S A FEROCIOUS MONSTER!

WE'RE UNDER ATTACK!

EVERYBODY RUN!

PEOPLE! STOP THE HYSTERICS!

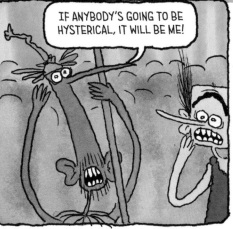

IF ANYBODY'S GOING TO BE HYSTERICAL, IT WILL BE ME!

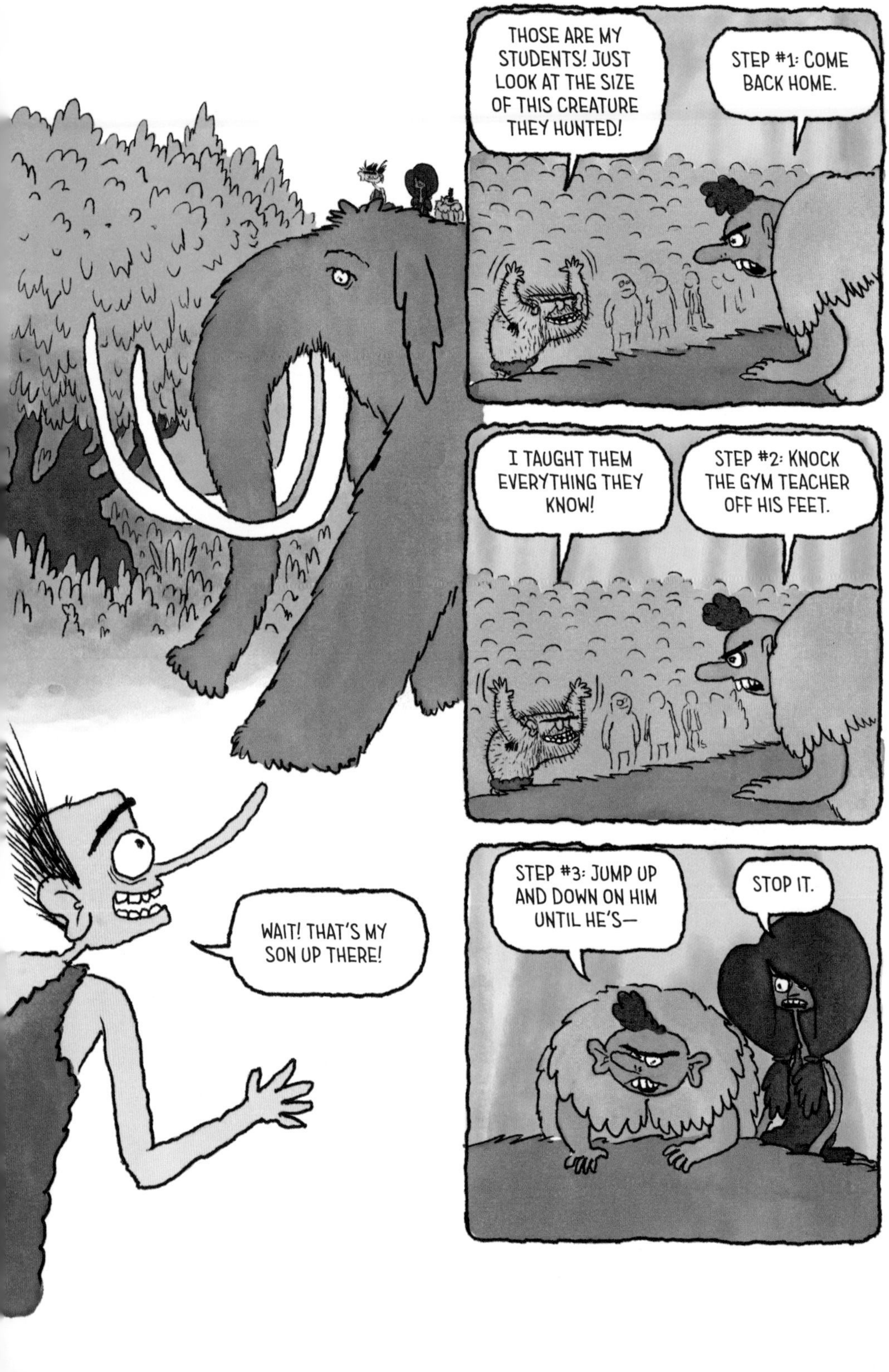
THOSE ARE MY STUDENTS! JUST LOOK AT THE SIZE OF THIS CREATURE THEY HUNTED!
STEP #1: COME BACK HOME.
I TAUGHT THEM EVERYTHING THEY KNOW!
STEP #2: KNOCK THE GYM TEACHER OFF HIS FEET.
WAIT! THAT'S MY SON UP THERE!
STEP #3: JUMP UP AND DOWN ON HIM UNTIL HE'S—
STOP IT.

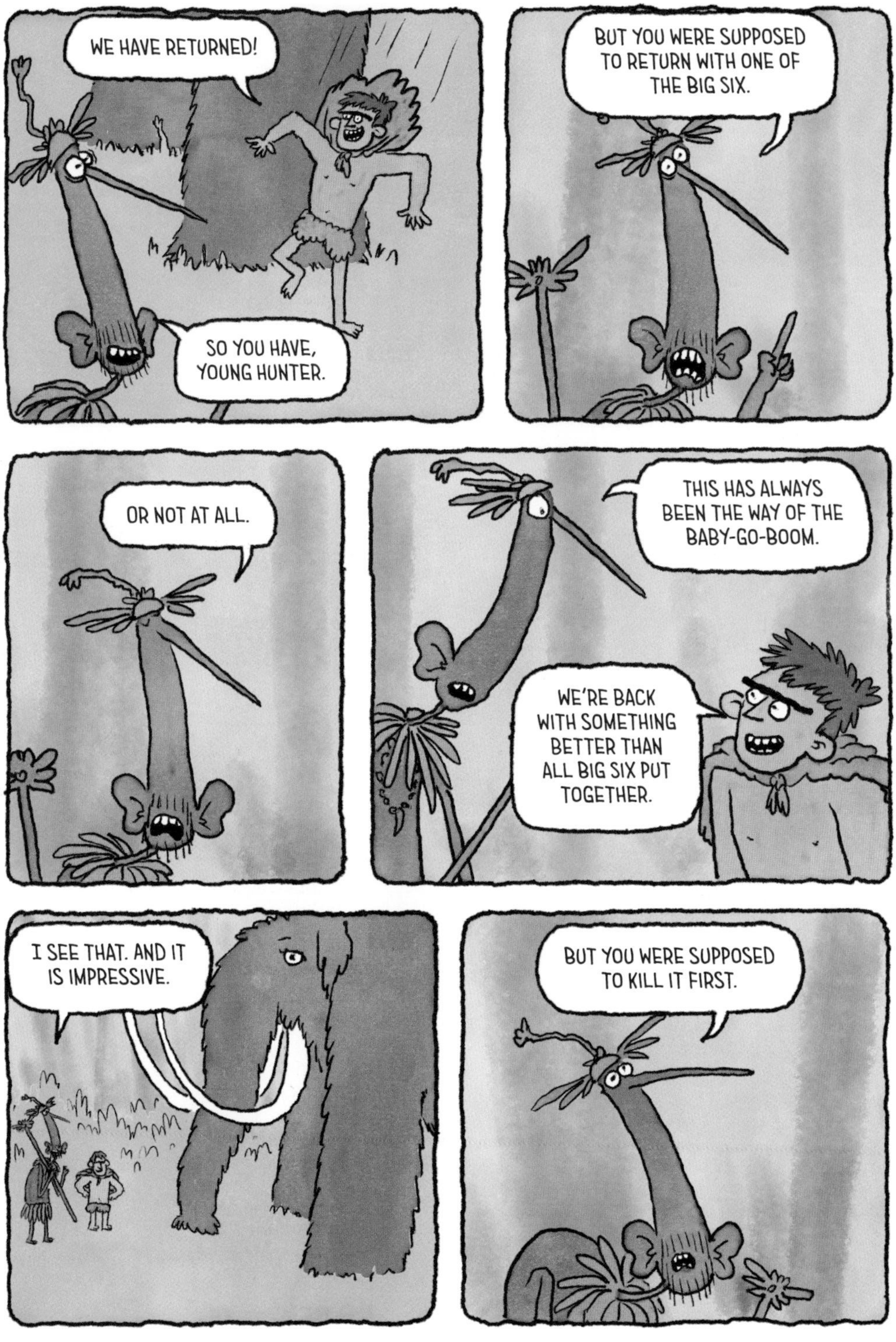
WE HAVE RETURNED!
SO YOU HAVE, YOUNG HUNTER.
BUT YOU WERE SUPPOSED TO RETURN WITH ONE OF THE BIG SIX.
OR NOT AT ALL.
THIS HAS ALWAYS BEEN THE WAY OF THE BABY-GO-BOOM.
WE'RE BACK WITH SOMETHING BETTER THAN ALL BIG SIX PUT TOGETHER.
I SEE THAT. AND IT IS IMPRESSIVE.
BUT YOU WERE SUPPOSED TO KILL IT FIRST.

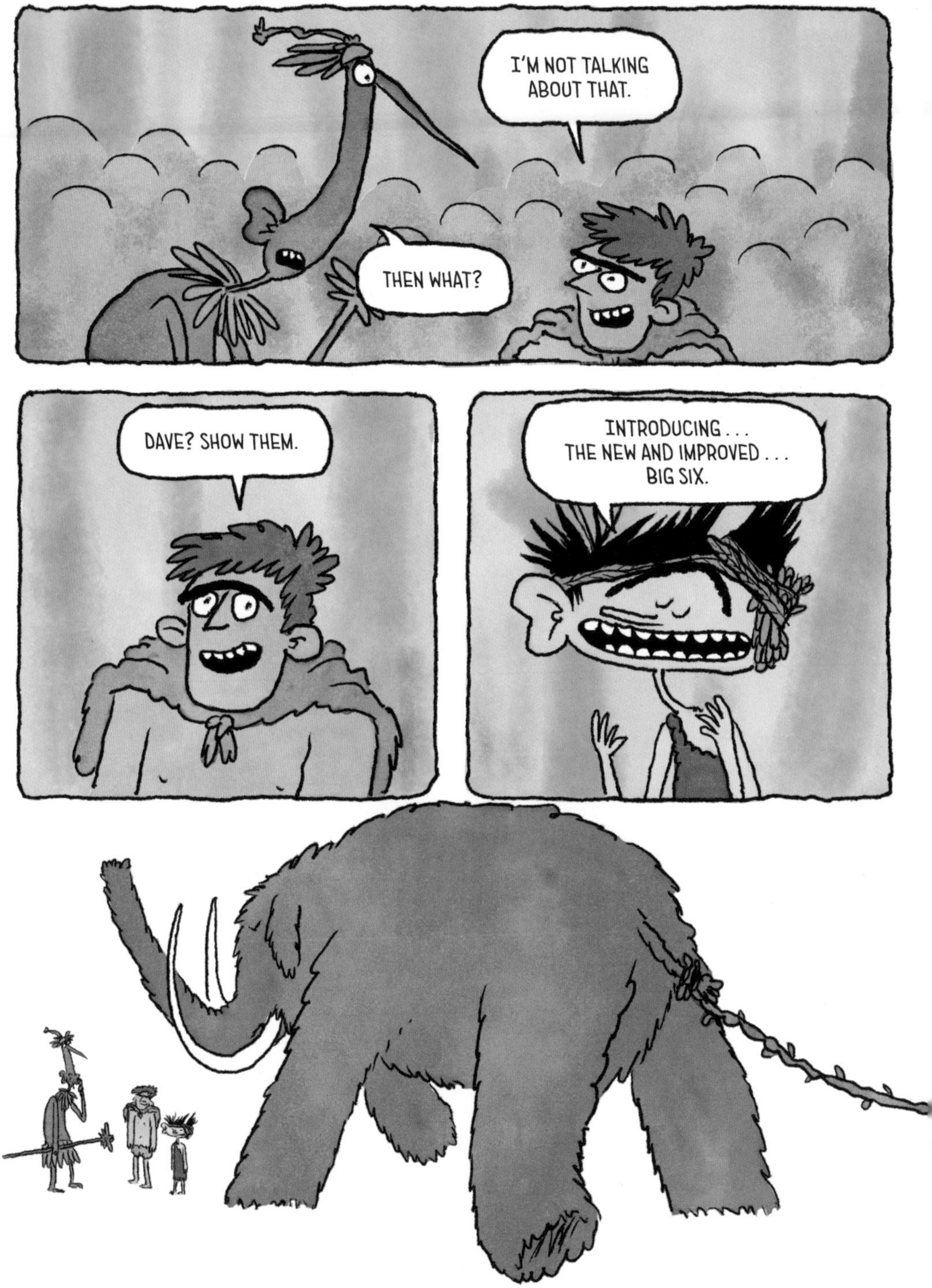
I'M NOT TALKING ABOUT THAT.
THEN WHAT?
DAVE? SHOW THEM.
INTRODUCING . . . THE NEW AND IMPROVED . . . BIG SIX.

FRESH FROM THE HUNT.

Mushrooms

Munch-munch leaf

(spinach)

Tree rocks

(walnuts)

Foody pebbles

(berries)

Toot-toots

(garbanzo beans)

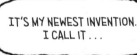

Leafmeat

(lettuce)

IT'S MY NEWEST INVENTION. I CALL IT . . .

The Salad Bar!

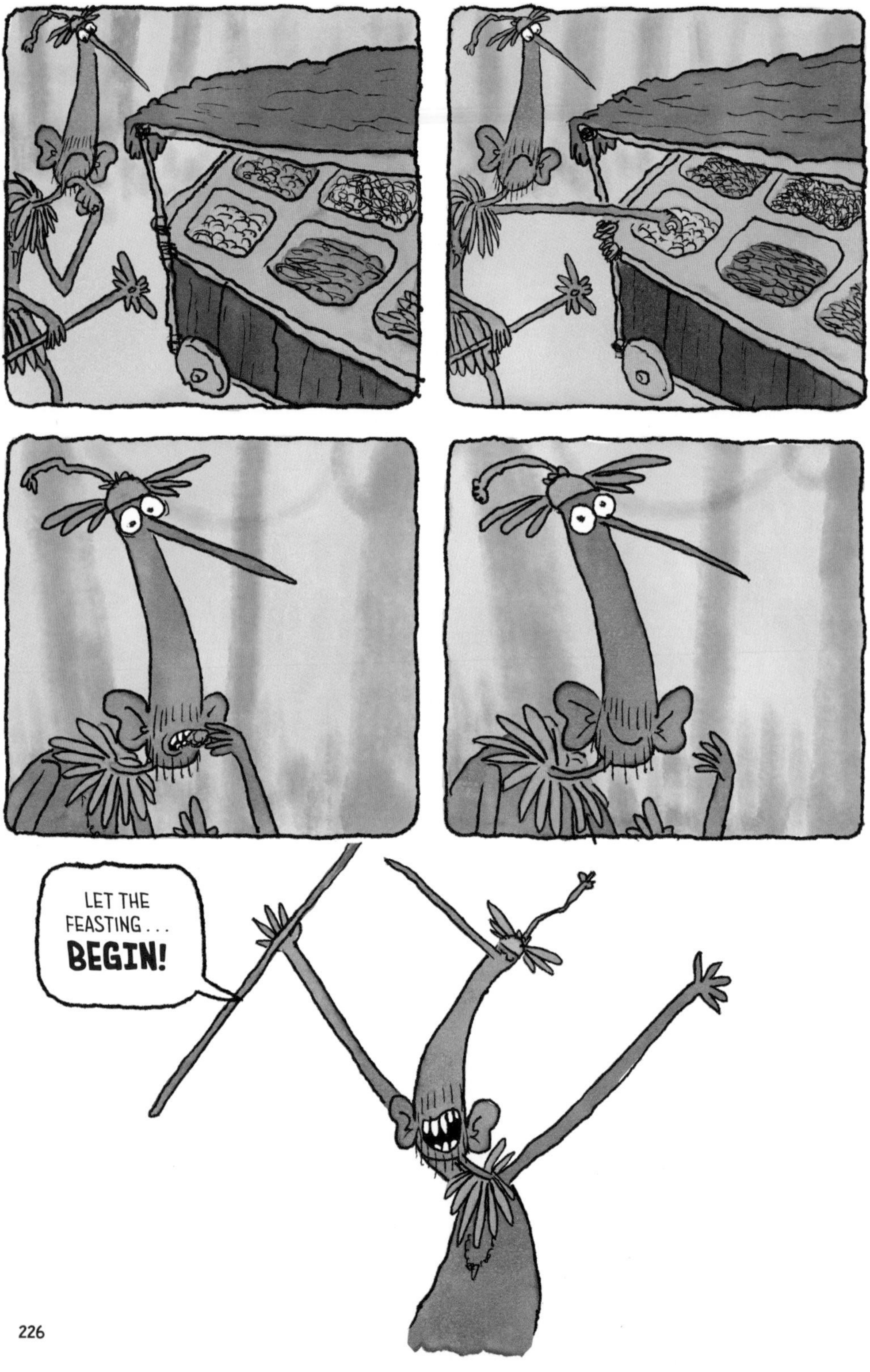
LET THE FEASTING . . . BEGIN!

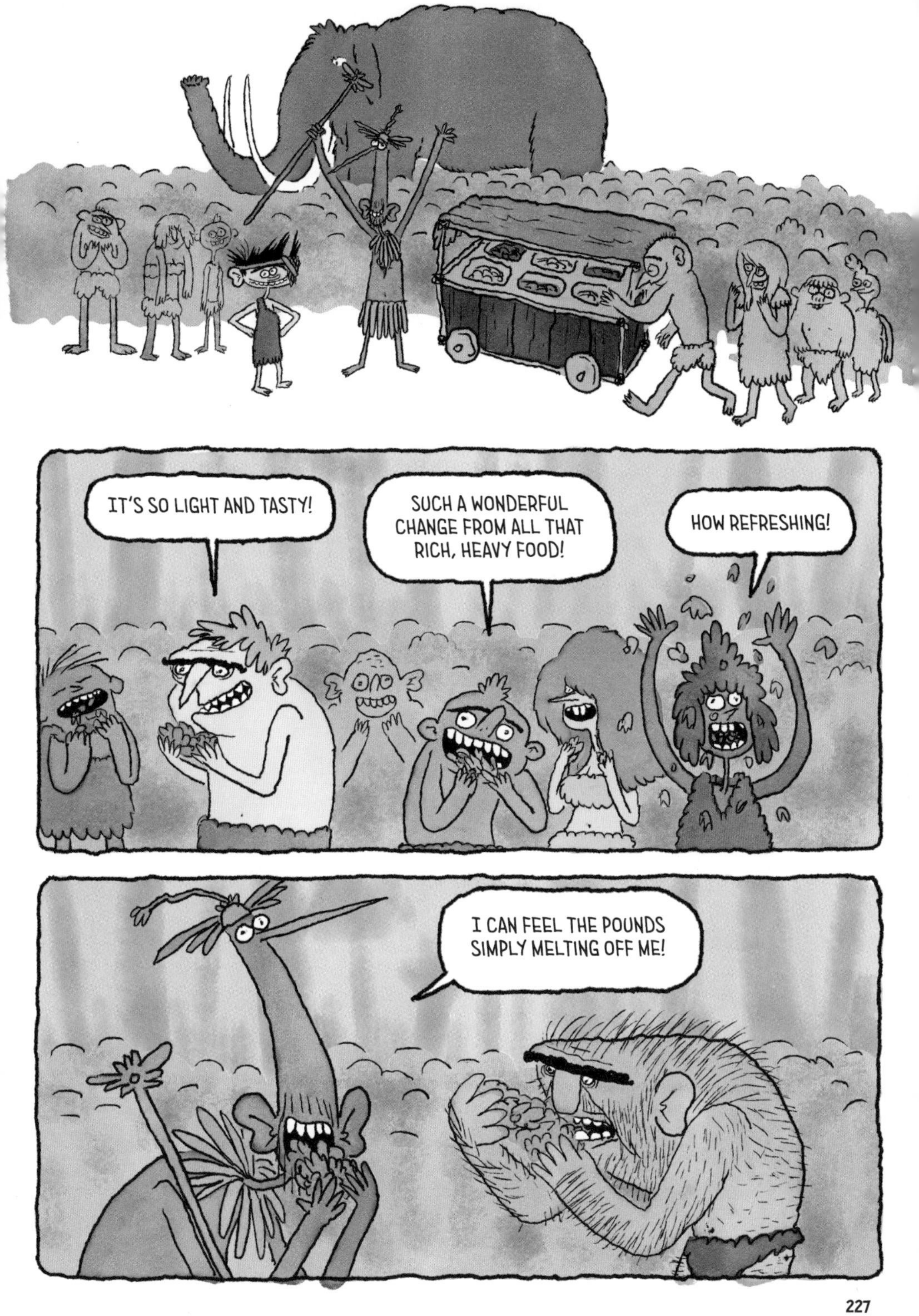
IT'S SO LIGHT AND TASTY!
SUCH A WONDERFUL CHANGE FROM ALL THAT RICH, HEAVY FOOD!
HOW REFRESHING!
I CAN FEEL THE POUNDS SIMPLY MELTING OFF ME!

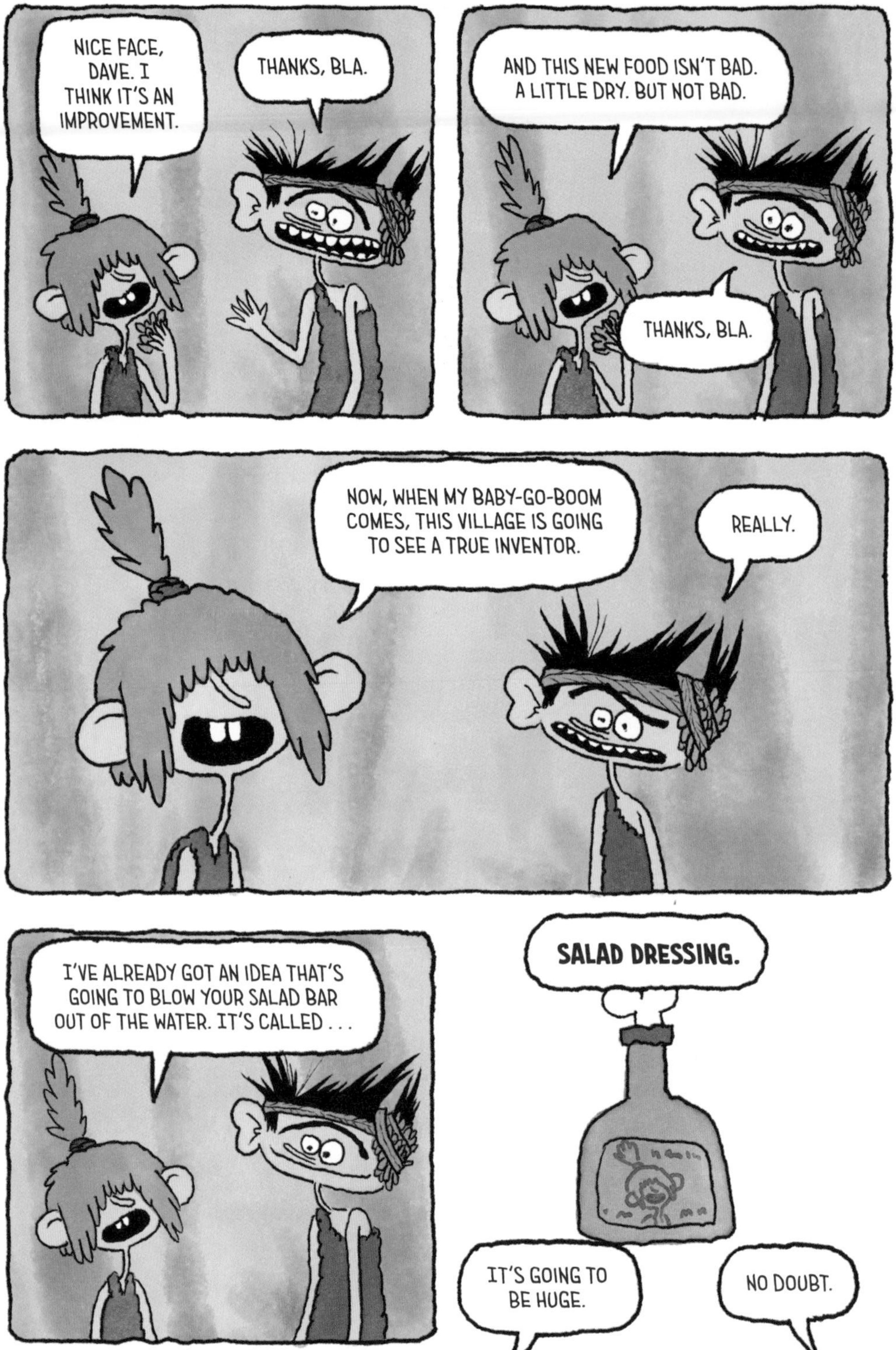
NICE FACE, DAVE. I THINK IT'S AN IMPROVEMENT.
THANKS, BLA.
AND THIS NEW FOOD ISN'T BAD. A LITTLE DRY. BUT NOT BAD.
THANKS, BLA.
NOW, WHEN MY BABY-GO-BOOM COMES, THIS VILLAGE IS GOING TO SEE A TRUE INVENTOR.
REALLY.
I'VE ALREADY GOT AN IDEA THAT'S GOING TO BLOW YOUR SALAD BAR OUT OF THE WATER. IT'S CALLED . . .
SALAD DRESSING.
IT'S GOING TO BE HUGE.
NO DOUBT.

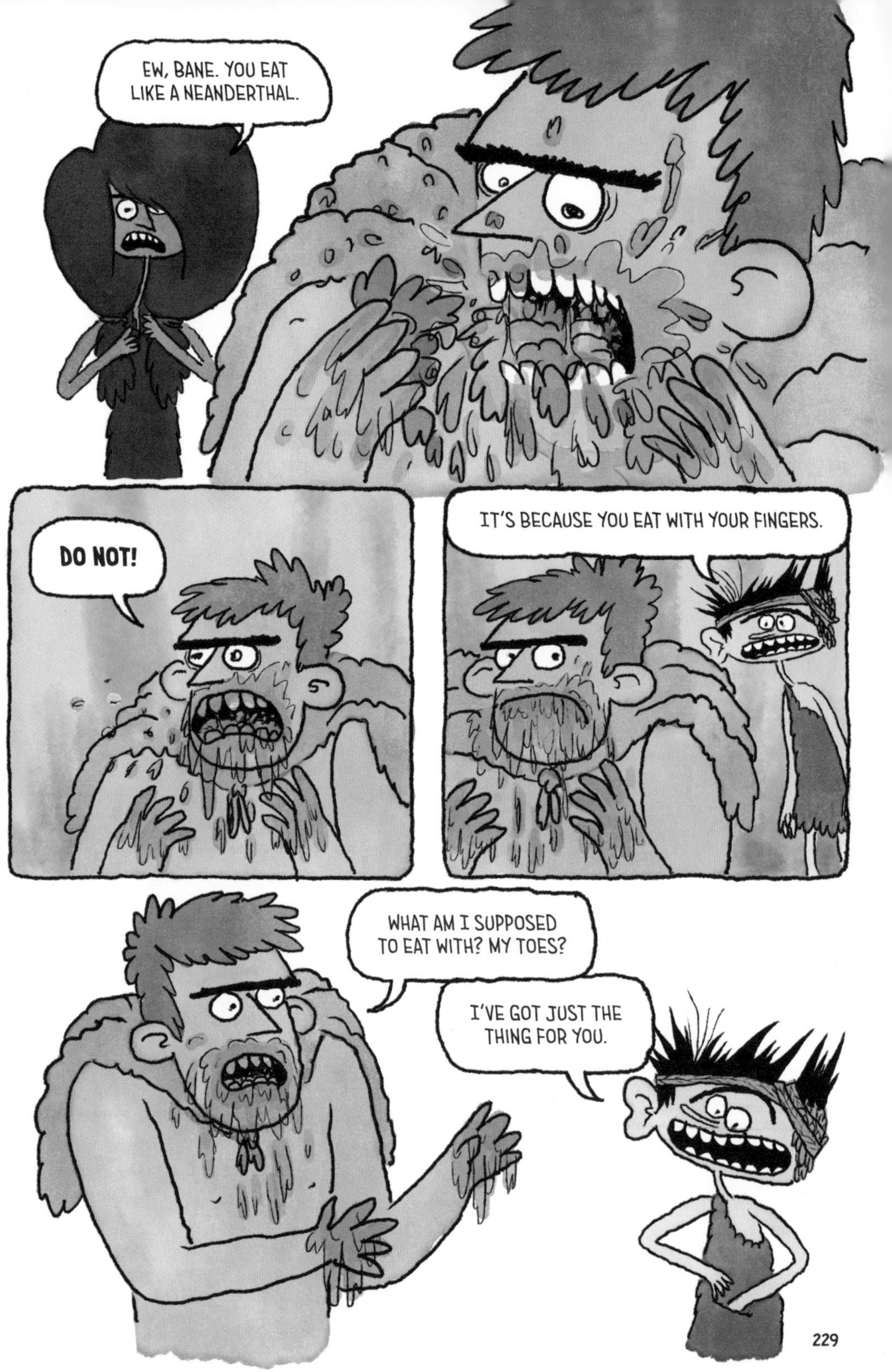
EW, BANE. YOU EAT LIKE A NEANDERTHAL.
DO NOT!
IT'S BECAUSE YOU EAT WITH YOUR FINGERS.
WHAT AM I SUPPOSED TO EAT WITH? MY TOES?
I'VE GOT JUST THE THING FOR YOU.

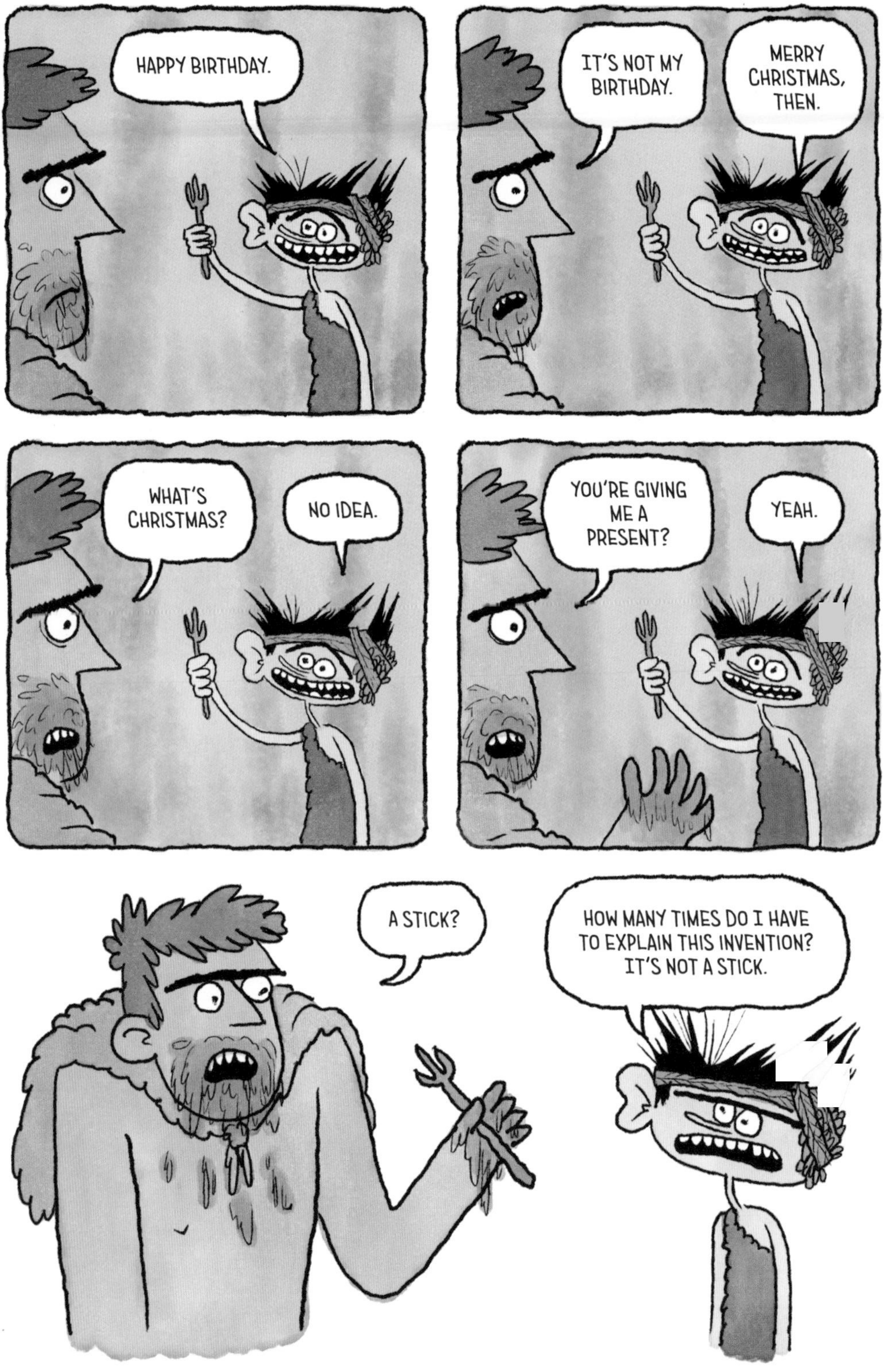
HAPPY BIRTHDAY.
IT'S NOT MY BIRTHDAY.
MERRY CHRISTMAS, THEN.
WHAT'S CHRISTMAS?
NO IDEA.
YOU'RE GIVING ME A PRESENT?
YEAH.
A STICK?
HOW MANY TIMES DO I HAVE TO EXPLAIN THIS INVENTION? IT'S NOT A STICK.

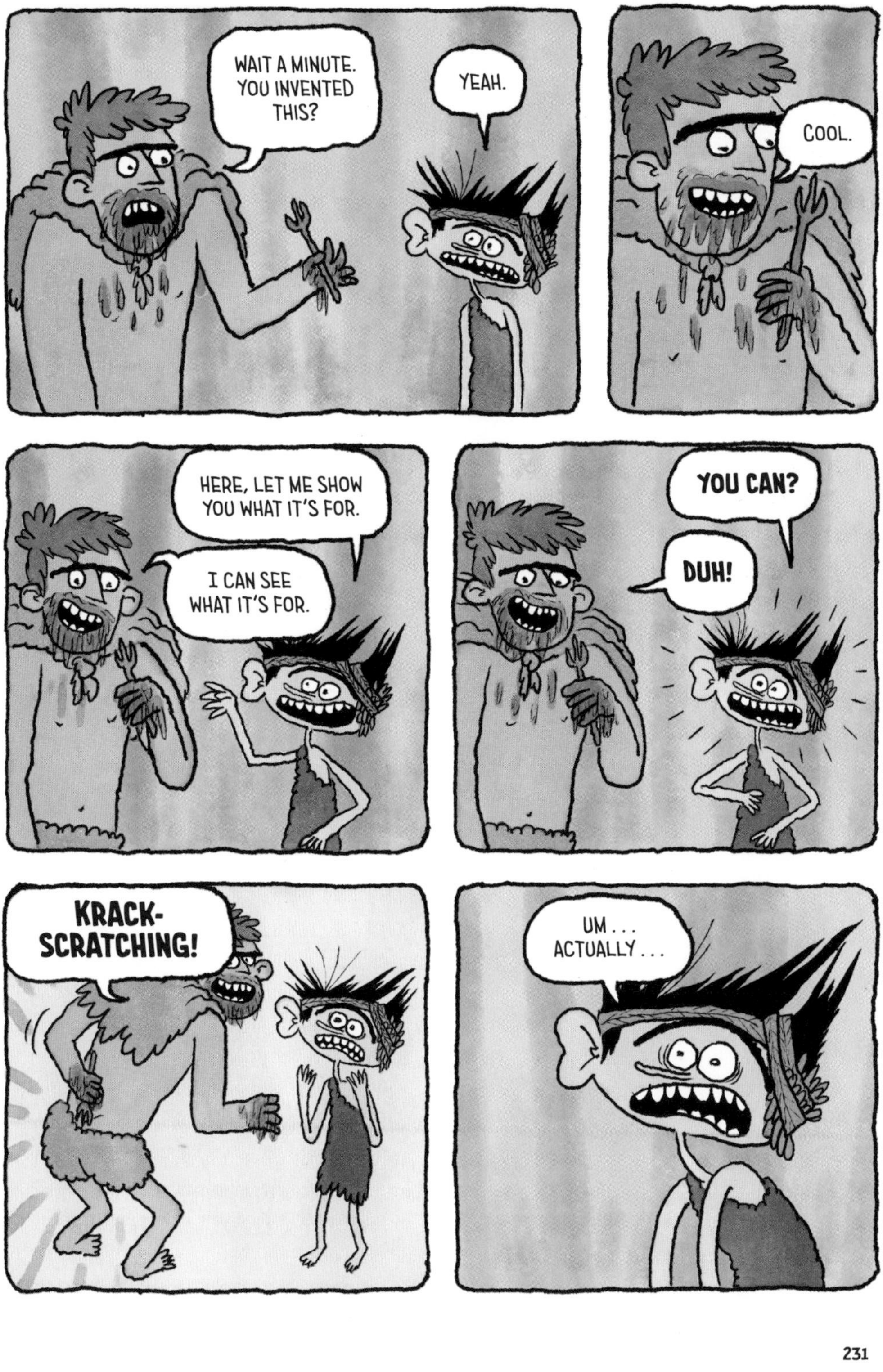
WAIT A MINUTE.
YOU INVENTED
THIS?
YEAH.
COOL.
HERE, LET ME SHOW
YOU WHAT IT'S FOR.
I CAN SEE
WHAT IT'S FOR.
YOU CAN?
DUH!
KRACK-
SCRATCHING!
UM . . .
ACTUALLY . . .

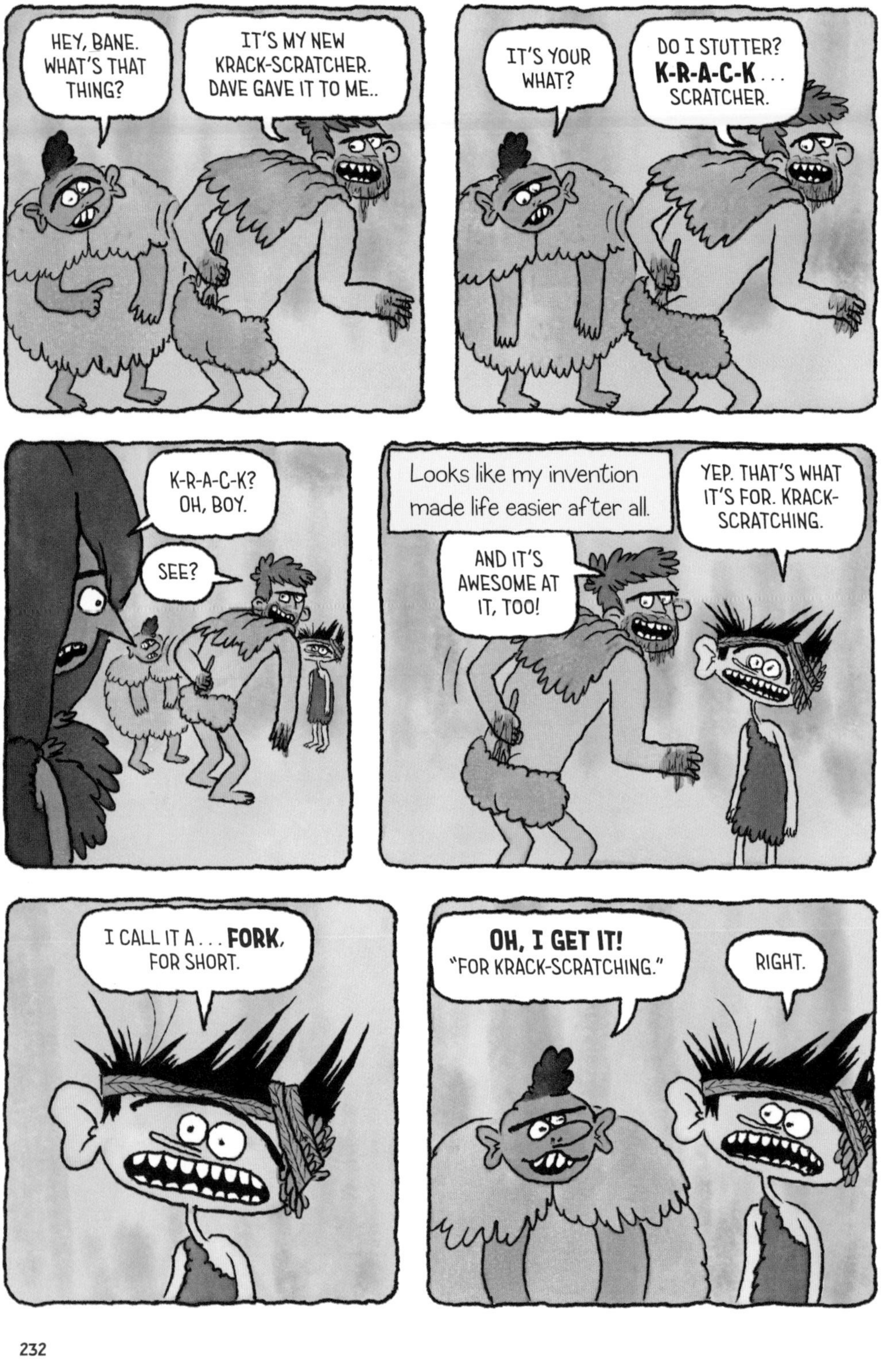
HEY, BANE. WHAT'S THAT THING?
IT'S MY NEW KRACK-SCRATCHER. DAVE GAVE IT TO ME..
IT'S YOUR WHAT?
DO I STUTTER? **K-R-A-C-K** . . . SCRATCHER.
K-R-A-C-K? OH, BOY.
SEE?
Looks like my invention made life easier after all.
YEP. THAT'S WHAT IT'S FOR. KRACK-SCRATCHING.
AND IT'S AWESOME AT IT, TOO!
I CALL IT A . . . **FORK**, FOR SHORT.
OH, I GET IT! "FOR KRACK-SCRATCHING."
RIGHT.

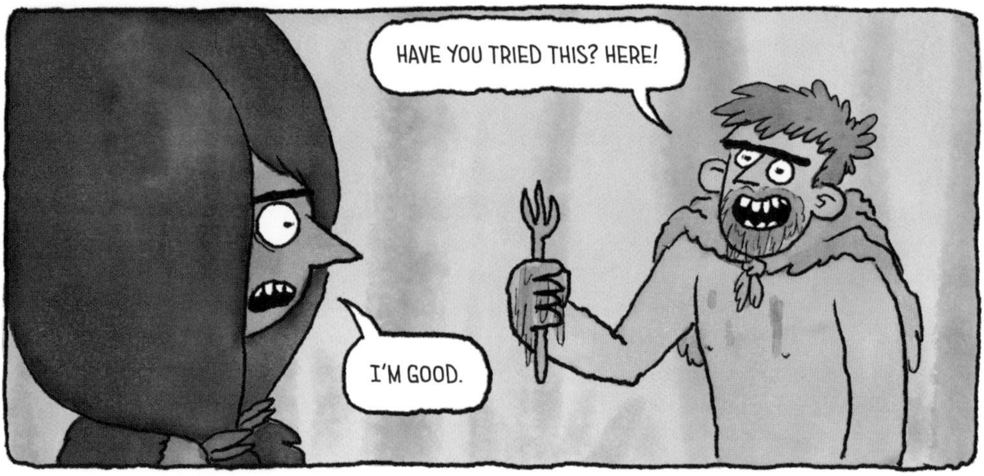
HAVE YOU TRIED THIS? HERE!
I'M GOOD.

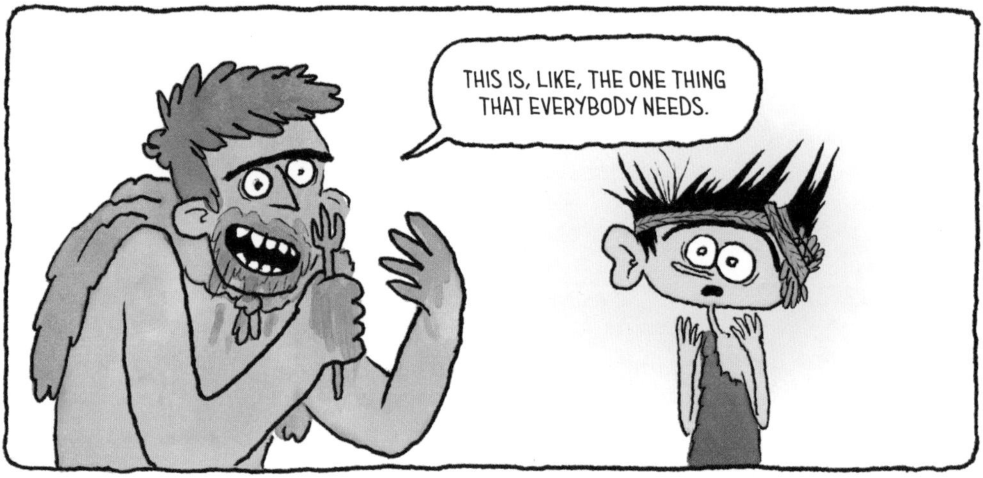
THIS IS, LIKE, THE ONE THING THAT EVERYBODY NEEDS.

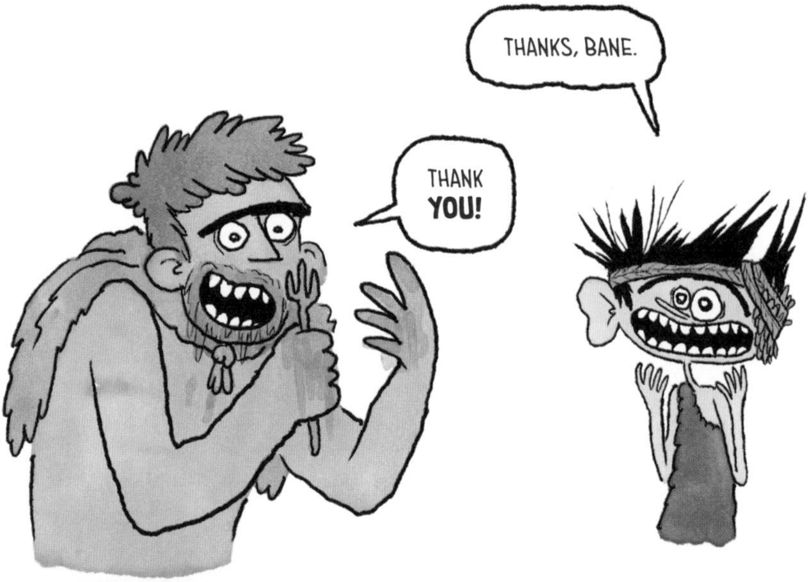
THANKS, BANE.
THANK **YOU!**

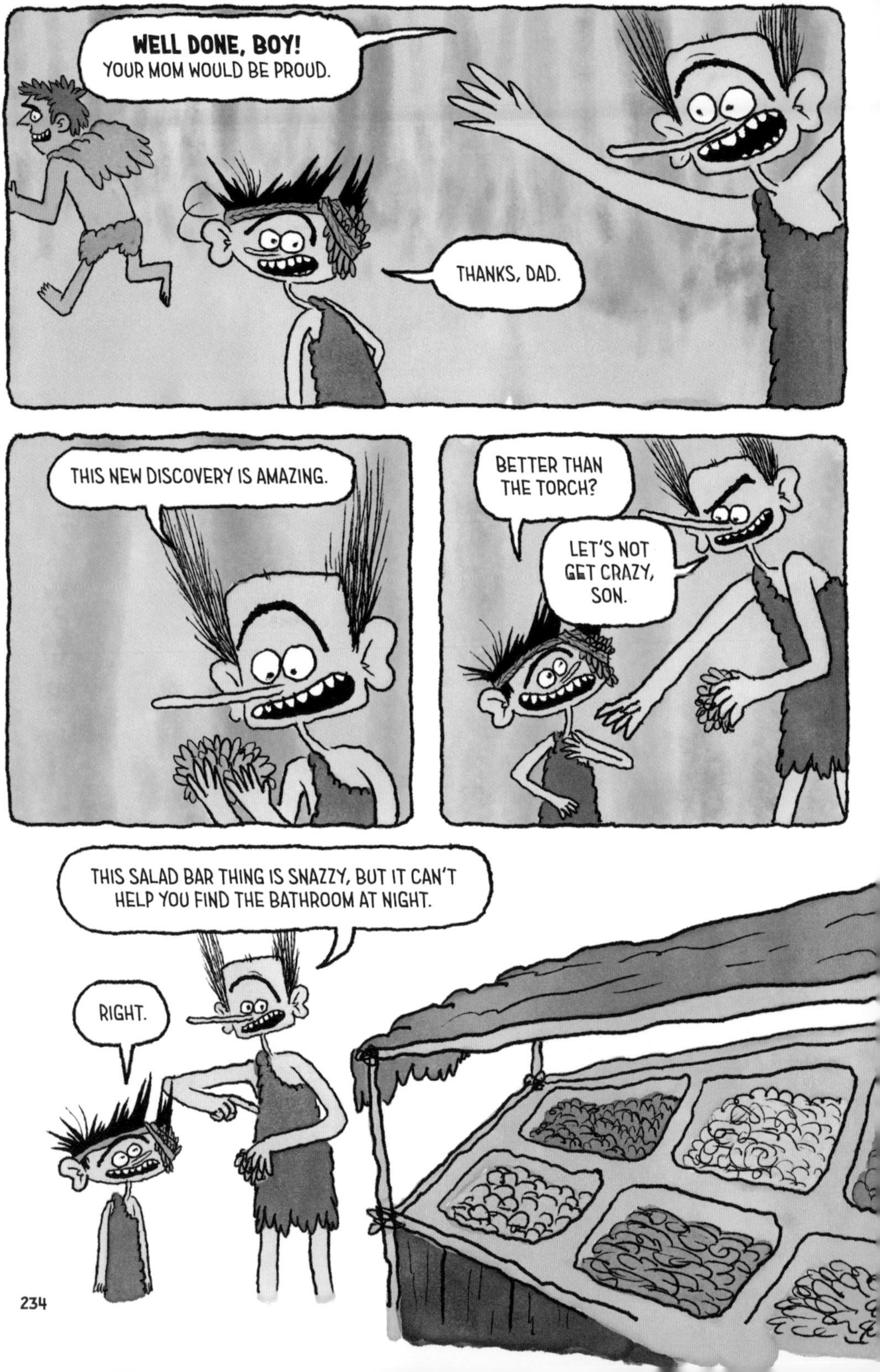
WELL DONE, BOY! YOUR MOM WOULD BE PROUD.
THANKS, DAD.
THIS NEW DISCOVERY IS AMAZING.
BETTER THAN THE TORCH?
LET'S NOT GET CRAZY, SON.
THIS SALAD BAR THING IS SNAZZY, BUT IT CAN'T HELP YOU FIND THE BATHROOM AT NIGHT.
RIGHT.

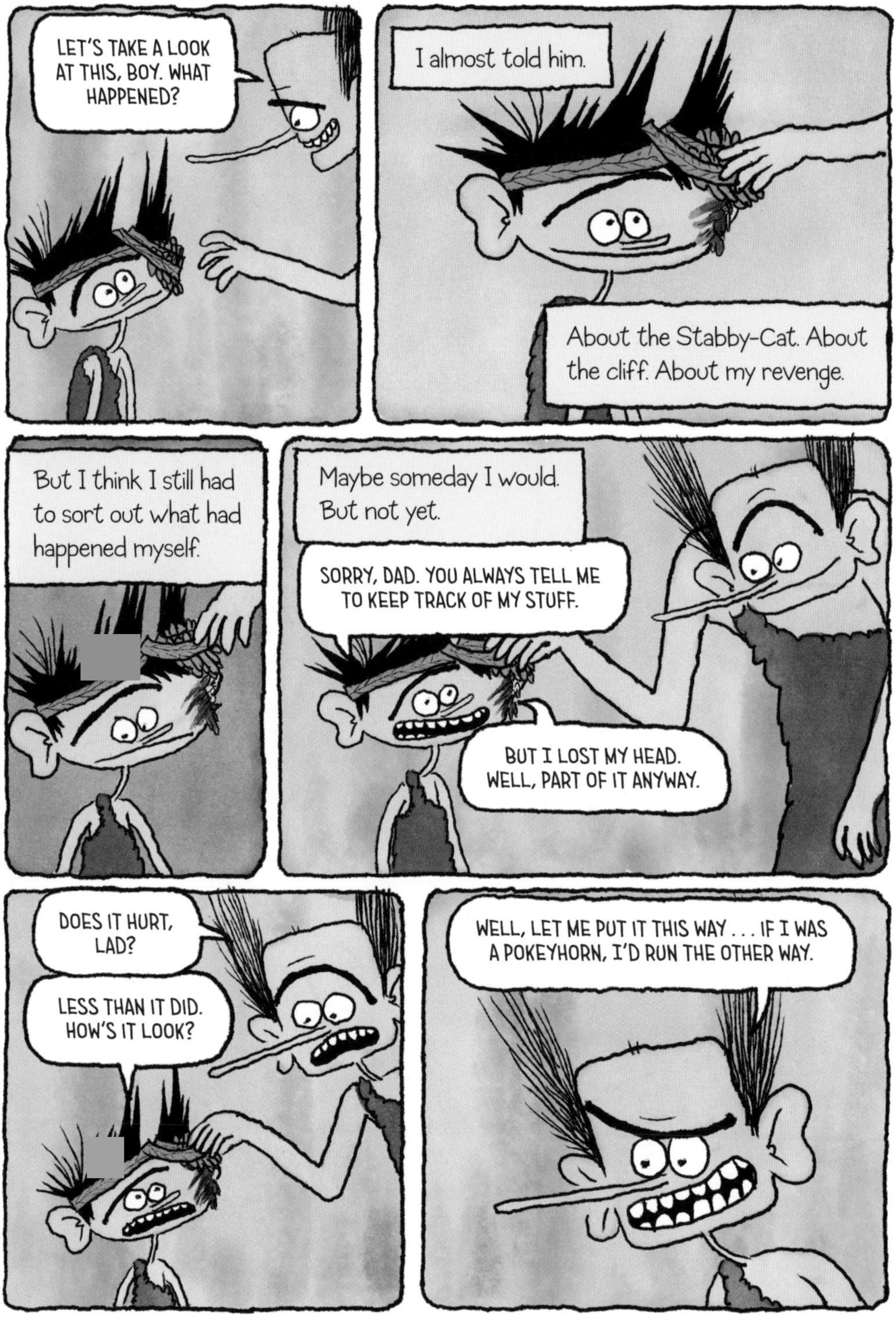
LET'S TAKE A LOOK AT THIS, BOY. WHAT HAPPENED?
I almost told him.
About the Stabby-Cat. About the cliff. About my revenge.
But I think I still had to sort out what had happened myself.
Maybe someday I would. But not yet.
SORRY, DAD. YOU ALWAYS TELL ME TO KEEP TRACK OF MY STUFF.
BUT I LOST MY HEAD. WELL, PART OF IT ANYWAY.
DOES IT HURT, LAD?
LESS THAN IT DID. HOW'S IT LOOK?
WELL, LET ME PUT IT THIS WAY . . . IF I WAS A POKEYHORN, I'D RUN THE OTHER WAY.

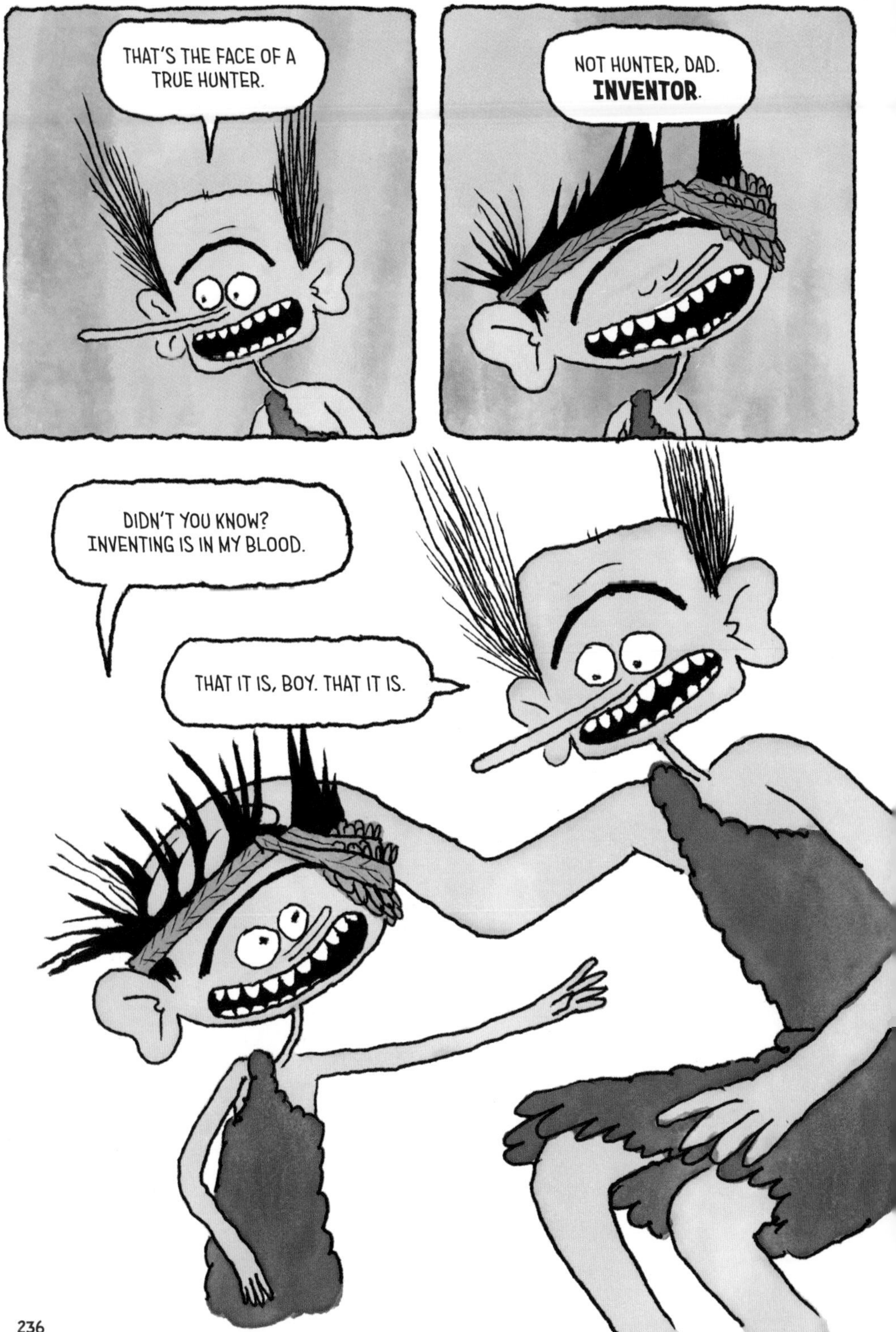
THAT'S THE FACE OF A TRUE HUNTER.
NOT HUNTER, DAD. **INVENTOR**.
DIDN'T YOU KNOW? INVENTING IS IN MY BLOOD.
THAT IT IS, BOY. THAT IT IS.

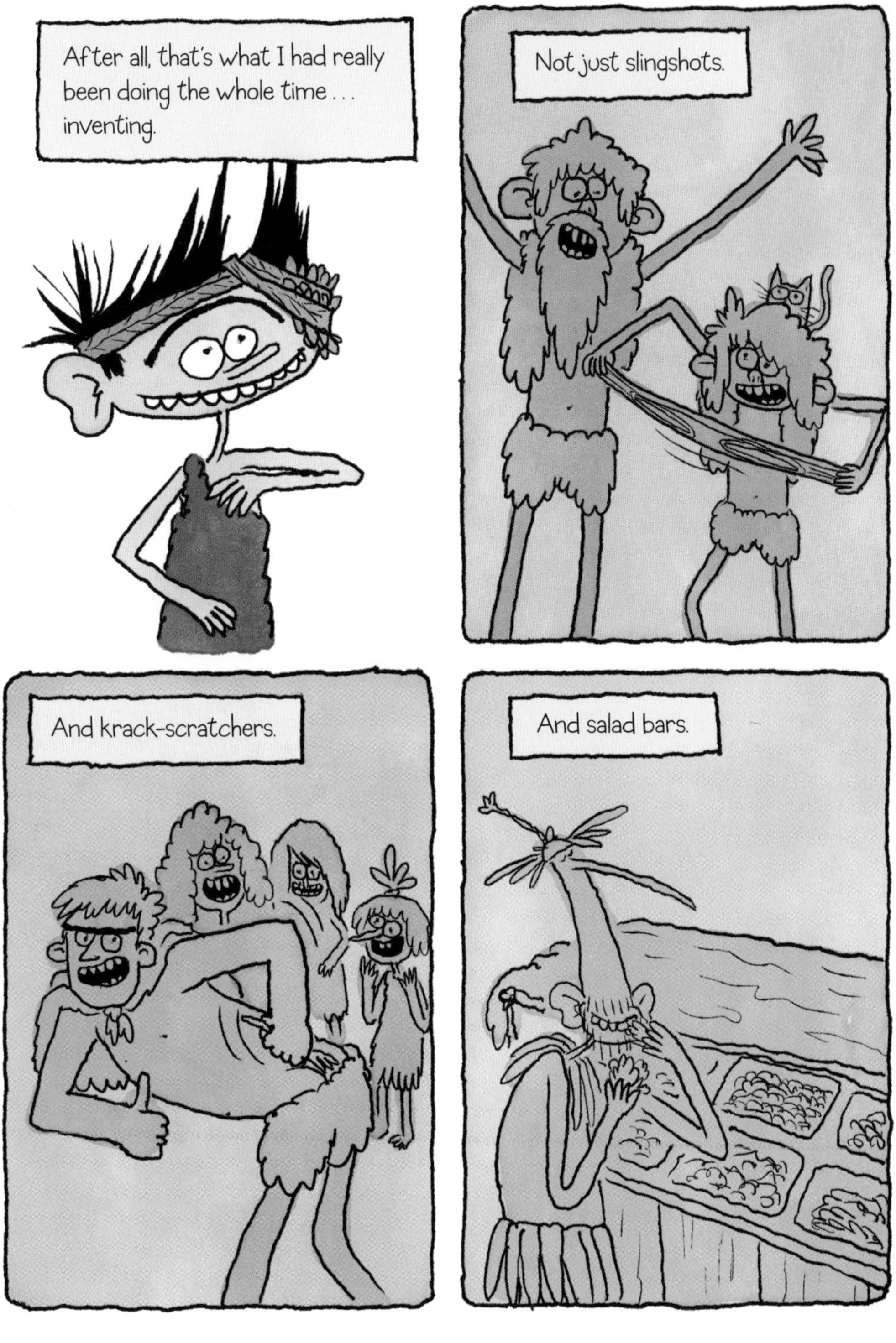
After all, that's what I had really been doing the whole time . . . inventing.
Not just slingshots.
And krack-scratchers.
And salad bars.

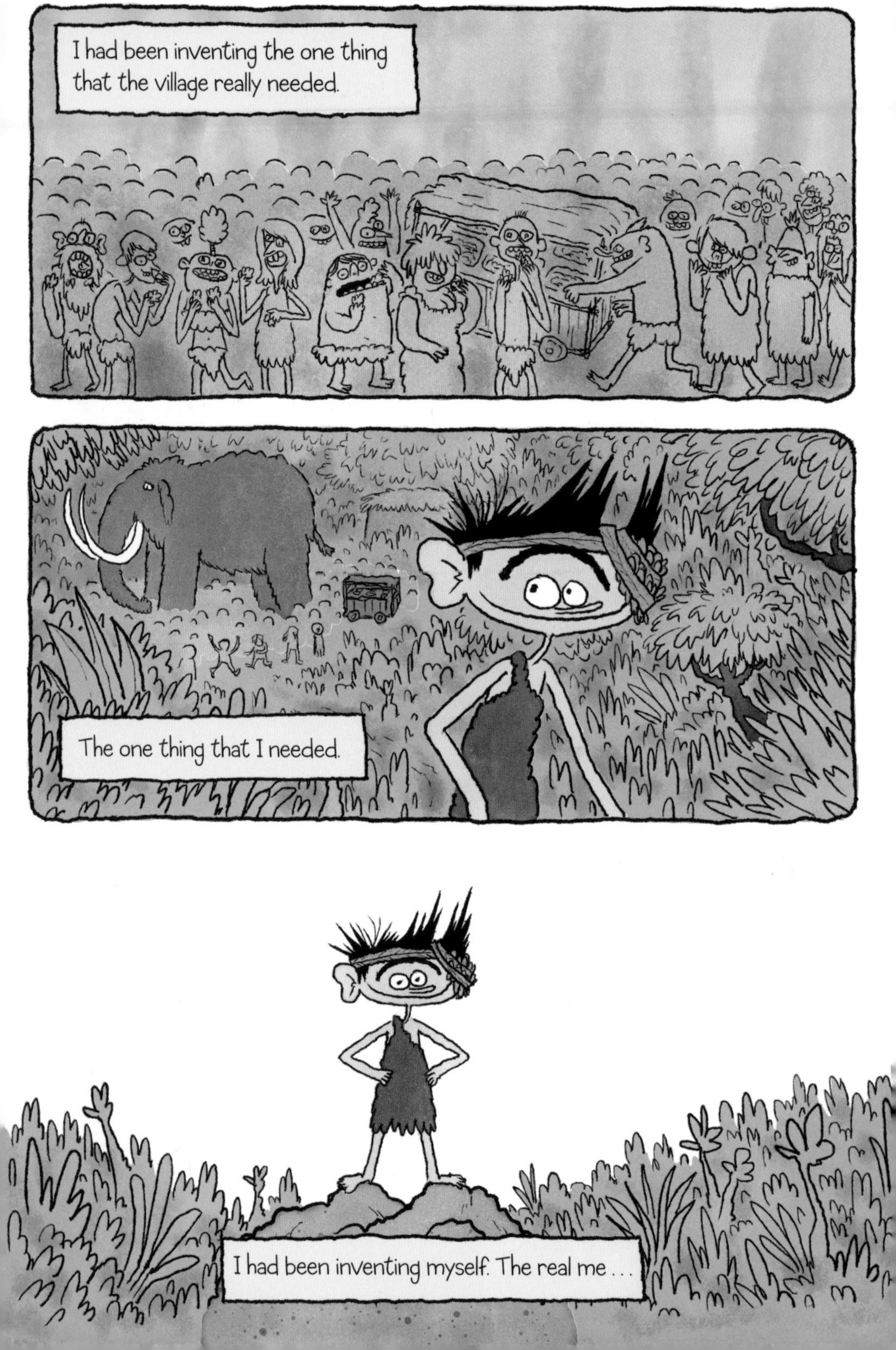
I had been inventing the one thing that the village really needed.
The one thing that I needed.
I had been inventing myself. The real me . . .

. . . Caveboy Dave.

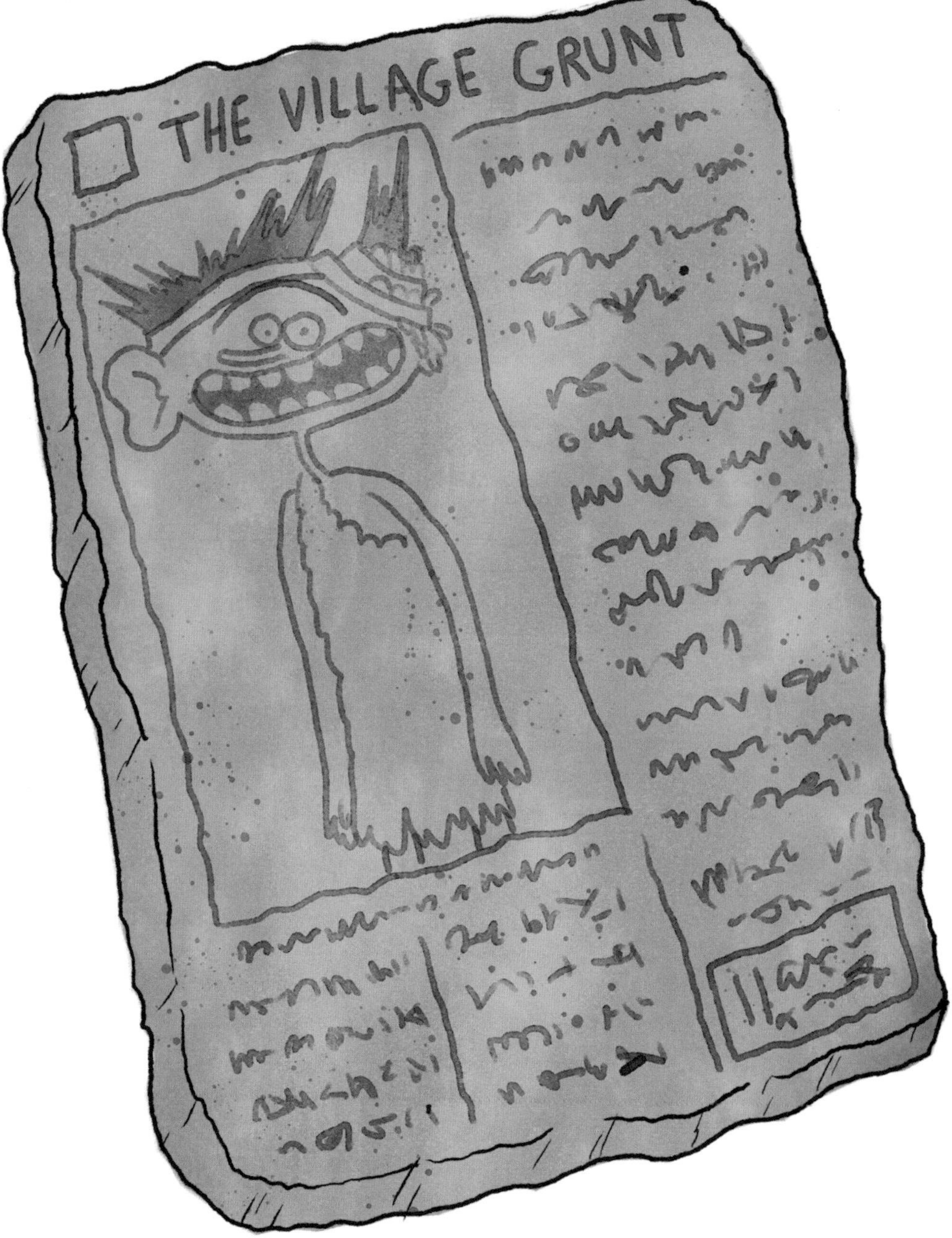
THE VILLAGE GRUNT

STARRING . . .

DAVE UNGA-BUNGA (Me!)

MR. UNGA-BUNGA
(My dad.)

BLA UNGA-BUNGA
(My sister.)

UG SMITH
(He's 100% Ug . . .)

ROCKIE FIREGOOD
(She keeps me on my toes.)

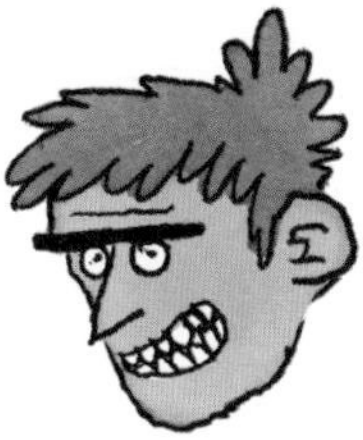

BANE BONESNAP
(Our best hunter . . .
and boy does he know it.)

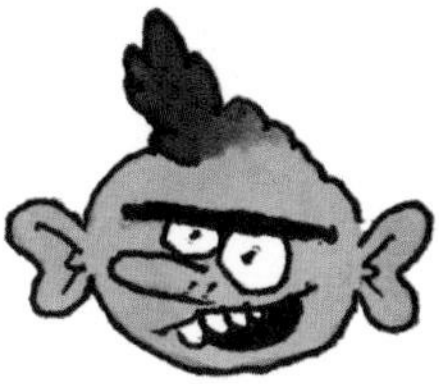

GAK CLUBBERSON
(Class clown.)

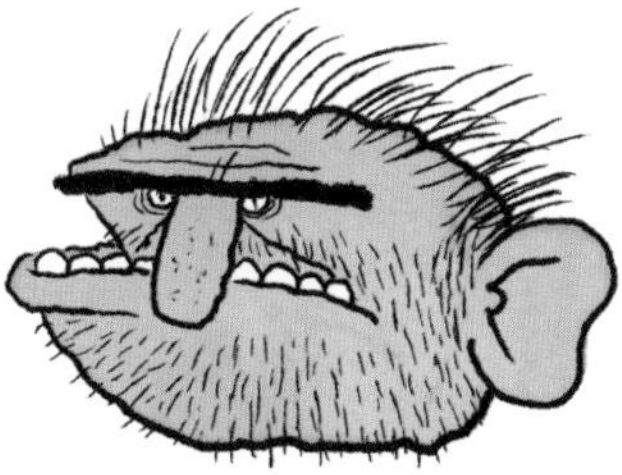

MR. GRONK
(Gym teacher
and soul crusher.)

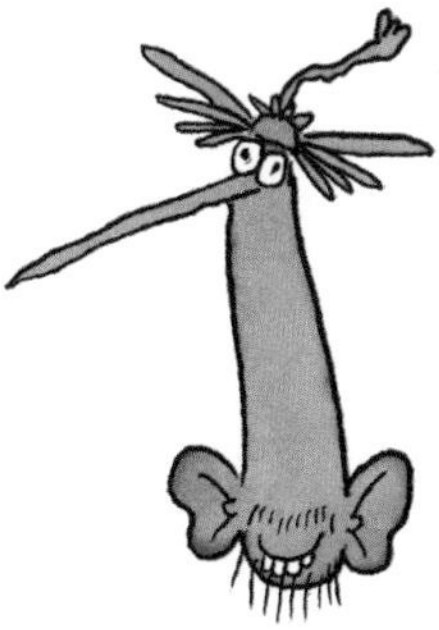

SHAMAN FABOO
(Our flashy and
fearless leader.)

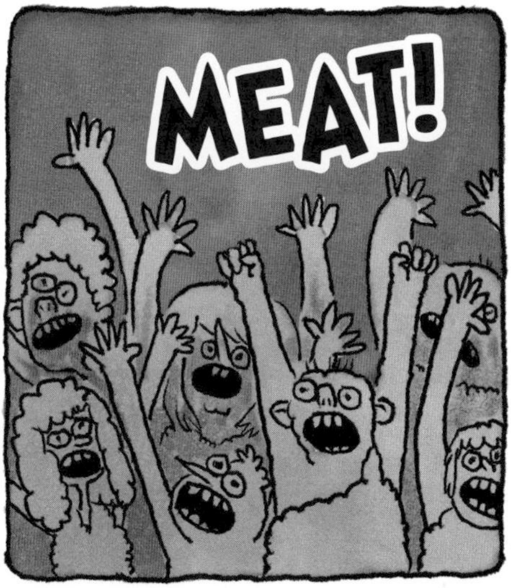
MEAT!

THE VILLAGE
(They like meat.)

Want more Caveboy Dave?

CAVEBOY DAVE
NOT SO FABOO

Coming soon!

When Dave Unga-Bunga discovers a column of smoke rising from the forest, he rushes to tell Shaman Faboo. Could this mean there's another village nearby? And are they *friendly* villagers or *evil* villagers?

The situation goes from curious to ominous when Shaman Faboo is nowhere to be found. Word gets out and panic floods the village. SHAMAN FABOO . . . HAS DISAPPEARED!

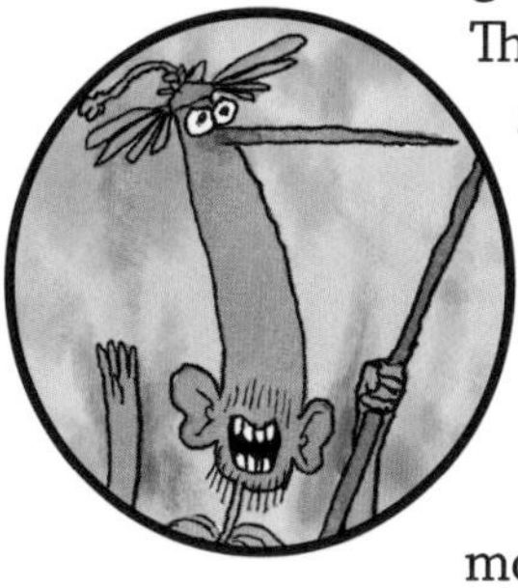

The villagers immediately look for somebody—anybody!—to tell them what to do. Dave's cool, rational thinking calms the crowd, and it becomes clear to the frightened villagers that Dave must lead . . . alongside two advisors, one of whom is Dave's dad.

Dave thinks this plan stinks worse than a month-old loincloth. He can't lead a village—he's only twelve! Will he successfully protect the village or inadvertently burn it to the ground? Will he ever find Faboo or is he stuck being the shaman forever? Is it possible to peacefully work with his dad or will they end up at each other's throats? And what about those other—most certainly sinister—villagers?

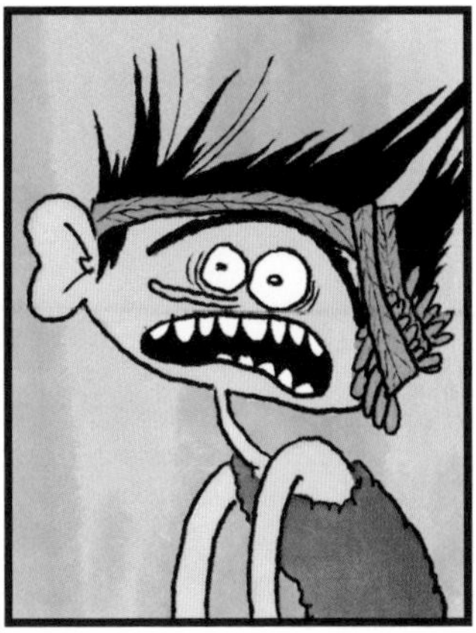

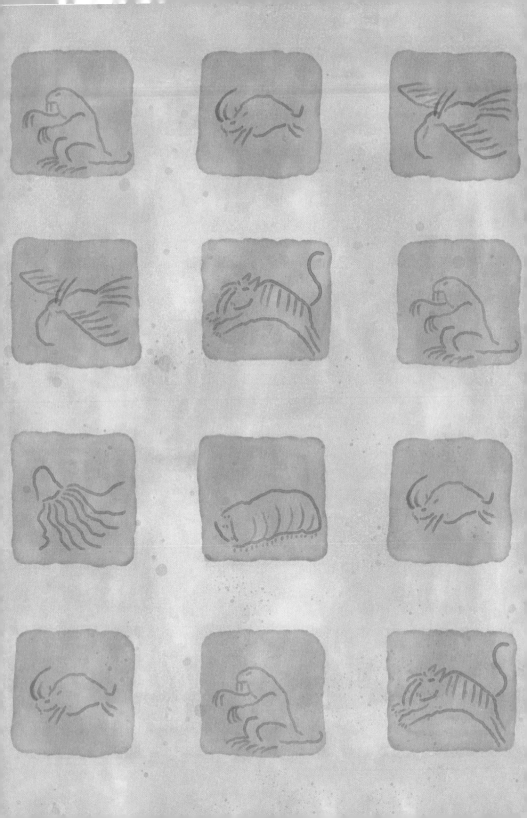

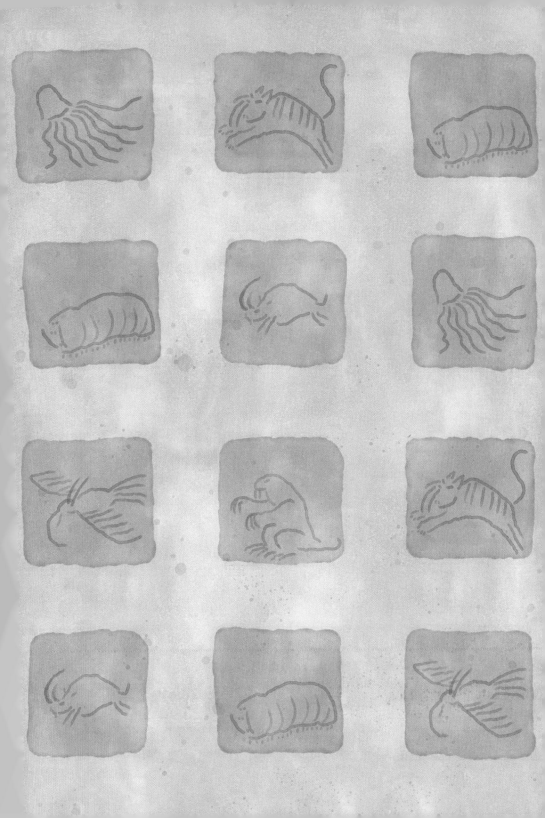

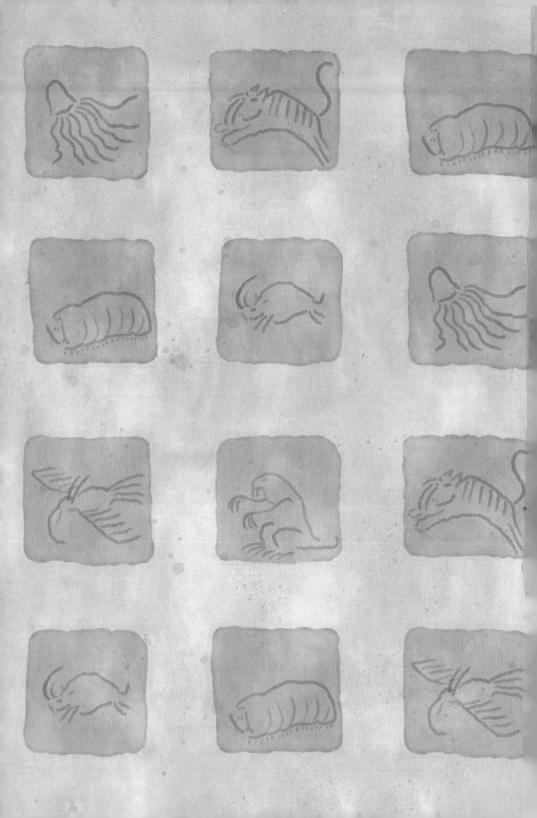